SelectEditions

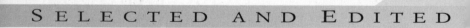
SELECTED AND EDITED

SelectEditions

BY READER'S DIGEST

THE READER'S DIGEST ASSOCIATION, INC.
MONTREAL • PLEASANTVILLE, NEW YORK

READER'S DIGEST SELECT EDITIONS

Vice President, Books & Home Entertainment: Deirdre Gilbert

CONTENTS

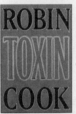

Mary Higgins Clark

You
Belong
to Me

*H*e is all she ever wanted: someone attractive, kind, and caring, someone to belong to.

And now her prayers are about to be answered. Now she will belong to him forever—but not in the way she expects. . . .

PROLOGUE

HE HAD played this same game before and had anticipated this time out it would be something of a letdown.
It came as a pleasant surprise, then, to find that it gave
him even more of a thrill.

He had boarded the ship in Perth, Australia, only yesterday, planning to sail as far as Kobe, Japan, but he had found her immediately, so the extra ports would not be necessary. She was seated at a
window table in the liner's paneled dining room, a discreetly elegant
space typical of the *Gabrielle*. The small luxury cruise ship was the
perfect size for his purposes, and he always chose a segment of a
deluxe world tour.

He was cautious by nature, although in truth there was little likelihood of his being recognized by previous shipmates. He had
become a master at altering his appearance, a talent he had discovered during his college drama club fling at acting.

He studied Regina Clausen. She was one of those fortyish women
who could have been quite attractive if she only knew how to present herself. Her ice-blue dinner suit made her look washed out.
Her light brown hair was so stiffly set that even from across the
wide room it seemed to age her.

He knew who she was. He had seen Clausen in action at a stockholders' meeting only a few months ago, and he had also watched her on CNBC in her capacity as a stock research analyst. Certainly in those venues she had come across as forceful and very sure of herself.

That was why, when he spotted her sitting wistfully alone at the table, he knew right away how easy it was going to be.

He raised his glass and, with the faintest movement in her direction, offered a silent toast.

Your prayers have been answered, Regina, he promised. From now on, you belong to me.

THREE YEARS LATER

1

BARRING a blizzard or something bordering on a hurricane, Dr. Susan Chandler walked to work from her brownstone apartment in Greenwich Village to her office in SoHo. A thirty-three-year-old clinical psychologist, she had a thriving private practice and at the same time had established something of a public persona as host of a popular radio program, *Ask Dr. Susan,* that aired each weekday.

The early morning air on this October day was crisp and breezy, and she was glad she had opted for a long-sleeved turtleneck sweater under her suit jacket. Her shoulder-length dark blond hair, still damp from the shower, was windblown, causing her to regret not wearing a scarf.

She stopped for a light at the corner of Mercer and Houston. It was only seven thirty, and the streets weren't crowded yet. In another hour they would be teeming with back-to-work New Yorkers.

Thank heaven the weekend's over, Susan said to herself. She had spent most of Saturday and Sunday in Rye with her mother, who was in low spirits—understandably so, Susan thought, since Sunday would have been her fortieth wedding anniversary. Then, not helping the situation, Susan had an encounter with her older sister, Dee, who was visiting from California.

Sunday afternoon, before coming home, Susan had made a courtesy call to her father's palatial home in nearby Bedford Hills, where he and his second wife, Binky, were throwing a cocktail party. Susan suspected that the timing of the party was Binky's doing.

I love my parents, Susan thought as she reached her office building, but there are times when I want to tell them to grow up.

Susan was usually the first to arrive on the top floor, so she was startled to see that the lights in the reception area and hallway were already on. She knew her old friend and mentor Nedda Harding must be the early bird.

She shook her head ruefully as she opened the outer door— which should have been locked—walked down the hallway, then stopped at the open door leading to Nedda's office.

One of the most respected defense attorneys in New York, Nedda's somewhat grandmotherly appearance offered little indication of the cleverness and aggressive energy she brought to her work. The two women had met and become friends ten years ago at N.Y.U. when Susan was a law student and Nedda a guest lecturer.

All Susan's friends, Nedda being the only exception, had been shocked when, after two years in the Westchester County District Attorney's Office, Susan quit her job as assistant D.A. to go back to school and earn her doctorate in psychology.

Sensing Susan's presence in her doorway, Nedda looked up. "Well, look who's here. Good weekend, Susan?"

Nedda knew about both Binky's party and the anniversary.

"It was predictable," Susan said. "Dee got to Mom's on Saturday, and the two of them ended up sobbing their hearts out. I told Dee her depression was making it harder for Mom to cope, and she blasted me. Said that if two years ago I had watched *my* husband swept to his death in an avalanche the way *she* had watched Jack die, I'd understand what she was going through.

"Then there was Dad and Binky's party, at that turreted mansion he built for her," she continued. "Incidentally, Dad now requests that I call him Charles, which says it all on *that* subject." She sighed deeply. "Another weekend like that, and I'll be the one who needs counseling."

Nedda eyed her sympathetically. She was the only one of Susan's friends who knew the full story about Jack and Dee, and about Susan's parents and the messy divorce. "Sounds to me as though you need a survival plan," she said.

Susan laughed. "Maybe you'll come up with one for me. Just put it on my tab along with all I owe you for getting me the radio job. Now I'd better get going. I've got to prepare for the show."

A year earlier Marge Mackin, a popular radio host and a close friend of Nedda's, had invited Susan to sit in on her program during a highly publicized trial to comment both as a legal expert and a psychologist. The success of that first on-air visit led to regular appearances on the program, and when Marge moved on to host a television program, Susan was invited to replace her on the daily radio talk show.

"Who's your guest today?" Nedda asked.

"This week I'll be concentrating on why women should be safety conscious in social situations. Donald Richards, a psychiatrist specializing in criminology, has written a book called *Vanishing Women.* Many of the disappearances he solved, but a number of interesting ones are still open. We'll discuss why an intelligent woman might get involved with a killer and how our listeners might avoid potentially dangerous situations."

"Good subject."

"I think so. I've decided to bring up the Regina Clausen disappearance. That one always intrigued me. Remember her? I used to watch her on CNBC and thought she was great."

Nedda looked up, frowning. "Regina Clausen disappeared about three years ago after disembarking from a world cruise in Hong Kong. I remember it very well. It got a lot of publicity at the time."

"That was after I left the district attorney's office," Susan said, "but I was visiting a friend there when Regina Clausen's mother, Jane—who lived in Scarsdale at that time—came in to talk to the

D.A. to see if he could help. There was no indication that Regina had ever left Hong Kong, so of course the Westchester County district attorney had no jurisdiction. The poor woman had pictures of Regina and kept saying how much her daughter had looked forward to that trip. I've never forgotten the case."

Nedda's expression softened. "I know Jane Clausen slightly. We graduated from Smith the same year. She lives on Beekman Place now. She was always quiet. I gather Regina was also shy socially."

Susan raised her eyebrows. "I wish I had known. You might have been able to arrange for me to speak with Mrs. Clausen."

Nedda frowned. "Maybe it's not too late. Doug Layton is the Clausen family lawyer. I've met him. Mid-thirties, lives on Park Avenue. I'll call him at nine and see if he'll put us in touch with her."

AT TEN after nine the intercom on Susan's desk buzzed. It was Janet, her secretary. "Douglas Layton is on line one."

As soon as Susan began to speak to the Clausen family lawyer, it became clear that he was not happy. "Dr. Chandler, we absolutely resent any exploitation of Mrs. Clausen's grief," he said brusquely. "Regina was her only child. It would be bad enough if her body had been found, but because it has not, Mrs. Clausen agonizes constantly, wondering under what circumstances her daughter may be living, if she is alive. I would have thought a friend of Nedda Harding would be above this kind of sensationalism."

When Susan spoke, her tone was chilly but calm. "Mr. Layton, you've already given the reason the case *should* be discussed. Neither the police in Hong Kong nor the private investigators Mrs. Clausen hired were able to uncover a single clue as to what Regina did or where she might have gone after she disembarked. My program is heard in five states. It's a long shot, I know, but *maybe* someone who is listening today was on that ship, or was visiting Hong Kong at the same time, and will call in to tell us something helpful. After all, Regina was on CNBC regularly, and some people have an excellent memory for faces."

Without waiting for a response, Susan hung up, leaned over, and turned on the radio. She had made promos for today's program, referring to her guest author and to the Clausen case. They had run briefly last Friday, and Jed Geany, her producer, had promised that the station would air them again this morning.

Twenty minutes later she heard the first of the promos. Now let's keep our fingers crossed that someone who knows something about the case is listening too, she thought.

IT WAS definitely a lucky stroke that his car radio had been tuned to the talk radio station on Friday; otherwise he'd never have heard the announcement. As it was, he was barely listening. But at the mention of the name Regina Clausen he had turned up the volume and concentrated intently.

Not that there was anything to worry about, of course. As always, he had taken every precaution. Hadn't he?

Now, hearing the promo again Monday morning, he became less sure. Next time he'd be especially careful. But then the next one would be the last. There had been four so far. One more to go. He'd select her next week, and once she was his, his mission would be complete and he would finally be at peace.

Angrily he listened again to the promo and to the warm, encouraging voice of Dr. Susan Chandler: "Regina Clausen was a renowned investment adviser. She was also a daughter, a friend, and a generous benefactor of charities. We'll be talking about her disappearance on my show today. We'd like to solve the mystery. Maybe one of you has a piece of the puzzle. Listen in, please."

He snapped off the radio. "Dr. Susan," he said aloud, "get off it and fast. All this is none of your business, and I warn you, if I have to make you my business, your days are numbered."

DR. DONALD Richards, author of *Vanishing Women,* was already in the studio when Susan arrived. He was tall and lean, with dark brown hair, and he appeared to be in his late thirties. He pulled off his reading glasses as he stood up to greet her. His blue eyes were warm and his smile brief as he took the hand she extended to him.

"Dr. Chandler," he said. "This is my first book. I'm new at this publicity business, and I'm nervous. If I get tongue-tied, promise you'll rescue me."

Susan laughed. "The name is Susan, and don't think about the microphone. Pretend we're hanging over the back fence, gossiping."

Who's he kidding? Susan wondered fifteen minutes later as Richards discussed with calm and easy authority the true-life cases in his book. She nodded in agreement as he said, "When someone vanishes—I'm talking now of an adult, not a child—the question the authorities first ask is if the disappearance was voluntary. As you know, Susan, it's surprising just how many people suddenly decide to do a U-turn on their way home and start a whole new life. The first step to tracing someone who has disappeared is to see if charges start to show up on their credit cards."

"Either charged by them or by someone who stole those cards," Susan interjected.

"That's right," Richards agreed. "Of course, *some* disappearances are not voluntary; some involve foul play. That, however, is not always easy to determine. It's very difficult, for example, to prove someone guilty of murder if the body is never found."

They discussed several of the open cases he'd covered in his book, instances in which the victim had never been found. Then Susan said, "Now I'd like your opinion, Dr. Richards, on a case that is not covered in your book—that of Regina Clausen. Let me fill our listeners in on the circumstances of her disappearance."

Susan did not need to consult her notes. "Regina Clausen was a highly respected investment adviser with Lang Taylor Securities. At the time of her disappearance she was forty-three years old and, according to those who knew her, very shy in her personal life. She lived alone and usually took vacations with her mother. Three years ago her mother was recovering from a broken ankle, so Regina went alone on a segment of the world cruise of the luxury liner *Gabrielle*. She embarked in Perth, Australia, planning to sail to Bali, Hong Kong, Taiwan, and Japan and disembark in Honolulu. However, in Hong Kong she got off the ship, saying that she was going to spend extra time there and rejoin the *Gabrielle* when it docked in Japan. Regina took only one suitcase and a carry-on with her when she disembarked, and she was reported to have appeared very happy. She took a cab to the Peninsula Hotel, checked in, dropped her bags in her room, and left the hotel immediately. She was never seen again. Dr. Richards, if you were just starting to investigate this case, what would you do?"

"I'd want to see that passenger list and find out if anyone else arranged to stay in Hong Kong," Richards said promptly. "I'd want to know if she received phone calls or faxes on the ship. I'd question her fellow passengers to see if anyone noticed that she had been getting particularly friendly with someone, most likely a man, also traveling alone." He paused. "That's for openers."

"All of that was done," Susan told him. "A thorough investigation. All that could be determined for certain was that Regina Clausen vanished the moment she left that hotel."

In her headphones Susan heard a signal from the producer. "Now, after these messages, let's go to the phones," she said.

She pulled off her earphones and said to Richards, "A couple of messages otherwise known as commercials. They pay the bills."

He nodded, then said, "I was out of the country when the Clausen case was in the news, but it *is* an interesting one. From the little I know of it, however, I'd guess it's a guy who's to blame. A shy, lonely woman is particularly vulnerable when she's out of a familiar environment in which she has the reassurance and security of her job and family."

You must know my mother and sister, Susan thought wryly. "Get ready," she said. "We're about to go back on air."

They put on their headphones, through which they heard the ten-second countdown. Then she began. "Dr. Susan Chandler with you again. My guest is Dr. Donald Richards, criminologist, psychiatrist, author of *Vanishing Women*—case studies of women who have vanished in the last ten years. Before the break we were discussing the case of socialite stockbroker Regina Clausen, who disappeared in Hong Kong three years ago while on a segment of a world cruise."

She looked at the monitor. "We have a call from Louise, in Fort Lee."

The calls were run of the mill: "How can such smart women make the mistake of being taken in by a killer?" "What does Dr. Richards think of the Jimmy Hoffa case?"

And then there was time for one more commercial and call.

During the break the producer spoke to Susan. "There's one final call I want to put through. I warn you, though, whoever it is, she's blocked off our caller ID from her end. But she says she may know something about Regina Clausen's disappearance. She said to call her Karen. It's not her name."

"Put her on," Susan said. As the on-air light flashed, she spoke into the microphone. "Karen is our last caller, and she may have something important to tell us. Hello, Karen."

The caller spoke with a husky voice, almost too low to hear. "Dr. Susan, I took a segment of a round-the-world cruise two years ago. I was feeling pretty rotten because I was in the middle of a divorce. My husband's jealousy had become intolerable. There was a man on the trip. He made a big play for me, but he did it in a quiet, even discreet way. At the places we docked, he'd have me meet him at some spot away from the ship, and we'd explore that port together. Then later we'd return to the ship separately. He said the reason for such secrecy was that he hated exposing us to gossip. He was quite charming and very attentive, something I needed badly at the time. He suggested that I leave the ship in Athens and spend more time there. Then we were going to fly to Algiers, and I could pick up the ship in Tangier."

Susan was reminded of the feeling she had gotten when she was in the prosecutor's office and was on the verge of learning something meaningful from a witness. "Did you do what this man suggested?" she asked.

"I was going to, but my husband phoned just then and begged me to give our marriage another chance. The man I was planning to meet had already disembarked. I tried to phone to say I was staying on the ship, but he wasn't registered at the hotel where he said he'd be staying, so I never saw him again. But I *do* have a photo with him in the background, and he gave me a turquoise ring that was inscribed 'You belong to me,' which I never got to return."

Susan chose her words carefully. "Karen, what you're telling us may be very important. Will you meet me and show me that ring and photograph?"

"I—I can't get involved. My husband would be furious."

"Karen, please come to my office at three o'clock," Susan said quickly. "Here's the address." She rattled it off, then added, her voice pleading, "Regina Clausen's mother needs to find out what happened to her daughter. I promise I'll protect your privacy."

"I'll be there at three." The connection was broken.

2

CAROLYN Wells turned off the radio and walked nervously to the window. Across the street the Metropolitan Museum of Art was blanketed in the quiet typical of Monday, its closing day.

Since making that phone call to the *Ask Dr. Susan* show, she'd been unable to shake off a terrible sense of foreboding.

If only we hadn't teased Pamela to do one of her readings for us, she thought, remembering the unsettling events of the previous Friday evening. She had cooked a fortieth birthday dinner for her former roommate Pamela Hastings and had invited as well the other two women with whom they used to share an apartment. They had decreed it to be a girls' night in, and the four of them had gossiped with the easy comfort of old friends.

Pamela, now a professor at Columbia, seemed to have the gift of second sight. Sometimes she was even called upon, discreetly, by the police in cases of kidnappings and missing persons. Her old friends hadn't asked her to do a reading for years. When they were younger, they had made a ritual of somewhat jokingly asking her to assess their future with a new boyfriend or a new job offer. After dinner last Friday, Pamela had agreed to do a quick reading for each of them. As usual, she asked each woman to choose a personal object for her to hold while she did the reading.

I was the last, Carolyn remembered. And why did I pick out that damn ring for her to hold? I don't even know why I've kept it.

The fact was that she had plucked the ring out of her costume-jewelry box that night because earlier in the day she had had Owen Adams, the man who gave it to her, on her mind. It was just two years ago that she had met him.

Pamela had noticed the almost illegible inscription inside the band. " 'You belong to me,' " she read, her tone half amused, half horrified. "A little strong in this day and age, isn't it, Carolyn? I hope Justin meant it as a joke."

"Justin doesn't know a thing about it. Back when we were separated, some guy gave it to me on a cruise. I've always been curious about what happened to him."

Pamela had closed her hand over the ring, and in an instant her whole body became tense, her face grave. "Carolyn, this ring could have been the cause of your death," she said. "It may *still* be. Whoever gave it to you meant to harm you." Then, as though it were burning her hand, she dropped the ring on the coffee table.

It was at that moment that the key turned in the door, and they all jumped like guilty schoolgirls. The separation was a taboo subject for Justin. Carolyn quickly scooped up the ring and put it in her pocket. It was still there.

Justin's excessive jealousy had been the cause of the breakup two years ago. The day he called her on the ship, he had promised to change. And I know he's *tried,* Carolyn thought, but if I get involved in this Dr. Susan thing, he'll think there really *was* something between Owen Adams and me, and we'll be back to square one.

She decided not to keep the appointment with Susan Chandler. Instead, she would send her the shipboard picture taken at the captain's cocktail party, the one showing Owen Adams in the background. She'd crop it so that she wasn't in the picture, and she'd send it, along with the ring and Owen's name, to Chandler.

If there was any tie between Owen Adams and Regina Clausen, it would be up to Chandler to find it.

SEVENTY-four-year-old Jane Clausen turned off the radio, then sat staring through her window at the swiftly flowing current of the East River. In the last three years, ever since her daughter Regina's disappearance, she had felt as if she were frozen inside.

She knew Regina was dead. In her heart it was a certainty. She had known it from the moment she received the call from the ship to say that Regina had not reboarded as planned.

This morning her lawyer, Douglas Layton, had phoned to warn her that Dr. Susan Chandler was going to discuss Regina's disappearance on the radio. "I tried to dissuade her," Douglas said, his voice tense, "but she insisted it would be a favor to you if the full truth came out."

Only Douglas Layton, the lawyer in the investment firm that handled the family assets, knew how desperately she had sought an answer to her daughter's disappearance. Topflight private investigators had searched thoroughly long after the police had given up.

But I've been wrong, Jane Clausen thought. I've convinced myself that Regina's death was an accident. That's made losing her more bearable. But then how to explain the phone call from Karen, who reported a man who had urged her to leave her cruise? She had talked about a ring—a ring with "You belong to me" inscribed on the inside of the band.

Jane Clausen had instantly recognized the phrase, and hearing the familiar words this morning chilled her to the bone. Regina had been scheduled to disembark from the *Gabrielle* in Honolulu. When she did not return to the ship, her clothes and effects that were left on board were shipped home. Going through the items, Jane had noticed the ring because it was so frivolous—a pretty, inexpensive turquoise thing, the kind tourists purchase on a whim. She was sure Regina either hadn't noticed the sentiment engraved inside the band or had ignored it. Turquoise was her birthstone.

But if this Karen had been given a similar ring only two years ago, did it mean that the person responsible for Regina's death might still be preying on other women?

Jane Clausen stood, waited for the pain in her back to ease, then walked slowly from the study to the room that she and her housekeeper carefully referred to as the guest room.

A year after the disappearance she had given up Regina's apartment, then sold her own too big house in Scarsdale. She had bought this five-room apartment on Beekman Place and furnished the second bedroom with Regina's own furniture and belongings.

Now she went to the dresser, opened the top drawer, and removed the leather box in which Regina had kept her jewelry.

The turquoise ring was in a velvet-lined compartment. She picked up the ring and slipped it on her finger.

She went to the telephone and phoned Douglas Layton. "Douglas," she said quietly, "today at quarter of three you and I are going to be in Dr. Susan Chandler's office. I assume you listened to the program?"

"Yes, I did, Mrs. Clausen."

"I intend to speak to that young woman who phoned in."

Jane Clausen replaced the receiver. Ever since she heard how little time she had left, she had contented herself that this terrible sense of loss soon would be over. But now she felt a blazing new need—to make sure that no other mother experienced the pain *she* had felt these past three years.

IN THE cab on the way back to her office Susan Chandler mentally reviewed the appointments she had scheduled for the day. In less than an hour, at one, she was supposed to conduct a psychological evaluation of a seventh grader who was showing signs of moderate depression. An hour later she was seeing a sixty-five-year-old woman who was about to retire and as a result was spending sleepless nights gripped with anxiety.

And at three o'clock she hoped she would be meeting the woman who called herself Karen. She had sounded so frightened when she phoned, though, that Susan worried she might change her mind. What did she have to be afraid of? Susan wondered.

As Susan opened the door to her office, her secretary, Janet, greeted her with an approving smile. "Good program, Doctor."

"Thanks," Susan said. "Any important messages?"

"Yes. Your sister phoned from the airport. She said she was sorry she missed you yesterday. She wanted to apologize for exploding at you Saturday. She also wanted to know what you thought of Alexander Wright. She met him at your dad's party after you left. She says he's terribly attractive." Janet handed her a message note.

Susan thought of the man who had overheard her father asking her to call him Charles. Fortyish, about six feet, sandy hair, an engaging smile. He had come over to her when her father turned away to greet a new arrival. "Don't let it get you down. It was probably Binky's idea," he had said encouragingly. "Let's get some champagne and go outside."

It had been one of those glorious early fall afternoons, and they stood on the terrace, languidly sipping from fluted glasses.

Susan asked Alex Wright how he knew her father.

"I didn't until today," he explained. "But I've known Binky for years." Then he asked her what she did and raised his eyebrows when she said she was a clinical psychologist.

"I'm really not so out of touch," he explained hurriedly. "It's just that I hear clinical psychologist and think of a rather serious older person, not a young and extremely attractive woman such as you, and the two things don't go together."

She was dressed in a dark green wool crepe sheath accented with an apple-green scarf.

"Most of my Sunday afternoons are spent in a bulky sweater and jeans," she told him. "Is that a more comfortable picture?"

Anxious to be away from the sight of her father gushing over Binky, and not anxious to run into her sister, Susan had left soon afterward—though not before one of her friends told her that Alex Wright was the son of the late Alexander Wright, the legendary philanthropist. "Wright Library, Wright Museum of Art, Wright

Center for the Performing Arts. Big, *big* bucks!" she had whispered.

Now Susan studied the message left by Dee. He *is* very attractive, Susan thought. Hmmm.

WHEN Susan's second patient left at quarter of three, Janet appeared with a container of chicken soup and a package of crackers. Less than a minute later Janet informed her that Regina Clausen's mother and her attorney, Douglas Layton, were in the reception area.

"I'll see them in the conference room," Susan said.

Impeccably dressed in a black suit, gray hair perfectly coiffed, Jane Clausen had about her an air of reserve that suggested breeding.

The lawyer, who had been so sharp on the telephone this morning, seemed almost apologetic. "Dr. Chandler, I hope we're not intruding. Mrs. Clausen has something important to show you, and she'd very much like having the opportunity to meet the woman who called in on your program this morning."

Susan detected a tinge of red beneath his deep tan. She glanced at her watch. It was ten of three. "Mrs. Clausen, I'm not sure the woman will show up. I'm going to see her in my office, and after I find out what she may know, I'll ask her to consider speaking with you. But if she does not agree, I can't allow you to infringe on her privacy."

Jane Clausen opened her purse, reached inside, and pulled out a turquoise band. "My daughter had this ring in her stateroom on the *Gabrielle*. I found it when her possessions were returned to me. Please show it to Karen. If it's like the one she has, she simply *must* talk to me." She handed the ring to Susan.

"Look at the inscription," Layton said.

Susan peered at the tiny lettering, squinting, turning it until she could read the words. She gasped and turned back to the woman who stood waiting. "Please sit down, Mrs. Clausen. My secretary will bring you tea or coffee. And just pray that Karen shows up."

"I'm afraid I can't stay," Layton said hurriedly. "Mrs. Clausen, I'm so sorry, but I was unable to cancel my appointment."

"I understand, Douglas." There was a slight but distinct edge in the woman's voice. "The car is waiting for me. I'll be fine."

SUSAN WATCHED WITH increasing frustration as the hands of the clock crawled to five after three, then ten after. Quarter past became three thirty, then quarter of four. She went to the conference room. Jane Clausen's face was ashen. She's in physical pain, Susan realized.

"I could use that tea now, if the offer is still open, Dr. Chandler," Mrs. Clausen said. Only a faint tremor in her voice revealed her acute disappointment.

AT FOUR o'clock Carolyn Wells was walking down Eighty-first Street toward the post office, a manila envelope addressed to Susan Chandler under her arm. Any temptation to keep the appointment with Dr. Susan had disappeared when her husband, Justin, phoned at one thirty.

"Honey, the craziest thing," he had said, a joking tone in his voice. "Barbara, the receptionist, had the radio on this morning, listening to some call-in advice program. Anyway, she said some woman named Karen was one of the callers and she sounded a lot like you and talked about meeting a guy on a cruise two years ago. Anything you haven't told me?"

Carolyn laughed it off, assuring Justin that she didn't have time to listen to the radio in the middle of the day. But given his past history of almost obsessive jealousy, she worried that she hadn't heard the last of this. Now all she wanted to do was to get this ring and this photo out of her life for good.

The traffic was unusually heavy, even for that time of day. At Park Avenue she waited at the front of an impatient throng of pedestrians as cars and vans spun around the corner.

A delivery van was turning, its brakes screeching. Instinctively she tried to step back, away from the curb. She could not retreat. Someone was standing directly behind her, blocking her way. Suddenly she felt a hand grab the envelope from under her arm just as another hand shoved against the small of her back.

Carolyn teetered on the edge of the sidewalk. Half turning, she glimpsed a familiar face and managed to whisper "No" as she tumbled forward and under the wheels of the van.

He HAD WAITED FOR HER outside the building in which Susan Chandler had her office. As the minutes ticked by and she still failed to appear, his emotions ran the gamut from relief to irritation—relief that she wasn't going to show up, and anger that he now would have to track her down.

Fortunately, he remembered her name and knew where she lived, so when Carolyn Wells didn't show up at Susan Chandler's office, he phoned her home and then hung up when she answered. He had gone to the Metropolitan Museum of Art and sat on the steps with the small crowd of students and tourists who were hanging around even though it was closed. From there he had a clear view of her apartment building.

At four o'clock his patience had been rewarded. She emerged carrying a small manila envelope under her arm.

The weather was so pleasant that the streets were filled with pedestrians. He had been able to walk closely behind her and even make out a few letters of the printing on the envelope: DR. SU . . .

He guessed that the envelope contained the ring and picture she had talked about when she called in to the program. He knew he had to stop her before she reached the post office. His opportunity came at the corner of Park and Eighty-first.

Carolyn had half turned when he shoved her, and their eyes met. She had known him as Owen Adams, a British businessman. On that trip he had sported a mustache and an auburn wig. Even so, he was sure he saw a flicker of recognition just before she fell.

With satisfaction he remembered the shrieks as observers watched her body disappear under the wheels of the van. It had been easy then to slip away, the envelope now hidden under his jacket.

He waited until he was in the safety of his office, with the doors locked, before he ripped open the envelope.

The ring and picture were enclosed in a plastic bag. There was no letter or note with them. He studied the picture carefully, remembering exactly where it had been taken—aboard ship in the grand salon, at the captain's cocktail party for the newcomers who had joined the cruise in Haifa. Of course he had avoided the ritual of having his picture taken with the captain, but clearly he had been careless. In circling his prey, he had made the mistake of getting too close to Carolyn and had ended up within camera range. He had sensed that aura of sadness about her, something he always required.

He looked carefully at the photograph. Even though he was in profile, the mustache obvious, someone studying that picture with a trained eye might recognize him.

He tossed the picture into the shredder and watched it transformed into unrecognizable strips. He slipped the ring on his pinkie finger. He admired it, looked closer, then frowned and reached for a handkerchief with which to polish it.

Another woman would very soon have the privilege of wearing this same ring, he told himself.

He smiled briefly as he thought of his next, his final, victim.

IT WAS four fifty when Justin Wells returned to his office in the architectural firm of Benner, Pierce and Wells, and tried to get back to work. In a characteristic gesture he ran his hand through his dark hair. Then he dropped his pen, shoved back his chair, and stood up. A big man, he nonetheless moved from the drafting table with easy, swift grace. She'll be furious if she finds out what I'm doing, he told himself as his fingers restlessly moved toward the phone on his desk.

Maybe Barbara, his receptionist, was wrong, he thought. Maybe it wasn't Carolyn who called in to that radio show. But Carolyn's voice was distinctive—well modulated, with a hint of an English accent thanks to childhood summers spent in England.

Justin shook his head. *"I have to know,"* he whispered.

He dialed the radio station and was put through to the office of Jed Geany, the producer of *Ask Dr. Susan.*

He gave the flimsy excuse that his mother had missed the program and he wanted a tape for her. Then, when asked if he wanted a tape for the whole program, he botched his story by blurting out, "Oh, just the listener call-ins," and then tried to correct himself by hurriedly adding, "I mean that's Mother's favorite part, but please make a tape of the whole program."

To make matters worse, Jed Geany himself got on the phone to say that they were glad to oblige, because it was good to hear that a listener was so involved. Then he asked for the name and address.

Feeling guilty and wretched, Justin Wells gave his name and the office address.

He had barely hung up when he received a call from Lenox Hill Hospital informing him that his wife had been gravely injured in an automobile accident.

3

WHEN Susan stopped by Nedda's office at six o'clock, she found her about to lock up her desk for the night.

"How about a glass of vino?" Nedda asked.

"Sounds like a great idea. I'll get it." Susan went down the corridor to the closet-size kitchen and opened the refrigerator. A bottle of pinot grigio was cooling there.

She opened the bottle, poured wine into two glasses, and returned to Nedda's office. "Cocktail hour," she announced.

Nedda looked at her steadily. "You're the psychologist, but if I can offer a nonprofessional opinion, you look pretty down."

Susan nodded. "I guess I am." She filled Nedda in on the angry phone call from Douglas Layton, as well as on the call on the program from the woman who identified herself as Karen, and then on Jane Clausen's surprise visit.

"I'm surprised about Doug Layton," Nedda said. "When I spoke to him, he didn't seem at all upset about the program."

"Well, he changed his mind," Susan said. "He came to my office with Mrs. Clausen, but he didn't stay. He said he had an appointment he couldn't break."

"If I were he, I'd have broken the appointment," Nedda said dryly. "Last year Jane made him a trustee of the Clausen Family

Trust. What was so important that he would leave her alone here, especially knowing that Jane might have been about to meet someone who could possibly describe the man responsible for her daughter's disappearance, perhaps even her murder?"

DONALD Richards's sprawling apartment on Central Park West was both his home and office. The rooms he used to see patients were accessible by a separate entrance from the corridor. The five rooms he reserved for himself had the distinctly masculine flavor of a home that had not known a woman's touch for a very long time. It had been four years since his wife, Kathy, a top model, died while on a photo shoot in the Catskills.

He was not there when it happened. Still, he had never stopped blaming himself. Most certainly he had never gotten over it.

The canoe in which Kathy was posing overturned. The boat with the photographer and his assistants was twenty feet away. The heavy turn-of-the-century gown she was wearing pulled her under before anyone could reach her.

Divers never recovered her body. "Even in summer that lake is so deep that it's icy on the bottom," he was told. He dreamed of her frequently. Sometimes he saw her lying trapped under a rocky ledge in the frigid water. At other times the dream changed. Her face dissolved, and others replaced it. And they all whispered, "It was your fault."

Following the *Ask Dr. Susan* program, he went directly home. Rena, his housekeeper, had lunch waiting when he got in.

As he ate, Don thought about Karen, the woman who had phoned during the broadcast. It was an intriguing situation. Regina Clausen had disappeared three years ago. The woman who called herself Karen had talked about being involved in a shipboard romance only two years ago. Clearly, Susan Chandler would make the inevitable connection that if only one man was involved with both these women, he might still be targeting victims.

Susan is stirring up a hornet's nest for herself, Donald Richards mused. He wondered what to do about it.

IN THE PLANE ON HER WAY back to California, Dee Chandler Harriman sipped a Perrier, slipped off her sandals, and leaned back, causing her honey-blond hair to spill around her shoulders. Long used to admiring glances, she deliberately avoided meeting the gaze of the man across the aisle who had twice attempted to start a conversation. There was no one seated next to her in the second row, for which she was grateful.

She had reached New York on Friday afternoon, stayed at the apartment her Belle Aire Modeling Agency maintained in the Essex House, and quietly met with two young models she was hoping to sign up. The meetings had gone well.

Too bad she couldn't say the same about Saturday, when she had gone to visit her mother. I shouldn't have been so nasty to Susan, she reflected. She's the one who was there with Mother, and who took the brunt of the separation and divorce.

But at least she's educated, Dee thought. Here I am at thirty-seven, thankful to have a high school diploma. But then from the time I was seventeen, the only thing I knew was modeling. They should have insisted I go to college. The two smart moves I made in my life were to marry Jack and to invest my savings in the agency.

Uncomfortably, she remembered how she had railed at Susan, telling her that she didn't understand what it was like to lose a husband. I'm sorry I missed her at Dad's party yesterday, Dee thought, but I'm glad I called her this morning. I meant it when I said that Alex Wright is terrific.

A smile played on Dee's lips as she thought of the good-looking man with the warm, intelligent eyes and appealing sense of humor. He had asked if Susan was involved with anyone.

Dee missed being married. The empty feeling that had begun this past weekend threatened to deepen. She wanted to live in New York again. It was there that Susan had introduced her to Jack, a commercial photographer. Shortly after they were married, they moved to Los Angeles.

They had five years together. Then, two years ago, he'd insisted on skiing one weekend.

Dee felt tears sting her eyes. I'm sick of being lonely, she thought angrily. Hastily she fished inside her shoulder bag and found what she was looking for: a brochure describing a two-week cruise through the Panama Canal.

Why not? she asked herself. I haven't taken a real vacation in two years. Her travel agent had told her that a good cabin was still available for the next slated cruise. Yesterday her father had urged her to go. "First class. On me, honey," he promised.

The ship was sailing from Costa Rica in a week. I'm going to be on it, Dee decided.

THE urgent sense of evil Pamela Hastings experienced when she held Carolyn's turquoise ring on Friday evening still frightened her. She hadn't spoken to Carolyn since then, but as Pamela turned the key in the lock of her apartment on Madison and Sixty-seventh, she made a mental note to call her friend and tell her to get rid of the ring.

She glanced at her watch. It was ten of five. She went straight to the bedroom, exchanged her dark blue suit for comfortable clothes, fixed a Scotch, and settled down to watch the news. Her husband was on a business trip, and her daughter was away at college. This was going to be a peaceful evening, just hers alone.

At five after five she stared at the image of the cordoned-off section of Park Avenue where crowds of spectators were observing a blood-spattered van with a smashed-in grill.

In stunned disbelief Pamela listened as the off-camera commentator said, "This was the scene at Park and Eighty-first, where forty-year-old interior designer Carolyn Wells fell into the path of a speeding van. She has been rushed to Lenox Hill Hospital with multiple head and internal injuries. Our reporter at the scene spoke with several of the eyewitnesses to the accident."

As Pamela jumped to her feet, she heard the smattering of comments: "That poor woman." "Terrible that people are allowed to drive like that." Then an elderly woman shouted, "You're all blind. She was pushed!"

Pamela stared as the reporter rushed a microphone to the woman. "Would you give us your name, ma'am?"

"Hilda Johnson. I was standing near her. She had an envelope under her arm. Some guy grabbed it. Then he pushed her."

"That's crazy. She fell," another bystander yelled.

The commentator came on again. "You have just heard the testimony of one eyewitness, Hilda Johnson, who claimed she saw a man push Carolyn Wells in front of the van just as he yanked what appeared to be an envelope from under her arm. While Ms. Johnson's report varies from the observations of all others at the scene, the police say they will take her statement into consideration. If her story holds up, it would mean that what seems to be a tragic accident is in fact a potential homicide."

Pamela ran for her coat, and fifteen minutes later she was sitting beside Justin Wells in the waiting room outside the intensive care unit of Lenox Hill Hospital. She slipped her hand into his.

"She's in surgery," Justin said, his tone flat and emotionless.

Three hours later a doctor came in to speak to them. "Your wife is in a coma," he told Justin. "It's simply too soon to tell if she's going to make it. But she seemed to be calling for someone. It sounded like Win. Who would that be?"

Pamela felt Justin's hand grip hers violently as in an anguished voice he haltingly whispered, "I don't know. I don't know."

THE sight of the crumpled, bleeding body on the pavement, the elegant suit marked with tire tracks, made eighty-year-old Hilda Johnson feel faint, but she recovered enough to speak to the reporter. Then she turned and with great difficulty made her way home to her apartment on East Eightieth Street. Once inside, she made tea and, hands shaking, sipped it slowly.

"That poor girl," she kept murmuring as she relived the incident over and over again. At least she had gotten a good look at the man before he disappeared through the crowd.

Finally she felt she had the strength to call the police station. The desk sergeant who answered was one she had spoken to several times in the past, usually when she reported panhandlers approaching pedestrians on Third Avenue. He listened to her story patiently.

"Hilda, you're mistaken," he said soothingly. "We already talked to a lot of the people who were on that corner when the accident happened. The press of the crowd when the light turned green caused Mrs. Wells to lose her balance, that's all."

"The pressure of a hand on her back deliberately pushing her forward caused her to fall," Hilda snapped. "I'll be in to see Captain Shea tomorrow morning. Eight o'clock sharp."

She hung up indignantly. It was only five o'clock, but she needed to go to bed. She felt a tightness in her chest that only a nitroglycerin tablet under her tongue and bed rest would ease.

A few minutes later she was dressed in her warm nightgown, her head propped up on the thick pillow that aided her breathing. The darting headache and chest pain were fading.

Hilda sighed with relief. A good night's rest, and she would go to the police station to give Captain Shea an earful and register a complaint about that boneheaded sergeant. Then she would insist on sitting down with the police artist and describing the man who had pushed that woman. Vile thing, she thought, remembering his face. The worst kind—well dressed, classy-looking, the type of person you would think you could trust.

That lunkhead sergeant had treated her like she was a child. Her final thought as she began to doze off was that in the morning she'd stir them all up. Sleep overcame her just as she began to say a Hail Mary for the gravely injured Carolyn Wells.

WHEN Susan left Nedda's office, she walked home through the twilight to her apartment on Downing Street. The penetrating chill of the early morning had returned. She picked up her pace.

She turned in to her own building, a three-story brownstone, and began the climb to her apartment on the top floor. It had a large living room, generous kitchen, oversized bedroom, and small den. Handsomely and comfortably furnished with the items her mother had offered when she moved to a luxury condo, it always felt warm and welcoming to Susan—almost like a physical embrace.

Tonight the place felt particularly soothing, Susan reflected, flipping the switch that turned on the gas-burning log fire in the fireplace. An at-home night, she decided emphatically as she changed into an aging velour caftan. She would make herself a salad and pasta and pour a glass of Chianti.

A short time later, as she was rinsing watercress, the phone rang. "Susan, how's my girl?"

It was her father. "I'm fine, Dad," Susan said, then grimaced. "I mean, I'm fine, Charles."

"Binky and I were sorry you had to leave so soon yesterday. You certainly caught Alex Wright's eye. He kept talking about you."

"I thought he seemed like a nice guy."

"He's a lot more than that. The Wright family is up there with the best of them. Let me put Binky on. She wants to tell you something."

Why me? Susan thought as the phone was handed over. Her stepmother's trilling "Hello" grated on her ear.

Before Susan could respond, Binky began to sing the praises of Alexander Wright. "I've known him for years, darling," she chirped. "Just the kind of man Charles and I envision you or Dee with. Never married, late thirties, and he's on everyone's A-list. He's on the board of the Wright Family Foundation. They give away tons of money every year. The most generous, most philanthropic person you'd ever want to meet. Not like these selfish people who only care for themselves."

I can't *believe* you said that, Susan thought.

"Darling, I did something that I hope you won't mind. Alex just phoned and practically demanded I give him your home number."

"I'd rather you didn't give out my home number, Binky," Susan said stiffly, then softened. "But in this case, I suppose it's all right."

She managed to cut short Binky's gushing reassurances and hung up feeling as though her evening had suddenly turned sour.

Less than ten minutes later Alexander Wright phoned. "I put the hit on Binky for your home number. I hope that was okay."

"I know," Susan said. "Charles and Binky just called."

"Why don't you refer to your father as Dad when we talk? It's okay with me."

Susan laughed. "You're very perceptive. I will do that."

"I caught your program today and thoroughly enjoyed it."

Susan was surprised to realize that she was pleased.

"I was seated at the same table as Regina Clausen at a Futures Industry dinner six or seven years ago. She struck me as a lovely person." Wright hesitated, then said apologetically, "I know this is last-minute, but I just finished a board of directors meeting at St. Clare's Hospital, and I'm hungry. If you haven't had dinner and don't have plans, could I possibly interest you in going out?"

Susan agreed to be picked up in about twenty minutes.

As she walked to the bedroom to change to a cashmere sweater and slacks, she convinced herself that the real reason she was going on this impromptu date was to hear any impressions Alex Wright might be able to offer about Regina Clausen.

4

ALEXANDER Wright spotted his car double-parked outside St. Clare's Hospital and was in the back seat before his driver was able to get out and open the door for him.

"A long meeting, sir," Jim Curley volunteered as he started the engine. "Where to now?" He spoke with the familiarity of a longtime employee, having been with the Wright family for thirty years.

"Jim, I'm happy to say that as of five minutes ago we're picking up a very attractive lady on Downing Street and going on to dinner at Il Mulino," Wright answered.

As the car made its way through the slow Ninth Avenue traffic, Curley glanced several times in the rearview mirror, observing with some concern that his boss had closed his eyes and leaned his head back against the soft leather of the headrest.

Whoever said that it can be as hard to give away money as it is to earn it was right, Curley thought compassionately. He knew that as chairman of the Alexander and Virginia Wright Family Foundation, Mr. Alex was constantly besieged by individuals and organizations pleading for grants. And he was so nice to everyone. Probably much too generous as well. Nothing like his father.

I hope this lady on Downing Street is fun, he thought. Alex Wright deserves to have some fun. He works too hard.

As USUAL, Il Mulino was busy. The scent of good food mingled with the cheerful voices of the diners. The overflowing harvest basket of vegetables at the entrance gave a countrylike coziness to the restaurant's simple decor.

The maître d' escorted them to a table. Alexander Wright immediately ordered a bottle of Chianti and one of chardonnay. At Susan's look of consternation he laughed. "You don't have to have more than a glass or two, but I promise you, you'll enjoy sipping both. I'm going to be honest. I skipped lunch, and I'm starving. Do you mind if we look at the menu right away?"

Susan decided on a salad and salmon. He chose oysters, pasta, and veal. "The pasta is what I would have had for lunch," he said.

As the captain poured wine, Susan raised her eyebrows. "I cannot believe that only an hour ago I was in my favorite, somewhat ragged caftan, planning a quiet evening at home," she told him.

"You could have worn the caftan," he suggested.

"Only if I was trying to impress you," she said, eliciting a laugh from Wright.

She studied him as he waved at someone across the room. He was dressed in a dark gray suit, a crisp white shirt, and a small-patterned gray-and-red tie. He was attractive and impressive.

Something was puzzling her about him. Alex Wright had the authority and poise that were the products of generations of breeding, but there was something else that intrigued her. I think he's a little shy, she decided. *That's* what it is. She liked that about him.

"I'm glad I went to the party yesterday," he told her quietly. "I'd decided to stay home and do the *Times* puzzle, but I'd accepted the invitation and didn't want to be rude. I want you to know I'm grateful to you for coming out to dine with me on such short notice."

"You said you've known Binky quite a long time?"

"Yes, but only the way you know people who go to the same parties. Small ones. I can't stand the biggies. I hope I'm not stepping on your toes when I say she's an airhead."

"A very *persuasive* airhead," Susan said ruefully. "What do you think of that Disney castle my father built for her?"

They laughed.

"But you're still hurt and uncomfortable about the situation?" he suggested.

When you don't want to give an answer, ask a question, Susan reminded herself. "You've met my father and sister," she countered. "What about you? Any siblings?"

He told her that he was an only child, the product of a late marriage. "My father was too busy making money to court anyone until he was in his forties," he explained. "Then he was too busy amassing wealth to pay much attention to me or my mother. But I must assure you that with the human misery I hear about every day at the foundation, I count myself very lucky."

"In the grand scheme of things, you are," Susan agreed. "Me too."

It wasn't until they were sipping espresso that Regina Clausen's name came up. Alex Wright couldn't tell her very much more than what he had said on the phone. He'd sat at the same table as Regina at a Futures Industry dinner. He found her to be a quiet, intelligent lady. It seemed impossible to think that someone with her background could just disappear.

"Do you put any stock in that call you got on the program?" he asked. "The one from the woman who sounded so nervous?"

Susan had decided that she would not discuss with anyone the ring Regina Clausen's mother had given her. That ring, with the same "You belong to me" inscription "Karen" had mentioned, was the only tangible object that might link Regina's disappearance and Karen's experience with a shipboard friendship.

"I just don't know," she told him. "It's too early to be sure."

"How did you ever happen to do a radio program in the first place?" he asked.

She found herself telling him how Nedda had introduced her to the former host, and about quitting her job in the Westchester County District Attorney's Office and going back to school.

Finally, over brandy, Susan said, "I'm the one who's usually the listener. Enough about me. *Much* too much about me, in fact."

Wright signaled for the check. "Not nearly enough," he said.

HILDA Johnson awoke at ten thirty p.m. feeling both refreshed and hungry. A cup of tea and a piece of toast would go down well, she decided, sitting up and reaching for her robe.

As she knotted the belt of her chenille robe, Hilda mentally reviewed the face of the man whom she had seen push Mrs. Wells. Now that the shock had worn off, she could remember his face even more clearly than she had seemed to at the time. In the morning she would give the police sketch artist a complete description of the man. His eyes had been far apart, and they narrowed as he focused on Carolyn Wells, his lashes long, his chin determined.

Hilda went into the kitchen to fill the kettle. She had just lit the gas beneath it when the buzzer sounded from downstairs. Who in the world was it at this hour? she wondered as she went into the tiny foyer and picked up the receiver of the intercom.

"Who is it?" She did not attempt to conceal her irritation.

"Miss Johnson, I'm so sorry to disturb you." The man's voice was low and pleasant. "I'm Detective Anders. We have a suspect in custody who may be the person you saw push Mrs. Wells."

"I thought no one believed me when I said someone pushed her," Hilda snapped.

"We didn't want it to leak that we were on the tail of a suspect. May I come up for just a minute?"

"I guess so." Hilda pushed the buzzer that unlocked the lobby door. She waited until Detective Anders rang the bell before she opened the door. Must be getting cold, she thought. His coat collar was turned up, and he wore a slouch hat pulled down low on his forehead. Plus he was wearing gloves.

"This will only take a minute, Miss Johnson," he said.

"Come in," Hilda said briskly. As she led the way to the living room, she did not hear the soft click of the closing door.

"I've got something to show you, Miss Johnson." The visitor laid down a driver's license with a photo ID.

Hilda gasped. "That's the face! That's the man I saw push that woman and grab the envelope."

For the first time, she looked directly up at Detective Anders. He had removed his hat, and his coat collar was no longer turned up around his neck.

Hilda's eyes widened in shock. Her mouth opened, but the only sound that came from it was a faint murmur. "Oh, no!" Her face went ghastly pale as she realized that she was trapped.

Beseechingly she raised her hands. Then in futile protest she turned her palms outward to shield herself from the knife her visitor was about to plunge into her chest.

He jumped back to avoid the spurting blood, then watched as her body sagged and crumpled to the threadbare carpet. A fixed, staring look began to settle in Hilda's eyes, but she managed to murmur, "God . . . won't . . . let you . . . get . . . away."

As he reached over her to take his driver's license, her body shuddered violently and her hand fell on his shoe.

Shaking the hand off, he walked calmly to the door, opened it, checked the hallway, and in four paces was at the fire exit staircase. When he reached the lobby, he opened that door a crack, saw no one coming, and an instant later was heading home.

Had her dying words put a curse on him? he wondered. They reminded him of the mistake he had made earlier today—the mistake that Susan Chandler, with her trained prosecutor's mind, might just possibly uncover.

He knew he couldn't let that happen.

SUSAN'S SLEEP WAS RESTLESS, filled with troubling dreams. When she awoke, she remembered fragments of scenes in which Jane Clausen and Dee and Jack and she were all present. At one point Jane Clausen had been pleading, "Susan, I want Regina," while Dee stretched out her hand and said, "Susan, I want Jack."

Well, you *had* him, Susan thought. She got out of bed and stretched, hoping to relieve the familiar clutch at her heart. It bothered her deeply that after all these years a dream like that could bring the memories flooding back. Memories of herself at twenty-three, a law student working part-time for Nedda. Jack, a twenty-eight-year-old commercial photographer, just beginning to make a name for himself. The two of them in love.

Enter Dee. Big sister. Darling of fashion photographers. Sophisticated. Amusing. Charming. Men in line wanting to marry her, but she had wanted Jack.

Susan went into the bathroom. She brushed her teeth briskly, as if by that action she could obliterate the bitter aftertaste. The crazy part, she thought, is that Dee and Jack were right for each other. They loved each other. Maybe even too much.

Susan turned on the hot water in the shower. On the other hand, she thought, if Jack and I had ended up together, I might have been caught in the avalanche and be dead too. Dee hates the cold, but I surely would have been on that slope with him.

By seven thirty Susan was having breakfast. She turned on *Good Day, New York* to catch the news. Not long after, a reporter began talking about an elderly woman who had been stabbed to death in her Upper East Side apartment. Susan was just about to turn off the TV, when the anchorman replayed the segment from the previous evening's news that included the report where Hilda Johnson, the murder victim, claimed that the woman who had been run over on Park Avenue was deliberately pushed during a mugging.

Susan stared at the television, realizing that the prosecutor in her was refusing to believe these two events were coincidental, while the psychologist in her was wondering what kind of out-of-control mind could commit *two* such brutal crimes.

HE SLEPT ONLY FITFULLY, awaking several times during the night. Each time, he turned on the TV, tuned to the local news station, and each time he heard the same thing: Carolyn Wells, the woman who had been run over at Park Avenue and Eighty-first Street, was in a coma; her condition was critical.

He knew that if by some unlucky circumstance she recovered, she would tell people that she had been pushed by Owen Adams, a man she met while on a cruise.

They couldn't trace Owen Adams to him. Of that he was certain. The British passport, like all the ones he used on his special journeys, was a fake. No, the real danger lay in the fact that he had been recognized by Carolyn Wells yesterday. Which meant that if she recovered, it wasn't impossible that they might run into each other in New York again someday. In a face-to-face situation she would recognize him again.

That must never happen. She could not be allowed to recover.

On the news at nine it was announced that an elderly woman had been found stabbed to death in her Upper East Side apartment. He braced himself for the anchorman's next words.

"As was reported yesterday, the murder victim, Hilda Johnson, claimed to have seen someone deliberately push the woman who was hit by a van at Park and Eighty-first yesterday."

Frowning, he pointed the remote control and turned off the television. If the police tied Hilda Johnson's death to Carolyn Wells's supposed accident, there would be a media stampede. It might even come out that Carolyn Wells was the one who phoned Susan Chandler's program and talked about a souvenir ring with the inscription "You belong to me." The little gnome who ran that rattrap of a cut-rate souvenir store in Greenwich Village might remember that on several occasions a particular gentleman whose name he knew had come in to purchase turquoise rings with the same inscription.

When he was young, he had heard the story of a woman who confessed to spreading scandal and was told that as her penance, she was to cut open a feather pillow on a windswept day, then retrieve all the feathers that were scattered. When she said it was impossible, she was told that it was just as impossible to find and correct all the people who had heard her lies.

It was a story that had amused him at the time, but now he thought of the feather pillow story in a different context. Pieces were escaping from the scenario he had planned so carefully.

Carolyn Wells. Hilda Johnson. Susan Chandler. The gnome.

He was safe from Hilda Johnson. But the other three were still like feathers in the wind.

5

 IT WAS one of those golden October mornings that some-times follow a particularly chilly day. The air felt fresh, and everything seemed to glow. Donald Richards decided to enjoy the morning by walking the distance between Central Park West and Eighty-eighth Street and the WOR radio studio at Forty-first and Broadway.

He was twenty minutes early for the program and was told by the receptionist that he could wait in the greenroom. In the corridor he ran into the producer, Jed Geany.

Geany gave him a quick greeting and was ready to rush past, when Richards stopped him. "I didn't think to ask for a tape of yesterday's program for my files," he said. "I'll be glad to pay for it, of course. Oh, and could you run one today as well?"

Geany shrugged. "Sure. Actually, I'm about to make a tape of yesterday's program for some guy who phoned in. Says he wants it for his mother. I'll run one for you too."

Geany held up the envelope he already had addressed. "Justin Wells. Why does that name sound familiar? I've been racking my brain trying to remember where I've heard it."

Donald Richards opted not to reply, but he had to force himself not to show how startled he was. He thought back to the one visit he had from Justin Wells. It had been the usual exploratory session, and Wells never came back.

Richards remembered that he had phoned Wells, urging him to get into treatment, saying that he needed help, a lot of help.

FOR the first part of Susan's radio program she and Dr. Donald Richards discussed how women could protect themselves and avoid getting into potentially dangerous situations.

"Look," Richards said, "most women realize that if they park their cars in a dark, unattended lot, they're risking big trouble. On the other hand, those same women can be careless when at home. The way life is today, if you leave your doors unlocked, no matter how seemingly safe the neighborhood is, you're increasing your chances that you'll be the victim of a burglary, or perhaps worse."

He has a nice manner, Susan thought. He's not preachy.

At the next commercial she told him, "I think I'd better look over my shoulder if I want to keep my job. You're good on air."

"Well, I'm finding I enjoy it," he acknowledged. "Although I have to admit that when I finish the publicity tour for this book, I'll be glad to go back to my mundane world."

"Not too mundane, I bet. Don't you do a lot of traveling?"

"A fair amount. I testify as an expert witness internationally."

"Ten seconds, Susan," the producer warned from the booth.

It was time to take calls from the listeners.

The first one was an inquiry about yesterday's show: "Did Karen keep her appointment at your office, Dr. Susan?"

"No, she did not," Susan said, "but if she's listening, I'm going to ask her please to get in touch with me, even if only by phone."

Several calls were directed to Donald Richards. Then Susan announced, "Our next call is from Tiffany in Yonkers. You're on, Tiffany."

"Dr. Susan, I love your program. I was listening yesterday, and you remember how that woman, Karen, talked about getting a souvenir turquoise ring from some guy and said that the inside of the band was inscribed 'You belong to me'?"

"Yes, I do," Susan said quickly. "Do you know something about the man?"

Tiffany began to giggle. "Only that he must be some cheapskate. Dr. Susan, my boyfriend bought a ring just like that for me as a joke one day last year when we were in Greenwich Village. It looked good, but it cost all of ten dollars."

"Where in the Village did you buy it?" Susan asked.

"I don't remember exactly. One of those dumpy souvenir stores that sell plastic Statues of Liberty and brass elephants."

"Tiffany, if you do remember where it was, or if any of our other listeners know, please call me," Susan urged.

"The little guy who runs the shop told us he made the rings himself," Tiffany said. "Listen, I broke up with my boyfriend, so you can have the ring. I'll mail it to you."

"Commercial," Jed warned into Susan's earphones.

"Many thanks, Tiffany," Susan said hurriedly. "And now for a message from our sponsors."

The moment the program was over, Donald Richards stood up. "Again, thanks, Susan, and forgive me if I rush off. I have a client waiting." Then he hesitated. "I'd like to have dinner with you sometime," he said quietly. "I'll call you at your office."

He was gone. Susan sat for a moment thinking about the last call. Was it possible that the souvenir ring Jane Clausen found among Regina's possessions had been purchased in the city? Did that mean the man responsible for her disappearance was from New York?

Deep in concentration, she got up and went into the control room. Geany was putting a cassette into an envelope. "Richards got out fast," he said. "I guess he forgot he had asked me to make tapes of the programs." He shrugged. "So I'll mail them with this one." He pointed to the envelope addressed to Justin Wells. "That guy phoned yesterday to get a tape of the program. Said his mother missed it."

"Flattering," Susan observed. "See you tomorrow."

In the cab on the way back to the office, she opened the newspaper. On page 3 of the *Post* there was a picture of Carolyn Wells, an interior designer who had been injured in the accident yesterday afternoon on Park Avenue. Susan read the story with keen interest. Further down the column she read, "Husband, well-known architect Justin Wells . . ."

A moment later she was on the cell phone to the station. She caught Jed Geany just as he was leaving for lunch. He agreed to send the package addressed to Justin Wells to her by messenger.

Susan mentally reviewed her day. She had back-to-back appointments all afternoon. But after that she would take the tape to Lenox Hill Hospital, where, according to the newspaper, Justin Wells was keeping vigil at his wife's bedside.

He may not want to talk to me, Susan thought, but there's no question—whatever reason he has for wanting a tape of yesterday's program, it isn't because his mother missed it.

JANE Clausen was not sure if she would be well enough to attend the board meeting of the Clausen Family Trust. It had been a pain-filled night, and she longed to spend the day resting quietly at home. Only the haunting knowledge that her time was running out gave her the drive necessary to get up and bathe and dress.

As she sipped coffee, she thought back to the previous afternoon. Her disappointment that Karen had not kept the appointment at Dr. Chandler's office continued to grow. Jane had many questions for the woman: What did the man you met look like? Did you have a sense of danger? Jane knew that Regina had a keen intuition. If she had met a man and been attracted enough to change her itinerary, he must have appeared to be aboveboard.

"Aboveboard." And now that word was bothering her because it raised questions about Douglas.

Douglas Layton bore a name of distinction, one that guaranteed his background. Jane Clausen had known the Philadelphia Laytons when they were quite young, but had lost touch over the years. Still, she remembered them well, and several times lately, when he mentioned them, Doug had mixed up their names. She had to wonder how close he really was to them.

Doug's scholastic background was excellent. There was no question he was very intelligent.

So what *is* bothering me? Jane Clausen asked herself.

It was what happened yesterday, she decided. It was the fact that Douglas Layton was too busy with someone else to wait with her at Dr. Chandler's office. She was sure he had been lying about his so-called appointment. But *why?*

This morning at the trustees' meeting they were going to decide on a number of substantial grants. It's hard to accept the recommendations of someone you are having doubts about, Jane Clausen thought. If Regina were here, we'd talk this over together. Regina used to say, "Two heads are better than one, Mother."

Susan Chandler. Remembering the compassion in Susan's eyes, Jane thought of how strong a liking she had taken to the young psychologist. She's both wise and kind. I've never had much use for the business of rushing to therapists, but she came across immediately as a friend. She knew how disappointed I was yesterday.

Jane Clausen stood up. It was time to go to the meeting. This afternoon I'll phone Dr. Chandler and make an appointment to see her, she decided.

She smiled as she thought, I know Regina would approve.

I MUST *go down to the seas again . . .*

The cadence of the words was a drumbeat in his head. He could see himself on the pier, showing his identification to a courteous crew member, hearing his greeting—"Welcome aboard, sir!"— walking up the metal gangway, being shown to his cabin.

He always took only the best accommodations, first class, with a private veranda. Once his presence had been established, he was free to prowl and select his prey.

The first voyage of that kind had been four years ago. Now the journey was almost over. Just one more to go. And it was time to find her. There were a number of appropriate ships going to the place that had been ordained for the death of this last lonely lady. He had decided on the identity he would assume, that of an investor who had been raised in Belgium, the son of an American mother and British diplomat father.

He couldn't wait to live the new role, to find the one, to let her fate be joined to Regina's, whose body, weighted with stones, rested beneath the busy waterway that was Kowloon bay—to meld her story with that of Veronica, whose bones were rotting in the Valley of the Kings; with Constance, who had replaced Carolyn in Algiers; with Monica in London; with all these sisters in death.

I must go down to the seas again. But first there was unfinished business to be attended to. This morning, listening once more to Dr. Susan's program, he decided that one of the feathers in the wind needed to be removed immediately.

IT HAD been fifty years since Abdul Parki first arrived in America, a shy, slender sixteen-year-old from New Delhi. Immediately he had begun working in his uncle's tiny souvenir shop on MacDougal Street in Greenwich Village. Now Abdul was the owner, but little else had changed. The store might have been frozen in time. Even the sign reading KHYEM SPECIALTY SHOP was an exact duplicate of the one his uncle had hung.

Abdul was still slender, and though he had of necessity overcome his shyness, he had a natural reserve that kept him distant from his customers. The only ones he ever talked to were those who appreciated the skill and effort he put into the inexpensive rings and bracelets he made himself. And though he had never inquired as to the reason, Abdul wondered about the man who came back on three different occasions to purchase turquoise rings with the inscription "You belong to me."

It amused Abdul, who himself had been married to his late wife for forty-five years, to think that this customer regularly changed girlfriends. The last time the man had been in, his business card had fallen from his wallet. Abdul had picked it up and glanced at it before returning it. Seeing the look of displeasure on his customer's face, he had apologized, calling the customer by name. Immediately he knew he had made a second mistake.

He doesn't want me to know who he is, and now he won't come back—that had been Abdul's immediate and regretful thought. And given the fact that a year had passed without a reappearance, he suspected that to be the case.

Abdul closed the shop every day at one o'clock, then went out for lunch. On this afternoon he was just about to put the sign—CLOSED. RETURN AT 2 P.M.—on the door when his mysterious customer appeared, came inside, and greeted him warmly.

Abdul smiled. "It's good to see you again, sir."

"Good to see *you*. I thought you'd have forgotten me by now."

"Oh, no, sir." He was careful not to use the man's name.

"Bet you can't remember my name," his customer said.

"Ah, I remember it, sir," Abdul said, and proved that he did.

"Good for you," his customer said warmly. "Abdul, I need another ring. You know the one I mean. Hope you have one in stock."

"I think I have three, sir."

"Well, maybe I'll take them all. But I'm keeping you from your lunch. Before any other customers show up, why don't we put the sign out and lock the door? Otherwise you'll never get out of here."

Abdul smiled again, pleased at the thoughtfulness of this remarkably friendly old customer. Willingly he handed him the sign and watched him turn the lock. It was then he noted that even though it was a mild day, his customer was wearing gloves.

Abdul went to the glass-topped counter and removed a tray. "Two of the rings are here, sir. There's one more on my workbench. I'll get it." Quickly he walked through the curtained area into the small workplace. Three girls at once, he thought, smiling to himself.

Abdul turned, the ring in his hand, then gasped in surprise. His customer had followed him.

"Did you find the ring?"

"Right here, sir." Abdul held it out, not understanding why he suddenly felt nervous and cornered.

When he saw the sudden flash of the knife, he understood. I was right to be afraid, he thought as he felt a sharp pain and then slipped into darkness.

AT TEN MINUTES OF THREE, just as her two-o'clock patient was leaving, Susan Chandler received a call from Jane Clausen. She immediately sensed the tension lurking beneath the quiet, well-bred voice and the request for an appointment. "I mean a *professional* visit," Mrs. Clausen said. "I need to discuss some problems I'm having. I'm afraid it's very important that I see you as soon as possible, even today, if that can be arranged."

Susan had clients coming in for appointments all afternoon. After that she had intended to go immediately to Lenox Hill Hospital. Obviously that would have to wait.

"I'll be free at six o'clock, Mrs. Clausen."

As soon as she broke the connection, Susan dialed Lenox Hill Hospital, having already looked up the number. When she finally got through to an operator, she explained that she was trying to reach the husband of a woman in intensive care.

"I'll connect you to the ICU waiting room," the operator said.

A woman answered. Susan asked if Justin Wells was there.

"Who's calling?"

The media must be hounding him, Susan thought. "Dr. Susan Chandler," she said. "Mr. Wells requested a tape of a radio program I did yesterday, and I wanted to bring it to him myself if he's still going to be at the hospital at seven thirty."

From the muffled sound in her ear Susan could tell that the woman had covered the receiver with her hand. Even so, she could make out the question being asked: "Justin, did you request a tape of Dr. Susan Chandler's program yesterday?"

She could hear the answer distinctly: "That's ridiculous, Pamela. Someone's playing a sick joke."

"Dr. Chandler, I'm afraid there's been a mistake."

"I apologize," Susan said. "That was the message I received from my producer. I'm terribly sorry to have bothered Mr. Wells at a time like this. May I ask how Mrs. Wells is?"

There was a brief pause. "Pray for her, Dr. Chandler."

The connection was broken.

Susan sat for a long minute staring at the phone. Had the request for the tape been intended as a practical joke—and if so, why? Or had Justin Wells made the call and now needed to deny it to the person he addressed as Pamela? And again, if so, why?

But these questions would have to wait. Janet was already announcing the arrival of her three-o'clock client.

Doug Layton stood outside the partly opened door of the small office Jane Clausen kept for herself in the Clausen Family Trust suite in the Chrysler Building. He didn't even have to strain to hear what she was saying on the phone to Dr. Susan Chandler.

As he listened, he began to perspire. He was fairly certain that *he* was the reason Mrs. Clausen wanted to meet with Chandler.

He knew he had bungled their meeting this morning. Mrs. Clausen was already there, studying the agenda for the trust meeting when he arrived. He had brought coffee to her, planning to smooth over any irritation she might still feel. "I don't care for any coffee," she told him, her eyes cool and dismissive. "I'll see you in the boardroom."

There was one file that had drawn her attention in particular, because she brought it up at the meeting, asking a lot of tough questions. The file contained information on moneys marked for use at a facility for orphaned children in Guatemala.

I had everything under control, Doug thought angrily, and then I blundered. Like an imbecile, hoping to head off any discussion, he had said, "That orphanage was particularly important to Regina, Mrs. Clausen. She once told me that."

Doug shivered, remembering the icy gaze Jane Clausen directed at him. He had tried to cover himself by adding hastily, "I mean, you quoted her as saying that yourself at one of our first meetings."

As usual, Hubert March, the chairman, was half asleep, but the other trustees stared at him appraisingly as Jane Clausen said coldly, "No, I never said any such thing." And now she was making a date to see Dr. Chandler.

Doug went to the men's room. There he dashed cold water on his face, combed his hair, straightened his tie, and looked in the mirror.

He was grateful for his appearance—dark blond hair, steel-gray eyes, and aristocratic nose.

Doug Layton looked the part of the trusted adviser who would handle the affairs of *the late* Jane Clausen in the manner she would have wanted. And there was no question that her condition was worsening. She was dying. On her death Hubert March would turn the running of the trust over to him.

Everything had gone so well until now. In her final days Jane Clausen could not be allowed to interfere with his master plan.

6

IN YONKERS, twenty-five-year-old Tiffany Smith was still stunned that she actually had gotten through to Dr. Susan Chandler and talked to her live, on air. Tiffany was a wiry, thin, teased-blond waitress on the evening shift at the Grotto, a neighborhood trattoria. She was famous for never forgetting a customer's face or what they had ordered at previous dinners.

Since her roommate's marriage Tiffany lived alone in a small apartment on the second floor of a two-family house. Her routine was to sleep till nearly ten each morning, then to listen to Dr. Susan in bed while she enjoyed her first cup of coffee.

Yesterday, when she heard Karen talk with Dr. Susan about the turquoise ring some guy had given her on a cruise, she thought about Matt Bauer, who had given her a similar ring. The phone call to Dr. Susan this morning had been an impulse, and immediately Tiffany regretted telling her that Matt was a cheapskate, just because the ring had only cost ten dollars. It actually was pretty, and she admitted to herself that she made that remark only because Matt had dropped her.

As the day wore on, Tiffany thought more and more about that afternoon she had spent with Matt in Greenwich Village last year. By four o'clock, as she got ready for work, fluffing her hair and applying her makeup, she realized that the name of the shop where they bought the ring was not going to come to her.

"Let's see," she said aloud to herself. "We had lunch at a sushi bar. Then we were walking around and passed that souvenir shop, and I said, 'Let's stop in.' Then Matt bought me a souvenir. We were trying to decide between a brass monkey and a miniature Taj Mahal when that classy guy came in."

She had noticed him right away. She had just turned away from Matt, who picked up something else and was reading the tag that said why it was special. The guy didn't seem to realize they were there, because they'd been standing behind a screen painted with camels and pyramids.

The customer was a doll, Tiffany reflected. She remembered the look of surprise on his face when he turned around and saw her standing there. After the man left, the store owner said, "That gentleman has purchased several of these rings for his lady friends. Maybe you'd like to see one."

It was pretty, Tiffany thought. Wistfully she looked at the turquoise ring she kept in a little ivory box. I'm not going to send it to Dr. Susan, she thought. Who knows? Maybe Matt will call me up sometime. Maybe he still doesn't have a steady girlfriend.

What Dr. Susan really seemed interested in was the *location* of the shop, Tiffany thought. So instead of sending the ring, maybe I can just narrow down the location enough to help her. I remember that there was a porno shop across the street, and I'm pretty sure it was only a couple of blocks away from a subway station. She's smart. She should be able to find it with that information.

Relieved that she had made the proper decision, Tiffany put on her blue dangle earrings. She would call Dr. Susan tomorrow. Once she was on the air, she could explain that she wanted to apologize for making that crack about the ring being cheap, that she only said it because she missed Matt so much. He was such a nice guy. Could Dr. Susan suggest some way they might get together again?

What's to lose? she asked herself. Maybe I'll get some free advice. Or maybe Matt's mother or one of her friends will be listening and tell him, and he'll be flattered and give me a call.

ALEX Wright lived in the four-story turn-of-the-century brownstone mansion on East Seventy-eighth Street that had been his home since childhood. It was still furnished as his mother had left it, with dark, heavy Victorian tables, buffets, and bookcases; overstuffed couches and chairs upholstered in rich brocades; antique Persian carpets and graceful *objets d'art*.

Even the fourth floor, most of which had been designed as a play area for Alex, remained the same. The built-ins, commissioned from F.A.O. Schwarz, had been featured in *Architectural Digest*.

Alex lived relatively simply, employing only Jim as chauffeur and Marguerite, a marvelously efficient and blessedly quiet housekeeper. She arrived at eight thirty each morning in time to prepare breakfast for Alex, and she stayed to cook dinner on those occasions when he planned to be home, which wasn't more than twice a week.

On Tuesday he spent the better part of the day at the foundation headquarters, then in the late afternoon played squash at the club. He hadn't been sure of his evening plans and had instructed Marguerite to prepare what he called a contingency dinner.

When he arrived home at six thirty, his first stop was to check the refrigerator. A bowl of Marguerite's excellent chicken soup was ready for the microwave oven, and lettuce and sliced chicken were prepared for a sandwich.

Nodding his approval, Alex went to the drinks table in the library, selected a bottle of Bordeaux, and poured himself a glass. He had just begun to sip when the phone rang.

He decided to let the answering machine screen his calls. He raised his eyebrows when Dee Chandler Harriman announced herself. Her voice, low and pleasing, was hesitant.

"Alex, I hope you don't mind. I asked Dad for your home number. I just wanted to thank you for being so nice to me the other day at Binky and Dad's cocktail party. I've been down a lot lately, and you really helped, just by being a nice guy. I'm going to try to kill the blues by going on a cruise in Costa Rica next week. My father's been pushing me to do it. Anyhow, thank you. I just had to let you know. Oh, by the way, for the record, my phone number is . . ."

I guess she doesn't know I asked her sister out to dinner, Alex thought. Dee is gorgeous, but Susan is much more interesting. He took another sip of his wine and closed his eyes.

In fact, Susan Chandler had been on his mind all day.

AT SIX o'clock Susan was in her office when Jane Clausen arrived for their meeting. The ashen complexion of her visitor reinforced Susan's realization of how seriously ill the woman was.

"Dr. Chandler," Mrs. Clausen began, then hesitated.

"Please call me Susan. Dr. Chandler sounds so formal."

Jane Clausen nodded, then looked directly at Susan. "You met my lawyer yesterday. Douglas Layton. Were you surprised that he didn't wait with me?"

"Yes, I was."

"Why were you surprised?"

Susan did not have to consider her answer. "Because it was entirely possible that you were going to meet a woman who might shed light on your daughter's disappearance. I would have expected him to stay with you for support."

Jane Clausen nodded. "Exactly. Susan, Douglas Layton told me all along that he did not know my daughter. Now, from something he said this morning, I think he *did* know her."

"Why would he lie about that?" Susan asked.

"I don't know." Jane Clausen spoke slowly, frowning in concentration. "Then later today I realized he was eavesdropping when I was speaking with you on the phone. The door was partially open, and I could see him reflected in the glass of the cabinet. Why would he do that? What reason has he to skulk around me?"

"Did you ask him?"

"No. I had a weak spell and wasn't up to confronting him. I am going to have one particular grant audited. It was one we were reviewing at today's meeting, an orphanage in Guatemala. Doug is scheduled to go there next week and then present a report at the next trustees meeting. I questioned the amounts we've been giving, and Douglas blurted out that Regina had told him it was one of her favorite charities."

"Yet he's denied knowing her."

"Yes. Susan, I needed to share this with you because I have suddenly realized one possible reason why Douglas Layton rushed out of this office yesterday."

Susan knew what Jane Clausen was about to tell her—that Layton had been afraid to come face to face with Karen.

Jane Clausen left a few minutes later. "I think that tomorrow my doctor will want me to go into the hospital for some further treatment," she said as she was departing. "I wanted to share this with you first. I know that you were once an assistant district attorney. In truth, I don't know whether I brought my suspicions to you to receive insight from a psychologist or to ask a former officer of the court how to open an inquiry."

DR. DONALD Richards left the studio right after the broadcast and belatedly realized that Rena would have prepared lunch.

He found a pay phone and dialed his home number. "I have to run an errand," he told Rena apologetically. "I'll be an hour or so."

When he reached his office an hour and a half later, Rena had his lunch ready. "I'll put the tray on your desk, Doctor," she said.

His two-o'clock appointment was a severely anorexic thirty-year-old businesswoman. It was her fourth visit, and Richards listened and jotted notes on a pad.

At ten of three, after he had seen the patient out, he phoned Susan Chandler, reasoning that she undoubtedly spaced appointments as he did—see a patient for fifty minutes, then take a ten-minute break before the next appointment.

Her secretary told him that Susan was on the phone. "I'll wait," he said.

Then Susan's voice, a bit breathless, came on. "Dr. Richards?"

"Just because you're in your office doesn't mean you can't call me Don."

Susan laughed. "I'm sorry. I'm glad you called. It's been a bit hectic here, and I wanted to thank you for being a great guest."

"And I want to thank you for all the great exposure." He glanced at his watch. "I've got a patient coming in, and you probably do too, so let's cut to the chase. Can you have dinner with me tonight?"

"Not tonight. I have to work late."

"Tomorrow night?"

"Yes, that would be nice."

"Let's say sevenish. I'll call you at the office tomorrow." A really planned date, he thought. Too late now.

"I'll be here all afternoon," Susan told him.

Richards jotted down the time—sevenish—and muttered a hasty good-bye. As he put down the receiver, he wondered just how much he should disclose to Susan Chandler.

DEE Chandler Harriman had phoned Alex Wright from the modeling agency office in Beverly Hills at quarter of four. That meant it was quarter of seven in New York, a time she thought he might be home. When he didn't pick up, she decided that if he was out to dinner, he might try to reach her later in the evening. With that hope Dee went directly from work to her condo in Palos Verdes, and at seven o'clock she was listlessly preparing herself a meal of a scrambled egg, toast, and coffee. She was bored and restless.

I'm tired of working, Dee admitted to herself. I'm ready to move back to New York. But not to get another job. "I can't even fix a decent scrambled egg," she complained aloud as she realized that the flame under the pan was too high and the egg was burning.

But anyone who married Alex Wright wouldn't have to worry about recipes and cooking, she told herself.

She decided to eat in the living room and was setting her tray on the coffee table when the phone rang. It was Alex Wright.

When she replaced the receiver ten minutes later, Dee was smiling. He had called because she sounded so down and he thought she might want to chat. He explained that he had enjoyed his evening with Susan and was about to invite her to a dinner Saturday night celebrating a recent grant from the Wright Foundation to the New York Public Library.

Dee congratulated herself on her quick thinking. She had told him that on the way to Costa Rica to board the cruise she was going to stop in New York over the weekend. Alex had taken the hint and invited her to the dinner too.

After all, Dee told herself as she picked up the tray with the now cold food, it isn't as if Susan is really involved with him yet.

AFTER Jane Clausen left her office on Tuesday evening, Susan went over paperwork until nearly seven, then phoned Jed Geany at home. "Problem," she announced briskly. "I called Justin Wells to see about getting the tape to yesterday's program to him, and he absolutely denies having requested it."

"Susan, I can tell you this. Whoever the guy was who called was nervous. Maybe Wells doesn't want anyone to know about his interest in the tape. At first he asked for just the call-in section of the program. I think that's actually the only thing he was interested in."

"The woman who was hit by a van on Park Avenue yesterday is his wife," Susan said.

"See what I mean? He has other things on his mind, poor guy."

"You're probably right. See you tomorrow." She hung up the phone and sat pondering the situation. Yesterday's calls were run of the mill, except for the one from the woman who identified herself as Karen and who talked about the turquoise ring.

That *has* to be the call Justin Wells—or whoever it was—is interested in, she thought, but it's been a long day, and I can't figure out why now. She collected her coat, turned off the lights, locked the office door, and started down the corridor to the elevator.

On the way home she thought through Jane Clausen's visit and the concern Jane had voiced about Douglas Layton.

It *was* possible that Layton had a meeting he couldn't change yesterday. But what about Mrs. Clausen's belief that he had known

Regina and lied about it? Chris Ryan's name jumped into Susan's mind. A retired FBI agent she had worked with when she was in the D.A.'s office, Chris now had his own security firm. He could do a little discreet digging about Layton.

Susan looked about her as she walked. The narrow streets of the Village never failed to fascinate her. She found herself glancing around to see if she could catch a glimpse of a souvenir shop like the one today's caller—Tiffany—had talked about. Tiffany said that her boyfriend bought a ring in Greenwich Village similar to the one Karen had discussed. Let her send it, please, Susan prayed. If I could just get to compare it with the one Mrs. Clausen gave me. Then, if it turned out that they were identical and were made right here, it might be a first step toward solving Regina's disappearance.

AMAZING how much a cold walk clears the brain, Susan thought as she opened the door to her apartment. It was eight o'clock. She changed into a caftan, reached into the cupboard for a package of linguine, and got the salad makings out of the refrigerator. While the water for the pasta was heating, she turned on her home computer and checked her E-mail. It was the usual stuff, except for a few comments on how interesting Dr. Richards was and suggestions that Susan should have him back as a guest. On impulse she checked to see if Richards had a Web site.

He did. With increasing interest Susan zeroed in on the personal information: Dr. Donald J. Richards, born in Darien, Connecticut, raised in Manhattan, attended Collegiate Prep, B.A. Yale, M.D. and Ph.D. clinical psychology Harvard, M.A. criminology N.Y.U. Married to Kathryn Carver (deceased).

A long list of published articles followed, as well as reviews of his book, *Vanishing Women.* Then Susan found information that raised her eyebrows. A brief biography stated that Dr. Richards had spent a year between his junior and senior years in college working on a round-the-world ocean liner as assistant cruise director and—under the heading of "recreation"—that he frequently took short cruises. As his favorite ship he had named the *Gabrielle,* noting that it was the one on which he had met his wife. Susan stared at the screen.

"But that's the same ship Regina Clausen was on when she disappeared," she said aloud.

SOMETIMES at night he took long walks. He did it when everything built up to the point that it became necessary to ease the tensions. This afternoon had gone easily. The old man in the souvenir shop had died quietly. There's been nothing about his death on the evening news, he thought, so the odds are that when the store didn't reopen, nobody cared enough to see if anything was wrong.

His goal tonight had been just to walk, however aimlessly, through the city streets, so he was almost surprised to find himself near Downing Street. Susan Chandler lived on Downing. Was she in now? he wondered. He realized that his walking here tonight, especially in a relatively unconscious state, was an indication that he could not allow her to keep making trouble. Since yesterday morning he'd had to eliminate two people—Hilda Johnson and Abdul Parki, neither of whom he had ever intended to kill. A third, Carolyn Wells, was either going to die or would have to be eliminated should she ever recover.

Of course, as long as she was in a coma, she posed no immediate danger. The real danger might be Tiffany, the girl who called in to Dr. Susan Chandler's program today. As he walked along Downing Street, he cursed himself. He remembered his visit last year to Parki's shop. He had thought it was empty. From the sidewalk he hadn't been able to see that young couple standing behind the screen.

The minute he noticed them, he knew he had made a mistake. The girl had been eyeing him, and he was sure she could recognize him if he saw her again. If Tiffany—the one who phoned in to *Ask Dr. Susan* about the ring—and that girl from the shop were the same person, she had to be silenced. Tomorrow he would find a way to learn from Susan Chandler if Tiffany had sent the ring, and if so, what she had written to accompany it.

Another feather in the wind. When would it end? One thing for certain. By next week Susan Chandler must be stopped.

7

ON WEDNESDAY morning Doug Layton set his strategy into place. He knew he had a long way to go to placate Jane Clausen before he left on the Guatemala trip, but during the sleepless early morning hours he had worked out a plan. This time the stakes were enormous.

In the taxi on the way to Beekman Place he carefully rehearsed the story he would give her. It shouldn't be difficult to calm her down.

The concierge insisted on announcing him even though he said not to bother, that he was expected. When he stepped out of the elevator, the housekeeper was waiting at the apartment door, holding it open only a little. She told him Mrs. Clausen wasn't feeling well.

"Vera, I *must* see Mrs. Clausen for just a minute," Doug said.

Seeing Vera's uncertain look, he whispered, "We both love her and want to take care of her." Then he put his hands under her elbows, forcing her to step aside. In four long strides he was through the French doors that led to the dining room.

Jane Clausen was reading the *Times*. At the sound of his footsteps she looked up with an expression akin to fear.

The situation is worse than I realized, he thought.

He did not give her a chance to speak. "Mrs. Clausen, I've been terribly troubled that you misunderstood me yesterday," he said, his voice soothing. "I was mistaken when I said Regina had told me the orphanage in Guatemala was a favorite charity of hers. The truth is that when he invited me to be on the board, Mr. March himself was the one who explained how Regina was so touched by the plight of the children there."

It was a safe enough story. March wouldn't remember having said it, of course, but he also would be afraid to deny it because of his growing awareness of his own forgetfulness.

"Hubert was the one who told you?" Jane Clausen said quietly. "He was like an uncle to Regina. It was just the sort of thing she would confide to him."

Doug knew instantly he was on the right track. "As you know, I'm going down there next week so the board can have a firsthand report on the progress of the orphanage. I know how precarious your health has been, but would you consider joining me so you could see for yourself the wonderful work the orphanage is doing for those poor kids? I promise I'd be at your side every moment."

Layton knew, of course, that there wasn't a chance in the world Jane Clausen could make the trip.

She shook her head. "I only wish I could go."

It was as though he were watching ice melt. She wants to believe me, Doug thought, mentally congratulating himself. There was just one more area he had to cover: "I have an apology to make about leaving you unescorted at Dr. Chandler's office on Monday," he said. "I did have an appointment of long standing, but I should have broken it. The problem was, I could not reach the client, and she was coming in from Connecticut to meet me."

"I gave you very short notice," Jane Clausen said. "I'm afraid that's getting to be a habit of mine. Yesterday I insisted another professional person see me almost instantly."

He knew she meant Susan Chandler. How much had she told that woman? he wondered.

When he left a few minutes later, she insisted on walking him out. Doug smiled as he rode down on the elevator. He was back in the good graces of Jane Clausen and once again on the road to the chairmanship of the Clausen Family Trust.

Leaving the building, he took care to exchange a few words with the concierge and to tip the doorman generously when he hailed a cab for him. There was always the chance that either or both would remark on how pleasant Mr. Layton was.

Once in the cab, however, the look of benign good humor vanished from Doug Layton's face. What had Jane Clausen talked about to Dr. Chandler? he wondered. Besides being a psychologist,

Chandler had a trained legal mind. She would be the first one to seize on something that didn't ring true.

He glanced at his watch. It was eight twenty. He should be at the office before nine. That would give him a good hour to get some paperwork out of the way before it was time to listen to today's installment of *Ask Dr. Susan*.

ON WEDNESDAY morning Susan woke at six, showered, and washed her hair, quickly blowing it dry with practiced ease. For a moment she studied her reflection, appraising herself dispassionately. Eyebrows, too heavy. She didn't like the idea of tweezing them. Skin, good. She could at least be proud of that. Mouth, like her eyebrows, too generous; nose, straight—that was okay; eyes, hazel like Mom's; chin, stubborn.

She thought about what Sister Beatrice had told her mother when she was a junior at Sacred Heart Academy: "Susan has a stubborn streak, and in her it's a virtue. That chin comes jutting out, and I know there's something she thinks needs fixing."

Right now I think a lot of things need fixing, or at least looking into, Susan thought, and I've got the list ready.

In the interest of saving time, she decided against her usual walk and took a cab to the office, arriving at seven fifteen. Entering her building, she was surprised to find that even though the lobby door was unlocked, the security desk was unmanned. The security in this place is nonexistent, she thought as she went up in the elevator. She got off the elevator to find the top floor completely dark. "This is ridiculous," she murmured under her breath as she searched for the corridor light switches.

But even the lights did not brighten the hallway adequately. No wonder, Susan thought, noting that two of the bulbs were missing. She made a mental note to speak to the superintendent later, but once she was in her office, the annoyance faded from her mind. She got to work immediately, and for the next hour she caught up on correspondence, then prepared to put in motion the plan she had made the night before.

She had decided to go to Justin Wells's office and confront him about the tape and about her belief that his wife was the mysterious caller. And if he was not there, she was going to play that segment of Monday's program for his secretary. The woman who called herself Karen just might be someone his staff knew, Susan thought. And could it be a mere coincidence that Justin Wells's wife was in an accident so soon after the phone call?

Susan scanned the rest of her notes, cataloguing points that still concerned her. "Elderly witness to Carolyn Wells's accident." Had Hilda Johnson been right when she declared that someone pushed Carolyn? Equally significant, was Johnson's murder a few hours later another coincidence? "Tiffany." She had called to say that she had a turquoise ring with an inscription identical to the ones Regina and Karen had. Would she send it in?

The next notation on her list was about Douglas Layton. He *had* acted suspiciously, Susan thought, the way he bolted minutes before Karen was due to arrive at the office. Was he afraid to meet her? And if so, why?

The last item concerned Donald Richards. Was it just a coincidence that his favorite cruise ship was the *Gabrielle* and that his book was about vanished women? Was there more to this seemingly pleasant man than met the eye?

Susan got up from her desk. Nedda would be in her office by now and would have coffee brewing. Susan locked the outer office door and, slipping her key in her pocket, went down the hall.

WHEN Susan got back to her own office, Janet was there and on the phone. "Oh, wait a minute. Here she is," Janet said. She covered the receiver with her hand. "Alex Wright."

Susan picked up the phone as Janet left the room. "Hello, Alex."

"I tried you at home half an hour ago. I assumed you got to your office around nine."

"I was here at seven thirty today. I like to get an early start."

"We're compatible. I'm an early riser too. My father's home training. He thought that anyone who slept past six a.m. was missing a chance to pile up more money. But some days, when I don't have a meeting, I pound the pillow or read the papers in bed, just because I know how much that would have irritated him."

Susan laughed. "Be careful. You're talking to a psychologist."

"Oh my gosh, I forgot. Actually, I didn't call to discuss my father, or to explain my sleeping habits. I just wanted to tell you that I had a very enjoyable time with you Monday evening, and I'm hoping you're free again on Saturday night. Our foundation has made a grant to the New York Public Library, and there's going to be a black-tie dinner in the McGraw Rotunda at the main library on Fifth Avenue. It's not a big affair—only about forty people. Originally I was going to beg off, but I really shouldn't, and if you come with me, I might actually enjoy it."

Susan listened, flattered to realize that Alex Wright's voice had taken on a coaxing tone.

"Yes, I am free, and I'd love to go," she said sincerely.

"That's great. I'll pick you up around six thirty, if that's okay."

"Fine."

His voice changed, suddenly hesitant. "Oh, Susan, by the way, I was talking to your sister."

"Dee?" Susan realized she sounded astonished.

"Yes. I met her at Binky's party after you left. She phoned my apartment last night and left a message for me, and I returned the call. She's going to be in New York this weekend. I told her I was inviting you to the dinner and asked her to join us."

"That was kind of you," Susan replied. When she got off the phone a moment later, she remembered how, seven years ago, Dee had phoned Jack, telling him how upset she was with her new publicity photos and asking him to look at them and advise her.

And that, Susan thought with a pang of bitterness, was the beginning of the end for Jack and me. Could history be repeating itself?

THE tension at the architectural firm of Benner, Pierce and Wells was the kind you could actually feel, Susan thought as she stood in the paneled entrance area and waited while a nervous young receptionist whose nameplate read BARBARA GINGRAS hesitantly informed Justin Wells of her presence.

She was not surprised when the young woman said, "Dr. Susan— I mean Dr. Chandler—Mr. Wells wasn't expecting you and can't see you now, I'm afraid."

Realizing the girl had recognized her name from the radio program, Susan decided to take a chance. "Mr. Wells phoned my producer and asked for a copy of Monday's *Ask Dr. Susan* program. I really just wanted to give it to him personally, Barbara."

"So he *did* believe me?" Barbara Gingras said, beaming. "I told him that Carolyn—that's his wife—had phoned you Monday. I was listening to your program when she called in. I know her voice, for heaven's sake. But Mr. Wells acted real annoyed when I told him about it, so I didn't say another word. Then his wife was in an awful accident, so the poor guy's been too upset for me to even have a chance to talk to him."

"I understand that," Susan said. She had the tape ready to play. Turning the cassette player on, she placed it on the receptionist's desk. "Barbara, could you listen for a moment?"

Susan kept the volume low as the troubled voice of the woman who had called herself Karen began to play.

As Susan watched, the receptionist bobbed her head excitedly. "Sure, that's Carolyn Wells," she confirmed. "And even what she's talking about makes sense. I started work here just about the time she and Mr. Wells were separated. I remember, because he was a basket case. Then, when he made up with her, it was like day and night. You never saw a guy so happy. Clearly, he's crazy about her. Now, since the accident, he's been a basket case again. I heard him tell one of his partners that the doctor told him her condition wasn't likely to change for a while."

The outer door opened, and two men entered. They looked at Susan curiously as they passed the reception area. Barbara Gingras seemed suddenly nervous. "Dr. Susan, if Mr. Wells comes out and catches us talking, he might get mad at me."

"I understand." Susan put away the tape recorder. "Just one

more thing, Barbara. The Wellses have a friend named Pamela. Have you ever met her?"

Barbara frowned in concentration; then her face cleared. "Oh, you mean Dr. Pamela Hastings. She teaches at Columbia. She and Mrs. Wells are great buddies. I know she's been at the hospital a lot with Mr. Wells."

Now Susan had learned everything she needed to know. "Thank you, Barbara."

"I really enjoy your program, Dr. Susan."

Susan smiled. "That's very nice of you." She waved and opened the door to the corridor. There she immediately pulled out her cellular phone and dialed information. "Columbia University, general directory, please," she said.

AT PRECISELY nine o'clock on Wednesday morning Dr. Donald Richards appeared at the reception desk on the fifteenth floor of 1440 Broadway. "I'm Dr. Richards. I was a guest on the *Ask Dr. Susan* program yesterday and Monday," he explained to the woman at the desk. "I asked to have tapes of the programs, but then I left without getting them. Is Mr. Geany—the producer—in yet?"

"I think I saw him," the receptionist replied. She picked up the phone and dialed a number. "Jed, Susan's guest from yesterday is here. He forgot the tapes he asked for." After listening a moment, she said, "He'll be right out. Take a seat."

Richards selected a chair near a coffee table on which lay copies of the morning newspapers.

Jed came out a moment later, a package in his hand. "Sorry I forgot to remind you yesterday, Doc. I was just about to send these down to the mailroom. At least you still want them and didn't change your mind like what's his name."

"Justin Wells?" Richards responded.

"Exactly. But he's going to get a surprise. Susan is dropping the tape from Monday's show at his office this morning."

Interesting, Richards mused. *Very* interesting. It can't be too often that the host of a popular radio show plays errand girl. After thanking Jed Geany, he put the small package in his briefcase and fifteen minutes later was getting out of a cab at the garage around the corner from his apartment.

AT TEN o'clock Donald Richards was driving north on the Palisades Parkway, toward Bear Mountain. He turned on the radio and tuned in *Ask Dr. Susan,* a program he had no intention of missing.

When he reached his destination, he remained in his car until the program was over. Then he sat quietly for several minutes longer before getting out of the car and opening the trunk. He took a narrow box from inside and walked to the water's edge.

The mountain air was cold and still. The lake surface shimmered under the autumn sun, but even so, there were dark areas that hinted at the water's depth.

For a long time he sat on the ground at the lakeside, his hands clasped over his knees. Tears glistened in his eyes, but he ignored them. Finally he opened the box and removed the dewy fresh long-stemmed roses that were nestled inside. One by one he tossed them on the water until all two dozen were floating there.

"Good-bye, Kathryn." He spoke aloud, his tone somber; then he turned and went back to the car.

AN HOUR later he was at the gatehouse at Tuxedo Park, the luxurious mountain hamlet that had at one time been the summer vacation retreat of New York City's very rich and very social. Now many, like his mother, Elizabeth Richards, were year-round residents. The security guard waved him by. "Good to see you, Dr. Richards," he shouted.

He found his mother in her studio. At age sixty she had taken up painting, and in twelve years of serious application her natural talent had developed into a genuine gift. She was seated at the easel, her back to him, totally absorbed in her work.

"Mother."

"Donald, I was beginning to give up on you." She rose and came to him, arms extended, but instead of embracing him, she brushed his cheek with her lips. "I don't want to get paint on you," she said.

Her arm linked in his, they walked down the wide staircase and through the foyer to the family dining room, which overlooked the gardens. "Where were you this morning?" she asked.

Don hedged. "I had to go by a radio studio."

"You went to the lake again, didn't you?" she asked.

"Yes."

His mother's face softened. She put her hand over his. "Don, I didn't forget that today is Kathy's anniversary, but it *has* been four years. You're going to be forty next month. You've got to move on, get on with your life. I want to see you meet a woman whose eyes will light up when you walk in the door at the end of the day."

"Maybe she'll have a job too," Don said. "There're not too many women who are just homemakers these days."

"Oh, stop it. You know what I mean. I want you to be happy again. Did you ever consider that even psychiatrists may need help recovering from a tragedy?"

He did not answer, but sat with his head down.

"And when was the last time you took a vacation?"

"Bingo!" Don said, brightening. "Next week, when I finish a book signing in Miami, I'm going to take six or seven days off."

"Don, you used to *love* going on cruises." His mother hesitated. "Remember how you and Kathy would take those spur-of-the-moment trips, having your travel agent book you on a segment of a long cruise? I want to see you do that sort of thing again. You haven't set foot on a cruise ship since Kathy died."

Dr. Donald Richards looked into the blue-gray eyes that reflected such genuine concern. Oh yes I have, Mother, he thought. Oh yes I have.

Susan got through to Pamela Hastings's office at Columbia but was told that Dr. Hastings was not expected there until shortly before eleven. Her first class was at eleven fifteen.

Chances are she stopped at Lenox Hill to visit Carolyn Wells, Susan thought. She left a message asking that Dr. Hastings call her at her office anytime after two o'clock, emphasizing that she needed to speak to her on a confidential and urgent matter.

She saw disapproval in Jed Geany's eyes when she arrived at the studio only ten minutes prior to broadcast time.

"You know, Susan, one of these days . . ." he began.

"I know. One of these days you'll be starting without me. It's a character flaw, Jed. I cut things too close timewise."

He gave her a reluctant half smile. "Your guest from yesterday, Dr. Richards, stopped by. He wanted to pick up the tapes of the programs he was on."

I'm seeing him tonight, Susan thought. I could have brought them. What was the big rush? she wondered as she went into the studio and put on her headphones.

When the engineer announced the thirty-seconds warning, she said quickly, "Jed, remember that call from Tiffany yesterday? I don't expect to hear from her, but if she does call in, be sure to record her phone number when it comes up on the ID."

"Okay."

"Ten seconds," the engineer warned.

In her earphones Susan heard, "And now stay tuned for *Ask Dr. Susan,*" followed by a brief musical bridge. She took a deep breath and began. "Hello and welcome. I'm Dr. Susan Chandler. Today we're going right to the phones to answer any questions you have in mind, so let's hear from you. Maybe between us we can put whatever is bothering you in perspective."

As usual, the time went quickly. Some of the calls were mundane: "Dr. Susan, there's someone in my office who's driving me crazy. If I wear a new outfit, she asks me where I bought it, then shows up wearing the exact same thing a few days later."

Other calls were complex: "I had to put my ninety-year-old mother in a nursing home," a woman said, her voice weary. "It killed me to do it, but physically she's helpless. And now she won't talk to me. I feel so guilty I can't function."

The show's time was almost up when Susan heard Jed announce, "Our next call is from Tiffany in Yonkers, Dr. Susan."

Susan looked up. Jed was nodding. He would copy Tiffany's phone number from the caller ID.

"Tiffany, I'm glad you called back today—" Susan began, but she was interrupted before she could continue.

"Dr. Susan," Tiffany said hurriedly, "I almost didn't have the courage to phone, because I may disappoint you. You see . . ."

Susan listened with dismay to an obviously rehearsed speech about why Tiffany couldn't send her the turquoise ring.

"So, like I said, Dr. Susan, I hope I'm not disappointing you, but Matt, my former boyfriend, gave it to me, and it kind of reminds me of all the fun times we had when we went out together."

"Tiffany, I wish you'd call me at my office," Susan said hurriedly, then had a sense of déjà vu. Hadn't she spoken almost those same words to Carolyn Wells forty-eight hours earlier?

"Dr. Susan, I won't change my mind about giving you the souvenir ring," Tiffany said. She had decided to add one more thing. "And if you don't mind, I want to tell you that I work at—"

"Please do not give your employer's name," Susan said firmly.

"I work at the Grotto, the best Italian restaurant in Yonkers," Tiffany said defiantly, almost shouting.

"Cut to commercials, Susan," Jed barked into her headphones.

At least now I know where to find her, Susan thought wryly.

When the program was over, she went into the control room. Jed had written Tiffany's phone number on the back of an envelope. "She sounds dumb, but she was smart enough to get in a free plug for her boss," he observed acidly. Self-promotion on the show was strictly forbidden.

Susan folded the envelope and put it in her jacket pocket. "She sounds lonely and very vulnerable. Suppose some nut was listening to the program and heard her and got ideas about her."

"Are you going to contact her about that ring?"

"Yes, I think so. I just need to compare it with the one Regina Clausen had. I know it's a long shot that they came from the same place, but I won't be sure unless I can check it out."

"Susan, those kinds of souvenir rings are a dime a dozen. Those guys who run the shops all claim their stuff is handmade, but who are they kidding? For ten bucks? No way."

"You're probably right," Susan said in agreement. "Besides . . ." she began, then stopped herself. She'd been about to tell Jed her suspicion that Justin Wells's critically injured wife was the mysterious Karen. No, she thought, it's better to wait until I see where that information leads me before I spread the word.

WHEN Nat Small noted that Abdul Parki's souvenir shop still hadn't opened at noon on Wednesday, he became concerned. Small's shop, Dark Delights, a porn emporium, was directly across the street from the Khyem Specialty Shop, and the two men had been friends for years.

Nat, a wiry fifty-year-old with hooded eyes, had one abiding credo, and it had served him well: Stay away from the cops. That was why he tried every other avenue available to him when he first became concerned about his friend's failure to open for business that Wednesday morning. First he tried peering in at the door of Abdul's shop. Seeing nothing, he then phoned Abdul at home. Not reaching him there, he tried phoning Abdul's landlord.

Finally, Nat did the one thing that showed the depth of his friendship. He called the local precinct and reported his concern that something might have happened to Abdul. The police checked Abdul's exquisitely neat apartment on Jane Street. A bouquet of drooping flowers lay next to the photo of his late wife. Otherwise there was no indication that he had been there recently. At that point they decided to go into the shop and investigate.

It was there they found the blood-soaked body of Abdul Parki.

Nat Small was not a suspect. The police knew Nat, and they all knew he didn't have a motive. In fact, the very absence of motive was the most troubling aspect of the case. There was nearly one hundred dollars in the cash register, and it didn't look as though the killer had even made an effort to open it.

What the police wanted from Nat and from other shopkeepers on the block was information. They did learn that Abdul had opened the shop as usual on Tuesday morning at nine o'clock and had been seen sweeping his sidewalk around eleven. "Nat," the detective said, "you're right across the street from Parki. Did you notice anyone going in or out of Abdul's shop sometime after eleven?"

By the time he was being questioned at three o'clock, Nat had had plenty of time to think and to remember. Around one yesterday he had been putting some display boxes in the front window. Although he hadn't actually stared at him, he had noticed a well-dressed guy standing on the sidewalk outside his shop. He seemed to be looking over the stuff already on display, but then he had crossed the street and gone directly into Abdul's shop.

Nat had a pretty good impression of what the guy looked like. But that well-dressed guy certainly wasn't the one who killed Abdul, Nat told himself. No, there was no use even mentioning him to the cops. If he did, he would end up wasting the whole afternoon in the precinct station with a cop-artist. No way.

"I seen nobody," Nat informed the cops. "But let me warn you guys," he added virtuously. "You gotta do something about the druggies round here. They'd kill their grandmothers for a fix. And you can tell the mayor I said so!"

8

JIM Curley was sure something was up when he picked up his boss at noon at the Wright Family Foundation and was told to stop by Irene Hayes Wadley & Smythe, an elegant Rockefeller Center florist. Once there, instead of sending Jim inside, Wright went into the shop holding a box under his arm. He returned fifteen minutes later trailed by a florist who carried a lavish bouquet in a large vase.

Wright instructed the florist to wedge the vase on the floor of the back seat, where he could be sure it wouldn't tip over.

With a smile the florist thanked Wright, then closed the door. Wright, his voice buoyant, said, "Next stop SoHo," then gave Jim an unfamiliar address and added, "We're going to Dr. Susan Chandler's office. Or at least *you're* going there to deliver these flowers. I'll wait in the car."

Over the years Jim had delivered flowers to many attractive women for his boss, but he never before had known Alex Wright to personally select them.

Jim took advantage of his long-established loyalty to ask a question. "Mr. Alex, isn't that the Waterford vase your mother brought back from Ireland?"

"You've got a good eye, Jim. The other night when I escorted Dr. Chandler to her door, I could see that she had a vase similar to that one, only smaller. I thought it could use a companion. Now you'd better step on it. I'll be late for lunch at The Plaza."

AT TWO thirty Alex was back at his desk at the offices of the Wright Family Foundation. At quarter of three his secretary announced a call from Dee Chandler Harriman.

"Put it through, Alice," he said, a note of curiosity in his voice.

Dee's voice was both warm and apologetic. "Alex, you're probably busy giving away five or six million dollars, so I won't keep you but a minute."

"I haven't given away that much money since yesterday afternoon," he assured her. "What can I do for you?"

"Nothing too difficult, I hope. Somewhere around dawn I made a momentous decision. It's time to move back to New York. My partners at the modeling agency out here are willing to buy me out. A neighbor will take my condo right off my hands. So here's why I'm calling. Can you recommend a good real estate agent? I'm in the market for a four- or five-room co-op on the East Side."

"I'm not going to be a lot of help, Dee. I've been living in the same house since I was born," Alex told her. "But I could inquire about a broker for you."

"Oh, thank you, that would be such a help. I hate to bother you, but I had the feeling you wouldn't mind. I'm arriving there tomorrow afternoon. That way I can start looking on Friday."

"I'll come up with a name for you by then."

"Then give it to me over a drink tomorrow night. My treat."

She hung up before he could respond. Alex Wright leaned back in his chair. This was an unexpected complication. He had heard the change in Susan's voice when he told her he'd invited her sister to the dinner at the library. That was why he sent the flowers today.

"Do I need this?" he muttered aloud. Then he remembered that his father had been fond of saying that any negative situation could be turned into a plus. The trick, Alex thought wryly, was to figure out how to make that happen in this case.

WITH weary resignation Jane Clausen entered the hospital room. As she suspected, her doctor had insisted that she go in for another bout of chemotherapy. The cancer that was inevitably winning the battle with her body seemed intent on not giving her the strength or the time to take care of all that needed tending to. Jane wished she could just say "No more treatment," but she wasn't ready to die— not quite yet. Not when she had a glimmer of hope that she might learn the truth about Regina's fate. If the woman who phoned in to Dr. Chandler's program would only come forward and show the picture of the man who had given her the turquoise ring, they would have a starting point at last.

When dinner was served, she accepted only a cup of tea and a slice of toast, then got into bed, took the painkiller the nurse brought her, and began to drift off.

"Mrs. Clausen."

She opened her eyes and saw Douglas Layton bending over her.

"I called you at home because we needed your signature on a tax form. When Vera told me you were here, I came right over."

"I thought I signed everything at the meeting," she murmured.

"One of the pages was overlooked, but it can wait."

"That's foolish. Give it to me." She reached for her glasses and glanced at the form Douglas was offering. "Oh, yes." She took the pen he gave her and wrote her signature, making an effort to keep it even on the line.

How quick she had been to mistrust Douglas yesterday, Jane thought. That was the trouble. Her illness and all the medication were robbing her of judgment. Tomorrow she would phone Dr. Chandler and tell her she had been wrong in her suspicions about Douglas—wrong, and terribly unfair to him.

"Mrs. Clausen, can I get you anything?"

"No, nothing at all, but thank you, Douglas."

She was asleep before he tiptoed from the room, but even had she been awake, given the darkness of the room, she probably would have been unaware of the satisfied smirk on his face.

AFTER her second phone call to *Ask Dr. Susan,* Tiffany was intensely pleased with herself. She had gotten across the message she wanted, and she hoped that someone would report her call to Matt. And she was sure her boss, Tony Sepeddi, would be thrilled when he heard about her plug for the Grotto.

She had just opened the door to leave her apartment for work when the phone rang. She ran across the small living room and managed to pick up the receiver on the third ring.

It was Matt's mother. She didn't bother with greetings. "Tiffany, I must insist that you stop talking about my son on the radio. He has just become engaged to a very attractive young woman. So please forget him, and do not talk about your dates with him, particularly where his friends or his fiancée will hear about it." A decisive click sounded in Tiffany's ear.

Shocked, she stood perfectly still for a full minute, feeling despair seep through her body. Then she slammed down the receiver. Tears streaming from her eyes, she ran out the door and down the stairs.

In the car, the hurt and disappointment washed over her. She wanted to pull over somewhere and cry it out of her system, but she knew she had to get hold of herself.

When she reached the Grotto, she chose a remote spot in the parking lot and sat for a moment in the car. Then she pulled out her compact. "Who needs him anyhow?" she asked out loud as she repaired her makeup.

On the way across the parking lot she passed the Dumpster. She paused for a moment and looked at it. In one sweeping gesture she pulled the turquoise ring from her finger and tossed it inside. "Lousy ring brought me nothing but lousy luck," Tiffany muttered, then ran to the kitchen door, pushed it open, and yelled, "Hi, guys. Has Tony heard about the big plug I gave this dump today?"

As SOON as Susan's two-o'clock patient left, Janet came in. "A Dr. Pamela Hastings phoned. She's anxious to talk with you."

"I'll call her right now."

"Aren't those flowers gorgeous?" Janet asked.

Susan had barely noticed the vase of flowers that sat on her credenza. Now, as she crossed to them, her eyes widened. "There must be a mistake," she said. "That vase is Waterford."

"No mistake," Janet assured her. "The guy who brought the bouquet said it was from his employer."

Of course she knew immediately who had sent them. Alex heard something in my voice after he told me he had invited Dee along on Saturday night, Susan thought. That explains a gesture as grand as this. How perceptive of him. And how stupid of me to allow my feelings to be so transparent.

For a moment she debated whether to call Alex right away to say that she couldn't possibly accept the vase. Then she shook her head. She could deal with all that later. Right now there were more pressing things. She reached for the phone.

The brief conversation ended with Pamela Hastings promising to be at Susan's office at nine o'clock the next morning.

A moment later Donald Richards phoned. "Just calling to confirm tonight, Susan. Seven o'clock at Palio—all right?"

After that call Susan realized she still had a few minutes before her next patient. She looked up Jane Clausen's number and quickly dialed it. There was no response, so she left a message for her on the answering machine.

IT WAS FIVE AFTER SIX BEFORE she'd seen her last patient out. Susan barely had time to freshen up at the office before she would have to take a taxi to the restaurant.

She had wanted to reach Tiffany at home earlier. The girl was surely at work now, and the restaurant probably was at the height of its dinner hour. I'll call her there later, when I get home, Susan thought. She probably stays fairly late.

Susan shuddered. Why did thinking about Tiffany give her such an uneasy feeling?

HE DIDN'T know Tiffany's last name, but even if he did, it wouldn't be wise to try to track her down at home. Besides, it wasn't necessary. She had told him where he could find her.

He phoned the Grotto in midafternoon and asked to speak to her. As anticipated, he was told that she wasn't there. She came on at five.

He had long ago learned that the best way to get information was to let someone correct an erroneous statement. "She gets off about eleven, right?" he suggested.

"Midnight. You wanna leave a message?"

"No, thanks. I'll try her at home again."

He couldn't wait for the time to pass until he could get to her. Tiffany had studied him. And probably, like many people in the restaurant business, she had a good memory for faces.

What about Tiffany's boyfriend—Matt?

Carefully he reviewed the scene in Parki's shop. It was when he turned to leave that he saw the couple. He had been directly in the girl's line of vision. The fellow she was with was looking over the junk on the shelves, his back turned. He wasn't a problem.

Parki was out of the way. And after tonight Tiffany too would no longer be a concern.

A line from "The Highwayman," a poem he had memorized as a child, ran through his mind: *I'll come to thee by moonlight, though hell should bar the way.*

He chuckled grimly at the thought.

DONALD RICHARDS WAS waiting at the bar at Palio when Susan arrived at ten after seven.

He cut short her apology, saying, "Traffic was terrible, and I just walked in the door myself. And you might be interested to hear that I had lunch with my mother today. She was listening to your program when I was on and was very impressed with you. However, she lectured me on the fact that I had arranged to meet you here. In her day a gentleman apparently always called for a young lady at home and escorted her to the restaurant."

Susan laughed. "Given the traffic in Manhattan, by the time you picked me up in the Village and then came back to midtown, the restaurants would be closed." She looked around. The horseshoe-shaped bar was busy and flanked on both sides by small tables. A magnificent mural depicting the famous horse race soared above them. The lighting was subdued, the atmosphere both warm and sophisticated. "I've never been here. It looks very nice," she said.

"Neither have I, but it comes highly recommended. The dining room is on the second floor."

She tried not to show how keenly she was studying Donald Richards. His hair was dark brown with just a touch of auburn. He was wearing wide glasses with a steel-gray frame. The lenses enhanced his gray-blue eyes—or were his eyes pure blue and their color subtly altered by the frame?

The elevator arrived. They got in and emerged on the second floor, where the maître d' greeted them and took them to their table. He asked for their drink orders, and Susan requested chardonnay. Donald Richards ordered a martini straight up.

"I don't usually have a 'see-through,'" he explained, "but it's been a heavy-duty day."

Was that because of lunch with your mother? Susan wondered. She warned herself not to seem curious about him. She couldn't let herself forget that he was a psychiatrist and would see through any effort to probe. She smiled warmly across the table. "A listener phoned today to say that after hearing you, she went out and bought your book and is thoroughly enjoying it."

"I heard her. Obviously a woman of great discrimination."

You heard her? Susan thought. Busy psychiatrists don't usually listen to two-hour advice programs.

Their drinks came. Richards raised his glass in a toast to her. "I'm grateful for the pleasure of your company."

She knew it was the sort of remark that people make over a cocktail. Still, Susan felt there was something behind the casual compliment—an intensity in the way he said it.

"Dr. Susan," he said, "I'm going to admit something. I looked you up on the Internet."

That makes *two* of us, Susan thought. Turnabout is fair play.

"You were raised in Westchester?" he asked.

"Yes. Larchmont, then Rye. But my grandmother always lived in Greenwich Village, and I spent a lot of weekends with her when I was growing up. I always loved it."

"Parents?"

"Divorced three years ago. And unfortunately, not one of those agree-to-disagree situations. My father met someone else and fell head over heels in love. My mother was devastated."

"How did you feel about it?"

"Sad. We were a happy family, or so I thought. We had fun together. After the divorce, though, *everything* changed. I sometimes think it was like a ship striking a reef and sinking, and while all on board survived, each of us got into a different lifeboat."

"What made you leave being an assistant district attorney and go back to school for a doctorate in clinical psychology?"

Susan found that an easy question to answer. "I got satisfaction from getting hardened criminals off the streets, but then I prosecuted a case where a woman killed her husband because he was about to leave her. She got fifteen years. I'll never forget the stunned, disbelieving look on her face when she heard the sentence. I could only think that if she had been caught in time, had gotten help, released that anger before it destroyed her . . ."

"Terrible grief can trigger terrible anger," he said quietly.

Susan nodded. "What took you into this field?"

"I always wanted to be a doctor. In medical school I realized to what extent the way the mind works affects physical health, and so I chose that path."

The maître d' arrived with menus, and after a few minutes of discussing various foods, they ordered their dinners.

Susan had hoped to steer the conversation more toward him, but he turned immediately to talk of her radio show.

"Did you ever hear anything more from Karen, the woman who called on Monday?" he asked casually.

"No, I didn't," Susan said.

Donald Richards broke off a piece of roll. "Did your producer send Justin Wells a copy of that program?"

It was not a question Susan had expected. "Do *you* know Justin Wells?" she asked, unable to keep her surprise from showing.

"I've met him—professionally."

"Were you treating him for excessive jealousy of his wife?"

"Why do you ask that?"

"Because if the answer is yes, I think you have a moral obligation to tell what you know about him to the police. It turns out that the woman who called herself Karen is Justin Wells's wife, whose real name is Carolyn, and she fell or was pushed in front of a van a few hours after she called me."

Donald Richards's expression was not so much surprised as grave and reflective. "I'm afraid you're probably right. I *should* speak to the police," he said grimly.

I was right, Susan thought. The obvious connection between what happened to Carolyn Wells and the phone call to me is her husband's jealousy.

"How's your salad?" Richards asked.

It was obvious he intended to change the subject. And rightly so, Susan thought with relief. Professional ethics. "Absolutely fine. And I've told you about myself. What about you? Any siblings?"

"No, I'm an only. Grew up in Manhattan. My father died ten years ago. That's when my mother decided to live in Tuxedo Park year-round. She's a painter, quite good, perhaps even *very* good. My father was a born sailor and used to take me along to crew for him."

Susan mentally crossed her fingers. "I was interested to see that you took a year off from college to work as an assistant cruise director. Your father's influence, I assume?"

He looked amused. "We both get information from the Internet, don't we? Yes, I enjoyed that year. Did the round-the-world cruise, taking in most of the major ports. Pretty much traveled the globe."

"What exactly does an assistant cruise director do?"

"Helps to organize the shipboard activities. Smooths ruffled feathers. Spots lonely or unhappy people and draws them out."

"According to your bio, you met your wife on the *Gabrielle*. That was the ship Regina Clausen was on when she disappeared."

"Yes. I never met Regina, of course, but I can understand why the *Gabrielle* would have been recommended to her. She's a wonderful ship."

They continued talking through the meal, niceties—comments on the food (highly favorable), comparisons with other favorite restaurants (New York City is a feast for diners)—interspersed among the more obviously probing questions.

They both decided to skip dessert and order espresso. After it arrived, Richards brought up Tiffany's name. "It was sad to listen to her today. She's terribly vulnerable, don't you think?"

"I think she wants desperately to fall in love and to be loved," Susan said in agreement. "She's given Matt's name to her need."

Richards nodded. "And I bet that if Matt *does* call her, it won't be because she's been making so much of his impulse to buy a souvenir ring. That would scare most guys off."

Is he downplaying the ring? Susan wondered.

When they left the restaurant, Richards hailed a cab. As they got in, he gave the driver her address. He looked at her sheepishly. "I'm not a mind reader. You're listed in the phone book."

Once they arrived at her apartment building, he had the cab wait while he escorted her upstairs.

"Your mother would be pleased," Susan told him. "A perfect gentleman." She thought of Alex Wright, who had done the same

81

thing two nights ago. Two gentlemen in three days, she reflected. Not bad.

Richards took her hand. "I think I said thank you for the pleasure of your company at the beginning of the evening. I say it again, even more emphatically." He looked soberly at her and added, "Don't be afraid of a compliment, Susan. You are, you know. Good night."

Then he was gone. Susan double-locked the door and leaned against it for a moment, trying to sort out her feelings. Then she crossed to the answering machine. There were two messages. The first was from her mother: "Phone me any time until midnight."

It was quarter of eleven. Without listening to the second message, Susan began to dial.

Her mother's nervousness was obvious as she began to stammer out the reason for her call. "Susan, this is crazy. I feel as though I'm being put in the position of choosing between my daughters."

Susan listened to her mother's fumbling explanation of how Alex Wright apparently had enjoyed meeting her at the party Sunday, but how Binky had been trying to set him up with Dee. "We know that Dee is lonely and restless, but I'd hate to see her interfere with a friendship you might be enjoying. . . ."

"You'd hate to see Dee move in again on someone who expressed interest in me. That's it, isn't it, Mom? Look, I had a very pleasant dinner with Alex Wright, but that's all. I gather Dee has been calling him. In fact, he's invited her to join us at a dinner party Saturday night. I'm not in competition with my sister. When I meet the right person for me, we'll both know it, and I won't have to worry about him straying when my sister crooks a finger at him."

"Just understand that poor Dee is so unhappy," her mother pleaded. "She called me this afternoon to say that she's moving back to New York. A bit sudden, even for Dee. She says she misses us, and she's tired of the modeling agency. Your father is treating her to a cruise next week. I hope that will pick up her spirits."

"I hope so too. Okay, Mom, talk to you soon."

The second message was from Alex Wright: "A business dinner was canceled, and I worked up the nerve to try you on short notice again. Not very good manners, I know, but I *did* want to see you. I'll give you a call tomorrow."

Smiling, Susan replayed the message. Now that's one compliment Dr. Richards wouldn't find me resisting, she thought. And I'm *mighty* glad Dee is signed up for a cruise next week.

WHEN she was in bed and drifting off to sleep, Susan remembered she had wanted to phone Tiffany at the Grotto. Turning on the light, she looked at the clock. It was quarter of twelve.

She got the phone number from information and dialed. The phone rang for a long time before it was picked up.

Susan asked for Tiffany, then waited several minutes before she came on. No sooner had she given her name than Tiffany exploded. "Dr. Susan, I never want to hear a word about that stupid ring again. Matt's mother phoned and told me to stop talking about him; she said that he's getting married. So I threw that dumb ring away! I wish Matt and I had never even gone in that souvenir shop. And I wish we hadn't been listening when the man who ran that dumb place told us the guy who'd just been in had bought these rings for several of his girlfriends."

Susan sat straight up in bed. "Tiffany, this is important. Did you *see* that man?"

"Sure I did. He was a doll. A class act. Not like Matt."

"Tiffany, I *have* to talk to you. Come into the city tomorrow. We'll have lunch together, and please tell me, is it possible to get your ring back?"

"Dr. Susan, by now it's under tons of chicken bones and pizza, and that's where it's gonna stay. I feel like such an idiot."

"Tiffany, have you remembered where you bought that ring?"

"I told you, in the Village. The West Village. I know it wasn't too far from a subway stop. The only thing I remember for certain is that there was a porn shop opposite. I gotta go. Bye, Dr. Susan."

Completely awake now, Susan replaced the receiver slowly. Tiffany had thrown away her turquoise ring, which was too bad, but she seemed to remember a man who apparently had bought several others. I was going to call Chris Ryan to run a check on Douglas Layton, she thought. I'll give him Tiffany's home phone number as well. He'll be able to get her address for me. And if he can't, then tomorrow evening I'll be sitting in the Grotto, having the best Italian food in Yonkers.

TIFFANY managed to get through the night. It helped that the Grotto was busy, and she hadn't had much time to think. There were only a couple of times that the hurt and anger came flooding back.

Around eleven o'clock some guy came in and sat at the bar. She could feel him undressing her with his eyes every time she passed him on the way to her tables.

Jerk, she thought.

At twenty of twelve he grabbed her hand and asked her to come have a drink at his place when she got off.

"Get lost, creep!" she told him.

Then he squeezed her hand so hard that she yelped in pain.

"Let go of her!" Joey, the bartender, had been around the bar in a shot. "Pay your bill and get out of here, mister."

The guy stood up. He was big, but Joey was bigger. Then the jerk threw some money on the bar and left.

Right after that, Dr. Susan phoned, and once again Tiffany was made aware of just how rotten she was feeling. All I want to do is go home and pull the covers over my head, she thought.

At five of twelve Joey called Tiffany over. "Listen, kid, I'll walk you to your car. That guy could be hanging around outside."

But then just as Tiffany was buttoning her coat to leave, a bowling team came in and the bar got busy.

"I'll be okay, Joey. See you tomorrow," she called to him, and darted out.

It wasn't until she was outside that she remembered leaving her car in the far corner of the parking lot. What a pain, Tiffany thought. If that guy *is* hanging around, he could be a problem. Carefully she scanned every inch of the lot. There was one person out there, a guy who looked like he had just gotten out of his car and was probably headed to the bar. Even in the shadowy light, though, she could tell he wasn't the jerk who had tried to come on to her. This guy was tall and thinner.

Still, something made her feel funny, made her want to get out of there as quickly as possible. As she walked rapidly toward her car, she fumbled in her bag for her keys. Her fingers closed over them. She was almost there.

Then suddenly the guy she had seen across the lot was standing in front of her. There was something shiny in his hand.

A knife. The realization made her freeze almost in mid step.

No! she thought, disbelieving, as she saw him move toward her.

"Please," she begged, incredulous that this was happening. *"Please!"*

Tiffany lived long enough to see her attacker's face, long enough for her excellent memory to help her recognize her killer as the classy guy she had glimpsed in that Village souvenir shop—the one who had bought those rings inscribed "You belong to me."

As HE drove back to the city along the Cross Bronx Expressway, he could feel the perspiration pouring from him. It had been a close call. He had just stepped over the low wall that separated the Grotto's property from the locked gas station where he had parked his car when he heard some guy yelling, "Tiffany!"

Fortunately, there was an incline, and he didn't have to start the engine until he reached the road. Once there, he turned right and merged with the traffic, so chances were no one had seen him.

Next week it would be all over, he reminded himself. He would choose someone to *See the jungle when it's wet with rain,* and his mission would be completed.

Veronica, so trusting—she had been the first—now buried in Egypt: *See the pyramids along the Nile.*

Regina, whose trust he had won in Bali: *Watch the sunrise on a tropic isle.*

Constance, who had replaced Carolyn in Algiers: *See the market-place in old Algiers.*

Fly the ocean in a silver plane. He thought of Monica, the timid heiress he had met on the flight to London.

The rings had been a mistake, of course. They were his private joke, like the connection between the names that he used on the special trips. He should have just kept his jokes to himself.

But Parki, who made the rings, was out of the way. Now Tiffany, who had seen him buying one, was gone. He was certain that, like Carolyn, she had recognized him at the end.

Well, these were feathers in the wind, and he could never recover them now, but surely they would blow away unnoticed. No matter how much he tried to stay out of camera range, it was inevitable that he had been caught in the background of some photos taken on the cruise ships.

After all, Carolyn Wells had been about to send a photo with him in the background to Susan Chandler. The thought of that narrow escape still unnerved him. He could imagine Susan opening the package, her eyes widening in surprise and horror when she recognized him.

A week from tonight all this will be over, he promised himself. By then I will have begun the last leg of my journey. Susan Chandler will have been eliminated, and I'll be starting my final cruise.

Once that was accomplished, the terrible burning inside him would go away, and finally he would be free—free to become the person his mother had always believed he was capable of being.

9

CHRIS Ryan had been an FBI agent for thirty years before he retired and set up his own small security firm. He and Susan became friends when the family of a murder victim hired him to try to solve the crime independently of the police. As an assistant district attorney, Susan was directly involved with the case, and information Chris uncovered and shared with her helped her obtain a confession.

They still saw each other for dinner every few months, so when Susan called him on Thursday morning, Chris was delighted. "Need a free meal?" he asked her genially. "There's a new steak house down the block. Forty-ninth and Third. When can you do it?"

"New steak house on Forty-ninth and Third, you say? Seems to me that's where Smith and Wollensky is located," Susan said. "And I happen to know it's been there about seventy years. Some people think you own it." She laughed. "Sure I'll go, but first I have to ask a favor, Chris. I need a fast check on someone."

"Who?"

"A lawyer, Douglas Layton. He's with Hubert March and Associates, a legal and investment advice kind of firm. He's also a director of the Clausen Family Trust."

"Sounds successful. Are you thinking of marrying him?"

"No, I'm not."

Susan filled him in on the background and explained that Jane Clausen had expressed concern to her about Layton. Then Susan told him about the events since the radio program on which Regina Clausen's disappearance was first discussed.

"And this guy did a disappearing act when you expected the woman who called herself Karen to show up in your office?"

"Yes. And something Layton said to Mrs. Clausen on Tuesday suggested he *knew* her daughter—a fact he's always denied."

"I'll get busy," Ryan promised. He reached for a pad and pen. "As of now, the clock is ticking. Where do I bill Mrs. Clausen?"

He caught the hesitation in Susan's voice. "It's not that simple, I'm afraid. I found a message from Mrs. Clausen on my machine this morning, saying she felt she had been unfair when she mentioned her suspicions about Layton to me. Clearly the implication was that I should forget about it, but I can't. I don't think she was unfair at all, and I'm worried for her. So bill it to me," Susan said.

Chris Ryan groaned. "Thank the Lord for my pension. Consider it done. I'll get back to you, Susie."

DOUG LAYTON'S SECRETARY, Leah, a no-nonsense woman in her early fifties, studied her boss with disapproving eyes. He looks as if he was out all night, she thought as Layton passed her and mumbled a perfunctory good-morning greeting.

Without asking, she went to the coffeemaker, poured him a cup, tapped on his door, then opened it. "I don't mean to spoil you, Doug," she said, "but you look like you could use this."

"Leah, Mrs. Clausen is back in the hospital," Doug said quietly. "I don't think she has very much time left."

"Oh, I'm so sorry." Leah suddenly felt guilty. "Will you still go to Guatemala next week?"

"Oh, absolutely. But I'm not going to wait to show her the surprise I was planning for her when I came back with my report."

"The orphanage?"

"Yes. She doesn't realize that the new wing is almost complete or that the people running the orphanage want to rename it for Regina. I don't think we should wait any longer to show the pictures to her. Get me the file, please."

Together they studied the eight-by-ten photos of the new section of the orphanage. "Room for two hundred more children," Doug said. "Equipped with a state-of-the-art clinic. You don't know how many of those infants arrive there malnourished." He opened his desk drawer. "Here's a rendition of the sign we're going to unveil at the dedication." The engraved and gilded lettering read THE REGINA CLAUSEN HOME.

"Oh, Doug, that will make Mrs. Clausen so happy!" Leah said, her eyes misting over. "It means that at least *something* good is coming out of her tragedy."

"Indeed it is," Douglas Layton agreed fervently.

IT WAS ten after nine when Susan's secretary buzzed her on the intercom. "Dr. Pamela Hastings to see you, Doctor."

Susan asked Janet to show her in.

The woman was distressed, her forehead creased with worry lines, her lips clamped together. But when she spoke, Susan instinctively liked her, sensing that she possessed both warmth and intelligence.

"Dr. Chandler, I feel that I must have sounded very rude to you the other night when you called the hospital. It was just that I was so surprised when you introduced yourself."

"And undoubtedly even more so when you heard why I was calling, Dr. Hastings." Susan reached out her hand. "Please, let's make it Susan and Pamela, if that's all right."

"Absolutely." Pamela Hastings shook Susan's hand, then sat down. "I can't stay long. I've been at the hospital so much that I'm really not prepared for my eleven fifteen class."

"And I go on the air in fifty minutes," Susan said, "so I guess we'd better get to the heart of it. Did you hear the phone call Carolyn Wells made to my program on Monday?"

"The one on the tape Justin denied requesting? No."

"I would like you to verify that it is indeed her voice on the tape. But let me tell you what she said."

Susan described talking about Regina Clausen's disappearance from a cruise and the call she had received from a listener who called herself Karen.

When Susan was finished, the other woman said, "I don't need to hear the tape. I saw a turquoise ring with that inscription last Friday night." She told Susan about the fortieth birthday party her friends had given her.

Susan opened the side drawer of her desk and pulled out her purse. "Regina Clausen's mother was listening to the program and heard Carolyn's call. Afterward she phoned me and came here with a souvenir ring that she said had been found among her daughter's possessions. Will you look at it, please?" She opened her purse and extracted the turquoise ring.

Pamela Hastings paled. She did not attempt to take the ring from Susan's hand but sat staring at it. Finally she said, "It looks exactly like the one Carolyn showed me. Is the inside of this band engraved with the sentiment 'You belong to me'?"

"Yes. Here, look at it closely."

Pamela shook her head. "No, I don't want to touch it. As a psychologist, you'll probably think I'm crazy, but I am gifted—or cursed, as the case may be—with very keen intuition, or second sight. When I touched the ring Carolyn had the other night, I warned her that it might be the cause of her death."

There was an awkward pause. Then Susan said, "There was very real fear in Carolyn Wells's voice when she called me on Monday. She sounded as though she was afraid of her husband."

"Justin is very possessive of Carolyn," Pamela said quietly.

It was obvious to Susan that Pamela Hastings was choosing her words carefully. "Possessive enough to hurt her?"

"I don't know." The words were anguished, as though they had been wrung from her. "Carolyn is unconscious, but I think I should tell you that she seems to be calling for someone."

"You mean someone you don't know?"

"A number of times she very clearly said, 'Win,' then, 'Oh, Win.' "

"You feel sure it was a name?"

"I asked her that yesterday as I stood next to her holding her hand, and she pressed my palm."

"Pamela, do you think Justin Wells is capable of hurting his wife in a jealous rage?"

Pamela thought for a moment. "I think he *was* capable of that," she said. "Maybe he still is. I don't know. He's been distraught since Monday night, and now the police have been talking to him."

Susan thought of Hilda Johnson, the elderly woman who claimed she saw someone push Carolyn Wells in front of the van—and who was murdered a scant few hours later. "Were you at the hospital Monday night with Justin Wells?"

Pamela Hastings nodded. "I was there from five thirty Monday evening to six o'clock Tuesday morning."

"Was he there that entire time?"

"Of course," she said, then hesitated. "No, actually not quite the whole time. After Carolyn came down from surgery—it was about ten thirty that night—Justin went out for a walk. He was afraid of getting one of his migraine headaches and wanted fresh air. But I remember that he was gone for less than an hour."

Hilda Johnson lived only blocks from Lenox Hill Hospital, Susan thought. "How did Justin seem when he came back to the hospital?" she asked.

"Much calmer," she said, then paused. "Almost too calm, if you know what I mean. I would say he was almost in shock."

WHEN Susan reached the studio, she poked her head into Jed Geany's office, already prepared for his reminder that one of these days she wasn't going to get there by broadcast time.

But today when he looked up at her, his face was grim. "I'm beginning to think we jinx our callers, Susan. That waitress, Tiffany, was stabbed to death last night when she was leaving work."

"She was *what?*" Susan felt as if she had been punched. She clutched the side of Jed's desk to steady herself.

"Easy. Take it easy," he cautioned, standing. "You've got a program to do in a couple of minutes."

Tiffany. Susan remembered their phone conversation late last night. The girl had been so anxious to get back with her boyfriend, so hurt when his mother phoned her. The poor girl, Susan thought.

"Remember how you tried to stop her from giving the name of the place she worked?" Jed said. "Well, apparently some guy went in looking for her. Made a pass at her. Got sore when she told him off. He's a bad apple. Has a record a mile long."

"Are they sure he did it?" Susan asked numbly.

"From what I hear, the cops have him dead to rights, although I don't think he has confessed or anything yet," Jed told her. "Come on, we've got to get into the studio."

Somehow Susan managed to get through the program. The lines were flooded with calls about Tiffany. At Susan's suggestion, during a commercial break Jed phoned the Grotto, and she spoke to the owner, Tony Sepeddi.

"Joey, our bartender, told Tiffany to wait, that he'd walk her out to her car," Sepeddi explained, his voice choked with emotion. "But he got busy, and she took off. When he saw she was gone, he ran out to make sure she was okay. That's when he saw a guy hurrying off in the direction of the gas station next door. By the time they found Tiffany's body, the guy was gone, but Joey is pretty sure it was the one who was bothering her in the bar."

Have they got the right man? This just doesn't seem like an isolated incident, Susan thought. Carolyn Wells phoned me, and a few hours later she was run over. Hilda Johnson swore for all the world to hear that she saw someone push Carolyn Wells; a few hours later she was murdered. Tiffany saw a man buying a turquoise "You belong to me" ring and called in to talk about it. Now she's been stabbed to death. Coincidence? I don't think so. But did the man in police custody kill Tiffany? And Hilda Johnson? And did he push Carolyn Wells?

As she was winding up the program, Susan told her listeners, "I'm grateful for all your calls. I think in those few times Tiffany spoke to me, we all felt we'd come to know her. Now I know many of you feel the same terrible regret I do at her death. If Tiffany's assailant went to that bar because she told us on air where she worked, it proves once more that we should never casually reveal such information to just anyone." Susan felt her voice breaking as she concluded, "Please, all of you, remember Tiffany and her family in your prayers. Our time is up. I'll be back with you tomorrow."

Immediately after signing off, she left the studio for her office. A contrite Janet told her that Alex Wright had phoned twice. "You had said to take messages when you were talking to Dr. Hastings, and then you ran out of here so fast I didn't remember to ask you to call him. Then he left a second message."

"I see." The first message was to please call Alex before the program. The second one Susan read and reread. Alex was meeting Dee at the St. Regis at five for drinks, and he wanted her to join them. Big sister, she thought, I love you, but there are limits. You not only got invited to the dinner Saturday night but you've managed to set up a meeting with him this evening as well.

As Janet watched, Susan tore up both notes and threw them in the wastebasket. She had no intention of joining Alex and Dee tonight for a drink or anything else.

It was twelve thirty. That gave her half an hour before her one-o'clock appointment. I can make some calls, she told herself.

The first one was to the Yonkers police. From her days in the Westchester County District Attorney's Office she knew several detectives there. She reached one of them, Pete Sanchez, and explained her interest in the murder of Tiffany Smith. From Sanchez she learned that the cops there were convinced they had their killer, and they expected it was just a matter of hours before the suspect, Sharkey Dion, an ex-con, confessed.

"When he was thrown out of the Grotto, a guy heard him say he'd be back to take care of her," Pete told her.

"That doesn't mean he killed her," Susan said. "Do you have the weapon?"

Sanchez sighed. "Not yet, but we impounded the Dumpster."

Then she told him about the turquoise rings, but he showed little interest. "Uh-huh. Give me your number. I'll let you know when Dion signs on the dotted line."

Susan put down the receiver and sat for a moment, deep in thought. The element connecting everything here is the turquoise ring. Regina Clausen had one and is dead. Carolyn Wells had one and may die. Tiffany Smith had one and is dead.

Tiffany told me that her ring was buried under tons of chicken bones and pizza, Susan thought. Did she mean in a Dumpster?

She called Sanchez again. She begged him to have the Dumpster sifted not only for the murder weapon but also for a turquoise ring with the inscription "You belong to me" inside the band.

THURSDAY was always a busy day for Dr. Donald Richards, and as usual, he had gotten an early start. His first patient came to him each week at eight o'clock and was followed at nine, ten, and eleven by other regular patients. Several of them expressed dismay when they learned that he would be out of town Thursday of next week, on a publicity tour for his book.

When Richards sat down at noon for a quick lunch, he was already weary, and he had a busy afternoon ahead of him. At one o'clock he had an appointment with Captain Tom Shea at the Nineteenth Precinct to talk about Justin Wells.

While Rena placed a cup of soup in front of him, he turned on the television to catch the local news. The lead story was the murder of the young waitress in Yonkers.

"This is the parking lot of the Grotto trattoria in Yonkers, where twenty-five-year-old Tiffany Smith was stabbed to death shortly after midnight," the anchorman said. "Sharkey Dion, a paroled killer who had been asked to leave the bar when he reportedly harassed Ms. Smith earlier in the evening, is in custody and is expected to be charged with the crime."

"Doctor, isn't that the woman who called in the other day when you were on that *Ask Dr. Susan* show?" Rena asked, shocked.

"Yes, it is," Richards said quietly. He pushed his chair back. "Rena, the soup looks delicious, but I'm afraid I'm not very hungry right now." His eyes lingered on the television screen as the camera panned to show a bright red pump with a stiletto heel.

That pathetic girl, he thought as he turned off the set. I know Susan will be upset. First Carolyn Wells and now Tiffany. I bet she's somehow blaming herself for both women's misfortunes.

IT WAS five minutes of four that afternoon before Donald Richards spoke to Susan. "I'm so sorry," he said.

"I'm heartsick," Susan told him. "I pray to God that if Sharkey Dion is the murderer, he didn't go into that bar looking for Tiffany because he heard her talking to me on air."

"From what I heard on the news earlier, the police don't seem to have much doubt about him being the killer," Richards said. "Susan, I doubt very much that the kind of man Sharkey Dion seems to be would be listening to an advice program."

"*If* he is the killer," Susan repeated tonelessly. "Don, I have a question you must answer. Do you think Justin Wells pushed his wife in front of that van?"

"No, I do not," Richards told her. "I think it much more likely that it was an accident. I went to see Captain Shea today and told him as much. True, Wells is obsessed about his wife, but part of that obsession is an extreme fear of losing her. In my opinion he would never hurt her deliberately."

As they talked further, Richards could tell how deeply disturbed Susan was by the recent events. "Look," he said, "this has been rotten for you. Why don't we grab a bite this evening. We'll find a restaurant somewhere around your place. I'll even pick you up."

"I'm afraid I can't," Susan told him. "I've set up a project for myself, and I don't know how long it will take."

It was four o'clock. Richards knew his last patient would be waiting in the reception room by now. "I'm good at projects," he said hurriedly. "Let me know if I can help."

He frowned when he put down the phone. Susan had politely but firmly refused his assistance. What was she up to? he wondered. It was a question he needed to have answered.

WHEN Pamela Hastings arrived at the hospital on Thursday night, Justin Wells was sitting at the far end of the intensive care waiting room, his back to her.

She tapped him on the shoulder, and he looked up at her. "Ahh, first friend," he said. "Have the police gotten to you yet?"

Pamela sank into the chair next to him. "I don't know what you mean, Justin. Why would the police want to talk to me?"

"They think I tried to kill Carolyn. Anything you want to contribute to help tighten the noose, old pal?"

She decided not to take the bait. "Justin, this isn't getting us anywhere. How do you think Carolyn is doing today?"

"I looked in on her, but only when the nurse was with me. Next thing you know, they'll accuse me of trying to pull the plug." He put his face in his hands and shook his head. "I don't *believe* this."

A nurse came to the door. "Dr. Susan Chandler is on the phone," she said. "She'd like to speak to you, Mr. Wells."

"Well, I don't want to speak to her," he snapped. "All this started with Carolyn making that call to her."

"Justin, please," Pamela said, standing and crossing to the waiting-room extension phone. "She's only trying to help." She picked up the receiver and held it out to him.

He stared at her for a moment, then walked over and took it. "Dr. Chandler," he said, "why are you hounding me? From what I understand, my wife wouldn't be in the hospital in the first place if she hadn't been on her way to you. Haven't you done enough harm? Please stay out of our lives."

He started to hang up but stopped with the receiver in midair.

"I don't think for one minute that you pushed your wife in front of that van!" Susan's voice was so loud that Pamela could hear it.

Justin Wells pressed the receiver against his ear. "And why do you say that?" he asked.

"Because I think someone else tried to kill her, and I think that person *did* kill Hilda Johnson, who was a witness to your wife's injury, and Tiffany Smith, another woman who called in to my show," Susan said. "I've got to meet with you. Please. You may have something I need."

Justin hung up a few minutes later. When he looked at Pamela, she saw only exhaustion in his face. "It may be just a trap to search our apartment without a warrant, but I'm going to meet her there at eight. Pam, she tells me that she thinks Carolyn is still in danger—but from the guy she met on that ship, not from me."

SUSAN didn't know what she expected Justin Wells to look like. Pamela Hastings and Don Richards had portrayed him as being excessively jealous. I guess I thought he would look sinister somehow, she realized as he opened the door to his apartment and she found herself looking into the troubled eyes of an attractive man in his early forties. Dark hair, broad shoulders, athletic build—he was downright good-looking, she decided. If looks were any criterion, certainly he was the last person whose appearance would indicate a man given to bouts of jealous rage.

"Come in, Dr. Chandler," said Wells. "Pam is here too. But first I'd like to apologize for the way I spoke to you earlier."

"It's Susan, not Dr. Chandler. And no apologies necessary."

The living room clearly reflected the fact that an architect and an interior designer lived there. The room had crown moldings, an intricately carved marble fireplace, satiny parquet floors, a delicately beautiful Persian carpet, comfortable-looking couches and chairs, and antique tables and lamps.

Pamela Hastings greeted Susan warmly. "This is very kind of you," she said. "I can't tell you what your coming here means to me personally."

She feels as though she's betrayed Justin Wells, Susan thought as she listened to Pamela's words. She gave the other woman a reassuring smile, then said, "Look, I know how spent you both have to be, so I'll get to the point. When Carolyn phoned me on Monday, she said she would come to my office and bring with her a turquoise ring and a picture of the man who gave it to her. We know now that she may have changed her mind and decided to mail those things to me instead. What I hope is that there are perhaps other things—souvenirs or whatever—that she kept from her cruise that would give us some indication of the mystery man she mentioned, the one who tried to convince her to leave the ship to go to Algiers. Remember she said that when she tried to phone him at the hotel where he was supposed to be staying, they said they'd never heard of him."

Wells's face flushed. "Doctor," he said, "you can understand that Carolyn and I didn't dwell on that trip, but as I told you on the phone, you are welcome to look for anything here that will help us to find the person who did this to Carolyn."

Susan noted an ominous quality in the tone of his voice.

CAROLYN Wells kept an office in the apartment, a large room complete with a spacious desk, a couch, a drafting board, and files. "She has a business office in the Design Building also," Wells explained to Susan. "But in fact, she does most of her creative work here, and certainly this is where she takes care of all of her personal mail." His voice was strained.

"Is the desk locked?" Susan asked.

"I don't know. I never touch it." Justin Wells turned away as though overwhelmed by emotion at the sight of his wife's desk.

Pamela Hastings put her hand on his arm. "Justin, why don't you wait for us in the living room? You don't need this."

"You're right. I don't." He got as far as the door before he turned. "But I insist on this: I want to know anything and everything you find, good or bad, that may be useful," he said. "Do I have your word?"

Both women nodded. When he turned to go down the hall, Susan turned to Pamela Hastings. "Let's get started," she said.

Hastings riffled through file drawers while Susan went through the desk. In the bottom desk drawer Susan found files with names written on them: MOM, JUSTIN, PAM.

Susan glanced in them just enough to see that they contained things like birthday cards, personal notes, and snapshots. She looked up and saw that Pamela Hastings had almost finished examining the three-drawer file. "How is it going?" Susan asked.

Pamela shrugged. "It isn't. From what I can see, Carolyn kept a mini-file here of her most recent jobs." Then she paused. "Wait a minute." She was holding a file marked SEAGODIVA. "That's the cruise ship Carolyn sailed on." She carried the file to the desk and pulled up a chair.

"Let's hope," Susan murmured as they began to go through it.

But the file seemed useless. It contained only the sort of information people save as mementos of a trip, things like the itinerary, the *Seagodiva*'s daily bulletins listing the activities of the day, and information about the approaching ports of call.

"Carolyn boarded the ship in Mumbai, but Algiers is where she almost went sightseeing with the mystery man," Pamela said. "Look at the date, October fifteenth. That's exactly two years ago next week."

Susan glanced through the bulletins. The last one described possible excursions from the ship. The headline was SEE THE MARKET-PLACE IN OLD ALGIERS.

That's a line in the song "You Belong to Me," she thought. Then she noticed that there was something written lightly in pencil on the last page. She bent down to examine it closely. It read, "Palace Hotel, 555-0634."

She showed it to Pamela. "Maybe that's where she was meeting the mystery man," she said quietly.

"Dear Lord, do you think he's Win, the one she is calling for now?" Pamela asked.

"I don't know. If only the picture she promised to give me was still here," Susan said. "I'll bet anything she kept it in this file." Her eyes swept the desk as though expecting the photograph to materialize. Then she noticed a sliver of bright blue cardboard next to a small pair of scissors.

"Does Carolyn have a housekeeper?" she asked.

"Yes. She comes in on Monday and Friday mornings. Why?"

"Because Carolyn phoned me shortly before twelve. Say a prayer that . . ." Susan did not finish the sentence as she reached under the desk for the wastebasket. Retrieving it, she dumped its contents on the rug. Bits of a blue cardboard folder scattered, and a photograph with an uneven border fell out.

Susan picked it up and studied it. "This is Carolyn, with the ship's captain, isn't it?"

"Yes, it is," Pamela said, "but why did she cut it like that?"

"My guess is she wanted to send only the part of the photograph that pictured the man who gave her the turquoise ring. She didn't want to be involved or identified herself."

"And now it's gone," Pamela said.

"It may be gone," Susan told her as she put together the scraps of cardboard, "but look at this. The name of the outfit in London that takes those pictures is printed on the folder, and there are instructions for ordering additional copies."

She pushed back the chair and stood up. "I'm going to call that outfit, and if they still have the negative of this photograph, I'm going to get it. Pamela," she said, her voice rising with excitement, "do you realize that if that's possible, we may be on our way to learning the identity of a serial killer?"

NAT SMALL WAS A LITTLE surprised at how much he actually missed his friend and fellow shop owner Abdul Parki. In the two days since Parki was murdered, the Khyem Specialty Shop had taken on a deserted look. You'd think it had been closed for years, Nat said to himself.

He grinned when he thought about the dopey-looking gift Parki gave him last year—a fat little guy with the head of an elephant, sitting on a throne.

It was Ganesha, Parki had told him in that singsong accent of his, "the god of wisdom, prosperity, and happiness."

Nat Small rarely yielded to a sentimental impulse, but in honor of his murdered friend he went back into the storage room, dug out the elephant god, and put it in the window, positioning it so that the elephant's trunk was pointed at Parki's store. I'll leave it there until somebody rents the place, he decided. It'll be a kind of memorial to a nice little guy.

DONALD Richards had told his housekeeper that he had dinner plans; then, not wanting to dine alone, he had phoned Mark Greenberg, a good friend and fellow psychiatrist whom he had seen professionally for a while after his wife's death. Greenberg was free for dinner. "Betsy is going with her mother to the opera," he said.

They met at Kennedy's, on West Fifty-seventh Street. Greenberg, a scholarly-looking man in his late forties, waited until their drinks arrived, then said, "Don, we haven't talked doctor to patient in a long time. How's it going?"

Richards smiled. "I'm restless. I guess that's a good sign."

"Still blame yourself for Kathy's death?" Greenberg asked.

"I'd like to believe I'm starting to get over that, but sometimes it still hits me hard. Mark, you've heard it from me enough times. Kathy didn't want to do that shoot. She was feeling queasy. Then she told me, 'I know what you're going to say, Don. It isn't fair to the others to pull out at the last minute.' I was always on her case about her habit of canceling plans at the last minute, especially work commitments. Well, listening to me cost her her life."

"But Kathy didn't tell you that she suspected she was pregnant," Greenberg reminded him. "Or you'd have urged her to stay home."

"No, she didn't tell me." Don Richards shrugged. "There're still rough times, but it's getting better. Maybe turning forty soon is making me realize that it's time to let go of the past."

"Have you considered taking a cruise—even a short one?"

"Actually, I am hoping to take one soon. I wrap up the publicity for the book next week in Miami, and I'm looking to see if I can find a cruise that I can fit in."

"That's good news," Greenberg said. "Last question: Are you dating anyone?"

"I had a date last night. Susan Chandler, a psychologist. She has a daily radio program as well as a private practice. Very attractive and interesting lady."

"Then I gather you plan to see her again?"

Don Richards smiled. "I'd say I have big plans for her, Mark."

WHEN Don Richards got home at ten o'clock, he debated calling Susan, then decided it wasn't too late to try.

She answered on the first ring.

"Susan, how do you feel?"

"Oh, better, I guess," Susan said. "I'm glad you called, Don. I wanted to ask you something."

"Go ahead."

"By any chance do you have any pictures that might have been taken on the *Gabrielle?* I'm hoping to learn the name of the photography outfit that works—or worked—the *Gabrielle.*"

"I'm sure I have some pictures."

"Would you mind checking? I'd really appreciate it."

"Hold on."

Donald Richards laid down the phone and went to the closet where he had stored pictures and mementos of his marriage. He pulled down a box from the top shelf that was marked VACATIONS and brought it back to the phone.

"Bear with me a minute," he told Susan. "If I have it, it'll be in the box I'm going through right now." He opened the top and looked at a picture of Kathy and himself at their table on the *Gabrielle*. He removed the picture from the folder and turned it over. On the back was information about reorders. His voice was steady as he read it to Susan.

"That's a real break," Susan said. "The same company handled the pictures on both the *Gabrielle* and the ship Carolyn sailed on. I might be able to get a copy of the picture we think Carolyn Wells was going to mail to me."

"You mean of the man who gave her the turquoise ring?"

Susan didn't answer directly. "I suppose I shouldn't be optimistic. They probably don't even have the negative any longer."

"Look, I'm going out of town Monday on the final leg of the publicity tour for my book," Don Richards said. "I'd really like to see you before I go. How's brunch, lunch, or dinner on Sunday?"

Susan laughed. "Let's make it dinner," she said.

After he hung up the phone, Donald Richards sat there for a while going through the pictures of the trips he and Kathy had taken together. It suddenly seemed a remote part of his life.

Clearly a change was due. In another week he might very well have put to rest all the torment of the past four years.

SUSAN looked at her watch. It was after ten. It had been a long day. Unfortunately, it wasn't going to be a long night. In less than six hours she had to be up and on the phone.

Four a.m. in New York would be nine a.m. in London. That's when she intended to call Ocean Cruise Pictures Ltd. and inquire about ordering photographs taken on the *Gabrielle* and the *Seagodiva* during those cruises when Regina Clausen and Carolyn Wells had been passengers. She put on a nightshirt, set the alarm clock for four, and went to bed.

WHEN the alarm went off, Susan struggled awake. She sat up in bed, then reached for the phone and pushed the long series of numbers that would connect her to the photography studio in London.

"Ocean Cruise Pictures Limited. How may I help you?"

A moment later Susan was talking to the reorder department. "We may indeed have the pictures from those cruises, madam. We keep the round-the-world photos a bit longer than the others."

But when Susan realized how many pictures had been taken between Mumbai and Athens on the *Seagodiva,* and between Perth and Hong Kong on the *Gabrielle,* she was shocked.

"You see, both ships were obviously quite full," the clerk explained. "So if you have seven hundred people on board, the odds are that while perhaps five hundred of them are couples, there still are many single passengers, and we try to take a number of photos of each person. We have photographers there while passengers are embarking on the ship, and many people want snaps taken at various ports of call, with the captain at the receptions, and at all the major social events. So you see there really are many opportunities for photographic keepsakes."

Hundreds of pictures, Susan thought; this could cost a fortune. "Wait a minute," she said. "The picture I want on the *Seagodiva* shows a single woman with the captain. Could you possibly go through those negatives and make a copy of all the pictures taken of a single woman posing with the captain?"

"On the leg from Mumbai to Athens in October two years ago?"

"That's right."

"We would, of course, need to be paid in advance."

"Of course," she said. "If the money is wired today, can you send the pictures by courier by tonight?"

"Certainly by tomorrow. You do realize we may be talking about as many as four hundred prints at twelve fifty U.S. each?"

"Yes, I do."

"I'm sure we'd be happy to offer a discount. I'll discuss it—"

Susan interrupted the clerk. "Look, just give me the information on the bank to which the money should be wired. It will be there by three o'clock your time today."

"Oh, then I really am afraid that we can't complete the job until tomorrow. But you'd still have the pictures on Monday."

10

ON FRIDAY morning Chris Ryan settled back in his ancient swivel chair and began to study the preliminary feedback he had gotten from his sources about Douglas Layton.

There was something funny about Layton, and one significant point stood out: For someone who was paid to both preserve and spend impressive sums of money, Layton seemed to have precious little of his own. "What gives?" Chris muttered to himself. Here's a guy in his mid-thirties, single, with no apparent financial responsibilities. He has worked with good companies for good bucks, yet it looks like he's worth nothing. His car is leased; his apartment's a rental. Checking account deposits just about cover monthly expenses. There's no savings account.

So what does Layton do with his money? Ryan wondered. There was definitely enough to justify a more probing investigation.

I'll give Susan a call, he decided. She'll probably derive a certain satisfaction from knowing she was right. As far as Doug Layton is concerned, there's something rotten in Denmark.

WHEN Susan arrived at her office, there was a call from Pete Sanchez waiting on the answering machine. She listened with a sense of triumph to the news that they had found the ring. This could be important, she thought as she reached for the phone.

"The D.A.'s office is grilling the suspect," Sanchez told her happily. "He'll break. Anyhow, what's with that crummy ring?"

Susan chose her words carefully. "Pete, I may be dead wrong, but I think these turquoise rings have everything to do with this case—"

Sanchez interrupted. "Susan, the guy who hit on Tiffany is in custody. I don't see where a ring has anything to do with it. We checked out the ex-boyfriend, Matt Bauer, the guy who bought her the ring. He's clear."

"Pete, trust me. That ring may be significant. Have you got it?"

"Right here."

"Any inscription on the inside?"

"Oh, yeah. It says, 'You belong to me.' "

"Pete," Susan begged, "please treat the ring as evidence and have your lab make enlarged photographs of it from every angle and fax them to me. And one more thing. I want to talk to Matt Bauer myself. Will you give me his phone number?"

"Susan, the guy's clean." Pete's tone was indulgent.

"Come on, Pete. I've done some favors for you."

After a moment of silence Sanchez gave her the number, then said, "Susan, if you're onto something, I want to know about it."

"It's a deal," Susan promised.

She had barely replaced the receiver before Janet announced a call from Chris Ryan, who filled her in on Douglas Layton.

He concluded by saying, "Susie, we're hot on the scent."

Yes, we are, Susan thought, and in more ways than you know. She asked Chris to keep her posted, then alerted Janet to be on the lookout for a fax from Yonkers.

IT WOULD have been too difficult and caused too much comment to break the morning's appointments, especially when he was going away in a few days' time, so he was able to catch only a little of Susan's radio program. As he had expected, the listeners were still anxious to talk about Tiffany's death.

"Dr. Susan, I live in Yonkers, and the guy they're questioning about Tiffany's murder is really bad. We all think he killed her."

"Dr. Susan, was Tiffany wearing the turquoise ring when she was murdered?"

This last was an interesting question, and one that disturbed him. *Had* she been wearing the ring? He didn't think so, but he wished now that he had thought to look for it.

Susan responded to the questions very much as he had expected:

There is a presumption of innocence, even in cases where a suspect has been convicted of a previous crime. She hadn't heard any mention of the ring in the media.

He knew what *that* meant. Susan wasn't buying the police theory as to Tiffany's murderer. She was too smart not to connect Tiffany's death to the others.

He wasn't worried. He had worked out the time frame for eliminating Susan. All that remained was to plan the details.

In the hidden compartment in his briefcase he was carrying the turquoise rings he had taken from Parki's shop—three of them plus the one Carolyn Wells had intended to mail to Susan. He needed only one, of course. The others he would toss in the ocean after he was finished with the final lonely lady. He would love to put one on Susan Chandler's finger once he had killed her, but then that would raise too many questions. No, he couldn't risk leaving it on her hand, but maybe for just a minute he would slip it on her finger to give himself the satisfaction of knowing that she, like the others, belonged to him.

"UNTIL Monday, this is Dr. Susan Chandler saying good-bye."

The red on-air signal over the studio door flashed off as Susan looked up at the control room, where Jed was taking off his headset. "How did it go?" she asked anxiously.

"Fine." Jed's voice softened. "It's been a tough couple of days. I know that. But things are looking up. Hey! You got to the studio today with twenty minutes to spare, and now it's the weekend!"

Susan made a face at him. "Cute," she said as she pushed back her chair and stood up. "See you Monday."

JANET handed Susan the faxes from Sanchez as soon as she walked through the door.

"Thanks, Janet," Susan said. She sat at her desk, laid out the faxes of the enlarged photos, and compared them with the ring Jane Clausen had given her. The photographer had managed to get some excellent shots of the inscription on the inside of the band. As

Susan expected, there were remarkable similarities between the ring in the photographs and the ring that had been Regina's.

I'm right, she thought. This *is* all about the rings. The one Mrs. Clausen gave me simply has to have been made by the same guy who made Tiffany's, which means it almost certainly was bought at the souvenir shop in the Village that Tiffany told me about. I'd stake my life that Tiffany was murdered because someone heard her talking to me on air about a man she had seen buying one of these rings, and he was afraid she could identify him.

Janet came into Susan's office, a bag from the luncheonette in hand. She placed it on Susan's desk. When Susan put down the turquoise ring, Janet picked it up and examined it. "What a nice sentiment," she said, squinting as she read the inscription. "My mother loves the old songs, and 'You Belong to Me' is one of her favorites."

In a voice that was low and only slightly off-key Janet began to sing: *"See the pyramids along the Nile / Watch the sunrise on a tropic isle."* She paused and hummed a few bars. "Then there's something about a *marketplace in old Algiers,* and something else about *photographs and souvenirs.* I don't remember how that part goes, but it's really a nice song."

"Yes, it is," Susan agreed absentmindedly. Like an alarm she couldn't shut off, the words of the song were sounding in her head. What is it about them? she wondered. She took the ring back and tucked it in her wallet.

It was ten of one. She should be preparing for her next session, but she didn't want to wait until two to try to reach Matt Bauer, the one other person who might be able to tell her the location of the souvenir shop at which he had bought the ring for Tiffany.

Susan dialed his office number but learned that Bauer was out. She left a message that it was urgent for him to call her.

MATT Bauer liked his job with Met Life. He intended to sit in one of the executive offices someday. That was why he was visibly distressed when he met Susan Chandler at five thirty in a coffee shop at Grand Central station.

Susan immediately liked the earnest-faced, clean-cut young man, and she was sympathetic when he explained why he did not want to get involved in a murder investigation.

"Dr. Chandler," he said, "I only went out with Tiffany a couple of times. She was fun, but I could tell right away there wasn't any spark between us, and I could tell right away that what she wanted was a serious relationship, not an occasional date."

The waitress poured their coffee, and Matt Bauer took a sip before continuing. "We went to see a film down in the Village. Afterward we just kind of walked around a little, looking in shop-windows. I don't know one end of the Village from the other."

"That was when you went into the souvenir shop?" Susan asked. Let him remember where it was, she prayed.

"Yes. Actually, Tiffany was the one who stopped when something in the window caught her eye."

"What do you remember about the shop, Matt?"

He thought a minute. "It was stuffed with cheap souvenirs, but it was still neat, if you know what I mean. The owner—or clerk, whichever—was from India, and in addition to the usual Statues of Liberty and T-shirts he had an array of brass elephants and Hindu gods—that sort of thing."

Susan opened her purse and took out the turquoise ring Regina Clausen's mother had given her. She showed it to Matt Bauer. "Do you recognize this?"

He studied the ring carefully. "Does it say 'You belong to me' on the inside of the band?"

"Yes, it does."

"Then I'd say, from what I remember, that it's the ring I gave Tiffany, or one just like it."

Susan said, "From what Tiffany told me, the reason you bought the ring was that some man came in and purchased one, and the clerk told you that the same man already had bought several others. Do you remember?"

"I remember it, but I never actually saw the guy," Matt said. "The shop was small to begin with, and there was a painted wooden screen that blocked my view of the counter. Also, as I recall, I was reading about one of the figurines. It had the head of an elephant and the body of a man, and it was supposed to be the god of wisdom, prosperity, and happiness. I showed Tiffany the elephant god, but she wasn't interested. The ring was the souvenir she wanted." Bauer shook his head. "It was only ten bucks, but you'd have thought I'd bought her an engagement ring."

"How often did you see her after that?"

"Only once." He looked at his watch. "Dr. Chandler, I'm sorry, but I honestly have to leave." He signaled for the check.

"This is on me," Susan said. She purposely had not asked about the location of the shop. She still held a faint hope that as Matt talked about what happened, something about the location would emerge from his subconscious.

When she did ask, the only thing he could tell her was that they were heading toward the subway stop at West Fourth and Sixth when they saw the souvenir shop.

"Matt, Tiffany mentioned a porn shop across the street from where you bought the ring. Do you remember that?"

As he got up to go, he shook his head. "No, I don't." He paused. "You know, underneath that tough exterior Tiffany was a sweet kid. I hope they find who did this to her. Good-bye."

Susan paid the check, picked up her shoulder bag, and took a cab downtown to West Fourth Street and Sixth Avenue. Her plan was to move out from the subway station along the haphazard streets of the Village until she found a souvenir store featuring Indian goods that was located across the street from a porn shop. It sounded simple enough. How many could there be?

She wasn't there yet, but she was narrowing the circle around the killer. She could *feel* it.

THE names of the streets she had walked echoed like a litany in her mind: Christopher, Grove, Barrow, Commerce, Morton. Unlike the grid of uptown Manhattan, the streets of the Village followed an irregular pattern all their own. Finally Susan gave up, bought the

Post, and dropped in to Tutta Pasta on Carmine for a late dinner.

She nibbled on warm bread dipped in olive oil and sipped a Chianti as she read the paper. On page 3 she saw a picture of Tiffany, taken from her senior yearbook, with a story on the progress of the murder investigation. Then on page 6 she was startled to see the photograph of Justin Wells and the report that he was being questioned about circumstances surrounding his wife's accident.

I'm not going to be able to convince anyone there's a connection between these two cases until I locate that souvenir shop and talk to the clerk, she thought. And show him that cruise picture that's supposed to arrive Monday.

She arrived home at ten o'clock and wearily went to the answering machine. The message light was blinking. Alex Wright had phoned at nine: "Just calling to say hello. Looking forward to tomorrow evening. In case we don't touch base during the day, I'll pick you up at six thirty."

He's letting me know that he's home tonight, Susan thought. That's good.

It's not going to be a shower tonight, she decided. After this day I need a long, hot soak in the tub. There isn't a physical or mental piece of me that isn't worried, sad, irritated, or aching.

Forty minutes later she opened the bedroom windows, her final task before getting into bed. When she glanced down into the street, she noticed that it was deserted except for a solitary stroller whose silhouette she could barely make out.

DESPITE—or perhaps because of—the exhaustion she had felt earlier, Susan was unable to sleep well. Three different times during the night she woke up and found herself listening intently for any sound that might suggest someone was in the apartment. The first time she woke, she thought she had heard the outer door opening. The sensation was so vivid that she got up and ran to the door, only to find that it was bolted. Then, feeling slightly foolish, she tested the locks on the windows in the living room, den, and kitchen.

She returned to her bedroom, haunted by the sensation that

something was amiss but determined not to close the bedroom windows. I am two flights up, she told herself sternly.

The temperature had dropped sharply since she went to bed, and the room was almost icy cold. She pulled the blankets around her neck, recalling the dream that had made her so uneasy and finally awakened her. In it she had seen Tiffany running out of a door and into a dimly lighted space. She had the turquoise ring and was tossing it in the air. A hand appeared out of the shadows and grabbed the ring, and Tiffany cried out, "No! Don't take it! I want to keep it!" Then her eyes widened in terror, and she screamed.

Susan shivered. And now Tiffany is dead because she called me, she thought. Oh, I'm so sorry.

Suddenly the window shade rattled, blown by a sharp breeze. That's what startled me, she realized, and she considered getting up and locking the window. Instead, she pulled the covers tighter against her chin and was asleep in just a few minutes.

The second time Susan awoke, she bolted up in bed, sure there had been someone at the window. Get a grip on yourself, she thought as she pulled the blankets almost over her head.

She awoke for the third time at six o'clock. She realized that her subconscious had been dwelling on the passenger list from the *Seagodiva,* which Justin Wells had allowed her to take.

Awake now, with no hope of going back to sleep, she decided that coffee would help to clear her brain. After the coffee was made, she brought a cup back to bed, propped herself up with pillows, and began to study the ship's manifest.

She noted that in the case of married couples the names were listed in alphabetical order, so that Mrs. Alice Jones was followed by Mr. Robert Jones, and so on. Eliminating all those who were clearly married couples, Susan went down the manifest, checking off the names of men who were listed without a woman's name preceding or following. The first name on the manifest that appeared to be that of a single man was Mr. Owen Adams.

Interesting, Susan thought when she finished running down the entire list of passengers. There were one hundred and twenty-five women listed singly, but only sixteen men who apparently were traveling alone. That narrowed it down a lot.

Then another thought struck her: Would the manifest of the *Gabrielle* be among Regina Clausen's effects? And if so, was it possible that one of those sixteen men from the *Seagodiva* had been a passenger on that ship too?

Susan tossed back the covers and headed to the shower. Even if Mrs. Clausen isn't up to seeing me, I'm going to ask her about the *Gabrielle* passenger list, she decided, and if it *was* returned with Regina's things, I'll beg her to let her housekeeper give it to me.

FEATHERS in the wind. Feathers in the wind. He could feel them scattering, dancing, mocking him. Now he knew he could never retrieve them all. He wished there was some way he could accelerate his plan, but it was too late. The steps had been laid out, and it couldn't be changed. He would leave on schedule, but then he would double back, and that's when he would eliminate her.

Last night, when he was walking past Susan's brownstone, she happened to come to the window. He knew she couldn't see him clearly, but it did make him realize that he must not take a risk like that again.

When he returned to New York, he would find a way to take care of her. He would not follow her and try to force her into traffic as he had with Carolyn Wells. No. He would have to corner Susan alone, as he had Tiffany. That would be best.

This afternoon, in the guise of a messenger, he would check out her office building. The thought of killing Susan there was eminently satisfying. He would honor her with the same form of death that he had accorded Veronica, Regina, Constance, and Monica— the same death that was awaiting his final victim, someone on a voyage to *see the jungle when it's wet with rain*.

He would overpower her, tie her up, and gag her, and as she watched, tortured with fear, he would slowly unwrap the long plastic bag, and inch by agonizing inch he would cover her with it. Once she was covered head to toe, he would seal the bag. There would be a little air inside—just enough so that she would have a few minutes to struggle. Then, as he saw the plastic begin to stick to her face and seal her mouth and nostrils, he would leave.

He would not be able to dispose of Susan's body as he had the others. The others he had buried in sand or weighted down with stones and watched them disappear into murky waters. Susan Chandler he would have to leave, but he could take comfort in the fact that after she was out of the way, the next—and final—victim would share the burial arrangement of her sisters in death.

11

SUSAN left her apartment at nine o'clock Saturday morning. Continuing her search, she explored all the blocks of the Village that slanted west toward the Hudson River. Most of these streets were largely residential, although she did find several souvenir shops. In none of them, however, did she see a sign of Indian-style objects.

At noon she used her cell phone to call Jane Clausen at Memorial Sloan-Kettering Hospital. To her surprise Mrs. Clausen readily agreed to Susan's request to visit her.

"I'll be there by four," Susan promised.

The day had started out overcast and chilly, but by early afternoon the sun broke through. She bought a pretzel and a cola from a street vendor and ate while she continued her search. She was exploring the area east of Sixth Avenue, and she turned onto Mac-Dougal Street. As she walked downtown from Washington Square, she stopped so suddenly that the teenager behind her bumped into her. "Sorry," he muttered.

Susan did not answer him. She was staring into the window of a shop she had just come upon. Over the entrance hung an oval-shaped sign that read DARK DELIGHTS.

Dark delights, indeed, she thought as she looked again at the display window. Inside, a red satin garter belt was draped over a pile of videotapes with crudely suggestive titles. But Susan's attention was riveted on an object in the center of the window: a turquoise-inlaid elephant god, its trunk facing outward.

She spun around. Across the street she saw a FOR RENT sign in the window of the Khyem Specialty Shop.

Oh, no! she thought. She crossed the narrow street to the shop, stood at the door, and peered inside. A counter with a cash register was visible directly in front of the entrance. To the left she could see a large painted screen that acted as a room divider. That must be the screen Matt described, she thought, the one behind which he and Tiffany had been standing when the man came into the shop to purchase a turquoise ring.

But where was the clerk who had been there that day?

Then she realized suddenly that there was one person who might know. She rushed back across the street to the porn shop. There appeared to be only one clerk, a thin, unattractive man who, like his surroundings, seemed a little seedy.

He looked at her nervously as she approached the counter. She realized instantly that he thought she might be a plainclothes policewoman. She pointed to the Khyem Specialty Shop across the street. "When did that store close?" she asked.

The clerk's nervous demeanor vanished.

"Lady, you haven't heard what happened? Abdul Parki, the guy who owned that place, was murdered Tuesday afternoon."

"Murdered!" Susan made no effort to hide the dismay in her voice. Another one, she thought. Another one. Tiffany talked about the shop's owner on my program.

"Did you know Parki?" the man asked. "He was a sweet guy."

She shook her head, struggling to compose herself. "A friend of mine recommended his shop," she said. "Someone gave her one of the turquoise rings he made." She opened her bag and pulled out the ring Jane Clausen had given her.

The man glanced at the ring and then at her. "Yeah, that's one of

Parki's rings, all right. By the way, I'm Nat Small. I own this place."

"I'm Susan Chandler." Susan held out her hand. "I can tell he was a good friend of yours. How did it happen?"

"Stabbed. The cops think it was druggies, although they didn't take nothing so far as anyone can tell."

Susan could see the genuine sadness in Nat Small's face. "Were there any witnesses?" she asked.

"Nobody seen nothing." Small looked away as he spoke.

"Actually, the woman who told me about Parki was stabbed to death on Wednesday night," Susan said quietly. "I think the person who killed both her and Parki is a customer who bought several of these rings from him over the past three or four years."

Nat Small's sallow complexion turned a deeper gray. "Parki told me about that guy. Said he was a real gentleman."

Susan took a chance. "Nat, I sense there's something you're not telling me. You've *got* to tell me before someone else dies."

Nat Small looked nervously toward the door. His voice was almost a whisper now. "Just before one o'clock Tuesday afternoon a guy was kind of hanging around, looking in my window. I figured maybe he was nervous about coming in here—he looked like a real uptown kind of guy—but then he went across the street and into Parki's shop. After that a customer came in here, and I didn't pay attention anymore."

"Did you report what you saw to the police?"

"That's what I didn't do. The police'd have me going through mug books, but it would be a waste. He was not the kind to be in mug books. He was classy-looking, in his late thirties."

"You think you'd recognize this man if I showed you his picture?"

"Yeah, I would. He had sunglasses on, but I got a good look at his profile. Listen, you gotta get out of here. You're bad for business. Guys don't want to shop with a classy-looking dame hanging around."

"Right away. Oh, and one more thing, Nat. Don't talk about this—not to anybody. For your own safety don't talk about it."

"Are you kidding? Of course I won't. I promise."

WHEN DOUGLAS LAYTON went into Jane Clausen's hospital room at three thirty, he found her sitting in a chair. She was dressed in a soft blue cashmere robe, and a blanket was tucked around her.

"Douglas," she said, weariness showing in her voice, "have you brought me my surprise? I've been trying to imagine what it could possibly be."

"Close your eyes, Mrs. Clausen," he said as he turned the framed sketch so she could see the rendering of the orphanage that showed Regina's name on the carved sign.

Jane Clausen opened her eyes, and for long moments she studied the picture. Only a tear in the corner of her left eye hinted at the emotion she was feeling. "How very lovely," she said. "I can't think of a nicer tribute to Regina."

"I'll be attending the dedication of the new wing next week. We were going to wait and show you this and the pictures from the ceremony at the same time, but my hunch was that it would give you a lift to see this one now."

"You mean you wanted me to see it before I die?" she said.

"No, I don't mean that, Mrs. Clausen."

"Doug, don't look so guilt stricken. I *am* going to die. We both know that. And seeing this does give me great happiness." She smiled sadly. "It's a comfort to me that the money Regina would have inherited is going to be used to help other people. In a way, it's as though she'll be living through the people whose lives are touched and bettered because of her."

"I can promise you, Mrs. Clausen, that every cent we spend in Regina's name will be carefully committed."

There was a soft tap at the door. Susan Chandler looked in. "Oh, Mrs. Clausen, I didn't know you had company. I'll stay in the waiting area while you two visit."

"Absolutely not. Come in, Susan. You remember Douglas Layton, don't you?"

"Yes," she said coolly. "How are you, Mr. Layton?"

"Very well, Dr. Chandler." She knows something, he thought.

A classy-looking guy in his late thirties, Susan thought, reflecting on the description Nat Small had given of the man he saw standing outside his shop on the day Abdul Parki was murdered. But then it fits many dozens of other men.

There was a tap on the door, and a nurse put her head in the room. "Mrs. Clausen, the doctor will be here in just a minute."

"Oh, dear. Susan, I'm afraid I've dragged you up here for nothing. Will you call me in the morning?"

"Of course."

"Before you go, you must see the surprise Doug had for me." She pointed to the framed sketch. "This is an orphanage in Guatemala that is being dedicated next week to Regina."

Susan examined it closely. "How lovely," she said sincerely. "I understand there's a desperate need for facilities like this in many countries, and especially in Central America."

"That's exactly right," Layton assured her. "And the Clausen Family Trust is helping to build them."

As she turned to leave, Susan noticed a familiar-looking bright blue folder on the nightstand next to the bed. She walked over and picked it up. As she had expected, the front of the folder displayed the logo of Ocean Cruise Pictures. She looked at Mrs. Clausen. "May I?"

"Absolutely. That was probably the last picture ever taken of Regina."

There was no mistaking that the woman in the picture was Jane Clausen's daughter. The same eyes and the same straight nose. Even the widow's peak on the hairline was similar.

"Regina was very attractive," Susan said sincerely.

"Yes, she was. I know that photograph was made two days before she disappeared," Jane Clausen said. "She looks very happy in it. Knowing that has been a comfort in some ways, a torment in others. I wonder if her happiness has to do with trusting the person responsible for her disappearance."

"Try not to think about it that way," Doug Layton suggested.

"I'm sorry I have to interrupt." The doctor was standing in the doorway. Clearly he expected them to leave.

Susan could not wait any longer for Layton to depart. "Mrs. Clausen," she said hurriedly, "do you remember if a passenger list from the cruise ship was among Regina's things?"

"I'm sure I saw one. Why, Susan?"

"Because if I may, I would very much like to borrow it for a few days. Could I pick it up tomorrow?"

"If it's important, you'd better get it now. I insisted that Vera take a few days off and visit her daughter, and she's planning to leave very early in the morning."

"I'd be happy to get it now if you don't mind," Susan said.

"Not at all," Jane Clausen said, her voice suddenly brisk. "Douglas, hand me my purse, please. It's in the night table."

She took out her wallet and pulled a card from inside. After jotting a note on it, she handed it to Susan. "I'll phone Vera to let her know you're coming, but you can take this note just in case; it has my address. We'll talk tomorrow," she said.

Douglas Layton left with Susan. Together they went down in the elevator and out to the street. "I'd be happy to go with you," he suggested. "Vera knows me very well."

"No, that's fine. Here's a cab. I'll grab it."

IT WAS five o'clock before Susan reached the Beekman Place address. Knowing that she was going to have to rush back to her apartment to get ready for the evening, she was grateful that Jane Clausen had phoned the housekeeper.

"These are all Regina's things," Vera explained as she took Susan into the elegant but inviting guest room. "The furniture is from her apartment. Mrs. Clausen sits in here by herself sometimes. It would make your heart break to see her."

Vera opened the top drawer of an antique desk and took out a legal-sized manila envelope. "All the papers found in Regina's stateroom are here."

Inside were the kinds of memorabilia that Carolyn Wells had also brought back from her cruise. In addition to the passenger list there were a half-dozen copies of the daily shipboard news bulletins, with information about the upcoming ports of call, and postcards that seemed to be from those ports.

Susan put the passenger list in her shoulder bag, then decided to take a quick look at the postcards and bulletins. She flipped through the cards, stopping when she noticed one from Bali that featured an outdoor restaurant. A table overlooking the ocean had been neatly circled in pen.

Why was it special? Susan wondered. She skimmed through the newsletters until she found the one about Bali. The headline read WATCH THE SUNRISE ON A TROPIC ISLE.

"I'm going to take this card and this bulletin," she told Vera. "I'm sure it will be all right with Mrs. Clausen."

It was twenty after five when she finally managed to hail a cab, and it was ten of six before she opened the door of her apartment. Forty minutes to get ready for the big date with Alex, she thought, and I haven't even decided what to wear.

PAMELA Hastings sat in the waiting room of the intensive care unit at Lenox Hill Hospital trying to comfort a sobbing Justin Wells. Just minutes ago the monitors in Carolyn's room had emitted a frantic warning, and code 9 had been activated. "I thought I'd lost her," he said, his voice breaking with emotion. "I thought I'd lost her."

"Carolyn's a fighter. She'll pull through," Pamela said reassuringly. "Justin, a Dr. Donald Richards phoned the hospital to inquire about Carolyn and about you. He left his number. Isn't he the psychiatrist you consulted when you and Carolyn had problems earlier?"

"The psychiatrist I was *supposed* to consult," Wells said. "I only saw him once."

"His message was that he'd be glad to help in any way possible." She paused, worried how he would react to what she was going to say next. "Justin, may I call him? I think you need to talk to someone." She felt his body stiffen.

"Pam, you still think I did that to Carolyn, don't you?"

"No, I don't," she said firmly. "I'll say it to you as straight as I can. I believe that Carolyn is going to make it, but I also know we are not out of the woods yet. If—God forbid—she doesn't make it, you're going to need help. Please let me call him."

Justin nodded slowly. "Okay."

When Pamela returned a few minutes later, she was smiling. "He's on his way over, Justin," she said. "He sounds like a nice man. Please let him help you if he can."

"YOU'RE early," Susan said when she answered the lobby intercom, dismay apparent in her voice.

"I won't get in your way, I promise," said Alex Wright. "I hate to wait in cars. Makes me feel like a taxi driver."

Susan laughed. "All right, come on up."

Of all the luck, she thought. Her hair was still wrapped in a towel. Her gown, a black tuxedo jacket with a long, narrow skirt, was hanging over the tub in the bathroom, an effort to steam out the last of the wrinkles. She was wearing the fuzzy white bathrobe that made her feel like an Easter bunny.

Alex laughed when she opened the door. "You look about ten years old," he told her. "Want to play doctor?"

She made a face. "Behave yourself and turn on the news." She closed the bedroom door, sat at the vanity, and pulled out the hair dryer. "I *am* late," she murmured as she turned the dryer onto the highest setting.

Fifteen minutes later she looked in the mirror. Her hair was fine, the makeup obscured the strain she had seen earlier in her face, so everything seemed to be in order. Yet somehow she didn't feel right. Had she been too worried, too rushed, or what? she asked herself as she picked up her evening bag.

She found Alex watching television as instructed. He looked at her and smiled. "You're lovely," he said.

"Thank you."

"I watched the news, so I'll tell you all about what went on in New York today once we're in the car."

"I can't wait."

SHE LOOKS GREAT, JIM CURLEY thought as he held open the car door. Really great. During the drive uptown to the library he kept his eyes on the traffic, but he focused his attention on the conversation in the back seat.

"Susan, there's one thing I'd like to clear up," Alex Wright said. "I had not planned to ask your sister to the dinner tonight."

"Please don't worry about that. Dee is my sister, and I love her."

"I'm sure you do. But I suspect you don't love Binky, and maybe I made a mistake inviting her and your father as well."

Oh, boy, Jim thought.

"I didn't know they were coming," Susan said, an edge of irritation apparent in her voice.

"Susan, please understand that I only wanted you with me tonight. Inviting Dee was not my intention, and when it happened, I thought that if I included your father and Binky and asked them to bring Dee, I'd be making a statement."

Good explanation, Jim thought. Now come on, Susan. Give the guy a break. He heard her laugh.

"Alex, please, I think I'm sending the wrong signals. I didn't mean to sound so irritable. You've got to forgive me. This has been a dreadful week."

"Tell me about it, then."

"Not now, but thanks for asking."

It's going to go okay, Jim thought with a sigh of relief.

"Susan, this is something I don't discuss much, but I do understand how you feel about Binky. I had a stepmother too, although in my case it was a little different. My father remarried after my mother died. Her name was Gerie."

He usually never talks about her, Jim thought. He really is opening up to Susan.

"What was your relationship with Gerie?" Susan inquired.

Don't ask, Jim thought.

ALTHOUGH she had been inside the huge Fifth Avenue branch of the New York Public Library many times, Susan Chandler didn't remember ever seeing the McGraw Rotunda, where the party was taking place. It was a magnificent space. With its soaring stone walls and life-size murals it made her feel as though she had been transported to another century.

Despite the setting and despite the fact that she really was enjoying Alex Wright's company, an hour later Susan found herself distracted and unable to relax. I should be enjoying a very pleasant evening, she thought, and here I am, preoccupied with thoughts of a very questionable man who runs a porn shop and who may be able to identify a murderer.

Maybe I should have stayed in the district attorney's office, she thought as she half listened to Gordon Mayberry, an elderly gentleman intent on telling her of the generosity of the Wright Family Foundation toward the New York Public Library.

Dee and her father and Binky came in minutes after she and Alex arrived. Dee, exquisite in a white sheath, had hugged her warmly. "Susie, have you heard I'm moving back to New York—lock, stock, and barrel? We'll have fun. I've missed not having you around."

I actually believe she *means* it, Susan thought. That's why what she's been trying to pull with Alex is so unfair.

"Have you seen the book that is being presented to Alex tonight?" Gordon Mayberry asked.

"No, I haven't," Susan replied, forcing herself to focus.

"A limited edition, of course. A copy will be given to all the guests, but you may enjoy taking a look at it before dinner. It will give you some idea of the enormous amount of good work the Wright Family Foundation has accomplished." He pointed to a stand near the entrance to the rotunda. "It's over there."

The book was open to the center pages, but Susan turned it back to the beginning. The table of contents showed that the book was divided into sections according to the various charities: hospitals, libraries, orphanages, research facilities.

She leafed through it at random. Then, thinking of Jane Clausen, she turned to the section that dealt with orphanages. Midway through those pages she stopped and studied a photograph of an orphanage. This must be a typical structure for that use, she thought. Typical kind of landscaping too.

"Really fascinating, isn't it?" Alex was at her side.

"Pretty impressive, I'd say," she told him.

"If you can tear yourself away, they're about to serve dinner."

Despite the elegance of the meal, Susan once again found herself distracted, so that she didn't notice what she was eating. I should have the pictures from Carolyn's cruise Monday, she thought. But what will I find? When Carolyn phoned the radio station and mentioned the photograph, she said the man who invited her to see Algiers was just in the background of that shot. And what about Regina's cruise? Maybe there are pictures from her trip that caught him. I should have ordered them as well, she thought.

The presentation of the book was made after the main course had been cleared. The director of the library spoke about the generosity of the Wright Family Foundation and about the grant to purchase and maintain rare books. She spoke also of the "modesty and dedication of Alexander Carter Wright, who so unselfishly devotes his life to running the foundation."

"See what a nice guy I am," Alex whispered to Susan as he stood to accept the book the director was presenting.

Alex was a good speaker, his manner easy and laced with a touch of humor. When he was seated again, Susan murmured, "Alex, do you mind if I switch places with Dee for dessert?"

"Susan, is anything wrong?"

"No, not at all. Peace in the family and all that. I can see that Dee is unhappy having her ear bent by Gordon Mayberry. Maybe if I rescue her, we'll bond a little." She laughed.

Alex's amused chuckle followed her as she walked to the nearby table and asked Dee to trade places. There's another reason to do this, she acknowledged to herself. If I'm going to start dating Alex, I want to be very sure that Dee won't be in the picture. If there is going to be a competition, I want to head it off before it can get started. I don't want to go through another situation like we had with Jack.

She waited until Mayberry had Binky's ear before giving in once more to a sense of foreboding.

I know Nat Small may be at risk, she thought. And he may not be the only one. There could be another person marked to receive one of those turquoise rings with "You belong to me" engraved inside the band.

Why did the lyrics of that song keep running through her head? Now she was hearing *Watch the sunrise on a tropic isle.*

Of course! Those words had been on the bulletin from the *Gabrielle* that she had found among Regina Clausen's effects.

I'll have the pictures from the *Seagodiva* on Monday, Susan thought. That means by Monday night I should have found Carolyn's picture. If the studio can make copies of the photographs from the *Gabrielle* by Tuesday afternoon, I'll have them Wednesday. I'll spend as much time as necessary going through them, even if I have to stay up all night.

"ON SUNDAY mornings Regina and I often attended services at St. Thomas's," Jane Clausen told Susan. "The music there is simply wonderful. I couldn't bring myself to go back for over a year after I lost her."

"I just came from the ten fifteen at St. Pat's," Susan told her. "The music is magnificent there as well." She had walked to the hospital from the cathedral. It was another beautiful fall day.

Jane Clausen clearly realized she had very little time left. It seemed to Susan that everything she said reflected that.

"It's very kind of you to stop by again today," Mrs. Clausen said. "Yesterday I didn't have the opportunity to speak with you privately, and I do need to do that. Douglas Layton has been very thoughtful, very kind. I told you that I felt I had misjudged him earlier and that my doubts about him were unfounded. On the other hand, if I make the move I'm contemplating—that is, asking the current director of the family trust to step aside and let Douglas take over—I will be giving him a great deal of authority over a substantial amount of money."

Don't do it! Susan thought.

Jane Clausen continued. "That's why I want to ask you to have Douglas Layton thoroughly investigated before I take this major step. I realize it's an imposition, but I've come to think of you as a trusted friend."

Susan knew it was not the moment to tell Jane Clausen that Layton already was being checked out. She chose her words carefully. "I think it's always wise to be very cautious before making major changes, Mrs. Clausen. I promise you I'll take care of it."

"Thank you. That relieves me greatly."

Susan searched for an appropriate way to explain her next request, but she realized she had best save explanations for later. "Mrs. Clausen, I have my camera with me. Would you mind if I took a few Polaroids of the sketch of the orphanage?"

Jane Clausen drew her shawl closer around her shoulders. "You have a reason for wanting that, Susan. What is it?"

"Will you let me tell you tomorrow?"

"I'd rather know now, of course, but I can wait. Tell me, Susan, did you ever hear from the young woman who phoned your program Monday morning, the one who said she had a turquoise ring like the one that belonged to Regina?"

Susan answered carefully. "You mean Karen? Yes and no. Her real name is Carolyn Wells. She was seriously injured a few hours after she made the call, and I haven't been able to speak to her, because she's in a coma."

"How terrible."

"She keeps calling for someone named Win. I think it might be the name of the man she met on the cruise ship, but I haven't been able to confirm it. Mrs. Clausen, did Regina ever phone you from the *Gabrielle?*"

"Several times."

"Did she ever mention anyone named Win?"

"No. She never discussed any of the passengers by name."

Susan, hearing the fatigue in Mrs. Clausen's voice, said, "I'm going to take those pictures and be on my way."

The sketch was propped on the bureau opposite the bed. Using her flash, Susan shot four pictures, watching them develop one by one. Satisfied that she had enough, she replaced the camera in her purse and quietly started for the door.

"Good-bye, Susan," Jane Clausen said, her voice heavy with sleep. "You know, you've just reminded me of something very pleasant. At my debut one of my escorts was named Owen. I hadn't thought of him in years, but I had quite a crush on him."

Owen, Susan thought. *That's* what Carolyn is saying. Not "Oh, Win," but "Owen."

She remembered there was an Owen Adams on the passenger list of the *Seagodiva*. He was the first man she had checked off as traveling without a wife.

Twenty minutes later Susan rushed into her apartment, ran to her desk, and grabbed the passenger list from the *Gabrielle*. Be here, she thought. Be here.

There was no Owen Adams listed, but realizing the man she was looking for might very well travel under a false name, she continued searching through the *Gabrielle*'s passenger list.

She was almost at the end when she found it. One of the very few passengers whose middle name appeared on that list was Henry Owen Young. There must be a connection, she thought.

ALEX Wright called Susan at her apartment at ten, eleven, and twelve before finally reaching her at one. "Tried you earlier, but you were out," he said. "I wanted to buy you brunch."

"Thanks, but I couldn't have made it," Susan told him. "I went to see a friend in the hospital. Which reminds me, Alex, is there any such thing as a standard orphanage in Central America?"

"Standard? I'm not sure what you mean. Why?"

"Because I have some pictures I need to show you," said Susan. "Are you going to be home for a while?"

"All afternoon."

"I'm on my way."

I know I'm right, Susan thought as she replaced the receiver.

These two buildings aren't just similar—they're the same. But this way I'll be absolutely sure.

The book about the Wright Family Foundation was lying on her desk, its pages open to the picture of the orphanage in Guatemala that had caught her eye. Line for line it appeared to be exactly like the sketch Jane Clausen had in her hospital room.

WHEN he studied the photographs, Alex saw something she had overlooked, but rather than distinguishing one building from the other, it confirmed the fact that they were the same. In the sketch Mrs. Clausen had, the artist had painted a small animal over the front door of the orphanage. "Look at this," Alex said. "That's an antelope. Look at the photograph in the book. It's there as well. The antelope is taken from our family crest; we always have one over the door of any building we fund." They were sitting side by side at the desk in Susan's den. "The sculpted sign in the sketch is definitely a phony, Susan. My guess is that someone is pocketing the money that was supposedly used to fund this building."

Susan closed the Wright Family Foundation book. "I'll show this photograph to Mrs. Clausen tomorrow. She's got to know as soon as possible." She looked at her desk, suddenly realizing how untidy it must seem in Alex's eyes.

"I'm not usually this messy," she explained. "I've been working on a couple of projects, and the papers have piled up."

Alex picked up the booklet with the passenger list from the *Seagodiva* and opened it. "Was this a cruise you were on?"

"No. I've never been on a cruise." Susan hoped Alex wouldn't ask any more questions about it. She didn't want to talk about what she was doing to anyone, not even him.

"Neither have I," he said as he dropped the booklet back on the desk. "I get seasick."

He stood up. "I should go. I've got a messy desk that should be cleared as well." He turned to her at the door. "Susan," he said, "tomorrow I'm going to Russia—St. Petersburg—to finalize the plans for the hospital we're building there. I'll be gone a week or ten days. Stay as busy as you want during that time, but after that don't get too booked up. Okay?"

Just as she closed the door behind him, the phone rang. It was Dee calling to say good-bye. "I'm leaving for Costa Rica tomorrow. I pick up the ship there," she said. "Wasn't last night fun?"

"It was great."

"I called Alex to thank him, but he's out."

Susan heard the question in her sister's voice, but she had no intention of explaining that Alex had been with her. "Maybe you'll catch him later. Have a marvelous time, Dee."

She hung up, painfully aware that the reason she could not take greater pleasure in being with Alex was that she still felt something could develop between him and Dee, especially if Dee kept pursuing him. And Susan had no intention of going through the distress of losing another man to her sister.

DON Richards had felt restless all day. Early Sunday morning he had run in Central Park. Afterward he came home and made a cheese omelette, reflecting that during his marriage he had been the regular Sunday-morning chef but had gotten out of the habit. He read the *Times* while he ate, but finally, after pouring a second cup of coffee, he found he was unable to concentrate, so he laid down the paper and walked into the bedroom.

He had to pack for his trip tomorrow, and the prospect irritated him. It was almost over, though. There was only one week more of publicity for the book, and then he was taking a week off to himself. The travel agent had faxed a list of cruise ships with empty first-class space that would accommodate his schedule.

He went back to his desk to look at it.

BY TWO o'clock he was in Tuxedo Park. His mother arrived home from having lunch at the club with friends to find him sitting on her porch steps. "Don, dear, why didn't you tell me you were coming?" she asked, feigning irritation.

"When I left, I wasn't sure that I was. You look nice, Mother."

"So do you. I like you in a sweater." She saw the suitcase beside him. "Are you moving in, dear?"

He smiled. "No. I just wanted to ask you to put this in the attic."

"Lots of room in the attic," Elizabeth Richards said.

"You're not going to ask me what's in it?"

"I suspect it has something to do with Kathy."

"I've taken every single thing that I still had of Kathy's out of the apartment, Mother. Does that shock you?"

"Don, I think you needed those reminders until now. I sense, though, that you're trying to go forward with your personal life—and you know Kathy can't be part of it. By the way, I know you have a key to the house. Why didn't you just go in?"

"I saw your car was gone, and I suddenly realized I didn't want to go into an empty house." He got up and stretched. "I'll have a cup of tea with you; then I'm off. I have a date tonight. That's two in a week with the same person. How about that?"

HE CALLED Susan from the vestibule of her building promptly at seven. "I apologize for not being on time," she told him when she let him into the apartment. "A couple of hours ago I closed my eyes for a few minutes and just woke up. I'll give you a glass of wine if you'll give me fifteen minutes to get myself ready."

"It's a deal."

She could see that he was openly studying the apartment. "You have very nice digs, Dr. Chandler," he said. "One of my patients is a real estate broker. She tells me that the minute she walks into a home, she gets vibrations about the people who live there."

"Well, I don't know what kind of vibrations this place sends out, but I'm mighty comfortable in it. Now let me get you that glass of wine, and you can look around while I get changed."

Don went into the kitchen with her. "Please don't get dressed up," he said. "As you can see, I didn't. I dropped in on my mother this afternoon, and she told me I looked good in a sweater, so I just put a jacket over it."

Susan walked into the bedroom. There is something strange

about Don Richards, she thought as she reached for her herring-bone jacket in her closet. I don't know what it is, but there's something about him that I just don't *get*.

She crossed from her room into the foyer and was about to say "I'm ready," when she saw Donald Richards standing at her desk, examining the two passenger lists from the cruise ships.

He had obviously heard her, because he looked up. "Any reason for collecting these, Susan?" he asked quietly.

She did not answer immediately, and he put them down. "Sorry if I overstepped your invitation to look around. This is a beautiful desk, and I wanted a closer look at it. The passenger lists didn't seem to be confidential material."

"You said you've often been a passenger on the *Gabrielle,* didn't you?" Susan asked. She didn't like the idea of his going through papers on her desk, but she decided to let it drop.

"Yes, many times. She's a beautiful ship." He walked over to Susan. "You look very nice, and I'm very hungry. Let's go."

THEY ate at an intimate seafood restaurant on Thompson Street. "The father of one of my patients owns it," he explained.

"That pompano was marvelous," Susan told him later as the waiter removed their plates.

"So was the salmon." He paused and took a sip of his wine. "Susan, you said the other night that after your parents' divorce you felt as though you'd all gotten into different lifeboats. Why is that?"

"Hey, don't analyze *me*," Susan protested.

"I'm asking as a friend."

"Then I'll answer. It's the usual thing that happens when there's a divorce: divided loyalties. My mother was heartbroken, and my father was running around saying he'd never been happier. Kind of made me question all the years when I was under the impression that we were a happy family."

"How about your sister? Are you close to her? You don't even have to answer. You should see the look on your face."

Susan heard herself saying, "Seven years ago I was about to get engaged. Then Dee came into the picture. Guess who got the guy and became a bride?"

"Your sister."

"That's right. Then Jack was killed in a skiing accident, and now she's in the process of trying to move in on someone I'm dating. Nice, huh?"

"Are you interested in this new guy?"

"It's much too soon to say. And now will you tell me why you were so interested in those passenger lists?"

The understanding warmth in Don Richards's eyes disappeared. "If you'll tell me why you checked off some names and circled two: Owen Adams and Henry Owen Young."

"Owen is one of my favorite names," Susan said. "It's getting late, Don. You're leaving early in the morning, and I have a very long day ahead of me."

She thought of the eight a.m. phone call she was going to make to Chris Ryan tomorrow, and the package of pictures she should be receiving from London in the afternoon.

12

ON MONDAY morning Chris Ryan unlocked his office door at eight twenty. He checked his messages and found several that warranted immediate attention. The first had been left on Saturday by a source in Atlantic City, and it contained interesting information about Douglas Layton. The second, from Susan Chandler, had come in earlier this morning. "Chris, it's Susan. Call me right away" was all it said.

She answered on the first ring. "Chris, I'm onto something, and I need you to check out two people for me. One was a passenger on a cruise ship, the *Gabrielle,* three years ago. The second was on another cruise ship, the *Seagodiva,* two years ago. The thing is, I don't think they're different people at all. They may be one and the same person, and if I am right, we're talking about a serial killer."

Chris grabbed for a sheet of paper. "Give me the names and dates." When he heard them, he commented, "Both mid-October."

"The dates have been in the back of my mind, Chris," Susan told him. "If mid-October is part of a pattern, then some woman could be in terrible danger right now."

"Let me get on it. My guys at the FBI can do a fast trace. Oh, Susan, I figured out why your pal Doug Layton doesn't have a nickel to his name. He's a compulsive gambler who's semi-notorious in Atlantic City. He lost big time there last week."

"What do you mean by big time?"

"Try four hundred thousand dollars. Hope he's got a rich aunt."

"The trouble is that he thinks he does." The sum of four hundred thousand dollars startled her. A man who can run up gambling losses that great is in *serious* trouble. He could also be desperate and dangerous. "Thanks, Chris," Susan said.

She hung up the phone and looked at her watch. She would have time to visit Mrs. Clausen before she went to the studio.

Jane's got to know about Layton immediately, Susan thought. If he owes that much money to gamblers, he'll need to cover it right away, and the Clausen Family Trust is where he'll go for it.

JANE Clausen knew something was seriously wrong when Susan phoned and requested such an early morning visit. She had also heard the tension in Douglas Layton's voice when he called a few minutes later to say he needed to stop by on his way to the airport. He said that another requisition concerning the orphanage required her signature.

"You'll have to wait till nine o'clock," she told him firmly.

"Mrs. Clausen, that might make me late for my plane."

"You should have thought of that sooner, Douglas. Susan Chandler is coming to see me in a few minutes." She paused, then added in a cool tone, "Yesterday Susan took some Polaroids of the sketch of the orphanage. I hope there's no problem."

"Of course not, Mrs. Clausen. Perhaps I can do without that signature for the present."

When Susan arrived, Jane Clausen said, "You don't have to worry about my reaction to anything you might tell me, Susan. I've come to believe that Douglas Layton is cheating or is trying to cheat me. But I would be interested in seeing the proof."

As Susan opened the book about the Wright Family Foundation, Jane Clausen made a call to Hubert March, who was still at home. "Hubert, get down to the office, call in your auditors, and make sure that Douglas Layton can't get his hands on any of our bank accounts or assets. And do it *now!*"

She put down the phone and studied the picture of the orphanage in the book on her lap.

"I'm sorry," Susan said quietly.

"Don't be. Even when Douglas was being so solicitous, that uneasy feeling about him just wouldn't go away."

DOUGLAS Layton now knew what it felt like to be trapped. He had called Jane Clausen from a phone near the hospital, anticipating that he could go right up and get the necessary signature.

You fool, he told himself. You've tipped her off.

He absolutely had to have the money. He shivered at the thought of what would happen to him if he didn't honor his debt to the casino. Susan Chandler was the problem. She was the one who had started everything. If only he hadn't felt lucky the other night . . .

He stood at the phone trying to decide what to do next.

There was one thing he could try that might work. But "might" wasn't good enough. It *had* to work.

His phone call caught Hubert March at home, just as he was leaving for the office. Hubert's salutatory question, "Douglas, what is this all about?" confirmed his suspicion that Mrs. Clausen had phoned him.

"I'm with Mrs. Clausen," Doug said. "I'm afraid she's in and out of reality. She thinks she may have just phoned you and apologizes for anything she said."

Hubert March's relieved laugh was balm to Douglas Layton's soul. "No apologies necessary to me, but I hope she apologized to you, my boy."

JIM Curley drove Alex Wright to Kennedy Airport and placed his bags on the curbside check-in line. "Awfully busy at this hour, Mr. Alex," he said as he glanced at the policewoman hovering about, threatening to ticket cars left too long at curbside.

"What do you expect at nine o'clock on Monday morning, Jim?" Alex Wright asked. "Take off before I'm stuck with paying a fine. And do you remember what I told you?"

"Phone Dr. Chandler and tell her that I'm at her disposal."

"Right," Alex said encouragingly. "And?"

"And she'll probably give me—what did you call it, sir?—the 'appropriate disclaimers' about how she doesn't need a car. That's my cue to say, 'Mr. Alex begs you to allow me to serve you, but with one proviso: Dr. Chandler may not bring a date in his car.' "

Alex Wright laughed. "I know I can count on you, Jim. Now get out of here. That cop has a book to fill, and she's heading for my car."

SUSAN finished her radio program and got back to the office a full hour and a half before her first appointment, at two o'clock.

She spent the time studying the file she had compiled as a result of the events of the past week. It included Regina Clausen's memorabilia from her cruise on the *Gabrielle*, Carolyn Wells's similar memorabilia from the *Seagodiva*, and the photographs of Tiffany's turquoise ring that Pete Sanchez had sent her.

Study as she might, however, they revealed nothing new to her.

She told Janet not to order lunch until after one o'clock. At one thirty Janet came in humming "You Belong to Me."

"Dr. Chandler," she said as she placed the lunch bag on Susan's desk, "that song has been going through my head all weekend. I just can't shake it. It was also driving me crazy because I couldn't remember all the lyrics, so I phoned my mother and she sang them to me. It really is a pretty song."

"Yes, it is," Susan agreed absentmindedly as she opened the paper bag and took out the soup of the day.

"See the pyramids along the Nile / Watch the sunrise on a tropic isle . . ."

Unasked, Janet was singing the lyrics of "You Belong to Me."

"See the marketplace in old Algiers . . ."

Susan suddenly forgot about the soup. "Stop for a minute, Janet," she said.

Janet looked embarrassed. "I'm sorry, Doctor."

"No, no," Susan said. "It's just that while listening to you, something occurred to me about that song."

Susan thought of the news bulletin from the *Gabrielle* that had referred to Bali as a tropic isle, and the postcard of a restaurant there, with a circle drawn around a dining table on the veranda. With a sinking feeling in the pit of her stomach Susan could sense that the pieces of the puzzle were falling into place.

Owen wanted to show Carolyn Wells around Algiers, she thought. *See the marketplace in old Algiers.*

"Janet, could you sing the rest of the lyrics, please?"

"If you want, Doctor. I'm not much of a singer. Let's see. *Fly the ocean in a silver plane . . ."*

Three years ago Regina disappeared after being in Bali, Susan thought. Two years ago it could have been Carolyn—and there may have been someone else chosen in her stead—in Algiers. Last year he may have met a woman on a plane rather than a cruise ship. What would have been before that? she asked herself. Let's go back: Did he meet a woman four years ago in Egypt? That would fit the pattern, she decided.

"See the jungle when it's wet with rain," Janet sang.

That could be the lyric for this year's victim, Susan thought. Somebody who has no idea she's being staked out for death.

"Just remember 'til you're home again"—Janet softened her voice as she concluded—*"You belong to me."*

Susan called Chris Ryan as soon as Janet left her office. "Chris, will you see if you can track something else down? I need to know if there are any reports of a woman—probably a tourist—who vanished in Egypt in mid-October four years ago."

"That shouldn't be too hard," Ryan assured her. "I was just about to call you anyhow. You remember those names you gave me this morning? The cruise ship passengers?"

"What about them?" Susan asked.

"Those guys don't exist. The passports they used were fakes."

I *knew* it! Susan thought. I *knew* it!

AT QUARTER of five that afternoon Susan broke a rule and left her patient alone to take an urgent phone call from Chris Ryan. "You're pushing the right buttons, Susan," Ryan said. "Four years ago a thirty-nine-year-old widow from Alabama disappeared in Egypt. She was on a Middle East cruise. She apparently had skipped the regular land tour and gone off by herself. Her body was never found, and it was assumed that, given Egypt's political unrest, she had met with foul play from a terrorist group."

"I'm fairly certain that had nothing to do with why she died, Chris," Susan said.

A few minutes later, as she was walking her patient to the door, a bulky Federal Express package was delivered. The sender was Ocean Cruise Pictures Ltd. of London.

"I'll open it, Doctor," Janet volunteered.

"No," Susan told her. "Just leave it. I'll get to it later."

Her day was filled with late appointments, and she wouldn't be finished with her last patient until seven. Then she finally would be able to go through the photographs that might reveal the face of the man who had killed Regina Clausen and so many others.

DONALD Richards arrived at West Palm Beach Airport at nine Monday morning. He was met there by an escort from his publisher and was driven to Liberty's in Boca Raton, where he was scheduled to autograph his book. When he arrived, he was pleasantly surprised to find people lined up and waiting for him.

Richards settled at the table set up for him, picked up his pen, and began to sign. He knew what lay ahead that day, and he knew as well what he had to do. A wild restlessness was making him desperate to bolt from the seat.

One hour and eighty signed books later he was on his way to Miami for another autographing at two o'clock.

"I'm sorry, but signatures only, no personal messages," he told the bookshop proprietor in Miami. "Something has come up, and I have to leave here promptly at three."

A few minutes after three he was back in the car.

"Next stop the Fontainebleau," the driver said cheerfully.

"Wrong. Next stop the airport," Don told him. There was a plane leaving for New York at four. He intended to be on it.

DEE arrived in Costa Rica on Monday morning and went directly from the airport to the harbor, where her cruise ship, the *Valerie,* had just docked.

Monday afternoon she halfheartedly joined the sight-seeing tour she had signed up for. When she impulsively decided to take this cruise, it had seemed a great idea. Now she wasn't so sure.

She returned to the *Valerie* bedraggled from a cloudburst in the rain forest and regretting that she hadn't canceled the trip. Yes, her stateroom on the sundeck was beautiful and had its own private veranda. Still, she felt restless, even anxious. She sensed that this just wasn't the time to be away from New York. Maybe she could catch a plane at Panama and fly back tomorrow, she decided.

As she headed for her stateroom, the room stewardess stopped her. "The most beautiful bouquet just arrived for you," she said. "I put it on your dresser."

Forgetting that she felt wet and clammy, Dee rushed to her room. There she found a vase holding two dozen pale gold roses. She quickly read the card. It was signed "Guess Who."

Dee didn't have to guess. She *knew* who had sent them.

At the dinner Saturday night, when she changed places with Susan, Alex Wright had said to her, "I'm glad Susan suggested you sit next to me. I can't abide seeing a beautiful woman be lonely. I guess I'm more like my father than I realized. My stepmother was beautiful like you, and also a lonely widow when my father met her on a cruise ship. He solved her loneliness by marrying her."

It's Jack all over again, Dee thought as she inhaled the scent of the roses. I didn't want to hurt Susan then, and I certainly don't want to hurt her now, but I don't think she's really that interested in Alex yet. She hardly *knows* him. I'm sure she'll understand.

Dee showered, washed her hair, and dressed for dinner, imagining what fun it would be if instead of his going to Russia, Alex were a passenger on the ship with her.

"THANK you, Dr. Chandler. I'll see you next week."

At ten of seven Susan escorted Anne Ketler, her last patient of the day, to the door. As she passed Janet's desk, Susan saw that the package of photographs had been opened, and the photos were stacked on the desk. Thou hast ears, but hear not, she thought.

She opened the office's outer door for Mrs. Ketler and from its easy click realized that it had been left unlocked.

"It's very dark out there," Mrs. Ketler said.

Susan looked over the woman's shoulder. Only a couple of lights illuminated the hallway, which was filled with shadows. "You're absolutely right," she told Mrs. Ketler. "Here, take my arm. I'll walk with you to the elevator."

After the elevator came, Susan hurried back down the corridor. Entering the reception area, she picked up the stacks of photographs from Janet's desk, not noticing the note that Janet had left under the phone for her. She crossed to her office, aware of both the silence in the building and the accelerated heartbeat she felt at the thought of finally seeing a picture of the man responsible for this series of murders. What am I so nervous about? she wondered as she passed the supply closet. The door was open a fraction, but with her arms full she didn't pause to close it.

As she set the photos on her desk, she accidentally hit the beautiful Waterford vase Alex Wright had given her, sending it crashing to the floor. What a shame, she thought as she swept up the shards of glass and loaded them into the wastebasket. It's the effect of everything that's been going on, she decided.

An hour later she was still going through the photographs, still searching for the one with Carolyn Wells. It *has* to be here, Susan thought. They said they were going to send every print they had of a woman posing with the captain.

She had the crumpled piece of a picture that Carolyn had thrown into her wastebasket, and she kept referring to it, searching for its match in the stacks of photographs she had spread out before her. But no matter how many times she went through them, she couldn't find it. That photograph simply wasn't there.

"Where is it?" she asked out loud, exasperation and disappointment threatening to overwhelm her. "Why, of all of them, is *that one* missing?"

"Because *I* have it, Susan," a familiar voice said in response.

Susan spun around in time to receive the blow of a paperweight smashing against the side of her head.

JUST as he had planned, he would follow the same procedure with Susan Chandler that he had used for all the others. He would bind her arms and hands to her sides, bind her legs together, truss her so that as she woke up and realized what was happening, she would be able to squirm a little—just enough to give her hope but not enough to save her.

While he twisted the rope around her limp body, he would explain to her why it was happening. He had explained it to the others, and while Susan's death was not a part of his original plan but more a matter of expedience, she nonetheless deserved to know that she too had become a part of the ritual he had undertaken to expiate the sins of his stepmother.

"You must understand, Susan," he began in a reasoning tone of voice, "I never would have harmed you if only you hadn't butted in. In fact, I quite *like* you. I do sincerely."

He began to wind the rope around her arms, lifting her body gently. She was lying on the floor beside her desk.

"Why did you have to talk about Regina Clausen on your radio program, Susan? You should have left it alone. She's been dead three years. Her body's at the bottom of Kowloon bay."

He crossed and crisscrossed the rope over her upper body. "For such a smart woman, it was remarkably easy to convince Regina to leave the ship. But that's what happens when you're lonely. You want to fall in love. Hong Kong is Regina's final resting place, but it was in Bali that she fell in love with me."

He began to tie Susan's legs. Lovely legs, he thought. Even though she was wearing a trouser suit, he could feel their shapeliness as he lifted them and wrapped the cord around them. "My father was easily duped as well, Susan. Isn't that funny?"

Susan was aware of a familiar voice just above her, but her head was splitting with pain, and she didn't dare open her eyes. What is happening to me? she wondered. Alex Wright *was* here, but who hit me? She had gotten just a glimpse of him before she blacked out. He had untidy, longish hair and was wearing a cap and a shabby sweat suit.

Wait, she thought, making herself focus. The voice is Alex's; that means he's still here. So why wasn't Alex helping her?

Then what she had been hearing sank in, and she opened her eyes. His face was only inches away from hers. His eyes were glittering, shining with the kind of madness she had seen in the eyes of patients in locked wards. He's mad! she thought. She could see now. It was Alex in that straggly wig. Alex, whose eyes were like sharp chips of turquoise slicing deeply into her.

"I have your shroud, Susan," he whispered. "Even though you were not one of the lonely ladies, I wanted you to have it. It's exactly the same as the ones the others wore."

He stood, and she could see that he was holding up a long plastic bag, much like the kind used to protect expensive gowns. Oh God! she thought. He's going to suffocate me!

"I do this slowly, Susan," he said. "It's my favorite part. I want to watch your face. I want you to anticipate that moment when the air is cut off and the final struggle begins. So I'll do it slowly, and I won't wrap it too tightly. That way it will take longer for you to die—a few minutes, at least."

He knelt in front of her and lifted her feet, sliding the plastic bag underneath her so that her feet and legs were inside. She tried to kick it away, but he leaned across her, staring into her eyes as he pulled it over her hips and then her waist. Her struggles had no effect. Finally, when he reached her neck, he paused.

"You see, soon after my mother died, my father took a cruise," he explained. "On it he met Virginia Marie Owen—Gerie—a lonely widow, or so she claimed. She was thirty-five years my father's junior, and attractive. He told me she liked to sing in his ear while they danced. Her favorite song was 'You Belong to Me.' You know how they spent their honeymoon? They followed the lyrics of that song, starting out in Egypt."

Susan watched Alex's face. He was clearly engrossed in his story now. But all the while his hands kept playing with the plastic, and Susan knew that at any moment he was going to pull it over her head. She thought of screaming, but who would hear? She was alone with him in an otherwise empty building.

"My stepmother hated me so much that she dedicated herself to persuading my father to establish the foundation rather than leave his money to me. It would then be my role in life to administer it. She pointed out to my father that I would have a generous salary while I gave away his money. *My money.* She told him that in that way their names would be immortalized. He resisted for a while but eventually gave in. I swore to myself I would get even. But then she died, right after my father, and I never had the chance. Can you imagine how frustrating that was? To hate her with such a passion and then for her to deprive me of the satisfaction of killing her?"

Susan studied his face as he knelt above her, a distant look in his eyes. He's *definitely* mad, she thought. He's mad, and he's going to kill me. Just the way he killed all the others.

BY EIGHT o'clock that night, Doug Layton was at a blackjack table in one of Atlantic City's slightly less fashionable casinos.

Through some rapid manipulation of funds he had been able to come up with the money he needed to cover the debts he had racked up during his last visit.

Doug felt a little relieved with how things were working out. Sooner or later the auditors would have caught up with him. Forewarned, and before it was too late, he planned now to get out with the half-million-dollar stake he had gotten hold of today. He already had made a reservation for a flight to St. Thomas. From there he would manage to get to one of the islands where there was no extradition policy with the U.S. It was what his father had done—and he never had been caught.

Half a million would buy a good start on a new life. Layton was determined to leave the country with that amount.

"You can't leave this place without trying your luck at least one more time," one of his friends told him.

Doug Layton acknowledged that he felt lucky. "Well, maybe a hand of blackjack," he said in agreement.

It was only nine o'clock when he left the casino. Barely aware of his surroundings, he walked onto the beach. There was no way to get the money he needed now, the money he owed to the guys who had staked him again today when his luck turned sour for the last time. It was all over for him. He knew what would follow. Conviction for embezzlement. Prison. Or worse.

He took off his suit jacket and laid his watch and his wallet on it. It was something he'd read about, and it seemed to make sense.

He could hear the surf pounding. A stiff, cold wind blew off the ocean, and the surf was high. He shivered in his shirtsleeves. He wondered how long it would take to drown and decided it was better not to know. It was one of those things that you wouldn't know about until you did it, like so much else in his life. He stepped into the water gingerly, then took another, bigger step.

It's all Susan Chandler's fault, he thought as the icy water lapped at his ankles. If only she had stayed out of it, no one would have known, and I'd have had years more at the trust.

He held his breath against the cold and plunged on until his feet were no longer touching bottom. A big wave caught him, and another. Then he was choking, lost in a world of cold and darkness, pummeled by the waves. He tried not to struggle.

Silently he cursed Susan Chandler. *I hope she dies.* It was Douglas Layton's last conscious thought.

DON Richards caught the plane to La Guardia with only minutes to spare. It had a layover in Atlanta, but that couldn't be helped. As soon as they cleared the airport and he was able to use the telephone, he called Susan Chandler's office.

"I'm sorry, Dr. Richards, but she's with a patient and can't be interrupted," her secretary informed him. "I'd be happy to take a message and leave it for her."

"How long will Dr. Chandler be there?" Don asked impatiently.

"Sir, she has patients until seven o'clock. She mentioned earlier that after that she's planning to do some paperwork."

"Then please take down this exact message: 'Don Richards needs to see you about Owen. His plane gets in about eight o'clock. He'll pick you up at your office. Wait for him.' "

"I'll leave it on my desk where she'll see it," Janet said.

And Susan would have if it hadn't been hidden under the phone.

The flight attendant was offering a drink and snacks. "Just coffee, please," Don Richards said. He knew he needed a clear head. Later Susan and I will have a drink and dinner, he thought. I'll tell her what I think she's already guessed—that the person poor Carolyn is trying to talk about is named Owen, not Win. Ever since he had seen the name Owen circled on both passenger lists on the desk in Susan's apartment, he had been turning this over in his mind, and he thought that was the most likely explanation.

He was desperate to get back to New York. Whoever Owen really was, he was very likely the killer. And if Don was right, Susan was in grave jeopardy.

She can't go this route alone any longer, Don vowed to himself. It's too dangerous. Much more dangerous than she knows.

Don got off the plane at eight ten. He rushed to a phone and called Susan's office. There was no answer, and he hung up without leaving a message. He got no response at her apartment either.

Maybe I should try again at the office, he thought. She may have just stepped out. But again he got no answer. This time, however, he decided to leave her a message. "Susan," he said, "I'm going to stop by your office. I hope you got the message I left earlier with your secretary and that you're still around. With luck I'll be there in half an hour."

"SUSAN, surely you can understand why I'm so angry. Gerie saw my having to run the family trust as a form of poetic justice. Every day I had to sign checks giving away money that belonged to *me*. Can you imagine? When the foundation was established sixteen years ago, it was worth one hundred million dollars. Now it's worth a billion, and I can take the credit for most of its growth. But no matter how much money there is in the coffers, I still get only my paltry salary."

I've got to keep him talking, Susan told herself. What time do the cleaning people come in? she wondered, then remembered with a sinking feeling that they had been emptying wastebaskets when Mrs. Ketler arrived at six. They were long gone.

His fingers were caressing her throat now. "I really think I could have been happy with you, Susan," he went on. "If I had married you, I might have tried to put the past behind me. But of course that wouldn't have worked, would it? The other night you sent Dee to take your place next to me at the table. You did it because you didn't want to be with me. You know that, don't you?"

"Alex," Susan said, her voice coaxing, "it's not going to do any good to kill me. There are hundreds more pictures being delivered to my office tomorrow. You're not going to be able to destroy them. The police will study them one by one. They'll study the people in the background."

"Feathers in the wind," Alex murmured, his tone dismissive.

I may be getting to him, Susan thought. "Someone will recognize you, Alex. You don't go to big parties, yet that first night, when I agreed to have dinner with you, you said you met Regina at a Futures Industry dinner. That's a big one, Alex. Something started troubling me about you that night."

"Feathers in the wind," he said again. "I know I can't go on much longer, Susan, but I *will* finish my mission before I'm stopped. Remember the song? *See the jungle when it's wet with rain.* You know who was in the jungle today? Dee. She was on a tour in the rain forest in Costa Rica. That's close enough. Tomorrow people will be grieving for you when your body is discovered. But that won't happen until nine o'clock or so. By then Dee and I will be having breakfast in Panama. Her ship docks at eight, and I will surprise her by joining her there. I have a turquoise ring for her. She'll read a great deal into it."

Slowly, very slowly, he was closing the bag. It was covering her chin. "Alex," Susan pleaded, trying to hide her desperation, "your luck is running out. You can save yourself if you stop now."

"But I don't *want* to stop," he said matter-of-factly. The ringing of the telephone made him jump. They both listened intently as Don Richards left a message saying he was on his way.

"It's time," Alex Wright said calmly. And with a sudden movement of his hand he pulled the bag the rest of the way over her head and sealed it. Then he pushed her under the desk.

He stood up and looked down at his handiwork. "You'll die long before Richards gets here. It will take about ten minutes." He paused to let his words sink in. "That's how long Regina lasted."

"Look, mister, I didn't invent traffic jams," the cabby told Don Richards. "The Midtown Tunnel is tied up. What else is new?"

"You've been on the phone with the dispatcher. Couldn't you have avoided this?"

"Mister, some guy has a fender bender. Thirty seconds later you got a tie-up and a traffic jam."

Arguing with him is not doing any good, Don cautioned himself. But it is *so* frustrating being stuck like this.

"Please, Susan," he half whispered, "be there, and be safe."

THE LITTLE AIR THAT HAD been trapped in the bag was almost gone. Susan felt herself getting light-headed.

Air. Air. The pain was starting to gather in her chest.

Don't pass out, she warned herself fiercely. She could feel her mind relaxing, as though ready to give up the fight.

Dee. Alex was going to meet her tomorrow. She was going to be his final victim.

I'm going to sleep, Susan thought. I can't stop myself.

I don't want to die. And I don't want Dee to die. Her mind struggled to continue, struggled to survive with no air.

She was wedged under the desk. With a sudden thrust she kicked her feet against the front panel and pushed her body out a few inches. She felt the wastebasket against her right side.

The wastebasket! The glass from the broken vase was in it!

Gasping now, Susan heaved her body to the side, felt the basket topple over, heard the broken glass scatter on the floor. As she twisted her head toward the sound, she felt the basket move away, felt blackness overwhelming her.

With one last effort she moved her head from side to side. A sudden, terrible pain hit her as the jagged glass, caught between the floor and her body, cut through the heavy plastic under her. Blood soaked her shoulder, but she could feel the plastic start to separate. She continued to gasp as she moved her body back and forth, back and forth, feeling the blood gush from her wound, but feeling also the first faint hint of air.

It was there, on the floor of her office, that Don Richards found her half an hour later. She was barely conscious. Her temple was bruised, her hair matted with blood. Her back was bleeding profusely, her arms and legs bruised and swollen from her struggles with the cord that bound her. Jagged glass lay all around her.

But she was alive! Alive!

ALEX Wright was waiting at the dock when the *Valerie* sailed into San Blas, Panama, on Tuesday morning. It was eight o'clock. He had left New York on Monday night, going directly to the airport from Susan Chandler's office. He wondered if Don Richards, who had phoned her asking that she wait for him, had finally given up. Alex had turned off all the lights when he left, so Richards must have assumed she simply hadn't waited for him. In all likelihood her secretary would find her body in another hour or so.

A good number of the passengers on the *Valerie* were standing on the deck. There was something magical about being aboard a ship as it steamed into harbor, he thought. But perhaps it was symbolic, because each new harbor signified an end of the journey for someone.

This would be Dee's final journey. She was his last lonely lady. And then he'd be on his way to Russia. That's where he'd be when he was notified of the tragic death of the two sisters who had been his guests on Saturday evening. Susan said that he might be spotted in some of the pictures from Regina's cruise. Maybe, he thought. But he looked very different on that cruise. Could anyone positively identify him? I don't think so, he decided confidently.

He spotted Dee standing on deck. She was smiling and waving at him. Or was she *pointing* to him?

He was suddenly aware that men had moved up to stand on either side of him. Then he heard a low, deep voice say, "You're under arrest, Mr. Wright. Please come with us quietly."

Alex Wright stifled his surprise and shrugged. Then he turned to go. He realized with a touch of bitter irony that this was the end of the journey for him.

Don Richards waited in the hospital lobby while Susan visited Jane Clausen. This morning Jane was lying in bed, a single pillow beneath her head. Her hands were folded on the coverlet. The shades were drawn.

Despite the room's darkness, she was quick to notice the bruise on Susan's temple. "What happened, Susan?" she asked.

"Oh, nothing. A bad bump, that's all." Susan felt tears come to her eyes as she bent to kiss Jane Clausen's cheek.

"How very dear you've become to me," Jane said. "Susan, I don't think I'll be here tomorrow, but at least yesterday I managed to take care of the trust. Some good, reliable people will watch over it for me. You've heard about Douglas?"

"Yes. I didn't know if you knew."

"I'm so sorry for him. He could have amounted to so much."

"Mrs. Clausen, there's no easy way to tell you this, but I think it's something you will want to know. The man who killed Regina, and at least four other people, has been arrested. There's overwhelming proof of his guilt. And your coming forward to talk to me when you did played a vital role in solving the crimes."

Susan saw the long shudder that went through the dying woman's body. "I'm glad. Did he talk about Regina? I mean, I wonder if she was very frightened."

Regina must have been terrified, Susan thought. I know I was. "I hope not," she said.

Jane Clausen looked up at her. "Susan, I'll be with her soon. Good-bye, my dear, and thank you for all your kindness."

As SUSAN rode down in the elevator, she thought back on the events of the preceding week. Could it really have been so short a time? she wondered. Was it really only nine days ago that I first met Jane Clausen? Yes, the mystery of Regina Clausen's disappearance had been solved, but in the process three other people had died and a fourth was seriously injured.

Susan thought of Carolyn Wells and her husband, Justin. She had talked to him this morning. Carolyn was out of her coma, and the doctors now were predicting a full, though protracted, recovery. Susan had started to apologize to him. After all, had it not been for her raising the whole subject of Regina Clausen's disappearance, none of these terrible things would have happened to either Carolyn or himself. Justin had insisted, however, that despite the agony of the past week, all things had happened for a reason. He was planning to go back into therapy with Dr. Richards, and he was hopeful that once his extreme jealousy was in check, the kind of fear that had driven Carolyn to be so secretive would no longer be a part of their lives.

At least he and Carolyn will be okay, Susan thought. But not poor Tiffany Smith nor the other two people whose deaths are tied to the case—Hilda Johnson and Abdul Parki.

It had all started so innocently. Susan had intended only to raise the issue of how lonely, unsuspecting women, despite their intelligence and apparent sophistication, can be lured into dubious and sometimes fatal relationships by men who prey on them. It was a great topic and had produced a few lively shows. And three murders, she thought. Then she asked herself: Will I be afraid to do that kind of investigative show in the future? I hope not. After all, a serial killer has been apprehended; who knows who else he might have killed—besides me and Dee—had he not been caught?

And a couple of good things had come out of it. She had gotten to know Jane Clausen and been a comfort to her. And she had met Don Richards. He was a strange bird, she thought—a psychiatrist who denied himself the help he offered on a daily basis, yet who finally summoned the strength to face his own demons.

I might have bled to death if I'd been lying there all night, she thought, wincing from the pain of the stitches in her shoulders and back. When Don got to her office and found it locked, some instinct had made him demand that the security guard open the door and check the office with him. I was never so glad to see anyone in my life, she thought. As he ripped the bag open and lifted her up, there was tenderness and relief on his face.

As Susan emerged from the elevator, Don Richards stood up and crossed to meet her. They looked at each other for a moment. Then Susan smiled at him, and he put his arm around her. It seemed to both of them the natural thing for him to do.

MARY
HIGGINS
CLARK

Mary Higgins Clark is an inveterate globe-trotter and a great fan of cruise ships, so she knows well the world she evokes in *You Belong to Me.* In fact, as soon as she completed the newest of her nineteen best sellers, she rewarded herself with a three-week cruise. Fortunately, unlike the solitary women travelers in her book, she wasn't alone. Her traveling companion? Her new husband, John J. Conheeney, a retired financial services executive.

Yet Clark says she does not expect her enormous literary success to ever lead to a life of leisure. "Someone once said, If you want to be happy for a year, win the lottery; if you want to be happy for a lifetime, love what you do. That's the way it is for me. I love to spin yarns."

John

American

Jakes

Dreams

It is the dawn of a
turbulent new century.
A time of dizzying progress
and sweeping change.
All of America is brimming
with possibilities.
And for a brother and sister
the dreams of a lifetime
are just beginning.

Part One   DREAMERS

Actress • Fritzi Crown flung her bike on the grass and ran down to the water's edge. She skipped across wet boulders strewn along the shore until she stood where the waves broke and showered her with bracing spray. It was first light, the dawn of a chill morning in early December 1906. Along the horizon the sky was orange as the maw of a steel furnace, metal gray above.

Remembering a recurring dream that had held her in the moments before she woke—a dream in which she stood on a Broadway stage while thunderous applause rolled over her—Fritzi threw her arms out, threw her head back like some pagan worshipper of the dawn. The wind streamed off Lake Michigan, out of the east, where lay the mysterious and alluring place that occupied her thoughts in most of her waking moments.

The waves crashed. The wind sang in her ears, a repeating litany that had grown more and more insistent in past weeks. Time to go. Time to go!

Red-faced, windblown but exhilarated, she stepped down from the rocks and turned toward the bike lying on the shriveled brown grass. The bike was a beautiful Fleetwing with a carmine enamel frame, gleaming silver rims and spokes.

Fritzi was a long-legged young woman with an oval face, a nose she considered too big, legs she considered too skinny, a bosom she considered flat. She was dressed for cold weather. Over long underwear she wore her bathing costume of heavy navy-blue alpaca cloth—a top with attached bloomers, a separate skirt. For added warmth she'd put on her younger brother's football sweater, a black cardigan with an orange letter P. He had bequeathed it to her after he was thrown out of Princeton. A knitted tam barely contained her long, unruly blond hair. Altogether it was the kind of costume that her father, General Joseph Crown, the Chicago millionaire brewer, disapproved of.

The spectacular sunrise burst over the lake and burnished a row of trees near the footpath. Wind tore the last withered leaves off the branches and flung them into fanciful whirlwinds. The leaf clouds spiraled up and up, like her buoyant spirits. There were great risks in the decision she must make. They started right here in Chicago, in her own family.

Returning to her bike, Fritzi stopped abruptly. In the evergreens planted behind the trees, a pair of eyes gleamed. They belonged to a man—a filthy, ragged tramp who'd been spying on her. He lurched out of the shrubbery, coming toward her. Fritzi was sharply aware of how early it was, how isolated she was here.

The tramp planted his feet a yard in front of her. "Hello, girlie."

Fritzi swallowed, thinking desperately. Even upwind of the man she caught his stupefying stench—mostly liquor and dirt.

He winked at her. "Girls out wanderin' by theyselves this time of morning, they're either runaways or little levee whores." He stuck out his arms with an oafish leer. "Come give us a kiss."

For want of her usual weapon of defense, a long hatpin, Fritzi called on her primary talent. She replied in a loud, perfect imitation of his wheezy baritone. "Don't let this long hair fool you, bub. You've got the wrong fellow."

The tramp's eyes bugged. He was confounded by the male bellow issuing from Fritzi. She'd always been a keen mimic. The tramp's confusion gave her the extra seconds she needed. She sprang to her bike and took off, pedaling madly.

Flashing a look back, she saw the tramp thumb his nose. She sped around a curve, snatched her tam off, and let her curly blond hair stream out. She laughed with relief, pumping harder. At least her talent proved to be worth something this morning. It could be worth a lot more in New York City.

As Fritzi pedaled away, she reflected on all the things that had driven her to the emotional epiphany by the lake.

Shapeless things, like the growing malaise of living day after day under the roof where she'd been raised but no longer belonged. Silly things, like a little easel card noticed on a cosmetic counter at the Fair Store—OVER TWENTY-FIVE? LUXOR CREME PREVENTS AGING! Ironic things, the most recent being a well-meant comment by her father at supper last night. Ilsa, Fritzi's mother, had remarked that she was still receiving compliments on the lavish anniversary party the Crowns gave in early October to celebrate thirty-seven years of marriage.

The General agreed that it was indeed a fine party. He then turned to his daughter. "Fritzi, my dear, your birthday will be on us in another month. We must plan. What do you want most?"

Fritzi sat to her father's right, on the long side of the dining table. Her older brother, Joey—Joe Crown, Jr.—sat opposite, in his customary vaguely sullen silence. Poor Joey was a permanent boarder. In 1901 he'd dragged himself home from the West Coast, crippled for life in a labor union brawl. Under a tense truce with his father, Joey worked at Brauerei Crown doing menial jobs. He and his father traveled to and from work separately, the General in his expensive Cadillac motorcar and Joey on the trolleys.

Fritzi thought about asking for motoring lessons, but the General believed women had no place at the wheel of an auto. She said, "I haven't an idea, Papa. I'll try to think of something."

"Please do. How old will you be?" It was a sincere question. Her elegant silver-haired father—who had been known as the General ever since his distinguished military service in the Spanish-American War—was, in his sixty-fourth year, occasionally forgetful. He had never lost the accent he'd brought with him as the immigrant boy Josef Kroner from Aalen, a little town in Württemberg, Germany.

"Twenty-six." Somehow it sounded like a sentence from a judge.

With this latest realization of her age thrust on her, Fritzi spent a restless night in her old room on the second floor—the room she'd occupied since she had returned to Chicago a year ago.

In 1905, during a late summer heat wave, the General had suffered a mild heart attack. Ilsa's telegram reached Fritzi in Palatka, Florida. She was appearing with Mortmain's Royal Shakespeare Combination, a seedy professional touring company with which she'd apprenticed in 1901. Moments after reading the telegram, Fritzi gave her notice. That night she caught a train for Chicago to help take care of her father.

Though Ilsa didn't ask her daughter to come home, Fritzi thought it her duty. Besides, after four years of repetitive visits to dreary mill and cotton and tobacco towns, Fritzi felt she'd learned as much as she could from her apprenticeship.

The General left his sickbed far too soon for Ilsa or his physician. He went back to driving to the brewery at six every morning to put in his usual twelve-hour day. Fritzi had planned on staying only a short time, and her father never invoked his illness to induce her to prolong her visit. Somehow it just happened.

THE wind raked her face and hummed in her ears as Fritzi pedaled into downtown Chicago, where sleepy citizens were dragging to work. The wind's murmur couldn't hide a faintly taunting inner voice.

You'd better get on, my girl.

The voice belonged to an imaginary companion who'd been with Fritzi for years. She was the magnificent and regal Ellen Terry, goddess of the international stage.

That Fritzi held silent dialogues with a nonexistent person didn't strike her as bizarre. She considered the conversations a natural part of the life of the imagination, and she had a very vivid one. Typically Ellen Terry offered comments about Fritzi's shortcomings, something like a personified conscience.

Remember how old you'll be next month.

Fritzi was annoyed. She needed no reminder that come January she would be but a scant four years from thirty, the threshold of spinsterhood, a state devoutly to be avoided by proper young women. Of course, proper young women didn't mount their bikes before daylight and go scorching off to greet the sunrise.

The yellow morning light fell on the city's busy commercial heart as she headed south along Michigan Boulevard. Fritzi quickly shot east two blocks to State, where she went south again. The sun was higher, splashing a storefront near Van Buren that had been converted into a five-cent theater showing pictures that moved. The place was exotically named the Bijou Dream.

Fritzi sniffed in disdain. Respectable people never set foot in such places. As for appearing in one of the crude little story pictures—she'd sooner die. She was, after all, a *legitimate* actress from the *professional* theater. Or would be again if she could summon the nerve to get out of town and follow her dream to New York.

Drifter • About the same hour, hundreds of miles to the east in Riverdale, a hamlet on the northern edge of New York City, Carl Crown was knocking on doors in search of work and food.

Fritzi's younger brother had turned twenty-four in November. He'd been wandering without direction ever since Princeton cast him out at the end of his junior year. "Bull" Crown had been a star on the Princeton football line but a failure in the classroom. He was smart enough, but not diligent or interested.

For a change Carl was shaved and barbered. In Poughkeepsie he'd swept out a barbershop in exchange for the barber's services. His clothes were reasonably clean—faded jeans, a blue flannel work shirt, a plaid winter coat, and hunter's boots laced on the sides.

All morning doors had slammed in his face. The afternoon was no different. As the wintry sun dropped near the great Hudson River, he was discouraged and famished. He knocked at the kitchen door of a neat cottage with a white picket fence.

A woman in her early thirties opened the door. "Yes?"

"Any work, ma'am? My name's Carl. I'm just passing through. I'm good with my hands."

The woman looked him up and down in the fading light. "Well, my daughter Hettie wrecked her cycle last Saturday. If you can repair it, I'll pay you thirty cents. I'm a widow, not mechanical at all. Tools are in the shed."

"Yes, ma'am. I'll get right to it while it's still light." Carl gave her one of the warm smiles that came naturally to him. He was good-looking in an unobtrusive way. He had his father's short legs, his mother's long upper body. His hair was thick like Ilsa's. His brown eyes shone bright like his sister's.

The woman smiled back. "Knock when you're done." She closed the door.

Carl found the damaged two-wheeler in the shed. It was a black Wright Safety Cycle, manufactured by the brothers who'd started in that business while they pursued their studies of aeronautics. Now the Wrights enjoyed worldwide fame as a result of their flights at Kitty Hawk, North Carolina. Airplanes and all the mechanical wonders of the age fascinated Carl.

He crouched with one hand resting on the bicycle's frame. After a minute of study he searched in the shed and found a shelf of old tools. He demounted the front wheel, patched a flat balloon tire, and straightened the bent fork.

Carl finished the job in twenty minutes. He didn't want to tell the widow how easy it was, so he wiped his greasy fingers on a rag and walked to the picket fence, gazing at the enormous western sky. The vista brought memories of the years spent in New Jersey during his disastrous college career.

He still remembered vividly the day it had ended. On a Friday in May 1904 Carl's father arrived in Princeton in response to a letter from the university president. The General stepped off the local from New York at two in the morning, grimy, tired, and in short temper. "I do not like to be taken away from business because of your scholastic failings," he said as Carl conducted him to the Nassau Inn for what remained of the night.

The General was calmer when he preceded a nervous Carl into the president's office the next morning. Dr. Woodrow Wilson, the son of a Presbyterian cleric, was a prim and austere man. The General took the visitors chair. Carl stood behind him.

Dr. Wilson reviewed Carl's record at the university. He had attended for four academic years and still had the status of a junior. The president's conclusion was dry and devoid of sympathy. "I am afraid we have no choice but to suspend Carl until such time as remedial work elsewhere merits his reinstatement."

Carl wanted to jump up and shout hurrah. He loved football and the sociability of college, but he didn't love academics.

The General placed both hands on the silver head of his cane. "I do want to observe that I've made substantial contributions to this school, Dr. Wilson."

"I am certainly aware of it, sir. Princeton is grateful. But failing grades are failing grades." He removed his eyeglasses. "I'm sorry."

At the depot afterward, as the New York local clanged and steamed in, the General said, "Many fathers would disown a son who behaved so recklessly. I did that to your brother Joe and regretted it later. I won't repeat my mistake. But neither will I support a son who has failed to repay my investment in his education. You may have a job at the brewery and earn your keep henceforth."

It took all of Carl's nerve to say, "I'm sorry, Pop. I don't want to work in the brewery the rest of my life."

The General's response was tightly reined anger. "Where, then, may I ask?"

"I don't know."

"Well, until you decide, you're on your own. You're a grown man, Carl. Matured physically if not in character as yet." That stung. "Look out for yourself. Maybe this spell will pass in a few weeks. If so, we have a place for you at home. You mean a great deal to your mother and me. Never forget that."

Father embraced son, the General boarded the car, and the train pulled out. . . .

At the picket fence Carl shook himself out of the reverie. He still believed in the possibilities represented by the new century and its wonderful new machines. But where did he belong?

He knocked at the kitchen door to tell the widow he'd finished the job. She paid him, then fed him supper and handed him two blankets. "You can sleep in the shed if you want, but the sheriff is hard on tramps. In the morning I'd advise you to move on."

"Sure," said Carl wryly. "I'm used to that."

Paul and His Wife • Across the Atlantic in London, Carl and Fritzi's cousin Paul was anxiously pacing on the north side of Derby Gate where it intersected Victoria Embankment by the river Thames. It was Friday; Parliament was not sitting. Most M.P.'s would be found in their offices in the building across the way.

"See them?" Paul asked his friend Michael Radcliffe, a reporter for the London *Light*.

"Not yet," Michael called from the corner. He was looking south toward the underground entrance, with Big Ben and the Gothic splendor of Westminster Palace just beyond.

Paul Crown was twenty-nine. He was a professional cameraman who filmed actualities—dramatic events and rare sights from all over the globe. He'd learned his trade in Chicago working for a profane genius named Colonel R. Sidney Shadow. Before the colonel died, he sold the assets of the American Luxograph Company to Lord Yorke, a British press baron, who kept the company name and its star camera operator. Paul had moved his family to London three years earlier.

Paul's camera stood on the curbstone amid a cluster of reporters and photographers. The WSPU march had not been publicized. But somehow word of it had reached the authorities and the press.

Another cameraman said, "Hey, Paul, what happens if they toss your missus in the clink?"

"Then I guess I'll feed the kiddies for a while," Paul said. He worried about Julie taking part in marches, but he knew better than to ask her to stay home. Julie was an ardent "new woman."

Michael hurried back. "They just came up from the tube."

Paul sprinted to the corner. He saw the women marching north in the middle of the road, twelve or fifteen of them in two ranks.

They walked like soldiers in long skirts and plumed hats. Each woman carried a rolled-up paper. Paul spied his beautiful wife in the second row. Julie and the others belonged to Mrs. Emmeline Pankhurst's Women's Social and Political Union. Their militant middle-aged leader marched in the front rank, flanked by her daughters Sylvia and Christabel.

Paul checked his tripod for steadiness. He sighted over the camera to the M.P. office building. A dozen policemen guarded the doors. Some of Mrs. Pankhurst's women—the *Daily Mail* had christened them suffragettes—had already been arrested and served short terms in prison for attempting to question speakers at Liberal Party meetings, among them the self-promoting Winston Churchill. Women weren't permitted to speak out or have any role in politics. Mrs. Pankhurst vowed to change that.

The marchers swung around the corner. Paul began cranking the camera with a practiced, steady rhythm. Julie saw him and waved. Paul waved back with his free hand.

On the Embankment, auto drivers sounded klaxons in derision. Men leaned from their cabs to swear and jeer at the suffragettes forming a semicircle in front of the constables. The policeman in charge strode forward to confront Mrs. Pankhurst. "Good day, madam. May I ask why you're interfering with traffic?"

Emmeline Pankhurst held up her rolled paper. "We are here with resolutions to be presented to members of Parliament."

The constable shook his head. "Can't be done, madam, and well you know it. You're not allowed to enter the building."

"We are going in," Mrs. Pankhurst announced. "Ladies? Forward." She walked past the dumbfounded constable, who was unprepared for disobedience. Mrs. Pankhurst bore down on the cordon of policemen blocking the doors. Two of the officers had no choice but to push her back, then grapple with her.

The women broke ranks. Paul cranked steadily but kept a wary eye on his wife. The horns, jeering, and cursing had risen to a bedlam. The police fended off the suffragettes with their hands and jabs of their truncheons. Antagonized by rough handling, some of the suffragettes punched and kicked. A truncheon opened a bloody gash in one lady's cheek. Another whacked Sylvia Pankhurst's ankle, sending her sprawling.

The exchange of blows went on for another minute or so. Then Mrs. Pankhurst rallied her troops with a cry. "All right! Retreat! We shall try another time. I want no serious injuries." Just that quickly the assault fell apart.

Paul kept cranking, thankful Julie hadn't been hurt. He watched her lean over with a piece of chalk. The WSPU often left messages for all to see: VOTES FOR WOMEN. END MALE DOMINANCE.

Julie had bent forward from the waist to write. The angry chief constable took note and delivered a vicious kick to her backside. Paul heard the sickening sound of Julie's head hitting the pavement. He abandoned the camera, charged across the street.

"Stand back, bucko," a bobby said, hanging on to Paul's lapels. "You've no call to—"

"Get out of my way. That's my wife." Paul punched the copper in the stomach and sent the man reeling. A policeman behind Paul smashed the small of his back with a truncheon, causing him to fly forward. Paul's temple hit the curb, jarring him. On hands and knees he crawled over to Julie. He pressed his mouth to hers frantically, felt her warm breathing. He groaned with relief.

Rough hands fastened on his neck and arms. He was dragged up, spun around. The policeman in charge fairly spat at him, "That's all, laddie. I saw you assault an officer. You're for the clink, sure."

But Paul didn't go to jail. Instead, mysteriously, he was released after three hours. He went home from Magistrate's Court to the flat in Chelsea. Julie was resting comfortably in bed. Philippa, the housemaid, was looking after the children—Joseph Shad Crown, called Shad, who was six, and Elizabeth, called Betsy, two.

Paul sat beside the bed while Julie drowsed. Presently she opened her eyes. "You must think I'm a dreadful fool."

He bent to kiss her cheek. "I think you're a remarkably brave woman mixed up with other women who tend to do foolish things for a noble cause." He squeezed her hand. "Sleep now."

NEXT MORNING PAUL WAS summoned from his office in Cecil Court to his boss's suite on the highest floor of the London Light building, in Fleet Street. Lord Yorke owned the *Light* as well as American Luxograph.

His Lordship was a short, round man, bald as an egg. "Well, sir?" he said, dwarfed by the great padded throne behind his desk. "What do you have to say for yourself?"

"I did what any husband would do if his wife was attacked."

"But her assailant was a police officer in pursuit of his duty."

"I come from America, Your Lordship. No one's above the law. Is it different here?"

With a raucous snort that substituted for a laugh, Lord Yorke slapped the chair arm. "Michael Radcliffe saved you. Before the film ran out, you caught that bobby kicking your wife in a most barbarous way. Michael hauled your cinematograph to safety before the coppers could smash it and then rang me. I called two persons in Whitehall who would not wish to have that kind of police behavior shown to the public. Of course, we've destroyed the offending section"—in light of his good fortune, Paul restrained a protest—"but that shall be our secret. You are a valuable employee, Paul. Try to stay out of trouble. Don't antagonize persons in authority."

"If I do that, I won't get good pictures."

Crankily Lord Yorke said, "The newsman's dilemma. Damned annoying sometimes. Good day."

Ilsa's Worry • Cold December rain created a virtual lake in Wells Street. Nicky Speers carefully parked the long maroon Benz touring car at the curb outside Restaurant Heidelberg and climbed out with arthritic slowness. Nicky was the family's chauffeur, loyal but elderly. He hobbled around to the passenger door to shepherd Fritzi, then Ilsa, to the ornate entrance.

"Thank you, Nicky," Ilsa said.

Ilsa Crown, fifty-nine, had matured into a stout, commanding woman. Her silvery gray hair, worn in a high pompadour, showed no trace of its original reddish brown color. She always dressed smartly and expensively, today in a white blouse with a large bow under a dark green tailored suit with a shoe-top hemline.

She had brought her daughter to the restaurant with serious intent. She knew Fritzi was unhappy. It was no sudden flash of insight; she'd known for months.

Ilsa regarded the menu through rimless bifocals. "Many fine specialties here, *Liebchen.* I really hope you will eat something substantial. If you don't mind my saying so, you are too thin."

Fritzi pulled a face. "You mean not enough chest."

"*Ach,* such bold language everyone uses these days."

It pleased Ilsa when Fritzi ordered a decent meal of beefsteak, potatoes, and string beans. Ilsa chose carp, preceded by noodle soup, and asked for a bottle of Liebfraumilch. She raised her first glass of the sweet wine, clinked it with Fritzi's. *"Prosit."* The wine slid down golden warm, buffing a little of the edge off her nerves. Ilsa was worried about Fritzi's future. She reached across to clasp her daughter's hand. "How I wish you felt better."

"Mama, I'm fine."

"No, no. I see the signs. A generous heart brought you home when your papa was ill, and you've stayed. But I know you're all at sea. Do amateur dramatics no longer interest you?"

"Truthfully, no."

Ilsa took another sip of wine and a deep breath, and leaped. "There is something your papa would like, you know. For you to settle down. He longs for a son-in-law, grandchildren."

Silence. Fritzi remained motionless with both hands on the stem of her glass. Ilsa had never pried into her daughter's romantic affairs. From scattered hints in letters she knew Fritzi had fallen madly for a young Georgia boy when Mortmain's company played two weeks in Savannah. The boy apparently liked her, but only that. The tone of Fritzi's letters had been sad for months.

At last Fritzi spoke. "Mama, I don't think it will ever happen."

"Why not? Is your mind made up against marriage?"

"No, but I know what I am. I'm an actress. I'm cut out for that and very little else. I love acting. That's why"—sudden spots of color in Fritzi's cheeks prepared Ilsa for something dire—"I've decided to go to New York after the first of the year."

"You would move to that awful place?"

Fritzi spoke earnestly. "You're a smart, cultured woman, Mama. You know perfectly well that theater, *real* theater, only happens in New York. If I try and fail, so be it. But I have to try."

"Have you told Papa?"

"Not yet, but I will soon."

"You know he may react badly." The catch in Ilsa's voice made Fritzi blink. "Please think it over. Think it over very carefully."

A Dream of Speed • At a coal stop in Maryland some miles above Baltimore, a railroad man rousted Carl from the southbound freight train. He'd headed south after the first snow whitened the Hudson Valley. In Maryland he found the milder weather he was seeking, though the sun was setting early.

He walked along dirt roads for a few miles, working up a ravenous appetite. He stopped at a country tavern and ordered pork roast and a stein of beer, paying with his last forty cents.

Carl wandered to a small table, pulled out the chair, and sat down heavily without judging the chair's fragility. The old dry wood protested noisily. Behind the bar the whale-size proprietor gave Carl a look. Carl jumped up and examined the chair.

"Nothing broken."

"Lucky for you. Furniture ain't cheap."

Presently the owner brought Carl's food and drink.

"Any idea where I could find some work?" Carl asked him.

"Try the track. Baltimore Downs. North edge of the city."

Carl slept that night underneath a bench in a park, half awake with his teeth chattering. In the morning he found the racetrack, a splendid one-mile layout with a big flag-bedecked grandstand. A groom pointed the way to the office. There a man named Reeves made short work of the interview. "You want a job? You game for mucking out the stables and whatever else needs doing?"

"I'm game for eating once in a while," Carl said.

Reeves liked that. "Well, the stables are clean and warm. You can sleep in an empty stall till you find a boardinghouse. Start tomorrow morning six sharp." As Carl thanked Reeves, he heard the deep growl of a motor.

"Sounds like a gasoline car," Carl said.

"Yep. When the ponies aren't running, there's a sporting crowd that will turn out for automobile races. Ever seen a race?"

"I saw the first one run in this country. Thanksgiving Day, 1895, in Chicago."

"The famous race in the snow," Reeves said with a nod.

"Fifty-four and three-tenths miles. Frank Duryea won it in ten hours and twenty-three minutes."

Since that wintry day when, as a wide-eyed boy, he had watched horseless carriages slipping and sliding along Michigan Avenue, Carl had carried on a constant if unfulfilled romance with autos. He often dreamed of driving fast. Back in Indianapolis, where he'd worked for three months earlier this year, the dream had become feverish. He bought a gallery seat for a musical play called *The Vanderbilt Cup*. It celebrated the great Long Island road race started in 1904 by the socialite William K. Vanderbilt. The show was touring with its original Broadway star, race driver Barney Oldfield.

Oldfield wasn't much of an actor, but he gave a convincing performance in the climactic scene in the second act. Two racecars, the Peerless Blue Streak and Barney's Peerless Green Dragon, raced side by side on treadmills while painted scenery flew by behind them. The cars spewed smoke and sparks. Barney wore his familiar forest-green driving suit, leather helmet, and goggles. Naturally, he won. He was the king of fast driving.

Carl's fever heated up again when Reeves said, "Two fellows in a Fiat are running practice laps for a hundred-mile race the end of the week. Go have a look."

Carl ran out into the pale winter sunshine to the track, where an engine roared in a cloud of dust. He stepped on the lower rail as the racecar sped toward the turn. It resembled half a tin can set forward on a chassis with unprotected wheels. The driver and his riding mechanic perched in bucket seats wearing goggles and fancy gauntlets.

On the back stretch the Fiat gathered speed. Carl's jaw dropped. "My Lord, they must be doing forty or fifty."

He hung on to the rail as the Fiat slewed through the turns, leaving a great rooster tail of dust behind. He watched for nearly an hour. To Reeves afterward he said, "I've got to learn to drive. I don't know where or how, but I'm going to do it. You can count on that."

Paul's Pictures • On the drive home from the restaurant Fritzi said little. Obviously her mother was upset about her decision.

The Crown mansion on Michigan Avenue and Twentieth Street was an enormous Victorian castle, twenty-six rooms, twice remodeled, and symbolic of its owner's success in the brewery trade. Ten minutes after Fritzi reached her room, Ilsa rushed in with a letter.

"*Liebchen!* See what came in the afternoon mail delivery? Pauli posted it in Gibraltar six weeks ago. He even sent a snapshot."

Ilsa gave her the Kodak print. A smile spread on Fritzi's face as she gazed at her cousin, photographed with his motion-picture camera and tripod on a hotel veranda. Paul had his usual cigar clenched in his teeth. One arm was hooked around his tripod; with his other hand he lifted his Panama hat to greet the lens.

Quickly Fritzi read through the letter. Paul had visited North Africa, photographing nomads and exotic locales in Morocco and the Sahara, then Gibraltar to film the new British warship H.M.S. *Dreadnought* steaming into the Mediterranean.

"We must find out who shows American Luxograph pictures," Ilsa said excitedly. "We'll go together, have another outing."

In one of those awful nickel theaters? Fritzi thought. She sighed a small inner sigh and said, "That would be lovely."

Fritzi and her mother bought their theater tickets at ten past two the next afternoon. The windows of the Bijou Dream were hung with green velvet drapes. The projector was shielded in a curtained booth at the rear of the long, rectangular room.

Instead of wooden benches there were chairs, a hundred or more. The Bijou Dream employed a piano player whose upright sat next to the screen, and a lecturer in a tuxedo, who introduced each batch of footage from a podium on the opposite side.

About twenty people attended the two-fifteen show. The operator switched off the tin-shaded ceiling lights, and a lantern slide appeared.

THE LATEST T. B. HARMS SONG HIT!
Words and Music by HARRY POLAND
As Featured by FLAVIA FARREL, the Irish Songbird

"Oh, it's Pauli's friend," Ilsa said, meaning the composer.

Two faces filled oval frames on either side of the slide copy. The Irish Songbird was a pouchy-eyed woman who must have been pretty before middle age. The man in the other frame, Harry Poland, had crossed the Atlantic in steerage with Paul in 1892. A Polish immigrant boy, he'd adopted a new name, found his way into the music business, and now wrote popular songs.

The first song slide appeared, illustrated by a photo of a man in goggles and a young woman in a big hat seated in an auto. Song lyrics were superimposed on the machine's long hood. The accompanist played the catchy tune: *That automobiling feeling is stealing over me.*

Ilsa sang along in her heavily accented voice. Fritzi found herself singing too. When the song slides ended, a clackety noise in the booth said the operator was turning the crank of the projector. A beam of light shot over the audience as a young woman with a leashed terrier paraded in a sunlit park. The lecturer announced, "*Mary's Mutt,* a comic novelty."

The three-minute sequence started with Mary accidentally letting go of the leash, then reacting with outrageous mugging as her dog dashed off. Chasing him, she enlisted a policeman, then a young gent eating a sandwich on a park bench. The crude film was no more than an excuse for the three actors to run around wildly, bumping into trees and each other.

"The latest from the American Luxograph," the lecturer said.

"Oh, here it is," Ilsa said, grabbing Fritzi's hand.

"Exotic sights of Morocco. Fierce Berber tribesmen." Men in sheetlike garments stalked past the camera, glowering and waving scimitars. This was followed by a camel race in the desert.

Next the clicking projector filled the screen with an image of a hotel veranda. British naval officers in white paraded in and out. With an unexplained jerk the scene changed. The audience had a glimpse of an immense battleship steaming past far below the camera. H.M.S. *Dreadnought?* The image stayed only a few seconds. A hand swooped over the lens, and the screen went black.

Another repetitive chase picture ended the fifteen-minute show. "That was thrilling, wasn't it?" Ilsa said as they left their seats. Fritzi agreed that Paul's pictures were worthwhile, in contrast to the cheap little comedies. Outside, she turned up her coat collar. The weather had worsened. A bitter wind blew off the lake.

"Pauli has seen so much of the world. What an exciting life he leads," Ilsa said.

"He should write a book about it," Fritzi said.

Ilsa and Fritzi bent into the wind, heading for the trolley stop. Ilsa had relieved Nicky of the duty of picking them up.

"Fritzi, those people in the little stories—are they actors?"

"They may think so. What they're doing isn't real acting, it's old-fashioned scenery chewing. The style of fifty years ago. Modern acting is—well, smaller. Intense but restrained."

"Would there be acting opportunities for you?"

Fritzi reacted emphatically. "Not me, Mama. I'll never have anything to do with that kind of entertainment."

The General and His Children • The General's new Cadillac started on the second spin of the crank. Black with matching leather seats, it had its winter hardtop latched in place. The machine had cost more than $3700, which put it in the luxury class. He slid under the wheel on the right side, put on his driving goggles, and drove out the brewery's east gate into Larrabee Street.

Creeping along congested streets, Joe cursed when horse dung splattered his fenders. He shook his fist at a Reo that swerved too close. In the east, clouds like gray granite slabs layered the sky. Sleet began to tick against the windshield.

The sleet had turned to snow by the time he drove into the garage at the rear of his property. In the house, Ilsa and the cook, Trudi, were mixing batter for stollen, the traditional raisin-and-sugar-dusted cakes of the season. Joe kissed his wife and said he'd be ready for *Abendessen*—the evening meal—by eight o'clock.

The Crown mansion reflected the season. A nine-foot fir tree stood beneath the huge electric chandelier in the two-story foyer. A marvelously detailed wooden crèche was arranged beneath. In the dining room two candles in the Advent wreath in the center of the long table were already lit.

At five past eight Joe proceeded to the dining room and sat at the head of the table. He heard his older son coming, announced by the scrape of his artificial foot. Joe Junior created fierce pity and anger in his father. The boy was a tragic misfit. Mired in socialist dogma, he'd taken part in a strike at a shingle factory out in Everett, Washington, where he worked for a time. The strikers fought a bloody brawl with hired goons. Two of the goons threw Joe Junior onto one of the buzz saws that split cedar blocks into shingles; the saw tore off his right foot. Only the quick action of a Norwegian woman, Anna Sieberson, kept him from bleeding to death. He later married Anna and was planning to adopt her son when influenza carried her off suddenly. The boy went to live with relatives, and Joe Junior slunk home to Chicago a bitter and defeated man.

"Good evening, Joe," the General said as his son limped in.

"Hello, Pop." Joe Junior took his seat and slouched, his right shoe stuck out as if to defiantly remind everyone of the cork foot it covered. Joe Junior was thirty. He'd resembled his father until beer and overeating ballooned his stomach.

Ilsa and Fritzi came in. Ilsa sat at the far end of the long walnut table. Fritzi took her place opposite Joe Junior on the side. Two serving girls set platters on the table.

Joe said to Fritzi, "Did you and your mother see Paul's pictures this afternoon?"

"We did. Paul's films are really remarkable. It's a shame his work is exhibited only in five-cent theaters. The other pictures, the ones that try to tell stories, are trash."

"We agree on that," her father said with a nod. "They offer nothing but low comedians chasing girls in scanty outfits—"

Loud knocking at the front door interrupted him. Ilsa looked toward the foyer. "Who on earth can be calling at this hour?"

The steward, Leopold, rushed in. "Sir, madam—it's your son."

"Carl?" Ilsa leaped up, ran past Leopold exclaiming, "Where did he come from?"

"Pittsburgh, Mama," Carl's voice boomed. "Pittsburgh and South Bend, on the boxcar Pullmans."

Elated but baffled, Joe followed his wife into the foyer. Snow was melting on Carl's hair. He hadn't shaved in several days.

Carl rushed to hug his mother. He then shook his father's hand. "Greetings, Papa. Hello, Joey. Fritzi, let me hug you."

Fritzi received a three-hundred-and-sixty-degree whirl. "No one expected you, Carl," she said.

"I'm on my way to Detroit to look for a job. I've been studying fast cars lately. I want to find out how they're built. I want to drive one."

Joe said, "You're looking for employment in an auto factory?"

Carl grinned, threw an arm over his father's shoulder, and leaned down to him. "Yes, Papa. Your wayward boy has found something he wants to do. It happened back east—Baltimore. Tell you all about it later."

"You'll be here for Christmas, won't you?" Fritzi asked.

"Through the holidays, but that's all," Carl said.

"This is wonderful news!" Ilsa exclaimed. "Come in, come in. There's plenty of food left," she said, fairly bubbling.

"Glad you're home, Carl," Joe Junior said as the others trooped back to the dining room. "But I'm bushed. We'll talk tomorrow."

Joe watched his son drag himself up the long staircase. He called for a bottle of schnapps and another place setting. Ilsa and Fritzi and Carl chattered away while he alternated sips of coffee and schnapps. Carl had given them a grand Christmas present.

Courage from Carl • Next morning everyone rose early. After breakfast Carl took himself out of the house to shop for presents, extracting a promise from Fritzi that they'd play some ball later. It was a pastime they'd enjoyed together when they were children.

That afternoon a burst of sunshine and warmth quickly melted an inch or two of snow from last night. Carl smacked his fist into his fielder's glove. "All right, Fritz, let's see if you have anything left in old age."

Fritzi wound up and delivered the hardball with a wild curve that took it over Carl's head. He stabbed his mitt up and neatly caught it. "Hey, you're not so creaky," he said, grinning.

They fired the ball back and forth, developing a rhythm.

"I'm thrilled you're going to Detroit, Carl."

"Pop made a point of congratulating me last night. He's happy too." That unnerved her. Would the General feel the same about her decision to leave? Doubtful. She was female.

"I made up my mind in Baltimore, where I watched that Fiat," he went on. "I hung out with the driver and his riding mechanic for three days. Learned a lot. I'll get a job in an auto plant. What about you? Haven't given up acting, have you?"

"Never." Fritzi smacked the ball into her mitt, took a deep breath, and threw. "I'm going to try Broadway."

Carl thought about that a moment, then broke into a smile. "Sure. It's the obvious place for someone as talented as you."

"It's a secret until I tell Papa."

"When are you leaving?"

Fritzi felt a chill that had nothing to do with the temperature. "Right after Christmas. I've told Mama. She doesn't like it, but she won't stand in the way. Papa's the obstacle. I dread it."

Carl tapped the ball into his glove, put his brawny arm around her. "I'm not too qualified to give advice, but I will anyway. You know Pop will probably rant. He's stuck in the past in some ways. Every woman needs a wedding ring and children, that kind of thing. Well, sure—if it suits you. But I think you're kind of like me, Fritzi. A maverick. We both have different dreams. They're not like Pop's when he came to this country, a poor boy eager to make a fortune. We're living in an incredible new century, and all the rules have changed, including Pop's. So don't be talked out of your dream." He pointed at the pale sky. "If your dream's there, sail out and find it."

Obligatory Scene • Wednesday of the week before Christmas, Fritzi went to the train depot to buy a ticket on the New York Central's *Empire State Express.* "One way, day coach, please."

She constantly rehearsed what she wanted to say to her father. She would do it Saturday before the family left to attend the annual party for employees of the brewery.

That day she dressed for the party about four in the afternoon. She struggled into her gown—red satin with a deep lace bertha—her stomach on fire, her palms already damp. Groping at the nape of her neck, she closed the clasp on the pearl choker borrowed from her mother. Then she yanked a comb through her tangled yellow hair.

A clock on her bedroom mantel showed half past four. Her father had announced their departure time as six o'clock. She heard a heavy tread in the upstairs hall, ran to the door.

"Papa! You're home early. Could I speak to you a moment?" Her heartbeat was thunder in her ears.

"Why, of course," he said with a smile. "Shall I come in?"

"It might be better if we go down to your office."

"Whatever you prefer." He offered his arm at the head of the stairs. "You look very fetching. You'll be the belle of the party."

"Hardly." Nervous, she almost stumbled twice on the long descent past the stunning Christmas tree.

In the office, Fritzi sat on the forward edge of the visitors chair, clasped her hands in her lap to keep them still.

"Now, my girl, what's on your mind?"

"Plans, Papa. I want to tell you my plans," she said. "I'm going to New York."

His forehead wrinkled. "You're going to shop?"

"To live. To look for work in the theater."

Joe Crown never changed his posture or expression, yet Fritzi fancied the blood left his cheeks. "I see." He crossed to the door, which stood open a few inches. He closed it with a dungeonlike bang, then stood with his back to the window. "When did you decide this?"

"Some time ago. I bought my railway ticket Wednesday."

"Let's discuss this reasonably."

"With all respect, Papa, discussion isn't necessary."

"Permit me to disagree. It isn't healthy for a girl your age to venture to New York for a career in a dubious profession."

"Carl's going to Detroit without the promise of a job."

"Carl is a man. It makes a difference."

"Oh, Papa, that's so old-fashioned."

His voice remained steady, controlled. "New York's a filthy, wretched city. I've seen it many times. It simply isn't safe, Fritzi. Please reconsider." He was adamant.

Well, so was she. "I've considered it carefully, Papa. I'm just informing you as a courtesy. You know Broadway is the only theater that matters. If I don't find out whether I can succeed there, I'll hate myself the rest of my life."

Joe Crown peered out the window, his profile etched by the dying daylight. "Please understand, Fritzi, I want the best for you. A husband. A home. Children."

"I'm hardly the kind of beauty a man's going to marry."

"You underrate yourself terribly. You'll find someone. In any case, a young woman of good character belongs—"

She jumped up. *"Kinder, Kirche, Küche?"* Children, church, kitchen. "Papa, that was your century. This is mine. My life."

"Your life! You must regard it very cheaply if you insist on consorting with low theatrical people."

His voice had risen. Fritzi clenched her hands. The scene was veering out of control. "How can you say that? You're the one who gave me permission to join the Mortmain company."

"I thought a year or two on the road would cure your ambition. You'd see the sordid lives of actors, and you'd give it up."

"You really thought that? You deliberately sent me out to fail?"

He took hold of her red satin sleeves. "Please calm down."

She wrenched free. "I'm not a child, to be patronized and pacified." Her color was high, her forehead hot.

"No, you misunderstand. I did *not* send you out to fail, only to get the theater out of your system. It appears I'm the one who failed. I must try again. I beg you not to go. You're a lovely girl"— she avoided his eyes—"but emotional. At this moment I would say slightly hysterical. Let me be plain. If you persist with this mad idea, you'll incur my deep displeasure."

"Then what, Papa? You'll disown me?"

"I dislike your tone of voice."

"I'm sorry. I'm a grown woman. I'll always be your daughter, but I'm not your slave."

"I forbid you to go. I forbid it!"

"You have nothing to say about it, Papa. Good-bye."

Fritzi was almost in tears. She dashed out, giving the office door a mighty slam. It was a splendid curtain cue for a play. The difference was, when a play ended, there were no consequences.

Eastbound • "*Liebchen,* don't do this," Ilsa said as Fritzi threw stockings and underwear into the tray of her steamer trunk.

"I'm going, Mama. He despises me."

"You're wrong—it's only the acting. And the thought of you alone in New York."

"What's the difference? That's what I am, an actress. Actresses belong in New York." She stuffed a pair of shoes into her leather bag on the bed. "Papa hasn't said three words to me since the party night before last. He's avoided me around the house. I never spent a worse Sunday. I'll be on the four-o'clock train."

"Fritzi, it's *Heiligabend.* Christmas Eve. We gather together, Papa lights the candles on the tree—"

"I'll celebrate by myself."

"Is there nothing I can do to change your mind?"

"Nothing. Carl's taking me to the depot—you won't have to bother."

"Bother? You are my child, my only girl."

"Well, don't worry. Your only girl will be fine in New York."

Ilsa dabbed her eyes with her handkerchief. "I have gifts for you. You must take your presents. Wait."

Fritzi went on packing. Moments later Ilsa returned with two white boxes—a large one and a smaller one, about six inches square. "Here, open them. Please."

Giving her mother a look that mingled affection and melancholy, Fritzi pulled the red ribbon off the larger box, unfolded the tissue paper. "Oh, Mama, how handsome."

"A winter coat. You need a new heavy coat."

Fritzi lifted it by the shoulders, admiring it. The coat was dark brown cheviot with a small black-and-brown plaid. The lining was bright yellow silk. A velvet collar ornamented the double-breasted cape. Fritzi held it against herself, secretly pleased.

"Perhaps the other gift will be useful as well," Ilsa said.

Fritzi opened the smaller box, discovered two white pads nested there. She poked one; it was stuffed with a spongy material. Ilsa said, "They call them gay deceivers. You pin them inside your—"

"Yes, Mama. I get the idea."

"You really don't need them, of course."

Fritzi dropped the pads into the trunk tray and hugged her mother. "Of course I need them. Thank you."

AT THE depot, amid travelers setting out on holiday journeys, Fritzi said good-bye to Carl and her mother. She was wearing her new brown coat. Under one arm she had a round tin of Ilsa's *Pfefferkuchen*—ginger-flavored Christmas cookies.

A freezing wind blew through the train shed, dispersing the steam billowing from under the cars. Carl walked up the platform to deliver her trunk and leather bag to the freight car. Ilsa said, "You must let me know at once that you are safe and settled. Telegraph collect."

"I will, Mama."

Carl returned. They all hugged and kissed and said their farewells. Inside the coach, Fritzi pressed her forehead against the glass and waved as the *Empire State Express* pulled out.

Part Two   STRIVING

Adrift in New York • At ten a.m. on a Monday morning in May 1908, in response to an audition notice in the *Dramatic Mirror,* Fritzi climbed the stairs of a building on Sixteenth Street a few doors from Union Square West. Her destination was the office of a casting agent. So far she'd auditioned for scores of parts without landing a role. At the Mehlman agency this morning she had read with eleven other actresses for the same small part, eighteen lines. The most brazen performance was given by a shapely redhead. At the end of an hour and a half—surprise!—Mehlman asked the redhead to stay and told the others to go.

Fritzi had another reading scheduled in the afternoon; perhaps that one would be better. But she couldn't help feeling discouraged. All she had to show for more than a year of effort was a walk-on, fifty cents a night, in a flop called *The Mongol's Bride.* It had lasted one week.

During much of her sixteen months in New York, Fritzi had supported herself as a waitress at a cheery restaurant called the Dutch Mill. Unfortunately, last month the Dutch Mill's owner decided to retire. The new owner immediately converted the restaurant to a five-cent theater—or nickelodeon, as the contemptible places were being called—and Fritzi was thrown back onto the streets she'd tramped for weeks before finding the waitress job.

At two o'clock Fritzi sat on a bench in the waiting room belonging to Shorty Lorenz, a little blond wart of a man. Crowded on the benches were six other nervous young women.

Shorty Lorenz breezed into the room at two fifteen clutching a batch of sides, which he handed out. "Okeydokey, girls. This here's a society drama called *Shall We Divorce?* The producer is Brutus

Brown." There were a few gasps. Brown was a noted philanderer. "His stage manager's inside," Lorenz continued. "He'll hear you one at a time."

Fritzi was third to read for the paunchy stage manager, who had a face like granite. She stumbled over words and pitched her voice too high; she made a mess of the reading. At the end, however, the granite face cracked, and the stage manager shook her hand with a fatherly smile. "Nice reading, Fritzi. We'll phone you tonight if we want you to come back."

Outside, rain pelted the street. She'd have to trudge home in that, all the way to First Avenue near Eighth Street. Paying for public transportation was out of the question.

When Fritzi got home, she saw light under her landlady's door, knocked softly. "I'm sorry to disturb you, Mrs. Perella."

"Not to worry. Was just reading the paper." Mrs. Perella was a Neapolitan woman who liked Fritzi and took messages on the downstairs hall telephone without complaint.

"Did I have any messages today?"

Mrs. Perella shook her head, saw Fritzi's disappointment, and squeezed her hand gently. Fritzi thanked her and trudged upstairs. Her room at the third-floor front was large, but that was about all you could say for it. Even with the jets unlit it smelled of gas. The building hadn't been modernized.

Weary and damp, she hung her sailor hat and coat in the wardrobe. An elevated train rumbled, approaching from the south. Fritzi pulled the blind and lit the gas mantle. She undressed, put on a cotton robe, and stretched on the bed, bedeviled by thoughts of a small rectangular tin box hidden in a drawer. Originally the box had contained lemon drops. Now it held all the money she had left— four dollars and change.

What did it take to succeed? She was still searching for the secret. What if she never discovered it? What if she woke up to find her dream of becoming an actress nothing more than an adolescent delusion she should have abandoned long ago?

She hardly dared think about that.

Smashup • In the twenty-second lap Artie Flugel, in the little Mason, deliberately whipped into a skid ahead of Carl, spewing dust over Carl's windscreen and blinding him. It was a dangerous trick of experienced drivers. Artie wanted to win not only the purse but a five-dollar side bet with Carl.

Coming out of the turn in a thick tan cloud, Carl took the middle of the straightaway by instinct alone. The dust blew away; the grandstand and pits loomed in the sunshine. Through the oil-specked lenses of his goggles Carl saw spectators sitting on the white rail fence at the turn beyond the stands. Damn fools.

The track was in a northern suburb of Detroit. The race was the closing event on a hot, dry Sunday in early summer. Carl worked six days a week at Henry Ford's auto plant; on the seventh day he raced.

Today four earlier races had rutted the track. A piece of hard soil flew up and hit the windscreen, cracking it. Above the engine roar Carl heard his riding mechanic yell a curse.

Four cars remained in the race—a Peugeot, a National, Artie's Mason, and Carl's Edmunds Special with lightning bolts painted on the cowl. The Peugeot and the National were a lap and a half behind. Carl was on Artie's tail, battling for the lead.

By now the race was taking its toll. Carl's rear end hurt, and his legs were killing him. He looked like a mummy: long-sleeved shirt, leather gauntlets, helmet, goggles, chamois face mask.

The first sections of the crowded grandstand flashed by on his right. Seated to his left, Jesse, his mechanic, was constantly in motion, peering at the gas and oil gauges, pumping up the gas pressure to spurt gas to the front carburetor from the rear tank, watching the four smooth rubber tires, especially the rear ones.

Halfway past the grandstand now, clocking close to fifty miles per hour. On the fence rail at the turn coming up, amid people wearing drab clothes, something bright white shone. Artie Flugel roared out of sight into the back turn. Carl shoved the accelerator pedal down. Jesse tapped Carl's knee frantically. *Tire going.*

Carl looked at Jesse for a second. Jesse stabbed a finger over his right shoulder. *Right rear.*

He knew he should slow down for the turn, but Artie was already showing him too much dust. Carl roared into the turn high up on the track near the fence where all those people roosted like crows on a wire. Jesse shouted a warning just before the right tire blew.

The Special began to slew and slide and headed straight for the fence sitters, who were screaming and trying to get down.

If Carl drove into the fence, people would die. At the fence's far end, hay bales were banked in the turn. He yanked the wheel over left, stood on the brake. The rear end juddered and slid. The Special just cleared the end of the fence. Carl shouted a pointless "Hang on, Jess" as the Special hit the hay bales, burst through, slammed down into a ditch, and threw them both out of the car.

Carl landed violently on his back in long grass, the wind knocked out of him. He ripped his goggles, helmet, and mask off, sucking air. The Special lay nose-down in the ditch, its front end crumpled. Oil smoke leaked out. The smell of gas was raw in the Sunday air. People were running from the grandstand—the racetrack vultures who'd loot any available souvenir from a smashed-up car.

Carl didn't see his mechanic. He had a queasy feeling that his friend lay in the ditch with a broken neck. "Jesse?"

Nothing but silence. The Special's owner, Hoot Edmunds, walked slowly toward the looters. Hoot's striped seersucker blazer was properly buttoned, and he twirled his malacca cane.

Then Carl saw the bright white person from the fence. The white was a shirtwaist, and the person was a girl with blond hair.

Curly black hair, a long-jawed head, coffee-and-cream skin poked up from the ditch. Blood ran from a gash over the man's left eye, dripping on his coveralls.

Jesse Shiner climbed out of the ditch with a dolorous expression. He was taller than Carl, starvation thin. He was colored, though clearly one or more ancestors had mixed a lot of white blood with his blackness. Jesse was ten years older than Carl and lucky to be riding as a mechanic. He had the job because Carl had insisted Jesse's color didn't matter, only his skill as a self-taught mechanic.

Jesse and Carl stood a foot apart, staring at each other. They came to the same realization at the same moment: They were miraculously whole. Both started to laugh wildly. Giddy in the wake of fear, they threw their arms around each other and slapped each other on the back. Hoot Edmunds strolled up, twirling his cane.

"Boys, are you in one piece?" Hoot liked to call them boys even though, at twenty-two, he was three years younger than Carl. Hoot was the son of Magnus Edmunds, a man who'd made a fortune manufacturing marine engines for Great Lakes steamers.

"Think so, Hoot," Carl said.

"That was a fine bit of driving at the last moment," Hoot said.

"Only thing to do." Carl's legs shook. He waved toward a giant sycamore tree. "Need to sit down." He sat with his spine against the bark. "I'm sorry I wrecked the car, Hoot."

"Don't worry. There's plenty of money to manufacture another."

"Why were those fools squatting on the rail?" Jesse complained. "Why didn't the stewards drive 'em off?"

"They tried," someone standing behind Hoot said in a sweet voice. "We refused to leave. It's an excellent vantage point."

The person behind Hoot stepped to one side so as to be visible. Sycamore leaves threw a lovely shadow pattern onto the full bosom of her bright white shirtwaist. "But you really did save lives. It was very brave," she said. Carl found himself looking at—drowning in—the loveliest dark blue eyes he'd ever seen.

Ever the prescient young gentleman, Hoot saw Carl's interest and excused himself. He strolled back to the crumpled Special. Jesse went the other way to roll himself a smoke.

The girl said, "You're a very accomplished driver. Have you been doing it long?"

"Started last summer. It isn't that hard. You need strong arms and shoulders, and you have to be willing to be killed before you're thirty." He said it smiling.

She laughed. "You need a lot more than that, sir. There's skill. In my estimation you possess a great deal of it."

Carl had never met a young woman quite so forward. She wasn't fresh, just plainspoken, direct. She was about his age, about his height. She had a pretty, round face, blond curls, and full lips. She was nicely though not expensively dressed, with a ribboned straw hat and a striped summer parasol.

He grabbed the sycamore trunk, stood, and walked to her. "Well, I do thank you for the compliment, Miss—"

"My name's Teresa. I prefer Tess."

"Carl. Carl Crown." He put out his hand, still encased in a greasy leather glove, which he peeled off with embarrassed haste. Her fingers were cool and firm.

"The kind of selflessness you exhibited should be rewarded in some way," the girl said. "Might I invite you to supper at our house? I'm sure my father would enjoy meeting you."

Surprised, Carl took a moment to react. "Sure, of course."

"I'm afraid you'll have to come a rather long way. Our residence is Woodward Avenue, but in the summer we live at Grosse Pointe."

"The electric cars run out there, don't they?"

"Indeed," she said. "Would Saturday evening be convenient?"

"Perfect!" he exclaimed. Then he grinned. "I don't think I've ever met a pretty young woman who likes racing."

"My father has a small connection with the auto business. That's how I got interested." She pulled out a slip of paper and wrote on it. "This is the address. Is seven o'clock convenient?"

"That should do fine, Miss—um, Tess."

"I'll see you then." Solemnly she shook his hand a second time, then walked away, opening her parasol.

Tess disappeared behind the grandstand, taking Carl down from the heights abruptly. He noticed Jesse talking to Hoot and walked over to them, legs and shoulders aching.

Hoot regarded him quizzically. Carl said, "Something funny?"

"That girl. You were quite friendly."

"Why not? She's pretty. She invited me to supper on Saturday."

"Really? I assume you know who she is?"

"Her name's Teresa. Should I know more than that?"

"I suppose not. You don't hang out with the Detroit elite. Teresa Clymer is Lorenzo Clymer's daughter."

"You mean Clymer as in Clymer, the Quality Car for Quality People?" said Jesse.

"That's the one."

"He owns the foundry I work at," Jesse said to Carl.

"Clymer doesn't actually run an auto plant," Hoot explained. "He merely lends his name to the company. Clymer's put money into auto ventures for some years now. I suggest you develop a sudden belly-ache Saturday night. He and the rest of his friends who make autos costing two thousand dollars think your employer is a man with stupid ideas. Clymer owned shares in Henry's second company, the one Henry walked away from. It's Cadillac now. Most of the Grosse Pointe crowd hates Henry's guts, and to my knowledge it's mutual."

Carl stood speechless. The Henry referred to was Ford, proprietor and resident genius of the Ford Motor Company.

Paul's Anchor • The Chelsea flat was quiet. Betsy, three, was napping. Seven-year-old Shad sat next to his father in the bay window seat, examining a book with a look of wonderment.

It was a warm Sunday in June. The boy traced a finger across his father's name under the book's title, *I Witness History*.

"You really wrote this, Papa?"

Paul smiled. "Every word, good or bad."

"Oh, it's all good, Papa, isn't it?" Shad was a bright-faced, sturdy boy whose dark brown eyes, from Paul, complemented the thick ink-black hair inherited from Julie.

"Well, people seem to think so."

Success had certainly surprised the first-time author. Paul had just signed a contract with a New York firm for an American edition.

Shad turned pages. "I can't read a lot of these big words."

Paul ruffled the boy's hair. "You'll understand them when you're a little older."

Like all youngsters, Shad kept his attention focused on one subject for only a few minutes. "Can we go to the zoo next week?"

"Saturday. My ship sails from Liverpool on Sunday."

"You're going back to America?"

"To make more pictures and to give a few lectures."

A man in New York, one William Schwimmer, at a company called American Platform Artists, had gotten a copy of his book and written to say he could arrange some lucrative auditorium appearances on Paul's next trip. Nervously Paul had agreed to try it.

"I'll see the family in Chicago, I hope," Paul went on. "Aunt Fritzi in New York, perhaps, and Uncle Carl in Detroit."

"Where's that?"

"In the state of Michigan." He shifted the position of the pillow at the small of his back. Some weeks ago in Morocco he'd lifted a crate the wrong way and wrenched something. Thirty years old and aching like Methuselah, he thought with considerable disgust. Julie was continually urging him to hire an assistant.

Shad started to ask another question, but the door opened. Julie peeked in from the hall. Shad sprang up to throw his arms around his mother. A moment later he slid out the door, grinning.

Julie was a slightly built woman with delicate fair skin and large, luminous gray eyes. Paul's heart leaped when he saw how fetching she looked in her afternoon dress—silk chiffon with pleated sleeves in a becoming shade of dusty rose.

Julie spied the book in the window seat. "I'm so proud of you, Paul."

"Without you I wouldn't have had the nerve to try the first paragraph."

She slipped her arms around his neck. "Just don't get so famous that hordes of women chase you."

"I only care for one," he said, drawing her into an ardent kiss. Her body strained into his. She rested her chin on his shoulder, sighing. "I'm losing you to the world again."

"Only for a few months." He kissed the warm curve of her throat. "Before you know it, I'll be back home with you and the children."

Three Witches and Four Actresses • Days went by. No jobs. Fritzi reduced her expenses to starvation level. For breakfast she ate two-day-old bakery bread and hot tea. Her main meal was another slice of stale bread, and once a week she bought a single oyster from a delicatessen and warmed it in a pan of broth on the gas ring in her room. She veiled her situation in every letter to her mother. "Everything fine! Prospects good!" In all the months since she'd left Chicago, she hadn't heard from the General or written to him.

By late August she had descended to a nadir of discouragement. One particularly difficult day—four ads answered, no job—she presented herself at a wicket at Grand Central Terminal.

"Schedule of passenger trains to Chicago, please."

Five minutes later she threw the schedule into a rubbish barrel. The image of Ellen Terry scolded her for even thinking of running home.

Footsore and depressed, she trudged downtown to Mrs. Perella's. Wasn't two years in New York enough? She set a deadline. If she couldn't find at least one good part by her birthday, next January 5, she would pack up, go home, and admit defeat to her father.

Fritzi stoically washed her face and put on her thin robe; then she pulled her chair under the gas mantle and opened one of the publications that regularly carried theatrical notices. She found a notice that made her breathe faster.

CASTING IMMEDIATELY: WITCHES, for new production of "THE SCOTTISH TRAGEDY" starring and personally presented by famed English tragedian HOBART MANCHESTER. Distinguished international company includes MRS. VAN SANT as Lady M. Readings 2:30–5 Wed., Novelty Theater, 48th St.

Fritzi experienced a delirious rush of excitement. She had played all three of the Weird Sisters in wretched Mortmain productions of "the Scottish tragedy." That and "the Scottish play" were theatrical euphemisms for the name of the Shakespearean drama actors regarded as a bad-luck vehicle. Horrible accidents happened to actors who played in *Macbeth,* it was said.

Fritzi laughed at such superstition. Even the presence of Beelzebub himself wouldn't keep her from showing up at the Novelty.

Next day she rode the Broadway cable car to Forty-eighth Street.

Walking east, she approached a garish marquee whose electric bulbs illuminated the name 5¢ VARIETY. In New York it seemed as though nickelodeons were opening on every block. Fritzi sniffed and hurried on to the Novelty.

"Sign the sheet and take a seat in the auditorium," said the old man who kept watch on the stage door. Fritzi picked up the pen. She blanched. She was looking at a sheet already filled with names. Horrified, she discovered a second full page underneath.

Ye gods, she thought, not the *Macbeth* curse already?

HER forty or so rivals were scattered throughout the orchestra. They eyed Fritzi as if she carried the plague. She took a seat on the aisle near the back, tried to compose herself.

Three more hopefuls came in. A minute later a flurry of conversation in the wings preceded the appearance of a fat middle-aged man wearing an English walking suit, a long opera cape, and a wide-brimmed soft hat. He carried a book and papers, which he put on a worktable onstage. He flung his hat away and came down to the footlights, fists on his hips. He shouted at the gallery.

"Is anyone awake up there? Let's have more light, sir." The man's voice surprised Fritzi with its baritone richness. From the high darkness a curse floated down. Instruments hanging on the front of the balcony blazed on. The fat man was fully lighted.

"Good afternoon, ladies." He made a courtier's bow. He unfastened his cape and whirled it away like a bullfighter. "I am Manchester." He beamed, as though expecting applause.

Fritzi didn't know what to make of the "famed English tragedian." She guessed his height at five feet six, his weight at two hundred pounds or more. He was decidedly bowlegged, with a face as red as a beef roast and shoulder-length hair. He strode to the table, picked up the signature sheets.

Manchester was a traditional actor-manager, a combination of producer and star. The great actor-managers had dominated the nineteenth-century stage, but their day was passing. New forces drove the modern theater: The director, a relatively new position in stagecraft. The producer, a powerful moneyman. The star, an actor people came to see. Mrs. Van Sant, Manchester's Lady Macbeth, was that sort of star.

At the footlights again, the great man addressed them. "We all know why we have gathered here, do we not? The call of Thespis. The lure of the lights, the claques, the crowd!"

An older actress in front of Fritzi half turned and whispered, "Full of himself, ain't he?"

Manchester touched the book on the table. "I trust I needn't summarize the famous work we are casting. We never speak the name of the play within a theater unless we utter it as it occurs in the text. Today we want three witches. We shall conduct the tryout here on the stage. Come up as I call your name."

So began Fritzi's ordeal of waiting through readings by actresses of every shape and disposition. When her turn came, at ten minutes past five, Manchester said, "This is act four. Begin with the speech at line twenty-two. I shall throw you the cue."

His magnificent voice rolled out. *"Double, double toil and trouble; Fire burn and cauldron bubble."*

"Scale of dragon, tooth of wolf, Witches' mummy, maw and gulf . . ." Fritzi read. *"Add thereto a tiger's chaudron . . ."* She hesitated; the word always threw her.

"Entrails!" Manchester exclaimed. "Guts! Pray continue."

"Thank you, um, *tiger's chaudron, For the ingredients of our cauldron.*"

"Excellent. Please be seated. Who is next?"

They finished at a quarter of six. Manchester studied comments he'd penciled on a separate sheet. "Permit me to thank you all for participating. Will the following four ladies kindly report back to this stage tomorrow morning, ten sharp? The Misses Sally Murphy, Cynthia Vole, Ida Whittemeyer, and Frederica Crown."

Fritzi let out a little squeal, then blushed. Four actresses for three roles. Miss Murphy was a soft-cheeked young woman with startling blue eyes. Miss Whittemeyer was older, with wild, spiky gray hair; she was sure to be cast. The third rival, Miss Vole, appeared the most formidable. She had a dark, almost demonic beauty and a husky voice. With a glacial smile Miss Vole strode up the aisle. She happened to glance over at Fritzi. That glance said she would if necessary kill someone to get a part.

ALL Fritzi had for breakfast the next day was a glass of water and two stale crackers. She donned her best suit, dark red silk. When she walked into the Novelty, Miss Vole was signing in.

"Oh, good morning, dear. That is the loveliest outfit. Let's wish each other well, shall we?" During this gush of goodwill Miss Vole continued to poke the nib of the pen at the open ink bottle. Somehow the nib tipped it. She cried, "Oh, dear," as the bottle rolled over, splashing ink on Fritzi's skirt. "Oh, horrors. I'm so sorry. Whatever can we do?"

Speechless, Fritzi stared at the stain. The doorkeeper said, "Try washing it out before it dries. C'mon, there's a dressing room."

"My dear, I am *so* terribly sorry," Miss Vole said as they left. She had laid out the rules for the contest: There weren't any.

In the dressing room, Fritzi worked valiantly but could wash away only some of the ink. "Sorry about the mishap," Manchester said when she walked onstage. "Don't let it throw you, my girl."

It already had, though Fritzi fought to hide it. Miss Vole hovered. "Whatever will you do if the stain won't come out?"

Fritzi smiled sweetly. "Oh, just put the suit in the ash can. I have many more." She wanted to break something. Like Miss Vole's neck.

Manchester passed out sides to the other three actresses. Fritzi watched while he auditioned them using the third scene of act one—the witches meeting Macbeth on the blasted heath. Manchester read both the title role and Banquo. Composed and confident, Miss Vole nearly matched him with her memorable huskiness.

Manchester gave Fritzi a side next. "Second Witch," he said.

They read the scene, then did it a second time with Fritzi as First Witch. After ten minutes Manchester called a halt and produced new sides. "Now for something completely different. This is act five. I would like each of you to read Lady Macbeth as the Doctor of Physic discovers her madness. Miss Murphy?" He pointed at the orchestra and said, "You ladies may await your turn down there."

Fritzi was all nerves. She'd never played Lady Macbeth. Miss Murphy read competently, Miss Whittemeyer too.

"Miss Crown, please."

She nearly tripped as she started up the steps. Behind her in the auditorium someone laughed.

As the doctor, Manchester read, *"Hark! She speaks. I will set down what comes from her, to satisfy my remembrance the more strongly."*

"Out, damned spot!" Fritzi read. *"Out, I say—"*

"Pardon me. Excuse me." The unmistakable voice came out of the dark. "I'm terribly sorry to interrupt, but I'm seated way back here and I can't hear Miss— What is her name?"

"Thank you, Miss Vole," Manchester said. He then whispered, "A little louder, can you?"

Completely thrown by the interruption, Fritzi struggled to the end. *"What's done cannot be undone. To bed, to bed, to bed."* And to hell with it. Disgusted with herself, she flung the side on the table. Manchester patted her arm and thanked her.

Of course, Miss Vole read magnificently. Manchester then took the stage for a final word.

"As you leave, please write down your correct address. I will send a note to the three chosen in tomorrow afternoon's mail."

BACK in her room, Fritzi shed a few tears. Then she wiped her eyes and worked on the inkstain. The more she thought of Cynthia Vole's sneaky tactics, the angrier she became. "I'm not going to be beaten by that witch." When she realized what she'd said, she laughed. Just like that, a beautiful idea popped into her head.

For a long time she paced the room. One moment she told herself the scheme was too wicked. The next moment she rehearsed aloud, saying the lines to get the huskiness just right.

Downstairs, at the wall telephone, she called the Novelty and asked for Manchester.

"His Lordship's gone. Try the Players Club down in Gramercy Park," the doorkeeper said.

"Thank you, I shall. It's urgent."

"Is that Miss Vole?"

Fritzi clicked the receiver on the hook and sank against the wall, eyes shut, hands trembling. Another tenant came off the street and tipped his derby. As soon as he went upstairs, she telephoned the actors club. She was in luck.

"Manchester here."

"It's Miss Vole, sir." Every syllable of the impersonation was a fight for control. "I regret to tell you I've been offered another role, which I've accepted."

"Oh, I'm so sorry. For the sake of my production, I mean to say. To you I offer congratulations. May I ask the vehicle in which you'll be appearing?"

She hadn't thought of that.

"Sir, I'm sorry. I didn't hear you. It's a bad hookup."

"Who is the producer? What is the play?"

Fritzi covered her mouth and said, "I can't hear you, Mr. Manchester. I'm very sorry. Good-bye." She rang off.

Next afternoon's delivery brought a note from Mr. Hobart Manchester informing Miss Crown that he desired her to play Second Witch in his forthcoming production.

Grosse Pointe Games • The Rapid Interurban carried Carl and a box of chocolates out to Grosse Pointe, a journey of almost ten miles. He got off across from the Country Club of Detroit. Nearly every big, imposing house that he passed was brightly lit in the soft darkness.

As he turned the corner from Grosse Pointe Drive onto Lakeland, a warm wind was blowing off Lake St. Clair. At the end of the street, by the water, the windows of a two-story rustic-shingle house laid yellow rectangles on the manicured lawn. A lacquered sign on the fence said VILLA CLYMER. If a place this fancy served as a summer cottage, what must their home be like? he wondered.

Carl had taken great care to be presentable. He wore a new neck-tie and his coat sweater of black ribbed wool.

A voice from the porch startled him. "Carl? Is that you?"

The sweet sound of it banished his anxiety. He charged up the walk. Tess stepped into the light from the open front door.

"You found us with no trouble?"

"Oh, yes, easy. Here, these are for you."

"Why, thank you. Chocolate creams are my favorite."

They gazed at each other in awkward silence. Tess was wearing a short fitted navy-blue jacket with a matching skirt and a filmy blouse. She'd fixed her hair in a chignon.

"Would you care to look at the lake? Supper won't be served until half past eight."

They strolled down the gently sloping lawn to a concrete seawall. A bright yellow half-moon hung above the lake.

She said, "We could play croquet if you like."

"Croquet? It's getting dark."

"Oh, Father's taken care of that. He installed brand-new lights for the back lawn. Come." She took his hand.

She stepped inside the four-bay garage behind the house. Bright lights on poles suddenly bathed the croquet court.

"I should caution you," Tess said as they walked to the mallet rack. "You mustn't be upset by Father's manner. He's rather blunt with everyone, me especially. He's ruled me with a strict hand ever since my mother died, when I was fifteen. At twenty-one I'm still trying to break him of that. Which color would you like?"

"Do you have a favorite?"

"Green."

He handed her a ball and mallet, took red for himself. They walked to the starting stake. "Is your father in the house?"

"Yes. He's meeting with his advertising agent, Wayne Sykes. Wayne's an old friend of the family. A Detroit boy. He handles the Clymer auto account. You go first."

The mallet felt small as a toothpick in his big hands. His stroke caromed the ball off the first of the two wickets, shooting it to one side. "Hell," he said without thinking. "Oh, sorry. I haven't played for a while."

"Just take your time. We're not competing for a prize," Tess said gently.

Still, she was adept at the game and competitive. She made clean strokes that went where she aimed. Behind from the start, Carl stayed behind, missing wickets and steadily losing ground.

By the time he hit the stake at the far end of the court, Tess was already back in front of the starting wickets. She bent over the ball, studied the path, hit. The ball rolled through the first wicket, struck the second, miraculously slid through.

"Good game. You beat me."

"Unfair advantage. I play golf. There's Father, with Wayne," she said, then turned off the lights. Carl saw two men on the porch, one with a lighted cigar; his voice carried.

"I'm just not sure of the advisability of featuring my portrait as the main illustration."

"Lorenzo, take my word. It's the right approach. Everyone knows you or has heard of you." The speaker had an unctuous voice Carl disliked at once.

"All right, but I definitely don't care for that fancy border on the ad. Show me a few other ideas. Tess, hello. I've asked Wayne to stay for supper. This is your guest? Good evening, young man. I'm Lorenzo Clymer."

Clymer shook Carl's hand with a firm grip. Wayne Sykes merely nodded. They went inside to a huge dining room, where two serving girls were placing platters of veal and side dishes and pouring wine. Clymer's fine white suit and the trim blazer and gray trousers worn by Wayne Sykes made Carl feel shabby. He stepped toward Tess's chair to hold it for her, but Sykes was quicker.

Under the glittering electric chandelier Carl could see the two men clearly. Lorenzo Clymer's features were unremarkable. He was short and slightly built, with small hands and sleek dark hair. Evidently Tess got her height from her mother.

Clymer said, "Tell us, Carl, where do you hail from?"

"Chicago. My father owns the Crown Brewery."

"Crown lager? Never tried it," Sykes said. "I'm a whiskey man. If not Kentucky bourbon, then French Champagne. Eh, Tess?"

He said it as though they shared a secret Carl couldn't possibly appreciate. Sykes—auburn-haired, slender, and tan, with mean black eyes—was a few years older than Carl.

"What college did you attend, old man?" Sykes asked.

"Princeton."

"Graduated when?"

"I didn't."

"Really? I'm Harvard '98 myself."

"And a bit uppity about it," Tess teased. "Like all Harvard men."

"Where do you work, Carl?" Clymer asked.

"I'm a driver for the Ford Motor Company, sir."

"Well." Sykes sat back, folding his arms. The single word conveyed a clear meaning: Carl had done himself in. To judge from the look on Lorenzo Clymer's face, he agreed.

"I don't expect you to condemn an employer, Carl, but neither will I hide my personal feelings about Henry Ford. The man's a bumpkin, with an ego big as a barn."

"A clown," Sykes said.

"Seven years ago, right here in Grosse Pointe, Henry's 999 race-car beat Alex Winton's Bullet," Clymer said. "On the strength of that victory the Henry Ford Company was organized. I put a considerable amount of money into it. In six months Henry damn near wrecked the company with his dilatory tinkering. The board got rid of him and put a good old Detroit name on the door—Cadillac. I made money when I sold out my interest, but I'll tell you, son, Henry's ideas are all wet. This new Model T won't amount to a thing after the first flurry of interest. Henry's a renegade in the auto business. A man of no education or breeding. He'll be gone in five years, if not sooner."

Tess looked uncomfortable. Clymer noticed and tried to lower the temperature of the discussion. "Tess tells me you race."

"I drive for Hoot Edmunds."

"I wouldn't suppose there's a great future in that."

Carl said, "I never worry too much about a future as long as I'm doing something I like."

"I see." Lorenzo Clymer looked at his daughter in what Carl took to be a pointed way.

The supper limped on, and the conversation shifted to the presidential election. Both Clymer and Sykes were Taft stalwarts, predicting a sure defeat for "that liberal radical Bryan," in Clymer's words. He said that the Socialist candidate, Eugene Debs, was an even worse menace and should be brought to heel, "preferably with tar and feathers."

"No, shoot him," Sykes said. Carl said he didn't know much about politics, but his older brother knew Gene Debs and considered him an honorable man devoted to change by nonviolent methods. Sykes looked at Carl as though he came from the moon.

Carl had had enough. He excused himself from coffee in the front parlor and rose to leave. Lorenzo Clymer shook his hand, thanked him for coming, said he'd be happy to see Carl anytime, which was an obvious lie. Carl walked out of the parlor with Tess.

She took his arm, steered him to the door. They hurried down the walk to the gate. "Oh, Carl, I do apologize. Neither of them was at all nice to you. Wayne was awful. I expect he thinks you're competition."

"For what?"

"Me," Tess said, linking her arm with his. They turned right toward the main avenue. "Did Wayne make you angry?"

"I wanted to pick up a chair and knock his brains out."

"Well, you're a true gentleman to hold back."

At the corner of Grosse Pointe Drive, Carl said, "I'll go on from here." He faced her in the leafy shadow of a moonlit tree and felt the warmth of her breath. He wanted to gather her in his arms, kiss her, but he dared not be too forward.

"Look, Tess, your father doesn't think I'm worth a nickel— No, let me finish. I'm just not his kind of person. If I'm going to see you again, we should meet somewhere else. Anywhere but here."

"I think so too. I know a dozen places in Detroit where we can be out in the open but by ourselves."

"Would you like that?"

She lifted her beautiful face in the moonlight. "I would."

"One way or another, I'll be in touch."

"Soon, I hope. Good night, Carl." On tiptoe she brushed her lips against his cheek, then turned and hurried away toward home.

Bad Omens • In a Ninth Avenue saloon Hobart Manchester ate stew and drank pale ale. Every farthing he'd salvaged after a string of West End flops in London was sunk in this New York production of the Scottish play. Expenses were strapping him, particularly the salary demands of his leading lady, Mrs. Van Sant.

He sopped up stew with stale bread and comforted himself with one fact. He had his cast. The last person, Miss Crown, had signed this morning. Charming child, Miss Crown. Not beautiful in the conventional sense, yet there was something attractive about her.

It had taken colossal nerve to mimic Miss Vole on the telephone. The impersonation had actually fooled him for a moment. He only hoped Miss Crown would be competent onstage.

FRITZI arrived at the Novelty at nine a.m. the following Monday, the first day of rehearsal. The doorkeeper looked out of the cubby. Fritzi introduced herself.

"Oh, I remember you, miss. Foy's the name. Most call me Pop. You're a whole hour early."

"I've learned it's a good idea to get the feel of a theater."

"Go on in. You're not the first."

By ten, when the full company had assembled, the stage manager, a string bean named Simkins, called them to order. As if on cue, Manchester bounded onstage.

"Good morning, good morning. All present, are we?"

"All but Mrs. Van Sant," Simkins said.

"We shall begin without her." Manchester strode to the apron. "Members of the ensemble, we are met in a great endeavor, about to labor together on one of the supreme works of stage literature. To ensure an auspicious start, this morning I donned the very tie I wore on the occasion of my professional debut in London." He touched his outdated cravat. A noise at the back of the hall interrupted him. Manchester peered. "Who is there?"

A galleon of a woman sailed down the aisle. Halfway to the stage she stopped and planted a tall ebony walking stick.

"You have two eyes, Hobart. Use 'em."

"Mrs. Van Sant, you are late."

"I was detained," the woman said in a foghorn voice. Eustacia Van Sant was English, about Manchester's age but a head taller. She had an enviable hourglass shape, and a squarish face softened by wide lips and brilliant dark eyes. Vivid hair of the shade Fritzi called Irish red contrasted dramatically with her black velvet cape and dress. Her hat was a large black velvet Gainsborough ornamented with ostrich plumes.

Manchester said, "Permit me to make something clear, madam. We have a mere five weeks until opening night. I expect all players to be present at the hour specified for rehearsal."

"Oh, stuff that, Hobart. I told you, I was detained. Some bookkeeper chap in the front office keeled over on top of his ledgers, dead as Jacob Marley. A copper refused to let me enter the building until the undertaker's men carried out the corpse."

A chill seemed to invade the theater. Manchester gasped, pulled out a big kerchief, and swabbed his cheeks. "Tragic. But it has nothing to do with us."

"It may," Ida Whittemeyer, who was playing one of the witches, whispered. "It's the Scottish play."

Manchester moved the actors to a semicircle of chairs onstage. They read the play from sides.

Fritzi was fascinated by Manchester's leading lady. She had great energy. Coupled with her deep voice, it achieved a powerful effect. During the lunch break she found Mrs. Van Sant in the theater's greenroom examining photographs of scenery.

"Will you look at these?" the older actress exclaimed. "I thought we were to have original designs. No! He's hauling this rubbish out of some warehouse." She thrust a photo at Fritzi. "I ask you, is that a blasted heath? It's a garden drop left over from some silly operetta. I was a fool to agree to this engagement."

Fritzi examined the photo, then another of a unit set that included high rostrums stage right and left and an even higher one center stage. "All those levels and ladders look dangerous."

"Of course it's dangerous. This is the most dangerous play Shakespeare ever wrote. Nearly everything happens at night, so the lighting's always wretched. Actors in armor rush about with swords. How could there not be accidents?" From her silver handbag she took a cheroot and a matchbox. "Care for a smoke?"

"No, thank you."

Mrs. Van Sant lit up. "What's your name again, dear?"

"Frederica Crown, but I'm called Fritzi."

"Frankly, Fritzi, I don't believe a lot of the superstition attached to *Mac*—our play. But I observe the rules as a courtesy. One never knows."

Reunions • Cunard's *Lusitania,* the world's largest ship, brought Paul into New York harbor. He thrilled again to the statue he'd seen for the first time in 1892. At the Hudson pier he supervised the unloading of trunks holding camera equipment, raw stock, and a dozen copies of the British edition of *I Witness History.* Cleared through customs, he telephoned Fritzi at the theater. She came on the line.

"Is that really you, Pauli? You're here?"

"Yes, but I have to catch a train tonight. Could we have a quick supper beforehand?"

They met in a restaurant at Times Square, hugging joyously before they settled down at the table. Paul apologized for leaving so quickly; he would be traveling when *Macbeth* opened. "I'll be sure to see it when I come back to New York to sail home."

A chunky man about Paul's age hailed him and approached the table. Paul stood. "Fritzi, let me present an old friend of mine, Billy Bitzer. We met in Cuba. Billy's a cameraman too."

"The Biograph studio," Bitzer said, shaking Fritzi's hand.

"Fritzi's in a play at the moment," Paul said.

"Shakespeare," she pointed out.

"That's swell," Bitzer said. "If you ever need some extra work, drop down to Fourteenth Street. I'll introduce you. It's great pay. Five dollars for a day's work."

"Thank you, Mr. Bitzer, but I'm afraid stage actors don't have time for the moving pictures."

Amiably he said, "Oh, we know all about that. The flickers are beneath you Broadway folks. You'll get over it as soon as we turn a few actors into stars. Offer's open anytime."

After Bitzer walked away, Paul said, "You were pretty hard on him."

Fritzi looked rueful. "I suppose I was. I'm sorry. It's the way I feel. I should have kept it to myself."

AFTER a day spent filming Niagara Falls, Paul delivered his first lecture in Buffalo—nervously, but with good response from the audience. Paul had only two more speaking engagements, Detroit and Louisville, but his lecture agent told Paul he was a "natural" and said he could book him for an extended tour whenever he returned. By the time Paul left Louisville to photograph the splendid horse farms near Lexington, he felt like a seasoned trouper.

A few days later Paul climbed aboard a train for Detroit, the new auto capital. The train arrived at the Michigan Central Depot on the shore of the Detroit River. Paul claimed his lacquered case from the baggage car, checked to be sure his camera had arrived unbroken, and hailed a hissing steam taxi. "Hotel Ponchartrain."

He had telegraphed asking Carl to meet him in the Ponchartrain bar when he got off work. Paul unpacked, then strolled around Cadillac Square for a half hour. At six thirty he put his foot on the brass bar rail and ordered a Crown lager.

"Paul!" Carl waved a cloth cap as he charged across the barroom. The cousins hugged each other.

Carl ordered a schooner of beer, then asked questions about Julie and the children. After Paul answered them, he said, "What about you? How are you doing at Ford's?"

"I love it. It's an exciting place." Carl planted his elbows on the bar. "Oh, I don't love everything about it. I hate the time clock. Job's taught me plenty about automobiles, though, and gotten me in with the racing crowd."

"What do you do exactly?"

"I'm a lowly utility driver. I drive Model T's down to the freight yards for shipment. Occasionally I take a car on a test run."

They proceeded to the Ponchartrain dining room, where they ate a huge meal of pot roast, potatoes, and corn on the cob. Paul asked how it happened that Detroit was becoming the auto center.

"They say it's because a lot of local people had experience building engines for the lake boats. Nobody had to start machine shops or foundries, because they were already here. And there's money all over the place. Millionaires whose fathers got rich building carriages or railroad cars are looking for another plunge."

"And you got on with Henry Ford with no trouble?"

"I wouldn't say that. I sure was nervous when he interviewed me."

"The head of the company talked to you personally?"

"Well, it doesn't usually work that way, but I wrote a letter to Mr. Ford. I couldn't believe it when he wrote back. He invited me to his house. Said there was something in my letter that he liked."

"What was it?"

With a smile Carl said, "I was kicked out of Princeton." Then he described his memorable first meeting with his employer.

ON THE night of the interview Carl had anxiously stood before a large but plain frame house, not at all what you'd expect of a man supposedly on his way to riches. Henry Ford had grown up poor in the country out by Dearborn—that much Carl knew.

A plain-faced woman answered his knock. "You must be the young man Henry's expecting. I'm Mrs. Ford. Won't you come in?"

The principal shareholder of the Ford Motor Company bounded into the hall to greet him. Ford's celluloid collar hung by one button; he'd discarded his tie. He was a tall, skinny man with big ears, piercing eyes, and a craggy face. Mid-forties, Carl judged.

"Come in, Carl. Have a seat. Care for a cup of coffee or a Malto Grape? That's a fruit drink. We serve nothing stronger."

The front parlor was furnished with a lot of old, dark, unpretentious furniture. As Carl sat down, Ford regarded him soberly. "So you want a job at our factory. Tell me why."

Carl drew a breath and delivered a halting but fervent statement about his fascination with machinery, autos in particular.

Ford asked whether he was a native Detroiter. No, Chicago. What was his father's trade? *Oh-oh.*

"He's a brewer, sir. Crown's beer."

Ford gave him another long, searching stare. "Heard of it. I won't hold it against you."

Mrs. Ford brought a tray with glasses of Malto Grape. Ford settled back and cracked a couple of jokes, complimenting Carl on being dismissed from Princeton. "I left school at fifteen, and I've done all right. Far as I'm concerned, college is mostly bunk. Emerson said, 'A man contains all that is needful to his government within himself.' Have you ever read Emerson?"

"No, sir, I'm afraid not."

"You should." Ford sprang out of his chair. "Let's sit on the porch while it's still light. I like to watch the birds." He led Carl out a side door. The wide porch bent around the corner of the house. Ford took the swing, Carl one of the white wicker chairs.

"You have any questions, Carl?"

"Well, could you tell me what kind of work I might do if—"

"We'll try to find you a driving job. I must warn you of one thing. I insist that men who work for me conduct themselves in a moral way at all times. No cursing, no carousing, nothing to bring shame on the organization or themselves. Clear about that?"

Carl said he was.

"Good." Ford launched into a monologue to which he clearly expected his visitor to pay heed. "There's a future at Ford. We're a dynamic company in a dynamic industry. Of course, my ideas are different from most of the other fellows turning out cars. They all want to cater to the well-to-do. I want to deliver a simple car, soundly made, speedy, dependable, but priced low enough for millions to afford it." He smiled. "They think I'm crazy, the rich boys from Grosse Pointe. We'll see. 'To be great is to be misunderstood'— that's what Emerson said. I was put into this life for a purpose. I've lived before, you know. We've all lived before, many times." Carl's hair almost stood up. Ford was saying mad things in a perfectly sane voice. "I believe in my last life I was a soldier, killed at Gettysburg the first or second of July, 1863. I was born into this present life at the end of that very same month, July 30. One life slipping into another, easy as the seasons changing." Carl sat in stupefied silence, having no idea how to reply.

He was reprieved when Ford shook his hand. "Report to the personnel department on Monday, seven a.m."

"Mr. Ford, thank you. Thanks very much."

"Don't be late. Just remember what I said about the behavior we expect. There are no exceptions. Oh, and don't forget. Go to the public library. Read some Emerson. Good night."

IN THE lobby of the Ponchartrain, Carl said good night to his cousin.

"I'll walk you home if it isn't in the next county," Paul said.

"Only about a mile. North of Gratiot. It's nothing to see. A lodging house for single men. The neighborhood's run-down."

"I was raised in a run-down neighborhood. Lead on."

They strolled past dark office blocks and lighted saloons. Carl said, "When will your book be published here?"

"You know about that?"

"Mama wrote me."

"It'll be next winter."

"That's wonderful. I can't wait to read it. I'm proud of you. The whole family's proud."

After reaching Carl's boardinghouse, Paul walked back to the Ponchartrain in the stillness of the night.

Tess • The weekend forecast promised unusually fine weather. During his Saturday lunch period Carl telephoned the Clymer residence and waited nervously while a servant summoned Tess to the phone.

"I thought you'd gone to China or forgotten me."

Carl laughed. "I'm a workingman. Last Sunday I had a race down in Monroe, which I lost. It'll be a fine day tomorrow. Would you like to go out to Belle Isle?"

"Yes."

She met him at the Third Street docks. He bought two round-trips, a total of twenty cents. It was a spectacular late summer afternoon, windless and fair. The one-fifteen ferry was packed with families carrying picnic hampers to the city's favorite playground.

Though it was Sunday, traffic on the Detroit River was heavy. Paddle-wheel ferries plowed back and forth between Windsor and Detroit. Carl and Tess leaned on the railing, Tess clutching her flat-crowned straw hat.

When the boat reached Belle Isle, the family groups dispersed to picnic tables. Carl and Tess followed the path to the canoe concession. He rented a canoe and handed her into it, grinning like a fool when she squeezed his hand and gave him a deep look with her beautiful blue eyes.

Carl paddled from one lagoon into another. "Seen anything of Wayne lately?" he asked.

"No. Why should you care about him?"

"You said he's keen on you."

"Oh, well, yes, but it's hopeless."

"What's hopeless?"

"The prospect of my marrying Wayne. Father brings it up often. Wayne proposed last year. He nearly burst a blood vessel when I turned him down. I wouldn't marry him if we were the only two people on earth."

"You're an independent sort. Where did that come from?"

"Not Grosse Pointe, I assure you." She unpinned her hat, laid it in her lap, and shook her golden hair free in the sunshine. "It was my mother. She taught fourth grade in the public schools. When Father began to make money and climb up the social ladder, he asked her to stop teaching. She wouldn't. Mama believed that whoever you were, you couldn't survive in this world if you were stupid. She said it took brains to defy conformity and find your own path. I took it to heart long before she died."

Carl beached the canoe. They strolled along a secluded path, isolated from the picnic crowds. In a patch of shade Carl took her hands in his. "I've got to tell you something. I'm keen for you."

She looked at him. "I like you too. A lot. But you don't strike me as a man who'd want a permanent attachment with a girl."

"I would—" Carl swallowed to clear a great lump in his windpipe. "I would if I fell in love with her."

A sudden joy sprang into her eyes. She gripped his hand fiercely, then kissed him—a long, ardent kiss.

He threw his arm around her, plunged his face into her sunwarmed hair. He felt her billowy breasts, her hips and legs, tight against him. "Oh, Lord," he whispered. "I'm shaky."

"Me too."

"How did this happen?"

"I don't know—it just did."

He held her tightly, bringing his right hand up to caress her hair. They heard voices coming near—broke apart, saw two youngsters, a boy and a girl, playing tag. They stepped away from each other. Both were red-faced.

For the rest of the afternoon they avoided the subject of their newly confessed feelings. Each seemed to understand that there was a degree of impossibility, impracticality, in a permanent relationship. Yet Carl had a strange conviction that he was already in the middle of one, excitingly but perhaps dangerously entrapped.

Jesse and Carl • Jesse Shiner worked at Clymer Foundry Number One on Detroit's east side. The foundry cast engine blocks for local car manufacturers. It was nasty, dangerous work. Clouds of soot filled the air. The melting furnaces were so hot, five minutes into his shift Jesse's clothes were glued to him and stayed that way all day. If a ladle tipped at the wrong moment, he could be roasted alive. Jesse endured the heat and grime because his weekly pay envelope let him live his life outside the foundry with some regularity and order.

When he was thirty, he had bought a frame cottage two blocks below the lodging house where Carl lived. He joined Ebenezer A.M.E. Church on Calhoun Street, where he met a handsome young black woman named Grace. They courted for a while, but she saw a better future with a young black dentist. She left Detroit as the dentist's bride and broke Jesse's heart.

Jesse stood foursquare for the rights of laboring men of whatever color. In a wave of strikes that swept the Detroit metal industry in 1907, mostly to promote closed union shops, Jesse picketed with his mates outside Clymer Number One. In return for that show of courage he got his head beaten by the clubs of strikebreakers.

The strike fizzled out; there would be no union shop at Clymer Number One. The irony was, the bosses had to rehire many of the strikers, including Jesse, because the inexperienced scabs quit after a few days in the hellish heat.

Jesse was self-educated and never stopped learning. He'd taught himself about gasoline engines by hanging around auto races on Sunday. He met Carl Crown that way.

In a small shed he built on the alley behind his house he installed an elaborate arrangement of drawers and bins for storing miscellaneous auto parts. To make extra money, working by the light of several coal oil lanterns, Jesse did repairs for local garages facing an overload. Of an evening Carl helped out.

One cool Monday night when Carl came over, Jesse noticed a change in his friend. Carl had a distracted, dreamy air. Jesse knew it was the girl, Clymer's daughter.

Carl and Jesse sat in the shed with a single large growler of beer between them and a fire burning in the small woodstove in the corner. Carl was patching a balloon tire inner tube.

"See Miss Tess again yesterday, did you?" Jesse asked.

Carl nodded as he roughed the tube surface with a little tin gadget in preparation for applying the cement.

"Pretty serious about her, are you?"

"I guess I am, yes."

"Speak out plain. You in love with her?"

Carl looked up. "Since you ask, yes."

"She feel the same way?"

"I think so."

"She want to marry up with you?"

"What is this, a police investigation?"

"Just having a friendly talk. You listen to me a minute."

Carl's eyes narrowed. He drank some warm beer.

"You marry that girl, for the rest of your natural life you'll be marrying one of those time clocks you hate so much. That is, if you want to do right by her. I just want to know, Carl. You got it in you to be a steady husband with a steady job? I'm not against folks marrying, but I'm against them marrying and then making each other miserable. Life's mean enough the way it is. You're my friend. Maybe the best friend I ever had. So be careful. Don't leap too quick. There's lots of other girls who—"

Carl's brown eyes flashed. "Shut up. There aren't any like Tess."

Jesse sighed. "Figured you might say something like that. Wasted my breath, did I?"

"Yes."

But he'd planted a seed.

Tragedy • On Monday in the third week of rehearsal Hobart Manchester stopped the seventh scene of act one to speak to Eustacia Van Sant. "Madam, your delivery is too slow. The wife of the Thane of Cawdor is the driving engine of this act. She pushes her husband forward relentlessly. He is the one who hesitates."

Eustacia was in no mood for a reprimand in front of the company. "I have my interpretation of the role."

"That may be, madam. But I remind you that I have the pen which signs the salary vouchers."

"See if I care, you dictatorial little s.o.b." She stormed off.

Fritzi hurried to Eustacia's dressing room and talked to her for ten minutes. "He's excitable," she said. "The whole weight of this production's on his shoulders, not just the leading role."

Eustacia returned to the stage in a half hour. Manchester shot an appreciative look at Fritzi, and the rehearsal went forward under a fragile truce. Fritzi wasn't comforted. Nerves were raw, tempers shorter and shorter as they careened toward opening night.

On the Monday they were to begin performances, Fritzi arrived at the Novelty Theater a whole hour before curtain. A drizzly September rain dampened the streets. She felt wretched.

Eustacia whispered that she'd seen Hobart. "His eyes are standing out of his head big as eggs. He encountered a funeral procession on his way here. Should have kept to the alleys, the fool. I'm beginning to have this dreadful feeling we're jinxed."

Putting on her makeup, Fritzi couldn't remember her first line. This had never happened before. She searched among the pots and tubes and sticks of makeup until she found her crumpled side for scene one. She folded it and tucked it under the frayed rope that belted her ugly dirt-colored smock.

Pop Foy mournfully told the actors the rain showers had become a downpour. The audience arrived sodden. People sneezed and complained. At twenty past seven Manchester called the company together. He did indeed look queasy and shaken. "I am delighted to report that the house is more than three-quarters subscribed. But I regret to announce that earlier today Mr. Entwistle sprained his back. The prompt table will be empty this evening. I am sure all of you will surmount this small problem with no difficulty."

Fritzi felt dizzy. Her teeth chattered. She'd experienced symptoms of stage fright many times before, but never so severely.

Simkins called places. Fritzi touched the curtain for luck. Ida Whittemeyer hugged each of her weird sisters. The other witch, Sally Murphy, squeezed their hands and said, "Break a leg."

The curtain rose. The tragedy began.

IN THE FIRST SCENE THE CHEAP electric fan in the trap shorted. With a squeal the blades stopped revolving. Smoke immediately thickened behind the cauldron. Ida Whittemeyer was convulsed by coughing for nearly half a minute.

Making his first entrance on the blasted heath, Hobart ripped his cloak on a nail. The sound, unfortunately loud, resembled a bodily function. It caused titters throughout the audience.

In Hobart's dagger speech the follow spot sputtered, sizzled, and expired.

One of the murderers fell off a ramp. It wasn't a graceful tumble but a pratfall. In the wings, Fritzi cringed at the laughter.

By the time the curtain rose on act three, everyone's timing was off. Lines were delivered at locomotive speed or dragged out unendurably. In the climactic duel Macduff's tinplate sword nicked the edge of a rostrum and bent like taffy. Completely thrown, the actor dropped the sword twice as he attempted to straighten it. Hobart tried to cover by staggering about, indicating pain from a wound. Since Macduff hadn't touched him yet, it looked more like an attack of indigestion. The audience hooted and whistled.

Hobart's prop claymore was made of stouter stuff: wood. When he finally struck a defensive blow, it snapped in half at the hilt. In the stunned silence Hobart could be heard to say, *"Oh, my Gawd."*

Hilarity reigned everywhere but onstage.

The audience fled the theater after one curtain call, which included a good many boos and catcalls. Fritzi wanted to weep. Their Scottish play was not a tragedy but a farce.

The New York *Rocket* was the first paper on the street. Mrs. Van Sant rose and read the notice aloud in a private room on the upstairs level of Charles Rector's swank Broadway restaurant. The cast had gathered for a party that had the atmosphere of a wake.

" 'Mr. Hobart Manchester's production at the Novelty suits the venue, as it is so novel, so unique in its particular badness, as to numb even the most insensitive devotee of the Bard. Miserably acted, it quickly descends into unintentional comedy. Evidence of penny-pinching is everywhere. Costumes appear to come from a ragbag, except for those worn by the English actress Mrs. Van Sant, which are more appropriate to the runway of a vaudeville house.' Bastard!" She threw the paper onto the floor.

Closed • Simkins posted the closing notice before Thursday night's performance. Late Friday afternoon Fritzi went uptown to the Novelty. The rain had let up only sporadically since Monday.

The theater had a sad, empty feeling. Backstage she met Sally Murphy and Ida Whittemeyer, both as dispirited as she was. They embraced and exchanged addresses. Mrs. Van Sant had already booked a cabin on the first available transatlantic ship, a Greek vessel sailing Monday for Cherbourg and Piraeus.

Simkins said pay vouchers would be ready at noon Saturday. Fritzi asked, "Is Mr. Manchester in the theater?"

"Yes, but he's incommunicado."

Outside, she stood under the marquee, pelted by blowing rain. She stared at the paper strip pasted diagonally on the poster: CLOSED. Her cheeks were wet but not from rain.

She'd looked on the *Macbeth* engagement as a benchmark, a full and final test of her ability to succeed in New York. She knew she wasn't personally responsible for the fiasco, but the result was the same. "What now?" she said to herself.

A lobby door swung open, and Hobart emerged. "Fritzi! What have you found? Any suitable auditions on the horizon?"

"Not immediately."

"Too bad. How are you fixed?"

"I won't starve for another two or three weeks."

"Ah, the cruelty of the profession. I am only slightly more solvent. I just settled with the scenery and costume houses. I didn't do it until I determined that we had enough to pay everyone full wages."

"I want to tell you how sorry I am."

"No sorrier than I, dear girl."

"Tuesday and Wednesday's performances were very good. Last night's was thrilling."

"Nevertheless, the curse on the play overtook us. I should have produced *A Midsummer Night's Dream.* Fairies are harmless. But we needn't say good-bye just yet. I have enough in my pocket for supper at Rector's—if you don't order too much." He opened his cape, pulled out his pocket watch. "We can't dine respectably for at least an hour. Let's go see some galloping tintypes."

"You mean pictures at a nickelodeon?"

"Yes. I enjoy them. Come." She didn't have the heart to tell him how much she disliked the cheap entertainment.

As they walked along, Fritzi said, "I understand the picture companies hire legitimate actors. Would you act in one?"

"I? Certainly not."

"I feel the same way."

Hobart paid for tickets to the 5¢ Variety. They found seats on a hard bench near the back. Soon the nickelodeon was full. The projector clattered, and a light beam pierced the dark.

In a one-reel melodrama lasting about fifteen minutes, a young society girl was abducted by kidnappers and rescued by the family chauffeur, with whom she finally eloped. Fritzi was a bit embarrassed to find herself caught up in the story. A sequence of actualities, the kind Paul photographed, came next. The program concluded with another reel, split between a pair of short comedies. Characters stepped into buckets and fell off ladders. All this the audience, Fritzi excepted, found hilarious.

Later, seated on the upstairs level of the restaurant, they ordered platters of fried oysters, a house specialty. Fritzi said, "What will you do? Try the West End again?"

Hobart fixed a melancholy eye on the ceiling. "No, I think not. I admire this country of yours. I'd like to stay here, mount another production in a year or two. Then I'll be right back on top."

She recognized the unreality of his optimism. Actors were universally guilty of deluding themselves. She was no exception.

"I've made a few inquiries already," he said. "William Gillette's taking his *Sherlock Holmes* on another extended tour, a year or more. I might do Moriarty. It's either that or an outing with James O'Neill's chestnut, *The Count of Monte Cristo.*"

Paul and Harry • In the last bright days of autumn Paul returned to New York. He checked into the small but smart Hotel Algonquin on Forty-fourth Street and telephoned Fritzi.

"Aunt Ilsa told me about the play," he said when she came on the line. "I'm really sorry. Are you in anything now?"

"My waitress oxfords," Fritzi replied with a laugh. "I'm back in another hash house. When can I see you? Tomorrow?"

"Sunday's grand."

He suggested a picnic in Central Park at twelve thirty. "With your permission I'll invite an old friend. I met him on *Rheinland* when I came over in '92. Herschel Wolinski was his name then. Now he's Harry Poland. He writes music."

"Oh, yes. I know his songs. I'd love to meet him." .

The next day Paul waited for his cousin by the great equestrian statue of General Sherman on Fifth Avenue. A big wicker hamper packed by the hotel kitchen rested on the pavement beside the lacquered case holding his stereoscopic camera. He checked his pocket watch. Twelve fifteen. Just then he heard, "Pauli! Here I am!"

Waving, Fritzi bounced on her toes on the opposite side of Fifty-ninth Street, then darted in front of a steamcar and threw herself into his arms. She wore a dark blue gored skirt and a long-sleeved shirtwaist, blue-and-white check with white piping. A navy-blue admiral's cap perched on her blond hair.

She kissed his cheek. "Don't you look wonderful."

"You too." Actually, he thought she looked pale and starved.

"Where's your friend?"

"He'll be here presently. He knows where to meet us."

"Tell me about him. How old is he?"

"Younger than I am. Twenty-seven, twenty-eight."

"Married?"

"I'm afraid so."

"Oh, too bad. Lives in Manhattan, I suppose?"

"He has an office in the Tin Pan Alley district on Twenty-ninth Street, but he lives in Port Chester. He's taking a noon train."

"Is he bringing his wife?"

"No. She's in a wheelchair." They entered the park and walked along a winding footpath. It had turned into a glorious day, clear and bracing. The trees showed vivid fall color.

"Harry's wife suffered a stroke some years ago," Paul continued. "She was a very successful singer, Flavia Farrel, twenty years older than Harry. He was her accompanist. Flavia helped Harry get his first musical job. When the stroke ended her career, he married her. He's cared for her ever since." Paul stopped, studying a rise to their left. "There's the place Harry described. Come on."

They climbed to the sunlit summit of the knoll. The next half hour passed in a rush of questions about his trip, his lectures, Julie, Shad, and Betsy. Paul took off his cap and coat. Fritzi laid her hat aside. He handed her something wrapped in brown paper, which she undid.

"Oh, Paul." She held up the book. "I'm dying to read it."

"It's the London edition— Oh, there's Harry."

On the footpath a tall, slender man with broad shoulders waved to them as he ran uphill with a canvas satchel. He wore a fine black suit with a faint gray check. His shoes had fancy kidskin tops and patent leather toes shiny as black mirrors.

Fritzi stood smiling while the two men hugged.

"So this is Fritzi the actress. Charmed." Harry swept off his derby, kissed her hand. Curly black hair gleamed in the sunshine. His blue eyes were merry. "I've heard so much about you."

"I can say the same, Mr. Poland."

"Please, it's Harry."

"You write very catchy songs."

"And his own words," Paul said. "Good ones too. Pretty remarkable for someone who spoke only Polish ten years ago."

"That's very kind of both of you. I love American music."

"How's Flavia?" Paul asked.

"Alas, no change." He explained to Fritzi. "My wife is paralyzed below the waist. For a year she couldn't speak."

"I'm sorry. That's sad."

"We're doing fine now. We have an excellent nurse-housekeeper, who lives in, and I look after Flavia when I'm home."

Paul opened the picnic hamper, spread a white cloth. "Started your own publishing company yet?"

Harry was busy with the clasps of his satchel. "I'm still working for other firms. Thinking a lot about it, though."

"Your automobile song's all over England."

Harry smiled. "Seven hundred and forty thousand copies world-wide—so far. I'm happy for the income, but I don't want to write topical novelties forever." He turned to Fritzi. "My dream is to write for the stage."

"I'm sure you will."

Harry's eyes sparkled. "As a matter of fact, so am I. There are no limits in this country." He pulled gaudy sheet music from the satchel. "Let me present you with two of my latest." Paul read the titles. "Statue of Liberty Rag." "Sadie Loves to Fox Trot."

Harry brought out a worn concertina. "I thought we should have music while we dine."

The hotel had packed cold chicken, liver pâté, crackers and cru-dités, potato salad, rye bread, and a bottle of claret.

Harry began to play "On a Sunday Afternoon." He followed it with "Take Me Out to the Ballgame." He's giving a concert for her, Paul thought with amazement. Fritzi was enchanted.

Harry played the first notes of "Meet Me in St. Louis" before he said, "I wish I'd written this. It's truly American."

Fritzi clasped her hands, swaying. Harry laughed and bobbed his head. "Yes. It fairly begs you to dance, doesn't it? Do so!"

Fritzi jumped up, lifted her skirts to show the ankles of her long legs. She began to turn, surrendering to the music. Nimbly she danced in the grass and sang while Harry played. When the song ended, she sprawled out and leaned on her elbows, laughing and breathing hard.

Soon it was four o'clock, and Harry announced that he had to catch a train. He took Fritzi's hand in a courtly way. "It's been a wonderful afternoon. What a pleasure to meet you." He bent slowly and kissed her hand once more, then picked up his satchel and quickly disappeared.

"I think he's keen for you, Fritz," Paul joked.

"He's charming, but he's married. I don't expect I'll see him again. Too bad. I liked him."

Boom Times • For Christmas, Carl spent much more than he could afford—nine dollars—for Tess's present. He couldn't resist the gold bracelet at Hudson's. It was a twist design, one of the golden strands smooth, the other embossed with tiny flowers.

Tess said she loved the bracelet. In return she gave him a wide leather belt and a fine steel razor with an onyx handle.

The gloomy Michigan winter dragged on. Carl was desperate for the March thaw, the chance to climb into the new Edmunds Special. Only Tess kept him sane, kept him trudging to the trolley stop through snow, fog, or rain to punch in at the Ford factory.

Through the winter their romance ripened, but Tess said the secrecy of their relationship was wearing her down. It went against her nature. She finally told her father she was seeing Carl. She didn't inform Carl until afterward.

Carl hid his annoyance. "Does he know we meet once or twice a week?"

"I didn't say so. I'm sure he can guess from all my absences. He hasn't spoken to me for two days. He'll get over it."

"I'm sorry I caused you trouble."

"Never say that." She laid her fingers on his lips. "Never. I'd walk through fire for you, Carl."

On their Sunday outings he and Tess sometimes took trolleys, but if the streets were clear of snow, she drove her red Clymer runabout. When they could find no other place for intimacy, they hid behind the isinglass side curtains. They kissed passionately in the front seat. Carl loved her and said so. She said she loved him. Each said it often. But Tess never mentioned the future, nor did he.

ONE night in April, Carl went to the repair shed to help Jesse but didn't find him. He sat down to wait, puzzling about an auto he'd noticed when he left his lodging house. It was a black two-passenger

Clymer, parked the wrong way on the other side of the street, the top closed, the motor running. As Carl walked to the front gate, the driver suddenly shot away. A corner streetlamp shone briefly on his face. Carl was almost sure it was Wayne Sykes.

After forty minutes Jesse walked in. A large gauze patch was taped below his left eye; a wound had bled through the bandage.

"Where the devil did you get that?"

"Foundry," Jesse said. "They had some boys waiting for a few of us when the whistle blew. Boys had brass knuckles."

"Are you stirring up the shop issue again?"

"Not *stirring up* anything," Jesse said with a flash of temper. "Just asking politely for what's fair. We got up a petition for a vote on a union shop. I signed. No demand like last time, no strike, just a democratic vote. You see anything wrong with that?"

"No, but obviously Clymer does. Tear up the petition."

"Hell we will."

"Guess you don't plan to live to a ripe old age." Carl reached for pliers. "You be careful. I don't want to scramble around for a new riding mechanic."

Speed King of the World • Berna Eli "Barney" Oldfield claimed to be the world's fastest driver. He held all kinds of speed records, had in fact broken many that he himself set. If someone thirty-one years old could be a legend, Barney Oldfield was legendary.

Automakers offered him fast cars and fat contracts if he'd drive for them. Wherever he appeared, he drew crowds. People loved him because he was fearless and colorful. He wore gaudy vests and striped shirts, a thousand-dollar ankle-length sealskin coat, a knockout of a diamond ring. He traveled in a private railway car with his wife, Bess, and his pet Irish terrier. When he raced, he chewed on a cigar. He had a reputation as a boozer, a woman chaser, a confirmed gambler with bad luck. He made three thousand dollars for an afternoon's exhibition—not bad for an unlettered kid born in a cabin in the woods of northwest Ohio.

On a Friday in May 1909 Barney and his entourage rolled into

Detroit in a private railcar for an exhibition that weekend. The mayor and several hundred citizens welcomed the Speed King. The papers printed photos and lengthy copy about the famous driver. Carl thought him a pretty ordinary-looking fellow, round-faced and dark-haired, though his smile had a certain pixie charm.

Carl invited Tess to the fairgrounds, but she declined, saying she didn't want to hold him back when he tried to meet Oldfield, as he said he wanted. Carl knew Tess well enough to suspect that she looked on the reckless world of auto racing as competition. She wasn't overt about it or bitter. But she was firm. It made him uneasy. He didn't want to face a choice between two loves.

Sunday turned out bright and beautiful, with the fairground's grandstand packed to capacity. Carl had a cheap seat, high up in the shade under the roof.

Trotting races took up the first hour, building the crowd's anticipation. After the last sulky left the track, Barney's advance man, Will Pickens, stepped in front of the grandstand with a megaphone.

"Ladies and gentlemen, here's the man you came to see. The Speed King of the World: *Barney Oldfield.*"

From behind the grandstand, pit mechanics pushed Barney's National racecar, painted with red and white stripes and white stars on a blue field. At the wheel of "Old Glory," Barney Oldfield waved to the crowd, a familiar figure from scores of news pictures: white coveralls, goggles, half-smoked cigar between his teeth.

"We are now ready for Barney's attempt on his one-mile speed record. Barney, are you all set?"

"All set, Mr. Pickens."

"Start your engine."

The crowd roared. The advance man lifted his starting pistol. Barney chomped his cigar. The pistol fired. The crowd screamed.

Barney sped away, spewing dust behind. The National circled the track and blazed past the grandstand, this time taking the green flag to signal the start of the test lap. Carl was on his feet, yelling. He tried to time Barney by taking his pulse but soon lost the count.

Barney took the checkered flag and slowed down. Just as he

chugged to a stop in front of the center stand, the advance man shouted through his megaphone, "Ladies and gentlemen, we have the official results. The Speed King of the World has just set a new record for the measured mile—forty-three and two-tenths seconds!"

Pandemonium. People tossed programs, threw confetti; Carl's head was draped with crepe paper streamers. In his excitement Tess was completely forgotten.

Barney and his team followed the speed run with three five-mile heat races. The competing cars were a Peerless and a Stearns. Barney took the first heat by two car lengths. In the second heat the driver of the Peerless, Red Fletcher, passed him going into the final lap, and the Peerless won by a length.

At the start of the final heat Barney looked grim. The race was a heart-stopping duel between the Peerless and "Old Glory," one nosing ahead, then the other, as they ran wheel to wheel, dangerously close. Going into the last lap, Barney drove relentlessly. He roared over the finish line half a length ahead of his rival.

Carl had a brief suspicion about the outcome. Was it rigged? Didn't matter—the spectacle was thrilling. Carl limped down the grandstand stairs exhausted. He now knew what he wanted to do with the rest of his life.

After the crowds dispersed, Carl loitered near the livestock barn being used as a garage. Eventually Barney emerged from the barn with his teammates, his pit mechanics, and his wife, a brunette with a lush figure and smoky good looks. Laughing and chattering, they all climbed into two Chalmers touring cars. Carl heard someone say there was a good roadhouse a half mile up the pike. The open autos drove away. Carl followed on foot.

At the roadhouse, Carl squeezed into a spot at the bar. Barney bought drinks for his crowd. The advance man started a stud poker game, and Barney's wife drew up a chair to watch. Carl saw his opportunity, walked up to Barney, and offered his hand.

"Can I talk to you a second? My name's Carl Crown."

"Hey there, Carl Crown. You know me—Barney Oldfield." Up close Barney's eyes had a filmy, not quite focused look.

"That was a great performance this afternoon," Carl said.

"Why, thanks. Enjoyed it myself."

"I've driven some races around here," Carl said. "Is there a chance I could get on your team?"

Barney eyed him up and down. "Tell you a little secret. Fellas who drive for me don't win unless I order it."

That answered Carl's earlier question. "Well, it would be okay with me. I just want to get out of Detroit and drive full-time."

"Sure you know what you're doing? I can't count the times I've crashed."

"I understand the risks."

"Then if you're not scared out of your drawers, you must be born to do it. Tell you what. In August, I'll be in Indianapolis to open the new motor speedway. I think my second driver, Red, may leave me in July. If he does and I haven't filled the opening, I'll try you out."

"I'll find you. Thanks."

"Good. What's your name again?"

"Crown. Carl Crown."

"Carl. Got it." Barney leaned back against the bar. "Step up and have a drink on Barney Oldfield."

A Desperate Call • Carl leaned in the doorway in his nightshirt, wakened by loud knocking. Mrs. Gibbs, his landlady, stood there with a candle set in a dish.

Carl knuckled his eyes. "What time is it?"

"Half past four." Tuesday, two days after he'd met Oldfield. "Not a decent hour for anyone to be calling."

"Calling?" His voice was fogged with sleep.

"Some female on the line says it's an emergency."

"Good Lord," Carl said, alert suddenly. "I'll be right there."

Mrs. Gibbs led him downstairs to the telephone. Carl took the earpiece, wondering, Had his mother or the General died suddenly?

"Carl, it's me. I can't talk long."

"Tess! What is it?" He heard a tremor in her voice.

"I wanted to wait until tomorrow, but I couldn't sleep."

"Tell me what's wrong."

"I can't go into it now. I'll tell you in the morning. I'll pick you up at half past eight."

"Tess, it's a workday."

"Call in sick. Half past eight." With a click the connection broke.

TESS arrived in her runabout fifteen minutes early. By the time Carl ran out the gate, she'd moved to the passenger side. He opened the door, stepped on the running board, and was horrified by the sight of her—cheeks raw from weeping. She wore a tan driving duster and a broad-brimmed hat tied under her chin with a red silk scarf.

"Where do you want to go?"

"Out in the country. Anywhere."

Ducking his head so as not to bang it on the top, he shut the door, grasped the wheel. "Did someone hurt you?"

"Not physically." She closed her eyes; tears squeezed onto her cheeks. "Just drive." He had never seen her this way.

He negotiated the busy morning traffic, heading west. Two miles past the city limits the brick pavement ended. The Clymer lurched along a road with deep ruts. Carl saw a track leading off through the tall grass of a fallow field and wheeled the Clymer into it. He braked and shut off the engine.

"I can't wait any longer, Tess. What's happened?"

"Let's walk." She left the car, blinked in the sunshine. He felt the warmth of the earth around them. She took her hat off but left her red silk scarf around her neck like a long, bright banner. Hand in hand they walked up the track toward a willow grove.

She began to talk. "It happened last night. After supper. Father asked to speak to me in his study. He said Wayne had been pressing him about marrying me." The hackles on Carl's neck rose.

"Father said he thought Wayne would be an ideal catch and I should say yes. I told him I couldn't possibly. We argued." There was strain in her voice. "I said I didn't love Wayne. He said it didn't matter. It was what he wanted for my own good. That's when my strength gave out. I told Father no, I wouldn't ever marry Wayne. I told him I'd marry you and no one else." A spasm twisted Carl's belly.

"Father leaned back in his big chair and just stared at me. You would think I'd said I wanted to marry a leper. He said he couldn't believe I was so willful and stupid." She dabbed her eyes. "I'm afraid I was pretty much of a wild creature by then. He was like stone. I knew he and Wayne must have conspired together. He said we'd talk about it when I came to my senses. He ordered me out, just like some clerk. That was about nine o'clock. I couldn't sleep, so I called you. What do we do, Carl?"

"Honestly, I don't know." He'd never been so deeply involved with a woman before or loved one the way he loved her. Jesse's words about a lifetime of responsibility haunted him.

Tess held his hand tightly. "Come on, let's sit in the shade."

Among the budding willows they came to a slow-moving brook. Carl sat down facing it with his back to a tree trunk. Tess cuddled against him, wrapped in his protecting arm like a child.

He held her and hoped he was comforting her with his presence; he wasn't a sophisticated person, didn't know the right words.

"Carl, do you love me?"

"More than anything."

"Make love to me."

"Tess—"

She put her palms against his face and brought her mouth near his. "I love you. We might never get another chance. *Please.*"

It was noon. They'd made passionate love twice. Now Tess looked at her small gold wristwatch. She said perhaps they'd better return to the city. Carl said she could drop him near the factory.

She let him out in front of a cigar store a block from the Ford plant. She seemed herself again, seated at the wheel, her hair more or less arranged. The sun in her blue eyes made them sparkle.

"Carl, believe me, I didn't set out to seduce you."

"Let's have none of that. I've wanted it ever since I met you. I just don't know what we're going to do. I have to think."

"Plenty of time for that." She caressed his face. "I won't marry Wayne, but I'd never force marriage on you."

With a smile she drew the red silk scarf from her neck, reached above him, and draped it over his shoulders.

"My shining knight on a gasoline charger. There's a token so you don't forget me."

"Forget you? I love you, Tess."

"Shall we plan a picnic on Sunday? I'll meet you at the Wayne Hotel. I'll bring the lunch basket. Eleven o'clock?"

"Perfect," he said. "I love you."

She kissed his cheek and drove away. Carl didn't know what to do now, except talk to Jesse. Ask his advice. Right away.

Savagery • "If you're this shining knight like she told you, don't you suppose you got to rescue her?" Sitting on a keg the next night, an oily rag in his hand, Jesse watched Carl. A coal oil lantern lit the shed as Carl paced back and forth.

"Yes, it's up to me," Carl agreed. He'd told his friend about Clymer's ultimatum to Tess and her reaction. "Barney Oldfield said he might have an opening on his team later this summer. If he'd hire me, and Tess would marry me, we could leave Detroit."

Jesse puckered his mouth. "To travel with that race crowd? You told me they're a pretty low bunch. I'd think real hard before dragging a high-class young lady away from all she's used to into a lot of barrooms and low-down hotels."

Carl started to speak, but a noise forestalled it. He heard footsteps in the backyard. "Somebody out there, Jess."

"Isn't your fight," Jesse said hoarsely. "Get into the alley." He grabbed a hammer from the tool bench.

"What fight? With who?"

A man in the yard gave a gruff order.

"The petition. Bosses must have sent somebody to—"

The door facing the yard flew open. Then a man was inside the shed, followed by another. The first man carried a fish gaff, the second an iron pipe. Just as Carl stepped in front of them, the door behind Jesse burst open. A man wearing a dirty driving coat and pea cap came in swinging a ball bat.

Carl shouted at the first two, "What are you doing here? Get—" A blow to his skull set lights dancing behind his eyes. The man with the bat had struck from behind. Carl fell forward.

The man with the gaff dodged Jesse's swinging hammer. The hook whirled and sank three inches into Jesse's left thigh. Pain glazed his face; the hammer flew out of his fingers. He sank to one knee. The second man raised the iron pipe to brain him, but the man in the driving coat screamed, "Elroy, you idiot, it's the other one!"

Carl was pulling himself up when he heard that. Clymer had told someone about Tess's refusal, and Carl knew who it was.

The ball bat smashed his legs. He fell on his face. As he rolled over, his attacker lifted the bat again. But the bat never came down. Just then Jesse broke the lamp over the man's head.

Coal oil soaked the man's neck and collar. The wick touched it off. His hair and cap burst into flames. More oil splattered a worktable and ignited. Fire ran up the flimsy wooden wall. The man with the gaff and the man with the iron pipe escaped into the alley. Screaming, the third man pulled his long coat over his head. Somehow he snuffed out the flames and ran after the others.

The wooden walls burned fast, popping like oily fatwood. "Jesse, get up." Jesse couldn't hear; he'd passed out. Carl dragged him outside. As a white man from next door rushed through a gate in the board fence, Carl yelled, "Call the fire station!"

"Already sent my boy. What happened to Mr. Shiner?"

"Man sunk a gaff hook in his leg. He needs a hospital."

The neighbor ran to hitch up his horse and buggy. Carl ripped a piece off his pants for an improvised tourniquet.

They left in the buggy seconds before the firehorses charged down the alley. Ten minutes later Carl and the white man carried Jesse through the emergency door of Samaritan Hospital on Jefferson Avenue. A doctor examined him immediately.

"We'll get him to the operating theater right away. Stitch him up. There's muscle damage—I don't know how much."

Attendants rolled Jesse away on a gurney. Filthy with sweat and grime, Carl sank down on a bench. He was still shaking.

The neighbor asked, "Why did those men attack Mr. Shiner?"

"It was a mistake. They were after me."

"Do you know where they came from?"

"I do. I know exactly where they came from."

SYKES & Looby, Advertising Agents, occupied two floors of the Penobscot Building on Fort Street West. The hushed reception lobby's forest-green color scheme had a studied quaintness.

"Where do I find Sykes?"

Carl's tone made the female typewriter draw back warily. "His offices are upstairs. But he never sees visitors without—"

Carl was already halfway to the next floor.

He pushed people aside, not seeing how they reacted to the sight of a man in workman's clothes stalking along glaring at the brass nameplate on each door. Carl found the plate that said F. WAYNE SYKES, JR. He pounded the door open with his fist.

Wayne Sykes, smartly dressed in a brown three-piece suit, sat at a mammoth desk. "What are you doing in this office?"

"Thought you'd like to know your hoodlums didn't do the job."

"Are you a madman? I don't know what you mean," Sykes said. "You'd better get out or I'll have you put away for ten years."

"I don't think so."

Sykes's eye shifted to ivory buttons on a box beside his phone. Carl pulled the box off the desk, broke its wire, threw it onto the floor. Then he tore the telephone loose and hurled it against the wall.

Sykes screamed, "Someone phone the police! Miss Rumford—"

Carl reached across the desk and hauled him up by his necktie. "So you like rough stuff, do you?"

He broke Sykes's nose with his first blow. Sykes collapsed, and Carl punched him twice in the gut. "Your thugs hurt my friend so bad he may not walk again."

"I'm sorry. I'm sorry." Sykes's tears ran into the blood dripping from his nose. "I love Tess. I had to do something."

Carl hauled him up and flung him against the wall. He wanted to hit him again, but he heard noises in the corridor. "In there, in there! He's killing Mr. Sykes!" Three policemen with hickory billy clubs piled through the door and beat Carl to the floor.

CARL spent the night in jail. He ached from the beating and was sure he'd go to prison for what he'd done, but to his astonishment they released him in the morning. No charges had been filed.

He visited Jesse in the charity ward. His friend was awake, drowsy, and falsely cheerful. As Carl left, a staff doctor confided to him that the damage to Jesse's leg was severe. He might be on crutches permanently.

"He works in a foundry," Carl said. "You can't work in a foundry on crutches."

"I'm sure that's true. He'll have to do something else."

At noon Carl punched the clock at the factory. The timekeeping clerk stared at his bruises. "Boss has been looking for you all over the place. You better hightail it up to the second floor."

On the staircase Carl felt everyone was looking at him. He walked to Ford's open door. Ford looked up from a blueprint.

"About time you showed up, Carl. Step in here." Ford rolled up the blueprint, snapped an elastic around it. He was about as friendly as a piece of iron bar stock. "Last night I had a phone call at home from Lorenzo Clymer. He told me you beat up a friend of his, Sykes. Young fellow in advertising. Is that the truth?"

"Yes, sir."

"They hauled you to jail, and you spent the night there?"

"Yes, sir. I wasn't charged with anything. Sykes deserved it. It's a personal matter."

Ford shook his head. "I don't make a habit of climbing out on a limb to hire somebody at your level. I made an exception because I thought you had potential, and you let me down. You let the whole company down. You violated the rules I described at my house. You're discharged. I'll give you a half hour to empty your locker and leave the plant." Ford glared at him like a wrathful preacher. "One more thing. Clymer said that if you set foot on his property, he'd put you away for five years."

Separation • Carl couldn't have afforded so much as a breakfast at "Detroit's finest," the Wayne Hotel, where he arrived Sunday morning at half past ten wearing his old brown corduroy coat with Tess's red silk scarf wound around his neck.

Tess appeared breathlessly at fifteen before eleven. She carried a small hamper and looked rested, refreshed. They walked down to the ferry terminal, where day-trippers lined up to board *Pleasure,* the gleaming white ferryboat.

"Father told me what you did to Wayne."

Fishing in his pocket for seventy cents, Carl looked at her for signs of condemnation, saw none. "I hurt him pretty badly. The men he sent spiked the leg of my riding mechanic with a fish gaff by mistake. You met Jess. He may never walk without crutches."

"Oh, that's dreadful."

"Damn right. And it's my fault."

He paid for two round-trip tickets, and they boarded *Pleasure.*

"Did Wayne admit he sent the men?"

"Yes, but I can't prove it to anyone. It's a terrible mess."

Tess sank down on a starboard bench. "Yes, it is. At the same time, these are the sweetest months I've ever known. Why is life always so mixed up, the good with the bad?"

"Maybe someone brainy like Emerson knows. I sure don't."

The Detroit River ran between two lakes for a distance of about thirty miles. Downstream from the city, opposite Amherstburg, lay Bois Blanc, one of the area's most popular island destinations.

When the ferry docked, Carl and Tess disembarked, then ate their picnic at a rustic table. She'd baked a loaf of oat bread for thick liverwurst sandwiches enhanced with strong Swiss cheese and hot German mustard. Unused to the deep waters he was treading, Carl was awkward in bringing up the subject that was bothering him so deeply.

He held her hand across the table. "Do you regret what we— what happened out in the country?" he said.

"Not for a minute. Do you?"

"No. Well, yes, if I took advantage of you."

"You didn't." She squeezed his hand. "You didn't."

He looked at her. "Will you marry me, Tess?"

"No."

Stunned, more than a little hurt, he sat back. "Why not? We could leave Detroit, settle down somewhere."

"Is this guilt talking?"

"It's *me* talking. I've told you over and over. I love you."

"And I love you. Which is exactly the reason I wouldn't say yes. You're not a factory man, a time-clock man. How often have you told me? I know some other things you are. Brave, kind—very exciting, because there's a wild streak in you. What's deeper than that, I'm not sure. Maybe you don't know either. But you won't discover the answer staying here out of some misguided sense of duty. I release you, Carl. I've never really had any hold on you or intended one. I want you to leave. Chase down Barney Oldfield. I know it's what you want."

"Tess, please let me—"

She stood up, smoothing her skirt. "Subject closed. Shall we walk? It's a lovely afternoon."

He mentioned marriage twice more during the afternoon, but she refused to discuss it. At five o'clock she said they should go.

He left her in Detroit's central square at the monument to the city's founder, Antoine de la Mothe Cadillac. As she rearranged the red scarf over the lapels of his coat, she said, "My shining knight. Off to chase the Saracens and dragons."

"The only dragon I know is the green one Oldfield drove. I can't go unless we settle—"

"Carl, we've settled it. Godspeed. Please don't try to see me again. My heart's breaking already."

She threw her arms around him, shocking the automobilists and buggy drivers passing in the twilight. He felt her tears as they kissed. She struggled to smile as she snatched up the basket and ran for the streetcar.

Postcard from Indianapolis • Fading summer wrapped Grosse Pointe in haze and lassitude. On a Saturday afternoon in late August, Tess sat in a canvas sling chair under a beach umbrella on the lawn near the seawall. She was writing a letter to Carl, never knowing when or whether she'd hear from him with a proper address. She felt that even if he wrote her once or twice, she would certainly never see him again. Ironically, she was at the same time enjoying a new sense of physical health. Her skin glowed. Father had remarked on it.

Emotionally she was far from whole. Often she cried for hours. The trauma of releasing Carl might fade but would never leave. She knew she couldn't have held him with the blackmail of love.

She interrupted the letter, turned the sheet of the tablet over to reveal a blank one. She drew on it with her pencil, a musing, almost whimsical smile on her face. Pensively she looked at what she'd sketched. Three initials, TCC, in fancy script.

Ice tinkling in a pitcher broke her reverie. Giselle, from the kitchen. "I thought you might like more lemonade, ma'am." Giselle set the dewy pitcher beside Tess's tumbler on the white iron table. "And this came in the afternoon post."

She handed Tess a gaudy postcard showing a cigar-store Indian and the words SOUVENIR OF INDIANAPOLIS. When Giselle left, Tess turned the card over, caught her breath. The message was one sentence: "Have a job with Barney O!"

She almost cried. For the message that said so little but set so many fears to rest, she was thankful. It made her decision easier to act upon.

Tess looked up and gazed at the lake, her dark blue eyes unreadable. Her father's long, graceful yacht, *Hiawatha,* had appeared.

Tess considered again what she'd planned to say to him. She firmed her resolve by gazing at the postcard one last time, then tore it up. If only the hurt in her heart could be disposed of so easily.

The yacht's captain docked *Hiawatha.* Lorenzo Clymer strode up the pier. His white linen suit and white hat broke the deep blue canvas of the lake. Tess rose, smoothed her skirt. How cross he looked. She was about to change that. "Father," she said, stepping to the head of the pier as he came stomping along.

"What is it?"

"I want to speak to you. I've changed my mind about Wayne. If you'll give your consent, I'll marry him."

Part Three   PICTURES

Biograph • During the spring and summer Fritzi continued to struggle. To stave off starvation, she worked as a waitress at a run-down restaurant, until it was destroyed by a mysterious fire; spent four weeks demonstrating a potato peeler at Woolworth's; and had just concluded two weeks as a typewriter for an insurance agency. Reluctantly she realized her future needed serious thought. She decided to investigate the only acting job she knew that paid fairly well.

Over the course of a week Fritzi left messages at the Biograph studio. On Sunday evening Mr. Bitzer returned her call.

"What can I do for you?" he asked.

"I'd like to accept your kind offer. When we met, I know I made a rather sharp comment about the pictures—"

"Nothing we haven't heard before. Forget it. I'll be glad to introduce you to our star director, Mr. Griffith."

"When should I be there?"

"Tomorrow morning, six thirty. Ask for Griffith. I'll set it up. One little tip. No snooty words about pictures to him, or you'll be out the door. Griffith wants people who take the business seriously. He thinks it's a new art form."

DAYLIGHT was rising above the East River when Fritzi came rushing along Fourteenth Street, a cardboard portfolio of programs and reviews clutched tightly in her gloved hand. At the correct address she stared up at a five-story brownstone. Staring right back at her were four would-be actors shivering on the stoop in the chill morning light. Fancy gold letters on a plate-glass window to the right of the high stoop said THE AMERICAN MUTOSCOPE & BIOGRAPH COMPANY.

She stepped aside to make way for men and women arriving with newspapers, lunchpails, makeup boxes. A young Irish-looking fellow said to a companion as they approached, "I don't care what the boss says. I think cops are funny." He winked at Fritzi, tipped his cap, and bounded up the steps.

Just as Fritzi prepared to go in, a man in a heavy football sweater came out. He studied a sheet of paper, then the actors. "Nothing today." He looked Fritzi up and down. "You're new."

"Yes, sir. I have an appointment with Mr. Griffith. Mr. Bitzer arranged it."

Though doubtful, he said, "All right. Come on in."

She started up the steps, and at that moment the imaginary Ellen Terry chose to hand down one of her opinions. *The galloping tintypes? Shameful. No good can come of this.* It might be true. Head high, Fritzi marched up the steps and into the building anyway.

The Biograph studio was one of the oddest, noisiest, grubbiest places she'd ever seen. The air reeked of paint and cigars. From upstairs came a din of hammering and sawing.

They climbed two flights to the second floor; there the din was worse. The man pointed at a bench. "Wait here. Don't go in—that's the main stage." When he disappeared through a wide archway, though, Fritzi promptly stepped over to peek.

It might have been the ballroom of the once fashionable town house. High-intensity overhead arc lights lit the room. On the floor, banks of glowing purplish tubes shed a different, more diffuse light on the peculiar scene. A canvas flat rose up before her eyes to establish a wall with patently fake table and chairs painted under an equally fake—in fact, horrible—landscape.

A door in the flat opened; a man walked out carrying two potted plants. A scene shifter unrolled a faded Turkey carpet. Off to one side a carpenter at a sawhorse sawed a two-by-four at maniacal speed. In another corner a wardrobe woman snatched garments out of a trunk. A young woman in Oriental pajamas bumped Fritzi from behind. To a stocky man wearing a straw hat the woman said, "Is the makeup okay, Billy?"

"Definitely not. The lip rouge is too heavy. You dames keep forgetting, red photographs black. Hey!" he exclaimed, noticing Fritzi. "Good morning. You made it."

"I did, Mr. Bitzer, thank you," she said. "I really do appreciate—"

"Swell. Got to rush. Good luck."

The man in the football sweater returned and led her into the big room. "Someone's with Mr. Griffith," he said. "Go in and wait till he speaks to you. Over there in the corner. Don't step on anything."

Half blinded by the lights, Fritzi squinted at a folding screen decorated with golden peacocks. Billy Bitzer left off polishing the lens of his camera and yelled at someone while the carpenter yelled at someone else and the wardrobe woman screamed epithets and yanked more costumes out of the trunk. What kind of crazy place was this? Fritzi had assumed that studios where silent pictures were made would be—well, silent.

Behind the screen a man held forth in a baritone voice. "I'm sick and tired of being hauled to the front office every week to explain how I cut my pictures." This must be Mr. Griffith.

Steeling herself, Fritzi stepped around the screen into an office improvised from a rolltop desk, two swivel chairs, and a gooseneck lamp. A tall, dignified man was speaking to the burly young Irishman who'd tipped his cap outside.

"Maybe I should look for another studio. Oh, good morning, my dear."

"Mr. Griffith?"

"Yes, I am David Griffith. This is Michael Sinnott, one of our actors with ambitions to direct."

"Only my kind of picture, boss." Sinnott gave Fritzi a little salute. "Pleased to meet you."

Griffith ushered him to the screen. "You make your nonsensical comedies, and I'll make five-reelers that tell a real story, and we'll see who wins." He said to Fritzi, "Please be seated."

She took the guest chair, fidgeting. Griffith was nearly six feet tall, in his early thirties. His hair was thick and brown, his sideburns long and full, his nose sharp. Unlike most of the raffish inmates of Biograph, he was smartly turned out in a suit, vest, and cravat.

He sat down and regarded her. "Now, my dear, to business. Billy Bitzer tells me you're an actress."

"Yes. Here are a few things I've done."

He examined the contents of the cardboard portfolio. "I've heard this *Macbeth* was execrable."

"I'm afraid that's too kind."

He smiled. Leaning back, he scrutinized her, oblivious to the shouting and banging on the other side of the screen. "Tell me something about your background, Fritzi."

She began with her Mortmain days. He drew her out with brief but precise questions. In his speech she heard the South.

"Thank you," he said when she'd finished. "Please don't be offended if I tell you motion-picture companies, particularly this one, are not fond of thespians who are merely slumming."

"Mr. Griffith, I'm serious about applying to work in pictures. I have no experience, but I learn quickly."

"Excellent. We've cleared the air. Please stand up, Fritzi."

Nervously she did.

"Turn toward me," he said. "That's fine. Turn again. Now sit. Stand. Register sadness. Let it become happiness."

She obeyed each instruction, feeling like a mugging chimpanzee.

"Now show elation. That's good. Scorn—oh, very nice. Hatred. Excellent." He stood suddenly, slipped his right hand forward to rest lightly just below her padded bosom. "Are you free this evening? We might discuss opportunities over supper."

Oh, no—he was *that* kind of director.

"Mr. Griffith, if that's the price of employment at the Biograph studio, I refuse to pay it, thank you very much." She pulled away and snatched her portfolio off the desk.

He cocked his head. "You don't strike me as a prude."

"I'm not, but the only thing I'm selling is whatever talent I may have."

There was a long, horrible moment of mutual staring. She was sure he was going to curse her. Instead, he laughed.

"Can't blame a fellow for trying, Fritzi. I'm sorry I have nothing for you at the moment. However, I do know of one opportunity. From time to time I hear from other directors in need of particular talent. In this case I'm speaking of a young fellow named Eddie Hearn. A Yale man, but don't hold that against him. He's working for Pelzer and Kelly, Pal Pictures. It's a blanket company."

"What's that?"

"Oh, just a technical term. Eddie is scheduled to start filming next week, but he hasn't found a suitable leading lady." *Leading lady?* Could she be hearing correctly? "If the weather's bad, it won't be too comfortable, I'm afraid. Eddie's shooting outdoors. But I'd be happy to recommend you."

Dumbfounded, she said, "May I ask why? I insulted you."

"You spoke frankly. I like actors with backbone." He scribbled on a memorandum pad. "I'll telephone Eddie this afternoon. You should go see him tomorrow. This is the address." He took Fritzi's hand between his. This time she didn't resist. "If Eddie hires you, here's a bit of advice. Make a friend of your cameraman. He'll know what lighting and makeup will show you to advantage."

"Yes, sir. Thank you for the advice. I'll remember it."

He patted her hand almost paternally. "I have a feeling you will. Oh, I should ask whether you can ride a horse."

"Why, yes. I rode a lot when I was growing up in Chicago."

"Good. Eddie's picture is a western."

"Western? Heavens, will I have to travel?"

He laughed. "No farther than the other side of the Hudson River. Fort Lee, New Jersey, is the western capital of America these days."

Westward Ho • David Griffith's bad handwriting directed Fritzi to something called the Klee & Thermal Film Exchange on Fourteenth Street. A front-office counter was staffed by a lone clerk.

"Can you direct me to Mr. Hearn's office?" Fritzi asked.

"Mr. Hearn's coat closet," the clerk corrected, "is that way, fourth on the left."

She plunged into a musty hall and proceeded to Hearn's open door. A coat closet, all right. Its poverty was slightly relieved by some magazine advertisements tacked to the wall. All included the words Pal Pictures and a logo, a racing palomino horse.

Eddie Hearn was absorbed in a sheet of yellow foolscap. Silver wire spectacles were set on the tip of his nose. Unruly black hair over his ears demanded a barber. He wore riding breeches tucked into scuffed brown cavalry boots whose heels rested on a desk.

She knocked on the doorjamb. Hearn glanced up, showing her a long, narrow face with vivid dark eyes behind the spectacles. "Golly, I didn't see you. Miss Crown?" He said it while swinging his feet off the desk. "Please come in."

At his invitation she took the visitors chair. He looked her over. He seemed friendly as a puppy. "I'm grateful to David for sending you over. Did he tell you what I'm doing?"

"A western picture."

"There's a strong market, domestically and in Europe. I love the West. I've seen Buffalo Bill's arena show at least twenty times. When I was little, I hid dime novels under my pillow. They weren't considered proper reading for rich boys in Greenwich."

"Connecticut?"

He nodded. "Born and bred. Pop's on Wall Street. He expected me to follow him there, but I fell in love with pictures." He leaned back. "What's your acting experience?" After she summarized it, he said, "Made any other pictures?"

"No, this would be my first. Can you tell me about the picture?"

"I grew up on Cooper's *Leather-Stocking Tales*. I wondered why an Indian should always be portrayed in pictures as the skulking villain. Why not a noble savage? A true Native American hero? So I wrote this scenario." He showed her the typed yellow foolscap. "My original title was *The Lone Indian*. Mr. Pelzer, one of the partners, approves all the scenarios. He wanted money in the title. He said everyone's interested in money."

Fritzi smiled sweetly. "Mr. Hearn, do I dare ask whether you have any interest in hiring me?"

"Yes! Definitely! I can offer two, possibly three days of work if we have fine weather. Wages are five dollars per day. Mr. Kelly also pays for trolleys, the ferry, and your lunch over in Jersey."

"Who is Mr. Kelly?"

"The other partner. In charge of the money. He squeezes a dollar ten cents out of every dollar we spend." From a drawer Hearn pulled another typed sheet, folded it, and handed it across the desk. "Please study the scenario. Tuesday morning report to the 129th Street ferry terminal at six thirty sharp. We'll meet our cameraman in Fort Lee, then proceed to Coytesville, a little hamlet several miles farther on. Dress warmly."

"Thank you, Mr. Hearn. Thank you very much."

"Everyone calls me Eddie. You must too. See you Tuesday."

Fritzi floated out of his office in a state of bliss. At a shop near Herald Square she treated herself to hot tea and a biscuit and unfolded the scenario: "*The Lone Indian's Gold* (1 reel). Scenario by Edw. B. Hearn, Jr."

The melodrama opened with Chief White Eagle of the Apache riding up to a general store. A "genial old-timer" ran the store, together with his "spunky daughter." The chief had a sack of gold from the "tribal mine." He'd ridden to town to have it assayed.

Three skulking badmen spied on the chief as he showed the gold to the storekeeper's daughter. The head ruffian demonstrated by "salacious leering" that he coveted the girl along with the gold. The badmen jumped the chief and fired pistols to make him "dance." With the Indian knocked unconscious, girl and gold were abducted. Of course, the chief found and rescued both. The girl clearly adored White Eagle, but he had other business. He rode off with a wave and an "expression of manly stoicism."

Fritzi sighed. Eddie Hearn of Greenwich and Yale had stuffed one too many dime novels under his pillow. The scenario was hokum, cheap blood and thunder. Did it matter? Shamelessly she felt that it did not. She had a part. She was going to *act* again.

Blanket Company • Tuesday's dawn was dark and foggy. Fritzi was in a state of nerves the moment she woke up.

She reached the ferry pier at six fifteen. Other actors came drifting out of the murk. Spears of light pierced the fog: a Stoddard-Dayton with headlamps blazing. Eddie Hearn was at the wheel. Seated next to him, arms folded, was a slight red-faced man in a high celluloid collar and a dark gray suit. He had thick white hair and a slit of a mouth. Kelly?

A deckhand waved the car onto the ferry. Eddie jumped out, summoned the others aboard, and performed introductions. The sour man was indeed Alfred A. Kelly. A young man with blond hair named Owen Stallings was playing the Lone Indian. He looked about as Indian as Leif Eriksson. After shaking Fritzi's hand, he sauntered to the rail and from there continued to smile at her, as though confident it would bowl her over. Handsome men were worse than beautiful women. The man playing Fritzi's father was Noble Royce, a jolly red-nosed old ham wearing a peacoat and a cap.

A Ford F Model touring car chugged out of the fog. Eddie hailed the stout and homely young man at the wheel. "Bill Nix, our chief carpenter and propman."

The bell rang, deckhands closed the stern gates, and the ferry churned into the Hudson, sounding its horn.

Soon the New Jersey Palisades loomed. The ferry docked, and the autos drove along a road for about three miles, bumping through pleasant countryside to Fort Lee. It wasn't much of a place—drab buildings along a dirt street. They reached a stable, where Eddie jumped out to greet a ruddy middle-aged man with orange hair. The man had arrived in a closed delivery wagon.

"Everybody, this is Jock Ferguson, our cameraman. Anyone follow you, Jock?"

"Don't think so, laddie. Hardly anyone's up at half past four but thieves and inebriates."

"We'll leave the wagon here."

"Aye." Ferguson opened the rear doors. He and Eddie unloaded something bulky wrapped in a bright red Navajo blanket. The two men lugged their mysterious burden to the Ford.

Then they left Fort Lee, bound for Coytesville. Fritzi said to Nell Spooner, the young girl who was in charge of wardrobe, "What are they hiding under the blanket?"

"The camera. Pal is a blanket company."

"So I heard. I thought it was a technical term."

"It's technical, all right. Mr. Kelly's partner, Mr. Pelzer, he designed the camera and sort of accidentally included some features Thomas Edison invented and patented. Mr. Ferguson told me Edison's even got a patent on the sprocket holes in the film. If your camera uses his inventions, you're supposed to pay royalty to something called the Motion Pictures Patents Company. It's a trust—most of the big studios belong. So do exhibitors. If they show pictures with a patented projector, they pay the trust two dollars a week."

"Does Biograph belong to the trust?"

"Yes. Blanket companies are independents that don't. They hide their cameras and move around a lot. The patents company keeps a flock of detectives hunting them to stop production. Worst one used to be a Pinkerton. Pearly Purvis is his name." Nell thought a moment before she added, "They carry guns."

Fritzi shivered. "Do they actually shoot at actors?"

"No," Nell said. "Generally they shoot the camera."

COYTESVILLE had a dusty main street. The little place could easily pass for a town out west. They parked at a frame building with a wide veranda. A sign above the porch eave identified it as RAMBO'S HOTEL. An assorted half-dozen males jumped up from benches on the porch and surrounded Eddie. "Any work today?"

"Two outlaws needed," Eddie said. A couple of the men fell into ludicrous poses of savagery. One flexed his biceps.

"You." Eddie pointed. "And you. Two and a half dollars per man for the day." He clapped for attention. "Actors! Dressing rooms are inside, upstairs. Dress quickly. We start in fifteen minutes."

A porter dragged the costume trunk upstairs. The men dressed in one room, Fritzi in another. Nell helped her into a cotton dress. Eddie came in with a wooden makeup box. He put Fritzi in a chair and worked quickly with grease sticks and powder while Nell, on her knees, sewed the hem of the dress. He then ran out, shouting, "Let's go, everyone. Time is money."

Fritzi walked down to the porch. Eddie strung sash cord to stakes, forming a rectangle directly in front of the steps. Jock Ferguson was setting up his camera in the street. A boy led a horse that Eddie had hired for the day around the corner of the hotel.

The extras came outside wearing fringed shirts and coonskin caps. Two minutes later Owen appeared in leggings, moccasins, a black wig with a center part and long braids. He'd darkened his face, arms, and brawny chest with reddish paint.

Eddie said, "We'll start with the storekeeper being dragged out by the badmen. Noble, they knock you out, and you fall down."

"Nothing to it," the old actor wheezed.

"All of you remember, you must stay in the roped area."

Fritzi's nerves were wound tight as Eddie chalked the name of the picture and a scene number on a school slate.

"Actors inside," Eddie ordered. Fritzi crowded through the door with the others. They hid on either side of grimy windows. "Everyone ready? Here we go, people. Camera. Action. Outlaws!"

Giving Noble a shove, the leader of the badmen snarled, "Let's go." In a moment Noble and the other outlaws were out the door.

"Rough him up. That's it, that's it. Bash him. Swell. On your knees, Noble—groggy, groggy! Daughter! Now!"

Fritzi ran out the door. She heard the camera grinding away, Eddie calling encouragement. Then disaster struck. As she rushed down from the porch, she stepped on her hem and went flying.

It would have been a bad fall had she not reacted instantly. She tucked her head, shot her hands out, landed on her palms, and somersaulted forward, springing up disheveled but unhurt. It was so surprising, everyone but Kelly burst out laughing.

Eddie shouted, "Cut. Fritzi, are you all right?"

Slapping dust off her sleeves, Fritzi said, "Oh, yes."

Al Kelly's face was wrathful. "This isn't the big top, sister. We aren't making a comedy."

"I apologize for spoiling the shot, Mr. Kelly."

"I thought it was funny," Eddie said. "Especially the expression on your face when you popped up on your feet. You looked as surprised as anyone. Catch your breath. We'll do the scene again."

Kelly said, "Hearn, get this. On the budgets I write, we don't have accidents. Your girlie better do it in one take every time, or we'll hire someone else."

Just then they all heard a chugging from the direction of Fort Lee. Fritzi turned around as a black Oldsmobile drove into sight. Jock Ferguson wiped his forehead with his sleeve.

"We're in for it now, laddie."

The patent detectives had found them.

As THE Oldsmobile chugged toward them, Fritzi was mesmerized. The man in the passenger seat casually draped his arm over the side. Sunshine gleamed on the silver-blue metal of a revolver.

Kelly stabbed a finger at her. "You. Stand next to the camera. Where's the other one?" He found Nell. "You too, the other side. They won't shoot women."

Eddie said, "Mr. Kelly, I have to protest."

"Protest all you want. I'm the boss." Turning back to Fritzi, he said, "Do it."

She looked at Nell, who gave a little shrug, as if to say, Who knows? Maybe he's right.

Her heart racing, Fritzi walked to the camera quickly, put her back against it. Nell positioned herself on the opposite side.

The Oldsmobile kicked up a cloud when the driver braked. He jumped out, strode forward with an air of authority. His helper, a hulk squeezed into a too tight suit, followed.

The detective glanced around. "Well, look here. Kelly and the forty thieves." He showed his teeth in a brilliant smile.

Kelly said, "Hello, Pearly."

"Do I get the camera without a fight, Al?"

"When hell freezes."

"Nuts." Pearly sighed. "It's too nice a day for rough stuff." So it was. The fog had lifted, and sunshine poured from the clear bright sky. The detective fanned back his coat to show a silver pistol hanging butt-forward in a harness. "Stand by, Buck." The hulk cocked his revolver, an ominous sound in the stillness.

The detective walked over to Fritzi. "Hello, miss. Earl Purvis is my name. I sure don't want to use force on a woman, but I mean to take possession of that illegal camera."

Let him smile all he wanted, she thought. He was the enemy, trying to throw her out of work.

"Step aside," he said.

Her stare registered unmistakable defiance. "No."

He blinked. Evidently he hadn't expected resistance from a woman. "Well. Sassy. I'll ask one last time. Move away from the camera."

"The devil I will."

He sighed again. "Buck, take the other one." When Purvis lunged and grabbed her shoulders, Fritzi shrieked. She stamped on his pointed black shoe. Her heel connected solidly.

He swore, hopping backward on the other foot. Meanwhile, Buck ran around to Nell. Seeing Fritzi's example, she seized his arm and bit his wrist. He screamed, firing his revolver into the dirt.

Purvis retreated a couple of steps, lowered his head like an annoyed bull. When he charged, Fritzi stabbed at his eyes with both index fingers and whipped her foot up in a high kick that hit him where it mattered. He cursed, doubled over.

Kelly yelled at Jock Ferguson, "The camera!" Ferguson threw the tripod over his shoulder and dashed to the Ford. He shouted to Eddie to follow and crank the engine.

Eddie whirled the crank so hard he could have broken his shoulder. The Ford's engine caught. Eddie leaped back, and the car careened down the street. Ferguson skidded left, around the corner of a general store and out of sight.

Buck stared at his tooth-marked wrist. He hauled his arm back to smash Nell's face with the gun barrel. From behind, Fritzi grabbed the gun. Eddie ran up, snatched it from her, and bashed Buck on the head twice. Buck sprawled against the porch rail, out of action.

By this time Purvis was upright again. He yanked the silver pistol out of its harness. Eddie stepped up beside Fritzi, pointed Buck's revolver at the detective. "Throw it down or I'll shoot."

Purvis's eyes were savage as he dropped the pistol in the dirt.

Kelly shouted, "Everybody in the car."

Owen Stallings and old Noble and the extras bumped each other like a pack of clowns to get to the Stoddard-Dayton. Eddie grasped Fritzi's elbow to move her along. Passing Purvis, she had a brief, terrifying look into his eyes.

"You did this, girlie. You'll pay for it."

"Shut up, you thug," Eddie said as they ran.

Kelly jumped into the car; Eddie spun the crank. Four spins and the engine started. Eddie took the passenger seat with Fritzi on his lap. Owen, the extras, and the carpenter jammed the back seat. Nell hung on to the left running board, Noble on to the right one. Kelly wheeled the Stoddard into a turn as Fritzi bounced up and down on Eddie's lap, her heart pounding, her blond hair flying.

THEY finished *The Lone Indian's Gold* in two days in the country near Mamaroneck, New York. No one troubled them. The patents company hadn't yet recruited a snitch corps in Westchester County.

After the excitement in Coytesville, filming was uneventful—in fact, dull. Eddie, who had praised Fritzi profusely for protecting the camera, invited her to join Kelly and his partner in the projection room to see the results—a thousand feet of film assembled into a coherent fifteen-minute story.

The room was cramped—just a few straight chairs and a screen. Eddie introduced Fritzi to the other partner, B. B. Pelzer, a short, round man with curly gray hair and a warm, paternal manner. ("People call him Benny, but never to his face," Eddie had warned ahead of time.) B.B. gave Fritzi's hand a vigorous shake before sitting down.

The operator switched off the lights and turned on the projector. The moment Fritzi saw herself, she let out a nervous giggle. She was mortified by her big feet, her flying hair. Fifteen minutes seemed like fifteen hours as she sat squirming in the dark.

At the fade-out Eddie said, "I spliced some extra footage on the end. I think you'll enjoy it."

Abruptly a new scene appeared—the shot in which Fritzi had rushed out the door and fallen. Horrified, she watched herself adjust in midair and finish with the somersault. All of them laughed, even Kelly.

As the projectionist put the lights on, Eddie patted her arm. "You're quite a comedienne."

"Not intentionally."

"Ought to be some way we can use it." *Let's hope not.*

B. B. Pelzer rushed up to her. "Say, Eddie's right. You're a sketch. I liked you in the picture. Like to see more of you at Pal."

THANKS to B.B.'s enthusiasm, Fritzi worked fairly regularly during the following winter and spring. Always wary of the detectives, they filmed in rented lofts in Manhattan and Brooklyn. For exteriors they went back to Mamaroneck or out to rural Long Island.

The Lone Indian's Gold had produced higher than usual rentals across the country, so Eddie concocted more offerings in the series. Late spring saw completion of *The Lone Indian's Courage*. They next returned to Westchester for *The Lone Indian's Battle*.

Reasonably steady work allowed Fritzi to spend $14.95 on something she'd wanted for a long time—a talking machine with a handsome golden oak cabinet and a beautifully sculpted flower horn. She splurged on a half-dozen twenty-cent records featuring anonymous vocalists performing with tinny orchestras. Her favorite was "A Girl in Central Park," a new hit composed by Paul's friend Harry Poland. After a long day's work she would slip off her shoes and listen to the soulful tenor: *"I met a girl in Central Park, fair as the morning's fair."*

The song was beautiful but melancholy; the gentleman never saw the girl again. By the second playing, her eyes misted. The seventh or eighth time through, tears were streaming down her cheeks.

New York Music • Harry Poland loved his adopted language. He thought of American speech as a giant tray of luscious appetizers, each with a special flavor suited to a special moment. A word he relished was "spiffy." He liked to wear spiffy clothes and was beginning to be able to afford them. If not yet a byword in Muncie or Boise, the name Harry Poland was well recognized in the tight little community of New York music publishing.

On a day in the spring of 1910, when Fritzi was making one of her first pictures, he took care to look spiffy for an afternoon visit with his wife. He chose a three-piece single-breasted suit, a blue-striped shirt, a rakish bowler hat, and a walking cane.

His destination was a rest home in the suburban village of Rye. The April afternoon brought a gentle, warm breeze off Long Island Sound. An attendant wheeled Flavia outdoors, and Harry sat with her under a sycamore tree, holding her hand while she stared vacantly into his eyes. Flavia's hair was thin, spiky, and white. At her doctor's urging, Harry had moved her to the home during the winter. He strove to be chipper as he related tidbits of news.

" 'Blue Evening' is doing well. And guess what? Tomorrow I'm seeing one of the biggest producers in New York. Ziegfeld. He called *me*. He's doing another *Follies* this year."

Each tidbit was received with the same fey, slightly bewildered smile that broke his heart.

When the shadows lengthened and the air turned cool, Harry signaled a man in white, rose, and kissed Flavia's forehead. "Goodbye, dear girl. I'll see you next week." And every week as long as she lived. Flavia had done so much for him, he could never desert her, even though he often thought of another woman. She was the one for whom he'd written "A Girl in Central Park."

Signs of Success • With some chagrin Fritzi found herself looking forward to each picture. It wasn't the artistry of the one-reelers she enjoyed—there wasn't any. It was the companionship. She liked Eddie, his wife, Rita, and their two children. She liked Nell Spooner, and on Griffith's advice she befriended the cameraman—solid, reflective Jock Ferguson. Sometimes, together, they accidentally made a scene that was almost respectable. Even so, she regarded the work as temporary, a source of income until she found the right stage role.

Fritzi began to notice certain signs of change at Pal Pictures. B. B. Pelzer started passing out fifty-cent cigars to favored visitors. The company moved to a bigger suite of rooms on Fourteenth Street. It suggested to her that she might improve her own living situation now that she had funds. She said good-bye to Mrs. Perella and relocated to two airy rooms on West Twenty-second Street.

B.B. proposed *The Lone Indian's Baby,* declaring that people loved babies almost as much as they loved money. This epic put Owen in the role of temporary father of an infant left in a basket outside his tepee. Owen had grown more conceited with each appearance as the heroic red man. He invited Fritzi out at least once a month, hinting that she was passing up a chance to dine with one of the screen's new luminaries. She cheerfully declined.

They risked filming the new Lone Indian picture near Fort Lee. In preparation Eddie bought a .32-caliber Smith & Wesson double-action revolver. "Damn thing scares me, but I won't go back to Jersey without a gun." Jock Ferguson hired an armed guard to accompany them and stand by the camera at all times.

Two weeks after the release of *The Lone Indian's Baby,* B. B. Pelzer summoned Fritzi to his new office.

"Fritzi, have a chair. I got something to show you." He looked happy. "You like working for Pal?"

"It certainly is interesting, Mr. Pelzer."

"Well, I'm telling you today, you got a great future with us. Magnificent. Here." He shoved a floridly decorated cigar box to her side of the desk. "Take a look."

She lifted the lid. Puzzled, she peered at two stacks of letters.

"You don't need to read 'em. I'll tell you what's in 'em. These people are crazy about the Lone Indian pictures, especially our latest one. Those letters are asking about the identity of our talent."

"I'm not surprised. Owen is a very attractive leading man."

"Forget Owen. Nobody asked about Owen!" He grinned. "They're asking who's the funny one who fights the badmen, falls off the horse, rocks the cradle at the end of the new picture."

Fritzi laughed in surprise and disbelief. "Seriously?"

"I'm telling you, Fritzi, they all want to know one thing—*who's the gel?* I said to Eddie this morning, next picture we raise you to six dollars a day. Heck, make it six fifty. Kelly wants to fight about it, I'm ready to go fifteen rounds."

HOME at half past nine, Fritzi was drawing a bath when the tenant of the first-floor flat pounded on the door to call her to the communal telephone. She ran downstairs.

"Hello? Is this Fritzi Crown?"

"It is. Who's this?"

"Harry Poland. Your cousin's friend, remember?"

"I couldn't forget. You're the man who's got half the country singing your songs."

"I finally found you," Harry said in an odd, bubbly voice. "I saw one of your pictures. The Pal office told me where to locate you. May I treat you to supper tomorrow evening? I'm not trying to be forward, Miss Crown. I only want to express my admiration for your talent. What do you say?"

"Well, since you're straightforward about it, and you're also the composer of my favorite song, I'll say yes."

They met at Rector's. Having arrived ahead of her, Harry leaped to his feet and waved from the rail of the second level when she walked in. How grand she looked gliding up the staircase. Her frock and hat were smart and new. He was intoxicated all over again by her blond ringlets, her brown eyes, her smile.

His hand trembled as he took her glove, pressing harder than he intended. "I saw you in a cowboy picture," he said after they sat down. "You were wonderful. Have you done many?"

"More than I'd like," she said with a rueful smile.

"Have you tried out for any musicals?"

"Oh, I don't have a voice for musicals, Harry."

"Wrong. I remember our picnic. Perhaps your voice isn't operatic, but it's strong. You can put over a song."

Laughing, she opened her menu. "I'll keep that in mind if all else fails." She ordered oysters on the half shell, a salad of fresh asparagus, a veal cutlet, and a stein of Crown lager.

He lit a cigarette, straining for nonchalance. "How is Paul?"

"Busy, I expect. I don't hear from him often. He's quite the celebrity now that he's written a book."

"Oh, I read it. I'm so proud to have him as a friend."

"He feels the same about you. So do we all. You know, you're the composer of my favorite song, 'A Girl in Central Park.' "

"Yes. It's really caught on," he said nervously. Did she know or even suspect how important she was to his creation? Though aching to tell her, he simply couldn't. "I wrote it for someone special. Someone very close to me."

Fritzi's smile saddened a little. "Your wife. I know you've been with her a long time. How is her health?"

"Not good, I'm afraid."

"No improvement?"

He shook his head, then looked away quickly, sure that she'd discover his secret. Part of him desperately wanted her to discover it. He longed to take her hand and ask her to let him make love to her. He couldn't even hint at it. To do so would betray the poor muddled woman in the rest home in Rye.

A second stein of beer overcame some of his shyness. He told Fritzi about his plans for his own music publishing company. She confided that she regarded picturemaking as temporary.

When they left the restaurant, Harry stopped abruptly under the marquee of a darkened theater. He touched her arm. "I want to say how much I enjoyed being with you. I don't know when I've enjoyed an evening more, Fritzi."

"Yes, it was delightful, thank you. Now I'd better find a taxi—"

With a sudden move that startled her, he swept his arms around her there in the shadows. For a few blissful seconds he tasted her warm mouth. Then she turned her head, pulled away, gasping.

"Harry, we can't do that."

"I couldn't help myself," he blurted. "You just don't know how much I—" Conscience choked off the rest.

Fritzi seemed more dismayed than angry. Giving him a curious, searching look, she took three rapid steps to the curb and flagged a taxi. Harry handed her into the cab red-faced.

Attack • Fritzi was still puzzling over Harry's romantic advances as she climbed the stairs to her flat. Although his behavior wasn't proper, his interest was flattering, and in the few seconds his mouth touched hers, something had stirred within her.

She unlocked the door and stepped in without immediately understanding what her senses told her. The window was open, bringing in night sounds—a couple arguing, an auto horn. Whenever she went out, she closed that window. Fritzi smelled barber's talc an instant before she saw the silhouetted head, torso, outstretched legs with heels resting on the table. The hair on her neck stood up.

"Hello, Miss Fritz. Don't be scared. It's Pearly Purvis."

"I recognize your voice." Fritzi's calm reply qualified as the performance of the week.

"Shut the door. Let's have some lights." Seated in a chair, Purvis sounded affable. With a shaky hand she snapped the switch.

Purvis was dressed up like a suitor. He'd shaved closely. His thick silver hair was parted in the center. His suit was a single-breasted tan corduroy with leather elbow patches. "Guess you're surprised to see me," he said.

"I'd like you to leave, Mr. Purvis." Fritzi's legs felt wobbly.

"Call me Earl. Or Pearly. Either's fine."

"Did you hear what I said? You broke into my room, and I want you out. If you don't go, I'll scream my head off."

He frowned. "Look, I'm really not here to do you harm." He pushed back both sides of his coat—no gun harness. "I'd just like us to get acquainted. I want to be friends."

Fritzi had a wild impulse to laugh. She sat on the sofa instead because she feared she'd fall over if she didn't. She unpinned her hat, laid hat and pin beside her. Fritzi pointed at the gold band on his fourth finger, right hand. "That's a wedding ring, isn't it?"

He touched it. "I keep it for sentiment. She's long gone. I caught her with another man. I divorced her after she got out of the hospital." He smiled, rubbed his knuckles. He wanted her to know exactly what he was capable of.

"I want you to go."

"When I'm good and ready." He eased himself up, stepped toward the sofa. Her mouth went dry. "Get this straight. The patents trust will nail your company, put it out of business. The only question is when. Be my pal, and you'll make it easy on yourself when it happens. Know what I'm saying?"

As he came near, she flung herself off the sofa, heading for the door. "I'm calling the police."

He was quick. He stood against the door and grabbed her left arm, pulling her forward against him. She wrenched away, toward the sofa. He held on. "You try that again, I'm liable to break your arm."

"Purvis, let go. Stop it."

"Sure, when you give me what I came for."

He pushed her backward; the sofa banged the backs of her legs. Uttering muted cries of fright, she groped behind her. He muffled her mouth with his left hand as he wedged his right knee between her legs. Finally she found the hatpin. With a vicious jab she drove it through corduroy into the side of his leg.

Purvis screeched in pain, and she gave him a shove. She ran to the window and leaned out. "Police! Help, help!"

He came at her, hit the back of her head with his fist. Dizziness and darkness took her for a second. Then she screamed. She heard people clamoring on the hall stairway.

Purvis heard them too. He gave Fritzi a hellish look that seemed to last forever. His yellow eyes promised terrible retribution. Then he ran to the door, tore it open, and roared down the stairs, kicking and punching.

Suddenly Fritzi's sitting room filled with people. She couldn't understand their shouted questions. Delayed shock hit her. She started shuddering, then hid her face in her hands and sobbed.

B.B. Decides • Al Kelly called Fritzi to his office two days later, the first of November. It had been snowing since daybreak, a heavy, wet snow that horses and auto tires had already converted to dirty slush down on Fourteenth Street.

"Come in, Fritzi," Kelly said. He dominated the room from his desk chair. B.B. sat holding his head.

Kelly cleared his throat. "Close the door, please."

"Have they found Pearly?" she asked.

Kelly shook his head. "My guess is, they never will."

Fritzi eased into a chair. "I handled it badly. I was scared out of my wits. I got rid of him the only way I could think of, but I just made him angrier. He swore he'd get us, the whole company."

"He can't hurt us if he can't find us," Kelly said. He fiddled with a cigar butt in a heavy glass ashtray. "What we want to tell you is, we've decided to close this office for a while."

"I decided," B.B. said. "I don't want any more trouble for the people who work for Pal. We're going to run away from it."

Kelly said, "California."

"Edison's a cheapskate," B.B. said. "Maybe he won't buy railroad tickets for his thugs. Maybe Purvis will leave us alone."

"Yeah, and maybe trees will grow dollar bills," Kelly said.

"Doesn't matter," B.B. said. "We're going—"

Fritzi interrupted. "Who is going?"

"The important folks," Kelly said.

"One of which is you," B.B. said.

Fritzi sat a moment, collecting herself. "Mr. Pelzer—Mr. Kelly— that's very kind, but I don't want to work in California."

"Why not?" B.B. said. "How can you beat it when you got sunshine every day? Biograph's gone west the past couple of winters, and I hear they may move for good."

Fritzi shook her head.

Kelly's voice took on a note of irascibility. "Don't be so quick to turn it down. You have a future with us."

"Right!" B.B. exclaimed. "This business is growing like a rabbit farm. The trade papers say there's ten thousand moving-picture theaters in the U.S., and eight or ten new ones open up every day. Can't make pictures fast enough for that kind of market. We're riding the crest, Fritzi. California's only the start. We need you."

"I appreciate it. I'm very grateful. But"—a deep breath—"I still want to make my career on the stage."

Kelly glowered at Fritzi. "So stay here. Just forget we were prepared to write a regular contract for your services. Hang around New York. Sling hash, sell hankies. Who cares?"

"Now, now," B.B. said. "Everybody calm down. Fritzi, did you catch what Al said about a contract? What do you make now?"

"Six fifty a day when I work."

"That's thirty-nine dollars if you work the regular six-day week. How does a guaranteed salary of seventy a week sound? We'll throw in some nice extras. Pay your rent for a month or two while you get settled. Say, do you know how to drive a motorcar?"

Taken aback, she said, "What?"

Kelly snatched the cigar out of his mouth. "A car? For heaven's sake, Benny, what is this? We didn't discuss a car."

"Al, you're overwrought," B.B. said. "What I'm talking about is a car available to be driven by all our important players, including this little gel. A Pal company car."

"Yeah? On whose money?"

"Ours, Al. And that's my final word. If Fritzi goes to California, and I am praying she does, she's going in style."

Kelly stomped to the window and glowered at the falling snow.

B.B. came over, grasped Fritzi's hands. "Don't forget Purvis. There's no guarantee we won't see Purvis in California, but it's a long way out there. You stay in this town, you'll be dealing with him forever. Do you want to live with that?"

Fritzi was surprised at the faintness of her voice when she said, "When will the company be leaving?"

"After Christmas," Kelly said.

"I'll think about it. I really will."

B.B. patted her shoulder. "Take your time. Take a whole day. Two if you need it. Come back, and we'll ink the contract on the spot. You'll be happy, Fritzi. I promise."

Fritzi's long face expressed considerable doubt.

In the Subway • Fritzi found herself supremely careful whenever she was on the crowded city streets. She scrutinized faces and looked behind her often, especially if she was out after dark.

Harry Poland telephoned three times, leaving messages. The third time, feeling sorry for him, she called him back. He asked for one more chance to see her, to make amends—to prove that he could be a complete gentleman.

Fritzi hesitated. "All right, yes—supper on Saturday. I'll tell you about my plans for the new year."

New York sparkled with colored lights as the stores decorated for the Christmas season. Harry called for her in a taxi, told the driver to take them to a restaurant called Bankers, just off lower Broadway a few blocks above Wall Street. As he helped her out of the cab, she saw headlights veer to the curb behind them. Someone clambered out of another taxi and faded into the shadow of a darkened building. She felt an odd tingle of alarm.

Bankers was swank and expensive. Their dinner conversation was lively, with no reference to what had happened last time. She told Harry about Pal's move to California for the winter and that she had decided to go with them.

"How grand for you, Fritzi—all that warm weather. One of these days I want to see the Pacific coast for myself. I'd be out there in a shot if you invited me."

"Harry," she said, raising her eyebrows.

"Sorry. You have that effect on me."

She smiled; she couldn't be angry. He was an attractive companion—charming, cultivated, yet with an air of Old World innocence. When they stepped outside, Fritzi had quite forgotten her earlier anxiety. Harry asked if she'd like to walk a bit, and she readily agreed, taking his arm. They turned north on Broadway.

After two blocks he said, "Let's finish the evening in style."

"What do you have in mind?"

"Riding the subway. The New York subway is one of the wonders of the age. The cars are clean, and you see all kinds of people on the subway, socialites to shopgirls—all for a nickel! Shall we?"

"All right, why not?"

Although it was nearly ten, there were still many people entering and leaving the City Hall station. Harry paid their fares. A rush of air and noise signaled the departure of a train.

"That was a local," Harry said, peering along the crowded platform. Fritzi hadn't ridden the subway in a while. She'd forgotten how attractive the stations were. Terra-cotta arches inlaid with colored tiles created a pleasing, airy effect above the platform.

Fritzi heard another train on its way to the station from the north. Someone bumped her, pushing her near the edge.

Harry glared at the man behind her. "You needn't stand so close. There's plenty of room."

Fritzi's eyes grew round. She heard strident breathing, watched as Harry turned with another annoyed look at the boorish passenger. *I know who it is. He's followed us.* Urgently she gripped Harry's arm. "Harry, let's leave." With her head turned slightly, she saw him from the edge of her vision—that damnable grin. A little cry of fear escaped her, unheard as the train came roaring along the tunnel.

Harry said something to the passenger, who grabbed him by the lapels and flung him aside. Pearly grabbed Fritzi's wrists, shoved her toward the edge as the train thundered closer. As one foot slipped off the platform, she twisted her hand, savagely dug her nails into Pearly's wrist. He cursed, and she pulled free, teetering.

Harry made a wild lunge to save her, shooting out his hand. She caught it and hung on. Pearly reached for his pistol under his jacket. People along the platform were screaming. Harry leaped at Pearly and shoved. Pearly swung the pistol to club him. The eight-car express hurtled from the tunnel just as Pearly stumbled, flailed in the air, and fell onto the tracks.

If Pearly cried out when the first car crushed him, no one heard. The train ground to a stop. A woman screamed. A uniformed ticket guard was frantically ringing an alarm gong.

Harry pulled Fritzi against his chest. "Don't look. He didn't stand a chance. Some crazy man—"

"Trying to kill me. It wasn't chance, Harry. I know him."

"Good Lord," he said with a look of horror. He pulled her close again, enfolding her in his strong arms while she trembled with fright and shock. It didn't matter that he was married; she wanted his arms around her.

AT POLICE headquarters Harry stayed with her while detectives questioned her. Pulled out of bed, B.B. arrived wearing an overcoat over his pajama bottoms. He quickly corroborated Fritzi's story of threats and harassment from the patents detective. She was released a little before one in the morning.

B.B. drove her to her flat on Twenty-second Street, with Harry riding along. "Poor defenseless gel," B.B. kept saying.

Harry saw her up to her door, gravely shook her hand, urged her to telephone if he could do anything at all. She thanked him, then hurried inside, hoping she'd feel safer, calmer, in her own bedroom.

She didn't. She lay awake, seeing those few seconds in the station again and again. Fritzi felt different about California now. She urgently wanted to flee, put this terrible night behind her.

Further Westward Ho • On her way out west Fritzi stopped in Chicago. She vowed to say nothing about Earl Purvis and the man's horrible end. Telling her parents would only confirm their fears about acting and the environment in which it was carried out.

When she arrived, rather than hiring a taxi to deliver her to the Crown mansion, Fritzi checked in at the Sherman House hotel. She felt sad about the decision but considered it prudent.

She telephoned her mother. "Mama? I'm here overnight. I'm on my way to California to make more pictures."

"Why didn't you telegraph, for heaven's sake?"

"I didn't know how I'd be received."

"Oh, *Liebchen*." It carried a sad, unspoken admission that she had reason for concern. "I'll leave now, take a taxi," Ilsa said.

"You mean I can't come to the house? I'd like to talk to Papa."

"Not such a good idea. I wouldn't advise it. Your father, I am sorry to tell you, is still angry."

"With me?"

"With you, with me—the world."

"But I've actually had some success. He predicted I wouldn't."

"All the more reason he's angry. You proved him wrong."

After a moment of pained silence Fritzi said, "Call the taxi, Mama. I'll reserve a table in the dining room."

DURING dinner Fritzi was still exercised. "Mama, what is the trouble with my father? What reason does he have to be angry?"

"Shall I make a list? Number one, he's a man. He's growing old and resents it. He's driven wild by the prohibition crowd. He's also, you know, a German. They are champion grudge holders."

"On Thursday, Mama, I had a birthday—"

"Oh, that's right. Congratulations. Child, I'm a little forgetful. How old are you now? Twenty-nine?"

"Thirty, Mama. Thirty years old. Do you know what that means? It means I'm old enough to have my father respect what I choose to do with my life."

"Oh, *Liebchen,* he does."

"That isn't true. You're just trying to make me feel good. But he will before I'm through." Fritzi pounded the table so hard the silver danced. "I promise you, he will."

Though the meal was sumptuous, and the meeting with her beloved mother comforting, Fritzi was emotionally devastated by her banishment. She boarded the westbound train next morning in a mood of deep melancholy.

Part Four

CALIFORNIA

Welcome to Los Angeles • "Glendale. All out for Glendale."

The Southern Pacific conductor sounded as tired as Fritzi felt. She stared out the window not with wonder, but with despair. Torrential rain hammered the glass and gushed off the red-tiled roof of the train depot.

"Conductor, what happened to the sunshine?"

"Rainy season. This way out."

She slipped and almost fell descending the metal steps. At the end of the platform four buggies and a muddy Pope-Toledo automobile awaited the arriving passengers. Across a street that resembled a lake, two pathetic palm trees shook and rattled. Where were the orange groves? Where were the suntanned natives?

"Excuse me," Fritzi said to a depot agent. "Someone from Los Angeles was supposed to meet me here. Has anyone asked for a Miss Crown?"

"Nope. Taxi man's yonder, by the far door," the agent said.

Fritzi picked up her valises and walked through the station. Outside, a man leaned against a dented Ford, holding an umbrella.

She consulted a crumpled paper. "I'm to go to the Hollywood Hotel, at Hollywood Boulevard and Highland Avenue."

"I know where it is, lady. Four dollars."

"That sounds like robbery."

"Then take another taxi." The driver flicked his eyes at puddles on either side of his black auto.

Fritzi kicked one of her valises. "The least you can do is load those for me."

His day's profit made, the taxi driver grew friendly. "Why, yes, ma'am, and we'll be off in a jiffy."

THE HOLLYWOOD HOTEL HAD a broad veranda and a comfortable, welcoming appearance. Its address was a misnomer, however. Hollywood "boulevard" was a dirt road. A trolley track ran down the center, and telephone poles marched away toward the city of Los Angeles, four or five miles behind them. Hollywood the town looked empty and rural, nothing but farmhouses and small citrus groves.

Fritzi gave the driver a tip and handed her bags to a bellhop. In her room she found a note of welcome from B. B. Pelzer's wife, Sophie, together with a small stack of flyers advertising rooms to let. Sophie had marked these and written a message on one: "All these areas are safe for young ladies. Mr. Pelzer made sure."

Next morning while Fritzi was at breakfast, B.B. showed up, apologizing for stranding her in Glendale. "I had this fella hired. He promised to be there, but when I didn't hear from him by six last night, I ran over to his garage. He said he wouldn't risk the car in the storm. By then I figured you'd either got here or hopped the next train back to New York, mad."

"The former," Fritzi said. "When may I start work?"

"Not until we finish the outdoor stage. I also want you to see the lot we leased for a studio. It's in a little neighborhood called Edendale—ain't far from here. But there's no point in you swimming through mud to do it. You might as well look for a room."

EVENTUALLY the rain stopped and the sun came out. Flyers in hand, Fritzi set out to find a place to live. The weather allowed her to walk. The homes she passed were conventional Victorian dwellings, widely scattered on the main and side streets.

She marched up the walk to the veranda of a handsome residence on Selma, checked the number in the flyer, and knocked.

"I've come about the room," she said to the elderly man who answered the door. "Is it still available?"

"Yes, 'tis. Won't you step in? I'm Mr. Moore," he said.

"Very pleased to know you. I'm Fritzi Crown."

"New in California, are you?" he asked.

"I am. I've come out to make pictures."

She saw his back stiffen. "Do I understand you're a movie?"

"I'm afraid I don't know that word, Mr. Moore."

"Movie—someone who performs in pictures. The pictures move—they're movies. The actors move too, one step ahead of the sheriff or the credit man. Never know whether they'll skip out in the night. Folks in this town don't like movies. You're not wanted here. Nothing personal, you understand."

"Oh, no, of course not. I'm sorry I troubled you."

In seven more tries over the next three days Fritzi found nothing except discouragement. At one house a placard had been tacked by the door to forestall conversation: NO JEWS. NO PETS. NO ACTORS.

One day as she ate lunch in the hotel dining room, Fritzi noticed a young woman watching her from another table. The girl had a round, plain face enlivened by striking blue eyes and a lot of curly red hair. She'd seen the young woman in the lobby the night before.

The girl walked over to Fritzi. "I've seen you reading ads for days. Are you looking for a place to live?"

"Yes, and I'm having no luck. It seems all the landlords in this town hate picture people. Movies, they call them now."

The girl nodded. "I had to go all the way to Venice to find a spot. But I did—the whole second floor of a nice house near the beach." She extended her hand. "My name's Lily Madison."

"Fritzi Crown. Are you an actress?"

"Oh, no. I write stories. That is, I'm trying. I just sold one to Nestor. I got fifteen dollars for it. Look, I don't mean to be forward, but I'm eager to find someone to share expenses."

"You mean your landlord would tolerate *two* movies?"

Lily laughed. "Yes, Mr. Hong will. His grandfather came to California from Canton, but Mr. Hong's still barred from all kinds of places. He understands having doors slammed in your face."

Fritzi pondered. "Isn't Venice a long way from town?"

"Not all that far by trolley. About a half hour. I guarantee you'd like Mr. Hong's house. There's a small room in front converted to a parlor, and two big bedrooms. Come look at it, won't you?"

"Yes, why not?" Fritzi said, pleased.

AT THE NEAT AND COMPACT house of Mr. and Mrs. Hong, Lily led Fritzi up the stairway to the front sitting room. Tall windows flooded the furniture with a golden patina. The smell of the salt sea blew in on the afternoon breeze.

"So much light—it's wonderful!" Fritzi exclaimed.

Lily grinned. "That's California."

Her spacious bedroom was on the left as you faced the front of the house. The other, on the right, was only half as large, but furnished with a good dresser, an upright wardrobe with a long mirror on the door, a chair, a bed, and three electric lamps.

Lily said, "Do you like it?"

Feeling good at last, Fritzi replied with an enthusiastic yes.

Wrong Turn • Carl drank from the double shot glass. The base of his skull ached. Whether it was nerves or the residual effect of his crash a few months ago, he didn't know. He'd been in Savannah, Georgia, for a road race and was out in front by two car lengths when the tire blew. He never remembered striking a tree headfirst.

He stared at the double whiskey, his fourth of the night. The tavern behind the sand dunes near Ormond Beach, Florida, was empty. The party had fallen apart when Barney went to the hospital.

Carl noticed the barkeep pouring liniment on a rag, which he rubbed on his wrist. Carl said, "Were you in the fight?"

"Nah. This is from pulling corks. I never pulled so many corks in so many quarts so fast in all my life."

"When Barney Oldfield celebrates, he celebrates."

"If that's what you call it," the barkeep said with a glance at the smashed chairs and tables. Carl drank again. How could a day so fine end so badly? It was Barney's temperament. Everywhere he went, he whored and gambled, drank and started fights.

That afternoon, in front of a roaring crowd that spilled over the Daytona dunes to watch, Barney had broken his own one-mile straightaway speed record of 132 miles per hour, set last year. Under a cloudless sky, Barney had driven his newest racer, a two-hundred-horsepower Benz with a gigantic four-cylinder engine. The crowd screamed when the chief judge shouted the new record—133.4.

Oil-spattered and grinning, Barney had signed autographs for nearly an hour. Then, as the sun dropped behind the western scrubland, he'd asked the location of the nearest saloon.

Two hours later Will Pickens, the team manager, had rushed him to a hospital with his scalp torn open. Carl stayed behind, drinking in the bar where the brawl had taken place.

Now it was dark. Carl's head buzzed. No hiding from the truth any longer. The dream he had chased to Indianapolis was a little dirty at the edges. He heard the beachside door open. A woman walked to the bar. He smelled her before he recognized her—the perfume she wore was something like lily of the valley. His eyes focused. "Bess."

"I hoped you might still be here." Barney's wife avoided a direct look at Carl as she put her purse on the bar. To the barkeep she said, "Give me a whiskey. Leave the bottle."

Carl said, "How's Barney?"

"Took the doctor two hours to sew up the worst, and he wasn't finished when I left. He'll be all right. Barney's got a hard head. He'll be good as new when the sun's up." She swallowed her whiskey, poured another, and swallowed that.

Carl pinched the inner corners of his eyes but couldn't clear his vision. Bess's pale, soft hand lay on his sleeve.

"Carl, I don't owe Barney anything anymore. He's cheated on me a million times. If you come right down to it, he isn't very original either. Just another dumb hick who got rich too fast and doesn't know how to handle it. You, though—you're different." She licked her lip. "Keep me company tonight."

Tempted, he gazed at her for a while before he said, "Don't think that's a good idea."

"The boss's wife? He'll never know."

"We would."

Anger made her sneer. "Little Lord Fauntleroy? I thought you were better than that." She slammed her glass on the bar. "You pay for the whiskey. I came all the way back here for nothing."

She walked out into the moonlight and disappeared.

Liberty Rising • Fritzi left the big red trolley car at Sunset Boulevard and Alessandro Street, in the district called Edendale. Following B.B.'s directions, she walked north in the morning sunshine. Edendale was rural, mostly stables. After nearly a mile she saw Pal's stout owner waving a hankie from the front of a weedy lot.

"Well, what do you think of it?" B.B. asked.

Fritzi shaded her eyes with her palm. "It's very—large."

"Three point eight acres. We got a good lease." He urged her forward through yellowed weeds that left tiny burs on her skirt.

They went up the rotted steps to the main house, a weather-battered relic with peeling paint. Out back, hammers rang.

"Offices will be in here," B.B. said in the entrance. "Al's already set up in the dining room. There's a study we'll fix up for a projection room. Hello, Al." B.B. waved at his partner. Kelly was seated at a dining-room table littered with bills and account books.

Kelly greeted them with a grunt, handed Fritzi a document. "Your contract. Look it over and sign before you go."

Fritzi examined it. "This contract's with something called Liberty Pictures."

"We got a new partner," Kelly said. "Name's Ham Hayman. He's bringing in a lot of working capital. Owns a string of theaters from Nevada to Colorado and down to Arizona."

Fritzi said, "That's fine, but why the name change?"

"For his capital Hayman gets some leverage."

"We already have a swell new symbol picked out," B.B. said.

"Let me guess. The Statue of Liberty?"

"Give the girl a prize," Kelly said. "Sign the contract today, Fritzi." He bent his head over a ledger, as if she didn't exist.

B.B. took her out through the kitchen to the rear of the lot. She saw carpenters on ladders and two familiar faces—Eddie Hearn and Jock Ferguson, who was tinkering with an unfamiliar camera. B.B. said, "We bought a new camera, a Bianchi. Jock says it's lousy. Breaks down all the time. But it don't violate any patents. We'll shoot with old faithful but keep this one for display. If detectives show up, it should keep them scratching their heads, huh?"

Jock kissed her cheek to welcome her. Eddie escorted her onto the stage, a large rectangular platform with a bare wooden floor. "We can shoot two interiors at the same time," he said. "Three if we crowd them together. B.B. and Kelly want to step up production to three reels a week—one comedy, one drama, one western. That's the standard for successful independents."

B.B. planted himself in front of Fritzi, cheerful as a cherub. "Well, my gel, what's your opinion now?"

Somewhat bewildered, she smiled. "There's a lot happening."

"And you're part of it. A big part."

For Fritzi's next picture, *The Lone Indian's Escape,* they filmed in the rugged and isolated area off North Highland known as Daisy Dell. About noon on the first day B.B. arrived in a taxi and hiked down a rough trail to where the company had set up Owen's tepee. Excited, he showed a picture postcard bearing a photograph of a hooknosed man in cowboy clothes.

"Found this yesterday, selling for a nickel at a theater. Ain't it a swell idea?" B.B. asked. Fritzi studied the legend with the photo: ESSANAY LEADING MAN "BRONCO BILLY" ANDERSON.

"Like it, Owen? Like to have your mug on one of these?"

"Anything you say, B.B." Owen folded his grease-painted arms and gave Fritzi a smug look. B.B. rushed around the crude camp table where the cast had been consuming sandwiches and tea.

"How about you, Fritzi?"

Before she could respond, Owen jumped up with all the feathers of his great warbonnet quivering. "Wait a minute. Who's the star of these pictures, may I ask?"

B.B.'s brow wrinkled in a studious way. "Why, Owen, based on the numbers of letters she gets, it's this little gel."

Owen turned a distinctly darker shade of reddish brown. "Oh, yes? Well, Mr. Pelzer, I'm not happy to hear that. I'm not happy at all." He tore off his warbonnet and threw it down. "We're having a talk about this, Mr. Pelzer. Right now."

B.B. sighed. "Okay." He and Owen hiked back up the trail. Owen's talk lasted forty-five minutes, putting them behind schedule. The talk resumed in the studio office when the company returned at sunset. It was never clear whether Pelzer fired Owen or he simply quit. Fritzi didn't learn the news until the next morning.

"I want to know how we finish the picture," Kelly said.

"We find another Big Chief Hot Air." B.B. captured Fritzi's hand. "This is the one we got to take care of, Al. This little gel is the star."

The *star?* No one had ever used the word in reference to Fritzi. She knew she should be thrilled. In a certain way she was. Mostly she was terrified.

Fritzi and Carl • The three cars—Barney Oldfield's white one, a green one, and Carl's yellow racer—took the starting flag and roared off for the final heat. Fritzi jumped up and down along with hundreds of others packed into the wooden amphitheater at Playa del Rey, within sight and sound of the Pacific. "Come on, Carl. Beat him, beat him."

This Sunday, in late April, Fritzi had no illusions about Carl beating Oldfield. He'd written to explain the rigged exhibition races. Even so, natural excitement drove her to cheer wildly.

Gas and oil fumes mingled in the exhaust smoke rising off the track. Two laps from the finish, Oldfield suddenly cut in front of Carl, clipping his left front fender as he passed. The impact sent Carl toward the grandstand wall, then into a spin when he corrected. Oldfield shot ahead. Carl finished a bad last.

Fritzi fought her way down the stairs through the crowd afterward. She spied Carl off by himself, climbing out of oil-stained coveralls. Fritzi caught her breath when she saw a nasty purplish bruise on his left cheek. "Carl?" She waved.

"Sis, how are you?" He flung his arms around her. She drew back, gently touched his bruised face. "What on earth is this?"

"A little fracas last night. Never mind, it isn't serious."

"How long will you be in town?" Fritzi asked.

"Till the end of the week. Give me five minutes to clean up, and we'll get out of here."

When he rejoined her, his face was washed, his hands too. He'd put on a jacket and wrapped a red silk scarf around his neck.

Back in Venice, Fritzi showed him where she lived. As daylight faded, they strolled through her neighborhood and found a small German restaurant for supper. Over platters of porkchops, cabbage, roast potatoes, and Crown's beer, they caught up on things.

Carl talked with enthusiasm of his new interest in learning to fly airplanes. Describing a driving exhibition in Denver, he mentioned a girl named Sissie. Fritzi said, "I also recall a Margaret and someone in El Paso. Forgive me for being a nosy sister, but are you ever going to marry one of them?"

Carl's face grew grave. "Not likely. There was one I really cared about in Detroit. Her name was Tess. I thought hard about staying, trying to make it work out, but— I don't know. Something pushed me on. How about your life? Any men in it?"

"Not presently, no."

"What about the actors? Aren't some of them pretty handsome?"

"Yes, but they all seem to fall into three categories. Married and happy. Married and cheating. Or madly in love with themselves."

He laughed. "Do you want to settle down sometime?"

"Well, I have my career to think about. The partners at Liberty feel that things are going so well out here that they've decided not to return to New York for the summer. But someday I'd like to try the theater again. I've always said picturemaking's temporary."

"Sis, answer the question."

"Of course I care about settling down."

To escape the subject, she opened her handbag and drew out a picture postcard. "Here, I've been meaning to show you."

When Carl saw the photo, he exclaimed, "Hey, it's you!" Indeed it was Fritzi, in a frilly dress and a picture hat, with printing beneath: FRITZI CROWN, A LIBERTY PICTURES FAVORITE.

Mickey Finn • Carl sat at a table with a plate of pickled sausages, a pencil, and a postcard. It was five o'clock, a day after his outing with Fritzi. He hadn't mailed a card to Tess in months, had no idea whether she would receive this one.

About a dozen men lined the long mahogany bar of the tavern. Carl wrote a line about his interest in airplanes. At ten past five the door opened and Barney swaggered in, chewing on a cigar. He spotted Carl. "Greetings, kid. How are you?"

"Doing all right, Barney. How about you?"

"Soon as I get a snootful, I'll be better." He hovered by the table. "Have a good visit with your sister?"

"Fine, thanks."

"Come on up to the bar. I'll buy a drink."

"I just had a beer. I don't think—"

"The boss wants to buy you a drink," Barney cut in. Reluctantly Carl slipped pencil and postcard into his coat pocket.

"Sure, I'll have one with you."

Customers greeted Barney as he and Carl stepped up to the rail. Barney waved his cold cigar. "Milo, give Carl a slug of that special stock we keep for friends. Make it doubles all around."

Barney leaned back, elbows on the bar. Without looking at Carl, he said, "My wife told me something I didn't like to hear, kid."

"What's that?"

"You talk about me behind my back. That true?"

Carl was surprised. "No."

Milo served two glasses of dark whiskey. With a little smile Barney said, "You wouldn't be calling Bess a liar, would you?"

Hell's fire. Ever since Carl had rebuffed Bess, she'd had it in for him. "No, Barney, I'm not saying a word against your wife. I'm only saying I don't talk behind your back."

"Well, we got two different stories here, don't we? Kind of hard to know which to believe. Gotta think it over. Drink up."

Carl took a big drink of the strong, faintly bitter whiskey. Barney finished his double in two gulps.

"We got to sort this out, Carl. I can't have a driver going around behind my back saying rotten things about the champ."

"Barney, let's talk about this some other—"

"Now." Barney shoved three stiffened fingers into Carl's chest. "We'll talk about it now."

Carl's ears erupted in buzzing. He saw two tiepins, not one, on Barney's cravat. Something sour churned in his throat.

Barney smiled. " 'Less you aren't feeling so good. You look a little green, kid."

So that was it. Nauseated and woozy, Carl crossed his arms over his heaving belly. Barney loved pranks, one of his favorites being knockout drops in a drink offered in friendship. Carl swung around, yelled at Milo. "Damn it, did you slip me a Mickey Finn?"

Milo dried a glass with a towel and didn't look up.

Swaying, Carl said to Barney, "You came in here to set me up."

"Yeah. I been meaning to settle accounts for weeks. Bess says you're a bum. A dirty lecher."

"Let me tell you"—Carl grabbed the bar as his knees went rubbery on him—"about your sweet, innocent wife."

Barney picked up his refilled glass and threw the liquor in Carl's face. "You say one word about her, I'll kill you."

Carl cocked his fist. But before he could swing, the room tilted and he felt himself going down. His head slammed the floor.

"You bum. Call my wife a liar, will you?" Barney kicked Carl's ribs. "You're through. You're fired." Conversation in the saloon had stopped. "Couple of you boys throw him in the alley," Barney said.

Rough hands seized Carl's wrists, dragged him across the floor. That was all he remembered.

CARL left his seedy downtown hotel that night, all his worldly possessions packed in one leather grip with a broken clasp. He had only four dollars. After turning up the collar of his coat, he trudged out of the central city. His head hurt. His mouth tasted like sewage. Around midnight he lay down in an orange grove and slept.

The next morning, dusty and sweaty, Carl raised his arm to hide the red sun. What he'd glimpsed from far down the road, distorted by wavy heat devils, took on clarity and detail.

The machine sat on its tail and two oversized solid wheels, next to a red barn. The biplane's yellow wings were patched in many places. The pilot's seat was small, directly in front of the pusher motor. In front of the seat was a control rod with a wheel. A sign on the barn advertised PROFESSIONAL AERONAUTICS INSTRUCTION: RIP RYAN, OWNER-AERONAUT.

From inside the barn came the sound of hammering. Carl discovered an open door. He walked in, saw a man on his knees with a hammer, trying to drive a nail with a misshapen hand. His fingers were gnarled as old roots.

"Hello," Carl said. "Got any work here?"

Rip Ryan of Riverside, California, was bent as a hilltop sapling tormented by the wind. Not much more than forty, he had a full head of white hair. He laid his hammer down and took a good ten seconds to rise.

"There might be work," he said after Carl introduced himself. "I know there's some coffee. Leave your grip and come on."

Carl followed him to a tiny cottage near the barn. It was slow going, for the small, wiry man listed to the left at every other step. Crooked fingers clutched the knob of a polished stick. "Arthritis," he said when he caught Carl staring. "Curse of my life."

They sat at a scarred table, and Ryan poured coffee from a blue enamel pot. Carl asked, "Who taught you to fly?"

"Pilot who knew Glenn Curtiss. You know who Curtiss is?"

Carl nodded. Like the Wright brothers, young Curtiss had owned a bicycle shop. Before he built and raced his own planes in competition with the Wrights, Curtiss was a familiar name in motorcycle racing—a chaser of land speed records, like Barney. Then Curtiss adapted his compact motorcycle engine for airplanes.

"His method is peculiar, but it works," Ryan said. "I soared like an angel. Forty-four years old and I felt life was just starting. Then"—he held up his malformed hands—"this. I can't fly anymore, but I can teach others. You have any desire to fly?"

"I do, definitely."

"Then I can teach you. No cost, but you'd have to help me build an addition to the barn."

"I'm your man," Carl said.

"Thought you might be when you walked in," Ryan said.

Carl Mows the Grass • Carl slept in Ryan's hayloft, warm and se-cure with blankets to cover him and straw to cushion him. The food was good. Rip Ryan loved to eat—huge meals of steak and eggs and local fruit and vegetables.

The barn addition went up fairly rapidly, thanks to Carl's strength and mobility. Once a week a local physician drove out for a flying lesson. Ryan was true to his word. He never touched the plane, just sat on a barrel by the landing strip, observing and instructing. At three thirty on a Tuesday, Carl took his first lesson.

"She's easier to pilot than a Wright plane," Ryan said as Carl climbed up on the small, hard seat in front of the motor. "Take the wheel in your hands. That's right. Push her forward, the plane will nose down. Pull back, she'll come up."

Ryan first had him get the feel of the controls by sitting in the plane with the motor off. Carl slipped into the shoulder harness connected to short ailerons mounted between the ends of the upper and lower wings. When he leaned left or right, the harness moved the ailerons.

His driving experience helped him learn quickly. In a matter of days Ryan fired up the engine and stood back while Carl taxied on the half-mile grass strip behind the barn. Ryan had wired the throt-tle so the plane couldn't lift off by accident. Carl bumped up and down the field. This exercise of beating back and forth Ryan called "mowing the grass."

When Ryan was satisfied with Carl's progress, he guided Carl through the installation of a special practice propeller that allowed the plane to race down the field and lift six or eight feet off the ground. Carl's first flight of about thirty-five feet set the blood singing in his ears and made him feel like a conqueror of gravity. His second flight carried him fifty feet, ten feet above the field.

Finally they mounted the regular flight propeller. With his belly knotted, Carl opened the throttle as he sped down the field, drew the wheel back, and felt the lift beneath the wings. The plane left the ground. He climbed slowly to two hundred feet, watching the world expand to an incredible panorama of orange groves and country lanes. For fifteen minutes he practiced long, slow turns, climbs into the sun, gliding descents. He landed with a feathery thump and a long roll, killing the motor six feet from his mentor.

Ryan hobbled over to the plane. "You've got the touch. A few more practice flights, the bird'll be ready to leave the nest."

ON A lazy June afternoon, with bees making noise in the flower beds Ryan cultivated near the cottage, they examined the new Dutch door in the barn's addition. Ryan slammed it several times, then declared the addition completed.

"So what now?" Ryan said as they returned to the cottage.

"I'd like to get a job flying airplanes. Are there any jobs like that?"

With one of his rare smiles Ryan said, "Sure, if you don't mind risking your life once or twice a day."

"I've done it before," Carl said.

In the kitchen Ryan fetched a smudged business card for RENE LEMAYE, CIRCUS OF THE AIR. The card bore a one-line address: GENERAL DELIVERY, EL PASO, TEXAS.

"This boyo passed through with his show last fall. Exhibition fliers. He told me pilots quit on him all the time because the stunts are dangerous."

"Frenchman?"

"Right. Lot of them interested in planes. This Rene told me the Sheldon Hotel in El Paso always knows where he's appearing."

"I'll look him up."

"Have you got money for a rail ticket?"

"I don't need a ticket. I jump on freights."

"Isn't that dangerous?"

"No more dangerous than flying." Or working for Barney.

"Well, you may be just the kind of crazy fool the Frenchman wants."

Ryan shuffled his way to the stove. They tore into a hearty meal of roast beef, snap beans, and homemade sourdough bread, washed down with some bourbon whiskey that Ryan kept for special occasions. He said, "I've liked your company. I'll hate to see you go."

"I appreciate what you taught me."

"Send a new aeronaut out into the world, it's like sending your-self. Well, almost." He saluted Carl with the whiskey, then knocked it back in swift gulps.

Loyal • Now and again Fritzi daydreamed of Harry Poland, his charm, his adoring looks—which ought to be reserved for his wife, she thought, bringing herself up short whenever she recalled him too fondly. Then in April 1912 something happened to banish memories of Paul's friend and fill her with happiness. It started, ironically enough, on a day when the papers were full of tragedy. The great liner *Titanic,* termed unsinkable by her builders, had struck an iceberg on her maiden crossing to New York and carried fifteen hundred people to their death.

Owen's replacement, Geoffrey Germann, and Fritzi were filming *The Lone Indian's Squaw* at Daisy Dell, the remote glen off North Highland. Eddie found it difficult to get cast and crew to concentrate. Nearly all of them, including Fritzi, had their noses in the *Times.*

"Let's go, let's go," Eddie stormed, clapping his hands. Sighing, Fritzi folded her paper. He was beginning to sound like Kelly.

For the first time she noticed the two extras hired to play outlaws in the picture. One was short, bowlegged, and forgettable, but the other caught her eye. He was tall, with a mahogany sunburn, gaunt cheeks, and a bold nose. His weathered jeans and shirt fit him nat-urally. Long brown hair hung down to his collar. Eddie introduced him as Loy—a strange name. She asked where he was from. "Texas," he said, touching his hatbrim. That was that. The man was polite, did what he was told, but didn't socialize.

The company returned to Edendale to finish a final day of shoot-ing on the stage, in front of flats representing the interior of a trad-ing post. Several buckets of rye flour stood in for a dirt floor.

Eddie's scenario included a switch on a scene already a western cliché: the badmen firing pistols to make the hapless tenderfoot dance. This time the victim was Fritzi, wearing a fringed and beaded Indian dress presented to her earlier in the story by the hero.

Loy and his partner shot blanks at Fritzi's feet. She fought back with an improvised dance that kicked dirt in their faces, then disarmed the badmen, ready to hand them over to the Lone Indian as he burst in. Eddie rehearsed the scene and filmed it in one take.

Since Kelly was nowhere to be seen, Eddie asked to do it again, urging Fritzi to "let yourself go." This time her dance for the stupefied outlaws lasted a full twenty seconds—a wild combination of ballet, soft shoe, clog, one-step, with a French cancan finish, ideal for kicking the tall Texan in the stomach. Jock Ferguson laughed so hard he had to signal his assistant to grab the crank. When Eddie called cut, Fritzi rushed to the Texan.

"I hope I didn't hurt you."

"No, ma'am, not a bit."

Eddie laughed. "Wasn't it swell?"

Loy beat his high-crowned Texas hat on his leg to knock off flour. "Sure was. This lady's mighty funny."

Eddie said, "We've known that for a long time. I'm trying to think up a comedy character for her."

"Oh, please," Fritzi said. "Let me be a serious actress for a few pictures."

Eddie shrugged. "If that's what you want. B.B. told me to keep you happy."

"That's a good thought," Loy said with a pleasant nod. He jumped down from the stage and walked off. Fritzi wanted to follow and talk to him. Unfortunately, Eddie said they were done. The extras strolled away toward the main house for their pay. Neither of them looked back or said good-bye.

COWBOYS were drawn to Los Angeles because the standard weekly output of almost every picture company consisted of a comedy, a drama, and a western. The cowboys came from all over the West. They hung out at Cahuenga and Hollywood Boulevard, a dusty corner already christened the Waterhole. Studios sent trucks to the Waterhole to pick up extras for the day.

At the end of the week of filming *The Lone Indian's Squaw,* Eddie didn't need her one afternoon, so Fritzi took the studio's new

Packard for a solo drive. By now she had completed a series of driving lessons, and she drove with confidence. But Fritzi knew nothing about the internal workings of autos, so she was alarmed when the Packard coughed and began to balk. She pulled to the curb alongside a horse trough. After one loud gasp the Packard quit. She looked around to see where fate had stranded her.

The Waterhole. Though it was too late in the day for hiring, a few cowboys were still loitering. Not wanting to look simple, she jumped out and started to unfasten the leather strap holding the hood shut. A shadow fell across the shiny blue metal. "Having trouble, little lady?"

From the unctuous tone she knew she wouldn't like the speaker even before she sized him up. He was a plump young man, wearing new jeans, a big white sombrero, and a flowing purple neckerchief. With a smarmy smile he took hold of her arm.

"You just sit back in the car, and I'll see to this tin horse."

"No, thank you," she said, flinging his hand off.

He grabbed her wrist. "Listen, lady, when someone tries to help and be nice, you ought—"

Someone walked around the corner; his long shadow fell in the street. The bold nose was familiar, as were the crow's-feet around his squinted eyes. The Texan strolled over to the Packard, where Fritzi stood wide-eyed. "Thad, why don't you light out of here and leave this lady be?"

The gaudy cowboy spun around. "What the devil you butting in for, Loy?"

"You're pestering a young lady who don't seem to want it."

Loy dismissively turned his back on him. Behind the Texan, Thad reddened. He slammed a fist into the back of Loy's head.

Loy fell forward, catching himself on the Packard fender. Thad regretted his sneak attack even before Loy turned to give him a look. In two quick strides the Texan had a wad of Thad's shirt in his fist. With his other hand he punched Thad's gut. Thad staggered sideways. His hat fell off. His eyes bulged. The Texan boomed a left under Thad's chin that dumped him into the horse trough.

Water splashed as Thad came up flailing. Loy grabbed his sopping shirt and said, "Don't let me catch you on this corner again."

The battered victim climbed out of the trough. He picked up his soaked sombrero and limped around the corner.

Loy came back over to Fritzi. "Some of these town dudes figure that if they dress the part, that's all it takes. Let's see the problem here. Can't get your machine to run?"

"No. I don't know what went wrong."

He unscrewed the lid of the round fuel tank and put his eye near the opening. "Dry as the Rio Grande in a drought. There's a store just up the way sells gas. I'll be right back."

Soon the tall man came loping back with a tin of gas. He poured it into the tank with a steady hand. "That should take you home."

"I'm very grateful to you. May I know your full name?"

"Loyal Hardin. Most call me Loy."

"I'm Fritzi Crown."

"Sure, I remember. Liberty."

"I must pay you for the gas and your trouble."

"Oh, no, ma'am. Glad I could help." He had a deep voice, an easy manner. She drank in details: his cracked boots, his worn leather vest. Just the sight of him made her hot and dizzy.

Heart racing, Fritzi spoke in a rush. "If you're looking for more picture work, I know we have another western starting in three weeks." She knew no such thing—she'd beg Eddie to write one.

"Three weeks? Afraid I won't be here. Catching a steamer for Alaska. Never seen that part of the world."

"Will you come back to Los Angeles?"

"I expect so. I like picture work."

"Perhaps we'll meet again."

"Sure, that'd be nice." Their eyes held for a second. He touched the brim of his hat. "Adios, Miss Crown." He went around the corner and on up Cahuenga.

Flying Circus • Carl rode the boxcars to El Paso and asked for Rene LeMaye at the Sheldon Hotel. He was told that LeMaye's aerial exhibition team was making an eight-week circuit of Arkansas and Oklahoma. Carl washed dishes in a restaurant for two months. At the end of that time LeMaye returned to his base. He interviewed Carl in the bar of the Sheldon.

Rene LeMaye was a small, squinty man of forty. He'd learned to fly in France. His remarks to Carl in fractured English were candid, not to say blunt. "I will try you out tomorrow on our oldest plane. If you don't crash it to pieces, I'll hire you. Our troupe is different from many touring your country. We are not demonstrating machines in order to sell them. We have nothing to sell but *le frisson.* The fluttering heart. The leaping stomach. Death-defying aerial stunts by daredevils. For the fliers too it is exciting—like drinking fine brandy or having a new woman. Can you deal with all that, *mon ami?*"

"I can," Carl said, with more hope than certainty.

After a successful tryout Rene hired him. In the weeks that followed, Carl discovered that the little man had spoken truthfully. The yells and cheers rising from a packed grandstand after a dangerous stunt were heady wine. Once, he had thought he should spend his life with racecars. Traveling from fairground to fairground with Rene's troupe, he realized he'd been wrong. He really belonged aloft, with the wind and clouds and air currents, challenged by a fragile machine that could carry him to spectacular heights or fail and kill him in an instant.

English Edgar • Fritzi and her roommate, Lily, rode the big red trolley to Edendale six, sometimes seven days a week. Lily had begun writing scenarios for Liberty Pictures. She was facile, quick; she had a gift for telling stories. Pelzer liked her work.

The Edendale neighborhood was growing busy. Michael Sinnott, whom Fritzi remembered meeting in D. W. Griffith's office in New York, had been rechristened Mack Sennett. He was now in California, directing cop comedies for Biograph on a lot up the street. Mack's company was called Keystone, after the logo of the Pennsylvania Railroad, which he freely appropriated. Mack had brought some dependable actors out west with him. He continued to produce the kind of zany police comedies Griffith had dismissed as silly.

Geoffrey Germann's wife worked as a freelance costumer for picture companies. In the late summer of 1913 she was employed at Mack Sennett's lot up the street. Geoff invited Fritzi to join them for an evening showing of a new picture, followed by a picnic.

Sennett's lot resembled Liberty's, though it had a more imposing entrance—a wooden arch with a large sign reading MACK SENNETT, KEYSTONE COMEDIES.

Sennett greeted Fritzi warmly by the picnic tables. She congratulated him on his success. "It's wonderful. You're a tycoon. Your very own studio."

"It isn't as grand as it looks. For the first time I'm responsible for a payroll. And a pile of debt." Despite his disclaimers, Sennett looked very successful in his fine three-piece linen suit.

"Mr. Griffith's moved here permanently, hasn't he?"

"Yes, and most of the old Biograph gang came too. Billy Bitzer, Lionel Barrymore, the Gish girls. Hey, there's my leading lady. Over here, Mabel."

He introduced Fritzi to a voluptuous five-foot brunette with snapping dark eyes. Fritzi and Mabel Normand hit it off and were soon chatting like old friends. As Fritzi listened to Mabel tell a joke, she was aware of the attention she was getting from a funny little fellow with wavy dark hair and bold eyes. Mabel introduced him as Charles Chaplin. "He's new. Our nickname for him's English Edgar."

"Charmed," said English Edgar, alias Chaplin. He kissed Fritzi's hand and batted his eyes. Then he tipped his derby and let it tumble brim over crown straight down his arm to his waiting hand. A show-off, but an amusing one.

Chaplin sat beside her on the grass during the showing of the new picture, *Fatty's Fabulous Feast.* A pastry cook, played by Roscoe "Fatty" Arbuckle, was pursued by Sennett's comic policemen, who mistook him for a jewel thief. Afterward, in the soft summer dark where fireflies winked, Chaplin tipped his hat once more, this time as a gesture of politeness. "Very enjoyable meeting you, Miss Crown. I hope I have the pleasure again."

Their paths were soon to cross. One Saturday night in September, Fritzi said yes to Lily's invitation to go to Poodles in Venice, where a colored jazz band played loud, peppy music. Not being welcome in established social circles, picture people entertained themselves with their own movable party. Every Thursday night the Hollywood Hotel rolled up its lobby rugs for dancing. Friday there was a picnic and dancing way out at Inceville, the ranch where director Thomas Ince filmed his westerns. Saturdays the party moved to Poodles.

The night out lifted Fritzi's spirits. A glass of Crown lager furthered the process. About nine o'clock Mack Sennett walked in with Mabel and Chaplin. As Mabel sat down, Mack saw Fritzi and waved. Chaplin came over, affecting a comic waddle that reminded Fritzi of a penguin. He let his hat tumble down his sleeve, bowed.

"Dear lady, care to step around the floor with me?"

"Yes, but what should I call you. Edgar or Charles?"

He led her by the hand. "Charlie, please."

The tune was "Oh, Gee," a Harry Poland fox-trot. Charlie was expert on his feet, whirling Fritzi until she began to feel giddy.

"Another lager?" he asked when the music stopped. "Or would you prefer a stroll on the pier? It's a lovely night."

"Yes. Let's go out."

The music of the band faded. On the long fishing pier a balmy breeze warmed Fritzi. The moonlit Pacific murmured.

"Allow me to pay you a compliment," Charlie said. "I saw *The Lone Indian's Escape* the other night. Very funny. You have crisp moves. Fine timing. You deserve better comic material."

"What, and get hit in the face with blueberry pies all my life?" Fritzi mugged. "I keep trying to be a serious actress."

"Nothing more serious than comedy, love. It requires precise planning and flawless execution." When he saw her reaction, he shrugged. "You've the wrong attitude. On the screen your face shines like a diamond. One can't help watching."

"That's silly. I'm not pretty."

"Pretty is common. Worth a penny or two. What you have, a kind of brightness—that's a thousand-dollar bill."

They reached the end of the pier and leaned on the railing. The full moon scattered needles of light on the sea. Charlie took her hand in his. "May I tell you something? I find you damnably attractive. Would you come back to my hotel room?"

Fritzi's heart raced. She was flattered. He couldn't know how the proposition had lifted her spirits. A respectable man found her worth looking at. Now, if only Loyal Hardin would . . .

Stroking her hand, he whispered, "My dear?"

"Charlie, I like you a lot, truly. But not enough to— Well, you understand. I hope you don't think I'm a terrible prude."

"If I thought that, I wouldn't have spoken in the first place. Is there someone else, may I ask?"

Fritzi gazed at the ocean. "I hope so."

"That's an odd answer."

"I know. I'm sorry. I hope we can still be friends."

"Well, my pride is damaged. I shall just have to take it in stride." He smiled and batted his eyes.

Fritzi laughed. She liked this brash little fellow.

Inceville • In March 1914 Pathé premièred the first episode of a chapter play called *The Perils of Pauline.* Overnight an actress named Pearl White became a star, and the serial form became the rage of Hollywood. Working together, Eddie and Lily wrote scenarios for twelve episodes of *The Adventures of Alice* by April, and they were rushed into production. Fritzi was dragooned for the title role, a spunky heiress whose villainous relative sought to do her out of her inheritance by doing her in.

She was tied to a moving buzz-saw belt, chained to a post, thrown from a runaway freight train (a dummy substituted), and subjected to other indignities. The shooting schedule ran into early summer. The first episodes, released in June, were instant hits.

On a golden summer Saturday, Fritzi met her new friend Charlie for lunch at a general store across the road from Mack's studio. They bought bologna sandwiches and sodas and retired to a trestle table in a sunny grape arbor next to the store.

Charlie's costume of the day consisted of oversized shoes, baggy pants, a too tight coat, a too small derby, and a cane. Fritzi commented on it, since she hadn't seen it before.

"Then you've missed my latest pictures, dear one. One morning a while back Sennett discovered a hole in the schedule. He gave me thirty minutes to come up with a character. I grabbed any wardrobe pieces I could find and added the mustache as a last touch. The picture I'm working on is my third as the little tramp."

"Have the others done well?"

"Smashingly. The theaters are clamoring for more. I'm very pleased. Say, I'm invited to a barbecue tomorrow. A special party for some actor Tom Ince has engaged. Care to go?"

Fritzi had laundry and mending waiting and a letter to write to her mother. "Thanks, but I don't think I should. Where is it?"

"Rather a long way. The Inceville ranch."

Cowboys? "I'll go. What time?"

THE next day Charlie hired a buggy. The June afternoon was glorious. The drive to northern Santa Monica took an hour.

Tom Ince had quickly become one of the town's premier directors. He filmed his big-scale westerns on eighteen thousand acres once part of a Spanish rancho.

They passed through an elaborate ranch gate and climbed a steep road to a bluff overlooking the Pacific. Fragrant mesquite smoke from a barbecue drifted over them as Charlie parked among similar buggies and a few autos. A large crowd, perhaps two hundred, were socializing around long food tables. Paper lanterns decorated an open-air stage, where a few couples were dancing to music provided by a fiddle and a squeezebox.

Charlie introduced Fritzi to Ince, a portly, genial man with dark hair and lively eyes. He in turn introduced them to his new player, a hawk-featured man named Bill Hart. Fritzi and Charlie filled their plates with shredded pork and potato salad. Cattle and oxen lowed in the ranch barn. Restless mustangs trotted around a horse corral.

The ranch fascinated Fritzi. Tough-looking men in cowboy clothes with a touch of swagger outnumbered women two or three to one. Quite a few of the men packed pistols in holsters.

Finished eating, Fritzi and Charlie strolled to the bluff and spent a while watching the sun descend to the Pacific. On their way back to the picnic tables Charlie excused himself to look for feminine diversion. Fritzi walked to the outdoor stage and sat on a nail keg. A half hour passed, when suddenly she noticed a tall cowboy walking out of the dark toward her.

Fritzi was alternately hot and cold. Thirty-three years old, and she felt twelve. Her legs wobbled. Her mouth dried up and so did her words.

"Howdy again, Fritzi. You 'member me?" Loy was bareheaded, his long, dark hair shiny where it curled over his collar.

"Oh, yes—yes, I do," she stammered. "You, ah, you've been away a long time, Mr. Hardin."

"Longer than I expected, that's true. After I poked around Alaska for six months, I went to Mexico till I hankered to hear English again." He smiled. "You here with anyone?"

"I came with Mr. Chaplin over there. He's an actor at Keystone." Charlie had gathered three young ladies and was mugging and cavorting for them. "Are you working for Mr. Ince?"

"I'm an extra in the new picture with that scissorbill Hart."

"Scissorbill?"

"Old Texas expression. Means somebody who can't throw a loop or do anything else the right way. A tenderfoot."

"That's right—you're from Texas."

"Yes'm. Little spot in the road called Muleshoe. You go to Lubbock; then you ask for a map." He smiled that melting smile. Fritzi was nearly delirious.

"Do you have family in Texas?"

His smile remained, but it seemed a little hollow. "One sister, that's all."

The squeezebox and fiddle swung into the waltz from *The Merry Widow.* Loy said, "Care to walk around the ranch?"

"Why don't we dance?"

"Well now, I must admit I don't know how to do that."

"You can learn. It isn't hard." She took his hand and led him to the crowded floor. "Right hand goes around my waist, left one up here in the air. Here we go. *One*-two-three, *one*-two-three—that's the idea."

A few seconds passed without mishap; he seemed to be getting the hang of it. Then suddenly his boot crushed down on Fritzi's left toe. Her leg nearly buckled.

"Oh, my Lord, I'm sorry," he said.

"It's nothing. I hardly felt it!" she cried, smiling to hide the pain. His grip on her waist strengthened. His hand held hers more firmly. He swung her, and they waltzed under the California stars. It was absurdly old-fashioned and deliriously romantic.

For the next hour she and Loy Hardin walked and talked. He soon dropped into an easy, conversational familiarity. He talked about all the cowboys pouring into Hollywood, most of whom he dismissed as scissorbills. He mentioned one cowboy friend, Tom Mix of Oklahoma, whom he respected as the genuine article.

Charlie came over with his arm around one of the girls, whom he introduced as Princess Laughing Water. She responded with a loony giggle.

"We should start back to town," Charlie said to Fritzi.

She hesitated. "I hope we'll see each other again, Loyal."

"That'd be fun." Fun? Was that all?

"Might work in one of your pictures. You never know," he added as he shook her hand.

On the drive back along the moonlit Pacific shore, Charlie said, "Is that cowboy the person you referred to when you told me there was someone else?" Fritzi nodded. "You fancy him, eh?"

"I do. I can't quite explain why."

"Who can explain *amour*? And why bother? Just enjoy it. What do you know about the fellow?"

"He's from Texas. He's footloose. That's about all."

"I'm not sure he's the marrying kind. Could be more the hotel-room kind. I'm an expert on that breed, being one myself."

She laughed and gigged him with her elbow. "Don't I know it."

· **The Day Things Slipped** • Eddie scheduled filming of *The Cowgirl and the Flivver* for the following Tuesday through Friday. As usual before starting a new picture, Fritzi slept poorly. By the time she reached Edendale, the sun was lighting the eastern mountains and carpenters were carrying their tools onto the lot. Liberty was undergoing a rapid and dramatic expansion.

Yellow pine framing for an addition to the main house was already standing. A new division of the company had been organized. Its product would consist exclusively of features—pictures of three to six reels. Studios believed short pictures would never go out of style, but features had a developing audience.

In a new building devoted to costumes and makeup, Fritzi changed into her cowgirl outfit, finding herself mostly thumbs. One of the pins holding the padding inside her one-piece combination brassiere and bloomers was open. She closed it hurriedly, fidgeting and jittering because Eddie had hired Loy for the picture.

Eddie said he couldn't hold him past Friday. "He's working on Griffith's big Civil War opus out in the valley. Sounds like Griffith's hired every horseman from here to Tijuana. Two dollars a day and a box lunch for wearing the blue or the gray. It must be some picture."

The morning's first shot took them to a stable a little way up the street. Eddie's assistant, a twenty-year-old beanpole named Morris Isenhour, or Mo, arrived driving a secondhand Model T, bought and repainted for the picture. He parked it by the fenced stable yard.

The three extras showed up on schedule, dressed like ranch hands. Loy strolled over to Fritzi, tipped his tall sugar-loaf hat. "How've you been, ma'am? Looking forward to this. Hear it's a comedy." With that, he walked off. She watched the way his old holster and highly realistic revolver rode on his right leg. The man excited her beyond belief.

The picture involved a modern-minded rancher who gave his daughter a Ford for her twenty-first birthday. The daughter resisted the idea of giving up her favorite mount, Old Paint, for the auto. Convinced it was a useless contraption, she struggled through various attempts to master the car the same way she'd break a horse.

In the first scene Fritzi had to try to mount the Model T like a horse. She approached the car, nervously aware of the three cowboys watching. About to raise her left foot as though to a stirrup, she saw a flicker of motion under the Model T. She heard a rattle.

Instinct told her not to move. Eddie said, "What's wrong? Go ahead and— Oh, my Lord."

The yellow-brown snake was four feet long. The diamond-shaped head came up with fangs dripping, eyes glittery as black ice.

Fritzi's legs quivered like willow wands. Behind her Loy said, "Stand still." She heard the click of a hammer cocking. He fired one shot, then, rapidly, three more. The snake was blown in half.

She collapsed in Eddie's arms. Everyone shouted questions at her. She said, "Yes, I'm all right. Just shaky."

"He was a real grandpa," Loy said. "Look at the length of his rattles." He walked over to Fritzi. "Sure you're all right?"

"Yes. You were quick with that pistol. You're no scissorbill."

He liked that and laughed.

In the afternoon they returned to the lot. B.B. brought his wife, Sophie, out to watch them shoot on the outdoor stage. The scene involved an exchange with Fritzi's troublesome ranch hand, Loy. When he got fresh, she fended him off with a wrench and a motor-oil can filled with chocolate syrup. At the end of the slapstick tussle he churlishly dumped the "motor oil" on her head.

After they shot the scene, Sophie elbowed her husband. "That cowboy's a handsome fella. Very manly, don't you think?"

"Didn't notice."

"Well, notice, notice. Ought to have a better part, that fella."

ORDINARILY Eddie Hearn didn't welcome visitors on his set. He made an exception when Fritzi's friend Charlie showed up unannounced on Thursday morning, looking debonair in a smart new suit. Fritzi expressed surprise that he wasn't working.

"But I am. For a new studio, Essanay. They offered me a lot more dough. I leave for San Francisco the end of the week. What happens here?" he asked with a nod at the flats representing the rear and side walls of a ranch-house parlor doubling as an office.

"The rustler's driven my cattle off. He's robbing the safe before he escapes. The Model T gets me back in time to stop him. I drive it through that wall, jump out, and foil him."

"Fascinating. Why not simply walk in the door?"

"Because he's put some kind of cactus paste in the gas tank. It makes the car loco."

Charlie rolled his eyes.

Fritzi was hot and uncomfortable in the summer heat. She tugged the front of her dress. The padding seemed loose. That damned pin again. Did she have time to run behind the stage and fix it? No. Eddie's voice boomed, "Everyone ready? Mo, start the car."

A few seconds later she heard the Model T puttering on a ramp behind the flat. Kelly had appeared from somewhere, folding his arms over his vest and planting himself next to the camera.

"Get it right the first time, Hearn. I'm not rebuilding this set."

Loy pulled his bandanna high on his nose to conceal his face and crouched down behind a black iron safe that stood open. Fritzi climbed into the Model T. Then Eddie called camera and action. She gritted her teeth and accelerated up the ramp, smashing through painted wallboards. She braked in a cloud of plaster dust.

On his knees at the safe, Loy reacted as Fritzi jumped out of the car, saying, "Caught you, Roy. This means jail." Eddie insisted on appropriate dialogue rather than improvisations such as "Stop hamming" or "What time's lunch?"

Fritzi started a dash across the room, but someone had set a footstool in the wrong place. Seeing it too late, she fell over it and broke it. She saved herself by shooting her hands out and turning a somersault. Jock Ferguson called, "Cut?"

"No, no. Keep rolling. That was funny," Eddie said.

"Wait a damn minute," Kelly protested. Eddie outshouted him. *"Jock, keep cranking."*

By now Fritzi had bounded up, only to discover that her gay deceivers had betrayed her—come unpinned and slipped down, so that she had one lump more or less in the middle of her chest, the other near her hip. It struck her as hilarious in a macabre way.

Impulsively she turned her back to the camera, reached under her collar and brassiere, and, with exaggerated wiggles of hips and shoulders, worked the padding upward to its right place. She turned around and smiled at the camera. Both bosoms promptly slid down to her waist.

She mugged, gave the padding a ferocious sideways wrench. The scene was beyond saving anyway. She popped her eyes at Loy, stuck out her index finger as a pistol, and cried, "Hands up." Caught between surprise and mirth, he raised both hands. Fritzi grabbed them and began to waltz. Not watching too carefully, she waltzed him into a chair. He bumped it, reeled away, and fell. Trying to help him stand, she lost her balance. Grabbing the shelf of a china cabinet to catch herself, she spilled and shattered plates, saucers, and cups. Playing along, Loy charged her but misjudged his position and went headfirst through an open window painted on the canvas flat. His legs stuck into the room, thrashing.

Caught up in the madness, Fritzi marched toward the camera. With a rueful smile she crossed her eyes, did a little curtsy, kicked up the hem of her skirt, and tripped out of the frame.

Kelly screamed, "Cut! Cut, Ferguson, or I'll break your arm."

Jock Ferguson let go of the crank. Everyone but Kelly was laughing. Charlie cocked his head and applauded.

Fritzi rushed to Loy, who'd extricated himself from the torn flat. "I'm sorry. I'm really sorry," she said, panting.

He managed to stop laughing. "You didn't hurt me. You're a sketch, you know that? I've never seen anything like it."

"I haven't either," Kelly said. "Will somebody tell me what's going on? Hearn, why didn't you cut?"

"Because she's hilarious."

Charlie said with a flourish of his cane, "You're all idiots if you don't put Fritzi in a picture doing exactly what she just did, only without the cowboy claptrap."

"We don't need advice from you, limey," Kelly shouted.

"Al, wait a minute," Eddie said. "Maybe Mr. Chaplin's got something. Maybe this is what we've been looking for. A character."

"Character, what character? I don't see any character. I see hundreds of dollars of lumber and props shot to hell."

"A character for Fritzi. A lovable imp who bangs up everything and everybody, and every time it makes the story come out right. I'm going to show this footage to B.B. and Hayman."

"This is some kind of conspiracy. I won't stand for it."

"Sure you will, Al," Eddie said with a cheery smile. "You want to make money. We all want to make money." He walked up on the littered stage, slipped his arm around Fritzi. Plaster dust blanched her face. Her gay deceivers hung crookedly inside her dress; the lumps at her waist gave her a total of four bosoms, all unsatisfactory.

And now he knows I wear padding. Oh, Lord.

Eddie squeezed her shoulder. "Money, Al—you keep telling us that's what it's all about. Well, take a look. You want to strike it rich, I'm standing next to the mother lode."

EVERY carpenter on the lot was dragooned to rebuild the set. It was ready by noon Friday, and this time Fritzi finished the scene as planned. Eddie made the last shot at half past four. He was thanking everyone when his wife arrived with the children and three hampers containing a picnic supper.

Fritzi helped Rita arrange the food. Rita said Eddie had worked most of the night writing a scenario for a new comedy inspired by yesterday's mishaps. He called it *Knockabout Nell.*

Eddie sidled up. "Fritzi, do I dare ask what slipped in your— That is, inside—"

Rita poked him. "No, you don't dare. Be a gentleman and eat this sandwich. It's liverwurst, your favorite."

B.B. came stumping out from the main building. He approached Loy. "Hardin, my wife saw you work this week. She likes your looks. Very manly, she said."

Loy smiled and dipped his head in polite acknowledgment. B.B. snatched his hand and wrung it. "Sophie knows talent. Why don't we shoot a little test, hey?"

"Mighty kind of you, Mr. Pelzer, but I've got to say no, thanks. I like what I'm doing now."

B.B.'s mouth dropped open. He ran over to Fritzi. "I offered him a part, and he turned it down. Can you feature that? I never heard of anybody turning down an offer to star in pictures."

Fritzi murmured that it was certainly strange, but before she could say more, Loy started his good-byes. "Excuse me!" she exclaimed, nearly knocking B.B. down as she dashed around him. "Loy, I still owe you for saving me from that snake. May I treat you to supper? Say, tomorrow evening?"

"Why, sure, that'd be fun. Tell you what. Come on out to the Universal ranch in the afternoon. Watch the big battle scene Griffith's shooting. Then we'll find some grub."

Fritzi almost leaped into the air. "I'll be there."

"Look forward to it. Don't dress fancy."

As he might say he looked forward to a good night's rest. Fritzi was disappointed again by his casual ways. She screwed up her determination. She'd make him fall for her no matter what.

Fritzi and Loy • *"Don't dress fancy,"* Loy had said. Fritzi wouldn't think of it. Saturday morning she spent a mere two hours trying on outfits in front of her mirror. Dissatisfied with every one, she ran out of time and chose a tailored white shirt with a dark blue silk scarf, a full skirt with vertical blue and white awning stripes, white buck shoes, and a smart Panama hat with a blue band.

She drove the studio Packard over the rough, winding road to the forty-acre Universal ranch in the San Fernando Valley; there Mr. Griffith was filming his version of Thomas Dixon's novel *The Clansman.*

Despite Eddie's advance comments about the size of the production, Fritzi was still agog at the reality. Five hundred men had been marshaled in authentic Civil War uniforms. Trenches had been dug, batteries of artillery put in place. She saw cameras on several hills for simultaneous filming.

The company was taking a late lunch on blankets spread on the grass. Fritzi assumed Loy was with the horsemen scattered across the location. She'd find him at the end of the day, or he'd spot her. That was one advantage of her costume—she looked like a yacht flag.

The battle staged that afternoon was spectacular and noisy. Griffith had worked out an elaborate signal system using assistant directors with semaphore flags and mirrors to cue masses of men on the battlefield. Cavalry charged and countercharged.

Late in the day Fritzi camped in the shade of a hilltop eucalyptus grove as the extras collected their pay and the crew loaded equipment into trucks. After about fifteen minutes Loy came tramping up the hillside. He stepped up to her with a tip of his hat.

"I thought you might not find me," Fritzi said.

"Spotted you an hour ago. Can't miss those stripes." When he touched her arm to help her stand, the sensation was like a charge of electricity. "Hungry? There's a roadhouse close by."

"I have the studio automobile. We can go anywhere."

"Well, aren't you something?" He kept his hand on her elbow, steadying her as they walked toward the access road. "I know a little cantina in south Los Angeles, if that isn't too far."

It took them about an hour to drive to the city. The cantina was a dim, quiet place. Candles lit the rough-hewn tables. Loy ordered for them—flour tortillas with a hot beef and bean filling and a wicker-covered jug of red wine.

"When did you come to California, Loy?"

"Let's see. 'Bout four years ago now. Family had a ranch in Bailey County near the New Mexico border. After our folks died, I got restless, and my sister—well, she couldn't handle the work anymore." Something unhappy clouded his eyes. "We sold out."

"You seem to be doing well in pictures."

"I reckon. Work's slowing down some. Week before I did the job where you got everyone laughing fit to bust, I was hired by Ince for another western. He had to shut it down after the first day."

"Why?"

"Not enough horses. Griffith's corralled a lot of them. European buyers are picking up the rest."

"What on earth for?"

"Cavalry and artillery. They say everybody's setting up for a war over there."

Fritzi shivered, upset by the mention of war. She wanted nothing to spoil the delicious feeling she got from Loy's nearness. Made bold by the wine, she asked, "Do you think you'll settle down sometime?"

He leaned back in his chair. "Doubt it. It's in my blood to drift."

"Will you go back to Texas?"

His mouth set. "Never."

"Not even to visit your sister?"

"Isn't much point. She wouldn't recognize me. She lives in a state hospital. Always will. Poor thing's not right in the head."

"Oh, Loy, I'm sorry. Has she always—"

He shook his head. "Something bad happened to her right before I left. Just as soon not talk about it."

The moment of warmth and intimacy was ruined. Loy pushed his plate away, emptied his wineglass, reached in his jeans for money.

Fritzi touched his wrist. "I'll pay. I promised I would."

He didn't argue.

She dropped him at a corner in downtown Los Angeles at half past nine. He walked around to her side of the auto, helped her out for a stretch on the curb. "You be all right driving home?"

"Just fine."

"Well then"—he extended his hand—"thanks so much. For the meal and the good time."

"Can we do it again? I'd like that."

"Why not? I'd like to count you a friend. I don't have a telephone where I live, but the gents at the Waterhole will get a message to me."

"Fine." Fritzi leaned forward, kissed his cheek. "Good night."

He smiled, gave her a long, warm look that melted her down to her toes. " 'Night." He tipped his hat, turned, and sauntered off.

That Sunday • B.B. called Fritzi to his office on Monday. "Hayman's wild for Eddie's comedy idea. When he saw the footage of you, he nearly fell out of his socks. He wants you in the picture."

"Am I only good for pratfalls, B.B.?"

"Now, now. Eddie feels this is a big opportunity. I'm pleading, Fritzi. Don't upset the applecart when we're in high cotton and the Liberty boat's riding the crest."

"All right. One more comedy. Then I want a dramatic part."

"That's my gel. That's my Knockabout Nell," he cried.

FRITZI hurled herself into the new picture. Eddie's scenario cast her as likable but clumsy Nell, a domestic at a posh mansion. The thin plot called for Nell to accidentally unmask a man pretending to be a European nobleman; he was in fact a yegg bent on lifting all the jewelry at a dress ball. One slapstick stunt followed another. A lot of pies were tossed. Nearly a whole crate of china was broken. The climax called for Fritzi to swing on a prop chandelier.

Liberty previewed Fritzi's picture at the Arcade, a theater on South Broadway. The two-reeler followed a showing of an Ince western, *Desert Gold.* Loy appeared as one of a hard-riding outlaw gang, though only in long shots, unrecognizable. He had to identify himself to Fritzi. She sat on his right, Eddie and Rita on her other side. The audience loved the western's thrilling action.

Fritzi's stomach knotted when the projector flashed the next title.

LIBERTY PICTURES INTERNATIONAL
presents
"KNOCKABOUT NELL"

Her hand flew over to clutch Loy's right arm. "I'm scared."

"Hush. It'll be fine." He put his left hand on top of hers.

Fritzi's eyes stayed on the flickering screen. She winced at some of her mugging, but the audience laughed at appropriate moments. At the end the camera irised in for a circular close-up of Nell delirious with happiness after receiving a kiss from the handsome young scion of the household. The audience applauded.

Later they bumped into Kelly in the lobby. He said, "It'll make money." From him that amounted to paragraphs of praise.

Fritzi held tightly to Loy's arm, elated by the picture's good reception. Eddie was excited too, chattering to Rita like a schoolboy. Outside, the summer evening was dry and warm. South Broadway was crowded. The people passing under the streetlamps seemed carefree, unworried by news of the unrest in Europe after the assassination of Austrian archduke Franz Ferdinand in the Balkans in June. A Russian army mobilization had already begun in response to Austria's declaration of war on Serbia earlier in the week. Russia stood with France and Britain, ostensibly allied against Germany and Austria.

As the foursome turned into a spaghetti house, Loy said to Fritzi, "We should celebrate the picture in style. I know a mighty fine place for a picnic on the coast above Inceville. Want to go tomorrow?"

"Do you need to ask?"

He grinned. "Didn't expect so. I'll borrow the Ford."

FRITZI sat with her legs tucked under her and her skirt wrapped tightly to keep it from blowing. The sun beat on her face with a sensual warmth. The ocean wind tossed her blond hair. Far below the hilltop where they'd spread their blue-and-white tablecloth and eaten fried chicken and coleslaw, the cobalt sea rolled in from Asia, breaking into fans of foam on shoreline rocks.

Loy held up their bottle of Buena Vista wine, checking the level against the sun. "There's some of this wine left."

"I don't need another drop. This place is so beautiful, it would make a cold-water prohibitionist tipsy. I want to stay here forever. I'm a hopeless romantic. Or haven't you noticed?"

"Fact is, I have. Never met anyone like you in Texas."

"I shouldn't imagine. Actresses are crazy."

"Oh, not you." In the sunshine his strong profile glowed like a bronze sculpture. Why didn't he lean over and kiss her?

Loy eased back on his elbows, squinting at the sea. She realized the initiative had to be hers.

"Loy, thank you for bringing me here." She rose on her knees, rested her right hand on his shoulder, and kissed him.

He threw one arm around her, pulled her to him for a harder kiss. Fritzi shivered, eyes shut, feeling her hair brush his face. He broke the embrace, giving her a swift, almost apologetic look.

Fritzi touched him again. "Do you know how I feel about you?"

"I've a mighty good idea."

"You probably think I'm a cheap hussy."

"I think you're a jewel, Fritzi. More modern than I'm used to, but a special woman. I'd like you to be my friend forever."

"Friend. It's always that kind of word."

He was silent a moment. "Can't be anything else."

"Why not? Because you're restless? I don't care. You can go to the South Pole, stay a year, if you'll just come back to me."

He gazed seaward again, his eyes melancholy. "There's more to it than that. I can't settle down, not even if I want to. I've been looking for the right time to tell you. I left Texas because I had to, Fritzi. I killed a man."

It had the effect of an earthquake. Her hands shook. "Oh, dear Lord. How did it happen? Who was it?"

"You don't need the details. That way, anybody ever shows up asking questions, you don't know a thing."

She jumped up, ran away from him. He scrambled to his feet and hurried after her with loping strides. His face seemed to smear, as though he stood on the other side of a rain-drenched window. *Please don't let me bawl.* "I think we should pack up."

"Sure. Can I still see you? I won't force it, but I'd like that."

Bitterly, "You just want me to be convenient, is that it? A *pal*—available whenever you decide to drop from the sky?" She hammered her fist on her skirt. "That's a lot to ask."

"But a while ago you said—"

"I know what I said. I said it before you told me about Texas. I'd have to grow old wondering every time you left whether I'd see or hear from you again, unless it was from some jail cell. Or maybe I'd never hear at all. What would they do if they—if—?"

"Hang me. The man was a Texas Ranger."

"Oh, my God." Fritzi fought to steady herself. "Let's go back to town."

The ride to the picnic site had been magical, electric with excitement. The return trip was hellishly long. Neither of them said a word. She'd never known such turmoil, disappointment, and anger.

They saw a vendor hawking newspapers on Sunset, unusual for this late on Sunday. "Must be an extra edition," Loy said. "I'll get one." He swung the Ford to the curb, got out and bought the paper, then walked rapidly back to the car. "It's what they've been jawing about for weeks. Kaiser Bill declared war on Russia yesterday."

A new war involving Germany. Fritzi wondered about her father's reaction. Loy gave her the *Times* as he took his seat.

FOUR POWERS AT WAR. FRANCE IS MOBILIZING.

GERMAN KAISER UNAFRAID, HIS BACK AGAINST THE WALL

Still numb from Loy's revelation, Fritzi laid the paper in her lap. "I hope the war has nothing to do with us."

"Don't see how it could," he said as he drove.

In Venice, Loy started to slide out to open her door.

"I'll go in by myself," Fritzi said.

"All right. Maybe I'll see you when I get back."

"Where are you going?"

"Arizona. For a month or more. Ince hired me for a chapter play that doesn't use many horses." He reached for her arm. "Fritzi—"

She opened the door and ran up the walk.

Part Five   BATTLEFIELDS

In Belgium • After August 1, 1914, the day Kaiser Wilhelm II of Germany went to war against Russia, the dominoes fell one after another. On August 3 Germany declared war against France. Next day Britain retaliated with a declaration of war against Germany, and a special tactical force of the German Second Army breached the Belgian border, violating her status of neutrality. Once Liège fell, the main armies could advance to the capital and on to Paris.

On August 6 Paul kissed Julie and the children good-bye. That day the transatlantic cables carried the text of Washington's official proclamation on the European war. The United States would maintain strict neutrality.

Persistent back trouble and Julie's gentle persuasion had finally convinced Paul that he should hire a helper. He engaged twenty-year-old Sammy Silverstone, who had grown up poor on the streets of London and was interested in photography.

Paul and Sammy crossed the Channel to Ostend and traveled on to Brussels with no difficulty. In Brussels the American ambassador arranged for a laissez-passer—an official document allowing unrestricted travel. That and their passports ensured Paul and Sammy's safety. Supposedly.

TALL poplars lined both sides of the road, like green, leafy banks of a river. In the riverbed flowed an unending tide of human misery. Refugees by the hundreds stretched to the horizon.

Paul set up his camera facing the oncoming throngs. Fear showed on every face. As Paul started to crank, Sammy said, "What a sight!"

Truly it was. The river carried men, women, and children on foot, riding bicycles with backpacks, driving old market wagons piled high. A grandmother dragged a dogcart without a dog to pull it. The cart held a small mountain of clothes, cook pots—the residue of a shattered life.

The river of terror flowed on for several hours, then thinned, then dried up altogether. Paul suspected that the German advance was close behind.

When the Germans arrived, Paul was staggered by their numbers, the splendid state of their equipment, and all the support units: horse-drawn kitchen wagons with smoking chimneys, hospital wagons, an open truck in which cobblers hammered away resoling boots, even a motorized post office.

Soon smoke clouds stained the horizons of Belgium. Where the Germans found resistance, they burned houses in retaliation.

Paul and Sammy drove an old abandoned horse cart through fields torn up by the iron wheels of caissons. They saw blue cottages with red-tiled roofs, all the windows smashed, doors ripped off the hinges. Paul filmed where he could, but the wooden Moy camera was bulky, easily spotted. They stayed off main roads to avoid confrontations in which their papers might be questioned.

Near one village they came upon soldiers working with horses and chains to drag tree trunks from a road. Fallen trees weren't the only roadblocks put up by the Belgians. A little farther on, flames licked around the gutted frame of an auto lying on its side.

Paul and Sammy hid the cart and approached the village on foot. Paul carried the camera wrapped in a blanket under his arm. Sammy had an extra magazine of film.

As they passed a barn and started to cross a field at the edge of the village, Sammy jerked Paul's arm. "Got to hide, gov." They ran into the barn and breathlessly climbed to the hayloft. From there Paul watched a squad of soldiers march three men and three women into the sunlit field. A young captain strutted in front of the civilians, all of whom had their wrists tied behind them.

"Ladies and gentlemen," the captain said loudly, "you have placed obstacles in the path of General von Kluck's First Army. I refer to the fallen trees, the burned auto." He spoke excellent French. "That kind of resistance can't be tolerated. We have our orders. Do you have anything to say before we carry them out?"

A young woman fell to her knees, weeping. Paul shoved the camera forward into the hayloft opening, checked the exposure. He cranked, wincing at the ratcheting noise. Could they hear it?

The captain tapped a cigarette on a metal case. "Sergeant, execute them."

The sergeant snapped orders. The soldiers raised their rifles. "No, no, not like that," the captain said. "We want a stronger lesson. Bayonets." He lit his cigarette.

The kneeling woman fell over in a faint. The soldiers looked at one another, hesitant.

The sergeant cleared his throat. "Fix bayonets."

Paul kept cranking as the soldiers marched forward and rammed their steel into the civilians. They kept stabbing until each Belgian was certifiably dead.

"Leave them," the captain said when all of them had fallen. His cigarette was down to a stub. As he started to toss it away, he happened to glance at the barn. There must have been a flare off the lens. He pointed. "Up there. I saw something. Surround the barn."

"Come on, gov." Sammy dived for the ladder.

"Give me the other magazine," Paul said.

Sammy obeyed. Hurrying, Paul removed the exposed footage, locked the other magazine on. He buried the exposed magazine under straw just as soldiers kicked the barn doors open.

Rifle bolts rattled down below. Paul shouted in German, "Don't fire. We're American citizens."

"Climb down, hands in the air." That was the captain.

Paul went first. The captain couldn't have been more than twenty-five. He had a soft baby face, mild blue eyes. He clicked his heels. "Captain Herman Kinder. You speak German."

"I emigrated from Berlin as a boy."

"Ah, *ein Landsmann.* Have you papers?"

"Yes." Paul pulled them out.

The captain studied the passport for an agonizing length of time. He next examined Paul's laissez-passer. "The Belgians no longer control this country. This document is worthless." He tore it in half and threw the pieces onto the ground. He eyed the ladder. Sammy had stopped halfway down. His face was pale, tense.

"What do you have up there? I saw a reflection."

"A news camera," Paul said. "I take pictures for theaters."

"Kino." The captain smiled briefly. "Bring it here."

Sammy lowered the camera to a soldier, then climbed down.

Captain Kinder asked, "You have pictures of what transpired in the field?" Paul nodded. To one of his men Kinder said, "Destroy it."

The soldier bore the camera out of the barn. Paul winced at the sound of the wooden case splintering.

"Since Germany and the United States are not belligerents, I am obliged to treat you courteously. But I advise you to leave the district at once. If you're seen here again, you will be shot."

"Yes, right, we'll go."

Paul and Sammy walked to the sunlit doorway and out. Sammy looked ready to burst with anger. Carefully Paul laid a finger across his lips, keeping his back to the barn. He walked quickly, without running. Any moment he expected a bullet in the back.

When they reached the far edge of the field, Paul risked a glance over his shoulder. Captain Kinder and his men were marching away toward the village. Paul pressed on toward a low stone wall. There he said, "It's all right, Sammy. They're gone."

He'd never seen Sammy's face so ugly. Sammy kicked the stone wall. "Bloody bastards. *Savages.*"

"Huns. That's the name I heard in the village. Like Attila's hordes." Paul rested on the wall and bent his head, sickened by the killings.

Sammy sat next to him. "Where next?"

"We'll make a run for Ostend and the Channel. I'll pay some fisherman to carry us across." They sat silent until Paul said, "I think it's safe now. We can go back for the film."

Troubled House • Fritzi was met on the platform at the Chicago train depot by the Crown family steward, Leopold.

"Welcome home, *Fräulein.*"

"Thank you, Leopold. I'm glad to be here."

"Your mother and father will be happy to see you."

Fritzi suspected only half of his remark was true.

The sky above the noisy street threatened rain. It was Friday, October 2, 1914, two days before Peace Sunday, proclaimed by the President as a national day of prayer to end the war.

Fritzi had come halfway across the country at her mother's urging. She was here to celebrate her parents' forty-fifth wedding anniversary. After some hesitation she had decided to venture home, hoping that the festive atmosphere would help her heal the rift with her father.

The family's maroon Benz touring car delivered her to Twentieth and Michigan at dusk. The servants were all new, unfamiliar. Her mother was still at a church committee meeting. The General was away in St. Louis and would return late tomorrow.

Unpacking in her old room, she turned suddenly, sensing someone in the doorway. "Joey!"

"Hello, sis." Joe Junior limped across the carpet; they hugged. Approaching forty, he was pasty and smelled of whiskey.

"Tell me, how are you?"

"How should I be? I'm the same. Go to the brewery six days a week, work at party headquarters on Sunday. I saw your new flicker, the one where you break everything. Funny."

"Glad you liked it," Fritzi said. "Has the war had any impact in Chicago? Out west people hardly know it's happening."

"German people are pretty worked up about it. Pop's hung a big map of Belgium and France in his office downstairs. Any day I expect to see him bring home a portrait of the Kaiser. He may be getting a little soft." Joe Junior tapped his head. "After all, he'll be seventy-three in March. Say, did anyone tell you? Carl's coming on a midnight train from Texas. He's on his way to France."

Carl's train was delayed, and he did not arrive at the house until half past four in the morning. He came bounding up the staircase with a worn-out gladstone in one hand and a bedraggled red scarf draped around his neck. In her nightclothes, Ilsa alternately hugged her younger son and urged him to be quiet. Fritzi yawned and waved at Carl from the door of her bedroom.

NOTHING ever changed. Saturday evening's meal was called punctually with a bell at seven forty-five. Working up her nerve at each step, Fritzi came into the dining room, a stiff smile on her face.

"Your father is in his office," Ilsa said. "I've sent Leopold to tell him we're sitting down." She clutched a lace hankie in her left hand, and Fritzi noticed that her knuckles were white.

Ilsa took her place at the end of the long dining table. Fritzi sat on one side, Joey and Carl on the other. She heard brisk steps, stood up without a second thought. Her palms were moist, her pulse beating fast. The General came in, slim and correct in his posture, though she was dismayed to see how frail he'd grown.

"Good evening, Fritzi," he said with a slight bow.

"Papa, I'm so glad to see you."

He marched down the other side of the table behind Carl and Joey and sat in his tall, thronelike chair. No kiss of greeting for her, not even a touch to demonstrate paternal affection.

Ilsa said, "Isn't it wonderful to have Fritzi here, Joe?"

"Very nice," he said. "I hope you are in good health, Fritzi."

Good health? Was that all he could think of to say?

Still with a false brightness Ilsa said, "Doesn't she look fine, Joe? She is so busy in California—"

"Making those pictures." He glanced at his daughter. "I have not seen any of them. I disapprove of a woman displaying herself to strangers. Paul's pictures, now—they reflect important events. They have value." Carl was frowning. The General went on, "I'm only grateful that few people in Chicago know what you are doing."

Joey laughed. "Pop, they know. Her new picture's a hit."

"No one has mentioned it at the brewery."

The serving girls brought platters and silver-domed dishes to the table. Everyone concentrated on filling their plates.

Ilsa's false cheer persisted. "After supper we all want to hear Fritzi tell us about California. It's such a fascinating place."

"Southern California's lovely," Fritzi agreed. "The climate is supposed to be as mild and sunny as the Mediterranean coast."

The General put his napkin down. "I don't believe I have time for a travelogue. Two gentlemen are coming here for a meeting."

"Here to this house?" Ilsa said. "You didn't mention it, Joe."

"We'll meet in my office. We won't trouble you." It was a curt dismissal.

Infuriated for the sake of his mother and sister, Carl threw his napkin onto the table. "What about me, Pop? Are you too busy to hear about my plans? I'm going to join the French air corps."

"As a mercenary." The General snorted. "Your mother informed me. Needless to say, I consider the idea barbarous and, in view of this country's official posture, unpatriotic. I am grossly ashamed of what you are doing."

Fritzi could take no more. "Carl ought to do what he wants, Papa. He's a grown man."

The General's glance withered her. "Of course you'd say that, living the kind of willful, selfish life that you do." He took a sip of beer, dabbed his mustache with his napkin, and stood. "You'll excuse me. The visitors will be here shortly."

He marched out.

DREARY rain fell on Sunday morning. Carl had vanished from the house before daylight without saying good-bye to anyone. Fritzi's train for California left at eleven. Leopold came for her valises at ten. She followed him downstairs, where the General and Ilsa met them in their church finery.

The General's expression was severe. He said, "I am one of the laypersons speaking at the eleven-o'clock service. We are unable to see you off. Leopold will drive you to the station."

"It isn't necessary. I can call a taxi."

"Must you quarrel with everything I say, Fritzi? Leopold will go with you!"

His anger beat on her like a tangible force. She drew a deep breath. "Fine, sir. Thank you."

She embraced Ilsa, who was in tears. The General stood apart, stiff when she kissed his cheek. She'd come home to heal the breach with her father and only made it worse. She left the house in despair.

Fritzi and Her Two Men • Shortly after Fritzi's return to Los Angeles, Eddie Hearn took her into his office and presented a typed scenario for *Paper Hanger Nell,* to start filming the following Monday. As Fritzi glanced over the two pages, B. B. Pelzer's typewriter, Miss Levy, tapped on Eddie's door. "There's a gent out front asking for you, Fritzi. Real slick fella."

Fritzi's brief rush of excitement didn't last—slick was not a word people would apply to Loy. At the doorway to the front porch she saw a shiny little red Reo parked in front. Not until she stepped out-side did she see him at the end of the porch.

"Harry? Is that you?"

"Yes, indeed. How are you, Fritzi?"

"What brings you to Los Angeles?" As if she had no inkling.

"Sight-seeing. I've been to San Francisco. Now I'd like to see your town. I have one more day before I must go back."

Fritzi wasn't sure slick was the right word to describe Harry Poland's appearance either. Smart would be better—smart and rich. His three-piece suit of striped gray wool was cut in the latest English style, buttoning high in front. His trousers had sharp center creases. His patent leather shoes shone, and a splashy yellow hankie bloomed in his breast pocket like an exotic flower.

"It's grand to see you," she said. "I'll be glad to give you a tour around—" She stopped, stunned. As Harry turned toward her, she saw a wide band of black crepe.

"Oh, no. Your wife?" she said instantly.

Gravely Harry nodded. "Flavia passed away five weeks ago."

"I'm so sorry to hear about it, Harry."

"My doctor suggested a change of scene, so I'm seeing the Pacific for the first time." The emotion in his eyes was unmistakable. "Also seeing you again. Will you have supper?"

"Of course." She would feel too guilty if she said no.

She introduced him to people on the lot, many of whom greeted him enthusiastically. They knew his songs. Harry laughed and charmed them. But standing off to one side, Fritzi saw clearly that his eyes were marked by fatigue.

He seemed to brighten at supper. They chatted about Paul's book, Harry's newfound success writing scores for Broadway, the war. When he drove her home in the rented Reo, he escorted her to the front door. "I can't tell you what a tonic you are, Fritzi. I feel better than I have for months."

On tiptoe Fritzi kissed him quickly on the cheek. "I'm glad." Then she asked a question that had occurred to her earlier. "Do you wear that armband all the time?"

"I'm determined to mourn Flavia properly." Harry's blue eyes locked with hers. "One year. Afterward I'll be a free man."

Fritzi knew she should tell him about Loy, to save him false hope and disappointment, but it seemed cruel after his loss. Light rain began whispering down. "I do give you my condolences," she said as they sheltered on the porch. "You've become a dear friend, Harry."

"Is that all?"

"For the present, yes. Yes, I'm afraid it is." He was a wonderful man; he just wasn't Loy. "Take care of yourself, Harry."

"I shall. Good-bye until we meet again." He turned and rushed down the steps as the rain fell harder.

ALL the next day the skies continued to pour. Rainy season's early, Fritzi thought as she wearily dragged herself home that night. She wandered into the parlor and sprawled on the horsehair love seat, too tired to go upstairs and change clothes right away. She sat while the rain hammered the roof and darkness fell.

Her head came up suddenly. She'd dozed. Fritzi noticed an auto parked outside, acetylene headlamps lighting the silvery raindrops. She ran to the front door, trying to see.

The car door opened and shut. The driver splashed through mud, passed through the beams of the headlights. She saw his sugar-loaf hat. She threw the door open, dashed to the edge of the porch. Loy bounded up the steps. Overwhelmed with emotion, she flung her arms around his neck. "I thought you were never coming back." She kissed him lightly. The wind blew rain onto the porch and over the two of them. "We should go inside," she said.

He laughed a soft laugh. "Sure. But that was a real fine welcome to a weary traveler. Wouldn't mind repeating it."

Fritzi almost swooned. She kissed him hard while her heart pounded. His arm circled her waist. She tugged his hand, drawing him to the front door. Loy looked into the house. "Who's at home?"

"No one."

He kissed her throat, the lobe of her ear. "I sure did miss your company. Can we go upstairs?"

"Yes. Oh, yes. And no strings, Loy, I promise," she cried, carried away by the feel of him, his hands, his mouth, the stormy darkness, all her months of yearning.

LATER, in the rumpled bed, Fritzi caressed him, smoothing down his long, damp hair. She studied him a moment, then exclaimed, "You forgot the headlights!"

He rolled toward the window. "Dang if I didn't. Got carried away. Too late now." He bent over to kiss her.

"How did you know when I'd be home?"

"Didn't. Didn't plan for this to happen either—you have to believe that." He was quiet awhile. Then he said, "I don't know how to say this exactly right, but I want you to know I like you a lot. But I wouldn't want you to expect—"

She pressed her fingers to his mouth. "I understand."

He leaned his cheek on her shoulder. "Wandering's in my blood, I guess. But there's more to it. My sister, Clara, in the institution. You're entitled to know the story."

"Loy, I'm not asking—"

"I want to tell you. Remember when Mr. Pelzer offered me a part and I said no? I turned him down because of Sis in that hospital. I pay for her care. If somebody should recognize me on picture screens in Texas, the authorities would know where to track me down. If I'm locked up, I can't send any more money to Sis. Her poor mind just crumbled away after a man took advantage of her by force—him and two friends. The man I killed was the one talked them into it."

Fritzi held his hand tightly. After a longer silence he went on.

"For about a year after they found Clara in her cottage, she lived off in some dreamworld. I had to sign papers to put her away. Every time I visited the hospital, I asked her who did the deed. She wouldn't say. I figured she'd tell me in her own good time, and she did. Afterward she said she could have revealed the name long before, but she was afraid I'd do something foolish. The ringleader couldn't be touched—he was above the law. He *was* the law."

"A Texas Ranger, you said."

"His name was Mercer Page. Sis was right. He couldn't be touched, not by me anyway. Didn't matter—I went to see him. Merce lived by himself, little cabin out in the country. I told him I knew he was the one who egged his friends into raping Clara when they came on her picking strawberries one afternoon when I was in Waco. Page didn't deny it. Brazen as you please, he said he and his pards had a jug of popskull that fired them up, and when they found Clara— Well, he took pleasure in telling me the things they did."

"Oh, Loy, that's terrible."

"Merce was one rotten apple. He said he didn't mind telling me 'cause he'd never liked me much, and what could I do about it, since Clara had gone crazy and wouldn't be a credible witness in court? About then I lost it. I pulled my pistol before he could grab his, and I killed him. That was my last day in Bailey County. I hopped a freight train to New Mexico and hid out. I swung up north to Idaho awhile, then drifted down to California." Loy leaned on his elbows, brought his hand up to cradle Fritzi's chin. "That's why I stay just so long in one place. It'll always be that way."

She pressed her mouth to his. "Even having you with me a little while is wonderful."

The rain fell, softer now, almost like a sigh. She heard but didn't see it. His headlights had gone out, the acetylene gas exhausted.

After they dressed, she saw him down to the door. On the porch he hugged her, kissed her quickly, and went down the walk whistling.

At the curb he raised his tall hat and waved. Fritzi sat in the porch swing until his car chugged away, without lights. She feared for his safety. He couldn't see what was ahead. As the car vanished in the dark, she realized she couldn't either.

Detroit Again • "Single room, sir?"

"The best you have. I'm only here for a couple of nights."

The haughty clerk scrutinized Carl's watch cap, cheap peacoat, the tattered scarf around his neck. "We prefer to settle the room charges in advance."

Carl shoved money across the marble counter and signed the register. There was satisfaction in returning to the Wayne Hotel as a paying guest, though it was an extravagance.

The Detroit weather was gray and dismal, with occasional rain. The boat horns on the foggy river seemed to mourn the coming of winter. After a hot bath and a breakfast of eggs, fried potatoes, and a sirloin steak, Carl wrapped the scarf around his neck and set out.

A black family lived in Jesse Shiner's cottage. A scrawny woman with an infant in her arms told Carl she didn't know where Jesse lived now, but he worked at Sport's, on the east side.

"That's a barbershop. For the colored," the woman added, to be sure he understood. Carl trudged away.

Sport's Tonsorial was a neat little establishment, four chairs. A stout man, blue-black and bald, stepped away from a customer in the first chair. "I think you got the wrong shop, brother."

From the rear someone said, "No, Sport. I know him."

"Jesse!" Carl tromped to the last chair. Jesse was little changed, spare as ever. When he hoisted himself out of his chair, he listed as he walked. It brought back that terrible night when the hoodlum had sunk the gaff hook in Jesse's leg. "How are you, Jess?"

"Surviving. Never expected you to show up again. Where you bound?"

Carl explained, then said, "I want to see Tess. Do you know anything about her?"

"Don't know much 'cept what I read now and then. Mrs. Sykes her name is."

Carl's face wrenched. "She married that s.o.b.?"

"Yeah, but he was killed a couple of years ago. Out joyriding with two roadhouse girls, all of 'em high. The car turned over."

"Anything more?"

"Don't think so. Oh, yeah—she and Sykes, they had a little boy. She's back in her pa's old house. He's in some kind of old folks' home. Clymer car company's gone. Competition got too fierce." Jesse puffed a cigarette. "From all I can tell, that Tess is a fine woman. I 'spect you were a fool to leave her."

THAT NIGHT, WITH A NORTH wind howling out of Canada, Carl shivered in front of the Clymer mansion. It was a splendid house, three stories, ablaze with lights. He was surprised and a little hurt that Tess had married Wayne Sykes, the man he'd beaten half to death. But he couldn't have expected Tess to be loyal when she assumed he was never coming back to her.

A man in livery answered the bell.

"I'm a friend of Mrs. Sykes's. If she's home, tell her Carl would like to see her."

The man shut the door. The autumn wind brought a few snowflakes whirling past the streetlamps. Carl shivered.

The door opened again. Tess stood there, stouter now, wearing reading spectacles. For a moment she seemed unsteady. "I never thought I'd see this moment, Carl."

Awkwardly, "Well, I didn't either. I'm passing through. Catching a boat in Montreal on my way to France."

"Always the wanderer. You must be frozen. Please come in."

As Tess closed the door against the wind, Carl saw the wedding band. He said, "My friend Jesse told me you'd gotten married but lost your husband. I'm awfully sorry to hear that."

Tess drew a long breath. "I never loved Wayne. I married him because Father always wanted it, and with you gone— Well, no need to bring up the past, is there?"

From the back of the house a small boy of five or six bounded through a swinging door. He raced up to Carl, looked him over, stuck out his hand. "Hello. What's your name?"

"Carl," he said, amused. They shook hands. The boy had brown eyes like Carl's, but Carl saw mostly Tess in his face.

"Henry's my name," the boy said with great seriousness.

"My Prince Hal," Tess said, ruffling his hair affectionately. "Bedtime." Henry ran up the stairs. She took Carl's hand, gently tugged him toward a parlor. "Tell me why you're off to Europe."

Tess rang for the manservant, who served Carl a whiskey, and hot tea for Tess. Her eyes were soft and warm as she indicated the scarf. "Still fighting the dragons and Saracens?"

"I guess you can say that. I'm going to fly in the French air corps. I've been piloting airplanes for a few years now."

"It's against the law for American citizens to involve themselves in the war, isn't it?"

Carl shrugged. "I don't think President Wilson will send detectives to arrest me, or anyone who helps the Allies. My friend Rene LeMaye—the man who talked me into this—convinced me we're wrong to stay neutral in this fight."

"But how can you join up when it's forbidden?"

"It isn't forbidden to join the French Foreign Legion. You sign up in Paris. They shuffle papers and reassign you to the air corps. Woodrow's content, thinking you're standing guard someplace in the desert." He gestured with the glass. "I had enough of that old fool when he threw me out of Princeton. Did I ever tell you about that?"

"How he lost his best football lineman? You did."

"We talked a lot, didn't we?"

"In such a short time," Tess said with a searching look. "How I wish it could have gone on, and on—" There was a rush of color in her cheeks. She averted her eyes to her teacup.

They reminisced for an hour. Then Carl rose to leave.

"You have a fine son," he said at the front door.

"Yes. I wish you could stay and get to know him." She sighed. "This war is terrible. Millions of boys are dying. Don't let one of them be you." Tears brimmed in her lovely eyes. "Kiss me good-bye for old times' sake?"

He swept her into his arms. It was all he could do to break the embrace, touch her smooth, soft cheek one last time, and go out into the bitter night.

Million-Dollar Carpet • Fritzi worked on her new comedy with such energy that she was ready to swoon from exhaustion every night. Unexpectedly, she liked making *Paper Hanger Nell*. She added some little tricks of technique she'd learned by studying Charlie's tramp comedies.

The whole country had come down with Chaplinitis. Dance orchestras were playing "That Charlie Chaplin Walk." Department stores filled their shelves with Chaplin dolls for Christmas. Charlie currently earned a well-publicized $1250 a week at Essanay. Fritzi's $150 a week was a pittance by comparison. A sense of injustice began to gnaw at her, especially since *Paper Hanger Nell* showed signs of being a hit. While the picture was still being edited, B.B. received orders for over 120 prints, and Eddie plunged into preparing *Firehouse Nell.*

The day that picture went before the camera, B.B. made his usual appearance to wish everyone well. Fritzi took the opportunity to corner him. "I'd like to discuss something with you and Al," she said. "May we have lunch today? It's important."

"Important, huh? Well, we got to take care of our star," he said, patting her arm. "Where do you want to eat?"

"The Palm Court at the Alexandria."

Kelly's chauffeur drove Fritzi and the two men downtown to the Alexandria Hotel at Sixth and Spring.

Entering the lobby, she said, "Let's not go to the restaurant just yet. Let's sit down over here." Kelly and B.B. exchanged looks as Fritzi led them across the Oriental carpet. Tall oak chairs were scattered about the perimeter. Fritzi sat between the partners.

B.B. scratched his nose. "Fritzi, you're pretty shrewd. I have a feeling this conversation will cost me money."

"What are you talking about?" Kelly said.

"This." B.B. tapped his foot. "The million-dollar carpet. They call it that because a lot of big deals are closed here. I got a hunch our little gel wants to discuss salary."

Fritzi's pulse was fast. "I know how many prints of *Paper Hanger Nell* were distributed to theaters," she began. "Exactly one hundred and twenty-four the first month."

"How do you know so much?" Kelly asked.

"I eat lunch with a bookkeeper once a week."

B.B. whipped out his silk pocket handkerchief and mopped his face. "I get the drift. You don't think we're treating you right. Three hundred and fifty a week. How's that sound?"

Fritzi wanted to leap up, dance a jig. She'd planned to ask for two hundred dollars. With a vaguely suicidal feeling she swallowed and said, "I was thinking of four hundred."

"*Four?*" Kelly nearly choked. "You think Liberty mints money?"

Sweetly Fritzi said, "No, but it seems the Nellie pictures do."

"Deal!" B.B. said, slapping his knees. "Yes, sir, and it's a bargain." Kelly flung one hand over his eyes to show his extreme pain. "We'd want to make it part of a new contract, though."

"Three years," Kelly said.

Fritzi was overwhelmed. The busy lobby seemed to tilt and blur. "That is very decent of you. But if we sign a new contract, I suppose I should have my own lawyer look it over."

Kelly waved it aside. "Not necessary."

B.B. jumped up. "Al, she can have her lawyer. Let's celebrate. French Champagne—the works."

The meal in the Palm Court was sumptuous and pleasant. Fritzi had never seen Kelly so cowed; he didn't say a word about the steep prices. They left the hotel at a quarter to three. Outside, a long, sleek Locomobile touring car, rich dark blue with wire-spoke wheels, was parked at the curb, unattended, with the top down.

"I don't see your car," Fritzi said to Kelly.

"We'll take this one," B.B. said.

"Whose is it?" Fritzi asked.

With a distant sourness Kelly said, "Yours."

"A present for our big star," B.B. said expansively. "You made quite a deal today, little gel. We bought the car for you last week to show our appreciation. Now you got the car and a big bump in pay. Quite a little businesswoman, ain't she, Al?"

"Yeah, swell," Kelly muttered.

Fritzi was lucky not to faint on the spot.

End of the Party • Fritzi was still euphoric when she and Loy motored up North Sycamore in her new car to a big party on Saturday night.

After they arrived, Loy didn't mingle. For over an hour he stood by himself, nursing his whiskey and rebuffing strangers who tried to chat. Finally Fritzi suggested they leave.

In the car, spatters of rain hit the windshield with increasing frequency. Fritzi turned her head slightly to study Loy's profile. His lips were tight together, his eyes carefully fixed on the road.

"Reckon I'd better close up the top," he said, sliding the long auto to the curb near a corner bungalow with lights shining in every window. Loy jumped out, pulled the canvas over, and fastened it. "Good enough light here, I guess." Seated again, he drew something out of his inside pocket. "See that all right?"

"Yes," Fritzi said, puzzled over why he wanted to show her a studio photograph. The rectangular image caught three men in chaps and tall hats riding past the camera lens. Loy's face was unmistakable as the rider in front.

"Director lined up a second camera for that chase shot. Never knew about it or saw it till I rode past. I'm on the screen clear as day for three, maybe four seconds. Anybody in Texas sees the picture, they'll be on me like a hound on a coon in hunting season."

Now she understood. "Don't worry. I'll speak to B.B. Maybe he can telephone someone and ask them to cut out—"

Loy's hand fell on her wrist quickly. "Never mind. Been thinking for a while that I should mosey on."

Fritzi leaned back against the seat cushion. "You're leaving town because your face is on the screen accidentally for a few seconds," she said. "Is this just a convenient excuse, Loy? Because you think I'm trying to tie you down?"

He gripped the steering wheel with both hands and stared through the streaked windshield. "I wonder that myself, a little."

Fritzi threw the picture into his lap. "So what does this mean? Good-bye?"

"Reckon so."

"When?"

"Tonight. I plan to light out north in the morning. Buy me a ticket to Frisco. Figure I'll stay there a day or two, then go have a look at Hawaii, where the pineapples grow."

Though Fritzi's emotional control was shattered, she managed to say, "May we drive on before I bawl my head off?"

Loy started to reply, thought better of it. On the long drive to his squalid house, behind a stable on Alessandro Street, she said nothing. When they arrived, he braked the car in the lane, stood outside with rain falling gently on his long hair. Fritzi pushed her door open and marched around the rear of the Locomobile. He stepped back respectfully, held the door to the driver's side as rain splashed into her eyes and mixed with tears.

"Are you steady enough to drive home?"

"What difference does it make?" She flounced into the seat.

With tenderness he said, "Makes a big difference. There's millions of folks out there in the wide world who think you're special. They love you."

"The only one I care about doesn't."

"Damn it, Fritzi—"

"Take your hand off the car, Loy. Good-bye."

She wheeled the Locomobile around in the lane and drove home. Loy had broken her heart beyond repair.

Winter of Discontent • December settled early darkness on the mountains and the shore of California. Fritzi hated to see the sun set because it meant sleep was much nearer, and sleep brought her frequent nightmares of loss, failure, even death.

She hated Christmas 1914—found no joy in it, only burdens: shopping, wrapping, posting, giving, all empty and sad.

Fritzi decided that too many bad memories lived in the room she rented. After settling what she owed the landlord, she leased a small house on a hilly side street in Hollywood. California Mediterranean, it pleased the eye with its golden stucco and half-round red roof tiles. She moved in two days after New Year's.

On February 8, 1915, D. W. Griffith premièred *The Clansman,* now subtitled *The Birth of a Nation,* downtown at Clune's Auditorium. Not long after that, Fritzi was summoned to a meeting one afternoon in B.B.'s office.

"I want to discuss how we can speed up production of pictures starring this little gel," B.B. said. Fritzi and Eddie sat in front of B.B.'s desk. Al Kelly hunched in a chair in the corner.

Eddie said, "Do we want to do that? We might glut the market."

Kelly snorted. "We could finish a two-reel Nellie every third day and not glut the market. People are screaming for them."

"Even in England, where they got the war to think about," B.B. agreed. "Scandinavians and Dutchmen are standing in line. I'm heading over there in a few weeks to check the situation personally. Negotiate some better percentages."

Fritzi said, "Is a trip like that a good idea with all those German submarines prowling?"

"You're a sweet gel to worry, but we got an investment to protect. Besides, there's a hundred ships crossing the Atlantic all the time, and only a few of those Hun subs. I got no worries. Sophie and I are taking that fabulous Cunard boat *Lusitania*."

Air War • The new plane was fine—light and maneuverable. Nicknamed the *Bébé,* it was a smaller version of Nieuport's two-seat reconnaissance ship. Today was the second time Carl had taken one up since three of them had been delivered to the N65 squadron operating in the skies over Nancy.

During his first months in the French flying corps Carl had piloted a slow Farman, spending most of his hours aloft buzzing back and forth with field glasses, observing German entrenchments. He was soon reassigned to the N65, a pursuit squadron devoted to chasing enemy planes. He'd left his friend Rene behind to shoot at German observation balloons, clumsy gasbags that could explode with deadly force.

Carl had rolled out of the hangar an hour before. He'd donned a fleece-lined coat. Tess's red silk scarf was knotted around his throat. The rest of his flight gear consisted of goggles and oil-stained motoring gauntlets. He wore no parachute.

New, hornlike streaks of white hair above Carl's ears testified to the strain of aerial duty. He had been flying three months and hadn't yet engaged an enemy plane, though he'd chased a few.

The *Bébé* clipped along at six thousand feet, the eighty-horsepower motor droning smoothly. Three other pilots were aloft with Carl. German artillery below the horizon was hammering again. French artillery replied from positions behind him.

He bent to adjust the air- and gas-mix levers, and when he looked up again, he panicked. His three wingmen had vanished into a towering cloud. Suddenly, two thousand feet below, an Aviatik two-seater with black wing crosses popped from under the same tall cloud, going the opposite way. An artillery spotter.

Quickly Carl planned his strategy: attack from underneath the Aviatik. A second German manning the rear-seat swivel gun made diving from above foolhardy.

A Fokker pursuit monoplane burst out of the cloud. The observer's escort. At once he changed his plan. Fokkers were deadly because their guns fired through the synchronized propeller. He must knock out the Fokker first.

As Carl went higher, he turned. He thrust the nose over into a dive and felt a heavy vibration in the wings. In seconds he was on the Fokker, pressing the button to fire the big Lewis gun mounted above him on the upper wing. His rounds missed. He dived past the Fokker, banked away underneath. The Fokker came after him.

Carl headed into the sun. The Fokker's fuselage-mounted machine guns chattered, and several rounds punched holes in the *Bébé*. He yanked the stick back, and the plane climbed. At the apex of the climb he put the nose over and descended steeply again; he'd gotten the Fokker off his tail.

Carl passed the German observation plane. When he was well in front of the Aviatik, the Fokker appeared behind it suddenly, dived beneath it, then zoomed up, closing fast on Carl's Nieuport.

Carl executed a *renversement*. He came out of it flying straight at the Fokker, his Lewis gun blazing. The Fokker returned fire and nicked Carl's propeller. One of Carl's incendiary rounds ignited the German's fuel tank. The explosion shook Carl's plane, and the red fireball scorched his face as it rolled toward him. Carl dived like a madman, just clearing the lethal smoke and flame. The Nieuport vibrated hellishly. Suddenly he was hurtling nose first to a crash. He fought to bring the Nieuport out of the dive.

A thousand feet above the earth, the plane responded. Carl flew with his eyes shut for a few seconds, feeling the wing vibration dampen and then disappear altogether. A glance overhead showed the Aviatik darting into clouds to hide.

After he landed, he turned the *Bébé* over to his flight mechanic and jogged toward an open staff car that would deliver him to the château where the squadron was billeted. Aviators rode and slept in style—dined that way too.

That evening in the mess Carl listened to his commanding officer, Major Despardieu. "Fine work today. Your colleague Rossay was above you during the dogfight. He verified the kill."

The mess in the château's great hall was crowded and smoky. Of the sixteen pilots who flew regularly, twelve were present. The major took the monocle out of his eye. "You do appreciate that the *Bébé*'s wings tend to crumple and shear off if it is pushed too hard?"

"Yes, sir. I got that idea today. I didn't think about it long—I was pretty busy."

"Of course." Despardieu clinked his brandy snifter against Carl's. "Still, *mon ami,* you needn't worsen your chances."

No other words were needed; Carl understood perfectly. The average life expectancy of a front-line aviator was three weeks.

In an abstract way he was proud of his success today, but he felt none of the heady exhilaration familiar from his days of race driving and stunt flying. Maybe it was because the brief duel at six thousand feet had ended with another man's death.

Carl reached for the brandy decanter to calm a bad case of nerves. Next morning when he looked into his shaving mirror, the hornlike streaks of white hair were thicker.

Torpedoed • On the last night out, Captain William Turner, a veteran of the Cunard Line, addressed hundreds of passengers in the grand lounge. Not all of them could crowd in; *Lusitania* carried more than nineteen hundred people on this crossing. Like all of the great ship's public rooms, the lounge was opulent. Heavy furniture complemented rich tapestries on polished mahogany walls. Captain Turner took a wide-legged stance, hands behind his back. "Ladies and gentlemen, while I do not wish to alarm you unduly, it is my duty to inform you that today we received an Admiralty signal advising us of submarine activity in the area of Fastnet Rock."

The dire announcement brought a gasp from B.B.'s wife, Sophie. She clutched the diamond choker glittering at her throat.

"In response we have altered course so as to clear Fastnet by a margin of more than twenty miles. Further, in the morning you will see an armed Royal Navy cruiser alongside—our escort to Liverpool. Meanwhile, we have taken certain precautionary measures. All lifeboats have been swung out on their davits, canvas covers removed, and provisions checked. Stewards have already blacked out the portholes of your cabins. We ask your indulgence in showing no unnecessary lights, particularly on the open decks. If you have questions, kindly consult one of the officers. Thank you for your attention."

B.B.'s dinner sat badly in his gut. He wasn't worried for himself, only Sophie, who looked pickle-faced with fear.

"Benny, are we in danger?"

"Definitely not. Hun subs are after merchant ships carrying ammunition and such stuff. Nobody attacks a floating hotel like this. Now stop fretting. Want to go dancing or play cards?"

Sophie wanted to do neither. B.B. helped her to their royal suite, the ship's finest accommodation. With Sophie settled in bed, he returned to promenade deck, staring at the star-flecked sky over the Atlantic and enjoying the balmy May air.

B.B. SAID, "Say, Alf, what's that white line in the water?"

Alfred Vanderbilt, the richest man on board, was one of B.B.'s new pals from first class. Vanderbilt peered at the bubbly streak lengthening under the surface as it sped toward the hull. The two gentlemen were taking the air on the starboard side of promenade deck. Sophie was resting.

It was a few minutes past two in the afternoon of May 7, Friday. An air of relief and anticipation had infused the ship. Although there was no sign of the promised Royal Navy cruiser, the Irish coast had been visible to starboard for some hours.

Vanderbilt craned over the rail as the white streak neared the ship. "That is very odd, Benny. You don't suppose it's—"

The explosion shook the ship from bow to stern. B.B. fell against the rail. Righting himself, he lunged past Vanderbilt to the nearest door. Alarms began to ring. People ran wildly.

The vessel listed to starboard. Deck chairs slid. A second explosion rocked the ship as B.B. lurched into the elevator lobby. Air ventilators in the wall suddenly gushed smoke. B.B. ran to the stairs. Alarms kept ringing—the seven short and one long that signaled disaster at sea. Another lurch to starboard hurled him against the wall of the stairwell. He stumbled downward, then ran along the corridor like a madman because of a horrible certainty. *Lusitania* was sinking.

The cabin door was stuck. B.B. kicked it open with strength he didn't know he possessed. He bolted into the room as the liner listed more. Sophie shrieked. Glassware toppled and broke.

"Sophie, we got to get to the boats."

"I'm ready." She'd dressed for shore in a dark brown dolman wrap with a mink collar, bought especially for the trip.

His heart was pounding. Screams were multiplying in the corridors. The ship listed more steeply every few seconds. B.B. flew into the passageway, pulling her with him. "Stay behind me."

He bowled toward the stairwell like a football lineman. If they reached the boat deck, they'd escape. Boat deck, station two, portside—that was his goal.

Smoke and soot from ventilators blinded them on the stairs. B.B. gripped Sophie's hand as she stumbled upward a step at a time. With a feeling of elation he burst through the doors to the boat deck.

Chaos! The port lifeboats, many of them half full, couldn't be lowered because the list to starboard swung them inward, over the rail. All around him B.B. heard terror. "Not enough life jackets!" "The bow's going down!"

The slanting deck hurled everyone forward. A lifeboat cable snapped at the pulley. Lifeboat two dropped, crushing the passengers in the collapsible boat beneath. Violently B.B. pushed Sophie back to the doors. "We can't get off this side."

B.B. fought his way to the starboard deck, saw a half-filled lifeboat to the left, dragged Sophie toward it. He forced her to climb the ship's rail and helped her into the boat.

Lusitania listed again. The lifeboat swung outward from the ship as B.B. climbed onto the rail. He teetered like a high-wire artist, windmilling his arms to keep his balance. Sophie stood in the lifeboat while other passengers screamed for her to sit down, and a deck officer shouted, "Number two boat, lower away."

"Benny, jump," Sophie cried.

B.B. jumped. For a moment he seemed to float like an aerialist above the sunlit sea. Then he fell into the boat, nearly knocked out when his forehead struck one of the thwarts. Sophie caught him by the belt and dragged his legs in.

The ship took another huge lurch forward, burying its prow in the waves. The lifeboat tilted seaward at a sharp angle. Those not hanging on tumbled out at the bow. B.B. grasped a thwart with one hand and reached for Sophie with the other, but she flew past him and dropped from sight. "Sophie!"

He tried to reach the bow through a tangle of arms and legs. The lifeboat tilted again, and a pulley gave way. B.B. fell out of the boat and dropped through space into the glinting green water.

Like an enormous steel fish, *Lusitania* was slowly diving bow first into the sea. Her stern rose high in the sunlight. Her hull stood nearly vertical. Passengers and crew continued to fall or jump, landing in the midst of furniture and wreckage as the ship sank.

The water was hellishly cold for spring. B.B. felt faint. He bit his lips till he tasted blood. He had to find Sophie. He dog-paddled and kicked, shouting repeatedly, "Sophie? Sophie?" At last he saw her, holding her head out of the water by grasping a dining table.

"Sophie, hang on. I'm coming." He nearly choked as a heavy wave threw salt water into his mouth. He spewed it out and swam hard, his soaked clothes slowing him. He was within ten yards of Sophie when she raised one hand to wave at him.

"Benny, hurry. I got awful cramps."

"Don't let go," he screamed. Somehow Sophie didn't understand that she needed to hold on to the table with both hands. Her gray hair hung over her eyes. Her twisted face bespoke agony.

"Oh, Benny, it hurts." She thrust both hands underwater, to her middle. A wave washed over her. Gasping, she hunted for the table, but it floated out of reach. She fell back and sank while B.B. was still six yards away.

"Sophie!"

With a great roar and final rush of water *Lusitania*'s stern disappeared under the waves, leaving a foaming whirlpool and a sea of drowning passengers and crew. The ship sank eighteen minutes after the torpedo struck. Sophie Pelzer disappeared with her.

Marching • A flotilla of fishing boats and tugs from Queenstown rescued 761 people from the Irish Sea. Of 1198 aboard *Lusitania* who died, 124 were American citizens, many of them notables including the theatrical producer Charles Frohman and Alfred Vanderbilt.

Germany celebrated it as a great victory. The Kaiser declared a national holiday. A wave of outrage swept the United States. *The Nation* condemned "a deed for which even a Hun must blush." Some editorialists wanted an immediate declaration of war.

German Americans nervously avoided public scrutiny. In some cities, shops owned by first- and second-generation Germans had their windows smashed. At Brauerei Crown an unknown vandal set a small fire at night, destroying a delivery wagon.

Liberty rushed *Racetrack Nell* to the theaters, but Fritzi was much too concerned for B.B. to worry about its fate. She wept when she heard the news of Sophie Pelzer's death.

Professional nurses hired by the studio brought B.B. home from England. Doctors placed him in Haven Hill, a private hospital surrounded by the orange groves of Riverside, California.

On the first Sunday after his arrival Fritzi drove out to visit. She found B.B. sitting alone outside the sanitarium on a bench beneath a palm tree, blankly staring at four patients playing croquet.

B.B.'s curly gray hair had turned white. A light woolen blanket covered his legs. Fritzi was distraught to see him so listless. "Hello, B.B.," she said gently. "How are you?"

"All right. How are you?" he said in a vacant way.

Fritzi took B.B.'s hand and pressed it between her palms, as he used to do. "We're all so terribly sorry about Sophie."

"Sophie." He pressed the fingers of his right hand to his brow, his classic worry pose. "Poor Sophie."

The conversation limped and lurched for another ten minutes. When Fritzi could stand no more, she patted B.B., kissed his pale, freckled forehead. "I'll come see you again."

SOPHIE Pelzer's cruel death had driven Fritzi from a remote interest in the war to a passionate conviction that Germany must be defeated. She might be alienated from her father forever if she took that stand, but principle had to prevail. When the local Preparedness League organized a parade and rally downtown, Fritzi intended to march. On the following Saturday afternoon three hundred marchers gathered in front of Morosco's Globe Theater on South Broadway. It was a mixed crowd of suffragettes, academics, Socialists, students, and little old ladies from temperance societies. Fritzi hoisted a placard saying ARM NOW! and swung into line as a five-piece marching band led off, blaring "The Battle Cry of Freedom."

Because the afternoon was cool and gray, she had put on a rather plain skirt and jacket of Scotch tweed. She'd chosen her hat carefully: a large black silk sailor whose wide brim partially concealed her face. Though Fritzi wanted to march, she wasn't overly keen on attracting attention personally, and she thought the hat would help. She was naïvely wrong. The parade hadn't gone a block when a ragamuffin on the sidewalk pointed at her. "Look, it's Nellie from the pitchers." Soon a small crowd was following her.

At the public square the president of the Preparedness League asked her to step up on the soapbox to say a few words. "Please," he said, "take off your hat so they can see you."

The sight of Fritzi's long face and frizzy blond locks touched off applause. "All right, you know who I am." The crowd laughed, and she smiled. "But in marching with you today, I'm just another American citizen. I'm here because I lost a dear friend on *Lusitania*. To attack a civilian ship was a heartless crime. I don't want to involve American boys in a foreign war, but we can't stand by and allow the Hun to destroy freedom and trample on everything that's right." The words came swiftly, up from the depths of her emotions.

"My heritage is German"—someone booed—"but I have no sympathy for a country that callously takes the lives of innocents. By the last count ninety-four children perished when *Lusitania* sank. Imagine them in that bitter sea, their minds on fire with fright as they sink once, then struggle, only to sink again, vainly searching for their parents." The crowd listened in rapt silence.

"Ladies and gentlemen, we must stand fast against those who would consign children to that kind of hell. We must have funds for our military. We must recruit thousands to show the Hun we are ready to intervene. And there is only one way we can accomplish that." She flung her arm over her head and clenched her hand into a fist. "Preparedness. Preparedness *now*. Thank you."

She jumped off the soapbox as the crowd whistled and cheered.

Troubled Nation • Paul's ship, *Caronia,* crossed without incident, though with marked strain on her passengers because of *Lusitania*. Upon his arrival in New York, he checked into the Hotel Astor on Times Square. A call from his lecture agent invited him to dinner.

Actually, the caller was his agent's widow. Bill Schwimmer had died in the summer of 1914. His wife, Marguerite, was a pale Nordic woman, striving to be tougher than any male competitor. She slapped Paul on the back when she met him at Lüchow's restaurant, on Fourteenth Street. She wore black trousers and a boxy double-breasted black jacket.

They drank beer under an indoor trellis lit by colored lanterns. "Any second thoughts on the title of the lecture?" Marguerite asked. "The auditorium manager in Minneapolis thinks 'Atrocities of War' will keep people away. Sure you won't change?"

"I'm sure."

"Well, you may be in for rough sledding. The farther west you go, the more they like Germans."

"Then I should be a hit, since I'm German. Look, Marguerite, the truth's the truth. The Kaiser and his gang are a bunch of maniacal militarists, and they're conducting the war like butchers."

"Paul, I'm warning you, that kind of sentiment isn't unanimous over here. There's still a big split in this country."

"Therefore I'm supposed to tone down the lecture?"

"I've booked a fine tour. First-class venues. If you want to alienate your audiences, it's up to you."

PAUL stood in the tight white circle of the carbon arc. His podium was set by the proscenium, stage right of the screen. Marguerite had booked him into New York City's famous old Academy of Music, on Fourteenth Street.

He spoke into darkness while images of the trenches flickered across the screen. "I must warn you about the concluding footage. I filmed it in Belgium last summer. If the pictures are too harrowing, please turn away. I assure you this is real."

As the first bayonet stabbed into the first victim, Paul heard gasps. Someone in the gallery cried, "No." A man in the third row dragged his wife to the aisle and left. Others stood in the orchestra gathering their wraps.

And this was pro-British New York.

The scene ended. The projection lamp darkened. Unnerved by the exodus, Paul started his brief closing remarks, but he stumbled over the words from his note cards and finished weakly. The curtain came down to feeble applause.

Paul started west by a southern route—Baltimore, Richmond, Charleston, Atlanta, New Orleans, the dusty cities of Texas. Managers of the halls greeted him with little enthusiasm. Every night people walked out. Others groaned or booed. In Houston he had twenty people in the audience. Cities along his northerly route, including Minneapolis and Des Moines, telegraphed cancellations.

When Paul's train arrived in Los Angeles, he asked a porter to arrange to send the film boxes directly to Clune's Auditorium, but an hour later he was contacted at his hotel and told the program had been canceled. He felt like he'd taken a body blow.

That evening Fritzi rushed home from Liberty after working all day on *Big Top Nell.*

"What will you do after the tour?" she asked at supper in her little Mediterranean house. Paul and Fritzi sat on a small terrace, cool now that the sun was hiding behind the hills. Fritzi refilled their wineglasses with an excellent Sonoma County red.

After a moment Paul said, "Why, I'll go home to Julie and the kids, then go back to the war zone. That's all I know how to do."

"I'm sorry you've had hostile crowds," Fritzi said.

"They just don't understand. I'm hanged if I know why."

After dark, in the small, cozy parlor, Paul set up Fritzi's projector and ran his film. When the six Belgian men and women died in the field, Fritzi wept.

Paul switched off the machine as Fritzi wiped her reddened eyes. "There's one person who must see this, Pauli. Papa."

"Chicago's canceled. I'm not stopping there."

"Please reconsider. For me."

"You've already told me how he feels about the war."

"Yes, but you might change his mind. Papa respects you. And you're family." She folded her hands in her lap. "You have to do it, Pauli."

He winced. "Give me some more wine while I think about it. I could wind up with the General despising us both forever."

Kelly Gives Orders • In his office Al Kelly wasted no time confronting Fritzi. "We pay you to perform at the studio. I hear you did an act downtown."

"I marched in the preparedness parade, if that's what you mean," Fritzi said.

"Made a big speech. It went all over the country on the press wires. I saw the *Times* write-up, and I didn't like what I read."

"I'm sorry. I spoke my mind."

"Take my advice. Don't get involved in causes."

Irked, Fritzi said, "There are more important things than being a picture star and signing autographs."

"Not in my cash book, sister. Take the wrong stand on a public issue like the war, your audience is liable to desert you. You can't afford that. Nor can Liberty. Don't make any more speeches. That's it. That's the order. I run this studio."

"You don't run me, Al. Not outside the gates."

"Then you're making your last picture as Nell."

"What?"

"You signed a contract binding you to work for Liberty for three years. We have to pay you, but we don't have to use you."

"Have you lost your mind? The Nell comedies make money."

"Sure, but watch them go the other way if you keep opening your bazoo about the war. Half the people in this country want no part of it. Get this straight, Fritzi. Liberty created the Nell pictures, and Liberty owns the character. We can hire any actress for the part. We can send you back to cowboy pictures."

"This is a bluff."

"Play the hand out and see." Kelly swiveled around in his chair and showed her his back.

Heat of the Moment • In the midst of a fiercely hot summer, a season of mounting war passions, Joe Crown felt himself a man besieged. The climate for German Americans steadily grew more hostile. Editorial cartoons portrayed all Germans as "cruel beasts" and "lying Huns." Though Joe didn't tell Ilsa, he worried endlessly about Carl, off in France in a fragile airplane, risking his life. And he was beset by physical ailments. His eyesight was failing. The winter had exacerbated pain in his arthritic hips. Since his seventy-third birthday, observed on March 31, things had slid downhill rapidly. Now, in the blaze of July, here was his nephew Paul fresh off the transcontinental train and eager to show him pictures.

"Why should I waste my time?" the General said after Ilsa had retired. He and his nephew sat with beer and cigars in the stuffy office on the first floor of the mansion.

"Because these pictures tell the truth about what's happening, and because I respect your integrity, Uncle Joe. If you see the truth, I know you won't try to deny it. You're not that kind of man."

The General chewed his cigar. "You said you were last in Los Angeles? Did Fritzi have a hand in your coming here?"

Paul didn't avoid his uncle's eye or even blink. "Yes. But I take responsibility. I made the decision to stop in Chicago."

The General said, "All right. For you, not her."

After footage from the trenches, the Belgian field appeared. The soldiers fixed bayonets and lunged forward, ramming the steel into the six victims. When they fell in postures of agony, the soldiers stabbed again and again, many more times than necessary.

Joe Crown's cold cigar dropped to the floor. He held the arms of his chair as the screen went black. *"Mein Gott in Himmel."* He staggered to his feet. "I need air."

He blundered to the door like a gored animal. Paul followed him through the darkened downstairs and down the front steps.

A pressure heavy as an iron anvil lay on Joe's chest suddenly. He leaned against an elm tree, struggling to breathe.

"Uncle, what is it?"

"A little pain. I have them occasionally. They pass."

This one took five minutes to pass.

"I'm all right now."

"Does Aunt Ilsa know about these pains?"

"No, she does not." He raised his fists in front of his nephew's face. "You must not tell her. I forbid you to say a word."

Profoundly shaken and disillusioned by Paul's pictures, Joe Crown slept badly that night.

At noon the next day, when he motored to the Union League Club for lunch, the temperature was already ninety-five degrees Fahrenheit. As Joe walked past crowded tables on his way to his customary small one by a window, he felt the racing of his heart. His step was unsteady. The General made a strange choking sound, clutched at his throat. "Catch him!" someone shouted as Joe toppled forward.

He flung his hands toward the nearest table, caught the white cloth, and pulled it down with him. China and crystal smashed. Half conscious, the General tried to rise but couldn't. He saw anxious faces peering down, then nothing.

IT MUST have been a hundred degrees in the room. And the smell! Fritzi knelt at the bedside, took her father's frail veined hand in hers. The General turned his head toward her.

White stubble covered his cheeks. He spoke from the right side of his mouth. *"Fritzchen."*

"Papa. *Wie bist du?"*

"Besser."

He didn't look better. "I'm so sorry it happened, Papa."

"Danke." He tried to touch her hair, but he was too feeble.

"You'll get well, Papa. This will pass." Out in the hall, she had heard the physician's verdict. Her father had survived the stroke and might walk again someday—but never unassisted.

"Ja, wirklich." Sure enough.

"I came as fast as I could. I need to ask forgiveness for making you angry for so long. I had to go to New York. I couldn't have done otherwise, but I know the pain that it caused you, and I'm sorry for it. No matter how we differ about things, I love you, always."

His papery fingers stirred ever so slightly in hers. *"Meine liebe Tochter."* My dear daughter. And then, like a benediction, he uttered one more word. *"Vergeben."*

Forgiven.

She touched his hand. "Rest, Papa. I'll look in again."

Casualties • In the late summer Carl shot down his second German plane. The kill wasn't any easier or less scary than the first, but it was different, less emotional.

He was depressed by the news of Rene LeMaye's sudden death. Rene had gone once too often against an observation balloon called a Drachen. Long lines of Drachens were strung along the German front. Rene had closed in on a balloon as usual, to fire incendiary rounds and ignite hydrogen in the bag above the observation basket. Somehow his guns jammed, and he attempted to finish the job by slashing the balloon with his wingtip. Rene accomplished that, only to disappear when some random spark set off the hydrogen, blowing up Rene and his airplane.

Then one beautiful October afternoon, about six miles into German-held territory, four planes from Carl's squadron encountered six triple-wing aircraft with red cowls. The Germans were soon swarming all over them.

One of the red Fokkers doggedly pursued Carl. No matter how he dodged and maneuvered, the German was always there. After an aerial fight that lasted nearly ten minutes with no victor, Carl took a burst that damaged his engine. He peered over the side to check his position. Enemy antiaircraft guns had swung around to bang away at the French planes. As black clouds bloomed and billowed, Carl signaled a wingman, pointing at his damaged engine, then banked and headed west.

The Fokker was right behind but withheld fire. Carl's broken fuel line spewed aviation gas behind the *Bébé*. The balloons that spotted for the German artillery were coming up ahead. Typically they were anchored three miles behind no-man's-land, which told him how far he had to fly to safety. He tilted the *Bébé* to slide between two of the Drachens.

Soon all his fuel was gone. The engine sputtered, coughed, died. Losing altitude, he looked back. The German was still there. Carl expected to be shot down. That was the mission of airmen, to down the other plane. But a certain code of honor prevailed on both sides. If one was feeling chivalrous and the enemy plane had been rendered useless, there was no absolute obligation to kill the airman too. Evidently the German pilot was in that mood. He swooped past Carl, saluted him with a smirk and a cheery wave of a leather gauntlet. He peeled away and was gone.

Carl held the *Bébé* aloft until he saw the German trenches and, beyond them in the distance, French balloons. He glided over the trenches at five hundred feet, drawing some ground fire that did no damage. He aimed the plane at a space between shell craters in no-man's-land, well short of the forward trenches on the French side. As carefully as he could, he brought the plane down.

The ground was rougher than it looked. Something caught the undercarriage, standing the plane on its nose and hurling Carl out of the cockpit. He tumbled through the air, landed violently on his left side, and blacked out.

He woke to feel excruciating pain in his arm. Germans were firing at him from their trenches. Carl dragged himself the other way. He felt no sensation in his left hand; his arm dangled like a broken twig. He crawled through loops of barbed wire, dragging himself with his right hand and pushing with his knees. Nearly unconscious, he fell over the edge of a trench and croaked his name to a French poilu before he sank into comforting darkness.

"Look," they said, bringing him a small hand mirror in the hospital ward.

His hair was completely white.

"Your left arm is crippled," they said. "If it is only damage to nerves, you may recover the use of it one day. Or perhaps not. In any case, you can no longer fly. We are sending you home."

In the Trenches • "Must be the funniest damn war in history," Sammy said minutes before the bombardment. "Blokes just standin' still lookin' and shootin' at each other." Sammy and Paul had photographed Allied troops for a week, then followed a circuitous route, via occupied Brussels, to the German front line.

The French howitzers fired their first rounds at four o'clock. Paul had given up filming much earlier, when the light of the winter afternoon was already failing. He and Sammy stood in a forward German fire trench, peering over a wooden revetment improvised from pieces of crate. The officer in charge of the sector, a Major Nagel, yelled into a field telephone.

Paul turned up his overcoat collar. Shells sent up geysers of earth in no-man's-land; dirt rained on them. The artillery barrage directed from observation balloons tore gaps in the barbed wire strung for miles in either direction. That was the purpose—to open the way for an infantry assault.

In no-man's-land a few shell-blasted trees stood like burned and amputated fingers. Major Nagel joined Paul and Sammy. "We should see them come over the top in about an hour. The same pattern has prevailed all month. The French call it nibbling us to death." Nagel was an overweight Bavarian, bewildered by this peculiar form of warfare and resentful of the conditions in which it placed his men.

Major Nagel's position was approximately eighty-five miles northeast of Paris, in the sector stretching from Châlons-sur-Marne west to Epernay, in the department of the Marne. The major and his men faced units of Marshal Foch's Ninth Army. On the way to the forward area Paul and Sammy had filmed German soldiers doing laundry, enjoying mess, marching and singing. Each scene was carefully arranged by senior officers to impress the outside world with German morale. Looking closely, however, Paul saw something else. The troops appeared wan and frightened.

As it grew dark, the bombardment continued. Nagel insisted Paul and Sammy go down into one of the dugouts. The earth above them shook as the French shells hit. Dirt fell into Paul's hair.

At the mouth of the dugout someone yelled, "They're coming." Paul heard rifle fire as the artillery ceased. Major Nagel had sent sharpshooters forward into the saps to enfilade the soldiers charging across no-man's-land. Machine guns stuttered.

The ground assault lasted forty minutes. The German position held. Finally quiet returned. Someone shouted down that it was all clear. Paul and Sammy climbed out of the dugout.

The French had gone back to their trenches. Under the cold, distant stars Nagel's men crept forward to drag bodies out of the saps and pile them in a heap several yards in front of the fire trench. Paul counted silently. Fifteen.

He slept half frozen in the dugout that night. At daybreak he loaded the camera, climbed out of the trench, and positioned himself to film the corpse heap.

A pale yellow sun shone through a thin morning fog. Paul was just setting up when Major Nagel came tearing out of the fire trench to confront him. "You can't do this. It isn't appropriate."

"Major, I have permission. I have papers signed by—"

"I don't care if they're signed by the Blessed Virgin," the distraught officer cried. "I lost good men last night. I lost my second, Captain Franz. What's left of him is scattered in little pieces. It isn't appropriate for you to photograph that. Do you hear me?"

Suddenly ashen, he threw his hands over his face and sobbed. As a sergeant led him away, a lieutenant explained to Paul, "You must understand about the major. He's a career man. The army's his life. He adopted Franz like a son; he was bringing him along. This filthy war is destroying all of us. I must ask you to take cover again. This ground is watched by snipers."

"All right," Paul grumbled. The winter cold had started his back aching again. Sammy trotted up and offered to take the camera. Paul gladly surrendered it.

"Keep low, please," the lieutenant said as he went ahead of them. Paul obliged, bending over. Sammy didn't hear the lieutenant. Talking around a cigarette in the corner of his mouth, he said he'd be thankful to retreat to someplace they could get a bath and a hot meal.

"And women. How can a bloke get on without—" A shot rang out, then two more. Paul watched the camera sail from Sammy's hand. Sammy pitched forward, his nose burying in the mud. The back of his skull was red with blood.

Paul dropped to his knees, picked up Sammy's shoulders, shook him. "Sammy. Sammy!" The sight of his friend's vacant eyes shocked him as few things ever had before.

"I must ask you to leave him until dark," the lieutenant said.

"Go to hell," Paul said, feeling tears on his dirty cheeks. "I'll bring him back when I'm ready."

The lieutenant retreated. Paul held Sammy against his overcoat, heedless of the blood. He cried. Sammy's death was the emblem of the nightmare that had enveloped Europe's golden summers of peace and confidence, turning them to winters of despair and ruin.

Under the pale sun, with the coils of wire growing visible again, Paul dragged Sammy's body to the fire trench. An hour later he buried the remains in alien ground.

He examined his camera. It was broken beyond repair. He felt the same way. He held the camera in his arms like a dead child, wondering how long the carnage would last—how many millions more would perish with their dreams.

The Boy • They stood in the same finely appointed parlor where they'd visited before he left for France. Carl looked bedraggled, underfed, in need of a barber. His lifeless left arm hung in a black sling. Using his other hand, he unwound the red scarf with its frayed ends. Gravely, with ceremony, he placed it around Tess's neck, drew it down over her shoulders, straightened it.

"The dragons and Saracens are all dead, Tess. I've come home to stay. With you if you'll have me."

Tess touched the scarf, holding back joyous tears. "I never wanted anything more. But what will you do? Work for your father? I'll live in Chicago if that's what you want."

He shook his head. "Prohibition's coming. Pop's recovering slowly from his stroke, but the brewery may not exist in a year or two. I'd rather make automobiles than beer. Automobiles and airplanes."

"The Clymer company's gone," Tess said. "But other manufacturers in Detroit are thriving. I know the right people. First, though—" She drew him to a horsehair sofa, sat close to him. He reveled in her nearness. "You remember my saying when you left the first time that I'd never let my love turn into guilt—or a rope to tie you down? For that reason there's something I've held back."

He took her hands between his. "What is it, Tess?"

"You haven't suspected? It's the boy. I married Wayne so he'd have a name, but his name really isn't Sykes, it's Carl Henry Crown. I changed it legally after Wayne died."

"He's my son?" Carl said. "All these years and I didn't—"

She kissed him ardently. "If there's any fault, it's mine."

"Does he know about me?"

"Yes. I explained. He's small but very quick. He didn't seem hurt, more curious. Principally about you. He asked a great many questions. He's waiting in the library." She took Carl's hand, tugged him toward the hall doors. "He's a fine boy. You'll like him."

They crossed the marble floor to an open doorway. The boy peered anxiously toward the sound of the footsteps. Carl saw the resemblance strongly now. He'd noticed it in the eyes before. His own eyes filled with tears.

"Hal, here's your father," Tess said with a loving smile. She stepped aside to let Carl pass. With excitement and a sudden strange sense of contentment he realized he was stepping into a new world where, one of these days, all his broken dreams might be mended.

The Unfinished Song • "Yes, Mr. Folger, I have it written down. Outdoor rallies in Eureka, Santa Rosa, Napa, Oakland. Then the parade and auditorium program in San Francisco. . . . No, I can't do any more after that. I've sublet my house. I've decided to return to New York. I'm tired of pictures, and the studio isn't using me. . . . No, Mr. Folger, I'm not joking. . . . Because of circumstances I can't explain. . . . All right. Thank you. Good-bye."

Fritzi hung the earpiece on the hook of the wall telephone.

At the front of the hall a stack of empty brown cartons nagged her about packing. The house had a still, dead feel. At two in the afternoon the December sun was already low. Fritzi pushed a strand of hair off her forehead and then lethargically moved away from the wall. She was scheduled to travel east in four days. She would visit her parents again, then continue on to New York and start over in the theater, shopworn and faded, and not a little jaded. Hmm, could

Harry Poland write a ditty about that? Probably, but who'd buy it?

In the front room Fritzi was annoyed by the clutter. She kicked her way through empty cartons and cranked up the Victrola. She played "A Girl in Central Park" five times loudly. Her status as a picture actress would open some doors on Broadway, but she suspected it would also restrict the parts she might be offered—loopy aunts and zany maids in farces, never Ophelia or Medea. She was typecast. After a while, as she reached forty, what parts would be offered? Any?

The loud music masked the arrival of a taxi. She saw it through the window. A man ran around to the curbside, opened the door to assist another passenger, feeble and white-haired. B. B. Pelzer.

Clinging to the arm of a man Fritzi recognized as an attendant from Haven Hill, B.B. came up the flagstone walk with short, tentative steps. Fritzi ran to the door.

"B.B., how wonderful to see you. How are you?"

"Who knows? My legs feel like toothpicks. You keep me standing here, they'll be broken toothpicks."

Fritzi helped him into the parlor, settled him in an easy chair. "I'll wait in the cab," the attendant said, leaving.

B.B. blinked at the packing boxes, the rolled-up rugs. "Eddie said nobody could stop you but me. You ain't going to do this, are you?"

"Yes. Kelly's holding me to the contract, but he won't put me in a picture. He hates my speeches."

"Eddie told me." All at once B.B. bristled with energy. "That Irish bully's out. He's out. I still got majority control. From here I'm driving straight to the studio to take care of it. Now let's talk about you. You belong in pictures. Liberty Pictures exclusively. You don't want to work on Broadway again. All those drafty theaters, cold dressing rooms—pfui. Eddie has just the picture for you. He told me. Say, you got any hot tea? I like English Breakfast."

"I'm afraid all I have is Earl Grey."

"That's British—that'll do."

Moments later Fritzi brought a tea tray into the parlor and served B.B. on a small lap tray.

"Ah, that's good." B.B. smacked his lips. "This is what I got to propose. Everyone loved you in the Lone Indian pictures. So how about two in one? Eddie's writing it now. He's nuts for it." B.B. held his breath. You could hear trumpets. "*Two Gun Nell.* Knocking them out in the Wild West! I know you had a terrible time, Fritzi. That cowboy vamoosing the way he did. Eddie told me. Work's good medicine, though. You want to work, we've got work."

Fritzi's eyes welled with tears. "Oh, B.B., I don't know if I can anymore."

"Sure, you can. You're a strong gel. You're professional, for heaven's sake. What do you say?"

Her old invisible friend Ellen Terry helped her out.

You say yes.

THE first thing Fritzi noticed on Monday morning was Al Kelly's office, padlocked. Her old friends welcomed her like a lost Queen of Sheba. The cameraman, Jock Ferguson, hugged her. No, he hadn't heard a word from Loy—probably never would.

Fritzi walked out of her makeup tent wobbling on high-heeled boots. Floppy sheepskin chaps over dungarees dragged in the dust. A blue-and-white gingham shirt fitted her nicely. She carried the huge sugar-loaf sombrero they'd given her, because as soon as she had put it on, it slipped down over her ears to the tip of her nose.

On the outdoor glass-enclosed stage, flats created a frontier saloon. B.B. sat to one side of the camera in a canvas-backed chair. Eddie approached her with his little megaphone.

"How do you feel, Fritzi?"

"I feel like an idiot in this getup." The truth was, she felt low. Little had changed; the same bleak questions persisted. Where was the laughter? There wasn't any. Just another performance. Oh, well. It was what she did. Maybe she'd love it again someday.

"Fritzi, you know the moves. You dash forward, but you don't see the cuspidor. You trip, you fall on the poker table, the legs break away, the three cardplayers tumble over backward in their chairs."

"I'm ready," Fritzi said in a weary voice.

Eddie called, "Camera." Jock started cranking. Standing by the flimsy batwing doors mounted in a cutout, Fritzi poised herself for the take. Sunlight falling on the greenhouse stage dazzled her a moment. She saw a tall, broad-shouldered man hurrying toward the stage, with a secretary pointing the way. Something about the man's build, his confident stride reminded her of—

No, she was wrong. It wasn't Loy. It was Harry Poland.

"Action!"

Identifying him as she started her run threw her timing off. Fritzi missed the cuspidor, banged into an empty table, lost her balance, and reeled into a canvas flat headfirst. The canvas tore, and her head poked through. Eddie yelled to Jock to stop cranking. Six feet in front of her, on the other side of the glass—yes, it was Harry, waving yellow roses wrapped in green tissue paper.

"What is going on here?" Eddie demanded.

Fritzi pulled her head out of the flat, unhurt. "It's an old friend, Eddie. I saw him, and it startled me."

Harry stepped in through the hinged glass door and tipped his hat. "Harry Poland," he said. "I remember some of you from my previous visit. I traveled a great distance to see Miss Crown. I sincerely apologize if my presence disrupted your work."

Rosetta, the girl who kept track of the scenario for Eddie, clasped her notebook to her bosom. "Harry Poland the music maestro? Oh, Eddie, he's famous."

"Yes, and I have a picture to make," Eddie said crankily. "All right, Fritzi, speak to your friend." He waved his megaphone at the others. "Take a half hour."

Fritzi dropped the oversized sombrero on a table and tried to rake tangles out of her frizzy blond hair. She felt a perfect fool in her cowboy regalia, especially with Harry looking so smart, as always. He tipped his hat a second time, presented the roses.

"Why, thank you. They're beautiful." She looked around for a vase, but of course there were no vases in a frontier saloon. Rosetta took the flowers, promising to put them in water right away.

Harry cleared his throat, meeting the inquisitive stares of the extras, the director, the cameramen, the carpenters and stagehands. He said in a stage whisper, "I wonder if we might go somewhere to talk?"

Fritzi pointed at the rear of the lot, still undeveloped and weedy. "There?"

"Fine. Lead on."

They stepped outside. Harry spied a rusting wheelbarrow, sat down on one side of the broken wheel while Fritzi sat on the other.

"I'm so happy to see you, Harry. Do you have business in Los Angeles, or is this another vacation?"

"Neither." He looked at her intently. "A year has gone by."

"So it has." She hadn't forgotten.

"A bit more than a year, actually. I've been in London, rehearsing my new show. I brought a song for you. Not perfect, not yet finished, it came to me in a rush, on the crossing."

Out came a folded music paper. He began to sing softly.

> *"I keep insisting, you keep resisting,*
> *Saying you can't love as I love you.*
> *Dearest, until the day that you do,*
> *I have love enough for two. . . ."*

Harry raised his head slowly, flushed. "You see why it's imperfect, don't you? *'Love enough'*—that's bad, difficult to articulate. Trouble is"—his blue eyes fixed on hers in a way that made the nape of her neck tingle—"trouble is, the words express the thought precisely."

"Harry, what are you trying to say?"

"I'm saying I love you, and I'm doing a damn bad job of it."

Fritzi was stunned by his fervor, and flattered. She noticed blurred faces pressed to the glass of the stage. She turned her back on them. "Now Harry—"

"Please, Fritzi"—he spoke in a rush—"let me say what I came thousands of miles to say. I dreamed of this country long before I saw it. I dreamed of all the possibilities in America, and when I got here, I discovered the freedom a man needs to make dreams come true. All my dreams have come true but one, and it's the most important. You, Fritzi. Having you as my own. Being with you as long as I live. I've dreamed of it from the day we met in Central Park. I fell in love with you that day, but I couldn't do a thing about it except write a song. Now I'm free. I want to know if there's the slightest chance for me."

"Harry, I don't want to hurt you. You're a fine, decent man, a dear man. You deserve honesty. I like you very much. I admire you enormously. But I don't love you the way you want."

Instead of disappointment he showed enthusiasm. "It isn't necessary! You will in time, I'll make certain of it. Don't you see?" He held out the paper. "I wrote the song to say that."

Fritzi rocked back on the wheelbarrow, laughing in spite of herself. "I must say, you're terribly confident."

"Yes, I am. In this country dreams come true." He tossed the music paper into the weeds, held her hand. "You're beautiful."

"Oh, Harry, that's not true."

"Beautiful—to me, from the very first."

Fritzi's blond hair tossed in the sunshine. "No one's ever said that to me."

"Then you are long overdue to hear it."

Looking at him with a new, wondering tenderness, she laughed again, deep in her throat. "You almost make me believe I might be, in another life, another century, perhaps."

"This life. This century." He drew her up from the rusted wheelbarrow. "Now."

"Harry, they're all watching—"

"I don't give a hang. I love you. You're beautiful. Believe it. I have love enough for two. Help me finish the song, Fritzi. Help me, and I'll make sure you never have a single regret," he said as he bent to kiss her.

JOHN JAKES

John Jakes is an American dreamer. And one of his first dreams was to become an actor, like Fritzi Crown, the pioneering movie star whose early career he chronicles in *American Dreams.* But during his freshman year at Northwestern University, Jakes began writing professionally and sold his first story for twenty-five dollars. "That check changed the direction of my life," he says. "I decided it was easier to go to the mailbox than to Broadway." And so began the career of one of America's most popular authors of historical fiction. Yet with more than sixty books to his name—including *Homeland,* the saga that introduced readers to the Crown family—Jakes has not forgotten his earlier theatrical ambitions. In his free time he both acts and directs in community theater productions.

What a treat!
For ten-year-old Becky Reggis,
going to the local Onion Ring
fast-food place was the best.
How could she know that
it would be hazardous
to her health?
How could anyone know?

**"An intelligent and timely
thriller."**

— San Francisco *Chronicle*

PROLOGUE

THE sky was an immense, inverted bowl of gray clouds that arched from one flat horizon to the other. It was the kind of sky that hovered over the American Midwest. In the summer the ground would be awash in a sea of corn and soybeans. But now, in the depths of winter, it was a frozen stubble, with patches of dirty snow and a few lonely, skeletal trees.

The leaden clouds had excreted a lazy drizzle all day. But by two o'clock the precipitation had abated, and the single functioning windshield wiper of the aged recycled UPS delivery van was no longer necessary as the vehicle negotiated a rutted dirt road.

"What did old man Oakly say?" Bart Winslow, the driver, asked. He and his partner, Willy Brown, sitting in the passenger seat, were in their fifties, their creased, leather faces witness to a lifetime of farm labor. Both were dressed in soiled and tattered overalls over layered sweatshirts, and both were chewing tobacco.

"Just said one of his cows woke up sick," Willy answered.

"How sick?" Bart asked.

"Sick enough to be a downer. Has the runs bad."

Over the years Bart and Willy had become what the local farmers called 4-D men. It was their job to pick up dead, dying, diseased, and disabled farm animals and take them to the rendering plant.

The van turned at a rusted mailbox and followed a muddy road that ran between barbed wire fences. A mile beyond, the road opened up at a small farm. Bart drove the van to the barn and backed up to the open barn door.

"Afternoon," Benton Oakly said. He was a tall, thin man. He kept his distance from Bart and Willy when they got out of the van.

Benton led his visitors into the depths of the dark barn. Stopping at a pen, he pointed over the rail. Bart and Willy ventured to the edge and looked in, wrinkling their noses. The area reeked of fresh manure. Within the pen an obviously sick cow was lying on its side. Raising a wobbly head, the cow gazed back at Bart and Willy. One of its pupils was the color of gray marble.

"What's with the eye, Benton?" Willy asked.

"Been that way since she was a calf. Got poked or something. I want her out before my other cows get sick. Is it still twenty-five bucks to haul her to the renderer?"

"Yup," Willy said. "But can we hose her off first?"

"Be my guest," Benton said.

Willy went and got the hose while Bart opened the gate to the pen. Trying to be careful where he put his feet, Bart gave the cow a few swats on its rump. Reluctantly it rose to its feet.

Willy came back with the hose and squirted the cow until it looked clean. Then he and Bart got behind it, and with added help from Benton they got it into the van. Willy closed the door.

"What d'ya got in there? About four head?" Benton asked.

"Yup," Willy said. "All four dead this morning. There's some kind of infection over at the Silverton Farm."

"Criminy," Benton said with alarm. He slapped a few wrinkled greenbacks into Bart's palm. "Get them the hell off my spread."

Bart and Willy drove the van out of the farm. When they reached the county road, Bart asked Willy, "You thinkin' what I'm thinkin'?"

"I imagine," Willy said. "That cow didn't look half bad after we hosed her down. Looks a mite better'n that one we sold to the slaughterhouse last week." He glanced at his watch. "Just about the right time, too."

The 4-D men did not speak again until they pulled off the county road onto the track that ran around a low-slung commercial building. A sign said HIGGINS AND HANCOCK. At the rear was an empty stockyard that was a sea of trampled mud.

"You wait here," Bart said as he pulled to a stop near the chute that led from the stockyard into the factory.

They got out of the van, and Bart disappeared down the chute. Five minutes later he reappeared with two burly men in long, bloodstained white coats, yellow plastic construction helmets, and yellow midcalf rubber boots. The heavier man's name tag said JED STREET, SUPERVISOR. The other man's said SALVATORE MORANO, QUALITY CONTROL. Jed had a clipboard.

Willy opened the van's rear door, and Salvatore and Jed covered their noses and peered inside. The sick cow raised its head.

Jed turned to Bart. "Can the animal stand?"

"Sure can. She can even walk a little."

Jed looked at Salvatore. "What do you think, Sal?"

"Where's the SME inspector?" Salvatore asked.

"Where do you think?" Jed said. "He's in the locker room, where he goes as soon as he thinks the last animal has come through."

Salvatore switched on a two-way radio and held it up to his lips. "Gary, did that last combo bin for Mercer Meats get filled?"

The answer came back accompanied by static. "Almost."

"Okay, we're sending in one more animal. That will more than do it." Salvatore switched off his radio and looked at Jed. "Let's do it."

Jed nodded and turned to Bart. "Looks like you got a deal, but we'll only pay fifty bucks."

Bart nodded. "Fifty bucks is okay."

While Bart and Willy climbed into the back of the van, Salvatore walked back down the chute, putting his earplugs in against the noise on the kill-floor area of the slaughterhouse. He approached Mark, the line supervisor.

"We got one more animal coming through," Salvatore yelled over the din. "But it's only for boneless beef. No carcass. Got it?"

Mark made a thumbs-up to indicate he understood.

Salvatore then passed through the soundproof door that led into the administrative area. Entering his office, he hung up his coat and construction helmet, sat down, and went back to his daily forms.

Concentrating as hard as he was, he wasn't sure how much time had passed when Jed suddenly appeared at his door. "We got a slight problem."

"Now what?" Salvatore asked.

"The head of that downer cow fell off the rail."

"Did any of the inspectors see it?" Salvatore asked.

"No," Jed said. "They're all in the locker room."

"Then put the head back on the rail and hose it off."

"Okay," Jed said. "I thought you should know."

"Absolutely," Salvatore said. "To cover ourselves, I'll even fill out a process-deficiency report. What's the lot and head number?"

Jed looked at his clipboard. "Lot thirty-six, head fifty-seven." He returned to the kill floor and motioned to two of his workers to heft the skinned, hundred-plus-pound cow's head from the floor onto one of the hooks on the moving overhead rail. He then trained a jet of high-pressure water on it as it moved along on the rail. Even to the hardened Jed the cataractous eye gave the skinned head a gruesome appearance. But he was pleased with how much filth came off. And by the time it passed into the head-boning room, it looked relatively clean.

CHAPTER ONE

Friday, January 16

THE Sterling Place Mall was aglow with the marble, brass, and polished wood of its upscale shops. Beautiful people milled about on this late Friday afternoon in their Gucci shoes and Armani coats to survey the offerings of the post-Christmas sales.

Under normal circumstances Kelly Anderson wouldn't have

minded spending a part of the afternoon at the mall. It was a far cry from the gritty beats she was usually assigned to as a TV journalist. But on this particular Friday the mall had not provided her with any promising candidates to interview.

Kelly blew out her breath in exasperation. "This is a joke," she said to Brian. Brian, a lanky, laid-back African American, was her cameraman of choice—the best WENE had to offer.

At thirty-four Kelly Anderson was a no-nonsense, intelligent, aggressive woman hoping to break into national news. Most people thought she had a good chance. She looked the part, with her sharp features and lively eyes framed by blond curls. To add to her professional image, she dressed impeccably.

Kelly checked her watch. "And to make matters worse, we're out of time. I have to pick up my daughter. Her skating lesson's over."

Kelly and Brian hoisted their equipment over their shoulders and started walking toward the center of the mall.

"What's becoming obvious," Kelly said, "is that people just aren't concerned about AmeriCare's merger of Samaritan Hospital and the University Med Center."

"It's not an easy subject to get people fired up about," Brian said. "It's not criminal or sexy, and there are no celebrities."

"All I know is that I shouldn't have scheduled this piece for tonight's eleven-o'clock news. I'm desperate."

Emerging from one of the corridors of the mall, Kelly and Brian arrived at the spacious epicenter. In the middle of the vast area, beneath a three-story-high skylight, was an oval skating rink. A dozen or so children along with several adults were all careering across the ice in various directions. The apparent chaos resulted from the conclusion of the intermediate lesson and the imminent commencement of the advanced lesson.

Seeing her nine-year-old daughter's bright red outfit, Kelly waved and called out. Caroline waved back and skated over. She stepped out of the rink and walked on the toes of her figure-skate blades to the bench and sat down. "I want to go to the Onion Ring for a burger. I'm starved."

"That's going to be up to your father, sweetie," Kelly said. "Mom's got a deadline." She bent down and got Caroline's shoes out of her knapsack and put them on the bench next to her daughter.

"Now, there's one heck of a skater," Brian said.

Kelly straightened up. "Where?"

"In the center," Brian said, pointing. "In the pink outfit."

A girl around the same age as Caroline was going through a warm-up exercise that caused some of the shoppers to watch.

"Whoa," Kelly said. "She looks professional. Who is she?"

"Her name is Becky Reggis," Caroline said, trying to yank off her skate. "She was the junior state champion last year. She's been invited to the Nationals this year."

"Reggis, huh? Could that be Dr. Kim Reggis's daughter?"

"I know her father's a doctor," Caroline said. "She goes to my school. She's a year ahead of me."

"Well, bingo," Kelly murmured. "I just had a brainstorm," she said to Brian. "Dr. Kim Reggis would be perfect for this merger story. He was chief of cardiac surgery at Samaritan before the merger, and then, bang, he became one of the Indians. I'd bet he'd have something to say."

"No doubt," Brian said. "But would he talk to you? He didn't come off too good in that *Poor Little Rich Kids* piece you did."

"He had it coming. I can't understand why cardiac surgeons, with their six-figure incomes, don't realize that moaning about Medicare reimbursement rates strikes a hollow chord with the public. Anyway, what do we have to lose?" Bending down to Caroline, Kelly added, "Sweetie, would you know if Becky's mother is here?"

Caroline pointed. "She's over there, in the red sweater."

"How convenient," Kelly said as she peered across the ice. "Listen, Chicken, get your shoes on. I'll be right back."

Kelly walked around the end of the skating rink and approached Becky's mother. The woman appeared to be about her own age. She was deeply absorbed in a textbook.

"Excuse me," Kelly said. "I hope I'm not disturbing you."

Becky's mother looked up. She was attractive, a dark brunette with auburn highlights. "It's quite all right," she said.

"Are you Mrs. Reggis?" Kelly asked.

"Please call me Tracy."

"Thanks," Kelly said. "That looks like serious reading for the skating rink."

Tracy flipped the book over to show its cover: *The Assessment of Child and Adolescent Personality.* "Before going back to school last semester, I was involved with therapy as a social worker, mostly with children, including adolescents."

"Interesting," Kelly said. "I should introduce myself. I'm Kelly Anderson of WENE News."

"I know who you are," Tracy said.

A pink blur raced past and drew their attention to the rink. Becky streaked backward. Then, to the delight of the impromptu audience, she executed a perfect triple axel.

Kelly let out a faint whistle. "Your daughter is phenomenal. My daughter says she's invited to the Nationals this year. That might make a good story for WENE."

"I don't think so," Tracy said. "She's decided not to go. Her father's not terribly happy about it, but to be honest, I'm relieved. That level of competition extracts a high price from anyone, much less a ten-year-old child. It's not always mentally healthy. It's a lot of risk without a lot of payoff."

"Hmmm," Kelly murmured. "I'll have to give that some thought. But meanwhile, I've got a more pressing problem. I'm trying to do a piece for tonight's eleven-o'clock news. Today's the six-month anniversary of AmeriCare's merger of Samaritan with the University Med Center. What I wanted was the community's reaction, but I've run into a lot of apathy. Do you think your husband would be willing to talk with me?"

"I really have no idea how he would feel," Tracy said. "You see, we've been divorced for a number of months."

"I'm sorry," Kelly said with sincerity.

"No need to be sorry. It was best for everyone, I'm afraid."

"Well, would you have any idea where I might find your former husband right now? I'd really like to talk with him."

"He's probably in surgery. With all the fighting for OR time at the med center, he's had to do all his weekly cases on Friday."

"Thank you. I'll see if I can catch him."

"You're welcome," Tracy said. She returned Kelly's wave and then murmured to herself, "Good luck."

OPERATING room 20 at the University Medical Center was one of two rooms used for open-heart surgery. At four fifteen it was still in full operation. With the perfusionists, anesthesiologists, scrub nurses, surgeons, and all the high-tech equipment, the room was quite crowded. At that moment the patient's heart, beating once again, was in full view, surrounded by a profusion of bloodstained tapes, trailing sutures, metal retractors, and pale green drapes.

"Okay, that's it," Dr. Kim Reggis said, and straightened up to relieve the stiffness in his back. He'd been operating since seven thirty that morning. This was his third and final case. "Let's go off bypass."

For the next twenty minutes communication wasn't necessary. Everyone on the team knew his job. After the split sternum had been wired together, Kim and Dr. Tom Bridges stepped back from the patient and began removing their sterile gowns, gloves, and plastic face shields. At the same time the thoracic residents moved in.

"I want a plastic repair on that incision," Kim called to the residents. "But don't make it your life's work. The patient has been under long enough."

"You got it, Dr. Reggis."

Kim and Tom emerged from the OR into the operating-room corridor. Both used the scrub sink to wash the talc off their hands. Like Kim, Tom Bridges was a cardiac surgeon. But whereas Kim's practice over the years had evolved into mostly valve replacement, Tom had gravitated more toward bypass procedures. They had been assisting each other for years and had become friends. They frequently covered for each other, especially on weekends. Kim was a trim six-foot-three athletic type who'd played football for Dartmouth. Now, at forty-three, because of the demands of time, his current exercise had been reduced to infrequent tennis and hours on a home exercise bike. Tom, too, had played football in college, but after years of no exercise the muscle bulk that he'd not lost had turned mostly to fat.

The two men started down the tiled corridor. Kim ran a hand through his dark brown hair and looked at his watch pinned to his scrub pants. "It's after five already, and I haven't even made rounds. I wish I didn't have to operate on Friday."

"It's sure not like it used to be," Tom said, "when you ran the department at Samaritan."

"Tell me about it," Kim said. "With AmeriCare calling the shots and with the current status of the profession, I wonder if I'd even go into medicine if I had it all to do over again."

"You and me both," Tom said. "Especially with these new Medicare rates. Last night I stayed up and did some figuring. I'm afraid I'm not going to have any money left after I pay my office overhead."

The two men stopped at the entrance to the recovery room just beyond the OR desk. "Hey, are you going to be around for the weekend?" Tom asked. "I might have to go back in on that case you helped me with Tuesday."

"Just page me. My ex is going away for the weekend. I think she's seeing someone. Becky and I will be hanging out together."

"How is Becky doing after the divorce?"

"Fantastic. Certainly better than I am. At this point she's the only bright light in my life."

"I guess kids are more resilient than we give them credit for. See you in the surgical locker room."

Kim stepped into the recovery room. He scanned the beds for his patients. The first one he saw was Sheila Donlon. She'd been his immediately preceding case and had been particularly difficult. She'd needed two valves instead of only one.

Kim walked over to the bed. One of the recovery-room nurses was busy changing an IV bottle. Kim's experienced eye first checked the patient's color and then glanced at the monitors. "Everything okay?" he asked as he read the chart.

"No problems," the nurse said. "Everything's stable."

Kim replaced the chart and moved alongside the bed. Gently he raised the sheet to see if there had been any unexpected bleeding. Satisfied, he looked for his other patient. Only about half the beds were occupied. "Where's Mr. Glick?" Kim asked. Glick had been his first case that day.

"Ask Mrs. Benson at the desk," the nurse responded.

Irritated at the lack of cooperation, Kim walked over to the central desk. "I don't see Mr. Glick," he said to Mrs. Benson, the head nurse.

"Mr. Glick was sent to his floor," Mrs. Benson said curtly.

Kim looked at the nurse and blinked. "But I specifically asked he be kept here until I finished my final case."

"The patient was stable. There was no need to tie up a bed."

"But you have tons of beds. It would have saved me time."

"Dr. Reggis, with all due respect, the recovery-room staff doesn't work for you. We work for AmeriCare. If you have a problem, I suggest you talk to one of the administrators."

Kim felt his face redden. Murmuring a few choice epithets, he walked out of the recovery room. Across the hall he stopped at the OR desk intercom and checked on the progress of his last case. The closure was proceeding on schedule.

Leaving the operating suite, Kim marched down the hall to the family lounge. By that time of day it was not crowded. He glanced around for Mrs. Gertrude Arnold, the wife of his last patient. He wasn't looking forward to talking with her. Her peppery personality was hard for him to bear. He found her in a far corner reading a magazine.

"Mrs. Arnold," Kim said, forcing himself to smile.

Startled, Gertrude looked up. "Well, it's about time," she snapped. "What happened? Is there a problem?"

"No problem at all," Kim assured her. "Quite the contrary. Your husband tolerated the procedure very well. He's being—"

"But it's almost six o'clock," Gertrude sputtered. "You said you'd be done by three."

"That was an estimate, Mrs. Arnold," Kim said, trying to keep his voice even. "Unfortunately, the previous case took longer than expected. We do the best we can."

"Yeah, well, let me tell you what else happened. AmeriCare isn't going to pay for my husband's first day in the hospital. They said he was supposed to be admitted this morning on the day of surgery and not the day before. What do you say to that?"

"This is an ongoing problem I'm having with the administration," Kim said. "When someone is as sick as your husband was before his surgery, I could not in good conscience allow him to be admitted the day of surgery. If AmeriCare persists, then I'll pay."

Gertrude's mouth dropped open. "You will?"

"It's come up before, and I've paid before," he said. "Now, about your husband. Soon he'll be in recovery. They'll keep him there until he's stable, and then he'll go to the cardiac floor. You'll be able to see him then."

Kim turned and walked from the room, pretending not to hear Mrs. Arnold calling his name. He retreated back up the hall and entered the surgical lounge. It was occupied by a handful of OR staff. Kim nodded to those few people he recognized. Having been working at the medical center only since the merger six months previously, he didn't know all the staff.

In the men's surgical locker room, Tom, who'd taken a shower, was putting on his shirt. Kim sat down on the bench in front of the bank of lockers and was about to pull off his scrubs when the door partially opened and one of the anesthesiologists from Samaritan, Dr. Jane Flanagan, called to Kim. "You have a visitor," she said, and the door closed.

"What now?" he questioned irritably. He pushed out into the lounge. Instantly he saw it was Kelly Anderson. A few steps behind her was her cameraman with a camcorder on his shoulder.

"Ah, Dr. Reggis!" Kelly exclaimed.

"How did you get in here?" Kim asked with indignation. The

surgical lounge was a sanctuary that even nonsurgical doctors were hesitant to violate.

"Brian and I knew you were here thanks to your former wife. And we were escorted here by Mr. Lindsey Noyes, from the AmeriCare–University Med Center PR department. We just need a moment of your time. We're doing a story commemorating the six-month anniversary of the hospital merger."

"Then talk to Mr. Noyes." Kim turned back to the locker room.

"Dr. Reggis, wait! I've already heard the AmeriCare side. We're interested in your view, from the trenches, so to speak."

Kim paused and looked back at Kelly Anderson. "After that piece you did on cardiac surgery?"

As Kim pushed open the locker-room door, Kelly called out again. "Dr. Reggis, just answer one question. Has the merger been as good for the community as AmeriCare contends? They say they did it for purely altruistic reasons. They insist it's the best thing that's happened to medical care in this city since the discovery of penicillin."

The absurdity of such a comment made it impossible for him not to respond. "The truth is that the entire rationale for the merger was to benefit AmeriCare's bottom line. Anything else they may tell you is pure bull."

When the locker-room door closed behind Kim, Kelly looked at Brian. Brian smiled. "I got it," he said.

Kelly smiled back. "Perfect. Just what the doctor ordered."

AFTER removing his scrubs and throwing them into the hamper, Kim had gotten into the shower. He'd not said a word to Tom.

"Aren't you going to tell me who was out there?" Tom said as he slipped on his long white hospital coat and Kim began to towel off after his shower.

"Kelly Anderson from WENE News. Can you believe it? She was dragged up here by one of the AmeriCare admin guys. My ex told her where to find me."

"Hey, what time were you supposed to pick up Becky?"

"Six o'clock," Kim said. "What time is it now?"

"You'd better get a move on. It's already six thirty."

"I haven't even done my rounds yet," Kim said. "What a life!"

IT WAS going on eight when Kim pulled his ten-year-old Mercedes up behind a yellow Lamborghini in front of his ex-wife's house in the university section of town. He leaped from the car and jogged up the front walk. The house was a modest Victorian. Kim took the front steps in twos to reach the columned porch, where he rang the bell. His breath steamed in the wintry chill.

Tracy opened the door and immediately put her hands on her hips. "Kim, it's almost eight."

"Sorry. My second case took longer than anticipated."

"I wish you'd at least called." Tracy motioned for him to step inside and closed the door behind him.

Kim glanced into the living room and saw a man in his mid-forties in a suede fringed jacket and ostrich cowboy boots. He was sitting on the couch with a cowboy hat in his hand.

"Luckily, we're not flying commercial," Tracy said.

"Flying?" Kim questioned. "Where are you going?"

"Aspen," Tracy said.

"Aspen for two days?"

"I feel it's time for me to have a little fun in my life. Not that you would know what that is, apart from your surgery, of course."

"By the way," Kim said, "thanks for sending Kelly Anderson to the surgical lounge. That was a pleasant surprise."

"I didn't send her," Tracy said. "I just told her I thought you were in surgery."

Over Kim's shoulder she saw her guest stand up. Sensing he was uncomfortable, she motioned to Kim to follow her into the living room. "Kim," she said, "I'd like you to meet a friend of mine, Carl Stahl."

The two men shook hands and eyed each other warily.

Tracy headed for the stairs. "I'll run up and make sure Becky has everything she needs."

Kim couldn't help feel some jealousy toward Tracy's apparent boyfriend, but at least Carl was several inches shorter, with significantly thinning hair. On the other hand, he was tanned in midwinter. He also appeared in reasonable physical shape.

Carl sat back down on the couch. Kim lowered himself into a facing club chair. "I saw that interview Kelly Anderson did with you a month or so ago," Carl said.

"I'm sorry," Kim said. "I was hoping most people missed it."

"I certainly didn't buy her premise. You guys earn every penny you get. I mean, I have a lot of respect for you doctors."

"Thank you. That's very reassuring. What do you do?" Kim asked. He was interested. The yellow Lamborghini outside had to belong to Carl.

"I'm CEO of Foodsmart. I'm sure you've heard of us."

"I can't say that I have," Kim said.

"It's a large agricultural business. Really more of a holding company. We're also the major stockholder in the Onion Ring burger chain."

"I've heard of them," Kim said. "I even own some stock."

"Good choice," Carl said.

A clatter of footfalls on the uncarpeted stairs heralded Becky's arrival. She dumped an overnight bag and her skates onto a chair in the front hall before racing into the living room. She made a beeline into Kim's arms and gave him an enthusiastic hug. Then without letting go, she leaned back and assumed a mock reproving expression. "You're late, Daddy."

Kim's aggravations of the day melted as he regarded his darling, precocious ten-year-old daughter who glowed with grace and energy. Her skin was flawless; her eyes were large and expressive. "I'm sorry, Pumpkin. You must be hungry."

"I'm starved," Becky said. "But look!" She turned her head from side to side. "See my new diamond earrings? Aren't they gorgeous? Carl gave them to me."

"Just chips," Carl said. "Sorta late Christmas present."

Kim was taken aback. "Very impressive," he managed.

Becky let go of Kim and went out into the foyer to get her things and her coat out of the front closet. Kim followed.

"Now, I want you in bed at your normal time, young lady," Tracy said. "You understand? The flu's making the rounds."

"Oh, Mom," Becky complained. "Don't be so nervous."

"I'll have a better time if I don't have to worry about you. You have the phone number I gave you?"

"Yeah, yeah," Becky intoned.

Becky ran to Carl, who was standing in the doorway to the living room. She gave him a hug and whispered, "Thanks for the earrings. I love them." She then gave Tracy a quick hug before dashing out the door, held open by Kim.

"SHE'S such a worrywart," Becky said as they got into Kim's car. Then she pointed ahead, through the windshield. "That's a Lamborghini. It's Carl's car, and it's awesome."

"I'm sure it is," Kim said, trying not to sound as if he cared.

"You should get one, Dad."

"Let's talk about food. How about the Onion Ring on Prairie Highway?"

"Fabulous!" Despite her seat belt, Becky managed to lean over and give Kim a peck on the cheek.

It being Friday night, the Onion Ring was mobbed. Most of the crowd were teenagers with competing boom boxes, but there were also lots of families. The noise level was considerable. The Onion Ring restaurants were particularly popular with children because the kids could doctor their own "gourmet" burgers with a bewildering display of condiments. They could also make their own sundaes.

"Isn't this an awesome place?" Becky commented as she and Kim got into one of the order lines.

"Just delightful," Kim teased. "Especially with the quiet classical music in the background."

"Oh, Dad," Becky moaned, and rolled her eyes.

"Did you ever come here with Carl?" Kim asked. He really didn't want to hear the answer.

"Sure. A couple of times. He owns the place."

"Not quite," Kim said with satisfaction. "Actually, the Onion Ring is a publicly owned company, which means a lot of people own stock. Even I own stock, so I'm one of the owners, too."

"Yeah, well, with Carl we didn't have to stand in line."

Kim took a deep breath and let it out. "Let's talk about something else. Have you thought any more about skating in the Nationals? The entry deadline is coming up."

"I'm not going to enter," Becky said without hesitation.

"Really?" Kim questioned. "You are such a natural."

"I like skating. I don't want to ruin it."

"But you could be the best. Gosh, Becky, I can't help but be a little disappointed. I'd be so proud of you."

"Mom said you would say something like that," Becky said.

"Oh, great. Your know-it-all therapist mother."

"She also said that I should do what I think is best for me."

Kim and Becky found themselves at the front of the line. Becky looked up at the menu mounted over the bank of cash registers. "Hmmm. I'll have a regular burger, fries, and a vanilla shake."

"And you, sir?" the teenage cashier asked.

"Let me see. Soup du jour and salad, I guess. And an iced tea."

Kim paid, and the cashier said, "Your number is twenty-seven."

It took some hunting, but Kim and Becky found a couple of empty seats at one of the picnic-style tables near the window.

THE level of activity in the kitchen and service area of the Onion Ring was controlled pandemonium. Roger Polo, the manager, regularly worked a double shift on Fridays and Saturdays, the Onion Ring's two busiest days. He was a nervous man in his late thirties who drove himself and his staff hard.

When the restaurant was this busy, Roger worked the line. He gave the burger and fries orders to the short-order cook, Paul; the soup and salad orders to Julia; and the drink orders to Claudia. All the restocking and ongoing cleanup was done by the gofer, Skip, who was new.

"Number twenty-seven coming up," Roger barked. "I want a soup and salad."

"Soup and salad," Julia echoed.

"Iced tea and vanilla shake," Roger called out.

"Coming up," Claudia said.

"Regular burger and medium fries," Roger ordered.

"Got it," Paul said.

Paul was considerably older than Roger. He had spent twenty years as a short-order cook on an oil rig in the Gulf.

Paul stood at the grill built into a central island behind the cash registers. At any given time he had a number of hamburger patties on the cooktop, each patty in response to an order. He organized the cooking by rotation so that all the burgers got the same amount of grill time. To fill the most recent wave of orders, Paul turned around and opened the chest-high refrigerator behind him. The patty box was empty. "Skip," he yelled. "Get me a box of burgers from the walk-in."

The walk-in freezer was at the very back of the kitchen. Skip stepped inside, and the heavy door closed behind him. The interior, about ten feet by twenty feet, was almost full of cardboard containers except for a central aisle. To the left were the large cartons full of frozen hamburger patties. To the right were boxes of frozen french fries, fish fillets, and chicken chunks. Skip flapped his arms against the sub-zero chill. He scraped away the frost from the label of the first carton to his left to make sure it was ground meat. It read MERCER MEATS. REG. 0.1 LB HAMBURGER PATTIES, EXTRA LEAN. LOT 6 BATCH 9-14. PRODUCTION: JAN. 12. USE BY APR. 12.

Skip tore open the carton and lifted out one of the inner boxes that contained fifteen dozen patties. He carried them back to the refrigerator behind Paul and put them in.

"You're back in business," Skip said.

Paul was too busy to respond. As soon as he could, he turned to the refrigerator, opened the patty box, and extracted the eight burgers he needed. But as he was about to close the door, his eye caught the label. "Skip," he yelled. "Get back here."

"What's wrong?" Skip questioned.

"You brought the wrong patties. These just came in today."

"What difference does it make?" Skip asked.

"Plenty," Paul said. "I'll show you in a second." He tossed the eight patties in his hand onto the grill and turned around to get the box of patties out of the refrigerator. As preoccupied as he was, he didn't notice that the first patty he threw ended up partially covering another patty that was already on the grill.

Paul motioned for Skip to follow him. "We get shipments of frozen hamburger every couple of weeks, but we use the older ones first." Paul opened the door to the walk-in freezer and was immediately confronted by the carton Skip had opened. Paul wedged the box he was carrying back into the carton and closed the lid.

"See this date?" Paul asked, pointing to the label. "Those other cartons back there have an older date. They have to be used first. Come on. Help me move these new ones to the back and the ones in the back to the front."

WHEN Paul returned from the freezer, an exasperated Roger demanded, "Where have you been? We're way behind."

"Don't worry," Paul said. "Everything is under control." He picked up his spatula and began slipping the fully cooked burgers into their buns. The patty that had been leaning up against another was pushed aside so that the one beneath could be removed.

"Ordering thirty," Roger barked. "Two regulars and one jumbo."

"Coming up," Paul said. He reached behind into the refrigerator, got the patties from the box he had brought back from the freezer, and tossed them onto the grill. He then flipped the patty that had been draped over another. It again landed so that it was leaning on another and not flat against the cooktop. Paul was about to adjust it when Roger got his attention.

"Paul, you screwed up. Number twenty-five is supposed to be two jumbos, not two regulars," Roger complained.

"Oops, sorry," Paul said. He got two jumbo patties from the refrigerator and tossed them onto the grill.

"Okay," Roger said. "Number twenty-seven's ready to go. Where's the burger and fries? Come on, Paul. Let's get on the ball."

"All right, already," Paul said. He used his spatula to scoop up the patty that had spent most of its grill time on top of two other patties, slipped it into a bun, and placed it on a paper plate. Then he filled a paper cone with french fries. The teenager on the distribution counter leaned over his microphone and said, "Pick up, number twenty-seven."

KIM stood up. "That's us. I'll get the food. You stay put."

"But I want to fix my own burger," Becky said.

"Oh, yeah," Kim said. "I forgot."

While Becky dressed her burger with an impressive layer of various toppings, Kim picked out the least offensive-looking salad dressing. Then father and daughter returned to their seats.

Kim was about to sample the soup when his cell phone rang against his chest. He took the phone out and put it to his ear.

"This is Nancy Warren," the nurse said. "Mr. Arnold is very anxious. And he says his pain medication isn't holding. He's also had a couple of premature ventricular contractions."

Becky used both hands to pick up her burger. Even so, a couple of sliced pickles fell out. Undaunted, she got her mouth around the behemoth and took a bite. She chewed for a moment, then examined the bitten surface. She reached out and tugged on Kim's arm, trying to get him to look at her burger. Kim motioned for her to wait. "Has he had a lot of PVCs?"

"No. But enough so that he's aware of them."

"Draw a potassium and double up on his pain meds. Check the potassium level and make sure there isn't any marked abdominal distension." He disconnected his call.

"Look at my hamburger," Becky said.

Kim glanced at Becky's burger and saw the ribbon of pink in the middle, but he was preoccupied and none too happy about the call he'd just gotten from the hospital. "Hmmm," he said. "That's the way I used to eat my hamburgers when I was your age."

"Really?" Becky questioned. "That's gross!"

"I ate my hamburgers medium rare and with a slice of raw onion, not with all that slop."

Becky looked at her burger, shrugged her shoulders, and then took another, more tentative bite. She had to admit it tasted fine.

CHAPTER TWO

Saturday, January 17

KIM turned into his drive and pulled up to the garage door. His house was a large Tudor on a generous wooded lot in a comfortable suburban township. At one time it had been an admirable house. Now it looked neglected. Most of the trim needed paint, and some of the shutters were awry. It was nine o'clock on an overcast, wintry Saturday morning; the neighborhood seemed deserted.

The interior of Kim's house reflected the exterior. It had been mostly stripped of rugs, accessories, and furniture since Tracy had taken what she wanted when she moved out. In addition, the house hadn't been properly cleaned in months. Kim tossed his keys onto a table in the foyer and passed through the dining room into the kitchen/family room. He called out Becky's name, but she didn't answer. He glanced into the sink. There were no dishes.

Having awakened a little after five, which was his custom, Kim had gone to the hospital to make his rounds. By the time he got home, he'd expected Becky to be up and ready to go.

"Becky, you lazy bum, where are you?" Kim called out while mounting the stairs. He heard Becky's door open. A moment later she was standing in the doorway, still in her nightgown. Her brown hair was a mop of tangled curls.

"What's going on?" he asked. "I thought you'd be raring to get to your skating lesson. Let's move it."

"I don't feel so good. I have a stomachache."

"Well, it's nothing, I'm sure. Does the pain come and go, or is it steady?"

"It comes and goes," Becky said.

"Where exactly do you feel it?" Kim asked.

Becky moved her hand around her abdomen.

"Any chills?" He put his hand on Becky's forehead. She shook her head.

"It's probably your poor stomach complaining about last night's junk food. You get dressed while I see to breakfast."

"I'm not hungry," Becky said.

"You will be. I'll see you downstairs."

Back in the kitchen, Kim got out cereal, milk, and juice. When Becky appeared, he asked, "Feel any better?"

Becky shook her head.

"Well, how about a shot of Pepto-Bismol?"

Becky screwed up her face in disgust. "I'll have a little juice."

THE stores in the mall were just beginning to lift their shutters as Kim and Becky made their way toward the skating rink. Kim was certain Becky was feeling better. She'd ended up eating some cereal after all, and in the car she'd been her usual talkative self.

"Are you going to stay while I have my lesson?" Becky asked.

"That's the plan," Kim said. "I'm looking forward to seeing that triple axel you've been telling me about."

As they approached the rink, a whistle sounded, indicating the end of the intermediate class. "Perfect timing," he said.

Becky sat down and started to unlace her sneakers. Kim glanced around at the other parents. A young girl about Becky's age skated over and exited the rink. She sat down next to Becky and said, "Hi." Becky returned the greeting. Kim turned, and to his distaste he found himself face to face with Kelly Anderson. Despite the early morning hour, she was dressed as if she were about to go to a fashion show. She smiled. "Have you met my daughter?" she asked.

Although he was reluctant to get into a conversation with Kelly, Kim greeted the young girl and introduced Becky to Kelly.

"What a delightful coincidence running into you again," Kelly said to Kim as she straightened up from shaking hands with Becky. "Did you see my segment last night on the eleven-o'clock news about the merger anniversary?"

"Can't say that I did."

"Shucks. Your 'bottom line' quote stole the show."

Kim shook his head in disgust.

Becky leaned over to Caroline. "I'll see ya," she said, then stood up, entered the rink, and skated off.

"Come on, Caroline," Kelly said. "Let's get your coat on."

Kelly and Caroline walked away, with Kelly carrying her daughter's skates and backpack. Then Becky, who'd been doing some warm-up exercises, skated back over to where Kim was standing.

"I can't take a lesson," she said. She stepped off the ice, sat down, and began quickly removing her skates.

"Why not?" Kim asked.

"My stomach is worse. And I have to use the bathroom—bad!"

Sunday, January 18

THE next day Kim finished his rounds at the hospital by eight in the morning. When the elevator arrived at his floor, Kim squeezed on. It was remarkably crowded for a Sunday morning. He found himself pressed up against a tall, bony resident whose name tag read JOHN MARKHAM, M.D., PEDIATRICS.

"Excuse me," Kim said. "Are there any enteric viruses making the rounds these days in school-age kids?"

"Not that I'm aware of," John said. "We've been seeing a pretty nasty strain of the flu, but it's all respiratory. Why do you ask?"

"My daughter's got a G.I. upset."

"What are the symptoms?" John asked.

"It started with cramps yesterday morning. Then diarrhea. I've treated her with some over-the-counter antidiarrheal agents."

"Has it helped?"

"At first. But then last night the symptoms returned."

"Any nausea and vomiting?"

"Some mild nausea but no vomiting—at least not yet. But she hasn't had much appetite either."

"Fever?"

"Nope. None at all."

"Who's her pediatrician?"

"It was George Turner. After the merger he was forced to leave town. He's back in Boston at Children's Hospital."

"I remember Dr. Turner," John said. "I rotated over to Samaritan. He was a good man. Anyway, about your daughter. It would be my guess she's got a touch of food poisoning, not a virus."

"Really? I thought food poisoning generally came on like gangbusters. You know, like the proverbial staph in the picnic potato salad."

"Not necessarily," John said. "Food poisoning can be present in countless ways. But if your daughter has had acute-onset diarrhea, statistically it's the most likely cause. To give you an idea of its prevalence, the Centers for Disease Control and Prevention estimates there are as many as eighty million cases a year."

The elevator stopped, and John disembarked. "I hope your daughter feels better," he said as the doors closed.

As he drove home, Kim continued to marvel at the idea of there being so many millions of cases of food poisoning every year in the United States. If such a statistic were true, it seemed incredible that he'd not come across it in any of his medical reading.

He was still mulling all this over as he came through his front door and tossed his keys onto the foyer table. He heard the sound of the TV coming from the family room. He walked in to find Becky sprawled on the couch, watching cartoons. She had a blanket drawn up around her neck. She looked slightly pale against the dark green wool.

They'd spent the previous evening at home because of Becky's condition, and she had gone to bed early.

"Hello," Kim called out. "I'm home." Becky didn't respond. When he got to the couch, he put his hand on her forehead.

"Feeling any better?" he asked. She felt warm, but he thought it might have been because his hand was cold.

"About the same," Becky said. "And I threw up."

"Is that right?" Kim asked. Vomiting was a new symptom.

"Just a little," she admitted.

"How about your cramps?"

"About the same. They come and go."

"What about your diarrhea?"

"Do we have to talk about this?" Becky asked. "I mean, it's, like, embarrassing."

"Okay, Pumpkin," Kim said. "I'm sure you'll be feeling your old self again in a few hours."

IT WAS dark by the time Kim pulled to the curb at Tracy's house. He went around to the passenger side and helped his daughter out of the car and up to the front door. Becky had herself wrapped up in a blanket so that it formed a hood over the top of her head. She'd spent the entire day on the family-room couch in front of the TV.

Kim rang the bell. When Tracy opened the door, she started to say hello, stopped, and frowned. "What's going on?" she asked. She turned back the edge of the blanket from Becky's face. "You're pale. Are you sick? Come in!"

Becky stepped inside. Kim followed. Tracy closed the door.

Tears formed in the corners of Becky's eyes. Tracy immediately enveloped her daughter in a protective hug. "What's the matter?"

"It's just a minor G.I. upset," Kim interjected. "Probably just a touch of food poisoning."

"If it's so minor, why is she so pale?" Tracy put her hand to Becky's forehead.

"She doesn't have a fever," Kim said. "Just some cramps and diarrhea. She's had Pepto-Bismol, and when that didn't seem to do the trick, I gave her some Imodium. It helped some."

"I have to go to the bathroom," Becky said.

"Okay, dear," Tracy said. "I'll be up in a minute."

Becky hoisted the edge of her blanket and hurried up the stairs.

Tracy turned to Kim. Her face was flushed. "Kim, you've only had her for less than forty-eight hours, and she's sick. I should have known better than to leave town."

"Oh, come off it," Kim said. "Becky could have gotten sick whether you left town or not. She's been feeling punk since Saturday morning. That means that if she's got food poisoning, then she probably got it from the Onion Ring out on Prairie Highway, the place that your new boyfriend bragged to Becky that he owned."

Tracy opened the front door. "Good night, Kim!"

Kim spun on his heels and left.

CHAPTER THREE

Monday, January 19

BY SIX a.m. Kim was already in his office dictating consult letters and writing checks for various expenses. At six forty-five he was in the hospital for teaching rounds and to see his own patients. Seven thirty was the daily hospital meeting. After that he met with the thoracic-surgery fellows he supervised, then went on to surgical grand rounds. By ten o'clock he was back at his office and already behind. The morning passed with nonstop patients. Lunch consisted of a sandwich that Ginger, his receptionist, had ordered in. Kim ate while he went over test results and X rays.

The afternoon was back-to-back patients, including a few emergencies. At four he dashed over to the hospital to handle a minor problem with one of his inpatients. While he was there, he quickly did afternoon rounds.

Back at the office several hours and a number of patients later, he collapsed into his desk chair and eyed the stack of phone messages he'd have to respond to before leaving.

The door to his office opened, and Ginger leaned in. "Tracy just called. She said to call."

"Okay, thanks," Kim said. He dialed. "What's up?" he asked with no preamble when Tracy answered.

"Becky is worse," Tracy said. "Her cramps are bad to the point of tears, and there's blood in her diarrhea."

"What color?" Kim asked.

"What do you mean what color?" Tracy demanded.

"Bright red or dark?"

"Bright red."

"How much?"

"How am I to tell?" Tracy responded irritably. "It's blood, and it's red, and it's scary. Isn't that enough?"

"It's not so abnormal to have a little blood in diarrhea."

"I don't like it," Tracy said. "I want her seen tonight!"

"Okay, okay," Kim said. "Calm down."

He paused to gather his thoughts. With George gone, he didn't have any handy contacts in pediatrics. He considered having one of his internal-medicine acquaintances take a peek at Becky, but it seemed excessive.

"I'll tell you what," Kim said. "When could you meet me over at the University Med Center emergency room?"

"I guess in about a half hour," Tracy said.

"I'll see you then."

AS THE major emergency room in a large midwestern city, the unit was so jammed it looked like an urban bus station. Monday nights tended to be particularly busy, a leftover effect from the weekend. Kim and Tracy steered Becky through the throng in the anteroom, where the main admitting desk was, and past the crowded waiting room. They were almost past the nurses desk when an enormous Brunhild-type nurse stepped out from behind the counter. Her name tag read MOLLY MCFADDEN.

"Sorry," Molly said. "You can't come in here on your own. You have to check in at the desk."

"Excuse me," Kim said. "I'm Dr. Reggis. I'm on the staff here, and I'm bringing my daughter in to be seen."

Molly gave a short laugh. "I don't care if you're Pope John whatever," she snorted. "Everyone, and I mean everyone, checks in at the front desk unless they're carried in here by the EMTs."

Kim was shocked. He could not believe that not only wasn't he being deferred to, he was being openly challenged.

Tracy sensed an impasse. Having an all-too-good idea of her former husband's temper, she took it upon herself to defuse the situation. "Come on, dear," Tracy said to Becky. "Let's get you checked in." She guided Becky back the way they'd come.

Kim shot a nasty look at Molly, then caught up to Tracy and Becky. They joined the line of patients waiting to check in.

"I'm going to complain about that woman," Kim fumed.

"She was only doing her job," Tracy replied. "If you'd taken Becky's complaints seriously over the weekend, we probably wouldn't have to be here now. You must have a thousand doctor friends. It wouldn't have been too much to ask."

"Wait a second," Kim said, struggling to control himself. "All Becky had was simple diarrhea and some cramps, both of short duration. And it was the weekend. I wasn't going to bother someone with such symptoms."

"Mommy," Becky said. "I have to go to the bathroom."

Tracy turned and put her arm over Becky's shoulder. "I'm sorry, dear. Sure. We'll find you a bathroom."

"Wait," Kim said. "We'll need a sample. I'll get a container."

"You must be joking," Tracy said. "She has to go now."

"Hold on, Becky," Kim said. "I'll be right back."

Kim walked quickly into the depths of the ER. Without Becky and Tracy he wasn't challenged as he passed the nurses desk. Like the outer waiting area, the ER was packed and chaotic. Every trauma room was occupied, and staff physicians, residents, nurses, and orderlies swirled between them in continuous motion.

Kim didn't see anyone he knew. He found a storeroom and retrieved two clear plastic bags with plastic containers inside.

He hurried back the way he'd come. Tracy and Becky were still in line. Becky had her eyes shut tight. Tears streaked her face. Kim handed one of the plastic bags to Tracy. She grabbed Becky's hand and led her to the rest room.

Kim held their place in line as it advanced by one more patient.

By NINE fifteen the ER waiting room was filled to overflowing. All the chairs were occupied. The rest of the people were leaning up against the walls or sprawled on the floor.

Kim, Tracy, and Becky had eventually checked in and found seats together. Becky had made several more trips to the rest room. Kim was holding the stool-sample container. Although there had been some spots of bright red blood originally, now the contents appeared a uniform light brown. Becky was miserable and mortified. Tracy was exasperated. Kim was still seething.

He glanced at his watch. "I don't believe this. We've been here an hour and a half."

"Welcome to the real world," Tracy said.

"This is what Kelly Anderson should have done her merger story about. AmeriCare closed the ER at Samaritan to cut costs and make everyone come here. Just to maximize profits."

"And maximize inconvenience," Tracy added.

"It's true," Kim agreed. "AmeriCare definitely wants to discourage emergency-room usage."

For the next hour Kim was sullenly silent. Every time one of the nurses or residents came to the waiting room to call out a name, Kim expected it to be Rebecca Reggis. Finally, after two and a half hours, they were taken into the ER.

A powerfully built, handsome African American man appeared, snapping latex gloves from his hands as he walked into the cubicle. The name tag pinned to his scrub top read DR. DAVID WASHINGTON, ACTING CHIEF, EMERGENCY DEPARTMENT.

Kim took a deep breath. "My sick child has been waiting for two and a half hours."

David stared at him for a beat. "What's the child's name?"

"Rebecca Reggis," Kim said.

David glanced at the sign-in sheet, then looked at his watch.

"You're right about the time. It's been close to three hours. That's too long to wait. You are on staff here?" he asked Kim.

"Since the merger. I'm one of the cardiac surgeons, although you'd never know it the way I've been treated here in the ER."

"We do the best we can," David said, and looked at Tracy. "Are you Mrs. Reggis?"

"I'm Rebecca Reggis's mother," Tracy said.

"How are you feeling, young lady?" David asked Becky.

"Not too good," Becky admitted. "I want to go home."

"I'm sure you do," David said. "But first let's check you out."

A half hour later Kim, Tracy, and Becky pushed through the exit door to the parking area. "Becky's blood count and electrolytes are fine," Dr. Washington had said. She was to be given broth and other fluids and to lay off dairy products.

Tuesday, January 20

THE OR door burst open, and Kim and Tom entered the scrub area outside OR number 20. They untied their face masks and rinsed off the talc from their hands. "Hey, thanks for lending a hand on such short notice," Tom said.

"Glad to help," Kim said flatly.

The two men started walking up the corridor toward the recovery room. "You seem in the dumps," Tom said. "Are you all right?"

"I suppose," Kim said without emotion. He then told Tom what had happened in the ER the night before.

"Whoa! What an awful experience. How's Becky doing today?"

"I don't know yet. But she's got to be doing better. Her blood work was fine, and she's been afebrile."

Kim and Tom parted ways at the recovery-room door. Kim went into the surgical locker room, took a shower, and mulled over in his mind the previous evening's experience. He was angry again. Of late it seemed to be his constant state of mind. Then, striding along a hallway, he practically ran head-on into Kelly Anderson and her cameraman, Brian.

"Ah, Dr. Reggis. Just the man I've been hoping to see."

Kim flashed a nasty glance at the TV journalist and continued down the corridor at a brisk pace. Kelly reversed directions and ran after him. Brian kept pace despite his burden of equipment.

"I don't have anything to say to you," Kim responded.

Kelly caught up to him. "Ah, but I think you do," she said. "Having to wait three hours in an emergency room with a sick child must have been a major aggravation."

Kim pulled up short and peered at Kelly in surprise. "How did you hear about that? And so quickly."

"Surprised you, huh?" she remarked with a self-satisfied smile. "But I'm sure you understand that I can't reveal my sources. You see, I do so many medical-related stories that I've developed a kind of fifth column here at the med center. Anyway, I think having to wait so long relates to the merger story. I believe it has something to do with AmeriCare's interest in profits. What do you think?"

Kim looked at Kelly. Her bright blue-green eyes sparkled. Kim had to admit that although she was a pain in the neck, she was also as smart as a whip.

"You said it, not me," Kim remarked. "So no quotes. My life right now is sufficiently messed up that I don't need you to make it worse. Good-bye, Miss Anderson." Kim left them and went through a pair of swinging doors.

IT WAS only eight o'clock, but it could have been midnight. There was no moon. With his arms full of paperwork he hoped to complete that evening, Kim made his way from the driveway toward the front door. He heard his phone even before he got into the house. Without knowing why, Kim felt a stab of panic. Tracy had said earlier in the day that there had been no changes. He rushed inside. With the help of the foyer light he dashed into the living room and answered the phone. It was Tracy.

"She's worse," she blurted. She sounded on the verge of tears.

"What's happened?" Kim's heart skipped a beat.

"She hemorrhaged," Tracy cried. "The toilet's full of blood."

"Can she walk? Is she dizzy?"

"She can walk okay."

"Get her into the car and back to the ER," Kim said. "I'll meet you there." He hung up the phone. Then he raced into the library and found George Turner's number. Taking out his cell phone, he entered the number and pressed SEND.

With the phone pressed to his ear, Kim retraced his route to the car. By the time George was on the line, he was already backing out of the driveway. "Sorry to bother you," Kim said. "It's just that Becky's sick with dysentery-like symptoms: cramps, diarrhea, and now some bleeding, but no fever. We never got another pediatrician after you left," he explained guiltily. "Tracy just called me to tell me Becky hemorrhaged. I'm on my way to meet them at the ER. Who should I have see her?"

"Hmmm," George intoned. "I don't think a pediatrician would be best. I'd recommend an infectious-disease specialist. Try to get Claude Faraday. You can't do better than him anyplace."

"Thanks, George."

"My pleasure. Sorry I'm not around. Keep me posted."

"I will," Kim said. He then used speed dialing to get the hospital. He had the operator patch him through to Claude Faraday. Kim explained the situation much as he did to George. Claude graciously agreed to come to the ER directly.

Kim pulled into the hospital parking area. He looked briefly for Tracy's Volvo. When he didn't see it, he went up the steps to the ER platform and pushed inside. The emergency room appeared nearly as busy as it did the night before. Kim bypassed the reception desk and went directly into the emergency room proper.

"Hey, where are you going?" Molly McFadden stood up and hurried after him.

Kim ignored her and found David Washington in a cubicle suturing a laceration on a child's hand. David was wearing two-plus oculars, and he regarded Kim over the top of them.

"My daughter's on her way in," Kim announced. "Now she's apparently passing frank blood."

"I'm sorry to hear that. What's her blood pressure and pulse?"

"I don't know yet. My ex-wife is bringing her in."

With his sterile, gloved hands raised in the air, David turned to Molly and asked her to get a room ready. She nodded and left.

"I want my daughter seen immediately," Kim ordered. "And I want her to have an infectious-disease consult."

"Dr. Reggis," David said, "let's try to be friends. It would help if you recognize I'm in charge here."

"I've already talked with Dr. Claude Faraday," Kim said as if he'd not heard David. "He's on his way. I presume you know him?"

"I know him. But the usual protocol is for us to order the consults if the patient does not have an AmeriCare gatekeeper."

"I want Dr. Faraday to see her."

"All right," David said. "But at least understand we are doing you a favor. This is not the way things are usually done here."

"Thank you," Kim said. He went out onto the receiving platform. Within minutes Tracy's station wagon appeared. Kim jumped down and opened the back door. Becky was lying on the seat on her side. Although she appeared pale, she smiled at him, and he felt relieved.

"Come on. Let me carry you," Kim said. He slid her out and hoisted her up. She put her arms around his neck. "Okay," he said soothingly. "Daddy has you."

Kim led the way. As he walked past reception, one of the clerks called out that they had to check in.

"You can get the information from last night's sign-in sheet," Kim called over his shoulder. The clerk paged David Washington.

Kim carried Becky into the first available cubicle and laid her on the gurney. Tracy came in and held Becky's hand. Kim took the blood-pressure cuff and wrapped it around her other arm. He put a stethoscope in his ears and started to inflate the cuff.

David Washington and Molly McFadden entered. David nodded a greeting to Tracy and waited for Kim to finish taking the blood pressure. "You have no respect for protocol," he commented.

"Her blood pressure is ninety over fifty," Kim said. "Let's get an IV going. I want her typed and cross-matched. Also—"

"Hold up!" David yelled, raising his hand for emphasis. Then in a calm voice he added, "Dr. Reggis, with all due respect, you've already forgotten that you are not in charge here."

"I'm just covering the basics," Kim said.

David went up to Kim. He wrapped one of his sizable hands around Kim's forearm. "I'm only going to ask you once," David said. "I want you to walk out of here and wait outside. It's in your daughter's best interest. I'm sure that if you just stop and think for a moment, you'll understand."

Kim's eyes narrowed as he stared at David. Slowly he looked down at David's hand clasped around his arm.

Tracy sensed the electricity in the air. "Please, Kim," she pleaded. "Let's let them do their thing."

Kim nodded to Tracy. "Okay," he said. David took his hand away. Then Kim turned back to Becky. "Daddy will be right outside, Pumpkin."

"Okay," Becky said reluctantly.

Tracy gave Becky's hand a squeeze and told her she would be with Kim and that they would be back in a few moments. Becky nodded, but she looked scared.

Tracy followed Kim out through the curtain surrounding Becky's gurney. She didn't say anything until they had passed the nurses desk. "Kim, calm down." She put her hand gently on his arm.

"David Washington drives me up a wall," Kim snapped.

"He's doing his job," Tracy said. "If you were taking care of his child, you wouldn't want him giving orders."

Kim pushed through the swinging doors to the platform outside. The blast of cold air felt good on his face. He took a deep breath. "It's hard for me to see Becky lying there so vulnerable," he said finally.

"I can imagine. It must be very difficult."

"You understand?" Kim asked.

"You're a surgeon. You are trained to act. For you the hardest thing is to see your own child in need and not do something."

"You're right," Kim said.

"Of course I am," Tracy said. "I'm always right."

In spite of himself, Kim smiled. "Now, I'm not going to go that far. Frequently maybe, but not always."

"DOES the IV bother you?" Kim asked Becky.

"I can't feel it at all," she said.

"That's the way it's supposed to be," he said.

David had carefully examined Becky, and although he'd yet to see the abdominal X rays, the blood and urine results were all normal. At that point he'd sent for Kim and Tracy.

Claude Faraday arrived a few minutes later. He was a slender dark-complexioned man with an intense manner. He listened to a full recounting of Becky's problem and did a rapid but thorough examination. "You seem okay to me, except for that slightly sore belly," he said at last. "Now, I'm going to step outside and talk to your parents. Okay?"

Becky nodded.

Tracy gave her daughter a kiss on the forehead before following Claude and Kim out through the curtain. David joined them.

"All in all, she looks good to me," Claude began. "She's a little pale, of course, and a bit dehydrated. There's also some generalized abdominal tenderness. Otherwise, on physical exam she's quite normal. I also went over her lab work. Compared to last night, there is a slight drop in her hemoglobin. It's not statistically significant, but in view of the mild dehydration it might be important, considering the history of the hemorrhage. There's also a slight drop in her platelets. Otherwise everything is within normal limits."

"What's your presumptive diagnosis?" Kim asked.

"I'd have to say foodborne bacterial illness," Claude said.

"But why no fever?"

"The fact that there has been no fever makes me think it is more a toxemia than an infection," Claude said. "Which also goes along with the normal white count."

"What about last night's culture?" Kim asked. "Is there a preliminary twenty-four-hour reading?"

"I didn't see a culture," Claude said. He looked at David.

"We didn't do a culture last night," David said.

Kim shook his head in disbelief. "What are you talking about?" he demanded. "I even gave you the sample."

"We don't do routine stool cultures for simple diarrhea here in the ER," David said.

Kim slapped his hand to his forehead. "Why wouldn't you do a culture? How else could you treat rationally?"

"AmeriCare utilization rules proscribe routine cultures in this kind of case," David said. "It's not cost-effective."

Kim reddened. "Cost-effective! What kind of excuse is that?"

"Calm down," Claude said. "It's okay. We'll run some cultures stat. We haven't lost that much, because I doubt we'd treat anyway."

"What kind of bacteria do you think is involved?" Tracy asked.

"Mainly salmonella, shigella, and some of the newer strains of *E. coli*," Claude said. "But it could be a lot of other things."

"Will she be admitted?" Tracy asked.

Claude looked at David.

"I think it is a good idea," David said. "She needs fluids. Then we can evaluate the possibility of anemia and make sure there's no more bleeding."

"What about antibiotics?" Tracy asked Claude.

"Not until we have a definitive diagnosis. If the offending agent turns out to be one of the aberrant strains of *E. coli,* antibiotics make the situation worse. They can decimate the normal flora and let the renegade *E. coli* flourish."

"Will she be admitted to your care?" Tracy asked Claude.

"No, that's not possible," he said. "AmeriCare requires a gate-keeper. But I'll be happy to look in on her."

"Since Becky does not have a staff pediatrician, she'll be admitted under the care of Claire Stevens," David said. "It's her rotation. I can give her a call."

"You can't do better than Claire," Claude remarked. "You're lucky. She takes care of my kids."

"Finally something seems to be going right," Kim said.

KIM turned into the hospital parking lot a little after six in the morning. He'd skipped stopping at his office. He was eager to make sure Becky was okay.

The previous night Dr. Claire Stevens had come into the ER within a half hour of being paged. She was a tall, thin woman about Kim's age, with sharp features that were belied by her gentle, reassuring manner. Her competence was immediately apparent, and she established instant rapport with Becky.

Kim pushed into Becky's room. There was a night-light near the floor, casting a gentle glow over the entire room. He advanced silently to the bedside and looked down at his sleeping daughter. Becky's breathing was regular and deep. Happy to see her resting so well, he quietly backed out.

At the nurses station, Kim withdrew Becky's chart. He glanced through Claire's admitting notes, then turned to the nurses' notes. Becky had been up twice during the night with diarrhea. She had reported some blood, but none of the nurses had seen it, because she had flushed the toilet out of embarrassment. Kim made a mental note to talk to Claire about that problem and to Becky as well. He then turned to the order sheet and was pleased to see that Claire had requested a pediatric gastroenterology consult for that day.

Kim went off to see his inpatients, then to hospital conferences, and finally hurried to his office. As usual, he was already behind schedule.

SHORTLY after he'd arrived at his office, Tracy called from the hospital. She thought Becky didn't look good—she was glassy-eyed and listless.

With a waiting room full of patients, Kim had instructed Tracy to page Claire and tell her. He also told Tracy to have the clerk call him when the gastroenterology consult arrived.

Kim went out into the corridor and lifted the heavy chart of the next patient out of the rack on the door to the examining room. Before he had even read the name, Ginger appeared at the end of the corridor. "I just got a call from the ward clerk on Becky's floor," she reported. "The G.I. consult is there."

"Then I'm out of here," Kim said quickly. "Tell the patients there's been an emergency. I'll probably be an hour and a half or so."

Ginger shook her head. She knew how upset they were going to be, especially the ones from out of town.

Kim dashed out to his car and drove to the hospital. Once on Becky's floor, he ran down the hall. When he entered her room, he was panting. He saw Tracy standing off to the side, talking with a woman in a long white coat. Even a quick glance told him that Tracy was distraught.

Becky was on her back with her head propped up against the pillow. Her dark eyes stared ahead. Kim stepped over to the side of the bed. "How are you doing, Pumpkin?" he asked. He grasped her hand and lifted it. There was little resistance.

"I'm tired," Becky offered.

"I'm sure you are, dear." Instinctively he felt her pulse. Her heart rate was on the high side. He could tell what Tracy had meant. There had been a change. "I'm going to talk to Mom," he said.

"All right," Becky answered.

Kim stepped over to Tracy. He could see she was trembling.

"This is Dr. Kathleen Morgan, the G.I. specialist," she said.

Kathleen was the physical antithesis of Claire Stevens. She couldn't have been much over five feet. Her face was round; her features were soft. She wore wire-rimmed glasses, and her dark hair was prematurely streaked with silver.

"Dr. Morgan has told me she thinks Becky's case is serious," Tracy managed.

"Serious, huh?" Kim remarked with obvious derision. "She wouldn't be in the hospital if it weren't serious."

"The lab will call me the moment they have a positive," Kathleen said warily. She was taken aback by Kim's response. "Until then our hands are tied."

"Have you examined her yet?" he demanded.

"Yes, I have," Kathleen said. "And I've gone over the laboratory results that are available. So far I agree with Dr. Faraday. Food-borne bacterial illness."

"She looks worse to me," Kim said.

"To me, too," Tracy added. "Just since last night."

Kathleen cast an uncomfortable glance over at Becky. She suggested they move out into the hallway.

"I want her more closely monitored," Kim said. "How about moving her into one of the isolation rooms in the ICU?"

"I'm only a consult," Kathleen said. "But to be truthful, I don't think your daughter needs the ICU. At least not yet."

"That's encouraging," Kim snapped. "In other words, you expect her to get worse while the lot of you do nothing."

"That's unfair, Dr. Reggis," Kathleen said, taking offense.

"Not from my point of view," Kim spat. "As a surgeon, I make a diagnosis; then I go in and I fix it."

"Stop it, Kim!" Tracy said, fighting tears. "This constant bickering with the doctors and the nurses is not helping."

"Dr. Reggis, please come with me," Kathleen said suddenly, and motioned with her hand as she started toward the nurses station.

"Go," Tracy encouraged. "Get a grasp on yourself."

As Tracy went back into Becky's room, Kim caught up with the striding Kathleen.

"I want to show you something," she said. "And I think we should talk, doctor to doctor." She took him to the chart room behind the nurses station, a windowless nook with built-in desks, an X-ray view box, and a communal coffeemaker.

Kathleen slipped some X rays from their folder and snapped them up onto the light box. The films were of Becky's abdomen.

Kim leaned forward to study the X rays. He was more adept at reading chest films, but he knew the basics. "The bowel looks uniformly edematous," he said after a moment.

"Exactly. The mucosal lining is swollen for most of its length."

"What does that tell you?" Kim asked.

"It makes me worry about *E. coli* O157:H7. You could see about the same X ray with shigella dysentery, but the patient would probably have fever. As you know, Becky doesn't have any."

"How do we make the diagnosis, then?"

"There is the possibility of testing for the toxin itself," Kathleen said. "Unfortunately, AmeriCare has not authorized our lab to do the test. It's one of those tests that is not used often enough for AmeriCare to justify its expense. But in this case I took it upon myself to have a sample sent out to Sherring Labs. We'll have the results in twenty-four to forty-eight hours."

"Thank you, and I apologize for saying you weren't doing anything."

"What do you know about this particular *E. coli* and its toxin?" Kathleen asked. "Assuming that it is indeed what Becky has."

"Not much. I didn't even know antibiotics weren't helpful. *E. coli* isn't something I've had to deal with in my practice."

"I think you and your wife should know that it can be a very bad bug."

"How so?" Kim asked nervously. He didn't like the sound of what she was saying. He didn't even bother to correct her misconception that he and Tracy were still married.

"Maybe you should sit down," Kathleen said.

Kim dutifully sat in one of the desk chairs. He was afraid not to.

"If *E. coli* is involved," Kathleen said, "I'm concerned about the drop in platelets Becky's had. There was only a slight drop last night, but after she's been rehydrated, the drop is more apparent and statistically significant. It makes me worry about HUS."

"HUS?" Kim questioned.

"Hemolytic uremic syndrome. It's associated with the shigella-like toxins *E. coli* O157:H7 is capable of producing. You see, this type of toxin can cause intravascular platelet coagulation as well as red-cell destruction. That in turn can lead to multiple-organ failure. Kidneys are the most commonly affected, and hence the name uremic syndrome."

Kim was stunned. For a moment all he could do was look at Kathleen. "You think Becky has HUS?" he asked.

"Let's put it this way: It's my concern. There's no proof yet."

Kim swallowed. His mouth had gone dry. "What can we do?"

"Not a lot, I'm afraid," Kathleen said. "I will suggest hematology and nephrology consults. Consult requests, of course, have to go through Claire Stevens. AmeriCare is very clear on this."

"Well, let's call her," Kim sputtered. He reached for the phone and pushed it in front of her.

While Kathleen made the call, Kim cradled his head in his hands. He felt weak with sudden anxiety. For the first time in his life he was on the patient's side of a major medical problem, one that he didn't even know much about.

"Claire's in full agreement," Kathleen announced as she replaced the receiver. "You are lucky to have her. She and I have handled several cases of HUS in the past."

"When will the consults see Becky?" Kim asked urgently. "I want them right away. This afternoon!"

"Dr. Reggis, you have to calm down," Kathleen said.

"I can't." He breathed out noisily. "How common is HUS?"

"Unfortunately, it's become relatively common. It's usually caused by *E. coli* O157:H7, of which there are about twenty thousand cases a year. It's become common enough to be the current major cause of acute kidney failure in children."

"Good Lord," Kim commented. He nervously massaged his scalp. "Twenty thousand cases a year?"

"That's the CDC estimate of the *E. coli* O157:H7 cases," Kathleen said. "It's only a percentage that go on to HUS."

"Is HUS ever fatal?" Kim forced himself to ask.

"Are you sure we should be talking about this aspect? The diagnosis has not been definitively made."

"Answer the question," Kim said hotly.

Kathleen sighed with resignation. "The CDC estimates between two hundred and five hundred people, mostly kids, die from *E. coli* O157:H7 every year," she said, "and it's usually from HUS."

Perspiration broke out on Kim's forehead. He was stunned anew. "Two to five hundred deaths a year," he repeated. "Unbelievable. How come all this isn't better known?"

"That I can't answer. There's been a couple of high-profile episodes with this *E. coli* strain, like the Jack-in-the-Box outbreak in '92 and the Hudson Foods recall in '97."

"I remember those two episodes. I suppose I just assumed the government and the USDA took care of the problems."

Kathleen laughed cynically. "I'm sure that's what the USDA and the beef industry hoped you'd believe."

"Is this mostly a problem with red meat?" Kim asked.

"Ground meat to be precise. Ground meat that is not cooked through and through. But some cases have been caused by such things as apple juice and apple cider and even unpasteurized milk. The key problem is contact with infected cow feces."

"I used to eat raw hamburger all the time."

"It's a relatively new situation," Kathleen said. "It's thought to have originated in the late '70s, perhaps in Argentina. The belief is that a shigella bacterium gave an *E. coli* bacterium the DNA necessary to make a shigella-like toxin."

"By bacterial conjugation," Kim suggested.

"Precisely. And today this new strain of *E. coli* bacterium exists in about three percent of bovine intestines. But nature probably didn't do it on its own. Man helped."

"How so?" Kim asked.

"I believe *E. coli* O157:H7 has come from the intense farming techniques in use today. The need for cheap protein to feed the animals has resulted in creative but disgusting solutions. Cows are fed rendered animals, including other cows. Even chicken manure is being widely used."

"You're joking!" Kim said.

"I wish," Kathleen said. "And on top of that the animals are given antibiotics. It creates a soup within the animals' intestines that fosters new strains. In fact, the *E. coli* O157:H7 was created when the shigella toxin DNA was transferred along with the DNA necessary for a particular antibiotic resistance."

Kim shook his head in disbelief. "The sum of all this is bovine fecal material particularly in ground beef."

"I think that's fair to say," Kathleen said.

"Then I know how Becky got it," Kim said angrily. "She had a rare hamburger at the Onion Ring Friday night."

"That would be consistent, although the incubation period is usually longer, sometimes as much as a week."

The door to the chart room banged open, causing both Kim and Kathleen to start. One of the nurses leaned in. She was flushed.

"Dr. Morgan," she said urgently, "there's an emergency with your consult Rebecca Reggis!"

As Kim came through Becky's door, he saw a nurse on either side of his daughter's bed. One was taking her blood pressure, the other her temperature. Becky was writhing in pain and whimpering. She appeared as pale as a ghost. Tracy was standing off to the side, a hand pressed to her mouth.

"What happened?" Kim demanded.

Kathleen came into the room behind Kim.

"I don't know," Tracy wailed. "Becky and I were talking when suddenly she cried out. She had a terrible pain in her stomach and her left shoulder. Then she had a shaking chill."

The nurse taking the blood pressure called out that it was ninety-five over sixty.

"Has Dr. Stevens been called?" Kathleen asked.

"Yes, immediately," one of the nurses said.

"Her temperature is one hundred and five," the other nurse said with dismay.

Kim nudged her away from the right side of Becky's bed. He was frantic. "Becky, what is it?" he demanded.

"My stomach hurts me," Becky managed amid groans. "It hurts me bad. Daddy, please!"

Kim pulled down Becky's blanket. He was shocked to see a swath of purplish subcutaneous bleeding on her chest. "Were you aware of this?" he asked, looking up at Kathleen. "It wasn't there last night."

Kathleen nodded. "Yes, I saw it earlier."

He looked back at Becky. "Tell Daddy where it hurts."

Becky pointed at her lower abdomen, to the right of the midline.

Kim gently placed the tips of his index, middle, and ring fingers on Becky's abdomen where she'd pointed.

Becky writhed. "Please don't touch me, Daddy," she pleaded.

Kim pulled his hand back sharply. Becky's eyes shot open, and a cry of pain issued from her parched lips. Such a response, called rebound tenderness, was a sign Kim did not want to see. It was a strong indication of peritonitis—inflammation of the lining of the abdominal cavity. Only one thing could cause such a catastrophe.

Kim straightened up. "She's perforated," he yelled, and pushed up to the head of the bed and released the wheels. "Someone get the rear wheels. We've got to get her to surgery."

"We should wait for Dr. Stevens," Kathleen said calmly.

"The hell with Dr. Stevens," Kim snapped. "This is a surgical emergency. We have to act."

Kathleen put her hand on Kim's arm, ignoring the wild look in his eyes. "Dr. Reggis, you have to calm—"

In his agitated frame of mind Kim swept her aside, inadvertently throwing her against the bedside table.

Tracy rushed over. "Kim, stop it," she sobbed. "Please!"

Several other nurses arrived, including the head nurse and a brawny male nurse. Finally overwhelmed, Kim let go of the bed. He yelled that anyone who didn't understand that Becky's condition was a surgical emergency was incompetent.

"HOW will they put me to sleep?" Becky asked with a voice already thick with sleep. She'd been premedicated, so her pain had abated, but she was anxious about facing surgery.

"They'll just put some medicine in your IV," Kim said. "The next thing you'll know is that you're awake and all better."

Becky was on a gurney in the anesthesia holding area of the OR. Kim was standing next to her. He was dressed in scrubs. He'd recovered his senses after the scene in Becky's room and apologized profusely to Kathleen. She'd graciously said she understood. Claire had arrived and immediately requested emergency surgery.

"Will I be all right, Daddy?" Becky asked.

"Of course," Kim said. "They're just going to open you up like a zipper, patch the little hole, and that will be it."

"Maybe I'm being punished for not signing up for the Nationals," Becky said. "I know you wanted me to."

Kim choked on tears that threatened to erupt. For a moment he looked off to compose himself. "Don't you worry about the Nationals. I don't care about them. I only care about you."

"Okay, Becky," a cheerful voice called out. "Time to fix you up."

Kim raised his head. Jane Flanagan, the anesthesiologist, and James O'Donnel, the gastrointestinal surgeon, had come over to Becky's gurney. Jane went to the head and released the wheel locks.

Becky gripped Kim's hand with surprising strength. "Will it hurt?" she asked.

"Not with Jane taking care of you," James said playfully, over-hearing the question. "She's the best sandwoman in the business."

"We'll even order you a good dream," Jane joked.

Kim knew and admired both these professionals. They maneuvered Becky toward the swinging double doors leading to the OR corridor. Kim walked alongside. Becky still had a grip on his hand. As they slid the gurney through, James reached out and grasped Kim's arm. "I heard what happened downstairs. I think it's best you don't come into the OR."

"The hell I'm not," Kim said. "This is my daughter."

"That's the point. You stay out, or I'm not doing the case."

Kim's face reddened. He felt cornered and confused. He desperately wanted James to do the surgery, but he was terrified to be apart from Becky.

"You have to make up your mind," James said. "The longer you agonize, the worse it is for Becky."

Kim snatched his arm free and strode away toward the surgical locker room. He was too distraught to look at the people in the lounge as he passed through, but he didn't go unnoticed.

In the locker room he went directly to the sink and splashed his face repeatedly with cold water. In the mirror, over his shoulder, he saw the pinched face of Forrester Biddle, chief of cardiac surgery. Biddle had the gaunt look of a Puritan preacher.

"I want to talk with you," Forrester said in his clipped voice.

"Talk," Kim said. He took a towel and briskly dried his face.

"I wasn't going to say anything about your quote Kelly Anderson gave during the Friday night news. Saying publicly that the rationale for the merger of the medical center and Samaritan was to benefit AmeriCare's bottom line hurts the reputation of this hospital. But I was appalled to hear Kelly Anderson again quote you on the eleven-o'clock news. She said it was your feeling that AmeriCare closed the Samaritan ER to cut costs and increase profits by forcing everyone to use the overburdened ER here."

"I didn't say that," Kim responded. "She did."

"She quoted you," Forrester said.

In his agitated state of mind Kim was not inclined to defend himself.

"I'm warning you," Forrester announced. "The administration and I myself only have so much forbearance."

"Fine. Consider me warned." Kim threw the towel into the hamper and walked out without giving Forrester another glance.

Knowing he could not just sit and wait while Becky was in surgery, Kim went to the hospital library. He had to learn what he could about *E. coli* O157:H7 and HUS.

IT WAS almost midnight. Kim looked at Becky and shuddered. A clear plastic tube snaked out of one of her nostrils and was attached to low suction. Her dark hair framed her otherwise angelic, pale face with soft waves. She was fast asleep.

Tracy was leaning back in one of the vinyl-covered chairs. She had her eyes closed, but Kim knew she was not asleep. She opened her eyes and glanced over at him. He looked wretched under the strain. His hair was a mess, and his face was covered with stubble. The single night-light near the floor accentuated the gauntness of his cheeks. Tracy sighed. "How's Becky doing?"

"She's holding her own," Kim said. "At least the surgery handled the immediate crisis."

"It was a major shock for Becky," Tracy said. "As was the tube in her nose. She's having a hard time coping. No one told her these things might happen."

"It couldn't be helped," Kim snapped. He sank into a chair and buried his face in his hands. He was exhausted mentally and physically.

Looking at Kim's dejected posture forced Tracy to think about the situation from his point of view. All at once her anger toward him melted. "Kim, maybe you should go home. You have to see patients tomorrow. I can stay. I'll just be skipping class."

"I wouldn't be able to sleep even if I did go home," Kim said without lifting his face from his hands. "Now I know too much."

During the entire time Becky had been in surgery, he had researched HUS in the hospital library. What he'd learned had been frightening. Everything Kathleen had said had been true. HUS could be a horrible illness, and now all he could hope was that Becky had something else. The problem was that everything was pointing in the direction of HUS.

Thursday, January 22

KIM ended up going home, but as he expected, he had not been able to sleep much. He was back in his car just after five in the morning.

In the hospital, he found Becky as he'd left her. She appeared deceptively peaceful in her slumber. Tracy was fast asleep as well, curled in the vinyl chair and covered with a blanket.

At the nurses station Kim came across the night nurse. "How was Becky's night? Anything I should know?"

"She's been stable. Her temperature has stayed normal."

"Thank God," Kim said. With nothing else to do, he drove to his office and busied himself with the mountain of paperwork. As he worked, he eyed the clock. When he thought the time appropriate, he phoned the nurses station on Becky's floor and asked for Tracy.

Tracy came on the line. "Becky seems a bit better," she said.

"Listen, I'm going to stay here, see a few patients, including the pre-ops for tomorrow. I hope you don't mind."

"I understand. I'll be here, so don't worry."

Throughout the morning Kim forced himself to concentrate on his patients, although his heart would race every time the phone rang.

In the middle of the afternoon he was talking with a cardiologist in Chicago when Ginger stuck her head in the door. "Tracy was on the other line. She was very upset. Becky has taken a sudden turn for the worse and has been moved to the ICU."

Kim's pulse quickened. He wound up the conversation with the doctor in Chicago, changed his jacket, and ran for the door.

"What should I do with the rest of the patients?" Ginger asked.

"Send them home," Kim said tersely.

Kim drove with determination. At the hospital, he moved as fast as he could. From the corridor on the ICU floor he caught sight of Tracy in the waiting room. She came forward and threw her arms around him, her eyes brimming with tears.

"What happened?" he asked. He was afraid to hear the answer.

"Her breathing. All of a sudden she couldn't get her breath."

Kim broke Tracy's hold, dashed across the hall, and entered the ICU. For a moment he scanned the room. Most of the beds were full. Nurses toiled at nearly every bedside. Banks of electronic monitoring equipment displayed vital data. The most activity was in one of the small rooms off to the side, where a group of doctors and nurses were attending to an acute situation. Kim walked over and stood in the doorway. He saw the respirator and heard its rhythmic cycling. A large tube stuck out of Becky's mouth and was taped to her cheek. She was being ventilated by a respirator.

Kim rushed to the bedside. Becky looked up at him with terrified eyes. She'd been sedated, but she was still conscious. He felt a crushing feeling in his chest.

"It's okay, Pumpkin. Daddy's here," he said, struggling to control his emotions. He looked around at the people present. He centered on Claire Stevens. "What happened?" he asked, keeping his voice calm.

"Perhaps we should go outside," Claire said.

Kim nodded. He gave Becky's hand a squeeze, and the doctors filed out into the ICU proper and formed a group off to the side. Kim folded his arms to hide his trembling.

"First let me introduce everyone," Claire said. "Of course you know Kathleen Morgan. And this is Dr. Arthur Horowitz, nephrologist, and Dr. Walter Ohanesian, hematologist." Then she turned to Kim. "I have to tell you we're definitely dealing with *E. coli* O157:H7. We'll have an idea of the particular strain tomorrow."

"Why is she intubated?" Kim asked.

"The toxemia is affecting her lungs," Claire said. "Her blood gases suddenly deteriorated."

"She's also in kidney failure," Arthur, the kidney specialist, said. "We've started peritoneal dialysis."

"Why not a dialysis machine?" Kim questioned.

"She should do fine with the peritoneal dialysis," Arthur said.

"But she just had surgery for a perforation."

"That was taken into consideration," Arthur said. "But Ameri-Care only offers dialysis machines at Suburban Hospital. We'd have to transfer the patient there, which we surely don't recommend."

"The other major problem is her platelet count," Walter, the blood specialist, said. "Her platelets have fallen precipitously to the point where we feel they must be replenished despite the inherent risks. Otherwise we might have a bleeding problem."

"There's also the problem with her liver," Claire said. "Liver enzymes have risen remarkably, suggesting . . ."

Kim's mind was on overload. He was no longer absorbing the information. He could see the doctors talking, but he didn't hear. A half hour later he stumbled out into the ICU waiting room. Tracy got up the moment she saw him. He looked like a broken man. For a moment they stared into each other's eyes. Now it was Kim's turn for tears. Tracy reached out, and they locked in a hug of fear and grief.

CHAPTER FIVE

Friday, January 23

KIM paused for a moment to get his breath. He glanced up at the OR clock. It was two in the afternoon. The scalpel trembled in his hand; he wondered if Tom noticed. They eyed each other, and Tom motioned with his head. Kim nodded, and they stepped away from the operating field.

"Kim, why don't you let me finish this last case?" Tom whispered. "You're understandably exhausted."

It was true. Kim had spent most of the night in the ICU waiting room with Tracy. "All right," he said at length.

The two surgeons returned to the operating table. With Tom at the helm the operation went smoothly. As soon as the sternum was closed, Tom suggested Kim should bow out. "Get over there and check on Becky," he said. "Jane and I will write the post-op orders. If there's anything else I can do, just call."

"I appreciate it," Kim said.

In the surgical locker room, he pulled on a long white coat over his scrubs. He was eager to get to the ICU and didn't want to take the time to change back into his street clothes.

Kim headed for the elevator. The closer he got to the ICU, the more nervous he became. Pausing at the waiting-room threshold, he saw Tracy sitting in a chair near the window. She spotted him and stood up. Fresh tears streaked her face. "What now?" he asked as she approached.

For a moment Tracy could not speak. She had to choke back new tears. "Dr. Stevens talked about a cascading pattern of major organ failure," Tracy managed. "Becky has had a stroke. They think she's blind."

Kim shut his eyes hard. Leaving Tracy in the waiting room, he strode across the hall and entered the ICU. A gaggle of doctors were pressed into Becky's cubicle. Kim pushed his way to the bedside and looked at his daughter. She was a pitiful shadow of her former self, lost within the wires and tubes as the screens flashed their information. Her eyes were closed. Her skin was a translucent bluish white.

"Becky, it's me, Dad," he whispered into her ear. He studied her frozen face. She didn't register any sign of hearing him. Kim straightened up and saw a new face: Dr. Sidney Hampton, neurology. "You think she's had a stroke?"

"Every indication suggests as much," Sidney said.

"The basic problem is that the toxin seems to be destroying her platelets as fast as we give them," Walter, the hematologist, said.

"It's true," Sidney said. "There's no way to know if this was an intracranial hemorrhage or a platelet embolus."

"Or a combination of the two," Walter suggested. "One way or another, the rapid destruction of her platelets must be forming a sludge in her microcirculation. We're into that cascading major organ failure situation we hate to see."

"Kidney and liver function is going down," Arthur, the kidney specialist, said. "The peritoneal dialysis is not keeping up."

Kim had to steel himself to curtail his anger and remain rational. "Well, we have to do something."

"I think we are doing all we can," Claire Stevens said. "We're actively supporting her respiratory and kidney functions and replacing her platelets. Dr. Reggis, I think it's only fair to tell you and your former wife that you should be preparing yourselves for all eventualities."

Kim saw red. He was in no frame of mind to "prepare himself."

"Do you understand what I'm saying?" Claire asked gently.

Kim didn't answer. In a suddenly clairvoyant moment he comprehended the absurdity of blaming these doctors for Becky's plight, especially when he knew where the fault lay. Without warning he rushed out of the ICU. Tracy was still in the waiting room. She spotted his hasty exit and ran down the hall to catch up to him. "Kim, stop! Where are you going?" She had to run merely to keep up with Kim's determined stride. The look on his face frightened her.

"I've got to do something. Right now I can't help Becky medically, but I'm going to find out how she got sick. A week ago I took Becky to the Onion Ring on Prairie Highway. She had a burger, and it was rare. That had to have been when she got sick."

"Right now it doesn't matter where Becky got sick," Tracy said. "What matters is that she is sick."

"It might not matter to you, but it matters to me."

"Kim, you're out of control," she said with exasperation. "You're not helping anyone by running off like this. At least wait until you have calmed down."

The elevator arrived, and Kim boarded. "I'm going," he said.

KIM pulled into the Onion Ring parking lot and took the first spot he came to. He sat in the car for a moment and looked out at the restaurant. It was as crowded as it had been a week earlier. The drive from the hospital had blunted the edge of his anger but not his determination. He got out of the car, went in the main entrance, and pushed his way to the front. He got the attention of one of the cash-register girls, whose name tag said HI, I'M DEBBIE.

"Excuse me," Kim said, forcing himself to sound calm. "I'd like to speak to the manager."

"He's, like, really busy right now," Debbie said. She turned her attention back to the person standing at the head of her line.

Kim slammed his open palm down on the countertop. The sound was like a shotgun blast. Debbie turned white. "I want the manager," he said.

Suddenly a man stepped forward from behind the row of cash registers. He was dressed in a two-tone Onion Ring uniform. His name tag said HI, I'M ROGER.

"I'm the manager," he said nervously. "What's the problem?"

"My daughter happens to be in a coma at the moment, fighting for her life, all from eating a hamburger here one week ago."

"I'm sorry to hear about your daughter," Roger said, "but there's no way she could have gotten sick here."

"This is the only place she had ground meat," Kim said. "And she's sick with *E. coli,* and that comes from hamburger."

"Well, I'm sorry," Roger said emphatically. "But our burgers are all cooked well done, and we've got strict rules about cleanliness. We're inspected regularly by the department of health."

"Her burger was rare. I saw it myself. It was pink in the middle."

"It couldn't have been pink," Roger interjected. "It's out of the question. Now, if you'll excuse me, I have to get back to work." He turned away.

Kim rounded the end of the counter, intending to talk directly with the cook. Roger, seeing Kim coming into the kitchen area, tried to confront him. "You can't come back here," he said gamely. "Only employees are allowed—"

Kim didn't give him time to finish. He simply shoved the manager out of the way, slamming him into the counter, sending him to the floor.

"Call the police!" Roger croaked as he scrambled to his feet.

Kim continued around the central island to confront Paul, the cook, who, like everyone else in the kitchen, hadn't moved from the moment Kim had pounded the counter.

"My daughter had a rare burger here a week ago," Kim growled. "I want to know how that could have happened."

Paul had seen people go crazy on oil rigs, and the look in Kim's eyes reminded him of these men. "Like Roger said, I cook all the burgers well done. It's policy."

"I'm telling you it was rare," Kim snapped. "I saw it."

"But I time them," Paul said. He pointed with his spatula to the

smoking patties on the grill. "We cook them to an inside temperature higher than the one proposed by the FDA."

"How do you know the inside temperature?" Kim asked.

"We gauge it with a special five-pronged thermometer several
times a day. It's always above a hundred and seventy degrees."

"Where do you store the patties before they're cooked?"

Paul turned around and opened the refrigerator, but Kim knew
he would see only a small portion of the meat on hand.

"Where's the bulk of them?" Kim questioned.

"In the walk-in freezer," Paul said.

"Show me," Kim commanded.

Paul turned and started to walk. Kim followed.

"Oh, no, you don't," Roger said. He'd caught up to Kim and
pulled on his arm. "Only employees are allowed in the freezer."

Kim tried to shake Roger off his arm, but Roger hung on. Frus-
trated, Kim backhanded the manager across the face and sent him
crashing to the floor. Without even a glance at the fallen manager,
Kim followed Paul into the freezer. Fearful of Kim's size and
impulsiveness, Paul gave him a wide berth.

Kim looked at the cartons lined up on the left side of the walk-in.
The first was open. The labels read MERCER MEATS: REG. 0.1 LB HAM-
BURGER PATTIES, EXTRA LEAN. LOT 2 BATCH 1-5. PRODUCTION: DEC.
29. USE BY MARCH 29.

"Would a hamburger last Friday night have come from this carton?" Kim asked.

Paul shrugged. "Probably, or one similar."

Kim stepped back into the depths of the freezer and saw another
open carton. He could see that the wrapping was also broken on
one of the inner boxes. "How come this carton is open?"

"It was a mistake. We're supposed to use the oldest patties first
so we never have to worry about the 'use by' date."

Kim looked at the label. This one said January 12. "Could a patty
have come from this one last Friday?"

"Possibly."

Slipping a pen and piece of paper from the pocket of his white coat, Kim wrote down the information from the two open cartons. Then he took a single patty from each, separated by sheets of wax paper, and pocketed them.

As Kim exited the freezer, he was vaguely aware of the muffled sound of a siren. "What's Mercer Meats?" he asked Paul.

Paul closed the freezer door. "It's a meat-processing company that supplies us with hamburger patties," he said. "In fact, they supply the entire Onion Ring chain."

"Is it in the state?" Kim asked.

"Sure is," Paul said. "Right outside of town, in Bartonville."

As Kim walked back into the kitchen area, the front door of the restaurant burst open. Two uniformed police officers came charging in. Their faces were grim. Roger trailed behind them, angrily gesturing toward Kim with his right hand while his left held a bloody napkin against his mouth.

Saturday, January 24

WEAK early morning sunlight slanted through the courtroom. Kim was standing in the beam and squinting from the glare. In front of him was Judge Harlowe, presiding in black judicial robes. Reading glasses were perched precariously on the judge's narrow knifelike nose. Kim was still attired in his long white coat over hospital scrubs, but the coat was no longer crisp and clean, since he'd slept in it overnight in jail.

"Doctor, I have great sympathy for you given that your daughter is ill," Harlowe said. "But in regard to trespassing and committing battery on a restaurant manager—this is unacceptable behavior no matter what the circumstances."

"Yes, Your Honor," Kim said resignedly.

"I hope you seek help, Doctor," the judge said. "I'm mystified by your actions, knowing that you're a renowned cardiac surgeon. At any rate, I'm releasing you on your own recognizance. You're to return for trial four weeks hence. See the court clerk."

Outside the courthouse, Kim caught a cab to pick up his car at the deserted Onion Ring parking lot. From there, en route to the hospital, he made a detour to Sherring Labs. At the receiving counter he fished the two hamburger patties, now defrosted, out of his pocket and handed them to a woman dressed in a lab coat. "I'd like these tested for E. coli O157:H7," he said. "Also for the toxin."

The technician eyed the discolored meat warily. "It might have been better if you'd refrigerated the samples. When meat's been at room temperature for more than a couple of hours, it's going to grow out a lot of bacteria."

"But I only want to know if E. coli O157:H7 is present."

The woman put on latex gloves and put each sample into a separate container. Then she took the billing details. Kim used his office account. "We'll have a final reading in forty-eight hours," she said. Kim thanked her, washed his hands in a rest room, and went back out to his car.

At the hospital, as he passed through the halls, people eyed him with curiosity. Kim could well understand, considering his appearance. Within the ICU, approaching Becky's cubicle, he found himself making a pact with God: If only Becky could be spared . . . He slipped in by her bedside. A nurse was changing her IV bottle. Kim gazed at his daughter. Any faint hope of improvement instantly vanished. Becky was obviously still in a coma. What was new were large, deep purple patches of subcutaneous bleeding in her face that made her look cadaverous.

Kim's trained ear drew his attention to the cardiac monitor screen. The beeping was irregular, as were the blips of the cursor.

"She has an arrhythmia! When did this develop?"

"It started last night," the nurse said. "She developed a cardiac effusion, which brought on symptoms of tamponade. She had to be tapped just after four this morning to relieve the compression."

Kim felt even more guilty for not having been available. Dealing with excess fluid around the heart was something he knew about. He walked down to the waiting room and found Tracy talking with Claire Stevens and Kathleen Morgan, the G.I. specialist. As soon as they saw him, their conversation stopped.

Tracy was clearly distraught. Her mouth was a grim line. "You're a mess. Where on earth have you been?"

"My visit to the Onion Ring took a lot longer than I thought it would." He looked at Claire. "So Becky has pericarditis."

"I'm afraid so," she said.

"We've confirmed that this is a particularly pathogenic strain of *E. coli* that produces not one but two extraordinarily potent toxins," Kathleen said. "What we're seeing is full-blown HUS. We're just trying to support her every way possible."

"Meaning you're sitting on your hands and treating complications," Kim spat.

Claire sighed and stood up. "I think it's time for me to see the rest of my inpatients. If I'm needed, just page me."

Kim collapsed into the chair vacated by Claire.

"Why did your visit to the Onion Ring take so long?" Tracy asked. She couldn't help but be concerned. He looked pitiful.

"Actually, I was in jail," Kim admitted.

"Jail!"

"You were right. I should have calmed down before I went. I lost my temper. I went there to find out about the possibility of tainted meat. The manager's denial drove me up the wall."

"I don't think it's the fast-food industry's fault," Kathleen offered. "With this *E. coli* problem the restaurants are as much a victim as the patrons. They get contaminated hamburger."

"But how can there be contaminated meat?" Tracy asked. "I mean, doesn't the USDA certify the meat?"

"They certify it," Kathleen said. "But unfortunately, the USDA has an inherent conflict of interest."

"How so?" Kim asked.

"It's because of the USDA's mandate," Kathleen said. "On the one hand, the agency is the official advocate for U.S. agriculture, which includes the powerful beef industry. That's actually the USDA's main job. On the other hand, it has inspectional obligations. Obviously the two roles don't mix. It's a case of asking the fox to guard the henhouse."

"This sounds incredible," Kim said.

"I'm afraid it's something I know about firsthand," Kathleen said. "I've been looking into the problem of food contamination for over a year. I've gotten active through a couple of consumer groups. Food contamination and the illness it causes have become a major part of my practice. And it's a problem that is getting worse. Furthermore, from what I've seen, the USDA and the beef industry are much too close. Particularly in middle-management positions, there's a kind of musical chairs, with people moving back and forth to make sure the industry is interfered with as little as possible."

"This is all for profit, no doubt," Kim said.

"To be sure. The beef industry is a multibillion-dollar business. Its goal is profit maximization, not the public weal."

"Wait a second," Tracy said. "The USDA has uncovered problems in the past. I mean, not that long ago with Hudson Foods—"

"Excuse me," Kathleen interrupted. "The USDA was not responsible for discovering the *E. coli* contamination involving Hudson Foods. It was an attentive public health official. Normally what happens is that the USDA is forced to make a show after an outbreak occurs. Then they make a big deal to the media. The USDA doesn't even have the power to recall meat it finds contaminated. It can only make a recommendation. And at Hudson Foods it was consumer groups that forced the USDA to up the recommended recall to over a million pounds. Perhaps the worst part is that when the USDA talks about inspecting for contamination, they're generally talking about gross contamination with visible feces. The industry has fought against any microscopic or bacteriologic inspection for years. Now there is supposed to be some culturing, but it is only a token. It's a sorry situation. With tragic consequences."

For a few moments no one spoke. A fresh tear streaked down Tracy's cheek.

"Well, that settles it," Kim said. He abruptly got to his feet.

"Settles what?" Tracy managed. "Where are you going now?"

"I'm going to pay a quick visit to Mercer Meats."

"I think you should stay here," Tracy said with exasperation. "You know Becky's condition is grave. There might be some difficult decisions to be made."

"Of course I know Becky's condition is grave," Kim snapped. "That's why I have so much trouble sitting here doing nothing. I said I was going to find out how she got sick. I'm going to follow this *E. coli* trail wherever it leads. At least I can do that for Becky."

"What if we need you?" Tracy asked.

"My cellular phone is in my car," he said as he started out of the ICU waiting room. "You can call me."

ONCE on the freeway, Kim called Tom.

"How's Becky?" Tom asked.

"To be honest, she's very bad," Kim said, fighting tears. "I'm not optimistic."

"I'm so sorry," Tom said. "What can I do to help?"

"Could you follow my inpatients for a couple of days?"

"No problem at all," Tom said. "I wish I could do more."

"Thanks, Tom," Kim said. "I owe you."

Bartonville was less than forty minutes out of town. Kim cruised down its main street and then followed the directions he'd gotten from a service station to Mercer Meats. It was a far bigger plant than he'd expected. The building was all white and modern. Immaculately landscaped, the whole complex projected an aura of high profitability. Kim parked in a visitor space. As he walked toward the entrance, he reminded himself not to lose his temper.

The reception area looked as if it belonged to an insurance company rather than a meatpacking concern, with plush wall-to-wall carpeting and framed prints on the walls. A matronly woman wearing a cordless headset sat at a circular desk in the center of the room. "May I help you?" she asked, eyeing Kim skeptically. His appearance was bordering on that of a homeless person.

"I hope so," he said. "Who's the president of Mercer Meats?"

"That would be Mr. Everett Sorenson," the woman said.

"Would you tell Mr. Sorenson that Dr. Reggis is here to see him?"

"Can I tell Mr. Sorenson what this is about?"

"Tell him it's about Mercer Meats selling contaminated hamburger to the Onion Ring restaurant chain. Or better yet, tell him I'd like to discuss the fact that my only daughter is fighting for her life after consuming a Mercer Meats patty."

"Perhaps you'd like to sit down," the receptionist said. She swallowed nervously. "I'll give the president your message."

"Thank you," Kim said, and retreated to one of the couches.

Kim waited until a man appeared with a long white coat not dissimilar to his own, except it was clean. On his head was a blue baseball hat emblazoned with MERCER MEATS. He came right up to Kim. "Dr. Reggis, I'm Jack Cartwright. I'm glad to meet you," he said with a slight smile. "Mr. Sorenson asked me to come out and talk with you. I'm vice president in charge of public relations." Jack was stocky, with a doughy face and a slightly upturned nose. "Listen," he said, "I'm sorry to hear your daughter is ill."

"She's fighting for her life against *E. coli* O157:H7. I imagine this is a bug you've heard of."

"Unfortunately, yes," Jack said. His smile vanished. "Everyone in the business is aware of it, especially after the Hudson Foods recall. In fact, we're so paranoid about it, we make an effort to exceed by far all USDA rules, regulations, and recommendations. We've never been cited for a single deficiency."

"I want to visit the hamburger-patty production area," Kim said. He wasn't interested in Jack's obviously canned spiel.

"You can't go onto the production floor, but we have a glassed-in observation walk so you can see the whole process."

"That's a start, I suppose," Kim said.

"Great!" Jack commented. "Follow me."

Jack led Kim along a corridor and started up some stairs. "I want to emphasize we're tigers about cleanliness here at Mercer Meats," he said. "The entire meat-production area gets cleaned every day, first with high-pressure steam and then with a quaternary ammonium compound. I mean, you could eat off the floor."

"Uh-huh," Kim intoned.

"The whole production area is kept at thirty-five degrees," Jack said. As they reached the top of the stairs, he pulled open a fire door, and they entered a glass-enclosed corridor perched a floor above the production area. It ran the entire length of the building. "Pretty impressive, wouldn't you say?"

Below, Kim could see workers dressed in white uniforms with white caps. They were also wearing gloves and shoe covers. Kim had to admit that the plant looked new and clean.

Jack had to speak loudly over the sound of the machinery. "Hamburger is usually a blend of fresh meat and frozen," he said. "It's coarse ground separately over there. After the coarse grind the fresh and the frozen meat are dumped into the formulation blender over there. Then the batch is finely ground in those big grinders." Jack pointed. "We do five batches per hour. The batches are then combined into a lot."

Kim pointed to a large rubber or plastic bin on wheels. "Does the fresh meat come in those containers?" he asked.

"Yup," Jack agreed. "They're called combo bins, and they hold two thousand pounds. We're very particular with our fresh meat. It has to be used within five days, and it's got to be kept below thirty-five degrees."

"What happens to the lot?" Kim asked.

"As soon as it comes out of the fine grinder, it goes by this conveyor below us to the patty-formulating machine over yonder."

Kim nodded. The formulating machine was in a separate room. They walked down the corridor until they were directly over it.

"How come it's in its own room?" Kim asked.

"To keep it extra clean and protect it," Jack said. "It's the workhorse of the plant. That baby puts out either regular tenth-of-a-pound patties or quarter-pound jumbos."

"What happens to the patties?"

"A conveyor takes them into the nitrogen freeze tunnel. Then they are hand-packed into boxes, and the boxes into cartons."

"Can you trace the origin of meat? I mean, if you know the lot number, the batch numbers, and the production date."

"Sure," Jack said. "That's all recorded in the patty-room log."

Kim withdrew from his pocket the paper with the information from the Onion Ring. He showed it to Jack. "I'd like to find out where the meat came from for these two dates and lots."

Jack shook his head. "Sorry. I can't give you that kind of information. It's confidential. Company policy."

"Then why keep the logs?" Kim asked.

"They are required by the USDA," Jack said.

"Sounds suspicious to me," Kim said, thinking about some of Kathleen's comments earlier that morning. "A public agency requires logs whose information is not available to the public?"

"I don't make the rules," Jack said lamely.

Kim let his eyes roam around the patty room. It was impressive, with its polished stainless steel equipment and lustrous tiled floor. There were three men and one woman tending to the machines. The woman was carrying a clipboard, on which she scribbled intermittently. In contrast to the men, she did not touch the machinery.

"Who's that woman?" Kim asked.

"That's Marsha Baldwin. She's a looker, isn't she?"

"What's she doing?" Kim asked.

"Inspecting," Jack said. "She's the USDA inspector assigned to us. She stops in here three, four, sometimes five times a week. She's a real stickler for details. She keeps us on our toes."

"I suppose she could trace the meat."

"Sure. She checks the patty-room log every time she's here. Come on," Jack said, motioning for Kim to follow him. "The only thing you haven't seen is the boxes being packed."

Kim knew he'd seen as much as he was likely to see.

"If you have any further questions," Jack said as they returned to the reception area, "just give a holler." He gave Kim a business card and flashed a winning smile.

Kim walked out of the building and got into his car. Instead of starting the engine, he turned on the radio. After making sure his cellular phone was on, he leaned back and tried to relax. He was feeling guilty about having abandoned Tracy in the ICU, but a little over an hour later his patience paid off: Marsha Baldwin walked out of Mercer Meats. She was dressed in a khaki coat and carried what looked like a government-issue briefcase.

Kim leaped out of his car and sprinted toward the woman. By the time he got to her, she was stowing her briefcase in her yellow Ford sedan. As she straightened up, Kim noticed her height. She had to be at least five feet ten. He estimated she couldn't have been much over twenty-five. "Marsha Baldwin?" he asked.

Surprised at being accosted by name in the parking lot, Marsha turned to Kim and gave him a once-over with her deep emerald-green eyes. "Yes, I'm Marsha Baldwin," she said hesitantly.

"I'm Dr. Kim Reggis. I was told you are a USDA inspector."

"What if I am?"

Kim extracted the paper he'd shown Cartwright. "I want you to find out where the meat came from for these two lots."

Marsha glanced at the paper. "What on earth for?"

"Because I believe one of these lots has made my daughter deathly sick with a bad strain of *E. coli,*" he said.

"Sorry. I can't get you that kind of information," Marsha said. "It's not my job to give such information to the public, and I'm sure it's against the rules." She started to get into her car.

Kim roughly grabbed her arm. "This is important," he insisted. "You're supposed to be protecting the public. Here's an opportunity to do just that."

Marsha didn't panic. She looked into Kim's indignant face. "Let go of me, or I'll scream bloody murder, you crank. I haven't done anything to you."

"Like hell you haven't," Kim said. "If you USDA people really inspected this meat industry, my daughter wouldn't be sick."

"Now just wait one minute," Marsha shot back. "I work hard at my job, and I take it very seriously."

"Bull," Kim spat. "I've been told that you people are in bed with the industry you're supposed to be inspecting."

Marsha's mouth dropped open. She was incensed. She climbed in behind the wheel and pulled her door shut.

Kim rapped on her window. "Wait a sec," he yelled. "I'm sorry. Please!" He ran a worried hand through his disheveled hair. "I'm desperate for your help. I didn't mean anything personal. Obviously I don't know you."

After a few seconds' deliberation Marsha rolled her window down and looked up at Kim. What had appeared to her as the visage of an eccentric oddball now looked like the face of a tortured man. "Are you really a doctor?" she asked.

"Yes. A cardiac surgeon to be exact."

"And your daughter is really sick?"

"Very very sick," Kim said with a voice that broke. "I'm almost positive it's from eating a rare hamburger. Will you help me for her sake? I can't help her medically, but I'm determined to find out how she got sick and maybe spare other kids from the same fate."

"Gosh, I don't know what to say," Marsha responded. She tapped the steering wheel as she debated with herself.

"I don't think there's any way for me to get this material without your help. At least not fast enough to make a difference."

"What about calling the department of public health?"

"That's an idea. But to tell you the truth, I wouldn't be optimistic going that route. I'd just be dealing with another bureaucracy, and it probably would take too long."

"I might be putting my job on the line," Marsha said. "Although maybe I could enlist the aid of my boss, Sterling Henderson, the district manager. The trouble with that is that he and I have never had what I would call a good working relationship."

"I'd prefer we just kept this between you and me," Kim said.

"Easy for you to say. It's my job, not yours."

"Tell me, have you ever seen a child ill with this *E. coli* problem?"

"No, I never have," Marsha admitted.

"Then come with me to see my daughter. After you see her, you can decide what to do. I'll accept whatever decision you make."

"Where is she?"

"At the University Med Center. The same hospital where I'm on staff. Call the hospital if you question what I'm saying."

"I believe you. When do you have in mind?"

"Right now," Kim said. "Just follow me."

"Okay," Marsha said warily, unsure of what she'd gotten herself into.

JACK Cartwright had been watching them through the window. He saw Marsha follow Kim's car out of the lot. Leaving the reception area, he hustled down the central corridor to the far end, where the administration offices were. He knocked on the president's closed door. A booming voice told him to come in.

Everett Sorenson had been successfully running Mercer Meats for almost twenty years. It had been under his leadership that the company had been bought out by Foodsmart and that the new plant had been constructed. Sorenson was a big man with a florid complexion, small ears, and a shiny bald pate.

"What the heck are you all wired up about?" Everett asked.

Jack took a chair in front of Everett's desk. "We've got a problem. You know that article in the paper this morning, the one about the crazy doctor carrying on about *E. coli* and getting arrested in the Onion Ring on Prairie Highway?"

"Of course," Everett said. "What about it?"

"He was just here. His name is Dr. Reggis. And I'll tell you, this guy is a nutcase. He's out of control, and he's convinced his daughter got her *E. coli* from one of our patties. I just watched him in our parking lot with Marsha Baldwin. Afterward they drove away in tandem."

"This is not what we need!" Everett slapped the surface of his desk. "That Baldwin woman has been a thorn in my side from the day she was hired. She's constantly filing these stupid deficiency reports. Thank goodness Sterling Henderson has been able to can them."

"Can't he get her fired or transferred or something?" Jack asked. "I mean, we're paying him as if he still works here."

"In his defense, it's a difficult situation," Everett said. "Apparently her father is connected in Washington."

"Which leaves us up the creek. Now we've got an overzealous inspector who doesn't play by the rules teamed up with a loose-cannon physician who's willing to get himself arrested at a fast-food restaurant just to make a point."

"I couldn't agree more," Everett said nervously. "Another *E. coli* fiasco would be devastating. Hudson didn't survive their run with the bug. But what can we do?"

"We've got to do damage control," Jack said. "And quickly. It seems to me we need to call on the newly formed prevention committee. I mean, this is what it was formed for. Maybe we can take advantage of Bo's dinner party tonight. That might speed things up."

"Good point," Everett said. He reached for his phone.

MARSHA saw they were following signs to the ICU. She sighed. This was going to be even worse than she'd feared.

Kim paused at the threshold of the ICU waiting room. He saw Tracy and motioned for Marsha to follow him. "Tracy, I'd like you to meet Marsha Baldwin. Marsha is a USDA inspector who I'm hoping will help me trace the meat Becky had."

Tracy didn't answer immediately. Kim instantly knew that something else had happened. "What now?" he asked grimly.

"Her heart stopped," Tracy said. "But they got it going again. I was in the room when it happened."

"Perhaps I should leave," Marsha said.

"No!" Kim said. "Stay, please. Let me go in and see what's happening." He turned and ran from the room.

Tracy and Marsha regarded each other uneasily.

"I'm so sorry about your daughter," Marsha said.

"Thank you," Tracy said. She dabbed at the corners of her eyes with a tissue. She'd cried so much that she was almost out of tears. "She's such a wonderful child."

"I wasn't aware your daughter was quite this ill," Marsha said. "It must be terrible."

"Unimaginable," Tracy said. "How can Kim even think about tracing meat? I'm having difficulty just breathing."

"It must be because he's a doctor. He's trying to prevent other children from getting the same problem. He's afraid there's a batch of contaminated meat out there."

"But why did he bring you here?"

"He asked me to help, but I was reluctant. His idea was that witnessing what this *E. coli* can do might change my mind."

"Seeing Becky might make you the most conscientious inspector in the world. Are you still interested? It'll take a bit of fortitude."

"I don't know. I don't want to intrude."

"You're not intruding. Come on. Let's make your visit."

Tracy led Marsha toward Becky's cubicle. Several of the nurses saw the women but said nothing. Tracy had become a fixture in the ICU.

Besides Kim, there were six doctors and two nurses packed into the tiny room. But it was Kim's voice that could be heard.

"I understand that she has arrested several times," he yelled. "What I'm asking is *why* it's happening."

"We don't know," Claire Stevens admitted. "There's no pericardial fluid, so it's not tamponade."

Kim stared at Jason Zimmerman, the pediatric cardiologist to whom he'd just been introduced.

"It seems to me it's something inherent in the myocardium itself," Jason said. "I need a real EKG."

Just then the monitor alarm sounded. The cursor swept across the screen, tracing a flat line. Becky had arrested again. "Code blue!" one of the nurses shouted. Jason immediately began external cardiac massage by putting his hands together and pumping on Becky's chest. Jane Flanagan, the anesthesiologist, upped the percentage of oxygen delivered by the respirator. ICU nurses brought the cardiac crash cart on the run. It was apparent that the heart had not just stopped beating but that all electrical activity had ceased.

Tracy clasped a hand to her face. She wanted to flee, but she couldn't, as if she were fated to watch every agonizing detail.

Marsha, fearful that she would be in the way, retreated to the waiting room, where she sat in shock and disbelief.

Kim initially stepped back, recoiling in horror at his daughter's pitiful body being savaged by the pediatric cardiologist.

"Epinephrine!" Jason yelled while he continued his efforts.

The nurses at the crash cart responded by filling a syringe with the medication and handing it off to Jason, who stopped his massage long enough to plunge the needle directly into Becky's heart. Tracy covered her eyes and moaned. Jason resumed the massage, but there was no change in the monitor's relentless tracking straight across the screen.

"Bring the paddles!" Jason yelled. "If that doesn't work, we're going to have to pace her, so be prepared." The nurses handed the paddles to Jason. "Everybody back!" he shouted. He positioned the paddles and pressed the discharge button.

Becky's pale body jerked. Everyone's eyes went to the monitor, but the cursor persisted in its straight, flat line.

Kim pushed forward. "More epinephrine!"

"No," Jason managed between pants. "I want calcium."

"Epinephrine," Kim repeated. His eyes were glued to the monitor cursor.

"Calcium!" Jason insisted. "We've got to see some electrical activity. There's got to be an ion imbalance."

"Calcium's coming up," Claire said.

"No!" Kim yelled.

"Hold it, everybody!" Jane shouted at the top of her lungs to get everyone's attention. "There's something very strange happening. Jason's getting good chest excursion, and I'm up to a hundred percent oxygen, and yet her pupils are dilating. For some reason there's no circulation."

No one moved or spoke except for Jason, who kept up with the massage. The doctors were stymied.

Kim was the first to respond. His training as a surgeon would not allow him to deliberate a moment longer. He knew what he had to do. With no circulation despite good chest excursion, there was only one alternative. He spun around to face the nurses at the crash cart. "Scalpel!" he barked.

"Oh, no!" Claire shouted.

"Scalpel!" Kim repeated more insistently.

"You can't!" Claire yelled.

"Scalpel!" Kim screamed. He lunged to the crash cart and snatched the glass tube containing the scalpel. He unscrewed the top with trembling fingers and extracted the sterile instrument, tossing the glass tube aside. It shattered on the tile floor. He picked up an alcohol swab and tore open its package with his teeth.

Kim reached the bedside and forced Jason out of the way. He swabbed Becky's chest with alcohol. Then he sliced open his daughter's thorax in one decisive, bloodless sweep.

A collective gasp rose from everyone present except for Tracy. Her response was more of a wail. She staggered back from the appalling scene.

Kim lost no time. Oblivious to the others in the tiny room, the consummate surgeon used both hands to pull Becky's slender ribs apart. Then he shoved his bare hand into his daughter's open chest and began rhythmically to compress her heart.

Kim's Herculean effort was short-lived. After only a few compressions he could feel that Becky's heart had perforated and was far from normal in texture. It seemed to squish between his fingers. Stunned, he withdrew his hand. In the process he also pulled out some of the foreign-feeling tissue. He brought the material up to his face to inspect it.

An agonized whine escaped from Kim's lips when he realized he was holding necrotic shreds of Becky's heart and pericardium. The toxin had been merciless. It was as if his daughter had been eaten from within.

Kim stood there, his hands bloodied, his eyes wild with grief. He tried to gently return the necrotic tissue to Becky's chest cavity. When he was finished with this futile gesture, he put his head back and let out a wail of anguish.

Blind to everyone and anything, he now shoved his way out of the cubicle and dashed across the ICU. Before anyone could respond, he was through the door. In the corridor, he went into headlong flight. People who saw him coming got out of the way.

Outside the hospital, Kim ran to his car. Gunning the engine, he shot out of the lot and drove like a madman out to Prairie Highway. When he turned into the Onion Ring parking lot, he brought the car to a screeching stop directly in front of the busy restaurant. Then he hesitated. A glimmer of rationality seeped into the corners of his brain. Kim had raced to the Onion Ring in search of a scapegoat, but now that he was there, he didn't get out of the car. Instead he raised his right hand and stared at it. Seeing his daughter's dark, dried blood confirmed the awful reality: Becky was dead. And he hadn't been able to do a thing to save her. He began to sob.

TRACY shook her head and ran her hand through her tangled hair as Marsha Baldwin patted her shoulder.

Right after Kim's precipitate departure Tracy had found herself paralyzed, unable even to cry. Claire and Kathleen had accompanied her to the ICU waiting room and had stayed with her to offer their sympathies and to explain what had happened. It wasn't until the two doctors had left that Tracy realized that Marsha was still there, and the two women began a long conversation. They sat in the far corner of the room by the window, where they'd pulled two chairs close together. Outside, the long shadows of a late wintry afternoon crept ever eastward.

"I want to thank you for staying here," Tracy said. "You've been a wonderful support. I hope I haven't bored you with all these Becky stories."

"She sounds like she was a wonderful child."

"The best," Tracy said wistfully. Then she took a fortifying breath and sat up straight in her chair. "You know, I'm worried about my ex-husband. I just hope he doesn't do something really crazy. He is basically a good man. How do you feel about helping him now?"

"I'd like to help very much," Marsha said.

MARSHA climbed into her car and sat there mulling over the events of this strange and terrible day. She wondered how to go about getting the information that Kim wanted. The source of meat for the various lots was recorded in the patty-room logs, but her job was just to confirm that the log was being kept, not to read specific entries. Knowing that someone was always looking over her shoulder, she decided to go after hours when only the cleaning crew was there. In fact, Saturday was ideal to try.

Marsha got out the address Tracy had given her and consulted the city map she had in the car. It didn't take long to find Kim's house, but when she arrived, she was dismayed there wasn't a single light to counteract the gathering gloom. She was about to leave when she caught sight of his car. She got out of her car and went to the front door. She noticed that the door was not fully closed. She rang the bell. There was no response. Marshaling her courage, she stepped into the foyer. Halfway across the hall she stopped dead. Kim was sitting in a club chair in an otherwise empty room, less than ten feet away. He looked like a specter in the half darkness. "Dr. Reggis?"

"What do you want?"

"Maybe I shouldn't have come. I just wanted to offer my help. I know it won't bring your daughter back, but I'd like to help you track the meat in those lots you think might be contaminated. I wasn't willing to admit it earlier, but every one of the deficiency reports I've filed has been suppressed by my district manager. He's all but told me to look the other way when there's a problem."

"Why didn't you say this to me before?" Kim asked.

"I don't know. Loyalty to my employer, I suppose. You see, I think the system could work. It just needs more people like me who want it to work."

"And meanwhile, meat gets contaminated and people get sick," Kim said. "And kids like Becky die."

"Unfortunately, that's true. But we in the business know where the problem is: in the slaughterhouses. It's profit over safe meat."

"When are you willing to help?" Kim asked.

"Right now. Actually, tonight would be a good time."

"All right," Kim said. "You're on. Let's go."

As TRACY approached her house, she could see Carl Stahl's yellow Lamborghini parked at the curb. She didn't know whether she'd be glad to see him or not. She felt shell-shocked. She wanted to fight it. At the same time, as a therapist, she knew she had to let herself grieve. Carl came down the steps to meet her, carrying flowers. Tracy stepped out of her car and into Carl's arms. "How did you find out?" she asked.

"Being on the hospital board, I hear all the news. I'm so sorry. Come on. Let's get you inside." They started walking up the pathway. "I hear Kim really lost it. That must make it extra tough on you. The man's clearly out of control. I tell you, the whole hospital is in an uproar."

Tracy opened the door, and she and Carl went in. "Kim's having a hard time," she said.

Carl took Tracy's coat and hung it in the hall closet. "That's an understatement. As usual, you're being generous. I'm not nearly so charitable. In fact, I could club him for carrying on the way he did in the Onion Ring. Did you see the article in the paper? It's going to have a big effect on the share price."

Tracy went into the living room and collapsed onto the couch.

Carl sat across from her. "I spoke to some other members of the Foodsmart board," he said. "We're thinking about suing him if the price falls."

"It wasn't an idle accusation on his part," Tracy said. "Becky had a rare burger there the night before she got sick."

"Oh, come on. Hundreds of thousands of burgers are made in the chain. No one gets sick. Besides, people have gotten the same *E. coli* from apple juice, lettuce, milk, even swimming in a contaminated pond." Tracy didn't say anything. Carl then said, "I'm sorry for carrying on like I am."

Tracy lowered her face into her hands. "Maybe it would be better for me to be alone tonight. I'm not very good company."

"Really?" Carl questioned. He was hurt.

"Yes, really." She raised her head. "I'm sure there's something else you should be doing."

"Well, there is the dinner at Bobby Bo Mason's house. He's one of the local cattle barons. Tonight's the celebration of his assuming the presidency of the American Beef Alliance."

"Sounds very important," Tracy said. "Don't let me keep you from it."

"You wouldn't mind? I'll have my cellular phone. You can call me, and I can be back here in twenty minutes tops."

"I wouldn't mind at all," she said. "In fact, I'd feel bad if you missed it on my account."

MARSHA and Kim drove in silence for quite a ways. Finally she was able to get him talking about Becky. She had a feeling it would be good for him. He regaled her with stories of Becky's skating exploits, something Tracy had not mentioned.

When the conversation about Becky lapsed, Marsha talked a little about herself. After veterinary school she'd become interested in the USDA and had vowed to join the agency to make a difference, but she discovered that the only entry-level positions available were with the inspectional services. It would take a year or so to be transferred to the veterinary side.

Marsha turned on the windshield wipers. It had started to rain. It was already as dark as pitch, though it was only a little after six.

"How are you going to get me into Mercer Meats?" Kim asked.

"I told you, it won't be a problem," she said. "They've never once even asked to see my ID. If it comes up, I'll say you're my supervisor. Or I'll say I'm training you."

Marsha exited the expressway and drove through Bartonville.

Moments later the white hulk of Mercer Meats loomed up. In

contrast to earlier that day, there were few cars. She pulled up close to the front of the building, turned off the engine, and got out. "Come on," she said.

The door was locked. Marsha rapped on it. Inside, the guard, an elderly man with a thin mustache, was seated at the round reception desk, reading a magazine. He rose and came to the door. "Mercer Meats is closed," he said through the glass.

Marsha held up her ID card. The guard squinted at it, then unlocked and opened the door. Marsha immediately pushed in. "Thanks," she said simply.

Kim followed. He could tell the guard looked at him suspiciously, but the man didn't say anything. He merely locked the door. Kim had to run to catch up to Marsha.

"What did I tell you?" she said. "It was no problem at all."

Once they were out of sight, the security guard returned to his desk and picked up the phone.

KIM stamped his feet and flapped his arms. The thirty-five-degree temperature of the patty room felt more like twenty-five.

Marsha had been leafing through the patty-room logbooks for more than fifteen minutes. There were two other people in the area, cleaning the patty-formulating machine with high-pressure steam.

"Ah, here we go," Marsha said triumphantly. "December twenty-ninth." She ran her finger down the column to lot two. Then, moving horizontally, she came to batches one through five.

"Uh-oh," she said. Kim came over to look. "Batches one through five were a mixture of fresh boneless beef from Higgins and Hancock and imported frozen ground beef. The imported stuff is impossible to trace other than maybe the country."

"What's Higgins and Hancock?"

"It's a local slaughterhouse. One of the bigger ones."

"What about the other lot?" Kim asked.

Marsha turned the page. "Here's the date. Lot six, batches nine through fourteen. Hey, we're in luck if the January twelfth production is the culprit. The entire lot was made from fresh beef produced on January ninth at Higgins and Hancock. Isn't there some way to narrow it down to one or the other?"

"Not according to the short-order cook at the Onion Ring," Kim said. "But I dropped off samples from both production dates at the lab. They should have the results by Monday."

"Until then we'll assume it's the January date," Marsha said, "because that's the only one that's going to be traceable. The next step is to go to Higgins and Hancock to trace the animals through purchase invoices back to the ranch or farm they came from."

"Give me that damn book," Jack Cartwright yelled.

Marsha and Kim leaped in fright as Jack lunged around Marsha and snatched up the ponderous logbooks. The noise from the high-pressure steam had kept them from hearing the Mercer Meats vice president enter the patty room.

"Now you have finally overstepped your bounds, Miss Baldwin," Jack sneered triumphantly.

Marsha tried to regain her composure. "What are you talking about?" she asked. "I have a right to examine the logs."

"You have the right to ascertain we keep the logs, but the logs themselves are private property of a private company. And more important, you do not have the right to bring in the public under the authority of the USDA to look at these logs."

"That's enough," Kim said. He stepped between the two.

Jack ignored him. "One thing I can assure you, Miss Baldwin, is that Sterling Henderson is going to hear about this violation of yours ASAP. I want you two out of here, before I have you arrested."

Kim glared back at Cartwright. Marsha had to pull on Kim's sleeve to get him to leave.

Jack watched them go. He hoisted the logs up onto their appropriate shelves. Then he walked down to the reception area. He got there in time to see Marsha's car leaving the lot.

He walked back to his office and phoned Everett Sorenson at home. "It was just as I suspected," Jack said. "They were looking at the patty-room logs. My worry is that this duo might end up at Higgins and Hancock. I heard them talking about it. I think Daryl

Webster should be warned." Daryl Webster was president of Higgins and Hancock.

"An excellent idea," Everett said. "I'll give him a quick call. See you at Bobby Bo's."

MARSHA turned into Kim's driveway and stopped directly behind his car. She left the motor running. "I appreciate what you've done," he said. "I'm sorry it didn't go more smoothly."

"It could have been worse," Marsha said brightly. "We'll just have to see how it plays out." She glanced at her watch. "By the time you get the lab results on Monday, I'd like to have the meat traced as much as possible. I'm going out to Higgins and Hancock. This might be my only chance."

"If you lose your job, I'm going to feel terrible."

"I knew the risk I was taking. Like you said, I'm supposed to be protecting the public."

"If you're going to the slaughterhouse now, then I'm coming along," Kim said. "I'm not going to let you go alone."

"Sorry, but it's out of the question. I'm not even assigned there. And slaughterhouses are akin to nuclear installations as far as visitors are concerned."

"What are the slaughterhouses hiding?" Kim asked.

"Their methods, mostly," Marsha said. "It's not a pretty sight in the best of circumstances, but particularly after the deregulation of the '80s, slaughterhouses have all pushed up the speed of their lines. Some of them run as much as two hundred fifty to three hundred animals an hour. At that speed contamination can't be avoided. It's inevitable. In fact, it is so inevitable that the industry sued the USDA when the agency considered officially calling meat with *E. coli* contaminated."

"You can't be serious. The industry knows that *E. coli* is in the meat, and they're contending it can't be helped?"

"Exactly," Marsha said. "Not in all meat. Just some of it."

"This is outrageous," Kim said. "I've got to see a slaughterhouse in operation."

"You'd never get in. Well, that's not entirely true. One of their biggest headaches is a constant shortage of help. So I suppose if you got tired of being a cardiac surgeon, you could get a job. Of course, it would help if you were some kind of vagrant, so they could pay you less than the minimum wage."

Kim shook his head in disbelief. "You know, this all makes me worry even more about you doing any more on my behalf."

"Listen," Marsha said, "what if I take my cellular phone with me and call you every fifteen or twenty minutes?"

"It's something, I guess." Kim wrote down the number. "I'm going to be waiting right by the phone, so you'd better call."

He slammed the car door and watched as she backed up, turned, and accelerated down the rain-slicked street. He then looked up at his dark, deserted house. Suddenly the reality of Becky's loss descended. The crushing melancholy flooded back.

IN KEEPING with his image of himself as well as his position in the industry, Bobby Bo Mason had built a house whose style was a monument to Roman Empire kitsch. Columned porticoes stretched off in bewildering directions. Imitation Roman and Greek statues dotted the grounds.

Everett Sorenson's Mercedes beat Daryl Webster's Lexus by less than a minute. The cars were whisked away by the valets, and the men and their wives started up the grand staircase.

"I trust you called your security," Everett said quietly.

"The moment after I spoke with you," Daryl said.

The front double doors were whisked open. In front of them stood Bobby Bo, framed by the massive granite jambs and lintel. Like Everett and Daryl, he was heavyset. He was impressively attired in a custom-tailored tuxedo.

"Welcome, folks," he said, beaming.

Music and laughter floated out from the living room. After the coats had been taken, Gladys Sorenson and Hazel, Daryl's wife, strolled into the party. Bobby Bo held back Everett and Daryl.

"We'll have a short meeting in my library," he said.

"I'd like Jack Cartwright to sit in on it," Everett said.

"Fine by me," Bobby Bo said. "Guess who else is here."

Everett looked at Daryl. Neither one wanted to guess.

"Carl Stahl," Bobby Bo said triumphantly.

A shadow of fear fell over Everett and Daryl.

"Come on," Bobby Bo teased. "All he can do is fire you."

THE windshield wipers tapped out a monotonous rhythm as Marsha turned into the deserted parking lot of Higgins and Hancock. The sprawling, low-slung plant looked ominous in the cold rain. Having visited the plant once during her orientation to the district, Marsha knew enough to drive around to the side to the unmarked employee entrance.

She parked and unhooked her cellular phone from its car cradle, checked the battery, and got out of the car.

She rang the night bell. After no response she rang again, and the door swung open. A man in a brown-and-black security uniform looked out at her. Marsha flashed her USDA card and tried to push into the building. The man held his position.

"Let me see that," he said.

Marsha handed the man the card. He inspected it carefully. "What are you doing here?" the man asked.

"What we inspectors always do," she said, feigning irritation. "I'm making sure federal rules are being followed."

The man finally backed up enough to allow her to enter. "There's only cleaning going on now," the guard commented.

"I understand," Marsha said. "Could I please have my ID?"

The guard handed back the card. "Where are you going?"

"I'll be in the USDA office," Marsha said over her shoulder. She was already on her way and didn't look back.

BOBBY Bo Mason pulled the library's paneled mahogany door closed and turned to face his tuxedo-clad colleagues, who were sprinkled around the room. Represented were most of the city's businesses associated with beef and beef products.

"Let's make this short so we can get back to more important things like eating and drinking," Bobby Bo said. His comment elicited some laughter. Bobby Bo enjoyed being the center of attention. "The issue here is Miss Marsha Baldwin. What's made this a crisis is her sudden association with this crank doctor who got the media's attention with his ruckus about *E. coli.*"

"It promises trouble," Everett said. "An hour ago we caught her and the doctor inside our patty room going through our logs. I'm afraid we're going to be facing another *E. coli* fiasco unless something is done."

The hushed jingle of a cellular phone sounded. It was Daryl's. He withdrew to the far corner to take the call.

"This *E. coli* nonsense is a pain in the neck," Bobby Bo sputtered. "You know what irks me about it? The poultry industry puts out a product that's swimming in salmonella, and nobody says boo. We, on the other hand, have a tiny problem with *E. coli* in two to three percent of our product, and everybody's up in arms."

Daryl rejoined the group. "That was my security out at Higgins and Hancock. Marsha Baldwin is there right now going through USDA records. She came in flashing her USDA card."

"There you go," Everett said. "Now I don't even think it's a topic for debate. I think our hand is forced."

"I agree," Bobby Bo said. "How does everyone else feel?"

There was a universal murmur of assent.

"Fine," Bobby Bo said. "Consider it done." He threw open the door. Laughter and music wafted into the room.

Except for Bobby Bo, the men filed out. He went to his phone and placed a quick internal call. Hardly had he replaced the receiver when Shanahan O'Brian leaned into the room. Shanahan was dressed in a dark suit and sported the kind of earphone a Secret Service agent might wear. He was a tall, dark-haired refugee of the turmoil in Northern Ireland. For the past five years he had been heading up Bobby Bo's security staff.

"Come in and close the door," Bobby Bo said. "The prevention committee has its first assignment."

TWENTY MINUTES LATER Shanahan pulled his new black Chero-kee into a rutted, gravel parking lot of a popular nightspot called El Toro. On top of the building was a life-size red neon outline of a bull. Even before Shanahan got near the entrance to the bar, he could hear the thundering bass of the loud music. The popular watering hole was crowded and smoke-filled.

Shanahan approached the busy bar. "I'm looking for Carlos Mateo," he yelled to the bartender. The bartender merely pointed to the back of the room and mimed shooting pool.

Shanahan had spent a good deal of time and effort recruiting for the proposed prevention committee. Carlos had escaped from prison in Mexico and had been on the run. Six months previously he'd come to Higgins and Hancock in desperate need of a job.

What had impressed Shanahan about the man was his cavalier attitude toward death. Shanahan learned that he'd been imprisoned in Mexico for knifing an acquaintance to death. In his job at Higgins and Hancock, Carlos was involved in the deaths of more than two thousand animals per day. Emotionally he seemed to view the activity of killing on par with cleaning his truck.

Carlos was a dark-haired, wiry man with a pencil-line mustache and hollow cheeks. His eyes were like black marbles. Over his bare torso he was wearing a black leather vest that showed off his lean musculature as well as his multiple flamboyant tattoos.

"I've got a job for you," Shanahan said. "You interested?"

"You pay me, I'm interested," Carlos said, lining up a shot.

"Come with me." Shanahan pointed toward the front door.

Carlos handed off his cue stick, gave a couple of crumpled bills to his complaining opponent, then followed Shanahan outside to the Cherokee. The two men climbed inside.

"Let's make this fast," Shanahan said. "The name is Marsha Bald-win. She's an attractive, tall blonde, about twenty-five."

Carlos's face twisted into a grin of pleasure.

"The reason you got to move fast," Shanahan explained, "is because at this very moment she's where you work."

"She's at Higgins and Hancock?" Carlos asked.

"That's right," Shanahan said. "She's in the admin section looking into records she's not supposed to. You won't be able to miss her. If you have trouble finding her, ask the guard. He's supposed to keep his eye on her." Shanahan reached into his jacket pocket and withdrew a crisp hundred-dollar bill. "Two hundred later if she disappears without a trace."

LIFTING her arms over her head, Marsha stretched. She'd been bending over the open file-cabinet drawer long enough to make her back stiff. She closed the drawer. Picking up her cellular phone, she headed out of the USDA office. While she walked down the silent hall, she punched in Kim's phone number.

"This better be you," he said without saying hello.

"That's a strange way to answer the phone," Marsha said with a nervous laugh. "I haven't had any luck so far. You have no idea how much paperwork the USDA requires. There's daily sanitation reports, process-deficiency records, kill-order reports, and purchase invoices. I've had to go through all of it for January ninth."

"What did you find?" Kim asked.

"Nothing out of the ordinary," Marsha said. She came to a door with a frosted-glass panel. Stenciled on the glass was the word RECORDS. The door was unlocked. She stepped inside, closed the door, and locked it behind her.

"Well, at least you looked. Now get yourself out of there."

"Not until I look at the company records," Marsha said. "It shouldn't take me much longer. I'm in the record room right now. I'll call you back in a half hour or so."

Marsha disconnected before Kim had a chance to object. She put the phone down. At the far end of the room was a second door. Marsha made sure it was locked. Feeling relatively secure, she walked over to a bank of file cabinets and yanked out the first drawer.

KIM was sitting in the club chair. The floor lamp next to it was the only light on in the house. On the table was the phone and an untouched glass of whiskey.

He had never felt worse in his life. Images of Becky kept flooding his mind and bringing forth new tears. The next instant he found himself denying the whole horrid experience and attributing it to a nightmare. The doorbell shocked him out of his stupor. Disoriented, he started to reach for the phone. He'd certainly not expected the door to chime. When the bell sounded again, followed by some knocking, Kim looked at his watch. It was a quarter to nine. He pushed himself out of the chair. To his utter surprise he found himself looking at Tracy.

"Are you okay?" she asked. She spoke quietly.

"I guess," he said.

Tracy stepped into the dimly lit foyer. Kim took her coat and rain hat. "I hope you don't mind my coming over here like this."

"It's okay," he said. He hung up Tracy's things.

"I didn't want to be with anyone," she explained. "But then I started thinking about you and worrying, especially with how agitated you were when you ran out of the hospital. I thought that since we've both lost the same daughter, we're the only ones that could have any idea of how we feel."

Kim breathed out heavily and swallowed as he choked back tears.

"Have you been sitting here in the living room?" Tracy asked.

He nodded. "I'll get a chair." He brought a dining-room chair in and placed it by the floor lamp.

Tracy sat down heavily, then leaned forward, cradling her chin in her hands with her elbows on her knees. Kim lowered himself into the club chair and looked at his former wife.

"There's also something I wanted to tell you," she said. "After I had a little time to think, I believe what you did today to Becky took a lot of courage."

"I appreciate your saying that," Kim said. "Open-heart massage is a desperate act in any circumstance."

"You did it out of love. Not hubris, like I thought at first."

"I did it because the external massage wasn't working," Kim said. "I couldn't let Becky just fade away. No one knew why she was arresting. Of course, now I know."

The phone's jangle startled them both. Kim snatched up the receiver.

"It's me again," Marsha said. "And this time I've found something. On January ninth there is a discrepancy between the USDA paperwork and Higgins and Hancock's."

"How so?" Kim asked. He motioned for Tracy to stay put.

"There was an extra animal slaughtered at the end of the day," Marsha said. "It means the animal wasn't seen by the USDA vet."

"So you mean it could have been unhealthy?" Kim questioned.

"That's a distinct possibility. The purchase invoice for this final animal indicates it was a dairy cow bought from a man named Bart Winslow. I recognize the name. Bart Winslow is a local guy who's what they call a four-D man. That means he goes around and picks up downers. Those are dead, diseased, dying, and disabled farm animals. He's supposed to take them to the renderer to be turned into fertilizer or animal feed."

"Don't tell me that they sometimes sell them to the slaughterhouse instead of the renderer."

"Apparently that's what happened. Head fifty-seven in lot thirty-six. It must have been a downer, probably sick. It gets worse," Marsha went on. "I found a deficiency report on the same animal that had nothing to do with its being sick or not having been seen by the vet. Something to do with the head. Are you ready for this? It's revolting."

"Tell me," Kim urged. He stood up.

"Uh-oh. Somebody's at the door. I got to get these papers back."

Kim heard the sound of a file-cabinet drawer being slammed shut. "Marsha!" Kim yelled. Marsha didn't come back on the line. Instead Kim heard shattering glass.

"Marsha!" Kim shouted again, but she didn't answer. He heard furniture crashing to the floor. Then there was a heavy silence. Kim looked at Tracy. His eyes reflected the terror he felt.

"What's going on? Was that Marsha Baldwin?"

"I think she's in danger," Kim blurted. "I have to go."

"Please, what's going on?" Tracy cried.

Kim simply spun on his heels and dashed from the house. "Stay here," he yelled. "I'll be right back." A moment later the car engine roared to life. Then he raced off into the night.

WITH the shattering of the door's glass panel, a gloved hand had reached in through the jagged edges and unlocked the door.

Marsha had let out a short shriek. She'd found herself facing a gaunt man wielding a long knife. She'd turned and fled, tipping over chairs behind her. Frantically she unlocked the rear door. Behind her she could hear cursing in Spanish and the crashing of chairs. She didn't dare look back. Out in the hall she ran headlong in search of the cleaning crew, anyone, even the intimidating guard.

She dashed past empty offices. At the end of the hall she hurried into a lunchroom. Behind her she could hear running footfalls. At the far end of the lunchroom a door stood open. With little choice, Marsha ran across the room, strewing her path with chairs. She ran through the open door and up a half flight of stairs that terminated at a stout fire door.

Yanking it open, Marsha darted into the vast, cold room beyond. This was the kill floor, and in the semidarkness created by widely spaced night-lights, it had a ghastly, alien look. Since it had been recently steam cleaned, a cold gray mist shrouded the ghostly metal catwalks and the sinister hooks hanging from the ceiling rails. The cleaning people had to be somewhere. She screamed for help, only to hear her voice reverberate against the walls.

Behind her the fire door banged open. Marsha took refuge behind a monstrous piece of equipment. A loud click made her start. An instant later the room was flooded with light. Her only chance now was to flee back the way she'd come. She sprinted to the fire door. Grabbing its handle, she yanked on it. The heavy door began to open, but then she could move it no farther. Marsha looked up. Over her shoulder was a tattooed arm.

She spun around and pressed her back against the door. With abject fear she stared into the man's cold black eyes.

"What do you want from me?" she screamed.

Carlos didn't answer. Instead he smiled coldly.

Marsha tried to duck around him, but she lost her footing and sprawled headfirst on the cold floor. Carlos was on her in an instant. She tried to grab the knife with both hands, but its razor-sharp edge sliced into her palms. She tried to scream, but he clasped his left hand over her mouth, raised his weapon, and dealt her a vicious blow with the heavy haft. Marsha went limp.

Carlos stood up. He crossed her arms so that her cut hands were on her stomach. He then dragged her by the feet across the kill-room floor to the grate at the termination of the cattle chute.

KIM drove like a madman, oblivious to the rain-slicked streets. He agonized about what could have happened to Marsha in the Higgins and Hancock record room. As he turned into the parking area in front of the immense plant, he saw Marsha's car among the few parked cars scattered around the lot.

Kim pulled up directly opposite the front door and leaped out. The door was locked. Cupping his hands around his face, he peered inside. All he could see was a dimly lit, deserted corridor. His anxiety mounted. Stepping back from the door, he surveyed the front of the building. There were a number of windows along the side of the building facing the parking lot. He tried each window. They were all locked. When he peered into the third window, he saw file cabinets, upended chairs, and what he guessed was Marsha's phone on the table. He picked up one of the stout rocks lining the edge of the parking area and hefted it through the window. The sound of shattering glass was followed by a tremendous crash as the rock bounced off the wooden floor.

Kim climbed in headfirst. He did his best to avoid the shards of broken glass and scanned the room. He saw a blinking red light on a motion detector, high in one corner and aimed at the window, but ignored it.

The abandoned cell phone, the upended chairs, as well as a broken panel of glass in the door to the front hall, convinced him that he was in the room from which Marsha had called him. He also noticed the open door at the rear. Dashing through this second door, Kim started down a deserted back hallway. At the far end he came to a lunchroom. Kim followed the trail of overturned chairs to the rear door, went up the steps, and yanked open the fire door.

He found himself in a room filled with a labyrinth of machinery and raised metal platforms that cast grotesque shadows.

"Marsha!" Kim yelled in desperation. "Marsha!"

There was no response. To his immediate right was a fire station with an extinguisher, a long flashlight, and a glass-paneled cabinet with a canvas fire hose. Kim snatched the flashlight from its bracket and turned it on. He set out in a clockwise direction past the machinery to explore more thoroughly.

After a few minutes the flashlight beam swept across a grate in the floor. Kim moved it back. Over the center of the grate was a dark smear. Advancing to the grate, he bent down and shone the light directly on the smear. Hesitantly he reached out and touched it. A chill went down his spine. It was blood.

FROM where Carlos was standing in the head-boning room, the place where cattle heads were stripped before being sent to the renderer, the sound of Kim's rock had come through as a muffled thump. Carlos stepped away from a flat conveyor belt that led to an ominous black hole, then turned out the light. He slipped off the bloody white coat and yellow rubber gloves he was wearing and stowed them under a sink. Picking up his knife, he pressed himself against the wall at the doorless opening to the kill-room floor.

Kim had come onto the kill-room floor. Carlos had no idea who this stranger was at first, but once the man yelled out Marsha's name, Carlos knew he'd have to kill him, just like he'd killed the woman. Cautiously he looked out. It was easy to keep track of the stranger now, thanks to the flashlight. He saw the man straighten up from the grate at Carlos's workstation at the end of the cattle chute.

All at once the flashlight shone directly at Carlos. He retreated from the beam. He held his breath as the stranger edged closer. The stranger was coming into the boning room.

KIM KNEW HE WAS IN A slaughterhouse that had been in operation that day, so finding blood shouldn't have come as a surprise. Yet the blood he'd found was unclotted and appeared fresh.

After having searched the kill floor, Kim decided to check other areas of the plant and headed into the only open passageway he'd seen. In the next instant, out of the corner of his eye, he detected sudden movement coming at him from the side. Reacting by reflex, he leaped ahead and used the long flashlight to parry a thrust.

Carlos had lunged from the shadows, hoping to skewer Kim in the side with a quick stab and then retreat, but the knife missed its mark and only succeeded in producing a shallow cut across the top of Kim's hand. As Carlos tried to regain his balance, Kim hit him on the shoulder with the flashlight and knocked him to the ground. Before Carlos could scramble to his feet, Kim took off. He ran through the head-boning room into the main boning room. This next room was almost the size of the kill floor and somewhat darker. It was filled with a maze of long, stainless steel tables and conveyor belts, where the carcasses were butchered into known cuts of meat.

Kim searched frantically for some kind of weapon to counter the long knife. Having turned off the flashlight and being afraid to turn it back on, he abandoned it and groped blindly along the tables. He found nothing. Looking back at the passageway into the head-boning room, he could see the silhouette of the man with the knife. Kim trembled with fear.

The sudden high-pitched sound heralding the start-up of electronic equipment made Kim jump. All around him the tangle of conveyor belts commenced their noisy operation. Simultaneously the room was flooded with bright fluorescent light. Kim crouched behind a plastic trash barrel. By looking beneath the boning tables, he saw the tattooed man pursuing him, advancing slowly, his right hand clasped around the knife that looked to Kim to be about the size of a machete.

Carlos was now only one aisle away. Impulsively Kim leaped to his feet and sprinted the length of the main boning room. He passed through a second doorless opening to find himself in a cold, misty, dimly lit forest of cattle carcasses. Then he heard the machinery suddenly stop.

Kim sprinted toward an EXIT sign, only to find that the door was secured with a chain and a heavy padlock. Hearing his pursuer's heels clicking against the concrete floor, he moved as quickly as he could along the narrow periphery of the carcass room and came to an interior door. He tried it, and to his relief it opened into a storeroom.

Kim ducked into the room, again hoping to find something to use as a weapon. The only sizable object was a broom. He picked it up. He was about to exit when he again heard the footfalls of his pursuer. The man was close.

Holding the broom in both hands by the tip of its handle, Kim flattened himself against the wall next to the door, which had closed.

The sound of the footsteps stopped just outside the door. The door began to move. The man was coming in! Kim's heart raced. He gritted his teeth and swung the broom. He hit the man full in the face, knocking him back through the door. The knife tumbled to the floor.

Still holding the broom in his left hand, Kim leaped for the knife. He seized it, only to discover it was a flashlight, not a knife. "Freeze!" a voice commanded.

Kim straightened up and looked into the blinding glare of another flashlight. Instinctively he raised his hand to shield his eyes. Now he could make out the man on the floor. It wasn't his pursuer. It was a security guard. Blood was coming out of his nose.

"Drop the broom," a voice behind the glare commanded.

Kim let go of the flashlight and the broom. Both clattered to the floor. The bright beam of the other flashlight was lowered, and to Kim's utter relief he found himself facing two uniformed policemen. One was pointing his pistol directly at him.

"Thank heavens," Kim managed.

"Shut up!" the policeman with the gun commanded. "Get out here and face the wall!"

Kim was only too happy to comply.

"Frisk him," the one with the pistol said to his partner.

Kim felt hands run up and down his arms, legs, and torso.

"He's clean."

"Turn around!" Kim did as he was told and quickly read the officers' name tags. The man with the gun was Douglas Foster. The other was named Leroy McHalverson. The security guard had gotten up and was dabbing at his nose with a handkerchief.

"Cuff him," Douglas said to Leroy.

"Hey, hold on," Kim said. "I'm not the one you should be cuffing. There's someone else in here. A dark, wiry-looking guy with tattoos and a huge knife."

"Really?" Douglas said scoffingly.

"I'm serious," Kim said. "The reason I'm here is because of a woman named Marsha Baldwin. She's a USDA inspector. She was here doing some work. I was talking with her by phone when someone surprised her. I heard breaking glass and a struggle. When I got here to help her, I was attacked by a man with a knife, presumably the man who attacked Marsha Baldwin."

The policemen remained skeptical.

"Look, I'm a surgeon at the University Med Center," Kim said. He produced his laminated hospital ID card.

"It looks authentic," Leroy said after a quick inspection.

"What about it, Curt?" Douglas asked the security man. "Was there a woman USDA inspector here or a dark, tattooed man?"

"Not while I've been on duty," Curt said. "And I came on at three this afternoon."

"Sorry, fella," Douglas said. "Nice try. Go ahead and cuff him."

"Wait a sec," Kim said. "There's blood in the other room that I'm afraid might have come from Ms. Baldwin."

"This is a slaughterhouse," Curt said. "There's always blood."

"This looked like fresh blood," Kim said.

"Cuff him, and we'll go see," Douglas said.

Kim allowed his wrists to be handcuffed behind his back. Then he directed them to the proper grate. But when Curt shone his flashlight, the blood was gone.

"It was here," Kim contended. "Somebody hosed it off. Wait. The telephone. She was talking to me on her cell phone. It's in the record room."

"That's creative," Douglas commented. "Let's take a look."

While Curt led the way to the record room, Leroy went out to the squad car to make contact with the station. At the record room Kim was immediately crestfallen. The chairs had been righted; the phone was gone. "It was here, I swear," he said. "And these chairs were upended."

"I didn't see any phone when I came in here to investigate the break-in," Curt said. "And the chairs were as you see them now."

Leroy returned from the squad car. A wry smile lit up his broad face. "They ran a quick check for me on the good doctor, and guess what. He's got a sheet. He was arrested just last night for trespassing and for assault and battery on a fast-food manager. Currently he's out of the slammer on his own recognizance."

"My, my," Douglas said. "A repeat offender. Okay, Doc. Enough of this nonsense. You're going downtown."

CHAPTER SEVEN

Sunday, January 25

KIM was back in the same courtroom with the same judge. He was seated at a scarred library table alongside Tracy. Standing before the bench was Justin Devereau, a lawyer and longtime friend of Kim's. He'd been fighting an uphill battle against Judge Harlowe's ire all morning.

Kim looked worse than ever, having spent yet another night in jail in the same outfit.

"I don't like to see the same face twice," Harlowe said with impatience. "It's an insult to my judgment for having allowed the individual his freedom after the first infraction."

"Dr. Reggis's daughter's recent death has caused him monumental stress, Your Honor," Justin persisted. "These were aberrant episodes that will not be repeated. As you have heard, Dr. Reggis is full of remorse for his rash actions."

Judge Harlowe had to admit the man did look penitent as well as pitiful. The judge looked at Tracy. The woman's presence and testimony had impressed him. "All right," he said. "I'll allow bail, but what has swayed me is not your bombast, Counselor, but the fact that Dr. Reggis's former wife has graciously consented to come before this court to attest to his character. Five thousand dollars bail and trial in four weeks. Next case!"

In less than a half hour the group emerged from the courthouse out into the overcast morning. "At first I was afraid Harlowe wasn't going to give you bail," Justin said. "As the judge implied, you should consider yourself lucky. And a word of advice, Kim. Don't get arrested again. If you do, I can guarantee you won't get bail."

"I understand," Kim said. "I'll be careful."

Kim and Tracy watched Justin walk away until he was out of earshot. They turned to each other.

"Now tell me what really happened," Tracy said.

"I'll tell you as much as I know," Kim said. "But I have to get my car. Would you mind giving me a ride out to Higgins and Hancock?"

"Not at all," Tracy said. "I'd planned as much."

"We'll talk in the car," he said.

The ride went quickly. Kim gave Tracy all the details. When he described the attack by the man with the knife, Tracy was aghast. He showed her the shallow slice across the top of his hand. "I think he was Mexican or at least Latin American. He had a lot of tattoos."

"Why didn't you tell all this to Justin?" she asked.

"It might have made things worse. It sounds so improbable."

"So you believe Marsha Baldwin is still in Higgins and Hancock?" Tracy asked. "Possibly being held against her wishes?"

"Worse. If it was human blood I found, she could have been killed."

"And you told all this to the police?" Tracy asked.

"Of course. But they think I'm some kind of nut. When I tried to show them the blood, it had been washed away. Even her car wasn't in the parking lot, where it had been when I got there."

"Do you know anything about her?" Tracy asked.

"I know almost nothing about her," Kim admitted, "except that she went to veterinary school."

"Too bad. If you could establish for sure whether she's missing, then the police would have to listen to you."

"You just gave me an idea," he said. "What do you think of my going to Kelly Anderson and getting her to help?"

"Now, that's not a bad idea," Tracy said. "She's caused you so much grief, it seems to me she owes you something. Maybe I can help you convince her."

Kim looked appreciatively at his former wife. "You know, Trace," he said, "I'm really thankful that you're willing to be with me after all that's happened."

Tracy looked over at him. The remark was out of character for him, yet seeing his eyes, she knew he was sincere. "That's a very nice thing to say," she told him.

"I mean it. I realize I've made a terrible mistake. I've focused too much on career and competition at the expense of family. And us. I've been selfish. It all makes me feel sad now. It also makes me want to apologize. I wish I could take back those wasted years."

"I'm surprised and overwhelmed," Tracy said. "But I accept."

"Thanks," Kim said simply. He stared out the windshield. They had turned onto the side road and were approaching Higgins and Hancock. "The entrance is coming up," he said.

Tracy pulled up alongside Kim's car, which was standing in total isolation. There were two other cars, but they were all the way at the end of the parking lot.

Kim pointed to the record-room window. It had been boarded up.

"What's the plan?" Tracy asked.

Kim sighed. "I've got to get to the hospital. Tom's agreed to look in on my patients, but I have to see them, too. Then I'll go see Kelly Anderson. I know where she lives."

"We have some decisions to make concerning Becky," Tracy said. "I know it is difficult, but we have to make funeral arrangements."

Kim nodded but looked off into the distance. Then he turned to face Tracy. There were tears in his eyes. "You're right," he admitted. "But I need a little more time. Would it be too much to ask for you to go ahead and make the arrangements? I know it's asking a lot. I'll agree to anything you decide."

Tracy tapped her fingers against the steering wheel. Her first thought was to say no and to tell him that he was just being selfish again, but then she reconsidered.

"All right. But promise to call me as soon as you get home."

"I promise," Kim said. He gave Tracy's forearm a squeeze before getting out of the car.

KIM was glad to get into the surgical locker room and away from inquiring faces. He was particularly pleased to find it vacant, and he lost no time. After removing his hospital ID plus a few papers and pens from the pockets, he pulled off the coat and the scrubs. Everything went into the laundry hamper.

Kim was shocked to catch his reflection in the mirror. He had significantly more than a five-o'clock shadow, and his hair was a mess. He quickly shaved and got into the shower with a vial of shampoo.

Kim had his head under the jet of water when he thought he heard his name called. He rinsed off the soap, then looked toward the shower entrance. Standing on the tiled threshold were Dr. Forrester Biddle, chief of cardiac surgery, and Dr. Robert Rathborn, acting chief of the medical staff.

"Dr. Reggis," Robert repeated. "It is my duty to inform you that your hospital privileges have been temporarily revoked."

"This is a curious conversation to have while I'm in the shower. You couldn't wait for five minutes?"

"We felt it was important enough to inform you as soon as possible," Robert said.

"What are the grounds?" Kim asked him.

"For obstructive behavior during your daughter's cardiac resuscitation attempt. Three doctors and two nurses have filed formal complaints."

"And I am appalled at your decision to perform open-heart cardiac massage on your own daughter," Forrester said. "It is beyond the pale of acceptable professional behavior."

"She was dying, Forrester," Kim hissed. "The closed-chest massage wasn't effective. Her pupils were dilating."

"There were other qualified people on the scene," Robert said.

"They weren't doing squat!" Kim snapped. "They didn't know what was going on. Nor did I until I got a look at her heart." His voice broke, and he looked away for a moment.

"There'll be a hearing," Robert said. "Meanwhile, you are not to practice any medicine within these walls."

"Well, it's good of you gentlemen to come into my office like this with such good news," Kim said.

"I wouldn't be so glib if I were you," Forrester warned. "You could very well find your medical license in jeopardy."

Without responding, Kim simply turned and went back to completing his shampoo.

THE El Toro bar looked like a completely different establishment in the daylight, ramshackle and abandoned. The rainy, foggy weather didn't help as it blanketed the area with a dense pall. Shanahan pulled his black Cherokee alongside Carlos's dilapidated pickup.

Carlos climbed out of his truck and came around to Shanahan's window. Shanahan handed Carlos a hundred-dollar bill.

"What's this?" Carlos said. "You told me two hundred. The woman's been taken care of, just like we talked about."

"You messed up. We heard about the doctor. You should have done him. You knew he was looking for the woman."

"I didn't have time," Carlos said. "He set off the silent alarm when he broke in, and the police got there before I could finish him. I was lucky to get rid of her blood and stuff."

"What did you do with her car?" Shanahan asked.

"It's in my cousin's garage," Carlos said.

"We'll pick it up," Shanahan said. "I don't want anybody using it. It's got to be junked. Does the doctor know what happened to the woman?"

"Probably," Carlos said. "He saw her blood."

"One way or the other, he's got to go. We'll pay you the other hundred plus three hundred extra to do the job."

"When?" Carlos asked.

"Tonight," Shanahan said.

DEFYING the revocation of his hospital privileges, Kim visited all his inpatients. By the time he left the hospital, it was midafternoon. He had considered trying to call Kelly Anderson to arrange a meeting but then decided it would be better just to drop in.

Kelly lived in a prairie-style house in the upscale Christie Heights section of town. Kim pulled up to the curb and gazed at the house. Coming to Kelly Anderson felt akin to conniving with the devil.

It was Caroline, Kelly's precocious daughter, who opened the door. For a moment Kim could not find his voice. The child brought back images of Becky. Kim heard a man's voice from inside asking Caroline who was there.

"I don't know," Caroline yelled back over her shoulder.

Edgar Anderson appeared behind his daughter. He looked like an academic, with heavy dark-rimmed glasses and an oversize cardigan sweater. "Can I help you?" he inquired.

Kim managed to say his name and asked to speak to Kelly.

Edgar invited Kim inside. He showed him into the living room. "I'll let her know you are here," he said.

To Kim's relief Caroline followed her father out.

"My, my, this is curious," Kelly intoned as she swept into the room. "The fox chasing the hound. Sit down, please." She plopped into a club chair. "And to what do I owe the pleasure of this unexpected visit?"

Kim started by telling her about Becky's death. Kelly's casual demeanor changed immediately. She was deeply moved.

Kim told Kelly the whole story, including the details of the discussions he'd had with Kathleen Morgan and Marsha Baldwin. When he finally fell silent, Kelly leaned back. She shook her head. "What a story. And what a tragedy for you. But what brings you to me?"

"I want you to do a report about all this. It's something the public needs to know. And I want to get the message out about Marsha Baldwin. The more I think about it, the more I'm convinced there's a conspiracy here."

Kelly pondered Kim's request. There were some intriguing elements to the story, but there were also some problems. After a few moments she shook her head. "Thank you for coming by and telling me all this, but I'm not interested, at least not at this time."

Kim's face fell. "Can you tell me why?"

"Sure," Kelly said. "As much as I sympathize with you about your tragic loss, it's not the kind of TV journalism I generally do. I go after harder, bigger stories."

"But this is a big story," Kim complained. "Becky died of *E. coli* O157:H7. This has become a worldwide problem."

"True," she admitted. "But it's only one case."

"Only one case so far. I'm afraid Becky's going to turn out to be the index case of what could be a big outbreak."

"But an outbreak hasn't happened," Kelly said. "You said yourself your daughter got sick over a week ago. I mean, one isolated case is not a story. Besides, what kind of proof do you have?"

"I don't have specific proof right now," he said. "That's what I expect you to find when you do the story. But all this was substantiated by Marsha Baldwin."

"Ah, of course," Kelly said dubiously. "How could I forget. The mysterious USDA inspector who you say has been missing for less than twenty-four hours. The one you feel has fallen victim to foul play."

"Exactly," Kim said. "They had to silence her."

Kelly wasn't sure she shouldn't be afraid of Kim, especially considering his double arrests. She had the sense his daughter's death had done something to his mind. He seemed paranoid, and she wanted him out of the house. She stood up. "Excuse me, Dr. Reggis. I'm afraid this is all hearsay. I'd like to help you, but I can't until you have something tangible."

Kim pushed himself up off the low couch. He could feel his anger rising, but he fought against it. He had to admit he understood Kelly's position, and the realization only renewed his determination. "All right," he said resolutely. "I'll get something substantive, and I'll be back."

"You do that," Kelly said, "and I'll do the story."

Kim exited the house and ran down to his car. He'd already decided what he was going to do. As soon as he made it onto the freeway, he punched in Tracy's number on his cellular phone. "Trace," he said with no preamble when she answered, "meet me at the mall."

There was a pause; then Tracy's voice came over the line. "I've made arrangements for a funeral service. It will be at the Sullivan Funeral Home on River Street, on Tuesday."

Kim sighed. "Thank you," he said at last. It was hard to find the words. "I appreciate your doing it without me."

"Do you want to hear the rest of the details?" she asked.

"You can tell me when I see you."

"Okay," she said with resignation. "Kim, what's going on?"

"I'll explain later," he said. "Meet me at Connolly Drugs as soon as you can."

SINCE it was late afternoon on a cold, rainy Sunday, there was no traffic, and Tracy made it to the mall in good time. She assiduously avoided looking at the skating rink. She located Kim in the hair-products section of the drugstore. He was carrying a box containing a pair of hair clippers and a bag from one of the clothing stores.

"Ah, Tracy," Kim said. "Just in time. I want you to help me. I've decided to go blond."

She lifted her hands onto her hips and regarded her former husband with bewilderment. "Are you all right?" she asked.

"There's nothing to worry about," he said. "All I want to do is disguise myself. I'm going undercover. I visited Kelly Anderson. She refuses to lend us her investigative journalistic skills until I supply her with some proof."

"Proof of what?" Tracy asked.

"Proof of the allegations Kathleen Morgan and Marsha Baldwin made about the meat industry and the USDA."

"And how are you going to do that?"

"Marsha Baldwin told me that Higgins and Hancock is always in need of help because turnover is so high. I need your help with the disguise. I want it to be good."

"I can't believe this. You mean you are going to try to get a job at Higgins and Hancock after someone tried to kill you there?"

"I've got to. For Becky's sake. It's a way to make her loss less meaningless." Kim suddenly felt tears spring to his eyes. "Besides, I have the time now. I'm on a forced leave from the hospital."

"Because of what happened in the ICU?"

"Uh-huh," Kim said. "Apparently you were the only person who thought my action was courageous."

"It *was* courageous," Tracy asserted. Without another word she turned to the shelving and walked along the aisle until she found the best bleaching rinse.

CARLOS turned off the single working headlight of his pickup before gliding to a stop beneath some trees lining the street. He switched off the ignition. From where he was parked, he could see the silhouette of Kim's house against the darkening sky.

Carlos waited in his truck for twenty minutes before he felt comfortable enough to get out. He heard a dog bark, but it sounded far away. He relaxed. He reached into his truck and extracted one of the long kill-floor knives from beneath the seat and slipped it under his coat.

AFTER parking his car in front of his garage, Kim gathered his bundles and went back to meet Tracy as she climbed from her car.

It was raining harder than ever. In total darkness they navigated the front walk. They entered the foyer and took off their coats. Then they carried their parcels into the kitchen.

"I'll tell you what," Tracy said while putting her bag of groceries onto the countertop. "I'm happy to make us something to eat and help you with your hair, but first I'd really like to take a shower and warm up. Would you mind?"

"Not at all. Help yourself. I'll start a fire in the fireplace. Maybe it will make this empty house a little less depressing."

While Tracy headed upstairs, Kim headed down to the basement, where the firewood was stored.

CARLOS heard the shower and smiled. This job was going to be easier than he'd imagined. He was standing in the walk-in closet in the master bedroom, intending to wait until Kim opened the door. But hearing the shower running, he thought that would be better. Escape would be impossible.

Carlos stepped out into the bedroom. He had his knife in his right hand. Moving like a cat advancing on its prey, Carlos inched forward. With each step he could see progressively more of the bathroom's interior through the open passageway connecting the rooms. He saw a hand flash by and drop clothing onto the counter.

Taking one more step, Carlos had a full view of the bathroom, and he froze. It wasn't Kim. Carlos was transfixed as Tracy turned her back toward him and climbed into the billowing mist coming from the shower stall. She closed the moisture-streaked glass door behind her and threw her towel over a bar at the shower's rear.

Carlos moved forward.

TRACY glanced at the soap dish and noticed it was empty. The bar was out at the sink. As she opened the door to get the soap, a flicker of light caught her attention. At first she couldn't believe her eyes. There was a man in black standing just within the bathroom. The flash had come from the blade of an enormous knife in the man's hand.

Tracy was the first to react. She let out a horrendous scream as she yanked the shower door shut. Then she snatched the tubular towel bar from its brackets and passed it through the U-shaped handle of the heavy glass door to prevent it from opening.

When Tracy's scream sounded through the house, Kim was on his way up the cellar stairs with his armload of firewood. His heart leaped into his throat. He dropped the firewood and raced up the stairs to the upper hallway door leading to the master bathroom. As he burst into the bathroom, he saw Carlos with his foot up against the glass shower stall, trying to open it. He saw the knife and immediately realized he should have brought something to defend himself.

Without hesitation Kim grabbed a table in the hallway and smashed it to free one of the legs. By the time Carlos turned to face him, Kim was brandishing the leg like a truncheon.

Carlos reacted by slashing out with the knife. As Kim backed up, Carlos bolted down the stairs.

Kim followed. Carlos threw open the front door and ran down across the front lawn. Kim was close behind, but he stopped when Tracy yelled for him. He looked back. She was standing in the doorway. She'd pulled on her coat.

"Come back," she yelled.

Kim turned in time to see Carlos leap into a truck parked in the shadows. An instant later the vehicle lurched forward and picked up speed.

Kim hurried back up to the house. Tracy was standing in the foyer. He enveloped her in his arms. "Was this the same man who attacked you last night?" she asked with astonishment.

"There's no doubt," he said.

Tracy shuddered and twisted out of Kim's grasp. "I'll call the police," she said.

Kim stopped her. "Don't bother. We'll end up spending a lot of time for nothing. They won't do anything. Undoubtedly they'll attribute this episode to a failed burglary, whereas we know what it is about."

"We do?" Tracy asked.

"Of course. Obviously what I was afraid had happened to Marsha did happen, and the people behind it are afraid of me. I feel so damn responsible. Because of me, one tragedy has led to another."

"I can understand how you feel," Tracy offered. "But Marsha was doing what she wanted to do, what she thought was right. It doesn't justify her death, but it's not your fault. I still think we should call the police."

"No!" Kim said emphatically. "Above all I don't want them interfering in my attempt to get evidence for Kelly Anderson. They think I'm a nutcase. Come on," he urged. "Let's get my gun. I doubt that guy will be back, but there's no sense taking any chances."

Tracy followed him up the stairs. "I'm having serious second thoughts about your getting more involved in all this."

"Not me," he said. "I feel even more committed." In the bedroom, he went directly to the bedside table and took out a small Smith & Wesson .38-caliber pistol. He slipped the gun into his jacket pocket.

"Please, Kim. I think we should forget about this whole thing."

"What would you have us do?" he asked. "Move away to some foreign country?"

"That's a thought," Tracy said.

Kim laughed mirthlessly. "Wait a sec," he said. "I was just kidding. Seriously? You'd go live in another country?"

"Yes. And given what happened to Becky, I'd like to be public about it—use the move to make a statement about the food situation in this country. And it certainly would be a lot less risky."

"I suppose," Kim said. He thought about the idea for a moment but then shook his head. "I think running away is too much of a cop-out. For Becky's sake I'm going to see this to the bitter end."

She took a nervous breath. "I still think getting a job in Higgins and Hancock just seems too dangerous."

"But there's no other choice. It's the only way to get the media involved, and the media is our only hope of doing anything about this sorry situation."

"Then I'm not going to allow you to go by yourself. I've got to help, even if I have to get a job, too."

"You're serious," Kim said. He was amazed.

"Of course I'm serious. Becky was my daughter, too. Maybe they could use me as a secretary or something."

"I've got a better idea," Kim said. "Remember Lee Cook, who worked for me back at Samaritan?"

"Wasn't he that technician who could fix anything electronic?"

"You got it. After the merger he retired, but I'm sure he could wire me up with a bug. You can be listening in the car in the parking lot. Then if need be you can use your cell phone to call for the cavalry."

"I could record what you say," Tracy said, warming to the idea.

"That's true," Kim agreed. "Let's call Lee right now. Come on. Get out of that coat and back into your clothes. We'll get the stuff we bought and get out of here. We can go on to your house if you wouldn't mind. I think we'll feel a lot safer there."

CHAPTER EIGHT

Monday, January 26

TRACY was leaning against the wall across from the guest bath.

"Well?" she called through the door.

"Are you ready?" Kim's voice answered.

"Ready," she said. The door squeaked open. Tracy's hand shot to her mouth, and she let out an involuntary giggle.

Kim looked completely different. She'd cut his hair short the night before, but now it was teased to stand mostly upward, and bleached platinum blond. His eyebrows matched his hair and formed a stark contrast with the dark stubble-covered face. He was dressed in black leather pants and a black T-shirt. Over that he was wearing a black corduroy shirt with the sleeves cut off. He had a black leather belt and matching bracelet decorated with stainless steel rivets. The outfit was topped off with a fake diamond-stud earring in his left earlobe and a fake tattoo on his right upper arm.

"So what do you think?" Kim asked.

"You look bizarre," Tracy said. "Where's the microphone?"

"Under my collar." He rolled over the upper edge of the shirt. A tiny microphone was pinned to the underside.

"Let's test the audio system," she suggested. "I want to make sure it's working as well as it did last night in Lee's garage."

Tracy went to her car and drove down to the corner while Kim moved around inside the house wearing his earphone. Lee had said the system would work for a distance of up to two hundred yards. Inside the car, Tracy slipped on a pair of stereo earphones that were attached to an old-style reel-to-reel tape recorder. After they talked, she rewound the tape and then played it. Both sides of the conversation came through perfectly clear.

They'd packed lunches and thermos bottles, banking on Kim's being hired on the spot. They stowed everything in the back seat. Kim climbed in the back, too, since the front passenger seat was taken up by the electronic equipment. Tracy slid behind the wheel.

"Wait a sec," he said. He was staring up at the house. "I was just thinking. It's not inconceivable that they could trace me here. On the way out to Higgins and Hancock we'll stop by the bank. We'll pull out our savings as a fallback. If we're being followed, credit cards aren't the best idea."

"In that case we might as well grab our passports, too."

"Let's do it," Kim said.

It was midmorning by the time they got on the freeway en route to Higgins and Hancock. The day that had started out so clear was already becoming veiled with high cirrus clouds.

"Let me ask you something," Tracy said after they'd driven for a few miles without conversation. "If all goes well, and we succeed in getting Kelly Anderson to cover the story, what would you hope would happen?"

"Well," Kim said, "I'd want the public to demand that meat and poultry inspection plus farm-animal feed approval be taken away from the USDA. It would be better if it were given to the FDA, which doesn't have a conflict of interest. Or better still, I'd like to see the system privatized so that there'd be a true competitive incentive for finding and eliminating contamination. We've got to get the media to make people understand that contamination must not be tolerated even if it means the product will cost a little more."

In the distance, stockyards came into view. It being a workday, herds of cattle could be seen milling about the muddy enclosure. Tracy turned into the parking lot, which was mostly full.

"How about dropping me off near the front entrance?" Kim said. "Then if you drive over to the end of the building, you won't be so noticeable, but you will be well within our two-hundred-yard range."

Tracy pulled over to the curb. They looked at each other and smiled nervously. Kim leaned toward her and gave her a kiss. It was the first time they'd kissed for longer than either cared to remember. Kim climbed out of the car.

Tracy watched Kim saunter brazenly toward the door in character with his outrageous disguise. Despite her apprehensions, she had to smile. She then drove down to the end of the plant and parked behind a van. With the headphones in place she immediately heard Kim's voice, with a southern accent.

"I need a job, any job," Kim was saying, drawing out his vowels. "I'm flat broke. I heard in town you were hiring."

Tracy hit the RECORD button, then tried to get comfortable.

KIM had been encouraged by the speed with which he'd been escorted into the office of the kill-floor supervisor. His name was Jed Street. He was a nondescript man with a slight paunch.

Jed had looked quizzically at Kim at first, but after a few moments he'd seemingly accepted Kim's appearance.

"Have you ever worked in a slaughterhouse before?" Jed asked. He rocked back in his desk chair.

"No," Kim said casually. "But there's always the first time."

"Do you have a Social Security number?" Jed asked.

"Nope," Kim said. "I was told I didn't need one."

"What's your name?" Jed asked.

"Joe."

"Where are you from?"

"Brownsville, Texas."

Jed rocked forward. "Look, this is hard, sloppy work. Are you ready for that?"

"I'm ready for anything," Kim said.

"When are you willing to start?"

"Hey, I'm ready to start right now."

"Okay, I'm going to have you start out sweeping the kill-room floor. It's five bucks an hour, cash. With no Social Security card, that's the best I can do."

"Sounds good," Kim said.

"One other thing," Jed said. "You gotta work the three-to-eleven cleanup shift, too, but just for tonight. One of the guys called in sick." He got to his feet. "Let's get you outfitted."

"I have to change clothes?" Kim could feel his gun against his thigh and the audio system's battery packs against his chest.

"Nah. You need a white coat, boots, hard hat, gloves, and a broom. You only have to change your shoes to get the boots on."

Kim followed Jed to one of the storerooms and got everything Jed had mentioned except the broom. Once Kim had on the yellow rubber boots, the hard hat, the yellow gauntlet-length gloves, and the white coat, he looked like he belonged.

Jed led Kim out through the lunchroom and up the half flight of stairs to the fire door. There he paused and handed Kim earplugs. "There's a lot of noise out on the kill floor. Your job is to move around and push the waste on the floor into the grates—cow manure, gore, whatever falls down from the line. And watch out for the moving carcasses suspended from the rails."

Kim nodded and swallowed.

Jed checked his watch. "It's less than an hour before we stop the line for the lunch break," he said. "But no matter. It'll give you a chance to get acclimated."

"Right," Kim said. He pushed the little spongy plugs into his ears and gave a thumbs-up sign to Jed.

Jed threw open the door. Even with the earplugs Kim was initially bowled over by the noise that exploded into the stairwell.

He followed Jed out onto the kill floor. Kim thought he'd prepared himself, but he turned green at the sight of the overhead conveyor carrying the thousand-plus-pound carcasses, the whine of the machinery, and the horrid smell. The air was thick with the stench of raw flesh, blood, and fresh feces.

Hundreds of workers in blood-spattered white coats were standing on the catwalks elbow to elbow, laboring on the carcasses as they streaked by.

Jed tapped Kim on the shoulder and pointed at the floor. Kim's eyes lowered. The kill floor was a literal sea of blood and offal. Jed was about to hand him a broom when he saw the color of Kim's face. Jed hastily pointed off to a door with a crudely painted sign that read GENTS. Kim made a beeline for the bathroom and retched into the sink. When he stopped, with trembling fingers he plucked out one of the earplugs and pushed in the earphone that he had coiled beneath his shirt.

"Tracy, are you there?" Kim questioned with a raspy voice.

"You sound terrible," Tracy said. "Are you all right?"

"I'm not great," he admitted. The sudden sound of a flushing toilet in one of the stalls made Kim jump. He tucked the earphone back under his shirt and turned to the sink to pretend he was washing. Behind him he heard the stall door bang open.

Kim worried what the stranger had heard. In the mirror he saw the man pass slowly behind him, studying him quizzically. Kim's heart leaped up into his throat. It was the man with the knife.

Slowly Kim turned around. The man had proceeded to the door but hadn't opened it. He was still staring at Kim with cold black impenetrable eyes. For an instant Kim locked eyes with the stranger; then, to Kim's relief, the man pushed open the door and disappeared. Kim exhaled. Bending his head down, he whispered into his microphone, "Good Lord, the knife-wielding madman was in one of the stalls. I don't know what he heard. He stared at me but didn't say anything. Let's hope he didn't recognize me."

After splashing some cold water on his face and replacing the earplug, Kim took a deep breath and returned to the kill floor. He caught sight of the stranger disappearing around a distant piece of machinery.

Jed was standing close by, obviously waiting for him. "You all right?" Jed shouted over the din. Kim nodded. Jed gave him a wry smile and handed him the long-handled, stiff-bristled broom. Then he patted Kim on the back before walking off.

Kim swallowed to stave off another wave of nausea. Grasping the broom in both hands, he tried to concentrate on pushing the offal that covered the floor toward one of the many grates.

"I don't know if you can hear me with all this noise," Kim said with his mouth close to his microphone. "Obviously the guy with the knife works here, which doesn't surprise me. I think I better locate him." He ducked as one of the carcasses brushed by him. Now his white coat had a bloodstain, just like everyone else's.

Kim straightened up, and after judging the speed of the carcasses, he stepped through the line, intent on following the route taken by the man who'd attacked him.

"Obviously I've been given the worst job in the place," Kim commented to Tracy. "But at least it gives me the opportunity to move around. It's like an assembly line for all the other workers. They stay in the same place while the carcasses move."

Kim moved around the monstrous piece of machinery he'd seen the stranger disappear behind. The floor in this area of the room was relatively clean. To Kim's left was a wall. He continued to sweep with his broom, although there was little debris on the floor. A new sound, like an air gun, emerged above the general noise.

"I've come to where the live animals enter the building," Kim said into his microphone. "When the lead animal comes abreast of an elevated platform, a man presses what looks like a jackhammer against the top of its head. It sounds like a nail gun. It must shoot a bolt into their skulls." Kim looked away, then forced himself to look back. "The cows collapse onto a large rotating drum that throws them forward and upends them," he continued. "Then a worker hooks them behind the Achilles tendon and they are hoisted up onto the overhead conveyor." Despite his revulsion about what he was witnessing, Kim forced himself to move forward. He now had an unobstructed view.

He stopped. Only twenty feet away was the knife-wielding stranger. Instantly he knew why the man favored knives. He was one of two people who stepped beneath the newly killed animal as it was hoisted up, and slit its throat just above a grate in the floor.

In the next second Kim's heart leaped in his chest. Someone tapped him on the shoulder. It was Jed, and he didn't look happy.

"What are you doing over here?" Jed shouted.

"I'm just trying to get oriented," Kim yelled.

Jed poked at him with an insistent finger. "I want you over where they're eviscerating." Jed motioned for Kim to follow him.

They soon came to the moving line of carcasses. "This is where I want you," Jed yelled, making a sweeping motion with his hand.

Kim nodded reluctantly. He lowered the head of his broom to the floor and started pushing the slop toward one of the many grates. His only solace was that his disguise must have been adequate. He was relatively confident that the man with the knife had not recognized him.

SHANAHAN was in his black Cherokee when a shrill beeping sound made him jump. He snapped the pager off his belt and glanced at the small LCD screen. He took out his cell phone and quickly dialed the number on the screen. It was Carlos.

"The doctor is here!" Carlos said in an excited, forced whisper. "At Higgins and Hancock. I'm using the phone in the lunchroom. The doctor is working here as a slop boy. He looks crazy, man. His hair's short and blond. It's him. I know it is."

"Did the doctor recognize you?" Shanahan asked.

"Sure, why not?" Carlos said. "He was staring at me. You want me to get him while he's here?"

"No!" Shanahan shouted. He took a deep breath and then spoke quietly and slowly. "Don't do anything. Pretend you don't know him. Just stay cool. I'll get word to you. Understand?"

KIM had moved all the way around the eviscerating area and now had a view of the whole slaughtering process. After the cows' throats were slit, they were skinned and decapitated, with the heads going off on a separate overhead conveyor system. After evisceration the carcasses were cut in half lengthwise by a saw.

Kim glanced at his watch to time the rapidity with which the animals were killed. He was astonished. "Marsha said the problem was profit over safety," he said into his microphone. "I just timed the activity here. They're slaughtering the cattle at the unbelievable rate of one every twelve seconds. At that speed there's no way to avoid gross contamination. And up on the catwalks there are a few inspectors, but they're hardly even looking at the carcasses as they whip by."

He suddenly caught sight of Jed Street. Kim recommenced sweeping, moving away from Jed in a counterclockwise direction, and soon found himself in the decapitation area. The beheading was done by a man with a saw. Another man caught the hundred-plus-pound head with a hook dangling from the conveyor rail. Kim followed the head conveyor into an adjoining room. He immediately recognized the room as the place where he'd been attacked Saturday night.

Kim took a chance that Jed wouldn't miss him and walked through the doorless opening into the head-boning room.

"I've come into the room where the heads go," Kim said into his microphone. "This is potentially important in how Becky got sick. Marsha had found something in the paperwork about the head of the last animal on the day the meat for Becky's hamburger might have been slaughtered."

Kim watched for a moment as the head conveyor dumped a head every twelve seconds onto a table, where it was attacked by a team of butchers. Then the heads were pushed onto a flat conveyor belt that dumped them ignominiously into a black hole that presumably led to the basement, where they were stored and then trucked to the rendering plant.

SO FAR it had been a good day as far as Jed Street was concerned despite its being Monday. He was confident that close to two thousand head would be processed by lunch. That made Jed happy. Wanting to catch up on his paperwork, he'd retreated to his office with a cup of coffee. He hadn't been working long when his phone rang.

"Jed, this is Daryl Webster. Do you have a moment?"

Jed had worked for Higgins and Hancock for fourteen years, and during that time the real boss had never called him. "Of course, Mr. Webster," he sputtered into the receiver.

"I got a call from one of Bobby Bo's people," Daryl explained. "He told me that we've employed a new slop boy just today."

"That's correct," Jed said. He felt his face heat up.

"Did he show you any identification?" Daryl asked.

"Not that I recall," Jed said evasively.

"What did he look like?"

"He is a little strange-looking. Kind of punk. Bleached hair, earring, tattoos, leather pants."

"Is he a fairly big guy?" Daryl asked.

"Yeah—over six feet for sure."

"Did he say where he was living?"

"No, and I didn't ask. I have to say he's been quite appreciative of getting the work. He's even agreed to work a shift and a half."

"You mean he's part of the cleanup crew?"

"Yup," Jed said. "Someone called in sick this morning."

"That's good," Daryl said. "Good job, Jed. Can I count on you to keep this conversation of ours confidential?"

"Absolutely, sir," Jed said.

NOT wanting to be caught in the head-boning room, where there was nothing to sweep, Kim went back to the evisceration area.

Despite his earplugs, he suddenly could hear a sustained raucous buzz of conversation. He saw that the cattle had been halted in the chute. The line was stopped. Workers started climbing down from the catwalks. Kim removed his earplugs and stopped one of the workers to ask him what was going on.

"Lunch break," the man said, hurrying away.

Kim watched as the workers lined up to pass through the fire door en route to the lunchroom and the locker area. The man who'd attacked him walked by without a glance to join the ever lengthening queue.

"Everybody's at lunch," Kim said into his microphone. "How anyone could eat is beyond me. I'm coming out. I need a breather."

TRACY soon saw Kim emerge from the front door and jog in her direction. He was dressed in a white coat and had a yellow plastic construction helmet on his head. He ran up to the car and climbed into the back seat.

"Why haven't you put your earphone in? It's been driving me crazy not to be able to talk to you."

"I can't risk the earphone except when I'm alone," he said.

"You're paler than I've ever seen you." Tracy was turned around in her seat as much as the steering wheel would allow. She reached out toward him. He took her hand and squeezed it.

Tracy sighed, then took her hand back and twisted around in the seat. "Can we get out of here now?"

"No," Kim said. "I've got to go back. I'm hoping that during the cleanup shift I can get into the record room. Marsha found what she called a deficiency report that involved the head of a sick animal. I want to find that paper. I don't think I'm taking any risk at this point. The guy with the knife looked me right in the eye in the men's room. If I was going to be recognized, that would have been the moment. In fact, I don't even want this gun anymore. Having it is more of a risk than a comfort."

Kim got the pistol out of his pants pocket and handed it to Tracy. Reluctantly she took it and put it down on the car floor.

"I want to follow this through," he said. "Would you call Sherring Labs with your cell phone? Ask about the results on the meat I dropped off. They should be ready now."

"Fine," Tracy said.

Kim gave her shoulder a squeeze. "Thanks," he said before climbing out. He closed the door, waved, and walked away.

CARLOS emerged into the afternoon rain along with an army of other workers heading for their vehicles. He saw the black Cherokee next to his truck. He headed toward the Cherokee and approached the driver's-side window.

The window went down. Shanahan smiled. "I got some good news," he said. "Come around and get in."

Carlos did as he was told. He shut the door behind him.

"You have another chance to do the doctor," Shanahan said. "He's working the cleanup tonight. It will be arranged that he will clean the men's room next to the record room. It will be late, probably after ten. Make sure you're there."

"I'll be there," Carlos promised.

"It should be easy," Shanahan said. "Just make sure the body disappears, like Marsha Baldwin."

"No problem," Carlos said.

CHAPTER NINE

Monday night, January 26

STRAIGHTENING up with a groan, Kim stretched his back. He was by himself, mopping the front hall, starting from the reception area. He had his earphone in, complaining to Tracy how exhausted he was. The cleaning had been extensive. The whole crew had started with high-pressure steam hoses on the kill floor. It was backbreaking work, since the hoses had to be hauled up onto the catwalks.

Cleaning the boning rooms had then taken until the dinner break at six. At that time Kim had gone back out to the car.

After the dinner break Kim had been sent out on his own on various jobs around the plant.

"I'm never going to complain about surgery being hard work again," he said into his microphone. "What time is it?"

"It's a little after ten."

"I haven't seen any of my cleaning colleagues for the last hour. It's time for the record room."

"Be quick!" Tracy urged.

Kim stuck the heavy-duty mop into his bucket and pushed the contraption down the hall to the record-room door. Its broken central panel was covered by a piece of thin plywood.

Kim tried the door. It opened with ease.

ELMER Conrad was the three-to-eleven cleaning-crew supervisor. His idea of work was to sweat like crazy for the first half of the shift and then coast. At that moment he was coasting, watching a Sony Watchman in the lunchroom with his feet up.

"You wanted to see me, boss?" Harry, one of the crew, asked, poking his head into the lunchroom.

"Yeah," Elmer said. "Where's that queer-looking temp guy?"

"I think he's out in the front hall, mopping," Harry said.

"Do you think he cleaned those two bathrooms out there?"

"I wouldn't know. You want me to check?"

"Thanks. I'll do it," Elmer said. "I told him twice he had to clean those heads before eleven. He's not leaving here until they're done." Elmer set out to find Kim. He'd received specific instructions from the front office that Kim was to clean the bathrooms in question, and he was to clean them alone.

"THIS isn't going to be so hard after all," Kim said into his microphone. "I found a whole drawer of process-deficiency reports. Now all I have to do is find January ninth."

"Hurry up, Kim. I'm starting to get nervous again."

"Relax, Trace," he said. "I told you I haven't seen a soul in an hour. I think they're all back in the lunchroom watching a ball game. Ah, here we are, January ninth. Hmmm. The folder's jammed full." Kim put it down on the library table.

"Pay dirt!" he said happily. "It's the whole group of papers Marsha talked about. Here's the purchase invoice from Bart Winslow for what must have been a sick cow." Kim spread out the other papers, finally picking one up. "Here's what I'm looking for. It's a process-deficiency report on the same cow."

"What does it say?" Tracy asked.

After a moment Kim said, "Well, the mystery has been solved. The last cow's head fell off the rail onto the floor. I know what that means after today. It probably fell in its own manure and then went in to be butchered for hamburger meat. This cow could have been infected with the *E. coli*. That's consistent with what you said you found out from Sherring Labs this afternoon indicating that the patty made from the meat butchered on January ninth was heavily contaminated."

In the next instant Kim was startled as the report was ripped from his hands. He spun around to find himself facing Elmer Conrad.

"What the hell are you doing with these papers?" Elmer demanded, his face beet red.

Kim felt his heart race. Not only had he been caught looking at confidential documents, but he had the earphone in his right ear. To keep the wire out of sight, he kept his head turned, looking at Elmer out of the corner of his eye.

"They were on the floor," Kim said, desperately trying to think of something. "I was trying to put them back."

Elmer glanced at the open file drawer, then back at Kim. "Who were you talking to?"

Kim gestured ineffectually at Elmer.

"Tell him you were talking to yourself," Tracy whispered.

"Okay," Kim said. "I was talking to myself."

Elmer looked askance at Kim. "You're one weird dude. Well,

you got more to do. I told you that you had to clean those two rest rooms next door."

"Sorry," Kim said. "I can get right to it."

Elmer tossed the report onto the table and roughly pushed all the papers together. While he was occupied, Kim pulled the earphone out and tucked it under his shirt.

"We'll leave these papers for the secretaries," Elmer said. He reached over and pushed the file drawer shut. "Now get out of here. You're not supposed to be in here in the first place."

Kim preceded Elmer out of the room. Elmer put out the light and closed the door. Taking out a large ring of keys, he locked it.

Kim was rinsing out his mop when Elmer turned to him. "I'm going to keep my eye on you, boy," Elmer warned. "And I'm going to inspect these two rest rooms after you're done, so don't cut corners." He gave him one final disapproving look before heading back toward the lunchroom.

Kim slipped his earphone back into his ear as soon as Elmer disappeared. "I want to get those papers," he said. "The problem is the bum locked the door. Anyway, it will have to wait until I make a stab at these two rest rooms. I better get busy."

Kim looked at the two doors. They faced each other across the hall. He pushed open the men's-room door. He gave his bucket a shove into the room and let the door close behind him.

The room was a generous size. In the middle of the far wall was a window that looked out onto the parking lot.

"At least this men's room isn't very dirty," Kim said. He wrung out the mop. Then he walked to the window and started mopping.

The door to the bathroom burst open. Kim's head shot up. To his utter shock he now found himself staring at the man who had attacked him, once again brandishing a kill-floor knife.

The man's lips slowly curled back into a cruel smile.

"Who are you?" Kim demanded. "Why are you doing this?"

"My name is Carlos. I've come to kill you. They pay me good for this."

"Kim, Kim!" Tracy shouted in Kim's ear. "What's going on?"

To help him think, Kim tore the earphone from his ear.

Carlos took a step into the room, holding up the knife. The door swung shut. Kim instinctively raised the mop. Carlos laughed.

Kim dashed into one of the toilet stalls and bolted the door. Carlos lunged forward and kicked the door fiercely. The stall shuddered under the impact, but the door held.

TRACY panicked. She started the car. Throwing the vehicle into gear, she stomped on the accelerator. Her only thought was to try to get to the men's room where Kim was cornered, apparently by the same man who'd been in his house the night before. She remembered the gun and swore at Kim for not having kept it with him.

Tracy brought her car to a shuddering halt opposite the record-room window. She snatched up the gun, jumped from the car, and ran over to the window. Remembering how Kim had gained entry, she put down the gun, and using both hands, she heaved one of the rocks against the plywood, knocking it free.

She grabbed the gun and went in headfirst. Once inside the dark room, she could hear intermittent thumps behind the wall to the right. The noise increased her frenzy. She moved as fast as the darkness would allow to the door to the hall.

She unlocked the door and made a right. After a few steps she saw the men's-room sign. Without a second's hesitation Tracy crashed through the door using her shoulder. She had the gun clasped in both hands and pointed it into the depths of the room.

She saw Carlos less than ten feet away, with one leg raised in preparation for kicking a toilet-stall door in. The door was already bent. As soon as he spotted her, Carlos made a flying leap for Tracy with his large knife.

She had no time to think. Closing her eyes against the hurling figure, she pulled the trigger in quick succession. Two shots rang out before Carlos careened into her, slamming her against the door and knocking the gun from her hand. She felt a stabbing pain in her chest as she crumpled beneath the man's weight. She desperately tried to breathe and to wriggle free, but he had her pinned against the floor. Then, to Tracy's surprise, the killer moved off her. She looked up, expecting to see him with his knife raised. Instead she was looking at Kim's distraught face.

"Oh, God!" Kim cried. "Tracy!" He'd pulled the killer off her and had thrown him aside. Frantic over the amount of blood spreading across Tracy's chest, he dropped to his knees and ripped open her blouse. As a thoracic surgeon, he'd treated stab wounds to the chest, and he knew what to expect. But what he found was a blood-soaked bra; Tracy's skin was intact.

"Are you all right?" Kim demanded.

Tracy nodded but couldn't speak. She was still struggling to catch the breath that had been knocked out of her.

Kim turned his attention to the killer. At such close range both of Tracy's wild shots had found their mark. One had gone through Carlos's skull. The other had hit him in the chest, which explained the blood all over Tracy.

"He's dead," Kim said.

Wincing against the pain in her chest, Tracy pushed herself to a sitting position. "I can't believe it," she managed to say. "I can't believe I killed someone."

"Where's the gun?" Kim demanded. Tracy couldn't take her eyes off Carlos. "The gun!" he snapped. He got down on his hands and knees. He found it. He grabbed a paper towel and wiped the weapon clean.

"What are you doing?" Tracy asked through anguished tears.

"Getting rid of your fingerprints. Whatever comes of this mess, I'm taking responsibility." He gripped the weapon, then tossed it aside. "Come on. We're getting out of here."

"No!" Tracy went after the gun. "I'm in this as much as you."

Kim grabbed her. "Don't be foolish! Let's go!"

"But it was in self-defense," she complained tearfully.

"We can't trust what kind of spin might be put on this. You're trespassing, and I'm here under false pretenses."

"Shouldn't we stay here until the police come?" Tracy asked.

"No way," Kim said. "I'm not going to sit in jail while this all gets sorted out. Come on now. Let's go before anybody gets here."

Tracy could tell that Kim's mind was made up. She let herself be led from the men's room. Kim looked up and down the hall, surprised that the shots had not brought anyone.

"How did you get in here?" he whispered.

"Through the record-room window," Tracy said.

Kim took Tracy's hand, and they dashed to the record room. Just as they were entering, they heard voices.

Kim quietly closed and locked the door. In the darkness he snatched up the incriminating papers. Then they made their way to the window. Kim climbed out, then Tracy. They ran for Tracy's car.

"Let me drive," Kim said. He jumped behind the wheel while Tracy got into the back seat. He started the car and drove quickly out of the parking lot.

For a while they drove in silence.

"Who could have guessed it would have turned out like this," Tracy said at last. "What do you think we should do?"

"Maybe you had the right idea back there," Kim said. "Maybe we should have called the police ourselves and faced the consequences. I suppose it's not too late, although I think we should call my lawyer, Justin Devereau, first."

"I've changed my mind," Tracy said. "I think your first instinct was correct. You'd certainly go to jail and probably me, too, and then who knows what would happen?"

"What are you implying?" Kim asked. He cast a quick glance at Tracy in the mirror. She never failed to surprise him.

"What we talked about last night. Let's go far away and deal with this mess from abroad. Someplace where the food is uncontaminated, so we could continue our fight against that issue as well."

"Are you serious?" Kim asked.

"Yes, I'm serious."

Kim shook his head. "You know what I like best about the idea of us going to a foreign country?" he said after a few minutes.

"What's that?" Tracy asked.

"That you're suggesting we do it together."

"Well, of course," Tracy said.

"You know, maybe we shouldn't have gotten divorced."

"I have to admit the idea has crossed my mind."

Silence again reigned for a time as the former lovers struggled with their emotions.

"How long do you think we will have before the authorities catch up with us?" Tracy asked.

"It's hard to say. Maybe forty-eight hours."

"At least that allows us time for Becky's service tomorrow," Tracy said, choking up all over again.

Kim felt tears arise in his own eyes with the mention of Becky's imminent funeral.

It was after eleven o'clock when they pulled into Tracy's driveway and parked behind Kim's car. They were both completely drained. They got out of the car. Arm in arm they walked up the path toward the house.

"Do you still think we should go to a foreign country?" Tracy asked.

Kim nodded. "At least I should. It seems I'm a marked man. In fact, after we change our clothes, let's not even stay here tonight."

"Where will we go?"

"Hotel, motel—what does it matter?"

Tuesday, January 27

DESPITE his exhaustion, Kim had slept fitfully and had awakened for the final time just after five. All night he'd agonized over what to do. The idea of being pursued by a hired killer was almost too much to comprehend. He eased out of bed to avoid disturbing Tracy, gathered up his clothes, and padded silently into the motel bathroom.

He shaved and showered. Brushing his hair down flat, he thought he appeared significantly more presentable. After pulling on his clothes, he scribbled a short note to Tracy that he'd gone to bring back some breakfast.

A few miles down the road was a doughnut shop, where Kim ordered two coffees, two orange juices, and an assortment of doughnuts. The place was nearly full of truckers and construction men.

On his way back to his car his eye saw the headline behind the window of the newspaper dispenser. It said in bold capital letters BERSERK DOCTOR SEEKS REVENGE BY MURDER!

A shiver of fear descended Kim's spine. He deposited the food and drink in the car, then went back to the dispenser. With a trembling hand he sought the proper coins from his pocket and got out one of the papers. Kim saw an old photo of himself below the headline.

Ducking back into the car, he found the story on page 2:

> Dr. Kim Reggis, a respected cardiac surgeon on staff at the University Medical Center, has taken the law into his own hands vigilante style. In response to the tragic death of his daughter on Saturday, he allegedly disguised himself with blond hair color, got a job at Higgins and Hancock under a false name, and then brutally murdered another worker by the name of Carlos Mateo. It is thought that the motive for this unprovoked killing is that Dr. Reggis believed his daughter died of meat slaughtered at Higgins and Hancock. Mr. Daryl Webster, the president of Higgins and Hancock, has said that this is a preposterous allegation. He also said that Mr. Mateo was a valued worker and a devoted Catholic, who tragically leaves behind an invalid wife and six young children.

Kim angrily tossed the paper onto the passenger seat and drove back to the motel.

Tracy heard him come in and poked her head around the bathroom door. She had just gotten out of the shower. "I heard you go out," she said. She stepped into the room while wrapping herself in a towel.

Kim held up the newspaper. "Read this," he said.

Tracy took the paper and slowly sank onto the edge of the bed. It didn't take her long. She looked at Kim. "What a character assassination," she said somberly. "They even included mention of your recent arrests and suspended hospital privileges."

"I didn't get that far," Kim said.

"I can't believe this has all happened so quickly," she said.

"When that man failed to kill me, the people who were paying him opted to destroy my credibility and possibly send me to jail for life. It gives you an idea of the power of the meat industry in this town that they can manage to distort the truth like this. I mean, there was no investigative reporting in this article. The paper just printed what they were told."

"This means we don't have forty-eight hours to decide what to do," Tracy said.

"I should say not. And for me it also means I'll fight this travesty but definitely from afar."

Tracy stood up and stepped over to Kim. "There's no question for me either. We'll go together and fight this together."

"Of course, it will mean we'll miss Becky's service," Kim said.

"I know."

"I think she'll understand."

"I hope so," Tracy managed. "I miss her so much."

"Me, too," Kim said.

Kim and Tracy looked into each other's eyes. Then he reached out and put his arms around his former wife, and they hugged as if they'd been involuntarily separated for years.

THE large wall clock in the WENE newsroom gave Kelly the exact time. It was 6:07. As usual, Kelly's pulse was racing. The director held up five fingers and gave the countdown, ending by pointing at Kelly. Simultaneously the camera in front of Kelly went live. "Good evening, everyone," Kelly said. "We have an in-depth report this evening concerning a sad local story. A year ago we had a picture-perfect family. The father was one of the country's most renowned cardiac surgeons; the mother, a psychotherapist, highly regarded in her own right; and the daughter, a darling, talented ten-year-old, considered a rising star in figure skating.

"The dénouement started presumably with the merger of the University Medical Center and Samaritan. Apparently this put pressure on the marriage. Soon after, a bitter divorce and custody battle ensued. Then a few days ago, on Saturday afternoon, the daughter died of a strain of *E. coli* that has surfaced in intermittent outbreaks around the country. Dr. Kim Reggis, the father, pushed to the limit by the sad disintegration of his life, decided that the local beef industry was responsible for his daughter's death. He became convinced that his daughter had contracted the *E. coli* from an Onion Ring restaurant in the area. The Onion Ring chain gets its burgers from Mercer Meats, and Mercer Meats gets a significant amount of its beef from Higgins and Hancock. The distraught Dr. Kim Reggis disguised himself as a blond drifter, obtained employment under an alias at Higgins and Hancock, and shot dead another Higgins and Hancock employee.

"WENE has learned from the authorities that a gun left at the scene had been registered to the doctor and that his fingerprints were found on it. Dr. Reggis is now a fugitive. In a bizarre twist to the story, his former wife, Tracy Reggis, has apparently joined him in flight. At this time it is unknown if she is being coerced or acting under her own volition.

"To follow up on this story, WENE interviewed Mr. Carl Stahl, CEO of Foodsmart. I asked Mr. Stahl if Becky Reggis could have contracted her *E. coli* from an Onion Ring restaurant."

Carl Stahl's face appeared on the studio's monitor. "Thank you, Kelly, for this opportunity to speak with your listeners," he said solemnly. "First let me say that having known Tracy and Becky Reggis personally, I'm crushed by this sad affair. But to answer your question, there is no way Miss Reggis could have contracted her illness from an Onion Ring restaurant. . . ."

THE house was quiet when Kelly got home after the newscast. She had expected to see Caroline sitting on the couch watching television, but the TV was off and Caroline was nowhere in sight. All Kelly could hear was the faint clicking of a computer keyboard coming from the library. She poked her head in. It was Edgar. She walked over and gave him a peck on the cheek.

"Interesting piece on Dr. Reggis," Edgar said.

"You think so?" Kelly said without a lot of enthusiasm. "Thanks. A year ago he could have been a poster boy for American success. As a heart surgeon, he had it all: respect, a beautiful family, a big home, all the trappings."

"But it was a house of cards," Edgar said.

"Apparently," Kelly said. She sighed. "What's with Caroline?"

"She wasn't feeling too good and wanted to go to bed."

"What's the trouble?" Kelly asked.

"Just some stomach upset with cramps."

Kelly left the room and climbed the stairs. Her face reflected her anxiety. She stopped outside Caroline's room and quietly opened the door. The room was dark. She stepped inside and silently walked over to her daughter's bedside.

Caroline was fast asleep. Her face looked particularly angelic. Her breathing was deep and regular. Kelly resisted the temptation to reach out and hug her daughter. Instead she just stood there in the semidarkness, thinking about how much she loved Caroline and how much Caroline meant to her. Such thoughts made her feel acutely vulnerable. Life was indeed a house of cards.

Kelly closed the door and returned to the library. She sat down on the leather couch and cleared her throat.

Edgar knew she wanted to talk. He switched off his computer. "What is it?" he asked.

"It's the Reggis story. I'm not satisfied with it. I said as much to the news director, but he overruled me, saying it was tabloid fodder, not hard news. But I'm going to do it anyway. There are some gnawing loose ends. The biggest involves a USDA inspector by the name of Marsha Baldwin. When Reggis stopped here on Sunday, he told me he thought the woman had disappeared. He implied foul play. I really didn't take him too seriously. As I told you, I thought he'd gone over the edge after his daughter's death, and according to him, the woman had only been missing for a few hours."

"But you still haven't found her," Edgar said.

"No. Monday I made a few calls, but I wasn't really into it. Today I called the USDA district office. When I asked about her, they insisted I talk to the district manager. But he just said that they hadn't seen her. After I hung up, I thought that it was curious that I had to speak to the head of the office to get that kind of information. So I called up later and asked specifically where she'd been assigned. Guess where."

"I haven't a clue," Edgar said.

"Mercer Meats," Kelly said.

"Interesting," Edgar said. "Well, I've learned to respect your intuition, so go for it."

"One other thing," Kelly said. "Keep Caroline out of the Onion Ring restaurants, particularly the one on Prairie Highway."

"How come?" Edgar asked. "She loves the food."

"For the moment let's just say it's my intuition."

The door chimes surprised both of them. Kelly glanced at her watch. "Who's ringing our bell at eight o'clock on a Tuesday?"

"Beats me," Edgar said. "Let me get it."

Kelly rubbed her temples as she thought about this Reggis situation. She heard Edgar talking with someone. A few minutes later he returned clutching a manila envelope. "You got a package," he said. He shook it. Something was moving around freely inside.

"Who's it from?" Kelly didn't like getting mystery packages.

"There's no return address," Edgar said. "Just the initials KR."

"KR," Kelly repeated. "Kim Reggis?" Edgar handed her the package. She felt through the paper. "Well, it doesn't feel dangerous." She tore open the envelope and pulled out a bunch of official-looking forms and a recording tape. Attached to the top of the tape was a Post-it. On it was written, "Kelly, you asked for documentation, and here it is. I'll be in touch. Kim Reggis."

"These are all papers from Higgins and Hancock," Edgar said. "With attached descriptions."

Kelly shook her head as she scanned the material. "I have a feeling my investigation just got off to a flying start."

EPILOGUE

Wednesday, February 11

THE dilapidated recycled UPS van coughed and sputtered, but the engine kept going as the van climbed a gradual incline along an isolated country road.

"I been thinking," Bart Winslow said to his partner, Willy Brown. "Benton Oakly's not going to have much of a farm if his cows keep getting the runs like the one we just picked up."

"Sure as shootin'," Willy said. "But you know, this one's not much sicker than the one we picked up a month ago. What do you say we take it to the slaughterhouse like we did the other one?"

"I suppose," Bart said. "The problem is we gotta drive all the way out to the VNB slaughterhouse in Loudersville."

"Yeah, I know. That TV lady got Higgins and Hancock to close for a couple of weeks for some kind of investigation."

"Well, the good part is that VNB is a lot less choosy than Higgins and Hancock," Bart said. "Remember that time we sold them those two cows deader than a Thanksgiving turkey?"

"Sure do," Willy said. "When you reckon Higgins and Hancock gonna reopen?"

"I hear by Monday next, 'cause they didn't find nothing but a handful of illegal aliens," Bart said.

"Figures. So what you think about this cow we got?"

"Let's do it," Bart said. "Fifty bucks is better'n twenty-five in anybody's book."

ROBIN COOK

"I'm not a vegetarian, nor am I suggesting that people should not eat meat," says Dr. Robin Cook about the health risks posed in *Toxin*. But, he says, the *E. coli* problem "is not going away—it's getting worse," and consumers need to protect themselves. "If [people] want to eat meat that's been professionally ground by a meat processor, they have to cook it *well done*. There's no buts, ifs, or maybes about it."

Toxin is Robin Cook's tenth appearance in this series. Trained as a surgeon, he published his first big medical thriller, *Coma,* in 1977. The book's success—and the popular film that followed—established him as the leading author of medical suspense. Today he is one of the world's most widely read novelists. Cook lives and works in Florida.

Firebird

JANICE GRAHAM

" When you are old and gray
and full of sleep,
And nodding by the fire,
take down this book . . ."

". . . And slowly read, and dream of the soft look
Your eyes had once, and of their shadows deep;

"How many loved your moments of glad grace,
And loved your beauty with love false or true,
But one man loved the pilgrim soul in you,
And loved the sorrows of your changing face. . . ."

—William Butler Yeats

chapter one

ETHAN Brown was in love with the Flint Hills. His father had been a railroad man, not a rancher, but the way he loved it, you would have thought he had been born into a dynasty of men connected to this eastern Kansas land. He loved it the way certain peoples love their homeland—with a spiritual dimension, like the Jews love Jerusalem and the Irish their Emerald Isle. He had never loved a woman quite like this, but that was about to change.

He was at this moment ruminating on the idea of marriage, as he sat in the passenger seat of the sheriff's car staring gloomily at the bloodied carcass of a calf lying in the glare of the headlights in the middle of the road. Ethan's long, muscular legs were thrust under the dashboard, and his hat brushed the roof every time he turned his head, but Clay's car was a lot warmer than Ethan's truck, which took forever to heat up. Ethan poured a cup of coffee from a scratched metal thermos and passed it to the sheriff.

"Thanks."

"You bet."

They looked over the dashboard at the calf.

"I had to shoot her. She was sufferin'," said Clay.

"You did the right thing. Tom'll be grateful to you."

"I sure appreciate your comin' out in the middle of the night.

I can't leave this mess out here. Just beggin' for another accident."

"The guy wasn't hurt?"

"Naw. A little shook up, but he had a big four-wheeler—just a little fender damage. He was comin' back from a huntin' trip."

It took the two men some mighty effort to heave the calf's carcass into the back of Ethan's truck. Then they headed home along the county road that wound through the prairie.

As Ethan drove along, his eyes fell on the bright pink hair clip on the dashboard. He had taken it out of Katie Anne's hair the night before. He remembered the way her hair fell around her face, the way it smelled, the way it curled softly over her naked shoulders. He began thinking about her again and forgot about the dead animal behind him in the bed of the truck.

As he turned onto the road toward the Mackey ranch, Ethan noticed the sky beginning to lighten. He had hoped he would be able to go back to bed, to draw his long, tired body up next to Katie Anne's, but there wouldn't be time now. He might as well make some eggs and another pot of coffee, because as soon as day broke, he would have to be out on the range looking for the downed fence where the calf had gotten loose, and there were thousands of miles of fence. Thousands of miles.

ETHAN Brown had met Katherine Anne Mackey when his father was dying of cancer, which was also the year Ethan turned forty. Katie Anne was twenty-seven—old enough to keep him interested and young enough to keep him entertained. She was the kind of girl Ethan had always avoided when he was younger. She was certainly nothing like Paula, his first wife. Katie Anne got rowdy, told dirty jokes, and wore sexy underwear. She lived on her father's ranch in the guesthouse, a beautiful limestone structure with wood-burning fireplaces, built against the south slope of one of the highest hills in western Chase County. Tom Mackey, her father, was a fifth-generation rancher whose ancestors had been among the first to raise cattle in the Flint Hills. Tom owned about half the Flint Hills, give or take a few hundred thousand acres, and, rumor had it, about half the state of Oklahoma, and he knew everything there was to know about cattle ranching.

Ethan had found himself drawn to Katie Anne's place. It was like a smaller version of the home he had always dreamed of building in the hills, and he would tear over there in his truck from his law office, his heart full and aching. Katie Anne would entertain him with her quick wit and her soft, sexy body, and he would leave in the morning, thinking how marvelous she was, with his heart still full and aching.

All that year Ethan had felt a terrible cloud over his head. He even quit wearing the cross and Saint Christopher's medal his mother had given him when he went away to college his freshman year, as though shedding the gold around his neck might lessen his spiritual burden. Then Katie Anne had come along, and the relief she brought enabled him to skim over the top of those painful months.

Once every two weeks he had visited his father in Abilene. Always, on the drive back home, he felt that troubling sensation grow like the cancer that was consuming his father. On several occasions he tried to speak about it to Katie Anne, but she would grow terribly distracted. In the middle of his sentence she would stand up and ask him if he wanted another beer. "I'm still listening," she would toss at him sweetly. He noticed her eyes glaze over, pulling her just out of range of hearing as soon as he broached the subject of his father. Ethan didn't like Katie Anne very much when her eyes began to dance away from him, when she fidgeted and pretended to be listening. And Ethan wanted very much to like Katie Anne. There was so much about her he did like.

Katie Anne, like her father, was devoted to the animals and the prairie lands that sustained them. Her knowledge of ranching almost equaled his. The Mackeys were an intelligent, educated family, and occasionally—on a quiet evening in her parents' company when the talk turned to more controversial issues, such as public access to the Flint Hills or environmentalism—she would surprise Ethan with her perspicacity. These occasional glimpses of a critical edge to her mind led him to believe there was another side to her nature that could, with time and the right influence, be brought out and nurtured.

So that summer while his father lay dying, Ethan and Katie Anne talked about ranching, about the land, about the new truck Ethan was going to buy. They drank a lot of beer and barbecued a lot of steaks with their friends, and Ethan even got used to watching her dance with other guys at the South Forty on weekends. Ethan hated to dance, but Katie Anne danced with a sexual energy he had never seen in a woman. She loved to be watched, and she was good. There wasn't a step she didn't know or a partner she couldn't keep up with. So Ethan would sit and drink with his buddies while Katie Anne danced, and the guys would talk about how lucky he was.

Then his father had died, and although Ethan was with him in those final hours, even though he'd held the old man's hand and cradled his mother's head against his strong chest while she grieved, there nevertheless lingered in Ethan's mind a sense of things unresolved, and Katie Anne somehow figured into it all.

Three years had passed since then, and everyone just assumed they would be married. Several times Katie Anne had casually proposed dates to him, none of which Ethan had taken seriously. As of yet, there was no formal engagement, but Ethan was making his plans. Assiduously, carefully, very cautiously, the way he proceeded in law, he was building the life he had always dreamed of. He had never moved from the rather inconvenient third-floor attic office in the old Salmon P. Chase house that he had leased upon his arrival in Cottonwood Falls fresh on the heels of his divorce, but this was no indication of his success. His practice had grown shamefully lucrative. Folks in Chase County loved Ethan Brown, not only for his impressive academic credentials and his faultless knowledge of the law but because he was a man of conscience. He was also a man's man, a strong man, with callused hands and strong legs that gripped the flanks of a horse with authority.

Now, at last, his dreams were coming true. From the earnings of his law practice he had purchased his land and was building his house. In a few years he would be able to buy a small herd. It was time to get married.

ETHAN looped the barbed wire around the stake. It was a windy day. The loose end of wire whipped him across the cheek, and he flinched. He nailed down the wire; then he removed his glove and wiped away the warm blood that trickled down his face.

As he untied his horse and swung up into the saddle, he thought he caught a whiff of fire. He lifted his head into the wind and sniffed the air, but the smell was gone as quickly as it had come. Perhaps he had only imagined it.

He dug his heels into the horse's ribs and took off at a trot, following the fence as it curved over the hills. This was not the burning season, yet the hills seemed to be aflame in their burnished October garb. The short copper-colored grasses stood out sharply against the fiercely blue sky.

From the other side of the fence, down the hill toward the highway, came a mooing sound. Not another one, he thought. It was past two, and he had a desk piled with work waiting for him in town, but he turned his horse around and rode her up to the top of the hill, where he could see down into the valley below.

He had forgotten all about Emma Fergusen's funeral until that moment, when he looked down on the old cemetery. It stood out in the middle of nowhere, but this afternoon the side of the road was lined with trucks and cars. The service was over, and as he watched, the cemetery emptied. Within a few minutes there were only the black limousine from the mortuary, and a little girl holding the hand of a woman in black, who stood looking down into the open grave. Ethan had meant to attend the funeral. He was handling Emma Fergusen's estate, and her will was sitting in a pile of folders in his office. But the dead calf had seized his attention. The loss, about five hundred dollars, was Tom Mackey's, but it was all the same to Ethan. Tom Mackey was like a father to him.

Ethan shifted his gaze and saw the heifer standing in a little tree-shaded gully just below the cemetery. To reach her, he would have to jump the fence or ride two miles to the next gate. He guided the mare back down the hill and stopped to study the ground to determine the best place to jump. The fence wasn't high, but the ground was treacherous. Ethan found a spot that looked safe. He got off his horse and walked the approach just to make sure. When he got back up on his horse, he glanced down at the cemetery again. He had hoped the woman and child would be gone, but they were still standing by the grave. That would be Emma's daughter and her granddaughter, he thought. He settled his mind and whispered to his horse. Then he kicked her flanks hard, and within a few seconds, with a mighty surge from her powerful hind legs, they sailed into the air.

The woman looked up just as the horse appeared in the sky, and she gasped. It seemed frozen there in space for the longest time, a black, deep-chested horse outlined against the blue sky, and then hoofs hit the ground with a thud, and the horse and rider thundered down the slope of the hill.

"*Maman!*" cried the child in awe. "*Tu as vu ça?*"

The woman was still staring, speechless, when she heard her father call from the limousine.

"Annette!"

She turned around.

"You can come back another time," Charlie Fergusen said in a pinched voice.

Annette took one last look at her mother's grave and knew she would never come back. She held out her hand to her daughter, and they walked together to the limousine.

ELIANA Zeldin got up on her knees and looked out the limousine's back window at the horse and rider pursuing the fleeing calf. She had an enthusiast's love of horses, and she could ride well, but this was another world, a world she knew only from picture books. When the rider tried to rope the calf and missed, she bounced with excitement and gripped her mother's shoulder.

"*Maman! Il faut que tu regardes ça!*"

"Sit back down and fasten your seat belt," thundered her grandfather.

The little girl turned sad eyes to her mother, eyes suddenly extinguished of all joy, and with painful remembrance Annette recognized herself in those eyes. She had a sudden urge to cry out, "Damn the seat belt!" but instead gently settled the little girl and tightened the belt, pinning her to the dark, dreary boredom of the limousine's interior.

Annette did not like being alone with her father. She feared him. She had never really wished to examine this fear, but when she read fear in the notes of a concerto, she played it with shivering intensity. Fear was not the only thing she played well. She played rapture and confusion, triumph and loss, shyness, sorrow and serenity all with equal beauty. The strings of her violin examined these hidden depths for her and brought her some measure of peace. It was the peace she yearned for—fame and glamour had been but perfumed petals on the water.

Riding in the back seat of the limousine with her father, her daughter between them, Annette felt anxiety rising in her chest. She hadn't seen him in five years, not since her parents had moved away from Wichita, which had been her father's last parish, and retired to the town of Cottonwood Falls, where her mother had been born and raised. Her mother had always been there, protecting her from his rages and rigid severity, and now Annette instinctively drew her daughter away from the man.

She need only endure it for a few weeks, she thought, to help her father get through the first stages of his mourning. Then they would be back in Paris, where Eliana could play in little square parks with tall old trees and dense flowering shrubs surrounded by high black wrought-iron fences that gave a strongly defined feeling of security. She would never come back to Kansas again.

The thought brought a sudden wave of relief—always drawn to this place, always obliged because her family was here. When her first recordings had been released, she had received all kinds of congratulatory notes from cousins and the like. Later, when her life had been shattered and she had withdrawn from public view, her family ties narrowed. Only her mother and father bound her to this Wonder-bread land. And now her mother was dead. This was not how she had wanted it to be. She had always wanted her father to go first, so she could have her mother back again.

The limousine followed a narrow blacktop that curved back through the Flint Hills, and Annette gazed at the smooth undulating lines. They reached the crest of a high hill and met with a glorious panorama. The swiftly scudding clouds cast moving shadows on the land below, and a string of cattle snaked through the copper-red valleys. She turned to her daughter.

"*Regarde,*" Annette whispered, tapping the window, and Eliana leaned over her mother's lap and peered out the window.

"I wish you'd teach that child some English," grumbled the old man. "It's just plain rude, always talking in French like that."

"She does know a little English, Dad."

"Then why doesn't she speak it?"

Annette stared silently out the window.

"I asked you a question, Annette," he said, irritated.

"I don't have an answer," she replied, and squeezed Eliana's hand. They rode in silence until the limousine arrived in Cottonwood Falls and deposited Charlie Fergusen, his daughter Annette Zeldin, and his granddaughter Eliana in front of the modest home of Nell Harshaw, who was hosting a reception for the family of her beloved friend, Emma Reilly Fergusen, deceased.

THE reception was a strain on Charlie Fergusen. He had never dealt particularly well with death, and the death of his wife was no exception. As a minister, Charlie would leave outdated little booklets about dealing with death with the families of the deceased, promise his prayers, then hurry away.

If Charlie was appreciated as a man of the cloth, it was not for his sermons, which, like his house calls, were dry and short, or for his spiritual guidance (if he had spiritual depth, he hid it well), but for his ability to raise and invest money for his church. The city leaders recognized his genius as a fund-raiser and so forgave him his inadequacies in the more traditional roles.

But the people who surrounded him this afternoon were not his parishioners. The people of Cottonwood Falls had known and loved Emma Reilly as a girl and had welcomed Emma Fergusen back to their fold when she returned at the age of sixty-five with her husband. They knew of Charlie only what they had seen for the past five years, and so his genius escaped them, and Charlie Fergusen felt very very alone.

The entire town of Cottonwood Falls flowed through Nell Harshaw's modest home that afternoon, and long before they had all departed, Eliana crawled up on her mother's lap and went to sleep. Annette carried her daughter home and laid her down on the spare bed in the back room of her father's house. The room was poorly heated, and Annette took off her long sable coat and covered the child. The little girl pulled the black fur up around her face.

"It smells like you," she murmured.

"Go to sleep, precious," Annette said, and kissed the child.

Eliana opened her eyes. "I heard a man in the kitchen at Nell's saying something mean about you, because of your coat."

Annette smiled gently at her daughter. "I suppose I shouldn't have worn it here. It's a bit too fancy for this place."

"I'm glad you wore it. I love it."

"So do I. When I wear it, I feel very safe and warm."

"That's the way it makes me feel, too." The little girl snuggled down under the coat. She had dark circles under her eyes, and as Annette ran her finger across her soft, downy cheek, Eliana's eyelids closed, and within a few breaths she was asleep.

ANNETTE took a shower and washed her hair, and she cried in the shower, where no one could hear her. When she came out, she sat on the edge of her bed in her nightgown, listening to her father open and close the drawers in his room next door. Suddenly she didn't want to be alone. She got up and went into the room where Eliana was sleeping. Upon their arrival, her father had shown them to the guest room, where they were to sleep, but while Annette was unpacking, Eliana had found this room and had insisted on sleeping here. In a vaguely dismissive tone of voice her father had referred to it as her mother's sewing room. Looking around the room, Annette understood what her daughter had sensed immediately. This was her mother's room, and she suspected her father never came in here.

The walls were covered with photographs of Annette and Eliana, framed press clippings from Annette's concerts, photographs of Annette shaking hands with the Queen of England and the Israeli prime minister. There was a sewing machine in a corner, and against the far wall stood her mother's piano, the keyboard open and music on the stand. There were postcards Annette had sent from cities around the world, which her mother had framed in elegant little gilded wooden frames. Then there were photographs of her mother's idols, the divas—Maria Callas and Joan Sutherland—and the younger Kiri Te Kanawa, whose voice sounded so much like her mother's had once.

Annette stood shivering in the middle of the room, listening to the Kansas wind, and thought of her mother's sweetly scented body lying alone in the cold ground in those lonely hills. Suddenly she had a frightening thought that spirits might have fetters just as bodies did. She knelt at the side of the bed and crossed herself, then offered up a prayer that her mother's spirit would not be bound to this land, that it would come away with her, away from this place and be free. Then she crawled into bed next to the child. She groped for her daughter's hand and held it in her own.

She tried to sleep, but every time she closed her eyes, she saw her mother's grave. Annette began to cry softly, and outdoors the wind rose to a piercing whistle. She rolled over and placed her hands over the child's ears so she would not be awakened.

After a while she thought she heard music. She listened carefully, trying to identify the tune, but it was masked by the wind that rattled the window. The music sounded faintly like a Schubert lied, one of her mother's favorites. She turned her head, thinking perhaps her father had turned on the radio in his room, but she could not locate the source.

The music intrigued her, and for a moment her grief was forgotten. It was the most beautiful sound she had ever heard, and as she descended into sleep, she wondered what this was and from where it came. She felt that something within the room was protecting her and her child from the world beyond.

Outside, the wind dropped quite suddenly, as though throttled by an unseen hand grown weary of its irascible ways, and the night was filled with the music of the spheres.

chapter Two

JERRY Meeker could pound in a fence stake with his bare hands and bring a wild horse to its knees with a single jerk on the lead, but he was having serious trouble getting a big leather club chair up the narrow stairs of the Salmon P. Chase house to Ethan's office. Ethan was at the top, and Jer was holding up the bottom, straining so hard his face had gone red and his bright blue eyes were swimming in tears.

"Set the thing down," gasped Ethan.

"Can't," grunted Jer through clenched teeth. "Keep goin'."

Ethan took another step and then another, and finally his heel touched the flat landing at the top of the stairs.

"Okay, buddy, we're here."

"Damn, this's heavy," said Jer as he wrangled his end up to the landing and then collapsed into the chair. "Nice, though."

Ethan wiped his brow. "Come on, let's get it in my office. I'm expectin' that French lady any minute now."

"You mean Emma's daughter?"

"That's right."

Jer rested his head on the chair back, and his eyes fell on the plaque that hung next to Ethan's door. Nothing identified the place as a law office. There was only one word on the plaque—WORDSWORTH—and below that, a framed quotation by the poet:

> *Where are your books?—that light bequeathed*
> *To Beings else forlorn and blind!*
> *Up! Up! and drink the spirit breathed*
> *From dead men to their kind.*

Inside the spacious attic office were walls of books, many having nothing to do with law. It was Ethan's sacred domain, and although Jer didn't understand it, he honored it and held his tongue.

Jer looked down at his stomach, where the sweat had soaked through the denim. "Well, I guess this won't make much of an impression on her, will it," he said, slowly getting up. "So I'll move. Just for her sake. Not yours."

"I'm supposed to be makin' an impression on madame, am I?"

"I met her at the funeral. She's a mighty pretty lady." Jer positioned his hands underneath the chair. "You'd probably like her."

"I doubt it," Ethan said as they lifted the chair. "She probably has one of those little yappy poodles with bows in his hair."

The office door, which was never locked, swung open as Ethan backed into it. "You doin' okay there, friend?" he asked.

"Yeah. Just take it easy," answered Jer.

"You remember the time they tried to put French crepes on the menu down at Hannah's?" said Ethan as they slowly inched the wide chair through the doorway. "It was on a Saturday night. Old Burt walked in, all spruced up in his good overalls, clean and pressed, and then he sat down and picked up the menu. He took one look at the Saturday Nite Special, slapped down the menu, and walked out. He's never been back to Hannah's since."

It was perhaps the physical exertion or just Ethan's remembrance of the look on old Burt's face, but mirth got the better of him, and his voice rose in a high-pitched, boisterous laugh that came straight from the heart, and tears swam down his face. It was not a mean laugh, for there was not a mean bone in Ethan Brown's body, but he was a Kansan, and his prejudices were deeply rooted in a proud conservatism and a cowardly lack of imagination.

"Better put this down before I drop it," Ethan said. He swept his hat from his head and wiped the tears from his cheeks. When he looked up, he saw that Jer was gaping at something over Ethan's shoulder. Ethan spun around.

In the middle of his office stood Annette Zeldin. Her soft brown eyes mirrored utter disbelief. She was holding a book.

"Excuse me. I'm looking for Mr. Brown. The attorney."

"I'm Ethan Brown."

The look in her eyes froze into a hardened stare. "I'm Annette Zeldin, Emma Fergusen's daughter. We had an appointment."

"Yes, yes, come in," boomed Ethan. With a frantic gesture he smoothed back his hair.

"I'll see ya around, Ethan. Good day, ma'am," Jer said, and disappeared out the door.

"Yeah, thanks, Jer," Ethan called after him. He turned back to Annette Zeldin and stepped forward, extending his broad hand to her, mustering an amiable smile. "Ethan Brown, attorney-at-law." It was the greeting he always used with folks out here, and they loved it. But Annette Zeldin ignored his outstretched hand.

"Please have a seat." He gestured to a chair in front of his desk. "Sorry to keep you waiting. I didn't see a car outside."

"I walked." She was still clutching the book. She had evidently taken it from his shelf, and Ethan recognized it immediately: *The Collected Poems of W. B. Yeats*. He started to comment on the book, but she spoke first. "You should put a sign up, Mr. Brown. Or do you only practice law as a hobby?"

Ethan's smile faded. "I apologize for that, ma'am. Everyone around here knows me by Wordsworth. Please sit down." Again he gestured to the chair, and Annette sat down.

Ethan sat and sifted through the jumble of files on his desk.

"I'm very sorry about your mama. She was a lovely lady."

Annette was unmoved. "My mother left me some land. I'd like to sell it," she replied coolly.

Ethan studied her for a moment. "You might want to reconsider. It's a real choice piece of property. Matter of fact, I just bought the property adjacent to it on the south. Some of the best grazing land in the hills. Nice place to raise a kid, too. And believe me, this kind of land just doesn't come up for sale—"

"Mr. Brown," she cut in, "I have a home. In Paris. I've lived there for seventeen years. I have no desire to move here."

"Have you ever seen this land?" he asked. "It's beautiful."

Pronouncing the words carefully, Annette said, "In these matters beauty is very much in the eye of the beholder, is it not?"

Ethan smiled, a kind of respectful acknowledgment of the subtle antagonism that sat rigid between them. "I'll be glad to take care of it for you," he said quietly. He quickly scanned through Emma Fergusen's will. "We'll need to get your father's written consent before you sell."

"Why? My mother left it to me."

"Under Kansas law the surviving spouse has a claim to half the property. But don't you worry about it. I don't anticipate any problems." Ethan closed the file. "I'll send the consent forms over to your house tomorrow morning. And we won't have any trouble finding a buyer for your land, I promise you."

Annette stood, and Ethan rose quickly to his feet. For a brief moment they stood only a few inches apart, Ethan towering over her. She noticed the clean smell of his starched shirt and judged him married, although he wore no wedding ring.

She started for the door, then noticed she still had the book of poetry in her hand. She looked back, glancing at his shelves. "At first I thought I'd walked into the city library," she said.

Ethan nodded proudly. "Best darn library in the county."

"Does anyone around here ever read Yeats?" she asked.

"Oh, a few of us starved souls do," he answered. From memory, in a gentle and expressive voice, he recited:

> *"When you are old and gray and full of sleep,*
> *And nodding by the fire, take down this book,*

And slowly read, and dream of the soft look
Your eyes had once, and of their shadows deep;

"How many loved your moments of glad grace,
And loved your beauty with love false or true,
But one man loved the pilgrim soul in you,
And loved the sorrows of your changing face. . . ."

He pointed at the book. "You keep hold of that till you go," he said. "I don't charge for the poetry, just the prose."

When she said good-bye, her eyes left him thinking he had, for a brief moment, impressed her.

After she left, Ethan dictated some notes to his secretary, Bonnie, then quickly closed up his office and headed for the Mackey place. Annette Zeldin had made him feel extremely uncomfortable. If he could just get out to the stable and saddle up his horse, he might well shake it off before she really got under his skin.

THAT evening, at the South Forty, Ethan sat alone watching Katie Anne dance. He reflected upon the events of the last few days. The idea of getting his hands on Emma Fergusen's property was a dream come true. Indeed, *all* his dreams were coming true. He should feel happy, contented, as though all was right with the world. He felt none of these things. What really annoyed him was that Mrs. Zeldin kept intruding upon his thoughts. He was relieved when Jer slid into the booth next to him.

"So what'd you think of Mrs. Zeldin?" Jer asked.

"One stuffy broad."

"I didn't think so. I talked to her at the reception at Nell's house. I liked her," Jer said quietly. "What d'ya have against her?"

"Vichy and de Gaulle, for starters."

"She just lives there."

"Yeah, by choice. That's my point. If you're born there, okay, I can make some allowances. But to make it your home!"

"Why're you gettin' all worked up about this?"

"I'm not all worked up."

Jer shrugged. "Okay. So you're not all worked up."

Ethan took a long draw on his beer. "I was thinkin' about asking Katie Anne to marry me."

Jer burst out laughing. "I knew somethin' was naggin' at you."

Ethan looked up to see Katie Anne approaching him, her soft brown hair curling in damp ringlets around her face the way it always did after she had worked up a sweat on the dance floor. She was always very appetizing then—her face flushed, her own scent mingling with the light floral perfume she wore.

"I'm outta here," Jer whispered, and slipped away.

Katie Anne slid in next to Ethan and put her hand on his leg, and Ethan forgot all about Mrs. Zeldin.

"Hi, handsome." She grinned. "Will you go get me a beer?"

"I can't," he answered gruffly. "Not right now."

She took a sip of Ethan's beer with her free hand. "I'll just drink yours," she said, her eyes dancing.

"How about April?" he asked.

"April who?"

"For our wedding."

Katie Anne grew still, but Ethan didn't notice. "The house should be finished by then," he continued.

She removed her hand from his leg.

"What's wrong?" he asked.

"Are you really serious this time?" she said.

"What do you mean?"

Katie Anne hesitated before replying. "Well, you keep finding reasons to put it off."

"No, I don't."

There was an edge of exasperation in her voice. "Ethan, this is the third time we've talked about setting a date."

"But we never set a date, and we haven't put it off."

She heaved a sigh. "Oh, whatever."

Ethan hated that expression. It made her sound juvenile and not very intelligent. "I just want us to have a house of our own," he said.

"We've been living together for over a year. Why do we need to wait until your house is built before we can get married?" She turned her back to him and watched the dancers.

Ethan was silent for a long time; then he said, "I sure didn't think this would turn so unpleasant."

"Is it unpleasant?" she said, her back still to him. Her voice sounded odd, and he wondered if she was crying.

"It is for me."

Ethan took a long swig of his beer. Finally he put his arm around Katie Anne and pulled her close to him. She laid her head on his shoulder and whispered, "April's fine."

As soon as she said it, Ethan felt a faint nausea sweep through him, but he attributed it to the unusually heavy cigarette smoke in the club that evening.

MEALTIME had never been an enjoyable part of the day in the Fergusen household, and the misery of those childhood moments crept over Annette as she picked away at her dinner. Charlie cast a severe glance at Eliana, and Annette unconsciously stiffened. What is she doing wrong? Annette wondered. What could a little six-year-old possibly be doing to annoy him?

"Annette, tell Eliana to put the salt back in the center of the table, where everyone can reach it."

Ah, that's it, thought Annette as she set the salt in front of her father's plate. Charlie, vindicated, went back to his dinner.

Eliana wiped her mouth and looked up at her mother. *"Est-ce que je peux aller jouer au dehors maintenant?"* she asked.

"Yes. But first take your plate to the sink."

Once Eliana was outside playing with the neighbor's dog through the chain-link fence, Annette relaxed. She was not expecting Charlie's next words.

"I don't want you to sell that land."

Annette faced him. "Why not?"

"I'll agree to sell it only if the money's put into a trust account for Eliana to use for her college education."

"Universities are free in France."

"Maybe she won't want to go to college in France."

"Dad, I need that money. The cost of living is very high in Paris, and it just keeps getting higher."

"Then why don't you move back here?"

"Because this isn't my home."

Charlie got up from the table and rinsed his dishes. "You can move back here and live in the house on the place, but if you sell it, you put the money into a trust. It's your choice."

"Dad, I'm not moving back here."

"Then I'll tell the attorney to set up the trust," he said as he dried his hands on a dish towel. He went into the living room and clicked on the television. She rose, went to the sink, and emptied her uneaten dinner into the garbage disposal.

chapter Three

ANNETTE sat in Ethan Brown's office with her hands quietly folded in her lap, listening to him apologize. When at last she spoke, her voice was cool and controlled. "Mr. Brown, I'm very disappointed in the way this has been handled. I was told you were one of the best civil law attorneys in the state."

"I don't know about that, ma'am. But I know I care a lot about the folks around here."

"I'm sure of that." Her voice softened suddenly, and the change arrested his attention. "You don't like me, do you?" she said. It took Ethan a moment to recover, and she went on. "But no matter. The point is, if you cared about my mother's final wishes, you would have handled this differently. My mother had nothing to leave me except this land. She was not rich. . . ." Her voice caught in her throat. "She left me great wealth, of course, but not in material things."

"Mrs. Zeldin, I did try to persuade her to get your father's written consent when the will was drawn up. But she didn't want to do it." Ethan paused. "She was afraid it would hurt him."

She stared blankly at Ethan for a moment, then looked down at her hands. "Yes," she said quietly. "Yes, I see."

ETHAN felt very uncomfortable with Mrs. Zeldin riding in his truck. He thought it was because she was wearing that fur coat and the same black dress she wore every time he saw her.

"Don't you have any jeans, ma'am?" he asked as he swerved around a pothole, and Eliana, sitting between them, clutched the dashboard and grinned.

"No."

"Don't women wear jeans in France?"

"The young ones do."

He wondered if she was inviting a compliment, but the serious, far-off look in her face told him her mind was far removed from such trivial games. For the first time he was aware of her beauty, the way she held her hands and her shoulders, the way her legs gracefully intertwined at the ankles. Her dark hair was very short and feminine, and her face bore only the faintest touch of makeup. He knew how old she was, he had all the statistics in her file, but only her hands betrayed her forty years. And her eyes.

Eliana twisted around to check on Traveler, Ethan's Border collie who rode in the back of the truck; then she said something to her mother in French. Her mother shook her head.

Ethan caught Annette's eye. "She can ride in the back if that's what she wants. Perfectly okay."

"I'd rather she didn't."

"I'd slow down."

Annette was caught off guard by his concern. He had read her mind. "Maybe on the way back," she said.

Eliana understood, and she smiled at them and bubbled over with enthusiastic French. Ethan understood not a word.

"Eliana, you have a dog at home?" he asked.

Eliana shook her head and replied that their dog had died when she was little and her mother didn't want another one. Ethan was surprised to hear her speak with a British accent.

"*Maman* doesn't like little yappy dogs," Eliana said. "She says we won't get a big dog until we can get a place in the country."

Ethan shot a quick look at Annette. She was looking out the window, trying to suppress a smile.

They reached the top of a hill, and Annette leaned forward. She had never imagined country this lovely in Kansas. She had been raised in the west, the flattest part of the state, but the low-flung Flint Hills were grasslands stretching as far as the eye could see, with the farther hills fading into a purple-blue haze. Cottonwoods and oaks struck bright dots of orange and gold.

Ethan turned off the dirt road onto a gravel entrance, the gravel quickly dissolving into tire tracks overgrown with grass. The truck climbed a steep hill, and as they pulled to a stop underneath a cluster of cottonwoods, Annette saw the old farmhouse. Although battered by the elements and overgrown with tall grasses, it was clearly once a noble house.

"All that land to the west. That's yours," said Ethan.

Eliana nudged her mother out of the truck. *"Allez, Maman."*

Ethan whistled to Traveler, and the dog sailed from the back of the truck and raced with Eliana down the gently sloping hillside.

"You've got over one thousand acres of this," said Ethan.

Annette was quiet as she gazed at the hills. Ethan had never known a woman who was comfortable with stillness. Katie Anne always seemed to be filling it up with words or gestures.

After a while Annette turned and walked toward the house. Ethan unlocked the front door, and she stepped inside. Her eyes passed over the rotted window frames and the uneven wood floor thick with years of dust.

The screen door banged in the wind, and Annette looked around to find Ethan Brown's eyes on her.

"It's still livable," he said. "And there's room for a big dog."

Annette laughed. She could see why he was so well liked. His thoughtfulness was sincere; he was earnest in his desire to please.

She asked, "Where's your land, Mr. Brown? Show it to me."

Ethan took her outside and pointed to the south.

"See that tallest hill over there? That's Jacob's Mound. That's the boundary. This time next year I hope to have a little herd of my own grazin' out there." He turned back to the north. "Up there, all that land belongs to the Mackeys. Tom Mackey."

"Aren't you engaged to his daughter?"

"Now how'd you hear that?"

"Nell Harshaw."

Ethan laughed pleasantly. "Word gets around."

They stood in the blustery wind, succumbing to the silence between them. Thunderheads darkened the horizon.

"Rain's movin' in. Where's your little girl?" asked Ethan.

Annette pointed to a gully below, where Eliana and Traveler were ambling along the dry creek bed. Ethan whistled, and Traveler came trotting, with Eliana close behind.

"I tell you what, Mr. Brown. It looks like I'm a thorn in your side. Why don't you buy me up? Then you can be one big happy family."

Ethan was silent, watching the girl and the dog.

"Don't you want this land?" she asked.

"Of course I do. If that's your decision—to sell."

"That's my decision. The money will go to my daughter."

"I guess I hate to see anybody give up something like this."

Annette watched her daughter approach. "That's exactly the way I feel about my home in Paris. About my life there."

Ethan looked at her face. She felt his gaze and turned to him.

"Forgive me, ma'am. I guess I forget that anybody can love anyplace else as much as I love this."

"They can. They do."

The wind blew at them, disrupting that subtle and wordless thing that made Annette's heart quicken and Ethan shuffle his feet and caused them both to look away at the approaching rain clouds.

IT WAS Ethan who made the arrangements for Eliana to ride later that week. Jer had only one horse that was trained for dressage, but he was a beauty—a big Arabian named Mike. When Jer saw Eliana working him, his respect for the horse and the child mushroomed into instant admiration. He was already a little awestruck around Annette, possibly because he occasionally listened to classical music and had seen her picture on the cover of a CD when he was looking for a Mozart violin concerto at a music store up in Kansas City.

"I got that horse for next to nothin'," Jer said as he leaned against the corral next to Annette.

"Is she okay out there?" asked Annette.

"Ma'am, Mike's in love with that little girl. I can tell you that right now. I ain't never seen him so mellow."

Annette smiled. "He does seem responsive," she said.

"I've just used him as a stud. To be quite honest with you, I've never seen him do this. He's eatin' it up."

"I suppose it seems silly to you, doesn't it? Out here horses have a practical function."

"Well, yes, they do. But to get these animals to obey you, whatever you ask 'em to do, sure ain't silly."

"I doubt if Mr. Brown would agree with you on that."

"Ethan and I don't always see eye to eye."

"I find that reassuring," she said with a smile.

THE week went by, and Charlie Fergusen would not be swayed, so Annette instructed Ethan to proceed with the sale of the property. To make matters worse, Charlie, who had little confidence in women when it came to managing business matters, named Ethan as cotrustee of the estate, with Annette, after his death. Wishing to leave as quickly as possible, Annette left the entire matter to Ethan to handle in her absence. He would purchase the land himself and promised her a very advantageous deal.

The night before they were to leave, Nell Harshaw invited them all to dinner. Annette begged off to stay at home with Eliana to pack. As soon as Charlie's car pulled out of the driveway, Eliana streaked through the house to the back room.

"Maman, il est parti!"

Annette swelled with relief. "Put on some music, precious."

They ate dinner in the sewing room, spreading a tablecloth on the floor and making a picnic with fried eggs and bacon and biscuits that Annette whipped up. They drank 7-Up out of crystal glasses and pretended it was Champagne. They played all her mother's old LPs, all the great divas, recordings of Joan Sutherland and Maria Callas. After dinner they worked on the puppet figures Eliana was making from cutouts in a coloring book, and so intent were they on their play and their music that they didn't hear Charlie come back until the door opened.

"I'm going to bed now. Keep it down, will you?" he said.

"I'm sorry, Dad. I didn't know you were home." Annette rose and turned off the record player. "How was your dinner?"

"Okay. Nell isn't the best cook in the world."

"I know, but she's a good friend." He turned to leave. "Dad? Would you mind if I took some of these recordings with me?"

"Don't ask me to make those kind of decisions now."

"But you never listen to this music."

Charlie's bloodshot eyes bulged with a tired rage. "They're still her things, and she left all her worldly possessions to me. After I'm dead, you can do as you damn well please with them." He slammed the door behind him.

Annette and Eliana sat still for a moment, hearing nothing but the pinched timbre of his voice echoing in the air. Then, their gaiety wilted, they wordlessly got ready for bed.

As Annette leaned down to kiss her daughter good night, Eliana said, "*Maman*, I'm going to miss Mike."

"Mike?"

"Mike! Big Mike!"

Big Mike, the horse. Of course. Annette smoothed back her child's soft hair. "What about the horses you ride back home?"

"Oh, *Maman*, they're nothing like Big Mike. He's fantastic! He does everything I ask him to do. He's so much fun to ride."

Annette kissed Eliana again. "So you don't think it would be so awful to live here?" she asked.

"Not if we didn't have to live with Grandpa."

"We'd live in your grandma's old house."

"Oh! Could we? I'd love that! Then we could have a dog, or two dogs, and I could ride Big Mike every day—"

"Honey, we're not going to live here. I'm sorry. I don't know why I even brought it up."

"I think it'd be fun."

"Wouldn't you miss your friends?"

Eliana thought for a moment. "My friends in Paris could come visit in the summer. They'd love it. They think cowboys are neat."

"That's because they only see them in the movies."

THE storm that had announced itself days earlier, as Annette stood beside Ethan Brown on the hilltop, unleashed its fury upon the plains that evening. Just after nightfall the temperature dropped below freezing, and on came a sudden rush of hail, pummeling the earth with dull thuds. After the hail the wind returned, and lightning and thunder rocked the hills late into the night.

Annette crawled into bed with Eliana, but the child slept through it all. Annette lay there listening to the storm, her eyes fixed on the piano. Sometime very late she heard that achingly beautiful music she had heard the other night. As she neared sleep, it brought her the message it had been sent to bear.

Annette awoke full of enthusiasm. In less than twenty-four hours she would be stepping off the plane in Paris, and already she longed for the gentle, dreary gloom of its gray skies.

She found her father in the dimly lit kitchen preparing his breakfast. He had slept poorly because of the storm and was ill humored. Annette bathed and dressed, then awoke Eliana and herded her through her morning routine. Charlie sat in his lounge chair reading his newspaper until Annette tactfully reminded him that they needed to leave shortly.

He looked up. His eyes were rimmed in red. "I won't be long," he said. He patted her hand, then shuffled off to his room.

Despite all her efforts, they were late getting out of the house.

Eliana went out back to say good-bye to the neighbor's dog and got her shoes caked in mud. The shoes had to be removed and cleaned. Meanwhile, Charlie had to take an important call from a trustee on the board of the Kansas Conference of Methodist Churches.

Annette went outside to wait. As she leaned against the hood of Charlie's old Buick, she looked around. Now that she was leaving, she could see the place with a more benevolent eye. It was a very picturesque town. An imposing slate-roofed Victorian courthouse towered over Main Street, which consisted of two blocks of the functional and the whimsical, notably a hardware store, a coffee shop, a small grocery store, an ice-cream parlor with a gazebo in its courtyard, an art gallery, and a 1930s movie house. The street dead-ended at a park looking out over the Cottonwood River and the falls from which the town took its name. Behind the courthouse spread the residential properties. Many were authentic turn-of-the-century Victorian and maintained proudly by their families.

Annette saw the town's charm, and thought perhaps she might return for a visit. Finally Charlie emerged from the house, and as Annette went off to look for Eliana, he started up the car.

They were all the way past Strong City, across the river, when Annette remembered the book.

"Dad, stop. I've got to go back."

"Back? What for?"

"That book the attorney lent me."

"Ethan? Forget it. He won't care."

"He will. Dad, go back, please."

"Annette, you'll miss the plane."

"No, we won't."

Charlie made a U-turn, and they drove back to the house.

As Annette scoured the house for the book, in the back of her mind she was wondering from where this bizarre compulsion came. She could send Ethan a book of Yeats's poetry from Paris. The longer she searched, the more obsessive she became. She knew she should stop and get back on the road, but she couldn't. She seemed no longer capable of rational thought or action.

Charlie honked his horn a few times; then he sent Eliana in. She found her mother sitting quietly in the sewing room.

"*Maman!* What are you doing?"

Annette looked up, and at the sight of her daughter a great peace washed over her. She smiled.

"Go. Go play outside in the mud."

A sly grin crept over Eliana's face. "Do you mean it?"

"Yes. Tomorrow we'll find you some jeans."

Annette heard her shouting the glorious news to Charlie before she sprang off through the backyard. Then she heard the car door slam and the slow purposeful steps as her father approached. She looked up at the old man in the doorway. He wore a peculiar expression of fear mixed with hope.

"I'll enroll Eliana in school and stay until spring," said Annette. "We'll go back then."

Charlie nodded. "Spring's the prettiest time of the year."

"I won't stay any longer. And I'm not doing this so you'll change your mind about the trust."

"That's good, because I'm not going to change my mind."

"Frankly, Dad, I don't care about the money anymore."

He gave her a rare smile. "I'll go put the car away."

Annette found Ethan Brown's book in her suitcase, where she had packed it by mistake.

chapter Four

KATIE Anne wanted to be married in white leather pants, a white fringed shirt, and a white cowboy hat, but her mother would not hear of it. Consequently, Katie Anne talked of nothing else. Ethan was quite used to tuning her out, and when they walked into the South Forty on Friday evening and looked up to see Katie Anne's best friend, Patti Boswell, waving to them from the bar,

Ethan knew what was in store for him. He looked around for Jer.

"Said he had a date," volunteered Whitey, who was standing next to Patti. Whitey was Katie Anne's regular dance partner.

"You're kiddin' me," replied Ethan. "With whom?"

"Wouldn't say."

They all got beers and found a booth in the corner. The guys argued K.U.'s chances of going to the Orange Bowl this year; the girls talked of Katie Anne's wedding. Ethan slid easily in and out of both discussions. Ethan, the same man who impressed his clients with his breadth of legal knowledge, was also at ease in the superficial and limited arena of conversation that flowed around this same booth every Friday night.

But this evening Ethan became acutely aware of the tedium of the conversation. Something hovered in the air, a cloud of discontent that had been growing since the evening he had asked Katie Anne to marry him. He found himself becoming irritated with her over little things, things he normally tolerated with humor.

A man more in tune with his feelings might have suspected that his discontent had as much to do with the specter of Annette Zeldin as with anything else. Like all men of his class and upbringing, even the ones of exceptional intelligence like himself, Ethan regarded women like her with a faint air of contempt. Women's liberation had very little effect on the way most men in these parts viewed women. Those like Mrs. Zeldin—brilliant, talented, and successful— did not tread the earth with a light step.

So when Jer walked in with Annette Zeldin at his side, the earth trembled.

"I hope he doesn't bring that snobby Frenchwoman over here," drawled Katie Anne.

"Hope he does," countered Whitey.

They approached slowly, stopping to chat with Jer's pals, and Ethan was struck by Annette's ease and graciousness as Jer introduced her to one man after another. She wore a loose, soft white blouse unbuttoned provocatively low and tucked into a black slim skirt that, although not as short as the swinging dance skirts worn by Katie Anne and Patti, molded her hips and thighs and accentuated the sensuality of her slow, unhurried movements.

Jer seemed to be under a spell. He guided Annette through the crowd to their table with a tender protectiveness he normally reserved for his animals. Ethan caught his eye and threw him a "What the hell?" look, which Jer pretended to ignore.

Jer seated Annette next to Ethan in the booth and drew up a chair for himself at the end of the table. There were whispers between Katie Anne and Patti. Then, with a rude abruptness, the girls got up to dance. Ethan refused to budge.

"You know I never dance," he replied to Katie Anne's urging. "Where's Whitey?"

"Dancing with Patti."

"Then stay here with me."

"I will not," she whispered emphatically in his ear, and stormed off. Jer, who had been looking around for their waitress, turned back and noticed the empty table.

"Where'd everybody go?"

Ethan gestured to the dance floor.

"Oh," Jer mumbled. He glanced nervously at Annette. "Would you like to dance?" he asked. Jer hated to dance. Annette declined, and he breathed relief. "What'll you have? I'll go get it," he said.

"Whatever you're having," replied Annette. She smiled warmly at him, which only aggravated his nervousness.

"Be right back," he said, patting her hand as he got up.

Annette and Ethan sat stiffly in each other's presence for a moment. Annette finally broke the silence.

"Jer's offered to give Eliana riding lessons."

"Jer's a good man."

"Yes, he is."

"I was a little surprised to hear you'd decided to stay."

"Just until spring. But that doesn't change anything about the land. I'm still selling if you're still buying."

"The documents are ready," Ethan said. "You can stop by the office to sign them whenever you like."

"I have that book, too. I need to return it."

"There's no rush. I have plenty more."

"Are they yours?"

Ethan wasn't quite sure he understood. "Are they mine?"

"Yes. I mean . . . I thought . . . Isn't it a library book?"

Ethan began to laugh. Jer sat down and placed a beer in front of Annette. Annette, who hated beer, smiled and thanked him.

"What's so funny?" asked Jer.

"She thinks my office is the town library."

Jer grinned. "Ethan's got a better library than Strong City. Only he don't lend 'em out."

Annette stole a questioning glance at Ethan, who was examining the sticky rings on the table.

"Ethan got his Ph.D. from Yale," Jer added. "Had one of those big scholarships, and he got an offer to go teach at Berkeley."

"Teach what?" asked Annette.

"English," answered Jer.

"Nineteenth century. The poets mainly," offered Ethan, finally warming, but only reluctantly, to the conversation.

"Wordsworth." Annette smiled.

Ethan returned her smile. "And Yeats." It was the first time their eyes had met since that moment on the hillside several weeks before.

They were both silent. Ethan played absentmindedly with his beer glass. Annette stared down at the table. Jer searched for something to say.

"And did you go to Berkeley?" she asked after a while.

Ethan shook his head. "I got homesick."

"So he threw it all in and came back here and went to law school at K.U.," said Jer.

"You got homesick?" asked Annette.

"I got homesick."

Ethan was so acutely uncomfortable now, he seized upon the first thought that rattled through his brain. "Would you like to dance, Mrs. Zeldin?"

Annette hesitated, then spoke very softly. "Yes."

Jer watched them move onto the dance floor with a relieved smile. He was glad to see them warming toward each other.

Once on his feet, Ethan's senses returned to him. He took Annette by the hand, and she followed him to the D.J.'s booth, where Ethan exchanged a few brief words with his friend. As they moved onto the floor, the music segued into a slow dance.

"That'll make it less painful for you," said Ethan as he took her in his arms. Annette laid her hand on his shoulder. Underneath the flannel shirt was hard muscle. It had been years since she had felt such strength in a man. His heat was tremendous. She felt it float over her as he wrapped his arm around her waist.

"You don't dance and you don't lend books," she said, rather more soberly than she had intended. She looked up into his face.

He replied, not as lightly as he would have wished, "That's right, ma'am," and tightened his arm around her.

Ethan was saved from the consequences of his rash behavior by a series of fortunate incidents. At just the moment he and Annette rose from the table to dance, Katie Anne and Patti left the dance floor for the ladies' room, and when they came out, Whitey caught them in the hallway and proposed they all go over to another bar called the Denim and Diamonds. By the time they had reached an agreement, Ethan was back and sitting alone at the table and Jer was dancing with Annette. Ethan left with Katie Anne and the crowd. Later that night he didn't know if the guilt he felt was for abandoning his friend or for dancing with Annette. It had been a long time since he had felt guilty about anything.

DESPITE his exposure to sophisticated tastes at Yale, Ethan had never been able to overcome his prejudice against classical music. His change of heart came in an unexpected way.

Ethan's attic office looked down onto the house of the Winegarner family, whose little boy had been severely burned in a prairie fire. After two years of painful plastic surgery and rehabilitation, the boy could just begin to use his hands and arms. He was still confined to a wheelchair. On sunny days his mother wheeled him into the backyard, where she read to him.

One Friday in late November, Ethan noticed Mrs. Zeldin entering the Winegarners' house with her violin. She returned the following Friday at the same time and left, as before, an hour later. The next morning Ethan ran into Mrs. Winegarner in the hardware store. Mrs. Winegarner, although younger than Ethan, had always reminded him somewhat of his own mother, perhaps because of her stoic silence and refusal to complain of life's hardships. He hesitated to ask about the visit from "that Frenchwoman," as the town had taken to calling Annette. To his surprise Mrs. Winegarner brought up the subject herself.

"She's giving Matthew violin lessons," she said quietly. Her mouth looked as though it wanted to smile. Ethan hadn't seen her smile in two years. "I'd heard she was giving lessons. I didn't think she'd be any good with kids. She always seemed so unfriendly."

"And is it working out?" he asked.

She looked away. "You know what she did?" She looked back at Ethan; tears glistened. "The first time she came, she just talked to him. She told him about this man named . . . Its . . . Its . . ."

"Itzhak Perlman?"

"Yes, Perlman. He plays the violin. And he's in a wheelchair. And she told us how he was so loved and admired by everyone. But that wasn't what . . ." She paused. "She brought her violin along. And she played for him." Mrs. Winegarner looked up into Ethan's eyes. "It was— Oh, it sounds silly."

"Tell me," said Ethan gently.

"I'd never heard anything so beautiful in all my life. And when I looked over at Matthew, he had this look in his eyes that I can't describe. It was like he was in heaven, listening to the angels." She took a deep breath. "You know what he said when she left? He said, 'Mama, this music makes me want to live.'"

She was trying to hold back her tears, then dug into her handbag for a tissue.

"She brought him a violin, one she'd rented for him. And she taught him how to care for it, and the names of the strings." Mrs. Winegarner turned away to blow her nose. "I shouldn't go on. I must be boring you."

Ethan laid his hand on her shoulder. "No, you're not."

"I was very wrong about her. She's awfully patient. And she seems to strike just that right note with kids." She took a deep breath and smiled. "We bought Matthew a new CD player. He can't seem to get enough of his music."

Ethan walked her to her car, and with uncharacteristic spontaneity Mrs. Winegarner hugged him.

The following Friday, Ethan thought he might time some errands to coincide with the end of Matthew's violin lesson. Then, as Mrs. Zeldin was on the front porch bidding good-bye to Mrs. Winegarner and he was pulling on his coat, his phone rang. His first inclination was to ignore it, but his good sense got the better of him, and he took the call. From his window he watched Mrs. Zeldin walk down the street, her violin case in her hand.

December was a tumultuous month for Ethan. The foundation for his house was laid, and because the weather had continued mild, he was able to start construction. Katie Anne set the date of their wedding for April 23, and the preliminary guest list totaled six hundred and thirty. Whenever there was a disagreement between Katie Anne and her mother, Betty Sue, he was dragged in to cast the deciding vote. He soon learned the best strategy was to side with his bride. But all this was no more than petty. Ethan's real tribulation came when his ex-wife, Paula, called from California to say their son, Jeremy, who was fifteen, had run away from home.

Ethan's perfect life suddenly caved in. That Katie Anne was no help to him in the matter came as no surprise. He mentioned the matter over dinner one evening, and in the midst of her prattle about a wedding shower, she paused, holding her fork in midair, and said sweetly, "Oh, honey, I'm so sorry. But you know he'll come back. Kids always do." Then she went on to ask him if his sister would be coming to the wedding shower.

That's when the nagging feelings began to come back—the same uneasiness that had stayed with him for so long after the death of his father. Katie Anne was no longer a mask for his pain, but neither had she become a balm. Ethan's soul paced through the day in anguish. Even Jer was of little comfort.

Not long before they discovered the cancer, Ethan's father had written him a letter. It was the only time he had ever mentioned the subject after Ethan's divorce from Paula. He wrote, "Ethan, I hope you'll find a way to return to the Holy Mother Church. I can't think you'd ever do anything like this because your dad asked you to do it. You need to find your own way back."

Ethan never answered the letter, and sometimes he thought that if he had, perhaps this nagging guilt wouldn't be bothering him now. Anyway, it was too late to do anything about it.

On the Wednesday after his call from Paula, Ethan went into Wichita to go to the courthouse. He was daydreaming and missed the turn onto Third Street and ended up on Central. The street took him by the big cathedral where he and Paula had been married and Jeremy had been baptized. He pulled over and stared at the pillared entrance and high wide steps for a long time. Then he got out of his truck and went in.

The old familiar ritual quickly seized him, and as he dipped his fingers into the marble font of cool water and touched his forehead, he began to smile inside. He walked slowly down the center aisle, genuflected, slipped onto a bench, and knelt, folding his hands in prayer the way he had done thousands of times as a child. But now there was no priest telling him what to pray, and he sat in the brilliant, sun-gloried silence and felt at peace. When he had been there several minutes, he heard someone enter the cathedral from the side door and kneel in a pew near the front.

After a while the peace began to fragment, and his worldly thoughts began clamoring for admission. Ethan stood, a little reluctantly, and as he did, the person at the front stood also. When she turned and came toward him, he recognized Mrs. Zeldin. She saw him and smiled warmly. He waited as she approached him.

"Mr. Brown," she said, and shook his hand.

"Mrs. Zeldin."

"Don't forget your hat," she said, smiling, and took it from the pew where he had left it.

"Thank you, ma'am."

Then she took his arm and gently leaned on him as they walked silently together down the long aisle toward the door.

Outside, she released his arm. Ethan turned and asked, "What's the daughter of a Methodist minister doing in a Catholic church?"

"I joined right after Eliana was born, to annoy my father." At first he thought she was serious—she had a dead-sober look on her face—then she broke into laughter.

She quickly changed the subject, asking him questions about his house and the wedding plans. She told him she was in town to do some Christmas shopping and run some errands.

"How about something to eat?" Ethan asked as they walked down the steps toward his truck.

"Okay. I'm starved," she replied.

"Hop in. I'll drive," he said.

Annette couldn't make it into the truck with her tight skirt, and she laughed as Ethan hoisted her up. "I'm just not made for this kind of life," she said as he closed the door for her.

"Sure you are," he said as he got in. "The clothes are the problem. Not the lady." He started the truck. "What sounds good?"

"Mr. Brown"—she grinned—"I don't expect we'll have the same taste in food, so just take me wherever you normally eat."

They settled on a Sonic Drive-In that took Annette's fancy as they drove by. She thought it would be fun to eat in the truck and have the waitress set their food on the window the way they used to do when she was a kid. Ethan was content. From the moment she leaned on his arm in the cathedral, the awkwardness between them had been swept away. Their conversation flowed easily now as she asked him questions about cattle ranching, and he talked at length about the soil of the Flint Hills and bluestem grass.

Ethan got a kick out of the way she handled the chili dog. She set it on her lap and used a knife and fork, cutting it up, bun and all, into bite-size pieces. After she finished, she asked for a chocolate milk shake. She looked at Ethan and smiled. "It reminds me of Eliana."

"You're lucky to have her," he said. Ethan ordered the shake for her. "I don't get to see my son much."

Annette looked surprised. "You have a son?"

"Jeremy. He's fifteen. He lives in Los Angeles with his mom. She moved out there after we got divorced."

"That's a dreadful place to raise kids."

The chocolate milk shake came. There was a long, hovering silence while Ethan stared at his steering wheel.

"He's run away from home," he said suddenly.

"Oh, Lord, no." She lifted her head, engaging his eyes with a look that held the promise of such comfort that Ethan blurted out all his misery. He was not accustomed to talking about himself, but Annette's eyes were never more focused than when he spoke to her about his son. The milk shake sat untouched on the tray. When he was through, she urged him to go to California.

"I wouldn't be able to do anything," he said. "I don't know who his friends are, where he hangs out . . . nothing."

"It doesn't make any difference. You're not a detective—you're his father. He needs to know you're looking for him."

Ethan studied her dark, luminous eyes and saw in them all the intense emotion he had trained himself to avoid.

Even the silence between them as he drove her back to her car was free of the discomfort of their previous times together. It was a silence that linked them in ways they did not yet know, with a bond that was not palpable, yet felt as strong and assured as a touch, a caress, a kiss.

EVERY Friday after Matthew Winegarner's violin lesson Annette Zeldin dropped in at Ethan Brown's office. Ostensibly she came to borrow his books. Initially their friendship seemed to be rooted in this mutual love of literature, but the seed of trust that had been planted at the Sonic Drive-In was buried much deeper than Wordsworth and Yeats. Jeremy, as it turned out, had returned home the day after their conversation, and Ethan was spared the anguish of flying to California. Instead, he was harboring the idea of bringing Jeremy to live with him. He had not yet spoken about it to his ex-wife, Paula, or to Katie Anne, but he did speak freely about it to Annette.

"I think it's a fabulous idea," she said, sitting in his office flipping through the pages of Willa Cather's *Great Short Works.* She laid the book down. "Do you think Paula would go for it?"

"Frankly, I think she'd jump at the chance. Jeremy's the problem. He'd have to give up his basketball, his friends."

"When's the last time he was out here?"

"Last Christmas. He'll be out here this Christmas, I hope."

She got up and poured herself some coffee. "I can't imagine your fiancée is the type of woman who'd like to share you with a fifteen-year-old boy." Annette never referred to Katie Anne by name.

"It won't be a problem."

Annette looked at him over her coffee cup.

THAT night he brought up the subject with Katie Anne. She stared at him in frozen horror, then rose without a word and went into the bedroom. Ethan knew she wanted him to follow her, but he loathed these histrionics. After a few minutes of silence he heard her on the phone with Whitey, making plans to go out dancing. Finally, reluctantly, Ethan went to find her.

She was thrashing around in her closet. "Where's my red skirt?"

"We need to talk about this."

She rummaged through a pile of clothes at the foot of their bed. "I don't know what there is to talk about. I mean, how can anybody be so . . . so dense as to think I'd want to spend my honeymoon with a fifteen-year-old brat."

"Jeremy's not a brat." His voice warned her to pull back.

"All fifteen-year-old kids are brats, Ethan. It goes with the territory," she said a little more gently.

"We've been living together for nearly two years now. It's not as if we haven't had time alone," he replied.

Katie Anne had a sudden urge to slap him for his stubborn, bullish refusal to understand. "Ethan, if Jeremy comes out here, I honestly don't think our marriage will last very long."

She turned her back to him, unzipped her jeans, and slowly slid them down over her hips. Suddenly Ethan was acutely aware of every curve of her back. He touched her and could feel the tension that ran through her into him. Then he pressed his lips to the back of her neck and felt her shudder. His eyes closed, he explored the delicate details of her body with his fingertips and smelled her perfume. He moved closer and pressed her against the wall.

Moments later, when she cried out his name, he barely heard her; her voice seemed far away, remote, distanced from that dark, mysterious thing that gripped him so steadfastly.

HE DIDN'T bring up the subject of Jeremy's visit again. He didn't really need to. Jeremy wrote him a stinging letter saying he didn't want to spend Christmas with them this year.

The next Sunday, Ethan quietly got dressed and drove twenty-eight miles to Council Grove to attend Mass. Annette Zeldin was there, as he had hoped. When he knelt behind her and her daughter and poked her in the back, she turned to him and grinned. "Ah, my prayers are working."

"Don't tell me I'm in your prayers."

"Of course you are."

They didn't speak to each other throughout Mass, except when Ethan whispered a comment about the soloist's resemblance to Kermit the Frog, which made Eliana giggle. He was quiet after that, but Annette felt his presence, and he felt hers.

What he had not anticipated was Katie Anne's reaction to this new habit of his. When she saw he intended to make a regular habit out of what she had thought was merely a seasonal twinge of conscience, she began to complain. Their Sunday mornings were now disrupted by Ethan who got up early, by Ethan who wasn't there to make Sunday morning love, by Ethan who made his breakfast closer to noon, by which time she wasn't hungry, having already fixed something.

But for Ethan it was worth it. Katie Anne's grumbling was a small price to pay for the inexpressible comfort he experienced every week sitting with Annette, Eliana between them, on a pew near the back of the little church in Council Grove. There was something undeniably familial about it. At first Ethan was concerned that his presence next to Annette might make tongues waggle, but Council Grove was just far enough removed from Cottonwood Falls to afford a modicum of anonymity.

KATIE Anne was expecting an engagement ring for Christmas. She had given up waiting for Ethan to take her into Kansas City to look for rings, and she had driven in with Patti and narrowed down her selection to a half-dozen gorgeous rings.

Three days before Christmas, Ethan called Jer in the closest thing to panic Jer had ever seen him exhibit.

"Pal, you've gotta do this for me."

"Ethan, you're crazy. If Katie Anne finds out, she'll be heartbroken. Worse than that, she'll call it off."

"She won't find out. You can tell me who sold it to you."

"This isn't like you, buddy. Why don't you just do it yourself?"

"I got too much work to do."

"You don't want to get married, do you?"

The startling effect of this straightforward cowboy reading between the lines jolted Ethan into silence.

Ethan replied after a long hesitation, "Well . . . will you come with me at least?"

"Sure. I'll come with ya," Jer said.

Ethan picked him up an hour later, and they reached the store a little after four o'clock. While the jeweler brought out the rings Katie Anne had selected, Jer's attention was caught by a display of gold necklaces.

"Pardon me, ma'am, but do you have any Saint Christopher medals in here?" asked Jer.

"Yes, we do," said the jeweler as she turned to help Jer.

"What do you want with that?" asked Ethan.

Jer ignored him. "It's for a lady," he said to the jeweler. "Needs to be small. Something feminine."

She selected a finely crafted solid-gold medal and arranged it on the black velvet cloth before him.

"Who are you buying this for?" demanded Ethan.

Jer turned and whispered in his ear, "Ethan, just go buy your ring and leave me to my business. Okay?"

The transaction was done quickly. Jer forked out nearly four hundred dollars in cash and quietly slipped the red velvet box into his pocket.

The jeweler turned back to Ethan and held up the first ring for him, describing the cut and quality of the stone, but Ethan cut her short, pointed to the ring with the largest stone, a two-carat marquise set in a circle of smaller diamonds, and said, "I'll take this one."

Ethan signed the credit card voucher. The ring was eighty-seven hundred dollars.

"You have impeccable taste, sir," said the woman simply.

Her commendation might as well have been a condolence, for the entire shopping episode hung over Ethan like a pall. As he and Jer drove back to Cottonwood Falls, not one word was spoken about Saint Christopher medals or engagement rings.

chapter Five

THE Sunday after Christmas, Annette and Eliana were late to Mass, and Ethan didn't see them until the service was over. As he caught up with them outside, he got a glimpse of the tiny gold medal against Annette's black sweater.

"Morning, ma'am. And a belated merry Christmas. Nice necklace." A startled look appeared in Annette's eyes for only a second; then it passed, but Ethan blushed solidly all the same.

"Merry Christmas to you, too, Mr. Brown."

"Ethan, look!" Eliana waved a child's white cowboy hat over her head. "Look what Jer gave me for Christmas!"

"Well, don't you look pretty!" In an unusual surge of playfulness he swung her up onto his shoulders. "How about a ride?" Ethan jogged off over the grass, with Eliana squealing and giggling, while Annette walked toward her car.

"Hey, hold on to that hat," said Ethan, circling back to the car. "We're dismounting." He lowered Eliana to the ground. As he did, he caught sight of the look on Annette's face. It was odd. Nothing he could figure out.

"Will you be in Friday?" she asked as she got into her car.

"You bet."

"Good. I'm glad. I'm looking forward to it."

Ethan turned toward his truck, and as they drove away, he heard Eliana call out, "Bye, Ethan!"

WHAT happened the following week was destined to change the nature of their relationship forever. On Tuesday, Annette was late getting to the school to pick up Eliana. She had taken the car into Strong City to have some work done on it, and when she got to the school, the grounds were already empty.

Her heart began to pound as she walked quickly down the hall to the principal's office. The sound of her high heels reverberated in the eerily empty hall. A terrifying nausea swept over her.

"I'm looking for Eliana. Eliana Zeldin," she said abruptly as she entered the office. "Do you know where she is?"

The startled secretary looked up. "Did you try the classroom?"

"It's locked."

The secretary rose and tapped on a closed door, then opened it and spoke softly. The principal emerged from her office. "I remember seeing Eliana leave the building, Mrs. Zeldin. But we had a little problem—a couple of the boys got in a scuffle on the bus—so I'm afraid we were a little distracted."

Annette spun the secretary's phone around and dialed her home. She let it ring, but no one answered. She raced out of the office, down the hall, and out to her car. Her hands were shaking so badly she had difficulty fitting the key into the ignition.

And then it began again. The cries. She knew it would. She jammed the accelerator to the floor, and the car skidded away from the curb, kicking up dirt. As she drove home, she looked for clues, anything that might help the police.

Annette pulled up in front of the house and ran to the backyard. She called her daughter's name. There was no answer. Inside, the house was dreary and silent. Her father was in Emporia for the day at a trustees meeting. She found some paper and scribbled a note: "Looking for you. Where are you? If you come home, please don't go out. Wait for me." She laid the note in a conspicuous place and ran out. The cries were incessant, startlingly clear, not at all like something imagined.

She got in the car and drove slowly, looking up and down each street through her tears. It was raining now. When she got to Ethan Brown's office, she stopped.

ETHAN looked up as Bonnie knocked loudly, then threw open his office door. "Ethan! Ethan! Come quickly!"

Ethan rose and followed his secretary down the stairs. At the foot of the staircase was Mrs. Zeldin.

The woman's frailty struck him forcefully as she turned her haunted brown eyes upon him. She wore no coat, and this vision of her glistening with rain and in despair wrenched his gentle heart more violently than any misery ever had done before.

"Bonnie, do we have any blankets?" he said as he rushed down to Annette.

"There's one in my trunk, I think. I'll get it."

Ethan put an arm around Annette and helped her up the stairs. Her skin was like ice, and she shook violently.

"What happened?"

"My daughter. She's gone," gasped Annette.

His strong arm around her seemed to release the tension in her, and she stumbled up the last few steps into his office. He let her down into a chair. Bonnie appeared with the blanket, and Ethan wrapped it around Annette. He thrust a twenty-dollar bill into Bonnie's hand and told her to run and get a pint of whiskey.

After she left, Ethan pulled another chair up to Annette's and sat down, taking her hands in his. They were thin and icy, and he gently pressed them between his own calloused, warm hands.

"Annette, take a deep breath and tell me what happened."

She nodded and inhaled deeply. "I was late picking her up. She wasn't at school. She's not at home. I've looked all over."

"This is Cottonwood Falls. Kids don't just disappear."

"It can't happen again, can it?"

"What do you mean?"

She looked down. "Oh, God . . ."

"Could she have gone to play with a friend?" he asked.

"Nobody's ever invited her over to play."

"Doesn't she have riding lessons after school sometimes?"

"Thursday. Jer picks her up on Thursday. This is Tuesday."

Ethan thought for a moment, rose, and went to his desk. He dialed a number, then looked over at Annette. Her eyes hung on him.

"Hey, Jer. You haven't seen Eliana, have you?" A smile crept over his face. He nodded to Annette. "Yeah, well, I guess she didn't get the message. We've got one worried mom over here."

Bonnie showed up with the whiskey just then, and Ethan motioned for her to set it down. She did, then left quietly.

"Yeah, sure. I'll tell her. Thanks, Jer." He hung up. "Jer said he called yesterday and left a message with your dad. Said he'd do the lesson today instead. I guess your dad forgot to tell you. Jer's got her in the indoor arena. He'll bring Eliana home in about an hour."

Annette stared at him blankly.

"Hey, did you hear me? She's okay."

Annette nodded. Ethan poured some whiskey into a coffee mug, and when he turned back to her, she had her hands over her ears. He held it out to her. "Annette?"

"Can you turn off the music?" she asked weakly.

Ethan set down the mug and gently peeled away her hands.

"There isn't any music." He held her hands in his. "See? There's no music playing. Now, what happened? Will you tell me?"

He held the mug of whiskey out to her. This time she took it and drank a little. After a long pause she shook her head sadly. Ethan waited patiently. She looked up into the gentle eyes of the man in front of her. The whiskey mollified her, and she reached out and touched his lips very lightly with the tips of her fingers. Her touch electrified him. He closed his eyes for a second, and when he opened them again, her hands were back in her lap, clasping the mug.

That afternoon Annette revealed her past to Ethan.

WHEN she had met the brilliant Israeli conductor David Zeldin nearly two decades ago, he had been finishing his season in Tel Aviv before taking up the baton at l'Orchestre de Paris. Although his career was to be envied, personal fulfillment had escaped him. David was forty-three, divorced, and childless. The morning he greeted Annette, a rising young violinist of twenty-three, at the airport in Tel Aviv and guided her to his car, intimations of his future began to shape themselves into clear thought. These thoughts were nurtured during the week as they rehearsed Mendelssohn's and Sibelius's violin concertos, as their music began to meld into a uniquely beautiful expression, and with it their hearts and souls.

David had never seen an artist respond so passionately to his direction, and Annette had never met a conductor who could draw genius from her with such ease. He took her back to his apartment after their final matinee performance, and they made love. As they lay there in the faded light of dusk, listening to the waves rushing onto the beach below, they both believed in happiness.

The next day Annette changed her ticket so that she could stay with him another week. The week turned into three, and she stayed to help him pack his books and paintings for the move to Paris. After the apartment was emptied, they flew together to Athens, where David was to transfer for his flight to Paris and she to New York. On their third day in Athens they were married by an American naval chaplain. A week later they arrived in Paris as husband and wife.

Annette detached herself from a past she had considered ill fitting and emerged the creature she was always meant to be. French soon became her dominant language.

When Violette was born to them four years later, Annette, who was a vibrant twenty-seven, took it in stride. David, then in his late forties, was profoundly altered. David Zeldin was not a nurturing man; rather, he was intensely cerebral. Yet some atavistic instinct emerged in him with the birth of his daughter—an immense love for her. If the weather was pleasant, he would come back early from rehearsals, command Maria, their Portuguese nanny, to ready the pram, and stroll off with his baby down Avenue Victor Hugo to the park. He wandered through toy stores, querying sales clerks in great detail, and then he would come home with, say, a small, pale blue stuffed bear because it matched the color of Violette's eyes.

When Violette was not yet one year old, Annette and David were invited to return to Israel as guest artists with the symphony orchestra for a special performance. Since Violette's birth David had turned down all engagements that required travel away from home, but this opportunity sorely tempted him. He missed his country. Finally they accepted. They would, of course, take the baby and Maria with them.

But Maria would not go. She was old and dreaded planes. They began looking for a nanny to accompany them, at last settling on Magda, a young Argentine girl who came highly recommended.

Violette did not take kindly to this changing of the guard. She was deeply attached to Maria. The new girl smiled and cooed and carried on easily, but she was a stranger. On the plane, when Violette mashed her plump little fist into Magda's smiling face, when she twisted her little body around and looked frantically for the faces of her mother or father or Maria, Annette and David said to each other, "It's just a question of time. She'll adjust in a day or two."

The first night in Jerusalem, at the King David Hotel, Magda assured them it would be all right, that they could go off to their cocktail reception, not to worry. In the back of the taxi, dressed elegantly in black, they reassured each other with observations about

Magda's maturity, her poise. She came from a good family—her father was mayor of a small town in Argentina. If an emergency should arise, she would handle it. She knew where to find them.

They were happy that evening. It was spring, and the air smelled of warm, rain-fed earth. In the taxi Annette draped one of her long, silky legs over David's. At the reception he kept noticing how beautiful she was, and when they returned home that evening and found Violette sleeping peacefully and Magda reading quietly, they slipped away to their bedroom and made love.

The next day Violette began running a fever. By late afternoon it ran high. They called in a doctor, who told them it was a result of an ear infection and that antibiotics would soon get it under control. Annette, dressed in her long black gown, bathed the baby continually during the hour before they left for the concert hall. David looked on. He could offer no soothing platitudes; his anxiety was as great as hers. Violette's eyes seemed a darker shade of blue. She would slowly turn her darkened gaze to him, then back to her mother. It was as if she wanted them to read something in her feverish eyes.

Annette didn't have time to call Magda until intermission. Despite her anxiety, she had played well. Her remarkable powers of concentration had carried her through the concert. David smiled at her from the podium, his brow slick with perspiration.

Magda was to expect their call shortly after nine o'clock. She answered immediately, in a whisper. Yes, Violette was finally sleeping. Her fever had finally broken. All was well.

WHEN David and Annette returned to their room that evening after the concert, their child was gone. Within minutes of David's call the hotel was invaded by detectives from every branch of service. Guests and employees were interrogated. A scenario was pieced together: Magda had left the hotel at approximately nine twenty p.m. with the stroller. The stroller was found abandoned in a side street several blocks away. Residents were interrogated. And then nothing. Their lives stopped there. Each of them bore pain so great that they could not console the other.

No ransom note ever arrived. No demands were made, no communication was ever attempted, and there was never a trace of Violette or Magda. After two weeks of futile waiting, all the while suffering the intense scrutiny of the press, David and Annette returned to Paris. Only much later did they learn there had been other cases similar to this, one in Greece and two in Italy.

Annette had already surmised her child's fate. The last night she spent in the King David Hotel she dreamed of a strange place, and she awakened to the sound of a baby's cry. That same night, far away, in a dark and dirty place, Violette opened her eyes. The cold and stench told her she was far from home. Her stricken soul grieved for her parents, and her tiny heart sent up such a desperate wail that even the angels cried.

ETHAN studied Annette Zeldin closely, without inhibition. She was calm now. The blanket had fallen from her shoulders, and he walked around behind her and quietly pulled it up over her arms. She reached for his hand.

"Ethan, she may have been adopted. Not a day goes by when I don't pray for her. I pray she is in a family, a good family. Someone who loves her. But then at times I have this feeling, this gut feeling, that the police were right. That she was sold. For awful reasons. And then I pray. . . . Oh, God, I pray. . . ."

She told him how David had wanted another child. Right away. But she only wanted to keep moving. She took any engagement she could get, anywhere in the world. She found respite from her misery only when she was performing. And she took pictures of Violette with her and looked for her daughter everywhere.

Steadily, quietly, their marriage fell apart. When they were home together, an inescapable emptiness blanketed their conversations. Overnight, it seemed, they became strangers. A year after Violette's disappearance Annette filed for divorce.

In Johannesburg, when the conductor Ernst Rodine saw her, he hardly recognized her as the same woman who had played with his symphony several years before. When Annette took her place onstage, he noticed the thin arms as she raised her instrument to her chin, the sunken, empty eyes, the raw smile.

After intermission, when they returned to the stage, Annette suddenly looked at the audience just as Rodine lifted his baton. He noticed the way she was holding her head, as if she were listening for something beyond the music.

Annette first heard it in the seconds of silence preceding the opening chords. It was faint but distinct. From that moment on, her hands and her heart were separate. She watched her fingers and her bow flying over the strings, but she heard not one note of the music she played. She heard only the sound of her baby's piercing cry. She remembered all the times she had heard that heart-wrenching wail and the ways she had rushed to calm it. But now the cries would not cease. There was nothing more she could do. So she listened, and she played on.

The orchestra stopped. Many had their heads lowered. An embarrassed murmur passed through the audience. The conductor's hands hung defeated at his sides. In the back of his mind he thought it rather amazing, really, that she was still going on at a delirious speed, and yet she was playing impeccably. Suddenly she stopped. She lowered her violin, and her bow slid from her hand. It clattered to the stage, and all the whispers and murmurs stopped. She raised her eyes to his and stepped toward him, her hand outstretched for help, and then she collapsed.

ANNETTE fidgeted with the silky blue binding on the blanket. "I don't know if she died then, or later, or maybe before. But I believe it was her spirit crying to me. I heard her, Ethan. Why it was given to me, that awful punishment of hearing her suffer, I don't know. But I believe she's at peace now." She looked up at him. "I know you think I'm crazy. Everyone else did."

"No, that's not what I think at all," Ethan said softly.

She told him how she went away to Switzerland after Johannesburg. It was a rest cure more than anything else. On the balcony of her hotel room she read voraciously and, through the power of words, was able to keep the ghosts of her own life in abeyance. At night she slept soundly, deeply.

Then, one Saturday morning, sometime after her third week there, she woke up restless. She dressed and went into town for coffee instead of taking it in her room as she usually did. It was still early, and the café in Montreux was deserted. She stared out over the lake, at the blue mountains on the other shore, and for perhaps the first time in her life she experienced a pang of wanderlust. Purpose had always guided her movements, and her purpose had been her music ever since she could remember. But for over a month now she had neither lifted a violin nor attended a concert. She had shut music out of her life as she had shut out David. It was the last link to the nightmare, and the nightmare was finally beginning to fade.

She walked down to the train station and stood for a long time looking at the schedule of departures. As she stood there, a train pulled into the station. With an impulse that made her smile to herself, she stepped up into the sleek silver machine. They were well out of Montreux when the conductor came for her ticket.

"I don't have a ticket," she said. "Where's this train going?"

"Lausanne," he replied curtly.

"Lausanne," she repeated. "Lausanne will be fine."

"You'll have to pay a surcharge."

"That's quite all right."

He was annoyed. It meant filling out forms in duplicate. As he flipped through his receipt book, a little square of carbon paper landed in the lap of the young man sitting opposite Annette. He picked it up and handed it to the conductor.

When the conductor had moved on, Annette turned toward the window. As the train wound through the verdant Swiss hills, the reflection of the young man opposite her drew her attention. He was resting his chin on his hand, his deep brown eyes fixed intently on the passing landscape. There was an air of dignity about the way he held himself, an unusual quality for someone his age, which she guessed to be about twenty.

The train emptied at Lausanne. With a polite nod to her, the young man stood, took his suitcase from the overhead rack, and inched his way down the aisle with the other passengers. When she got off the train, he had disappeared into the crowd.

She made her way to the station exit. She stood at the top of the steps and looked at the sparkling city rising up on the mountainside before her. Her senses were overwhelmed.

Suddenly he stood beside her.

"Excuse me," he muttered, a little shyly and very respectfully. "I can suggest a hotel if . . ."

"Yes, thank you," she said. "I would appreciate that."

He looked at her then, warmly, an intensely honest gaze. His eyes were very dark and very bright. "It's not far, just up the hill."

They both dined at the hotel that evening, and he asked the waiter to invite her to his table for coffee. He was an engineering student, and he had come to Lausanne to meet his mother, who would be arriving the next day from St.-Moritz. Annette gave him her maiden name and told him she was on vacation. He was a mature young man, very well bred, intelligent and gracious in his conversation. Over Cognac they energetically argued politics, and they were the last ones to leave the dining room. On the way up the stairs he slipped his hand into hers. There was something reassuring about his decisiveness, and she did not hesitate when he drew her into his room.

She never saw him again after that night. He asked for her address, but she would not give it to him. She was surprised to find herself crying as she took the train back to Montreux the next morning.

Three weeks later she learned she was pregnant. A profound peace settled over her, a serenity. She questioned nothing, and she had no fears. She named the baby Eliana, which in Hebrew meant "God has answered me."

When she had finished telling Ethan all these things, they sat quietly for a long while. Ethan didn't know what to say, and she looked so tired. Without thinking, he leaned forward and kissed her silently on the lips. A light came into her eyes.

chapter six

ANNETTE was holding on the line for Ethan when he walked into work the next morning. He ignored Bonnie's look as he closed the door to his office and picked up the phone.

"Ethan?" Her voice was bright. "Can I still get in my mother's old house?"

"Sure. I haven't done a thing to it," he answered.

"Would you mind terribly if I went out there sometimes?"

"Course not. I keep it locked, though. There's still some boxes up in the attic. Stuff for a garage sale, your mother said."

"I didn't know that. Could I come by and get the key?"

"Anytime. I'm here."

When she entered his office later that morning, dressed in jeans and wearing her sable coat, Ethan thought she looked like a movie star, but all he said was, "Lady, you could use a good old sheepskin-lined parka."

"You're such a cowboy," she replied. The fondness in her voice was unmistakable.

"So what's all the excitement?" he asked.

"I can't tell you. If I do, it might go away." She smiled and took the key he held out to her.

ANNETTE enjoyed the drive out to the old house. Even the bleak winter landscape didn't seem to oppress her, and as she opened the front door of her mother's family home, it struck her that she was falling in love with Ethan Brown. She stood motionless in the doorway with the cold wind blowing at her back; then she walked inside and closed the door behind her.

She laid her violin case on an old dusty table, opened it, and carefully removed the instrument. As she tuned it and tightened the bow, thoughts of Ethan crowded her mind. She marveled at how such an extraordinary man could be so much at home in this place. And yet she could envision him nowhere else.

She began to play, and gradually the wind ceased its roar. The demons withdrew into silence, and music calmed the land.

THE next day Ethan reined in his mare at the top of Jacob's Mound and looked down at the old Reilly house. How many times had he ridden by the place without so much as a thought for its past or its future? He'd thought only if he could ever get his hands on Mrs. Fergusen's little strip of prairie that cut like a ribbon between the Mackey land and his own, then his cattle would have access to the richest bluestem in the state of Kansas.

Today such thoughts were far from his mind. This strip of land was his, and Katie Anne would soon be his wife. Another obstacle, much more threatening, now stood here. For a moment he cursed the fate that had brought her here; then he pressed his heels into his horse's flanks and galloped down the hill.

When Annette heard the sound of his boots on the porch, she stopped playing her violin. Ethan opened the door hesitantly and removed his hat. She was smiling at him, and he thought her eyes looked different, happier maybe, but he wasn't sure.

"Don't stop," he said quietly, a shade embarrassed. He sat down at the table. Then he listened and gave himself up to the unbearable sweetness of the sound.

When she had finished, she laid the instrument back in its case. Ethan sat quietly with his hands folded between his knees.

"You want some hot coffee?" she asked.

"Sure."

She poured some coffee into a thermos cup and passed it to him. As he took the cup, he commented on her fingerless gloves.

"I thought those things went out with Charles Dickens."

"We wore them quite a lot in Europe. Places like Prague and Budapest. The concert halls were never heated."

He reached out and took her hand and turned it over, examining the glove. He grazed the tips of her naked fingers with his thumb.

"Are you going to make a habit out of this?" he asked.

"Out of what?"

He grinned. "Coming out here and serenading my cows."

She replied brightly, "I'm planning on it."

"Then I'd better have the electric company turn on the juice."

"You don't need to. I've rehearsed under worse conditions."

Her hand had settled in his comfortably. "Rehearse. Does that mean you're going to start performing again?"

She smiled. "I hope so."

"Was that your secret?"

"Yes. This morning I called my old booking agent in London. I didn't know if I was still worth anything. She seems to think I am."

As she spoke, it struck him how emotions danced across her face like the shadows of the clouds across the plains.

"What was that you were playing?"

"Beethoven's violin concerto."

He shook his head slowly. "You're a pretty amazing woman."

"And you're a pretty amazing man."

"I'm just a cowboy."

"Sure."

"I think the phone lines are still working. You want the phone connected?" he asked.

"Oh, heavens no. I don't want anyone to find me out here."

"Even me?"

"Except you."

For a long while they sat without speaking. They stared silently at their intertwined hands, heads lowered.

"I love you," he said softly.

She grew very still. He could not see her face.

"Annette?" He lifted her chin. "Look at me."

Her eyes told him all he needed to know.

AFTER that day, Ethan rode out to see her several times a week, and in those bleak, bare surroundings they looked upon each other with new eyes. There were only the one table and two stiff wooden chairs. And her violin stand with her music. So when they were together, they sat in stiff-backed chairs and talked about reviews of films they wished they could see, about articles Ethan had read in *The New Yorker,* about Annette's father and Ethan's mother, about favorite poets such as Yeats and Wordsworth, and about places they longed to visit, such as Wordsworth's glorious Windermere, in England's Lake District. And when Ethan could bear it no longer, he would lean across the table and kiss her, or stand and hold her for long, painful minutes. And then he would leave.

When they were apart, they blindly planned their futures. Responses to Annette's comeback were far beyond her modest hopes. Her winter schedule was already shaping up with guest performances in Lyon, The Hague, Heidelberg, and Munich, and her agent was pushing her to start as early as October. Ethan began to focus on the details of his house. Evenings he would earnestly solicit Katie Anne's advice on kitchen countertops and cabinet finishes. She was flattered and took it as a sign of his growing commitment. His lovemaking became more urgent, more passionate, and afterward he was more reflective. Katie Anne fell in love with him all over again.

ETHAN got a cold blast of reality late one evening while playing pool with Jer at the Beto Junction Truck Stop. Jer had wanted to quit much earlier, but Ethan had begged him to stay, so Jer kept his beer-drinking buddy company. He chalked up his stick and leaned over the table.

"Six ball in the side pocket," Jer said. He made the shot and walked around to the other side of the table. "You're gonna get yourself in too deep if you let this thing go on."

"What can I do, buddy? You're on a roll." Ethan laughed.

"That's not what I mean. Don't play dumb." Jer bent down to eyeball his next shot. "You've been with Annette." The balls cracked, and the seven ball dropped into the corner pocket.

Ethan laid his cue across the table and looked Jer in the eye. "You know nothin' about it, Jer."

Jer glared back at him. "You can't make enemies around here," he said, putting down his cue. "You make enemies with Tom Mackey and you won't have a friend in all of Chase County." He took his coat and hat from the rack. As he buttoned up his coat, he said, "Katie Anne's been askin' questions. She ain't as blind as you think."

After Jer left, a sobered-up Ethan sat at the counter drinking coffee with the truckers. When he got home much later, Katie Anne was asleep, but there was a note on the kitchen table: "Daddy called about tomorrow. He'll pick you up at seven."

ETHAN liked working cattle with Tom Mackey. He liked the man, envied him his down-to-earth simplicity. Tom dealt in numbers, in deeds, hide and meat. When Ethan was riding the range with him, he was able to laugh at that other side of himself that sat up in his office late at night reading poetry. He stole a glance at the man now.

"There he is," said Tom Mackey, pointing to a big Black Angus bull staring at them.

"You're not figurin' on sellin' him, are you?" asked Ethan.

"Hell no. Old Paco's the best breeding bull I've ever had."

The two men slowly eased their horses through the herd, scattering the cows.

"I'm gonna give him away."

Ethan felt his horse shudder. "Give him away?"

"Well, I figure now you've got your fencin' finished on Emma Fergusen's property, I could go ahead and give you your wedding present. I want you and Katie Anne to come out here tomorrow and cut fifteen cows outta this herd and put 'em to pasture with Old Paco on your place."

Tom reached over and slapped Ethan firmly on the back.

"Welcome to Chase County," he said.

The next morning Katie Anne said she wasn't feeling well, so Ethan cut the cows with Tom and one of the cowhands. They drove the small herd back over Jacob's Mound, and at the top of the hill Ethan thought he could hear the strains of a violin in the distance. But he kept his eyes fastened on the cows and would not look toward the east. By the time he got home, Katie Anne had already gone down to the main ranch house for dinner.

Tom Mackey was unusually voluble that evening. He had just taken delivery on a new Cessna airplane, and when Ethan arrived, Tom opened up a bottle of Champagne he'd chilled for the occasion. Katie Anne looked especially pretty. She flashed around the two-carat marquise he'd given her at Christmas, throwing shy, seductive smiles at him when her parents weren't looking.

During dinner Ethan drank too much Champagne, and Katie Anne drank nothing at all. He got the impression she was watching him without looking at him, and the more he drank, the more uncomfortable he became.

After dinner Ethan glued himself to Tom. They went into Tom's office to look over the prospectus on the new Cessna, and Katie Anne stood in the doorway watching them. After a moment she walked over to her father and wrapped her arms around his neck.

"Guys, I'm tired. I'm gonna take my Jeep and go on home." She glanced at Ethan. "You mind, honey?"

He looked up at her and found himself trapped in a gaze of startling transparency. In her eyes shimmered all those confounding things of the heart that Ethan so feared. He looked away.

"I'll take you home," he muttered, and started to rise.

"No," she answered quickly. "Stay with Dad." She kissed her father's cheek. "You guys look like you're havin' fun."

AFTER she left, Ethan had a hard time focusing on his conversation with Tom. Betty Sue made him down several cups of hot coffee before she let him go home.

When Ethan walked up the front steps to the guesthouse, the lights were off, but he saw a ghostly flicker from the television set coming from the bedroom, and he knew she was still awake. He was just hoping to get through one more evening.

He undressed and got into bed next to her.

The remote control was lying on her stomach. For a long time he watched the thin black box rise and fall with her breathing.

"Katie Anne?"

"Yeah?"

"We need to talk."

She picked up the remote control and turned off the television. Then, without a word, she pulled the blankets up around her neck and curled up with her back to him.

Ethan was quiet. He lay staring at the dark ceiling for a long time; then he turned his back to her and fell asleep.

Thunder woke him in the night, and he looked over and saw she wasn't there. He found her sitting on the front porch steps, her knees pulled up under her chin, her robe wrapped around her.

"What're you doing? It's cold," he said from the doorway.

Lightning crackled in the distance; then thunder shook the earth. Ethan looked down to see Traveler come padding up and quietly sit down next to him. He reached down and scratched the animal behind his ears. Katie Anne had never taken much of a liking to the dog, and so he never went to her. But tonight Traveler did something extraordinary. He left Ethan and went and lay down next to Katie Anne. Absentmindedly, without thinking, she reached out her hand and stroked his back. Ethan saw her shoulders shake, and he knew she was crying.

"I'm sorry, hon," he said quietly. That's all he said. He couldn't find the words to say more.

Ethan turned and went back inside. Traveler watched him go, but he stayed next to Katie Anne. Only when he heard the truck engine start up did he jump up and trot around the house and wait, sitting, alert, until Ethan whistled and he sailed over the tailgate into the back of the truck.

Ethan threw down his sleeping bag onto the hard wooden floor of his new house, and Traveler lay down beside him. He slept late, long after sunrise, and was awakened by one of the construction workers. He went down to the old Reilly house and took a cold shower; then he sat on the porch in the cold March wind and waited for Annette.

"Mornin', ma'am," he said as she got out of the car and walked toward him, violin case in one hand and a thermos in the other. She wore an old sheepskin jacket he had found in his closet and given her. He loved seeing her in it. It made her belong to him.

"You haven't shaved," she said as she stood over him.

"Nope," he said.

She drew her fingers down his cheek. He caught her hand and pressed the open palm to his lips. A wave of desire passed through her. She pulled away. He rose and followed her inside the house.

She poured steaming coffee. They sat at the table and looked at each other as they sipped their coffee.

"You've never seen the house I'm building, have you?"

She smiled. "I've sneaked a look from time to time."

"What do you think of it?"

"It's big. It's not finished. What can I say?" she teased.

He looked down at the placid surface of the coffee, feeling the blood pounding through his veins.

"Why?" she asked softly. "Is it important what I think?"

Thunder rolled in the distance, and Ethan looked out the window to see dark, heavy clouds scudding swiftly through the sky.

"We sure need some rain." He sighed.

His face drew up, as if he were in great pain. She touched his cheek. "Ethan, why is it important?" she whispered.

"I've done more soul-searchin' these past few months than I've ever done in my life," he said.

"Ethan, what have you done?" Now she held his hand, running her fingers through his. The feel of his skin against hers made her ache. "Ethan," she murmured. "Ethan."

Purposefully he stood and came around the table to her. He lifted her out of her chair and gathered her up tightly in his arms, and it seemed that she was drawing him in with her whole body.

"Is this . . ." She paused. Her voice was a throaty whisper. "Is this all we'll ever have?"

His eyes met hers. "Do you want more?" he asked.

Suddenly her face became like a child's, full of tenderness and vulnerability, and in the moments that followed, Ethan felt bound to her like to no other thing on the face of the earth.

A COLD RAIN HAD BEGUN TO fall so lightly that it landed with all the stillness of snow. Ethan and Annette, wrapped in their coats, lay together on the floor in front of the dark fireplace.

"This has changed everything," she said, her head on his chest. "That's why I was hoping to get away. Before this happened."

Ethan was quiet for a long time, but he held her close to him. "What's changed?" he asked finally.

She hesitated. "The way I see this place. Maybe I'm beginning to see it the way you do."

"Annette," he began. His voice was tight in his throat. "Annette, could you live here? With me?"

She shivered. "I'm cold." She started to get up, but he stopped her. "Answer me."

"I think I could," she said as she knelt before him.

Suddenly Ethan felt tears sting his eyes. He turned away.

"Then I'm all yours," he said quietly. "You've had my heart and soul for a long time. Just give me some time to work things out."

She looked down at him. "Will you come here again?"

"Every day. And I'll bring a bed next time I come." He grinned. "Say, would you mind if I slept out here?"

She laughed. "For heaven's sake, Ethan, it's your house."

"Could you sleep out here sometimes?" he asked.

"I'd have to come late. And leave early." She caught the look in his eyes and kissed him tenderly. "I love you," she whispered.

The rain came down heavily now, and they fell silent. Ethan thought what a mess his life was and how gloriously happy he was.

HE GOT into the office around ten. He was unshaven and his shirt was wrinkled. Bonnie stared at him, but he kept her busy and got away at noon without having to answer any questions. He got up his courage to go back to the guesthouse to pick up some clothing and some of his things. He relaxed when he saw that Katie Anne's Wrangler was gone. He didn't want to run into her like this, like a thief in the night. He wanted her to sit down and listen to him.

He had to drive up to Emporia to get the bed. With the help of the warehouse man he loaded the thing onto his truck and then drove the back roads through the hills to the Reilly house, hoping he wouldn't pass anyone he knew. As he drove along, he had a sudden flash of what his life would be. How all the habits and customs he'd built over the years would be halted abruptly, dealt a death-blow. His ordered life was in upheaval.

After he'd set up the bed, he went back to work in his office. It was quiet and Bonnie was gone, and there was no one to ask him any questions. When he came back to the old house, it was almost eleven. Annette was sitting on the bed reading a book. A bare bulb shed a faint light.

"This is brand-new, isn't it?" she commented as he walked in. "Why'd you get such a big one?" she said with a grin.

"Don't you think we'll use it?"

"Is it for sleeping?"

"Eventually. When we're old and gray."

"*And full of sleep / And nodding by the fire,*" she said.

He took the book from her hands and stretched out alongside her. *"Take down this book / And slowly read, and dream of the soft look / Your eyes had once . . ."*

For a long while they looked at each other in silence. Then they turned off the light and pulled the sleeping bag over them and buried themselves deep in each other's warmth.

chapter Seven

ANNETTE awoke in the pitch-dark to the sound of her name—Annie. Only her mother had ever called her Annie. She lay awake, listening, but she heard only the wind.

She rose and pulled on her jeans. Ethan awoke.

"What time is it?" he asked. He stroked the side of her arm while she put on her boots.

"I don't know. I can't see my watch."

"Is something wrong?"

"I'm worried. If Eliana should wake up and find me gone . . ."

Ethan sat up. "You want me to follow you into town?"

"I'll be fine." She kissed him. "When will I see you?"

"I'll come by around lunchtime," he said. "I want you to come over to see the house."

Ethan lay awake and worried about her after she had gone. He'd have the phone connected the next day. He'd come early in the evening and make a fire in the fireplace, and he'd bring some sheets and blankets. It struck him that he had never bothered with this kind of thing before. Not ever. Not for any woman.

He went back to Katie Anne's place later that morning. She was standing in the kitchen boiling water as he walked in, and she turned her back to him and cinched up her bathrobe. He sat down at the table.

"We're going to have to talk," he said finally.

"No. Correction. Excuse me. *You're* gonna talk." She poured some water into a mug and turned to face him.

"I can't do this," he said. "I can't marry you."

She dipped a tea bag in the water, but said nothing. Finally she turned, went into the bedroom, and closed the door.

Ethan took his shower, shaved, and dressed. When he came out of the bathroom, Katie Anne walked up to him and laid her hand on his chest. "Let's just put it off," she said. "It's not too late. I mean, it'll be a nightmare, after all the plans Mom and Dad have made. But we can still do it." She wrapped her arms around him. "I know how scared you get. Come back home. Please."

She felt so familiar to him. So known. He stroked her back and closed his eyes, wishing himself away from this moment.

Suddenly all her pain burst forth in long, strangled sobs. He let go of her and turned away.

"Look at me, damn you!" she wailed, and when he looked around, she slapped him hard on the face. Her eyes were swollen and red, and tears streamed down her cheeks. Never had he seen her so enraged. "I never cry in front of you, 'cause you can't stand it. But boy, if you only knew! I hid it from you because I knew it'd just scare you away. Well, take a look at me now. And remember what it looks like. When you're lookin' into her eyes, you remember mine!"

She ran back into the bedroom and slammed the door. Ethan stood in stunned silence, listening to her cry. Then he gathered up all the papers on his desk and walked out of the house. He was numb but cleansed. Purged. Her anger had done it for him. He was deeply grateful to her for that.

ETHAN pulled up in front of the old house a little after noon, and Annette ran out and hopped into the truck. She was breathless and exuberant. So very different from the woman who had been waiting to greet him in his office five months before.

He made a quick turn around the yard and headed back to the road. "I was worried about you this morning."

"I'm fine." She turned a smile on him, and the joy on her face swept away all his guilt and pain.

"And Eliana?"

"She woke up just after I got home. She was having a nightmare. She doesn't have nightmares very often."

It was a clear, cold day. The sky was a seamless pale blue against the dry, brown winter hills.

"It's beautiful, all this," she said. She waved at the immense land that stretched around her.

"You think you could handle it?" Ethan asked.

"Yes." She nodded. "I could. I know I could."

"It's a different life. You won't get bored?"

"With you?" She laughed, then said, "I love you desperately."

"Move over here next to me," he said softly.

She slid over next to him and laid her head on his shoulder. "Have you told her?" she asked quietly.

"Yeah. I didn't handle it too well. I'm not very good at that kind of thing. I don't like hurting people."

"I'm afraid for you, Ethan. I'm afraid of what they'll all do to you."

"What do you mean?"

"Jer told me Tom Mackey's one of your biggest clients."

"Now why would Jer be talking to you about Tom Mackey?"

"It came up in conversation after one of Eliana's lessons."

"Well, Tom Mackey's a big client, but he's not my only client. I have clients all throughout the state. People who don't even know Tom Mackey."

"I'm afraid you'll regret it."

"And what about you? Will you regret it?"

"I'll be homesick, I suppose. And I'll never really fit in."

"I don't think I'd ever want you to." Ethan came to the crest of a hill, and the house came into view. He slowed and turned off onto a narrow dirt road. "What about your career?" he asked.

She reflected. "Maybe I could still tour. A little."

"You bet you could. It's not big-time like you're used to, but there are plenty of good orchestras in the region."

"I just want to perform again."

"Well, I want you to think about it all before it's too late."

"When is too late?"

"When you marry me."

She grew quiet.

"You will marry me, won't you?" he said.

She looked up at him. "When?"

He put his arm around her and whispered, "Tomorrow."

"Ethan!"

"I'm afraid I'll lose you."

"You're not going to lose me. I'm not going anywhere."

Ethan pulled up and stopped in front of his house. It was built on the back of the hill, with the top floor facing south and the two lower floors looking north. The view was spectacular.

"It's almost finished." He turned to look at her. "You think you'll like it?"

She grinned. "Do you know how often I've driven out here?"

"You told me you'd never been out here."

"What I said was, I'd sneaked a look from time to time." She tugged on his sleeve. "Now show me the kitchen."

WHEN Ethan got back to the office, there was a note on his desk from Katie Anne. Ethan sat down to read it.

Dearest Ethan,

I know I should have talked about this to you this morning, but I just couldn't. I couldn't stand to see your face when I told you. I've known for a long time that something was wrong. I was just hoping you'd get over it.

Ethan, I'm going to have a baby. I didn't do this on purpose. You know I'm not ready to have kids. You know I'm not even really crazy about kids.

Nobody's going to force you to marry me. I haven't told anybody yet. But I want you to know that I'm going to keep it. I couldn't possibly do anything else. If this is all I'll have of you, then I'm going to have to love him twice as much, to make up for not being able to love you.

Katie Anne

Ethan's phone was ringing, but he didn't answer it. His stomach felt as if it had caved in, and he found it difficult to swallow.

Bonnie looked in. "It's Mrs. McNeil. Can you take it?"

Ethan shook his head and motioned her away.

"Ethan, are you okay?" she asked.

"Take messages for me. I need to go out." He grabbed his hat and coat and stuffed the letter into his pocket.

HE HEADED east along dirt roads through the hills until he ran into the interstate and took it to Beto Junction. It was snowing heavily when he pulled into the truck stop. For a long time he sat in the parking lot. The thoughts that danced into his mind reeled with the same chaotic confusion as the snow. Rational thought abandoned him. He was aware of a heaviness that seemed to cut his breath short and hobble every movement. His spirit lay inert.

He sat until he was stiff and cold. Then finally he started the engine and headed back into the storm. He knew Annette would be waiting for him by now.

His decision that night was made, quite literally, at the fork of a road. Afterward he made himself believe that there was some hand of fate at work here, but he knew this was not true. What lurked deep and nameless inside him was the ugly face of cowardice, and Ethan was too proud to recognize it. And so he continued straight, down the old county road that he had traveled countless times and would travel until the end of his life. He drove on in the night, the miles between them increasing with each minute, and the more he tried to imagine his life without Annette, the stronger her image burned into his mind. Countless times he stopped the car and started to go back, but each time the ugliness seemed to loom up around him, and his heart would start pounding in his chest. So he drove on, cautiously, for the road was barely visible through the blinding snow. Gradually a veil descended upon his heart, and it grew distant and cold, retreating deep into the cavernous recesses of his soul. He willed it so.

When he finally reached the guesthouse, it was nearly two in the morning. Katie Anne was in bed, asleep. He undressed and crawled in next to her, and she awoke and put her arms around him, snuggling up against his back.

"You're cold," she whispered.

"Yes," he replied, and Annette burst out of his heart, flooding him with her presence the way fireworks explode in a summer sky, with fleeting colors and beauty before they dissipate and float away on the night breeze. "Yes," he repeated, "I'm cold," and with his back to her he curled up, like a little boy protecting a secret treasure buried deep in his chest.

Katie Anne drew her fingers down his back, but when he did not respond, she quietly rolled over to her own side of the bed.

AFTER the night of his return Katie Anne handled Ethan with deft skill. She gave him nothing to worry about and nothing to dispute. He worked at his office every day, including Sundays, for he showed no more interest in Mass. She ate alone each evening without so much as a sigh of complaint, for he returned late at night.

There was no more intimacy between them. Ethan slept in the guest room and was often gone before she awoke. Katie Anne told him she preferred not to tell her parents, or anyone else, about her pregnancy until after the wedding. Ethan agreed, and nothing else was ever said about the subject.

Ethan called Jer a week before the wedding and asked him for help moving all his furniture into his new house from the storage where he had kept it while he had been living with Katie Anne.

When his mother and sister arrived in town the afternoon before the wedding, Ethan put them up at his new house. He spent the night there with them, which vexed Katie Anne, but she never breathed a word of displeasure to him. His mother's presence was a balm to Ethan. When she kissed him on the top of his head and went off to bed, Ethan allowed himself to imagine an encounter between the two of them—Annette and his mother. He saw Annette standing there at the top of the stairs, all deference and respect, listening to his mother with that quiet, intense way she had to let others know she was all there, all theirs. Then the vision departed, and he turned off the light and went upstairs to bed.

At ten o'clock the next morning Ethan, dressed in his tux, deposited his mother and sister at the Mackey ranch, where the eleven-o'clock ceremony was to take place, with the understanding that he would pick up Jer and be back by ten thirty. By ten fifty, when Ethan had not yet shown up at his house, Jer went to find him. Only by chance did Jer catch a glimpse of Ethan's truck sitting in the parking lot of the South Forty.

The South Forty was an ugly place in the morning, and it looked particularly ugly to Ethan after his fifth beer. The owner was running a vacuum somewhere behind him, so that Ethan didn't hear Jer when he came in.

"Come on, buddy," said Jer. "Let's go."

The sight of Jer in a tux brought a glimmer of amusement into Ethan's eyes. "Finally got you into that penguin suit, didn't she?"

"I'm doin' it for you, pal," said Jer.

"Well, if you're doin' it for me, who am I doin' it for?"

"Let's go, Ethan. Everybody's waitin'."

"I'm comin'," he mumbled.

Jer couldn't get the owner's attention over the roar of the vacuum, so he went behind the counter and found two mugs and filled them with hot coffee. He slid one over to Ethan.

"Is she there?" Ethan asked, staring down at the mug.

"She's there. Waitin'. A little ticked off."

"I mean Annette."

"No." Jer blew on his coffee. "You didn't expect her, did you?"

"Katie Anne sent her an invitation."

"Yeah. Well, that's Katie Anne for ya."

Ethan sipped the coffee. "Thanks for comin', Jer."

"I was worried, buddy. I've never seen you like this before."

"I've never been like this before." Ethan gulped the coffee.

"You gonna make it?" asked Jer.

"Yeah. I'll be okay." Ethan gave him a level gaze. He suddenly looked very sober. "When's she leaving?"

"End of the week. Friday," answered Jer.

Ethan nodded.

"Things'll be better when she's gone."

"Yeah." Ethan sighed. "Yeah, you're right."

At that moment Ethan was on the verge of telling Jer all that had happened: how he had lifted the phone countless times to call her, even dialed the number; how he had driven by her house, lurking like a lovesick kid in the dark. But as time went on, it had seemed so much easier to withdraw behind a wall of silence and let the others wrestle with truth and pain.

Ethan picked up his jacket. "Let's go, buddy," he said to Jer.

FROM that moment on, Ethan was swept along by events. He pledged to love and honor Katie Anne in sickness and in health and to forsake all others. When he said the last part, it seemed to him her smile quivered slightly, or maybe it was just a movement of her veil from her breath.

Ethan had expected the ceremony to make a difference. But to his surprise he awoke Sunday morning still longing for Annette. He finally admitted to himself that his love for Katie Anne had died. He thought that one day he might be able to tolerate her again, even enjoy her, but never love her.

FOR years Ethan had helped his neighbors with their spring burn, and this year was no exception. It was no way to spend a honeymoon, as more than one friend commented, but Ethan was too engrossed in strategy to pay much attention to local gossip. There were the backfires to plan, the cattle to move to safer ground, the neighbors and authorities to notify.

The ranchers worked in parallel lines, stringing fire across the prairie, igniting the brown winter grass with friendly napalm dripping from ten-foot pipes. Ethan worked the mop-up crew, beating out little fingers of unruly fire with paddles and rakes. When they were done, he always looked out at the blackened hills and marveled at the potency of fire and the phoenixlike regenerative power of nature. For in less than a week tiny new green sprouts of bluestem would appear underneath the blackened crust. Then they'd turn the cattle loose again, and the beasts would nudge aside the charred earth and nibble on the green juicy blades that tasted better than anything else in the world.

Soon it was Ethan's turn to burn his land. With Tom Mackey's help he had assessed the weather and the wind and planned the burn with military precision. It was a spectacular sight, with the red flames outlining the hills against the night sky. The burn went well, and the county firefighting crew that had been in a state of readiness throughout the day was now preparing to move on.

"How're we doing?" Ethan asked the fire chief.

"Looks good. It was touch 'n' go there for a while. Sure felt like that wind was changin' on us. We're leavin' one truck over there next to the firebreak, where you've still got some flames."

"Good enough."

When Ethan stepped under the shower that night, he realized he had not thought of Annette all day. The physical labor had drained his body and mind. For the first time in months it felt as though chaos no longer threatened the orderliness of his world.

chapter Eight

IT WAS dark in the kitchen. Dawn had not yet tinted the eastern sky. Annette sat at the small yellow Formica table, the same one at which she had eaten as a girl. The coffeemaker spurted its last few drops into the glass carafe, and she rose, poured herself a cup of coffee, then opened the window. It would be a warm day, but she would be gone before the end of it. Everything was ready; their suitcases were packed.

She had waited that wintry night, waited until the snow covered Charlie's old Buick in a wispy white blanket, and then she had written a note to Ethan and gone back home. She had called the next morning and left a message with Bonnie, but her call was never returned. For many days she waited for him, rehearsing there in the old house for hours on end, her sadness carried on the waves of the gradually warming spring air.

Finally she broke down and called him again. This time Bonnie was cool and evasive. Annette left another message. This, too, went unanswered. After that she quit going to the old house. The bed still sat in the living room. He never came to get it.

When the wedding invitation came in the mail, she made up her mind to go back home to Paris. Her strength began to grow from that moment on. She planned a recital for her students and scheduled it for Sunday afternoon, the day after Ethan's wedding, at the Winegarners' large house. To her astonishment all her students and their parents attended. Matthew Winegarner performed in his wheelchair to a hushed audience. It was a surprisingly pleasant occasion, and afterward, when everyone had gone and Annette was washing the punch bowl, Mrs. Winegarner broke down in tears. The two women sat together at the kitchen table and cried while Eliana pushed Matthew around the backyard in his wheelchair.

A LAST thing remained to be done. Annette had put it off because she could not bear to return to the old house. Surely, if there was anything of value left in the attic, her mother would have said so. Ethan had said they were things intended for a garage sale, but perhaps there was something overlooked, forgotten.

Annette finished her coffee and wrote a note telling her father and daughter where she was going and that she would be back shortly, even perhaps before they awoke. Then she took the keys to the Buick and left.

As she drove out to the country, she saw giant pillars of smoke rising from the fields. She had been alarmed last night when she saw long ribbons of fire consuming the prairie, but her father explained how they did it every year. A planned burn, he had called it.

Annette pulled into the driveway of the old house. She sat in the car, with the engine idling, for a long time, watching the columns of smoke move across the horizon with the wind. Finally she regained her senses. She would not allow memories of Ethan to interfere.

The bed was still there. Everything was as she had left it. She averted her eyes and dragged her legs up the stairs to the attic.

THE call had come at four a.m. Ethan had only been asleep a few hours. It was the county sheriff. The worst possible scenario had been realized. The wind had come up unexpectedly and carried embers from smoldering cow chips into dry, brown winter pasture that had not been burned. Livestock was threatened.

When Ethan had dressed, he found Katie Anne in the kitchen filling a thermos full of hot coffee.

"I heard," she mumbled groggily. "What's the wind speed?"

"Around twenty-two," he said. "And the sun's not even up yet."

She shook her head in despair.

"Your dad's going to take the Cessna up as soon as day breaks," he said. "We're gonna need a firebreak somewhere up north of here. Pick up the disc tractor. He'll tell you by radio where to plow."

Ethan could smell it as he sat on the porch pulling on his boots— the woodsy, autumnlike smell of burning leaves. It grew stronger as he drove up the road, the window down. The pungent air was cluttered with flying ashes. He passed the road to the old Reilly house and had a sudden urge to turn onto it. He had not returned since the night he had spent there with Annette. A brief memory of that night exploded in his brain, and he squeezed his eyes shut. He accelerated and sped north toward the fire. Let it burn to the ground, he thought.

KATIE Anne had Jacob's Mound in her sight. A few more miles and the firebreak would be finished. Ethan's land would be protected. In a few minutes her father would be taking up his plane, and they would have a better assessment of the scope of the fire. But they all knew one thing: It was moving fast. Too fast.

Katie Anne turned around to look at the mark she had made on the earth. The disc tractor had torn up a fifteen-foot-wide stretch of prairie, plowing under the dried winter grass, bringing to the surface cool, moist earth that defied fire. When she reached Jacob's Mound, she would turn around and come back right alongside this line, widening the break another fifteen feet.

The air was cluttered with flying ashes, and the sun was barely visible through the haze. It suddenly occurred to her that the old Reilly house that Ethan had bought was right in the path of the fire. The place where Ethan had betrayed her. Let it burn.

She looked up, and her heart seemed to freeze in her chest. There was a patch of fire on top of Jacob's Mound, only a few hundred feet in front of her. She watched its movements. Within a few seconds it was down the slope of the mound and moving toward her. She turned the heavy tractor southward and gave it full throttle, its mammoth engine whining, while the fire rushed steadily forward. The wind, impatient, blew the smoke ahead of the fire line. Katie

Anne saw the blue sky in front of her grow dim, and then the prairie disappeared into a dark cloud of smoke.

ANNETTE had been sitting in the cool, dark attic with her flashlight, oblivious to the passing time and the delicate arrival of dawn. She was totally perplexed by what she had found. Letters to and from a friend named Beth she had never heard her mother mention before. A friend her mother had gone to school with here in Cottonwood Falls and who had moved to Los Angeles to study painting. Beth had written letter after letter, pleading with Emma Reilly to leave her husband. And Emma had been so tempted. From the very first months of her marriage she had recognized her folly. Charles Fergusen's persuasive charm had soured to a frighteningly oppressive severity. His demands that she adhere to his rigid authority were enforced with cold cruelty.

After Annette was born, he became even more demanding. He ridiculed his wife's attempts to breast-feed the baby, insisting she would pervert the child. When Annette was only two months old, he contracted pneumonia and was in bed for three weeks. Whenever the baby cried to be fed or changed or simply held, he would ring the bell he kept at his bedside table to summon his wife. And Emma Reilly Fergusen would run to her husband and wait on him, and the baby's cries would go unheeded. Her heart, like her breasts, swelled, ached, and then grew dry. From that time on she learned how to love her daughter silently, without passion.

Annette cried as she read the letters. The pungent smell of smoke did not penetrate the attic, and the sirens remained at a distance. The fire alighted upon the house quickly, and Annette, her mind alive with the past, did not hear the crackling flames.

Annie.

She jumped, her hand flew to her heart, and she turned to see a pale light on the attic stairs. Then she smelled the smoke.

She rushed to the window and drew back the curtains. The prairie was gone, obscured by a tidal wave of smoke trailing behind a thin red line of fire that was eating its way toward the house, licking up the brown grasses like an insatiable dragon. Annette scrambled down the narrow attic stairs. She lost her left shoe near the bottom, stumbled, and fell against the door. It flew open, and she landed on her knees on the second-floor landing. Pale gray smoke was creeping stealthily along the floor and up the stairs toward her. Think clearly!

Annie.

She ran to the second-floor bathroom and looked for a towel, a rag. But there was nothing. She stripped off her sweater, jammed it underneath the faucet, and turned on the water. Only a trickle came forth. She cried and cursed at the old house, and the smoke swirled soundlessly around her legs. Covering her face with the sweater, she hobbled on one shoe to the stairs. As her left foot hit the second step, her stocking slipped on the old wood. There was a sharp crack and wrenching pain as her ankle bent underneath her, and in that last second of her life she flew downward through the air to the bottom of the stairs, where the flames ate their way toward her.

ANNETTE stared down at her crumpled burning body with calm curiosity. She recognized herself as if she were another. The fire no longer seemed to be her enemy, but something ravishingly beautiful and energetic that belonged to the earth and had its place there. The voice behind that persistent *Annie* was now clearly revealed. Her mother was there with her.

Annette's spirit ascended above the old house, and she saw all things at once. She saw the prairie and the fire and the people struggling to contain it. She saw the huge lumbering tractor throwing up dirt as it raced across the field to escape the flames, and she saw the smoke overcome it. She saw the pretty young woman jump off it and run down a narrow corridor of grass with walls of fire on each side, and she saw her stumble and fall, the smoke overwhelming her. She saw the airplane emerge from the smoke and set down, and the father, masked and coated in yellow armor, race through the narrowing corridor and throw himself upon the burning body of his beloved daughter. She saw him carry his child in his arms and stride through the flames like a god. She saw the airplane take off and disappear into the sky.

Mama, stay close to me.

I'm taking you home, Annie.

How beautiful you are, Mama.

It's my love you see, Annie. There's nothing to restrain it now.

What is this, Mama? This darkness? I can touch it.

We're on our way home. There. Can you see the light? Can you feel the light?

Oh, yes. It feels like your arms around me when I was little.

It's much greater than that, Annie.

Slow down, Mama. Don't go so fast.

Annie . . .

Mama!

As Annette called out, she felt an ache throb through her. She felt her mother move toward the light, faster, faster, and yet she herself slowed and seemed to slip backward, away from the light. Suddenly her mother's presence was gone, and she found herself in her daughter's bedroom. Eliana was asleep, her glorious mane of hair swept over her pillow in artless beauty. Annette looked upon her daughter's peaceful face, and an anguish now consumed her soul.

I will not leave you. Not for all the beauty of heaven. I cannot leave you, cannot leave this earth. I love you too much.

A dull peace settled over Annette now. It had none of the beauty she had known earlier, but the anguish was gone. She knew she was earthbound. She would never again see the light. But as she looked upon her daughter's face, her lonely spirit rejoiced.

IT WAS late in the afternoon by the time Ethan got to the hospital. He had been setting backfires with a few brave hands up north of the main fire. A local sheriff had been sent to track him down.

Ethan was overcome with guilt. As he sped down the interstate toward Kansas City, he muttered inarticulate prayers, and his eyes, already inflamed, burned with tears that never fell. Katie Anne's vanity and selfishness now seemed to him like small blemishes on a character that was ultimately sound and good. He tried to prepare himself for the worst about her. But nothing could have prepared him for the looks on the faces of Tom and Betty Sue Mackey when he came rushing down the corridor. Their eyes were flooded with the kind of pain he had spent a lifetime avoiding.

"How is she?" Ethan whispered.

It was Betty Sue who spoke. "She was burned pretty badly. Her face . . ." She broke down sobbing, and Tom finished.

"It's the smoke. She inhaled so much smoke."

After a moment Ethan went down the hall to Katie Anne's room. She had an oxygen tube down her throat and an IV in each arm, and her face seemed to be wearing a mask of some sort. He could tell that most of her hair was gone.

"Mr. Brown?"

Ethan turned and saw a woman in a white jacket.

"I'm Dr. Eagleton. We still haven't got her stabilized, but I think we'll be able to pull her through."

"She's pregnant," Ethan blurted out. "About eight weeks, I think. I'm the only one who knows about it."

"I understand. We'll do an ultrasound right away."

Ethan waited in the hallway while they wheeled in the equipment. For the first time since the news of the accident he allowed himself to think about Annette. She would be gone now. Her plane would have already departed.

"Mr. Brown, can you come in here, please?"

As Ethan entered the room, he forced himself to look closely at Katie Anne. One side of her face was black and crusty from third-degree burns. The other side was blistered. Her eyes were swollen shut. Her arms and chest were wrapped in bandages.

"Mr. Brown, I want you to see this." The doctor guided Ethan's attention to the monitor while she passed a detector over Katie Anne's stomach. "Your wife's not pregnant."

Ethan stared at the black-and-white image of Katie Anne's womb. "You mean she's lost it?"

"If she did, it wasn't recently. There's no sign of a fetus."

Ethan stared at the snowy image. "I don't understand."

"Did she have positive test results?" She spoke quietly.

"I don't know what kind of tests she had done."

"Were you married recently?"

"Just last week."

"It's possible she missed a period or two. That's a very stressful time for young women." Dr. Eagleton placed a gentle hand on his arm. "We're going to do everything we can for her."

Ethan slipped out of Katie Anne's room and down the corridor. He couldn't face Tom and Betty Sue just now, so he went into a stairwell and sat on the steps. It had been such an elaborate lie—morning sickness, loss of appetite, the secrecy. For a long time he sat there staring at the wide gold wedding band on his finger.

ELIANA crept quietly out of bed and felt her way along the dark hallway to the kitchen. She groped along the wall until she found the light. The kitchen was spotless, as her mother had left it early the night before. Only her mug sat on the kitchen table where she had sat that morning when she was still alive. Eliana's eyes flooded instantly with tears at the sight of the mug. But the tears did no good, and she was tired of crying.

That morning Eliana had stood in the doorway and heard the sheriff tell her grandfather that her mother had been killed in the fire, and she had seen the sheriff's pained look when he saw her standing there. After his visit Charlie Fergusen had locked the front door and closed himself in his bedroom. For a long time Eliana had lain in her bed. Her tears seemed never ending.

Sometime in the early afternoon she knocked on her grandfather's bedroom door, but there was no answer. So she went back to her bedroom, closed the door, lay down on her bed, and prayed for God to let her die. She did not die, but finally she fell asleep.

She was very hungry now; she had eaten nothing all day. She poured herself the last of the milk and sat down and ate some graham crackers. She was still hungry, however, so she climbed up on the counter and opened the cabinet. She saw some cans on the top shelf, but she couldn't quite read the labels, so she tried to pull herself up by the shelf. As Eliana lodged her weight against it, the shelf tilted toward her, sending the entire contents onto her head. Eliana screamed and covered her head with her hands, and when the terrible noise had finally stopped, she looked up to see her grandfather standing in the doorway.

"What are you doing in here!" he bellowed, and his voice seemed even more terrible to her than the crashing tins and glass. "Clean it all up!" he commanded, shaking his gnarly finger.

"Yes, Grandpa," whispered Eliana. Her heart pounded in her little chest as she scurried down from the counter. When he left, she quickly began picking up the tins and broken glass. Her shoulders shook with silent grief, and her delicate features were distorted into a mask of sadness and pain. As she worked, her resolve grew. She turned off the kitchen light and tiptoed back to her mother's room. Their suitcases lay open on the bed, neatly packed, as her mother had left them. Eliana slipped on her jeans and cowboy boots, put on her white cowboy hat, picked up her mother's violin, and turned out the light. Within minutes she was outside and racing down the road as though ghosts were at her feet.

Chapter Nine

JER stood at the entrance of the hospital cafeteria looking for Ethan. He found him in a booth at the back, concealed by an artificial ficus. Ethan had a cup of coffee in front of him and a piece of apple pie pushed to the side. The coffee looked cold.

Jer slid into the booth. "How's she doin'?" he asked.

"Hangin' in there."

"How about Tom and Betty Sue?"

"They've checked into a hotel across the street. I told Tom I'd call him if . . . if there was any change."

An awkward silence stretched between them.

"Get yourself a cup of coffee," said Ethan. "They're still open."

"Naw, thanks. I can't stay long. We're still moppin' up."

"How's it going?"

"We got it licked. Finally."

"Anybody else get hurt?"

Jer took a deep breath. "Yeah," he replied. "One of the volunteers from Strong City. Smoke inhalation, but they released him."

"How about property?"

"Your house is safe," Jer said. "But the Reilly house . . ."

"Did it go?"

"Yeah." Jer could hardly hear his own voice.

"Just as well," mumbled Ethan. He stood up. "I'm gonna get a hot refill. Sure you don't want something?"

"No, thanks." Jer caught him by the sleeve. "Ethan?"

"Yeah?"

Jer's mouth felt like cotton. "Annette was in the house."

The coffee cup that dangled from Ethan's finger slipped to the floor and shattered. He slowly turned to look at his friend.

"What?" His voice was but a whisper.

"She was in the house when it burned. Charlie Fergusen said she went off early that morning and planned on being back before everyone woke up. They found her—" Jer's voice broke suddenly, and a strange high whine burst from his chest. It was the first time Ethan had ever heard him cry.

ETHAN walked quickly through the hospital corridors, looking for a way out. If he could just hold it in until he got outside. Where's the outside? He stopped a nurse and muttered at her angrily, wanting to know the way out, but he didn't wait for her reply. He felt it beginning to rise in his chest, and he hurried away before she had finished. She called after him that he was going the wrong way, but he ignored her. He tried to control his breathing, but he could no longer stop the tears. They flooded down his face, soundlessly.

He walked for a long time down long, endless corridors of sickness and health. He cried until his face was soft and tender, like a child's, and when at last he saw a rest room, he went in and shut the door. As he blew his nose on some toilet paper, he caught sight of his face in the mirror—bloated, streaked with pink, his nose red—and it shocked him. It looked just like Katie Anne's had looked the night he left her. It looked the way Annette's must have when she waited and he never returned.

It was a long time before he could return to Katie Anne's room. He stopped at the door and looked in on her. The woman on the bed now seemed to him like someone else's wife. It was a tragic incident, but not his own. He turned and thought he saw Dr. Eagleton at the end of the corridor just as the door was closing behind her. He had a sudden urge to speak to her, and he hurried down the corridor after her. She had gone out through the emergency exit. Ethan opened the door and looked up and down the stairwell, but there was no sound of a door closing or of feet on the stairs. As he turned, disappointed, his hand on the door, he paused. He had heard no sound, but he knew he was not alone. A chill ran through him, and he turned to see Annette standing on the landing below him.

The first thing he noticed was her beauty, although afterward he could recall nothing about the way she dressed or how she looked. All he knew was that she was there. He felt her love pouring through him like heat from the sun. It was as though an aura, like a net, arose from her and descended upon him, drawing them together. She spoke to him. She told him that he must take charge of Eliana, be the child's guardian. That Eliana had run away from her grandfather's house and should not be forced to return. She told him that for all the beauty of heaven, she could not leave this earth. That she loved him.

Ethan heard a shout, then the sound of running feet. He glanced toward the door, and when he looked back, Annette was gone. He called her name; then he ran down the stairs after her, three flights, but they were empty. His heart pounded as he walked back up. He tried to rationalize what he had seen. Perhaps it was his overwrought imagination, his distress.

As he neared the third floor, he could hear shouting again and what sounded like equipment being rolled in the hall. He opened the door and looked down the corridor; the commotion was outside Katie Anne's room. He rushed through the corridor and slipped into the room.

"We're not getting a heartbeat!" Dr. Eagleton said. She was pumping Katie Anne's chest while a nurse pumped the air bag, forcing air into her lungs. Another nurse watched the monitor. Ethan could see it. It was flat. Lifeless.

"Still nothing," said the nurse.

"Okay. Repeat the atropine."

The nurse slapped a needle into the doctor's hand, and she injected the atropine.

The others stood in silent watch as Dr. Eagleton continued pumping Katie Anne's chest and the nurse pumped the air bag. They worked together in perfect cadence, but the cadence slowed gradually, and finally they stopped.

ANNETTE saw all of this. She saw Ethan in the corner of the room and the valiant doctor and all the dedicated people. *It's too late. Her spirit left her long ago. She's gone.* Suddenly Annette felt a presence with her, a strong, powerful friend. As she looked upon the blackened, lifeless shell—the body that would inspire no love, the face that people would turn away from—the anguish of choice overwhelmed her again. It came upon her all at once, and she had a vision of her life far into the future, what would be her struggle, her suffering, her glory. She also knew in that timeless moment that all this knowledge that she now had would be taken away from her. She felt this knowledge come to her from her friend, and she understood then the frailty and limitations of man. She had one fragile glimpse into eternity, and then she plunged into darkness.

Dr. Eagleton jumped with fright when the lifeless body beneath her suddenly shuddered, as though jolted by a powerful electric shock. The patient's chest moved.

"Get her back on the ventilator!"

The room burst into activity. As the staff worked, they hid their awe behind masks of professionalism, but each of them knew he had just witnessed a miracle. Then Katie Anne opened her swollen eyes, and a sound came from deep within her body.

"Eth . . ."

"She's conscious!"

Ethan pushed his way through them and bent over the bed. Her whisper, barely audible, was little more than a breath passing through her black lips. "Eth . . . Ethan."

"I'm here. I'm here."

"Eli . . ." She fell back into sleep.

WHEN Jer opened the stable door in the cold light of dawn, he immediately noticed an open gate on one of the empty stalls. He picked up a flashlight and slowly made his way down the corridor. As he cautiously peered around the stall gate, he made out a dark form in the corner on a low pile of hay. He shone the light on it, then knelt down and pulled back the horse blanket. When he saw the long, pale hair full of straw, the white cowboy hat, the violin case, his heart lurched. He gently gathered the sleeping child in his arms and walked toward the house.

"DOES her grandfather even know she's gone?" asked Ethan. He was watching Jer whip up batter for pancakes, his strong, callused hand flying in even strokes around the big metal bowl.

"Sure he does. Sheriff went around to tell him." Jer lifted the skillet and tilted it to spread the hot oil over the surface. "He didn't call. He knows she's here. He just doesn't give a damn." He poured the thick batter into the skillet. "You eatin' with us?"

"I'm not hungry."

"Well, maybe not, but stay." He broke some eggs into a bowl. "You send her back home and she'll just run away again. Hell, the kid never knew her daddy, and now her ma—" Jer's voice broke. He beat the eggs with a fury.

Ethan rose to leave. "I'd better be gettin' on home."

Jer pointed the wire whip at him. "You stay where you are!"

Ethan stared at him in amazement.

"You're one sorry bastard, Ethan Brown," Jer went on. "You could've had her, you know."

"What are you talking about? You're the one who told me that I wouldn't have a friend in all of Chase County. . . ."

"Maybe I did, but that was my head talkin', not my heart."

Jer looked up all of a sudden, and Ethan turned around to see Eliana standing in the doorway rubbing her eyes. She looked confused and afraid.

"Where's my mama?" she asked in a clear voice.

The two men only stared back at her.

"She isn't really dead, is she?"

They didn't answer her, and so she knew this horrible nightmare was real and her mother wasn't ever coming back. Her pretty little face, worn and tired, suddenly dissolved in tears. Ethan stood frozen in front of her. He had never felt grief so real and pain so utterly tangible as he did at that moment.

Jer rushed over and swept her up in his arms. "Hey! How 'bout goin' out and sayin' hello to Big Mike before we eat? Okay?"

Eliana nodded and clung to him, burying her wet face in his big neck as he carried her out the back door. Ethan watched them from the window. Jer had forgotten the pancakes, and Ethan had the good sense to pick up the spatula and flip them.

THE legal aspects of Eliana's guardianship were relatively simple for Ethan. When, after five days, Charlie Fergusen had made no attempt to contact his granddaughter, Ethan paid him a visit with legal papers. He expected a battle. Instead, Charlie Fergusen, without a word, signed the custody documents where Ethan indicated. Ethan took the documents and left quickly. His own loneliness was all he could bear. He had no stomach for Charlie's misery.

When Ethan had walked into the county coroner's office and requested they turn over to him the charred remains of Annette Zeldin, they did so with respectful deference. And when he took her remains in the back of his truck to have them cremated, no one questioned his authority. And despite the fact that the plot next to Emma Reilly Fergusen was destined for her husband, Charles, no one dared contradict him when he gave instructions for a small grave to be dug, just large enough for the urn. He did it all alone.

Word gets around, however, in a town like Cottonwood Falls, and that morning, while Ethan stood watching them dig her grave and recalling how he had first seen her standing here less than a year before, other people arrived. Jer showed up with Nell Harshaw and Eliana. A little later Mrs. Winegarner arrived with her husband and Matthew. Matthew's father carried the boy to a limestone bench; then Mrs. Winegarner took Matthew's violin out of the car. Ethan watched as Matthew reverently opened the case. He took only a moment to tune the strings and then played "Amazing Grace," followed by an Irish lullaby. The little boy's playing was remarkably clear and melodious. When he had finished, he put his violin away, and his father carried him back to the car.

Over the next few days several floral arrangements appeared on the grave, sent by Annette's students. But at the end of the week a windstorm passed through eastern Kansas, and Annette's grave was swept clean of every trace of human remembrance.

DR. EAGLETON personally believed Katie Anne's progress was as miraculous as her return to life, but to Ethan she gave a subdued report tempered with professionalism. From the time she had told him about the false pregnancy, she sensed there was something broken between the couple, and although she knew better, she nonetheless carried a personal burden for it. Her patient had taken to confiding in her, and although Dr. Eagleton tried to maintain her distance, she had developed a fondness for the young woman.

She had worked with many burn patients, and she got so she could read the pain in their eyes or in the way they gripped with their hands. But this young woman was unusual. She continually struggled to be free of her pain, as though she were able to live in the future and distance herself from the gruesome and tedious task of healing her body. And this future, for her, seemed to be full of hope, although her husband gave her little of that.

"ETHAN was in love with her," said Katie Anne one day as Dr. Eagleton carefully removed a layer of bandages from her back.

"With whom?"

"With the little girl's mother."

With deft, precise movements Dr. Eagleton lifted the gauze squares and dropped them into a metal basin. "Your skin is looking good. I don't see any infection." She continued peeling the gauze. "And now she's coming to live with you?"

"Yes." Katie Anne winced when a patch of gauze stuck to her.

"Sorry about that. So, about the little girl . . ."

"Eliana."

"That's a pretty name." Katie Anne was silent as Dr. Eagleton began applying fresh sterile bandages. "I think you'll be able to start some therapy in a few days."

"When can I go home?"

"When you've got new skin."

"I wasn't really pregnant, you know," Katie Anne said suddenly. "I did it to keep him. It was a pretty awful thing to do."

"Katie Anne . . ." Dr. Eagleton studied the young woman. The redness on one side of her face had gone a shade purple, and there were still bandages on the other side, where she had third-degree burns. Her hair had been cut short all over, but there were still patches where there was only stubble. She had lost her left ear.

"What?"

"You don't believe this was a punishment, do you?"

Katie Anne stared into the doctor's cool blue eyes with her own deep dark ones. "I don't know. But I do think that this little girl, Eliana, is my savior."

THAT night Katie Anne had a dream about a beautiful woman with pure white hair. The woman sang her a song that seemed very familiar, and in the dream the woman called her Annie. When Katie

Anne awoke in the night, she lay there in bed, feeling the pain in her body and fondling this name in her thoughts. It was only suitable that she have a new name. She would have a new face and a new family.

As the weeks in the hospital went by, she began to feel more and more that she was a new being. This newness was as fragile as her new skin. Her flesh had burned, she was regenerated, transformed, and from the flames, phoenixlike, rose a new person, someone profoundly aware of having been given a twelfth-hour gift of life.

JER drove Eliana and her two suitcases, one of which was filled with her mother's things, over to Ethan's ranch one spring evening. At Ethan's request Big Mike, the horse, had already been installed in Ethan's new stable.

Ethan stood waiting for them on the front porch as they drove up, escorted by Traveler, who raced alongside the truck, barking and leaping at Eliana's hand as she reached for him through the open window. It was, in appearance, an enthusiastic and joyous arrival, but the little girl trembled inside and the man on the porch smiled too much. As Ethan showed her around the house, he kept glancing at her for signs of approval, but there were none. He noticed then how different the child was, as if the light had been torn from her eyes. They brought her bags up to the room Ethan had thought of as Jeremy's. Then they left her alone.

Eliana sat on the bed and looked around. The room seemed dull to her. The entire house lacked the vibrancy that had surrounded her growing up. She was only seven, but she knew what was beautiful and what was ugly. This house was not ugly, but it was anemic. In her mind she pictured her home back in Paris, filled with exotic objects her mother had brought back from her concert tours. Her mother had always seemed to make everything so beautiful, even when they had little money. The house had always been awash in color and music and things that smelled good. A terrible wave of homesickness came over Eliana, and she curled up on the bed and stared at the beige wall.

THE THOUGHTS THAT HOVERED in Katie Anne's mind more persistently than any others now were thoughts about Eliana. She began to query Ethan when he came to visit her.

"Have you fixed up her room yet?"

"Not yet. I had to move cattle last weekend. I haven't had time."

"Then take the time. Go buy her a pretty pink bedspread. No, not pink. She probably doesn't like pink."

"She doesn't. She already told me as much."

"Well, take her with you. Bring her into Kansas City and take her to a department store or a mall. And don't be stingy, Ethan."

He smiled at her. A real smile. It warmed Katie Anne.

"Are you getting her to school on time?"

"Yep."

"Where does she go for lunch?"

"She walks over to Nell's. Nell fixes her lunch every day."

"Why don't you take her out sometime? You could pick her up and take her out to lunch. She'd like that."

Ethan sighed. "I don't know. She doesn't feel real comfortable around me. I don't think she likes me."

"Well, you broke her mother's heart."

There was no malice in her voice. They were silent, and for the first time since the fire, he felt at ease with her.

Chapter Ten

AFTER two months Ethan drove Katie Anne home from the hospital in Kansas City. She was quiet in the truck as she gazed at the hills. Everything looked fresh and new to her, as though vibrating with an inner light. Ethan sensed something unusual about her that afternoon, a serenity that was apparent in the way her hands lay quietly in her lap, the way her head turned slowly in response to his questions. Before today he had thought it was the pain that made her move like this, but now he thought otherwise.

When they arrived, Katie Anne didn't want to go in the house.

"Let me just sit on the steps out here for a little while," she said as he helped her out of the truck. She walked with a cane, and she lowered herself gently onto the top step while Traveler approached her. "I look funny, don't I, boy? Smell me. I haven't changed."

Ethan watched as she scratched the dog behind the ears and under the chin. He remembered the only other moment he had ever seen her pet the dog—the night when he left her.

"Where's Eliana?" she asked, looking up at him. Her face had healed well, although there was still a discoloration of the skin on one side, and her hair was growing back unevenly. She wore a black scarf around her head to cover her missing ear. Ethan noticed with a sudden pang of pity that she was wearing just a touch of makeup, and he remembered how she always used to labor over her makeup, agonizing over the color of her lipstick or eyeshadow.

She turned away, suddenly self-conscious under his gaze. Her heart sank whenever Ethan looked at her. "Why are you staring at me?" she said to him. "Do I look so different out here?"

"No," he lied. "It's Traveler. You never liked him much before."

"Yeah, well, that was my loss. Wasn't it, fella?" she said to the dog as she stroked him. "Where's Eliana?" she asked again.

"I don't know. Jer's truck is here. Maybe in the stable."

"I'll go find her." She picked up her cane.

She met Jer coming from the stable. A big grin broke out on his face. "Can I hug you?" he asked.

"You bet," she said, smiling.

He put his arms gently around her, and she laid her head on his chest. "Oh, Jer, you feel so good." She sighed as she slipped her arms around him. Ethan had not shown her this much affection, she thought with a sudden clarity that chilled her like a cold wind. She realized it would be a long time before he would touch her again. "Jer, do I look too awfully scary?" she asked.

"No," he whispered, still holding her. "You look great."

"Where is Eliana?"

"She's out in the stable, brushin' down Big Mike. We just came in from a ride."

"What'd she say about me coming home today?"

"Nothin'. She's not much of a talker. At least not anymore."

AT THE entrance to the stable Katie Anne closed her eyes and breathed in the sharp odor of animal, straw, and leather. It was late June now, and the warm late-day sun laid a gentle hand on her back. She walked through the stable, talking to the horses. Big Mike was tied up at the end of the corridor, and she found Eliana mucking out his stall. She had never seen the child before this moment.

"That's no fun, is it?" she said.

"I like it," replied Eliana without looking up.

"Then you're a good horsewoman."

Eliana worked on, scooping up the manure.

"I'm Annie," said Katie Anne.

There was something about the way she said it that made Eliana pause and look up. In the dim light of the stable, with the black scarf on her head, she did not look hideous, the way Eliana imagined she would look. She was leaning on a cane.

"I know," replied Eliana.

"I'm glad you're all right. I was worried about you," she said, and she lowered herself down onto an upturned bucket. Eliana found it a little odd that this strange woman should be worried about her, but she said nothing, only went back to mucking out the stall; then she spread fresh straw down. When it was neat and clean, she brought in the horse and took off his halter.

"You really love that big guy, don't you?" said Katie Anne.

"Yes. More than anyone in the world. Him and Traveler."

"Two very worthy creatures."

Eliana carried the halter to the front of the barn and hung it up with the rest of the tack, then called back from the door, "I'm going inside now."

"You go on. I'm gonna sit out here for a while," Katie Anne replied from the stall.

Eliana stood quietly at the entrance for a moment, then turned and walked back to the house. To her surprise she had felt at ease in the woman's presence, and her face was not all that frightening. What Eliana particularly liked was the fact that the woman had not tried to make friends with her or ask her a lot of boring questions. She just seemed to want to sit there and have her company. Eliana thought that was okay, and she broke out into a run and then skipped all the way back to the house.

ETHAN and Katie Anne slept together in the same bed that first night, and Katie Anne lay awake much of the night, hoping for him to move next to her, to reach out for her, to touch her. The memories of their lovemaking surged into her thoughts, and thinking Ethan was asleep, she nestled up behind him. She slid her arm around him, and as soon as she touched him, she felt him grow tense. His shoulder was hard to her, like a wall.

"Katie Anne . . ."

"Are you ever going to touch me again?" she whispered.

He sighed deeply, and he gently moved her arm away.

"Katie Anne, I've filed for an annulment."

She drew back as though he were fire.

She knew something had been troubling him, saw how he had smiled at her only with his mouth, not his eyes, during her recovery, his care bolstered with platitudes, not love. But his words hung like a heavy sword in the air, cutting off his breath. Katie Anne saw this was just the beginning. All the pain from her body was nothing compared to the tribulations she would endure from now on. Ethan was not a vengeful man, but he could not forget, it seemed, what had happened between them.

For a long while she lay there in the bed, her heart beating wildly. In the darkness everything whirled around her.

"I'm sorry." His voice was flat.

"I'm sorry for what I did, Ethan." She rolled away from him, and the tears flowed quietly down her face, drowning her eyes, empty- ing her heart. When he made no reply, she added, "I guess I don't belong here anymore. But I love you. I love you more than I ever did before, and different somehow. I'll never get over you."

He wanted to say, "Yes, you will," but the words never rose from his throat. He lay there, blocking out his feelings, and said, "I want you to know, it doesn't have anything to do with . . . with what's happened to you. With the way you look. It's not that. I'm not that callous." But what he thought was this: If you were Annette, you could be deformed, hideous, and I'd take you in my arms and love you until the sun quit shining.

THE next morning Ethan found Katie Anne in the kitchen, making pancakes. Eliana soon appeared in her nightgown, and Katie Anne ushered her off to the bathroom and saw to it she washed her hair. When Ethan left for work, he heard laughter coming from the bathroom, and he wondered what on earth they could be laughing about. Jer was sitting on the front porch as Ethan came out, drinking a cup of coffee.

"I think you need to give the girl some credit, Ethan. I'll be the first to admit, I never thought Katie Anne had it in her to pull off something like this, the way she's done," Jer said. "She used to whine about a chipped nail, and now she's hobblin' up and down the stairs with a face any kid would die for on Halloween, and I never hear her complain. And she seems to have really taken a liking to having Eliana around—"

"That's all put on," interrupted Ethan. "Katie Anne can play a role up to the hilt. Underneath that generous soul is a . . ." He didn't finish his sentence.

Jer was staring at him. "You used to love her."

"I guess I thought I did." He paused. "I'm going to try to find some of Annette's relatives and see if one of them'll take Eliana. And I'm going to get my marriage annulled."

"On what grounds?"

"I have good reason."

"You want to tell me why?"

"Nope."

Jer noticed a tone of voice Ethan had never used with him before. There was animosity behind his words.

"Okay," he said to Ethan. "And then you're gonna live out here all alone with your horses and your cattle and your land."

"That's right," Ethan said, and he got into his truck and drove off to work.

WHEN Katie Anne had dried the child's hair, she offered to braid it for her. Eliana was delighted.

"I used to practice on my Barbie dolls," Katie Anne confessed. "Once I cut the hair on one of them, and I cried for days afterward because I couldn't braid it."

When the braid was finished, Eliana looked at it in the mirror and smiled. "This is the way my mama used to do it."

"You look very much like your mother right now," said Katie Anne softly. The little girl turned around to face her, and Katie Anne thought she'd never seen such a grave child.

"I thought you'd hate me," Eliana said quietly.

"Why would . . ." she began, and then she caught herself. She took a deep breath. "I don't hate you at all. On the contrary, I . . ." She paused. She sat down on the bed and stared at the brush. It was a strange kind of brush, and she wondered if it was French. "Eliana, you should know this. Ethan doesn't want to be married to me anymore. He's getting the marriage annulled."

"What does that mean?"

"Well, it's like the marriage never really took place."

"But how can you say something didn't happen when it did?"

"Ethan loved your mommy. That's who he wanted to marry."

"Really?"

"You didn't know that?"

"No," she answered quietly, shaking her head. "My mommy cried a lot the month before she died. She was very sad."

Katie Anne studied the hairbrush. She could not bear to see all the heartache in the child's eyes. "I don't think he's ever going to forget your mommy. That's how much he loved her."

"Do you still love him?"

Katie Anne took a deep breath. "I can't remember when I didn't love him." She got up and placed the brush on the dresser. "This room is so bare."

"All my toys are still in Paris."

"I'll talk to Ethan about that."

ELIANA and Jer helped move Katie Anne's things to the downstairs bedroom. When they were done, Katie Anne lay down and rested, and Jer took Eliana out to check on his herd. She was real proud of her braid, Jer told Katie Anne later in the day. You could tell by the way she held up her head.

Nothing else was said about the annulment. That Katie Anne had taken the initiative and moved herself downstairs seemed to be a concession of sorts, but she made no pretense of moving out of the house, and Ethan thought it was best not to press the matter until the annulment was final.

Several nights after her return Ethan knocked on her door.

"Come in," she answered.

He opened the door. She was sitting up in bed, reading.

"You need anything?" he asked.

"No, nothing. Thanks."

He stood there awkwardly in the middle of the room; then he asked, "What are you reading?"

She held the book up to show him. "I can't pronounce it." She smiled a little self-consciously. It was a copy of Victor Hugo's immense *Les Misérables*. "Dr. Eagleton gave it to me. It was kind of a joke, really. The title, you know. But it's really good."

Ethan had never known Katie Anne to read a book. "You want me to bring the television down from my bedroom?"

"No. I won't watch it at night," she said.

"You used to. You used to be glued to that screen."

"I know." She laid the book down and passed her finger along the spine. "Maybe because I watched so much of it in the hospital when I couldn't move very much, after a while it just all seemed so . . .

so pointless." She fingered the pages. Ethan sensed she wanted to talk about the book, but didn't know how.

"Are you sleeping okay down here?" he asked finally.

"Yes, fine," she replied, and she went back to her book, shutting him out of her world.

He left, mumbling a quiet "Good night."

THEN one afternoon he came home and found her in the kitchen listening to her Walkman. She was washing lettuce in the sink, and she didn't hear him come in. She turned and jumped and let out a squeal that cut through to his heart, so much it reminded him of her laughter when they had first met.

"Sorry," he said, grinning. "Didn't mean to come up on you like that."

She nervously rushed to dry her hands and turn off the music, but not before strains of violin had reached Ethan's ears.

"I thought I'd try something different tonight," she blurted out. "I got some salmon steaks, and I thought we could grill them."

Ethan hated fish, and Katie Anne knew it, but he was too distracted by her nervousness to comment on it. He said, "Whatever you want." As he left the room, he noticed the cassette case on the counter. It was Annette's recording of Sibelius's violin concerto, and there, on the front, was a picture of Annette and David Zeldin.

"Where'd you get this?" he asked, and the still, cold emptiness of his voice made her heart stop. In all the years she had known Ethan, Katie Anne had never heard him speak to anyone like this.

"I bought it."

"You *bought* it? Why?" His body was tense with rage.

"I . . . I bought it with Eliana."

"Why are you listening to her music?" He shook the box now.

"I bought it for Eliana!" she yelled at him, and tears welled up in her eyes. "We were looking at music, and she saw it, and she wanted it, so I bought it for her. Ethan, she doesn't have anything left! You haven't done anything about her stuff, her toys. The things her mother owned are still sitting in Paris. Why?"

"Because she's not staying here! That's why! I've been in contact with her relatives, some cousins I located, and they're gonna take custody of her. They're coming to get her at the end of July."

Katie Anne felt as though he had knocked the breath out of her. "You can't do that," she whispered.

"I'm her guardian. I can do whatever I think is best for her."

She pulled out a chair from the kitchen table and sat down. Her chest felt tight. "Please. Don't do this," she whispered.

"Why? I don't know why you're so concerned."

She took a moment to answer. "I don't know. I honestly don't. I just don't want her to go."

"If you think it's going to make a difference about us . . ."

"That's not it."

"Well, I'm still pursuing the annulment. Regardless of what happens with Eliana."

"I know." She broke into tears then, and Ethan left the room.

SEVERAL nights after that Katie Anne was awakened in the middle of the night by a cry. She sat up and listened.

"Maman!" came the child's cry again.

A primordial response surged from deep within her. She sprang up, and her arm swept the bedside lamp to the floor. Groping through the darkness for the door, feeling the broken glass underneath her bare feet, she hobbled toward the cries.

"I'm coming! I'm coming, precious!"

She found Eliana sitting up in bed, wide-eyed and terrified.

"It's okay. It's okay, honey." Katie Anne rushed to the bed and took the child in her arms. "It's just a nightmare. It's okay. I'm here." Katie Anne held her as tightly as she could, and slowly, with the child in her arms, her heart began to calm. "It's okay. It's okay," she repeated over and over. She wondered what had made her panic like this. What child is this, she thought, that moves me with her sorrow? That heals me with her love?

"It's over now," she whispered, rocking the little girl in her arms, back and forth. "It's over." As she spoke, Eliana's arms fixed themselves around her waist, and Katie Anne kissed her silky hair. "It's okay, precious," she whispered.

She looked around to see Ethan standing in the doorway, drawing the sash of his robe around his waist. "She okay?"

"Yeah. She just had a bad dream. I'll take care of her."

"You sure?"

She nodded. "I'm sure. You go on back to bed."

For a long time she sat there holding the child. She tried to remember some nursery rhymes, but all she could remember were some lyrics from country-and-western songs. She hummed one as she rocked the little girl to sleep in her arms. Afterward Katie Anne lay down on the bed next to her. She leaned close and inhaled the child's sweet smell. She knew the smell of spring on the prairie, the smell of a newborn calf, and she knew the smell of fire. But this was new. She lay there for a long time and finally fell asleep. She awoke several hours later and got up and went back downstairs to her own room.

In the morning she awoke to find Eliana standing in her room, watching her. "Did you come into my room last night?"

"You were having a nightmare." Katie Anne tossed back the sheets. Eliana crawled into bed and lay down next to her.

"I dreamed I was looking for my mother and I couldn't find her," said the child. "It was very sad. That's all I remember."

They lay there next to each other. Katie Anne noticed how lovely the little girl's hands were.

"The worst ones are when I find her and I'm happy. Then when I wake up, it's worse."

Katie Anne took her hand. "If you ever wake up and get scared again, and if I don't hear you, come crawl into bed with me."

"You sure you won't mind?"

"Not at all."

KATIE Anne became a virtual recluse after the fire. Ethan urged her to invite people to the house, but she discouraged visits from friends like Patti Boswell and Whitey, and she inevitably cut short telephone conversations with them. When she ventured to Cottonwood Falls or Strong City for groceries or other needs, she always took Eliana with her, and the little girl was always the focus of her attention. They seemed to form an island in a sea of curious faces. They turned their eyes toward each other and saw only each other, shutting out the cruel world around them. They seemed to need no one.

Then one hot Friday morning in early July, only an hour after he had left for work, Ethan came back home. Katie Anne heard his truck and went out on the front porch to meet him.

"Where's Eliana?" he asked Katie Anne as he walked toward her.

"She's out back. Why? What's wrong?"

Ethan removed his hat and wiped the sweat from his forehead. "Charlie Fergusen's dead. He committed suicide. Hung himself."

Katie Anne stared at him blankly. "Suicide?" she said.

"I thought I'd better let you know. We'll have to tell Eliana. But I don't think she should know it was suicide."

Katie Anne sat down on the porch swing. She looked away from Ethan, out toward the hills.

"Katie Anne?" He sat down beside her. "Are you okay?"

"It's my fault," she whispered. "I should have taken Eliana and gone to see him. She hasn't been to see him since she ran away."

He gently laid a hand on her shoulder. She was crying. "You didn't have any obligation to him."

She turned toward him, and it looked as if she wanted to contradict him, but she didn't speak. She got up and went inside.

Ethan didn't follow her inside, and she was glad. She had a desperate urge to kneel. She went into her bedroom and knelt at the side of her bed.

That evening she had a violent argument with Ethan. She didn't want Eliana to know her grandfather was dead. Ethan had never seen her so opposed to him. When he finally conceded, she went to bed, and the following morning she took Eliana off to Kansas City on a shopping trip. She called him that evening and told him they had decided to stay for the weekend and would be back Monday morning after the funeral.

Ethan did not see them until he came home from work Monday afternoon. He was surprised to find that he had missed them.

For the next several days he was exceptionally gentle, and Katie Anne felt herself open up to him again. For the first time since the accident she hoped he might be having a change of heart.

Then one evening later in the week Katie Anne found Ethan out on the porch, sitting alone. It was one of those rare summer evenings when only a mild breeze stirred the grasses.

Katie Anne sat down next to him. "Can I join you?"

"You bet," he said congenially. It was hard to read him without looking into his eyes. He was always so pleasant, she thought. Even when he's breaking your heart, he's so damn nice.

She sat there without speaking, basking in his presence, imagining that somewhere in his heart there still lurked some love for her. He had said nothing more about the annulment, and she was hoping he had changed his mind. She had longed to ask him but was afraid. "I wish everything could stay like this," she whispered.

His breathing changed, and she thought perhaps he was going to say something. She waited.

"I died, didn't I?" she blurted out. The thought had come to her all of a sudden. Ethan turned to her in the darkness.

"Yes, you did. You were . . . Technically you were dead."

"How long?"

He shook his head. "I don't know. Several minutes maybe."

"What brought me back?"

"I don't know. They'd taken you off all the life support."

"I think I remember heaven. I remember something so terribly beautiful. But for all the beauty of heaven, I could not leave this earth." She turned and looked at him. "I love you too much."

She sat there, willing him with every nerve, every fiber in her body to reach out and take her in his arms. When he made no move toward her, she reached out and laid her hand on his knee. "Ethan," she whispered, "until you learn to forgive me, you'll never see how much I've changed."

"I know you've changed," he replied. "I know how hard you're trying." He suddenly got to his feet and walked down the steps. The night was aglitter with stars, and there stood Ethan, so desolate and alone. "But that's the trouble," he went on. His voice grew to a high pitch as he spoke, strained. "You think if you act like her, you think I'll love you. But I'll never—"

She rose to her feet. "That's not true, Ethan!"

"Be able to love you like I loved her."

"I'm not trying to act like anybody!"

"The hell you aren't. I can see right through you."

She stared at his back in the darkness. How he trivialized what she had gone through—the emptiness, the confusion, the sense of having lost something and the miracle of having found it again. "You have no idea what I'm feeling inside," she said.

He wanted to tell her he didn't care. She stood behind him, and he could hear her breath as she tried to calm her tears.

"Ethan," she whispered finally, "don't drive us away. You've already made one mistake you'll regret for the rest of your life. Don't make another one."

Then she turned and went into the house.

ETHAN walked down past the stable and out onto the prairie. She had taken him by surprise. She had not flailed her arms or screamed at him. Instead, she had cut through his defenses with razorlike insight. It bled him, and as he walked through the grass, he felt as if he were drowning in emotions. Suddenly a mournful cry heaved from his throat. He bellowed out all his rage, his pain, his losses, his loves. He roared and roared and found he could not stop. He came upon a hedgerow and fell to his knees. His shoulders shook mightily, and he cried.

When he could cry no more, he lay there in the dark and let his mind rest. After a while, into this emptiness came an infinitesimal truth, a flicker so fine and faint that, had he not been perfectly still, he would never have heard it.

But for all the beauty of heaven, I could not leave this earth. I love you too much.

He tried to recognize the voices. Katie Anne's he could recall, but the other hung so faint in his memory, and it had been the voice of a spirit, and how does one recall the voice of a spirit?

His mind summoned memories, and he began to see something, something that frightened him, that thrilled him, something he could almost believe. He got up and began to walk back toward the ranch. He had come miles in the darkness, and he had been gone for hours. As he walked, he tried to recall the odd incident, the words, the gestures, those subtle changes he had so firmly discredited that had taken place over the months. As great as his disbelief was, nothing else made sense except this. He needed some time now, time to observe her, to listen. To test her. As he grew closer to the house, he saw the lights on upstairs in Eliana's bedroom. He broke into a run.

They were gone. Suitcases had been dragged out and packed hurriedly. Toys still lay in the middle of the floor in Eliana's room, and the book Katie Anne had been reading, *Jane Eyre,* lay open on the coffee table in the living room. But they were gone.

Ethan called Tom and Betty Sue Mackey. They were polite, but they would not tell him where she was.

"She called us, Ethan, and told us she was leaving on a little trip, but she didn't say where. She said not to worry."

Two days later Tom Mackey called and said he had heard from her. They were in Paris.

Chapter Eleven

ETHAN rode his horses hard that summer, and he drove his cattle all over the Flint Hills, as if he were a fugitive looking for somewhere to hide out in the endless waves of prairie. Word gets around, of course, in a town like Cottonwood Falls, and everyone knew that Katie Anne had walked out on him and taken Eliana, but Ethan wouldn't talk about it. He never showed his face around the South Forty anymore, and unless he had some business in town, he stayed away from his office. He gave Bonnie a month's paid vacation and took his legal files out to the ranch and worked from his home office. But people liked Ethan Brown, and his absence was felt in Cottonwood Falls. His bright-eyed charm and his deep laughter were conspicuously missing.

Ethan had over ten thousand head of cattle to care for that summer, and he worked himself and his cowhands summer hours from dawn to dusk, mending fences, carrying out vet checks, vaccinating, rounding up strays, and generally watching over the huge brutish babies like a mother while they doubled their weight and ate their way to a healthy profit. He was content as long as he was working, but the evenings spent alone at his ranch were unbearable. He took to sleeping out on the range with the wind and the rattlesnakes. Sometimes Jer or one of the cowhands stayed out with him, and once Tom Mackey drove out at dusk to join them. On those nights Ethan could pretend the world was a solid place, fortified by staunch male defenses. They talked cattle and cursed the politicians in Washington and ate pan-fried steak and fried potatoes cooked over a Coleman stove; then they stretched out in their sleeping bags and gazed at the stars until they fell asleep. But even this ploy worked only temporarily. After a while the earth became hard under Ethan's back. One night at around midnight he packed up and drove back to his ranch.

His beloved hills had turned dark and sour on him. The jagged rocks just below their smiling green surface seemed to puncture his old joy, deflating him. They stretched before him in the starlit night like the pouting curves on the cheeks of a sullen child. They appeared to him now in the dark light in which so many others had seen them. Impenetrable, they gave up so little of themselves. He recalled Willa Cather's words: "Between that earth and that sky I felt erased, blotted out." His beloved hills. For the first time in his life they afforded him no peace.

For weeks he waited for a word from Katie Anne, but none

came. He would find reasons to call Tom and Betty Sue, and he would work into the conversation a question or two about her, but they were vague. Yes, she was fine. She had called them just yesterday. Katie Anne was having some cosmetic surgery done at a Swiss clinic; Eliana was planning a week at a summer camp in the mountains. Ethan didn't ask when she was coming home.

He finally sat down and wrote her a letter. It was the kind of letter one would expect of him—articulate and intelligent, full of wit and artful turns of phrases. But there was nothing to betray the terrifying loneliness he was living. He looked at the letter and prided himself on how it sounded, how happy, solid, unperturbed it sounded. If I just keep a good attitude about it all, he said to himself, the world won't come crashing in on me. But his world *had* crashed in on him. His house stood strong and tall around him, and yet his life was splintered timber. Still, he believed he could will Katie Anne to come back with his happiness.

His letter went unanswered. The fear that she might never return began to grow as the days passed and he did not hear from her. This was no ploy, no elaborate scheme to win his heart back. Ethan knew that now.

Betty Sue had shared one of her letters with him. She had stopped by one evening when Tom was gone, and brought it for him to read. She did this against her husband's wishes, for although Tom loved Ethan Brown like a son, he loved his daughter much more, and he felt that his child must have been deeply wounded to run so far away to a place she had never aspired to, with a little girl who was not even her own.

Dearest Mom and Dad,

I know I just called, but I feel I have things that need to be said with paper and pen.

I'm learning a little French, but my pronunciation is dreadful. Of course, Eliana does much of the talking for us. I have long since given up trying to explain who I am. So now she just introduces me as her mother, which I don't mind.

Eliana's affection for me (if I'm not mistaken) seems to grow stronger. She is very protective of me. When people stop and stare at me in the street, she presses my hand more tightly. Even though the plastic surgery has done wonders, I still feel like a walking curio, one of those knickknacks you find in the antique stores here that invite long, studious examination. But it doesn't bother me so much anymore. Not like it did back home. Here I am in Paris, so far away from all I cherish, but I feel safe. Can you imagine that? This city is nothing like anything I have ever known or imagined. It has made an overwhelming impression on me with its grandness and its misery. There are holes gouged out of the huge stone blocks, from machine-gun fire during the last war. The city seems to weep with joy. I think I could find anything here.

Betty Sue waited quietly while Ethan finished the letter. He handed it back to her. He had grown very solemn.

"I never knew she could write like that."

"Oh, I did," said Betty Sue as she very carefully folded the letter. "When she was in high school, she used to write the most beautiful poetry. At least I thought it was beautiful. But I guess it was just a phase. When she got out of school, she lost interest in it." She hesitated for a moment. "Ethan, I think she intends to stay for a while." She stood up and went to the door. "But she seems so much happier than she did here. I was really worried about her. I'm not so worried now." She smiled brightly. "Besides, Tom and I are going to visit her in October. I'm excited about it. I've never been to Paris."

Several days later Ethan took a piece of his business stationery with WORDSWORTH at the top, and wrote:

> Dear Katie Anne,
>   I'm a mess. Please come home.
>   Love,
>   Ethan

For the next few days after he mailed it, he was happy. He called Jer, and they went out for a beer, and he told him things were going to be okay. But when two weeks had gone by and Ethan still hadn't received an answer, he called Betty Sue and asked for Katie Anne's telephone number.

"She got your letter, Ethan."

"She did?"

"Yes. She got it last week." He was silent. "Ethan, she asked us not to give you her number. She doesn't want to talk to you."

The next week Ethan received the notice that the annulment was final. It was a shock. He had completely forgotten about it. But now it sat on his desk, reminding him of what he had done.

THE night before Tom and Betty Sue left for Paris, Ethan stopped by. He knocked, and Tom came to the door.

"Evenin', Tom."

"Ethan. Come on in."

Ethan stepped inside, but he remained at the entrance. "I just wanted to drop this by. It's something for Katie Anne. A book I thought she might like to have. Please make sure she gets it as soon as you get there." Then he turned and walked back to his truck. Tom Mackey watched him go.

"What is it?" asked Betty Sue as she walked up behind him.

"Something Ethan brought by. It's for Katie Anne."

He opened the front cover and saw this note:

I'm going to Windermere at last. Please come.

Love,
Ethan

He gave it to his wife and looked out at the dust trail left by Ethan's truck. "God bless his soul," sighed Tom, and he shut the door.

FROM the window of the Continental Airlines jet Ethan could see Kansas City sprawled below him, but then the city passed from view, and below him stretched a bank of green treetops. His own land was barren now, the color of rust, deep coppery red against the bluest of skies, the color it took on every autumn.

He changed planes in Chicago. The price he was willing to pay for his ticket was sufficient testimony to his ardor—the only seats available were first class. He was served dinner on a linen-covered tray and wiped his mouth on a white starched-linen napkin. He cut his meat with a silver knife and ate colorful vegetables with a silver fork. Coffee, served in a china cup, was taken with his apple tart. He fell asleep partway into an English film about a mad English king and awoke when the stewardess was setting up his breakfast tray and daylight was creeping in around the shades of the portholes.

As HE lugged his suitcase off the revolving baggage carousel and set it down at his feet, a wave of self-consciousness washed over Ethan. Standing there in a sea of Europeans, his new chocolate-brown alligator boots all of a sudden seemed very wrong. He picked up his suitcase and followed the crowd of passengers marching toward customs, and then the taxis beyond.

The train station was a nightmare. He kept reminding himself it could be worse—this could be France and he wouldn't understand anything. He got lost, of course, several times. He was not used to train stations. He was used to prairies. He knew where everything was on the prairie.

When he finally got his ticket and found his train, he was sweating. At least the people were friendly to him. They helped him find his seat, and he settled into it like a hare in a burrow. He caught his breath and then struggled out of his coat. He tried reading the section on England in his AAA guidebook, but it made him nervous. A while later he slept, the swaying metal hips of the train lulling him to sleep as it curved northward through town and country. Several passengers sat next to him, but he wasn't aware of them.

Ethan awoke with a start and looked out the window. He was stunned to see his hills. Rockier perhaps, and rising higher to mountains in the distance, and too green for this time of year, but his hills nonetheless. Anxiously he looked around. People were standing in the aisles, lifting down their luggage. Ethan caught the eye of another passenger and asked where they were.

"Windermere," he answered. "End of the line."

ETHAN had only glimpses of the town from the station. What he saw mostly was tourists. This was not what he had expected, this crush of people and cameras. He waited patiently in front of the station and watched them. Occasionally he would glance up at the hills—fells they were called in this part of the world. Finally he saw his name on a sign waving in the air above the crowd. It was being held aloft by a young man leaning against the door of a roadster. Ethan approached him.

"I'm Ethan Brown."

The young man stared at him curiously. He noticed the cowboy boots and grinned. "I say, I thought that might be you. I'm from the Drunken Duck. Here, let me take your bag."

The young man upended the suitcase in the narrow back seat of the roadster, and Ethan slid into the front next to him.

ETHAN had wanted accommodations in Grasmere, a village a few miles down the road from Windermere and the home of the poet Wordsworth, but there was nothing available on such short notice, and so he was booked into an old coaching inn called the Drunken Duck.

The inn was miles away from the train station at Windermere, but from the moment he set foot inside, Ethan found himself succumbing to the grandeur and charm of the old place. Despite its isolation, the inn was not wanting for patrons. At the entrance stood a boot rack full of muddied rubber walking and hiking boots, and above it hung an assortment of hats. To the right was the pub, and through its open door Ethan glimpsed a roaring fire in a high stone fireplace and the gleam of bright wood endlessly polished by tweeds and wools.

For most of the evening he was able to forget the purpose of his journey. The Drunken Duck was a highly sociable place. Ethan drank a very good lager the bartender recommended, ate his beef and potatoes, and had his first taste of English trifle.

He stayed until the pub closed and then went to his room. The maid had shown him how to close the shutters so that the morning light would not disturb him, and before he shut them and went to bed, he pulled back the curtains and gazed out at the blackness of the hills. A new moon cast faint light across this corner of England. Ethan felt a connection to English soil, to this unknown land.

He lay in the strange bed that night with his eyes wide open, staring at the dark. Then he fell asleep as if lulled by the swaying motion of a train.

ETHAN was driven back into Windermere the next day after lunch, and he waited at the station all afternoon, meeting all the trains arriving from London, but Katie Anne was not on any of them. Between trains he sat at the pub across from the station and read some brochures about Wordsworth's home in Grasmere.

On the second day he became restless, and between trains he wandered the streets of Windermere. It was Monday and the weekenders had gone, and he was beginning to feel at ease in the village. For lunch he discovered another pub, the White Hart, an establishment fashionable with walkers. Later, after the third train had come and gone and Katie Anne had not arrived, he left a note for her with the stationmaster detailing where he was staying. Then he ventured back to a bookstore and bought himself a handsomely bound edition of Wordsworth's poetry. That afternoon, fortified by his lager at the White Hart and determined to shake off the despondency that was growing in his chest like a hard lump, he followed a long walking trail that led back to the Drunken Duck, but his boots were made to gouge the ribs of a horse, not for walking.

On his third morning, rested from an early evening brought about by his hike up the fell, he was able to get up at dawn and catch a ride into town. He was directed to a good shop that specialized in walking boots, and Ethan gently folded his cowboy boots into a plastic bag and walked down to the White Hart for lunch in his new boots. This established a rhythm for the next few days, and despite his growing disappointment at Katie Anne's silence, he looked forward to his trips into Windermere each day.

IT WAS on his fifth evening, after he had returned to the inn from his walk and taken his seat at the bar, that he made the decision to leave. She had not responded to his plea. He had hoped that the book he had asked Tom to deliver might kindle something in her— a memory, long forgotten. He allowed himself to think back to the night she had left, and he tried to recall the way she had looked when she had spoken to him.

Don't drive us away. You've already made one mistake you'll regret for the rest of your life. . . .

He tried that evening to recall other words, too.

For all the beauty of heaven, I could not leave this earth. . . .

The words he recalled perfectly, but what was fading from his memory was where and when he had heard them. Visions that had once blinded him with truth now seemed like faint shadows in his mind. She had been dead only six months, but he could no longer conjure the whole of her face, just her lips. That was all he could see now in his memory—her mouth when she held it just a certain way. Everything else was fading. Tears stung his eyes.

He didn't know how long the woman had been sitting next to him, perhaps seconds, perhaps minutes. He hadn't noticed when she had slid up on the barstool. But now he felt her presence, and the emptiness that seemed like a huge cavern in his soul was suddenly flooded with warmth. That's how he knew it was her. The tears that had been stinging his eyes rolled down his cheeks, and he kept his head lowered and tried to brush them off. She didn't speak to him, nor did he speak to her. After a moment he took her hand and held it gently on his lap, warming it in his large, rough hands. It nestled there, and he sighed a deep sigh that shook his chest. They sat that way for a long time.

"Well, is this the Mrs. Brown we've been waiting for all this time?" asked the bartender with a smile.

"This is she," said Ethan quietly.

"Welcome to the Drunken Duck, madam," the bartender said. "How do you like our country?"

"It's lovely," she said, and Ethan thrilled at the sound of her voice.

"Will you be stayin' longer now, Mr. Brown? You'll not be goin' on to Paris tomorrow?"

"No. Not now."

"Well, I'm glad to hear that. Will you have another lager? And what would you be havin', madam?"

"The same, please."

As the bartender moved aside, Ethan caught their reflections in the mirror behind the bar. She was staring at him. The light from the fire touched her hair with streaks of golden red, and her skin glistened milk-white in the darkness. He looked at her mouth. He studied closely the way she held it, and without turning, he raised his hand to her lips and touched them lightly with his fingers.

"Do you see me now?" she whispered faintly, and he almost didn't hear.

"Yes. I see you now. Yes."

"Am I still so terribly ugly to you?"

His hand moved across her face, touching the skin.

"You're beautiful." His hand moved down her neck. She caught it and kissed it. "I was afraid you wouldn't come," he said gruffly.

"I almost didn't."

"Why did you?"

She waited for a long time before she spoke. "Why did you send me that book?"

He looked at her face in the mirror. He could see her eyes.

Take a look at me now. And remember what it looks like. When you're lookin' into her eyes, remember mine!

She had screamed those words at him once. Long ago. The shame of that moment, of the pain he had given her, washed over him, and he had to look away.

"I thought that book might mean something to you," he said.

"Should it?"

He shrugged. "Only if you want it to." He shook off a sudden ugly flash of doubt. It didn't matter, really, if it meant anything to her or not. What mattered was this: Whoever this woman was, he loved her to the very depth of his soul.

Her hand found his under the bar, in the darkness, and they clung to each other.

"You were coming to Paris?" she said.

"Yes."

"How were you going to find me?"

"I don't know." He paused. "But I wasn't going to go back home until I had."

After a while he rose from the stool. "Come with me."

She hesitated.

He laid his hand on her shoulder, standing behind her, looking at her in the mirror. Her eyes tortured him.

"It's all right. Come."

IN THE room, he moved a chair over to the window for her to sit. Then he turned off all the lights and opened the shutters. The cold sweet air rushed in on them. Ethan stood behind her with his hands resting gently on her shoulders.

"What do you see out there?"

She was very still, and finally, after a long silence, she sighed. "Oh, Ethan. What is it you expect from me? I feel like . . . like if I give the wrong answer, I'll lose you."

Ethan was momentarily stilled by her blow. He felt her shiver, and he leaned down and wrapped his strong arms around her fragile body, protecting her.

"Then I will ask you one last question, and whatever you answer, regardless, I will lay you down in my bed, and I will make love to you." Her body shifted ever so slightly, and he could see her breasts rise, full and soft. "Will you marry me?"

He kissed her then, to stop her reply, for he feared he might lose her again.

Epilogue

THE English bed was high and very deep and soft. As they lay in each other's arms that night, they could see, sparkling in the distance, the lights from Grasmere, the home of Ethan's beloved poet, William Wordsworth.

Ethan never asked her again about the book he had sent her. It was not, strangely enough, Wordsworth, but Yeats. Nor did he ever ask her what she did with it. They lived many years together as man and wife, although not as many as Ethan would have liked. And although he knew his wife intimately and profoundly, knew the scars on her body and on her soul, he never knew the whereabouts of his book of Yeats's poetry, the book he had asked her father to deliver to her in Paris. It was, of course, the same book Annette Zeldin had borrowed from him and kept until her death, when Ethan retrieved it from Charlie Fergusen's home.

MUCH to his profound regret, Ethan outlived his wife.

By the time she died, his face was deeply lined from sun and wind, but he was still healthy, and his heart was strong. Several days after his wife's funeral Eliana, who now lived in New York with her husband, sent him a package. Her note said:

Dear Daddy,

I'm so sorry I had to leave so quickly after the funeral. I hope you are getting along all right. At least Adam's not far, although I know his studies keep him too busy to spend much time with you. All the same, we are only a phone call away.

Let yourself grieve. If Mama taught you anything, let it be this. But do not let your grief pull you down. You have two sons and a daughter who need you, and we all love you dearly.

We will of course be back for Adam's graduation in the spring. I'm so sorry Mama didn't live to see him go this far. He'll make such a fine vet. And, Lord knows, you need a new vet in Cottonwood Falls.

The enclosed is something Mama wanted you to have after she died. She was very careful to keep it hidden from you all those years. Give my love to Jeremy.

Your loving daughter,
Eliana

P.S. The page that is marked is the one she marked for you. She said it would mean something to you.

Ethan carried the book outside and sat down in his chair on the porch. It was a still morning, without a trace of wind. With trembling hands he opened the book to the marked page. Although his eyes were blinded by tears, he knew the poem by heart.

> *When you are old and gray and full of sleep,*
> *And nodding by the fire, take down this book,*
> *And slowly read, and dream of the soft look*
> *Your eyes had once, and of their shadows deep;*
>
> *How many loved your moments of glad grace,*
> *And loved your beauty with love false or true,*
> *But one man loved the pilgrim soul in you,*
> *And loved the sorrows of your changing face. . . .*

When his eyes cleared, Ethan noticed the tops of the cottonwoods in the grove down by the stream were perfectly still.